Rushton Medley

MEMORIES OF MABUHAY

- MIDDAYPRESS -

ISBN: 978-1-66788-889-7 (softcover)
ISBN: 978-1-66788-890-3 (eBook)

Printed in the United States of America

First printing, 2023

For
Joe Emi
and
Chiyomi

TABLE OF CONTENTS

Chapter 1
Major Kaiishi Kojima
Luzon
1945

General Yamashita stood before the dusty dress mirror, doing his best to smooth out the creases of his tunic. His sword lay across his desk. He had spent the last hour ensuring it was gleaming to perfection. It was to be handed over to the Americans as part of the final symbolic act of surrender. On September 2, 1945, it still seemed like we were all sleepwalking through the worst kind of nightmare. We had been camped in Bangbang in the mountains of northern Luzon. The campaign had been going against us for months. We had been in retreat ever since abandoning Manila. Our "strategic" withdrawal to Baguio was the beginning of the end. We were soon pushed farther into the field, where we were forced to take advantage of the high ground and "dug in" along the Cordillera Range for a long campaign of attrition.

In another of life's cruel ironies, Bangbang was the most fitting name imaginable for our final stand. Just a day earlier, the general was making strategic plans for long-term guerrilla warfare when the call to surrender arms came. Events back in the homeland had dictated that we end hostilities. The Emperor had spoken. It was the first time his voice had been heard. He had called for us to desist in our actions. He told us that "the war had not turned in

Japan's favour." He asked us all to "endure the unendurable and bear the unbearable." For all of us who were still alive and fighting, his words seemed like an affirmation of our daily existence.

At this most desolate of times I kept as close to the general as possible. I feared he might be unable to surrender and that he might choose another, more "honourable" option. He looked tired and worn, but remained stoic. The general assured me he would not take his own life. To do so would mean another man would have to be chosen to take the blame. The terms and arrangements for our surrender and placement into American custody had been delivered only a few hours earlier. General Yamashita had finally run out of options. He was ordered to command our forces to lay down all arms with immediate effect.

Despite this new turn of events we were still receiving reports of heavy fighting along the Cordillera Mountains. Some commanders were unable to accept surrender and felt duty bound to give their lives. It was the code of Bushido, the way of the warrior. To die with honour in the field of battle was a far nobler ending than being confronted with the humiliation of surrender and captivity. It was estimated that we had fifty thousand men still under arms, though nobody knew for sure, because our losses were horrendous. More than two hundred thousand men had fallen, their blood soaking the fetid ground. Fate had determined that we were not to join them. No warriors' ending would await us. In the morning at first light we were to take that long, humiliating walk down the mountainside and give ourselves up into enemy custody. The Americans had offered the general a dignified escort and a modicum of courtesy, befitting his rank. He refused outright and said he would lead what was left of his command and personally walk at the head of the column.

Dawn broke, and we gathered in the clearing outside the general's tented command area. A light breeze bore the smell of cordite from ongoing skirmishes. We were about thirty in number, each one of us making our best effort to find the conviction to make this final walk. The general emerged from his command post accompanied by his chief of staff, Lieutenant General Muto. We immediately stood to attention, only for the general himself to put us at ease. Military protocol was being relaxed in the final hours of our army. General Yamashita walked along the lines and thanked each of us for our brave service and loyalty to the Emperor. Finally we all turned to face the rising sun and cried, "*Tennoheika banzai*" three times. "Long live the Emperor." As the real sun rose, cresting the Luzon mountains, our rising-sun battle flags were lowered for the last time, folded with precise drill, and packed, ready to be handed over to our victors. Another symbolic act demanded by the Americans. Surrender means shame etched into the heart, now and forever. Then, without a word of command the general turned on his heels and started out on the descent down the mountainside to the village of Kiangon, where the American surrender committee would be waiting. We dutifully followed down the rocky tracks to captivity. If I were to be truly honest, I would have to admit to a feeling of relief that the doors of hell had been unlocked.

The route down the mountainside was lined with heavily armed American marines who kept their weapons trained on us at all times. It must have been a surreal moment for them, to be so close to the men who were their despised enemy. I expected a shot to ring out at any moment. I thought some war-shocked soldier would be unable to resist the opportunity to kill, to take some kind of revenge for the comrades they had lost. It was not to be. They just stared at us with cold, hate-filled eyes.

After a walk of about thirty minutes we reached a stony track where we could see the American surrender committee waiting ahead. The general raised his arm and we halted. A group of American staff officers walked towards us. Their commanding officer, Major Caposto, ordered all of us to be searched for any concealed weapons. Even the general was body searched. He was allowed to keep his sword at his side, but I noticed that an American officer with an unholstered sidearm stood in close attendance. Caposto ordered us forward, and we walked the short distance to a small wooden building that had once been a schoolhouse. Standing outside on the veranda was General Wainwright, the very same man who had suffered defeat at our hands earlier in the war. The two generals came face-to-face. Wainwright refused to shake the outstretched hand offered him. Our general was ushered into the schoolroom along with Muto. The rest of us were told to sit on the ground and place our hands on our heads. And wait to be processed. Several long trestle tables had been set up with officers seated and ready to take our details. I was dragged to my feet and led to a table by two American marines and roughly pushed into the seat opposite a young officer flanked by a translator. I was read my rights as a captured enemy combatant in accordance with the Geneva Conventions. When asked my name, I replied, "Kojima, Kaiishi." Rank, "Major." Unit, "staff officer, General Yamashita's command."

I was forced to stand. My hands were bound behind my back, and a young marine removed my military insignia and decorations from my tunic and placed them in a bag on which he wrote my name. I was pushed towards a jeep and roughly aided into the rear seat, where I sat between two marines. I was driven away, alone and separated from my fellow captives, who were being transported together on an army truck. I did not understand why.

I was driven along the battle-scarred tracks and roads. I stared out in sickened fascination. What I saw was the grim testimony of battle. There was war damage everywhere. At one point we slowed down to allow civilian trucks to pass by—open trucks piled with corpses. The local men had been given the grisly task of body collection. It was a shocking indictment of the total waste of life. The fighting had ended; so many men had died, and now in this moment of defeat came the realisation that life held no value. We passed large areas of burnt forest and still-smouldering buildings. The landscape was devastated. In the course of our retreat from Baguio to the mountains, our army had burnt buildings and torched crops. We did not want anything of value to be left behind for enemy use. Now, I felt shame for those actions. Mothers cradling infants watched passively from their wooden shacks. How the hell had they managed to survive this?

It took us about four hours to reach Manila. From time to time we had to slow to an almost walking pace to navigate the wreckage strewn all over the rutted tracks that passed as roads. Blackened buildings lined our route, and piles of rubble stood as testament to what had stood there before. When we finally arrived on the outskirts of the capital, the sight before my eyes was beyond my understanding. I stared with incredulity at the burnt-out shell of a once proud and fine city. It was unrecognisable from the place we had left almost six months earlier. At that time General Yamashita had decided to withdraw from Manila and concentrate our efforts farther north. I had stood alongside him as he gave the orders to Vice Admiral Okochi. It was specific. Okochi was to destroy port facilities, declare Manila an open city, and then arrange for his naval personnel to reinforce our numbers in the north. It was made plain that he was to avoid direct contact with the enemy. The general believed Manila to be of little value from a strategic point of view. There was no room for any misinterpretation of his directives. What had happened here was something truly evil.

The marine lieutenant riding in the front turned to me and spoke. I couldn't understand his words, but he spoke with hate, and his anger and loathing were plain to see. Street urchins, kids as young as three years of age, were all over the place. One little girl approached our jeep and gave the lieutenant a white flower. She saw me and ran away shouting, "Nippon, Nippon." Soon, about thirty kids were following us, chanting and running alongside, making faces and running away. We picked up speed and left them standing in the road, their chants and abuse fading in the distance.

We arrived at our destination—some kind of fortified compound—without ceremony. A Philippine guard came to check us. The lieutenant handed over some papers, and the guard signalled for a pair of massive iron gates to be opened. We drove into the wide dust bowl of Los Baños Internment Camp, where gangs of men, shackled around the ankles, shuffled along in the afternoon heat. Guards stood idly by, cradling shotguns, smoking, and shouting abuse at their captives. My American "escort" handed me over to two such guards, local men who looked more like bandits than officers. One of the guards pulled my head back and cursed into my ear. His fetid breath made me retch. They each grabbed me by my arms and dragged me to a corner of the compound. My arms were freed, and I was told to strip naked. Guards crowded around and made obscene gestures. I was kicked to the floor. Buckets of cold water were thrown over me. Then I was cuffed again and led away down a corridor inside the prison to a small bare stone cell. All the other cells I passed were empty. I was isolated. A stinking prison uniform of coarse brown material was thrown at me. The guards didn't say a word to me. The doors banged shut, and I was left in the gloom. The air was vile, thick with flies and mosquitoes. There was a thin rattan mat on the floor and a wooden bucket for toilet use. I put on the prison clothes and waited and waited and waited.

I spent the first three days of captivity in my cell, allowed out only to empty my toilet bucket. Food and drink was passed to me through a tiny opening at the bottom of the cell door. It was always the same: rice, taro roots, and banana. My guards were always thoughtful enough to mash cockroaches and lice into the mush. I drank water which always tasted of piss. My guards may have thought this a cruelty, but it wasn't much worse than what our troops had eaten to survive in the battlefield.

On the fourth day I was brought out of my cell for questioning. An American soldier of Japanese descent named Hamamoto had been ordered to act as a translator. A tall American in civilian clothes, who identified himself as Mr Robert Rushton, was also waiting for me in the small but brightly lit interrogation room. A plain wooden table separated us. He was polite and civil, well groomed and relaxed in his crumpled linen suit and necktie. He looked out of place in this wretched place. Rushton began by telling me a little about his background. He said he had been a newspaper man before the war. Being too old for the first draft, he had decided to serve his country in other areas. He told me he was grateful for the chance to help put right some of the damage done by the war. His demeanour changed as he fixed me with an icy stare and said that was what he was doing now and he wouldn't stop until justice had been served.

Rushton was placing his markers, setting out his position. I thought he was using me to get information about the general. I was wrong. Rushton told me that General Yamashita had been arraigned on various charges related to his conduct during his time as commander of the Japanese army in the Philippines. He would answer his charges along with his senior staff before a military court of law. Rushton studied me intently to gauge my reaction to this news. There was silence for a few minutes whilst Rushton shuffled the papers that were before him. "Major Kojima, I am a reasonable man trying his damnedest to do a very difficult job. You see, I have to find the information that will give us all some understanding of why we have all found ourselves in this place. I have some questions, and I know you have the answers to these questions." Hamamoto translated his words, and I nodded to show my understanding. Rushton was reading the papers. Without looking up he continued to speak. "I expect you to fully co-operate with our enquiry into the conduct of your army during the war here in the Philippines. In return for your co-operation I will personally enter a leniency plea on your behalf should you subsequently be charged with any crimes. Do you understand?" I said yes. Rushton signalled to the guard that the session was over, and I was led back to my cell, where I was left for seven or eight days without contact except with the guards when I had to clean my toilet.

I was brought back for interrogation. The loneliness and isolation had left me feeling weak and agitated. Rushton was waiting as before. Hamamoto sat beside him. Without looking up from the papers in front of him, Rushton's voice sounded harder than before. "Kojima, I have given you time to think and to reflect. I hope you are now ready to answer some of my questions." I said nothing, just stared blankly. "We have intelligence that you along with others are involved in a great crime and that you have played a part in a great conspiracy to steal and conceal valuable assets belonging to sovereign states." Rushton's opening statement had taken me completely by surprise. He continued in his relaxed monotone. "Major Kojima. Have you assisted or been ordered to assist in the concealment of any kind of sovereign assets? Do you have any knowledge of such a conspiracy?" Rushton probed further. "Did General Yamashita order the looting of Manila?"

It was an absurd question, and I showed my contempt by sneering back at the man opposite me. However, Rushton was tenacious. This was to be his tack for days on end. He constantly probed me about looting and about missing treasures, about conspiracies to steal and conceal valuable artworks and gold. I said nothing other than to explain my daily duties. I was the general's driver, and as a member of his command headquarters, served as a link between him and other officers in the field. I said time after time that I had never heard of any conspiracy to loot, steal, and/or hide valuable assets.

Day after day we continued this monotonous verbal sparring. Rushton rarely showed any signs of anger; he would get impatient at times but always managed to keep himself controlled. He constantly told me that this was his job and he would take it to its conclusion. He would try to catch me out. At times he would talk about the general. He kept me informed about his health and well-being. He told me that the case against him was being prepared and that he would soon face a military tribunal in Manila. Rushton informed me that it was yet undecided if I was to stand trial myself. He would talk often about how I could still help myself. Rushton said he knew that I had a lot of ground to cover but that he thought I was in self-denial and shock about my nation's capitulation. He constantly encouraged me to unburden myself, to give myself the feeling of release and free my soul from torment—to allow myself to be at one with the truth.

The truth. What is it? One man's truth is another man's lies. This was the end of war. Truth was what the victors wanted it to be. I didn't know whether Rushton was a man of faith, but he pursued me with almost religious zeal. He wanted my confession. After facing each other over this table for hours and days, Rushton was beginning to show signs of weariness. My stony silences and his constant probing were becoming the routine. I hoped he would start to think he was chasing shadows and accept my innocence. It was not to be.

It was on September 20 that the course of my interrogation changed. I was brought from my cell at first light. The guards had taken to waking me at every hour on the hour around the clock. I was weakening, and my nerves were jagged. Insufficient food and constant thirst were taking their toll on my body. I was dragged along to the room I had come to know and hate so well. Rushton sat opposite me as usual. In spite of the early hour he was well dressed. His pencil-thin moustache and immaculate greased-back black hair were a contrast to my own pathetic state. We were around the same age, and yet I must have looked twenty years older. I hadn't seen a mirror since the day of our surrender. How long ago had that been?

Rushton sat passively, but his silence spoke volumes. He was giving me a final chance to "unburden myself." I stared back mutely. The silence between us was oppressive, as if a black cloud hung above the table that separated us. Suddenly, Rushton brought his hand down heavily on the table. This uncharacteristic action jolted me to what little remained of my senses. "Kojima, it's time to introduce you to one of my colleagues. May God help you."

Rushton stared pityingly at me. After a minute or so the door opened, and in came a tall, wiry Filipino man. He had a hard face, with features that looked as if they had been carved from ebony.

His forearms were like twisted whipcord, all sinew and laced with muscle. He looked like a darker and more evil version of Rushton himself. Including the interpreter, there were now four of us crowded into that tiny hot, stale room. Rushton spoke. "Kojima, this is Mr Santa Romana of the Philippine National Council. He will be conducting your questioning from now on." Rushton stood and left the room. To my surprise Hamamoto followed him out.

I was left alone in the room with Romana. To my greater surprise, Romana had no need for the interpreter. He spoke Japanese. Not perfectly, but well enough for him to go about his business. Romana took Rushton's seat. His presence was threatening; he carried an aura of menace. He reached into his pocket and removed a small photograph, then pushed it across the table for me to study. It was a black-and-white picture of a handsome young man, smiling, dressed in a barong white dress shirt. "Major Kojima, this is a picture of my son, Raul. My lovely and only son, who was a brave young man and a soldier not unlike yourself. Raul was headstrong, as most young men his age are. He followed his instincts and his heart without question. He was noble and strong, and I was ever so proud of him. In 1942 he joined the Philippine Liberation Army and fought in the campaign to liberate our country from your illegal occupation of our homeland. Before the Americans came to help our cause, Raul and the men like him were the only thing that stood in your way as you sought to murder and enslave our people as you saw fit. Raul was a brave man and a good son."

Romana took the picture back and looked at it for a long moment. When he looked up at me, tears were welling in his eyes. He didn't care to hide his emotion. He took out another picture and passed it over. There was a close-up of a face, but not a face.

Where the eyes should have been were only black hollows. The nose had been cut off, and the ears were missing. Romana was staring at me. The tears had gone, and he had steeled himself to speak. His sadness was gone, replaced by raw hate and anger, and his mouth twitched as he fought to control his venomous snarl. "This is my Raul. This is how he was returned to me after being captured by your army. This is what you did to my son."

Cracked with hate, his voice rose to a devilish pitch. He slammed his fist down onto the table and leaned closer to me. His breath reeked of stale fish. "Let me tell you what you did to my boy, my only boy, my beautiful son. He was captured by one of your reconnaissance patrols along with nine other brave men. The patrol commander decided that five would live and five would die. They were divided into two groups. Raul was chosen to die. He was tied to a tree, as were the others. Their comrades were forced at gunpoint to kneel before them and watch the horror about to befall their friends. Each member of the patrol took turns taking a part of my son. First Raul's left ear was cut off, then his left eye was gouged out, and then his nose was sliced off with a bayonet knife. Then his right ear was cut off. He remained conscious. The screams and sobs from the mutilated and the spared alike filled the air. Then his tongue was cut out of his mouth. He may have been dead by this point. My God, I lie awake each night praying that he was released to our dear Lord well before. Finally, his clothes were shredded off his body and his penis was hacked off and stuffed into his blood-filled mouth and down his throat. It was the same for all the others chosen to die.

"Your army didn't want information. No, there was no chance for Raul. Your army wanted to send a message to our brave freedom fighters, to break our spirit and resolve. That was why their comrades had been spared. They had to deliver that message.

Each of them had to carry one of their mutilated comrade's broken bodies back and bear witness to what had happened. My Raul was used as a message. He was carried back to the arms of his family by his comrade in arms, a young man by the name of Hector Ramirez. I was told everything that happened that day, and believe me, there is no room for doubt. Oh, one more thing. Hector and his 'spared' comrades had their fingers cut off before being released. That was to make sure they couldn't continue the fight. You can't fire a gun without fingers. Hector is now my junior staff officer and is looking forward to meeting you." Romana stood up, kissed the photograph, and made a show of carefully replacing it into his wallet. He then left the room without as much as another word. The guards returned, and I was roughly dragged to my feet and thrown into my cell.

I was left to myself, numbed by the images I had seen in those two pictures. Romana's raw emotion had seared itself into my consciousness. I closed my eyes, but the mutilated face of a once handsome young man would not leave me. Santa Romana had a vendetta to carry out, and I was his quarry. I knew nothing would stop him, that he wouldn't let anything stand in his path. I wasn't left alone for long, maybe twenty minutes. Just long enough for those brutal images to be seared deeply into my mind. The guards rattled open my cell door, kicked me to my feet, and manhandled me back to that dreaded interrogation room. So it was with unfettered fear that I came face-to-face with Romana for the second time. Here was a man who had lost all that he held precious in the most foul, brutal, and heinous of ways. He despised me and what I represented. He had a personal agenda that would not be denied.

There was no small talk. Romana came straight to the point. "Kojima, I have it on excellent authority that you conspired with others to conceal the whereabouts of stolen items of great value. Now, it is simple. I want you to tell me where those things are hidden, and I want to know who was involved in the operation to conceal them. Do you understand?" I said nothing.

Romana stood and shouted, "Guards." Two men in plain-clothes came and dragged me out of the room and into another room across the corridor. My arms were roughly bound to my sides by tight leather straps. My legs were bound, too, around the thighs and at the ankles. I was forced to lie on a low narrow wooden table that tilted my head back. Romana stood over me and placed a rough towel over my face. I lay there motionless for about five minutes. Then I felt a stream of cold water being poured over my face. The steady flow of water started to fill my nose. It was impossible to breathe. I was coughing, retching and choking all in one. As my body filled with water, I could feel myself slipping away. It went on and on. I could no longer find the will to stay alive. I was giving way to the water. I had a sense of slipping under the water. I didn't feel pain. I embraced its sweet release. Then I died. I was brought back to life by Romana, who sat on my stomach and bounced on my body. As he pressed me, I vomited back water. It was streaming out of my mouth, nose, and ears. The pressure in my head was unbearable. I was tipped off the table and left on the floor writhing in convulsions, gasping for air, unable to fill my lungs.

They picked me up and put me back on the table. Romana put another towel over my face and started the water torture again. This time I was unable to keep myself together. I let myself go and prayed for death. To die now would be a most merciful thing. Romana turned out to be a good judge of a man's mortality and stopped the water flow as I was meeting the gods. Again he put pressure on my chest and stomach. The agonizing cycle of drowning and recovery was repeated over and over. I died five times and was brought back from the dead each time by the "black angel," Santa Romana.

They didn't bother to move me, just left me where I lay. They removed my restraints and left me semi-conscious on the floor, lying in pools of watery vomit. I prayed that my resolve wouldn't desert me. My only hope was that Romana would accept that I didn't know anything. I was left alone for the rest of the day, water leaking out of every orifice of my body. As dusk fell, the bare light bulb high up on the ceiling started to flicker on and off. It was constant and added to my misery. Sleep of any kind was not possible. Some kind of machine was put outside my door that made high-pitched screeching noises. It went on like this for more than a day.

Finally, two guards came into the room, followed by Romana. I was totally at their mercy, my will to resist gone—sleep deprived, starving, and thirsty. Any sound at all made me shake and jump. My nerves were destroyed. The guards forced me up and into a seated position with my back against the wall. They bound my legs and arms as before. I could hear the sound of running water. Romana threw a towel down in front of me. "Kojima, are you ready to tell me what I need to know?" I said nothing, hardly able to comprehend his words. "Very well. I won't waste time, I'm a busy man. I had hoped you would be a bit more forthcoming by now." I felt beyond struggle. I prayed for my death. The guards blindfolded me, and I was forced onto the table and my head tilted back. I waited for the downpour that would bring agony and eventually sweet release. I felt something being fixed to my chest, like a cold, tight belt. Some kind of clips were fixed to my fingers. My pants were pulled down, and clips were attached to my testicles. The pain was excruciating. I was left alone in that position for more than ten minutes—left to dread what would surely come. Then it started. First, a slow trickle of water was poured over me, slowly building up to a heavy flow. I gasped for air, only to find water. It was beyond me; I gave up and waited to die. But the water stopped, leaving me on the edge of death. Then a massive burst of pain sent an involuntary scream from the deep depths of my soul. Water bilged out from my mouth and nose, and I could smell burning. Then again came the agonising jolts of unbearable pain. I felt somebody was peeling my spine away. Every fibre of my body was pulverised. I was "shocked" four or five times, and then I lost all feelings.

I came round in my cell. I was naked and shaking uncontrollably. It was impossible to tell how long I had been lying there in a pool of vomit, piss, and liquid shit. I dragged my body over to the wall and leaned against it and cried great, sobbing tears. The guards came in and swilled me with buckets of cold water. Again I was left alone. After a few hours the door was opened and the usual stinking brown prison clothes were thrown at me. I was ordered to dress, but I couldn't move. I had lost control of my body. The guards finally lost patience and dragged the clothes onto my body, roughly pulling my hair and twisting my arms and legs as though I were a rag doll. They hoisted me upright and, with my legs trailing, dragged me back to Romana's room.

Romana was sitting there waiting for me, along with another man, who placed a writing ledger on the table. Romana looked at me impassively and asked me if I was ready. I looked at him and just nodded. "Very well," Romana said. "Let's begin."

He wanted to know everything from the very beginning. I had been on the general's staff since our deployment in 1944. I told him of my duties and of the relationship I had with General Yamashita. Most of it I had already told to Rushton. Romana was "softening" me up. He was getting me used to talking after so many weeks of being within myself. Once I started talking, I felt as if I couldn't stop. Seeing another human being encouraged by my words felt liberating. Rushton was right: It did feel good to finally unburden my soul. The other man took notes. Romana asked questions and listened. He directed me if he thought I was being evasive. I kept telling him that my duties were primarily logistical and administrative, but Romana was interested in my personal relationship with the general. He asked if the general had ever confided in me about military or personal matters. I said I hoped I had gained his trust and that occasionally the general would rage at his orders from Imperial Military Headquarters and ask what I thought of them. I wouldn't go as far as to say he valued my opinion, but he never discouraged me from expressing myself. I said I thought we had a good relationship with respect to the obvious difference in our ranks. As a member of the general's command, I did my duty as I was ordered.

Romana just nodded passively. "Of course you did, but that is not why you are sitting across from me now. Your daily regimen is of little interest to me other than to fill in the details. It is those 'details' that I want from you." It was plain that Romana was losing patience with my meanderings. "Intelligence has come into our possession that concerns matters of a serious criminal nature. It is my belief that your 'beloved' general and, by implication, you, were involved in an elaborate conspiracy to conceal articles of value that were looted from occupied territories by your army. We know that a great deal of those looted assets remain here in the Philippine Islands. It is my duty to recover them and return them to their sovereign owners." There was silence between us for a few minutes. "Kojima, we can play around like this or I can go back to giving your memory a little help, and believe me, I will make you beg to tell me."

I had lost all will to resist. Romana had broken me. The words came out of my mouth almost without my thinking. "There was a meeting."

Romana leaned back in his chair, put his hands behind his head, and stretched. He had won the battle of wills and was closing in on his prize. "Kojima, now it is time to tell. Leave nothing out, for I will be the judge of what is important." I told him of a meeting that had taken place more than a year earlier whilst we were still headquartered in Manila, one that resulted in my duties being changed. General Yamashita was accustomed to receiving military delegations and officials from Tokyo. One day in September 1944, his chief of staff, Lieutenant General Muto, informed me that a delegation from Tokyo was to arrive at command headquarters that very evening. They were to meet with the general under the tightest secrecy and security. The details of this secret meeting and the agenda were highly classified. I was not told whom to expect. Muto told me to clear the command headquarters of all immediate personnel and ordered me to stand by on security detail. Earlier that same day the general had mentioned this meeting to me. He had expressed hope that this delegation would bring him news about resupply and reinforcements for the imminent battles that lay ahead. The general was constantly demanding that Tokyo take direct action, but so far his requests had gone unheeded. He was of the belief that the evening's delegation was from Imperial Headquarters.

The "guests" arrived later than expected, maybe about eight o'clock. General Yamashita stayed in his study. Muto told me to join him in the foyer to welcome our visitors. Two staff cars drew up to the main entrance, and out stepped the delegation. Travelling in the first car was an elderly gentleman around seventy years old; he was accompanied by a shaved-headed man of stout formality, possibly army but wearing civilian clothes. I didn't know or recognise either man. I wasn't introduced, and they passed me by without any formalities at all. The second car was carrying four people, including the driver, who got out first to open the rear door. Then a man in military uniform got out and stood to rigid attention, followed by the last two men. Both Muto and I were left speechless. Somehow the guests looked familiar, and yet I couldn't name them. They were wearing a kind of ceremonial court uniform of a type I had never seen before. I have to say that they carried themselves with that certain bearing of people born into the highest of orders, yet they looked bewildered to find themselves in such a place. They looked slightly lost and waited for the uniformed officer to lead the way. "Your Excellencies," he said, and escorted them into the general's office. The driver followed from the rear. He walked backwards, checking back from time to time to watch his step. It was obvious that he was a bodyguard of some sort.

Muto and I were left to take up the rear. As we were about to enter, the driver held out a hand and said, "With the greatest of respect, sirs, the meeting and dinner this evening are to be held with the minimum of personnel." Meaning we were to be totally excluded. Muto's indignation was plain for all to see. Being told what to do by a mere driver was more than he could bear. He left without words and went to his study. The uniformed officer came out of the office and talked with the guard. They asked for chairs to be placed on either side of the door and remained there the entire time. The four guests and the general were "in conference" for around five hours. I went to my own office on the second floor and waited in case my assistance was required. The residence was unusually quiet; I had dismissed the staff as instructed.

The evening was surreal. From my window above, I overheard the arrangements being made for the delegation's departure. I heard the name Hamazaki spoken. The two "distinguished" guests left first. I watched them from my window as they took their leave, quietly slipping into the night with their guards. The elderly man, whom I took to be Hamazaki, left alone in the second car. That left the shaved-headed man still in conference with General Yamashita. I went downstairs to enquire if the general required any form of assistance before retiring. I was surprised to see him still talking with the remaining guest. Upon seeing me, the general called me into the office. "Major Kojima, this is Lieutenant Colonel Nishii, of the Kempeitai. He will be staying with us for some time. He will require a great deal of assistance, and I have told him that you are a fine administrator. You will help him with whatever he requires."

Nishii looked at me with a contemptuous stare. "Major Kojima, I thank you in advance for your help. I believe you and I will co-operate together to great effect." Nishii bowed slightly, the general dismissed me, and I retired for the evening.

The next morning staff headquarters had resumed its normal operational routine. Army "runner" vehicles were constantly coming and going, bringing updates from the field. General Yamashita was busy in tactical briefings with his field commanders. The American invasion was imminent, and the tension was beginning to show. It was around midmorning when I was called to Nishii's quarters. He had commandeered two rooms at the back of the building. Nishii greeted me with a sullen and very cold manner. He told me to sit down in the chair before his desk, where he was looking through a file. "Major Kojima, you have a fine record of dedicated service, and General Yamashita speaks very highly of you. He informs me that your loyalty is unquestioned. Is that true?" I looked him straight in the eye and said my loyalty to the Emperor and my army were absolute. Nishii sighed and looked down at the papers, and then pushed them aside. "Kojima, you have been chosen to assist me in a matter of great national importance that will have a positive bearing on the future of our nation. Now is the time to prove your loyalty. This is what is required of you. I need you to identify the most loyal, brave, and trustworthy officers in the Fourteenth Area Army. These officers will be pulled from regular combat duty and reassigned to special operations under my command. In total I require five teams of men. Each team is to be led by a captain, with a lieutenant as second in command. They will lead a team of ten men selected from the ranks."

So, in total he needed five teams of twelve men. "I want you to select those men and arrange for them to be transferred here for tasking on these dates." He passed over a sheet of paper. The first group was set to be tasked in November, two months from receiving my orders. Each group was to report at two-month intervals. Nishii was studying my reaction. I asked him if I would need the general's sanction to re-deploy men from the field. Nishii told me not to talk with the general about these matters. He would deal with any issues that concerned the general personally. I was told to start selecting the men for Nishii's task without delay. All my other duties were to be suspended until my orders had been accomplished. I wasn't told what their operational duties would be, but I knew it was a highly classified operation.

Nishii then made it plain and personal. "Kojima, this operation must succeed. The very future of our nation will depend on its success. I take it as read that you will have realised on whose authority this operation has been sanctioned. The very presence of those esteemed visitors we had the honour of 'entertaining' last evening would confirm that this goes higher than General Yamashita. The mission has the full support of Tokyo." Nishii let this information hang in the air for a few moments and then continued. "You will speak of operational matters and communications between the two of us to no other man. That includes the general. Indiscretion of any kind will be seen as a traitorous act punishable by death." Nishii once more looked at me with his cold stare. His dark eyes bore into me, defying me to betray any sign of insubordination. I said I understood. Nishii then went back to the file on the desk. "You have a wife and young daughter back home, do you not? It would be regrettable for their sakes to have to inform them that you had died a traitor. The life of a traitor's family can be particularly harsh." I felt my anger boil. I had to keep control of myself as Nishii kept his unblinking stare burning into my thoughts. I said again that my loyalty was true. As I sat there, I realised that I too had been singled out for this operation. Nishii had researched my background. He was a cold and cruel man bereft of heart and devoid of compassion.

I had been talking for a long time, and Romana had been a good listener. His aide had recorded all of what I had said. I told Romana that I was unaware of Nishii's objectives and wasn't allowed any knowledge of the operational deployment or specifics regarding the mission. My duty was to supply Nishii with the manpower he needed and to make sure they were ready for deployment on those specified dates. Romana looked at me with the same disbelief he had maintained throughout my torture and questioning. I told him I had resisted telling him this information during our earlier "sessions" out of fear for my family's safety.

Romana became angry and stood up and put his face close to mine. "Your fucking family! Don't make me sick. I am sick of your fucking story. Tell me what I want to know or I will fucking personally arrange to kill your family. Just as you killed mine." He pulled my hair back and gave me an almighty slap across the face. My nose streamed with blood, but Romana wasn't finished. "You speak of loyalty and devotion. Who is loyal to you, Kojima? The war is over. You lost. This Nishii cannot do anything now. I can, and I will if you don't tell me. This is your last fucking chance to talk. We are going out now, and I will be back in a short while. When I come back, you will tell me. Do you understand?" He and the writer left the room, leaving me alone to think. Romana was right. The war was over. Perhaps Nishii was dead. I hoped with all my heart that it was so. I kept asking myself the same question over and over. How did Rushton and Romana know about me? I could only think that some of the men I had recruited for Nishii had been captured and had talked. I wasn't in any shape to offer any further resistance. I waited for Romana to return. I had lost all fear. My hopes of ever being reunited with my family were gone. I knew I would never get out of this country alive.

Romana came back alone. He sat down, folded his arms, and stared at me in silence—a silence that spoke volumes. I broke down and finally, in a fit of shameful tears, told Romana the rest.

It must have been around the end of November when the first group of men assembled at command headquarters. They had been chosen by me personally and given a final vetting by Nishii himself. He took command of the men. He took the two officers into his private quarters for some kind of deployment briefing. I wasn't required to attend. Nishii had requested only light equipment, standard infantry kit, and the latest pathfinding devices.

Combat had yet to break out, so I guess Nishii wasn't concerned about enemy contact. A troop truck was ordered, and Nishii and his men set off into the night. I watched them drive away. I had tried to avoid all thoughts about what was in store for those men. I couldn't help thinking they were being used like pieces in a game, a game of death.

Nishii returned alone to headquarters about five days later. I don't know how he got back. He just seemed to reappear, like a spectre. The same procedure was followed again and again, except we had now moved on to Baguio as fighting had broken out around the area of Leyte and the Americans were pressing their superiority. We were now farther into the field and on higher ground, but Nishii carried on his tasks regardless. It was the final tasking that was giving Nishii some kind of problem. Two days before the men arrived for briefing, Nishii had to urgently deal with some matter. He was agitated, and prone to flying into abusive and violent rages. One morning he ordered me to get a jeep and drive him out to some location. We were now stationed in Bangbang, our final holdout up in the mountains. Nishii navigated and gave me directions from a field map he was holding. Driving was proving difficult. Constant heavy rains had quelled some of the fighting, but we could hear artillery and mortar fire in the distance. Now and again an explosive flash would light up the grim grey sky. Nishii told me to stop the jeep and said we would tackle the last mile on foot. It turned out to be about an hour's trek. Nishii reminded me of the loyalty I had pledged and talked of unswerving devotion to duty. He was compromising himself by allowing me into his plans. I reassured him that my devotion to any cause that would help our nation was sound.

We eventually came to a small clearing where trees had been removed. A group of workmen—all bare-chested local men—were moving rafts of earth and rocks. They were overseen by armed guards, our men. A large winch and pulley system was set up over an opening. Chains were clattering and straining to move something from below the ground. Nishii ordered me to stay put whilst he went over to one of the guards. The guard pointed him to a group of men gathered over what seemed to be plans of some sort. I heard Nishii call out a name—Saito, I think. This Saito and Nishii went down the hole in the ground and were there for around an hour. Eventually they emerged. Nishii seemed satisfied with what he had seen. He called for me, and we set off back to Bangbang. Neither of us said a word on the return journey.

Romana seemed satisfied with my answer. I silently prayed he would let me be. I desperately wanted to close my eyes. "Kojima, tomorrow you will take me to this place. I take it you can remember?" I said I thought so, but that it might be with some difficulty. I saw Romana smile for the first time. "Major Kojima, I suggest you go and have a long rest, for tomorrow you will remember—oh yes, you will." He leaned back in his chair, hands clasped behind his head. His smile suddenly disappeared, and the look of pure evil was back. He called for the guards, and I was taken back to my cell. My rattan mat had been returned, and a pitcher of cold water had been left on the floor. After a few moments the guard opened the little flap at the bottom of the iron door and pushed in some food. It was the usual rice and taro served on a banana leaf, but I was also given a bar of chocolate. Was this my reward for turning traitor? I ate like a ravenous dog but vomited back most of the food into the toilet bucket. My stomach had gotten used to being empty. Real food was hard to take. I collapsed onto the mat and watched a gecko scuttle up the wall, casually picking insects off with a lightning flick of its tongue. Romana was a gecko and I just a tiny fly.

25

I stared at the ceiling and wondered what would happen to me after the next day. Would I be charged and found guilty and executed? Rushton had offered to plead for leniency for me. Would that still stand? Thoughts and fears crashed around my head. I couldn't sleep, and sweated and shivered the night away.

As first light was starting to make its way through the tiny barred window, I heard a commotion outside in the corridor. My door was flung open, and Romana stood there in military fatigues and Chinese-style sunglasses. He threw an old army uniform down at me and told me to hurry and get dressed. He stared at me as I did my best to get my aching limbs into the clothes. A guard came in with breakfast. It was some kind of sweet cake and cold tea. I had drunk only water since my surrender; the tea tasted bitter and burnt my throat.

Romana was in a hurry to get going. He called the guard to handcuff me, and my arms were pinned tightly behind my back. I was pushed forward down the corridor and out into the prison yard, where two jeeps were waiting. The rear jeep was full of local soldiers who looked more like bandits with their long hair and moustaches. Romana got into the lead jeep next to the driver, and I was put between two guards in the rear seat. It was the first time I had been outside in more than three months, and the early morning light singed my eyes. We waited in the yard, engines powered, ready to move. Everyone was on edge and waiting for the order to set off. A door opened, and a line of prisoners shuffled out, chained together at the ankles and waist. My heart lurched. There in the middle of the line was the general. My general. Chained and manacled like a petty criminal. My entire being wanted to cry out to him. I was unable to control my emotions. I tried to stand, but the guards forced me down into my seat. My tears started to flow. I stared at the general and shouted, "Banzai, Tennoheika, banzai!"

"Long live the Emperor." The general looked over at me for a few seconds, then hung his head.

I heard laughing. It was Romana. He turned round in his seat. "Banzai, banzai, banzai. In our language we say '*mabuhay*.' It has a similar meaning, except most Filipinos translate it as 'stay alive.' Kojima, your general was tried in court and found guilty. He is to die in this prison by hanging, along with his criminal officers." Romana removed his sunglasses and looked me in the eye. "Mabuhay, General Yamashita. I think not." Romana ordered the driver to go, and we sped off, leaving the general choking in the trail of dust behind us.

The route was the same as I had taken after surrender except in reverse. Six months earlier, we had driven through hell. Now the madness had given way to sanity. The debris of war had been pushed aside, and the business of daily survival took precedence. There were far more people and vehicles about the place. Chaos ruled. The American army had taken a step back to let the local people enjoy their new freedom. Nobody bothered to pay us a second glance as we made swift progress over the dirt tracks and potholed roads.

It took all of two hours to reach Bangbang, and from there I had to play my part and show the route I had taken with Nishii six months earlier. It was surprising how little I could remember from that rain-sodden day. By luck or by divine chance, I found the track and we found ourselves at the point where Nishii had ordered me to stop the jeep and walk. It was near impossible to recall the direction. I was torn between two paths, finally choosing the one that led into the thickest undergrowth. Romana ordered two of his men to take "point," and the rest were staggered along the track evenly. Romana walked at my shoulder, prompting me all the time with questions and threats. It was difficult to keep my balance with my hands cuffed behind my back. I stumbled countless times, only to be picked up by a guard and pushed forward. It took around an hour to reach our destination, the same place Nishii had directed me to.

Only it wasn't the same place anymore. It was completely different. It was like being in a familiar place and then again being totally lost in that place. I was certain this was the same clearing. Looking up at the mountains and taking in the landscape only made me more convinced.

I told Romana this was the place but that it had changed. He looked at me as if I had lost my mind. I waited for his anger to come down on me, but he was very calm and calculated. "Kojima, where was the hole in the ground?" I pointed to the huge banyan tree that dominated the area. It looked like it had stood there for hundreds of years. "Are you sure?" It was impossible to be sure, and yet I was as sure as uncertainty allowed. It was surreal. Romana called his guards over and told them to handcuff me to a tree. Then he ordered them to spread out and do a search of the area and the perimeter. Romana himself went over to the tree. I watched him as he examined the leaves, picking some and squeezing them in his fist. He shook a branch, and a hail of leaves fluttered to the ground. He went over to a different banyan tree and shook it vigorously, but not even a single leaf fell to the ground. Romana called over one of his men, and they talked for a few minutes. The guard pointed in my direction. It was plain to see that they were talking about me. The guard signalled for me to be untied, and I was marched back along the track we had come. Romana didn't follow.

I was "escorted" by three guards. It was a relief to see the jeeps. My body was doubling up with stomach pain and muscle cramps. I was standing, waiting to get into the jeep, when my feet were kicked from under me with one nasty, violent movement. I was felled, and gripped from behind. A blindfold was tied tightly around my eyes, and I was forced into a kneeling position. I knew this was the end of my time here. I wasn't afraid. I had died inside a long time ago.

The guards were shouting in Tagalog. One of them had his face close to mine. I could smell his stale tobacco breath. My hair was pulled back, and a pistol barrel was pushed into my mouth. I heard a voice talking softly in my ear. "You killed my family. You raped my wife and burnt my house. You cut my best friend to pieces in front of my eyes. Now it is your turn to die."

I raised my head to speak. The gun was pulled out of my mouth, taking a tooth with it. I strained to find the words. "Hector. 'Mabuhay.'" Then blows and boots rained down on me, and finally a mighty crack on the jaw sent me into oblivion.

I came around in my cell. It was impossible to say how long I had been out or how I had come to be back here at Los Baños. My whole body ached, and breathing caused agonising pains. I had broken ribs on my left side, and my neck couldn't support my head. I could only lie down and wait. I was too weak to even call out for help. Why hadn't they killed me there? It would have been a mercy. How long would this go on? Beyond all hope and rational thought, death was a thing of beauty to be welcomed with open arms. Yet its sweet embrace was still denying me. I tried to stop breathing, willing myself to die. There was no release for me. After a few hours—or maybe days, it was impossible to tell—a medical orderly came into the cell and treated my body. I was cleaned, bandaged, and given some kind of medicine on a spoon that made me drowsy. I was in and out of life for a few days. I was unable to eat or drink unaided, but someone poured water down me from time to time.

Time passed slowly, and I spent every minute of it in my cell, never once let out. My body was recovering from the almighty beating I had taken. The pain had started to ease, but standing was still impossible. I was leaning against the wall of my cell. A shadow of the man I once was. My wife used to tease me about how portly I was. Now my arms were the same thickness from wrist to shoulder, and my legs were loose skin on bone. I had only three teeth left.

Then one day the door was opened, and to my surprise Rushton came in, accompanied by a young uniformed officer. I barely had the strength to look up. Rushton was visibly shocked by what he saw. But he went about his business. The uniformed officer translated. Rushton read from a piece of paper he was holding. "Major Kojima of the former Imperial Japanese Army: You are charged with failing to discharge your duties as a combatant in an appropriate manner. That you did willingly, between the dates of October 2, 1944, and September 2, 1945, steal and conceal precious artefacts and other items. That you did also conspire with person or persons unknown in the theft and concealment of said items. You are also charged with participation, along with other persons, in that you did commit high crimes against the sovereign peoples of the Philippines and the United States of America."

Rushton waited for the interpreter to finish and then said, "Do you understand the charges laid against you?" I said nothing. Speech of any kind was too painful. Rushton wrote something on his paper and dropped it down to me. "Sign there or make your mark." I couldn't hold a pen, so the interpreter roughly took my hand and rolled my thumb on an ink pad and then pressed it onto the paper. Rushton looked down at the paper and then at me. "Kojima, you have to a certain extent co-operated with our enquiries into crimes committed by your forces during the illegal occupation of the Philippine Islands, and in recognition of your co-operation I will ask for some leniency to be shown. However, I have to say that you have been charged with the most serious of crimes. The maximum penalty for such crimes is death by hanging. There is no guarantee that leniency will be shown to you. Your trial date is set for February 18, 1946. You will be assigned an officer from the Allied Military Command who will represent you and act as your defence counsel. You are also allowed to act on your own behalf if you so wish."

I stayed slumped against the wall, beyond caring what was to happen to me. Rushton's voice and the interpreter's words just bounced off the cell's walls like a distant echo. "Your trial date is set for four weeks from today. You may still be able to help yourself. If you have any other information on the whereabouts of other stolen property, now is the time to offer that information. Kojima, I ask you for the final time to do what is right. Your loyalty may be something to be admired, but who is loyal to you? At least give yourself the chance to be with your family again."

Rushton waited for my response. When none was forthcoming, he gave a sigh of resignation. "Kojima, you and I are finished. We will not talk anymore. If you have a change of heart and decide to talk, then and only then I am willing to listen, and I promise to do what I can to help you." Rushton and the interpreter left. The cell door was banged shut, and the outside bolts and keys locked out my final chance of leniency.

My trial date was set for February 18, 1946, as Rushton had said. It was four weeks away, and I remained in solitary confinement for the entire period. I never had any visits from my defence counsel. I wasn't given any pens and paper to write any form of defence. Neither Rushton nor Romana came to question me. Food was passed to me through the door hatch, and I was allowed to clean my toilet each morning. That was my life each and every day in the run-up to my trial. I began to think I had been forgotten. I was an insignificant player in a big game. Rushton's offer of leniency was of no use to me: I didn't know the locations of any other sites.

I lost all track of time, each day merging into the next. I marked the passing of each day by watching the shadow cast by the sun as it moved slowly past the tiny barred window.

After what seemed like an eternity of waiting, the day of my trial came. Without any notice I was led out of my cell to the washing rooms and there told to clean myself. A barber was called to shave my head and beard. I was kept under armed guard the whole time. My body still ached, but I could move slowly. My old uniform, which had been washed but still stank, was given back to me, and I was told that I would stand trial wearing my combatant uniform minus any insignia. The tunic that I was once so proud of was now many sizes too big and hung off my bony shoulders like a cape. The guard gave me some twine to make a belt.

After I was dressed, I was placed in restraints, chained around the ankles and feet, and marched, barefoot, outside to a waiting truck that would transport me on the short drive to the Manila Supreme Court, where I was to stand trial. Nobody spoke to me at all. On arrival at the courthouse I was put in a holding cell and waited to be called up. After a few moments an American officer, who identified himself as Captain Andrews, came to the cell. He looked very young, maybe even young enough to be my son, and was accompanied by the same nameless interpreter Rushton had used. Andrews said he was my appointed defence counsel and asked if I would require his services. He pointed out that I was free to conduct my own defence if I so wished. I accepted Andrews as my counsel. He called for a table and some chairs to be brought into the cell, and we stood in awkward silence while some work-men set them up. After we were seated, Andrews took out some papers and briefly shuffled them about. He looked up and asked me if he had my consent to enter a guilty plea on my behalf, explaining that the judge would be more likely to be merciful if I showed willingness to accept my "crimes." If I agreed, Andrews said, he would then plead for some leniency.

He studied the papers once more and without looking up said the evidence against me was irrefutable and that he strongly advised me to plead guilty. I looked him straight in the eye and said I was ready to accept whatever fate the court had determined for me. Andrews said nothing had been determined and that the court gave all men a fair and equal chance to prove their inno-cence. If that is so, I said, then why should I plead guilty? Andrews said the case against me was strong, and urged me to follow his advice. He avoided eye contact with me as he said, "All I can do is try to save your life," to which I replied, "I don't have a life worth saving." Andrews took this as my consent to plead guilty, and once the translator had finished his words, I had given myself into the hands of the court.

An American military police officer banged on the door and shouted "Time." We were led out and up a narrow stone staircase that led straight into the courtroom. I was put into a raised wooden dock flanked on either side by two of the largest men I had ever seen. My chains were removed, and I took in my surroundings. The room was smaller than I had expected. I was before three American uniformed officers, one of whom was a general, and a Filipino man dressed in civilian clothes. None of them were for-mally identified to me. Captain Andrews and his interpreter sat lower down in front of me. To their right was a small Filipino man who stood and read the charges. The general looked down at his papers and without looking up asked how I pleaded. Andrews stood up and identified himself for the court and said he had my permission to act as my defence representative and that, acting in that capacity, had my consent to enter a plea of guilty. The general looked at me for the first time and asked, "Is that so?"

I said yes it was. The general then said, "Enter for the record that Major Kojima has pleaded guilty to all the charges laid against him and that his guilty plea has been made of his own volition." There was a brief pause whilst the tribunal conferred. One of the other officers, sitting next to the general, said, "Captain Andrews, let us be clear: The charges against this prisoner are most serious and carry a maximum penalty of execution by hanging. Does the prisoner understand this?"

Andrews replied, "He does fully understand, sir."

The officer continued. "Very well. In light of the evidence placed before this tribunal and the prisoner's plea, we will adjourn for a short recess. The prisoner is to be taken back down and brought back when summoned for sentencing. Take him away." I was chained again and led back down to the holding cell. The guards pushed me inside, and the door was banged shut behind me. I wasn't alone: Seated and waiting for me was Santa Romana.

He told me to sit opposite him. The guards hadn't removed my chains. I shuffled forward and slumped down onto the chair. Romana was smoking a long thin cigar; he blew smoke into my face. "Kojima, in a few minutes the guards will take you back up and the judge will find you guilty and sentence you to die by hanging, a punishment you deserve." I said nothing, because what was there to be said?

There was a large envelope on the table, and Romana was drumming his fingers on it. His stare burnt deep into me. The cavernous silence between us went on for a few minutes. Then

Romana opened the envelope and took out some photographs. "You should see these pictures. They were taken at the site you led us to—the very same place where you and your friends tried to hide your dirty secrets. It took us some time to reach, but we got there. We found your little hell on earth." He passed over a picture for me to study. Rows of skeletal, decomposing corpses were laid out side by side alongside a great mound of earth. Workers stood around with cloths tied over their noses and mouths. Romana laid out more pictures on the table. Close-ups of rotting faces with absurdly big teeth. Skulls with full heads of hair staring back out of the pictures. "Do you recognise any of them?" Romana asked me with venomous contempt. The emotion was starting to rise in his voice. "Kojima, they are your friends. You chose them personally. You sent them down that hole to their death. You are the one who chose them to die."

I looked at the pictures, not fully able to believe what I was looking at. Romana shouted for the guard. The door opened, and the guard came in carrying a small cloth bag, which he handed to Romana. After the guard left, Romana tipped the contents out onto the table. A pile of identification tags. Japanese Imperial Army tags all tangled up together. "These were taken from the necks of the men in these pictures. Look at the names; these are the men you selected for your mission, men betrayed by you. Gassed and shot to death." Romana was banging his fist down onto the table. I looked at the tags and read the names, twelve brave men I had chosen for Nishii's special mission. Their names, their infantry regiments. Shame burnt my eyes like hot needles. I too had been betrayed. Tears started to roll down my face as I held the tags.

I looked at Romana. "No, no, no. It was Nishii." I put my head down. "I am ready to die. I want to die."

Romana stood up and walked around the table. "You talk about this Nishii man. Who is he? I don't think there is such a man. It is all lies, Kojima. You are Nishii. You sent those men to die. What did they die for? For this?" Romana showed me another picture. It was a pile of blocks, each about the size of a brick. "Gold, Kojima, gold—your gold."

"No!" I shouted out.

"Kojima, I understand men. I understand war too. So too does your judge. He has seen these pictures, and as God is my witness, he will send you to your death without thinking twice. I, on the other hand, take a different view. War takes over our minds and corrupts our souls. I understand. In war we have to become a different man. We have to get through, we have to survive." I felt a hand on my shoulder, and Romana got closer to my ear and said, "Tell me what I need to know, and you have my word that you will not die. Give me something, and I will give you something in return. If you talk now, I will get your trial suspended and I can arrange for charges to be dropped and for your repatriation to your country. You owe this to your wife and daughter. Give them the chance to see you again. I need something from you, and I need it now."

Romana took out some papers from his envelope. He passed them over for me to study. The first page was titled "Request for Suspension of Trial" and stamped "secret"; it had been translated into Japanese and set out the special conditions that need to be applied. I looked at Romana and told him I didn't know where the other sites were. It was the truth. I told him that as the gods bore witness to my fate, I didn't know. I could face my executioner with a clear conscience. Yes, I chose those men, although at the time I didn't know for what purpose. I had been ordered to do so.

It was my duty, and I had carried it out. For what had happened to those men I too deserved to die, and I was ready.

Romana looked resigned to finally accepting that I was telling the truth. He shook his head slowly and started to put the papers back into the envelope. Before I had time to regret my words, I said, "Stop. There is something you will want to know. I don't know if it is of any value to your investigation, but if it offers me a chance of salvation, then I will sign your papers." Romana considered my words and then without question took the papers out again and gave me a pen. With some difficulty, as my hands were still bound, I signed in three places. Romana called for a guard and passed him the papers, and told him to take them straight to the general presiding over my trial. Then he told me to tell him what I knew.

It was two months before our surrender. We were camped high in the mountains of Bangbang. The fighting was closing in. Enemy mortar fire was becoming more accurate by the day, and we were in constant danger. With all that was going on, I was surprised to find Mr Hamazaki once more back at our headquarters. He must have undertaken his journey at tremendous risk, because he had to navigate around American lines and cover some distance on foot. Not an easy task for a fit, highly trained soldier, let alone a man of advancing years like Mr Hamazaki.

He was accompanied on this visit by a small contingent of ten heavily armed men. Hamazaki had dressed himself in our regular battle dress. My obvious thought was that he had returned to consult with Nishii, but Nishii was away on his final mission. Hamazaki went straight in to command headquarters to confer with General Yamashita. After a short while I too was called in to the general's office. Hamazaki was seated with a glass of brandy in his hand. The general told me that Hamazaki had something to say. Hamazaki thanked me for assisting Nishii in his tasks and said my loyalty and devotion to duty would be honoured. I thanked him. Then Hamazaki passed me a paper and told me to read the names on it. I read it aloud. "Lieutenant Tanaka, Forty-Eighth Infantry Division of the Fourteenth Area Army. Lieutenant Ogawa, Special Operations Unit of the Fourteenth Area Army." Hamazaki told me to find these two men and order their immediate return to command headquarters for a special assignment. He told me these two had been specially chosen. He didn't say by whom. He went on to tell me that time was the most crucial factor now. Then he told me that this mission was to be conducted on a strictly need-to-know basis and that did not include Lieutenant Colonel Nishii or any person associated with him. Hamazaki also stressed that his clandestine visit here was to remain a secret. Nishii was not to know.

Hamazaki then took a sealed envelope from a locked box and passed it to the general. "General Yamashita holds the orders for this operation, which shall be known as Golden Lily. He will personally brief Tanaka and Ogawa personally upon their arrival here. You, Kojima, are to locate those officers, just as you did for Nishii. Do I have your sworn vow to secrecy?" I told him that he did.

Hamazaki was a man of forceful persuasion who carried an air of authority that none would dare question. After all, he was probably the third-most-powerful man in Japan behind the Emperor and the prime minister. Yes, I had realised who he was. Hamazaki was the armaments minister and also minister for war. It seemed as if the world had gone mad. The minister for war was actually in the middle of a war. Just what he was doing here in the middle of all-out battle was beyond my understanding. The general, who had been listening in silence, passed the orders to me and then told me to go about finding these two men. He also told Hamazaki that they were both more than likely dead, if recent casualty reports were accurate. I was told to pass the paper back to Hamazaki and to repeat the names of those officers. I said them aloud: "Lieutenants Tanaka and Ogawa." I was ordered to set about locating them and then dismissed.

I went straight to the communications area and ordered one of the radio operatives to try to reach one of our field commanders, Colonel Sugiyama, who was commanding the Forty-Eighth. The static rendered the reception almost inaudible. The Americans had developed methods of scrambling our communications, forcing us to regularly change frequencies. This often led to units in the field being cut off. The operative told me that the Forty-Eighth had been in contact only a few hours earlier. They had requested resupply of ammunition to be brought up to the lines. I knew that such requests would be next to useless, because supply lines had all been cut off. I told the operator to keep trying and raise anybody at Forty-Eighth.

I was resigned to having to send a runner out to the lines when after ten or fifteen minutes the crackling, desperate voice of someone in the midst of battle drifted back. I ordered the operative out of the room and tried to get my message through. Eventually, after several frustrating and gut-wrenching minutes I was talking to Sugiyama. I told him that Lieutenants Tanaka and Ogawa were to be withdrawn from the field on the orders of the highest authority and were to report to General Yamashita for a personal briefing. Sugiyama's anger was evident, but he held back as he tried to explain that such an order would be nigh impossible to execute, as our defence lines had been fractured and communication along the lines had all but broken down. I told him that the general insisted that his orders be carried out with the most urgent priority. Failure to do so would leave me with no alternative but to report back to the general at that moment. Sugiyama's broken voice streamed back, saying he would do his best to find the whereabouts of these officers but also to expect the worst news. Casualties were high, and some units were reduced to being commanded by sergeants. Sugiyama gave his regards to the general and salutations to the Emperor, and then the line went dead.

I stayed in the communications area for about an hour, waiting for news. None came. Eventually I went back to the command area. The general was there as usual, studying the latest reports from the field and giving out orders to runners and messengers. He saw me and called me over. He told me he had received a direct communication from the front lines from Colonel Sugiyama, who was able to report that Lieutenants Tanaka and Ogawa were alive and had been tasked as instructed to report to command headquarters at the earliest opportunity. It was plain that Sugiyama had doubted my instructions and taken the opportunity to gain favour with the general. Even in the face of death, men still played little power games. Nonetheless, the general expressed his thanks to me for my expedient actions in locating them.

Romana quickly scrawled down the details on a small piece of notepaper. He asked me why these men had been specially chosen. I said I had no knowledge of that. He asked me if I had met them at all. I told him I had not. General Yamashita had ordered senior staff, including me, to an adjacent area so that in case of a direct hit from incoming enemy fire, we would still be able to maintain some form of command structure. Nishii was still absent from headquarters. I believe Tanaka and Ogawa reported to the general the next morning. I neither saw them nor was privy to their orders.

Later that same morning the general informed me that our "business" from the previous evening had been concluded and we were never to refer to it as long as we lived. To my shame I was now breaking that pledge. "I break that pledge in the name of all my fallen comrades and to pacify the spirits of the men who lost their lives because I chose them," I said.

Romana nodded. "Kojima, for the first time since we met, I believe you have told me all you know. I expect the tribunal to allow my directive and to rule in favour of suspending your trial. I will do my utmost to see that your co-operation is recognised."

He left me alone to wait to be called back up before the court to hear my fate. Romana had given me some hope that I might be spared execution, but I felt empty inside. I had lost the will to care. After a few moments the guards came to escort me back up the staircase and into the dock. The American general and his tribunal were not in the room. Only my guards and the Filipino court clerk waited along with me. There was no sign of Andrews, my defence counsel. We were kept waiting for more than thirty minutes. Eventually the American general and his tribunal team entered the court. I was dragged back to my feet. The general ordered my restraints to be removed. Deep inside my heart, I hoped this was a sign that I would eventually be freed from this captive misery. The interpreter arrived at my side just as the general was readying himself to speak. The general looked at me and said, "Major Kaiishi Kojima. We have considered the evidence placed before us, and it is the unanimous verdict of this tribunal, notwithstanding your plea of guilty, that the charges against you have been proved beyond any reasonable doubt. These charges are of the most serious nature and carry the ultimate punishment of death by hanging. The tribunal has not received any form of mitigation, either written or verbal, about the sentence you will receive. I see your defence counsel is absent from court. Do you wish to personally address the court?" After the interpreter had finished his translation, I kept my head bowed and remained silent. "Very well. Kaiishi Kojima, this military tribunal finds you guilty as charged on all counts. I have taken into account your plea of guilty, for which this court in turn spares your life. It is now my duty to pass sentence upon you. You are to serve no less than thirty years in prison. The first five years of your incarceration are to be served under a regimen of hard labour. Take him away."

I was chained and led straight out to a waiting truck. I was to be taken back to Los Baños, where I would await transfer to a severe penal unit. My trial had taken no more than thirty minutes. That was how long I had actually stood before the judge. I remembered Andrews telling me that nothing had been determined. Hollow words indeed. Romana never made any representation on my behalf. To him I was just an object for which he had no further use.

I spent the next four days alone in my cell. I had been given lice-infested prison clothes to wear. The guards were now all local men and didn't try to hide their disgust and contempt. One guard took pleasure in spitting into my food each time he brought it in. Los Baños had been my hell for nearly six months. But now it was time to descend to an altogether different hell. Thirty years was a death sentence. I would die in this country as so many of my comrades had done. In my heart I was still a soldier, and my *kami*—spirit—was pure. I was told by the guards that my new place was just like heaven. They tried to outdo each other with stories and obscene gestures about what lay ahead for me.

Eventually it was time for my transfer. It was the middle of the night. The guards restrained me with the usual belts and chains, and then each took an arm and they dragged me out. They didn't take me towards the quadrant, as I expected, but to a different area of the prison compound. I was forced up a wooden staircase of about twenty steps. At the top was a plain door that was opened from the inside. I was pushed forward. The sight before me took my breath away. We were in the prison gallows. The thick rope was noosed and swaying gently. On the rampart to my left was a Catholic priest leading a column of five men dressed in simple, plain army uniforms that had been stripped of rank and insignia. A Buddhist priest wailed a high-pitched chant and swung a burning lantern of incense. Behind him, walking with head bowed, was General Yamashita. My general. Standing before the gallows he looked ahead, proud and defiant. I bowed my head, but the guards grabbed my hair and pulled my head up, forcing me to watch. The general was urged forward, and a uniformed American officer bound his wrists and ankles. The officer asked the general if he had any last words. The general spoke, and his words cut through the wretched air and straight into my heart. "I pray for the Emperor and his family and for national prosperity. I pray that all our children will be better educated. I forgive my executioner. My dear mother and father, it is time to go by your side."

A black hood was placed over his head, and then the noose with its thick knot placed under the general's left ear was pulled tight. I wanted to cry out. I could see the general tense, and his chest expanded as he took a great gasp of air. Then with one swift motion the officer brought down a sharp blade and cut the rope holding the counterweight, and General Yamashita was sent crashing down through the floor. We could see only the top of the rope, which jerked and twitched for a few moments and then became deathly still. The priest was no longer chanting. We all stood still. My body convulsed in great sobs. The man I loved and respected more than any other on this earth was now gone.

I was pushed back to the door to leave. I turned my head and through my tears looked at the rope one last time. Then I noticed a line of men assembled there to witness the last moments and final breath of General Yamashita. Romana was there, dressed in a fine white suit. Standing next to him, looking relaxed and elegant, twirling a Panama hat around his finger, was the devil himself. Lieutenant Colonel Nishii. Our eyes met, and he gave me a stare as cold as marble in winter. I wanted to scream out, but words wouldn't come. Nishii said something to Romana, who looked over in my direction. He had a big smile on his face and gave me a cutthroat gesture. I was pushed towards the door and my new hell.

I looked over my shoulder again. Romana had his arm on Nishii's shoulder. They were easy with each other like two old friends. Two demons together.

Chapter 2
Elias Cohen
Virginia
1948

Elias Cohen brought his fist down onto his desk so hard that his penholder almost hit the ceiling and stationery scattered across the small space that served as an office. Even old Miss Mills, who had seen and heard it all before, stopped tapping her keys and peered over her half-moons, giving Cohen a pitying and at the same time reproachful look. She would wait a full five minutes before clearing up the detritus of his anger. It was not her place to enquire what had brought about her boss's ire this morning, but she knew it was something among the despatches that had arrived earlier.

She had come to dread the daily delivery of confidential papers sent over from headquarters each morning. With military precision she could almost set her watch by the sound of the heavy boots on the landing outside as the two military policemen performed their regular delivery drill. They saluted Cohen before depositing the thin steel case on his desk and making a smart about-turn, then exited in a fashion that always seemed comical to Miss Mills's old eyes. She always waited for the sound of their jeep's engine to rattle away into the distance before looking up to gauge the mood of the man sitting across the room from her. These were the most important few minutes of the day, for what that case contained would determine Cohen's mood as they were cocooned together in the tiny space. There was no escaping his sourness. Yet despite all the misgivings she harboured, she knew deep down that Cohen was a decent man at heart. It was the demons inside that drove him to work eighteen-hour days and spend countless nights sleeping under his desk. Those same demons were responsible for souring his soul.

Miss Mills herself had come from hard times. Her chances of making something of her life had been all but blighted by the Great Depression. Those hard times had never really left her, and she still felt a surge of pride in the fact that somebody paid for her labour each and every month. These too were hard times, and not many women of her generation were in any kind of employment at all. Despite the local economy showing signs of improvement, soup kitchens were still open all over the state of Virginia, and decent office jobs were nearly impossible to find. The euphoria of victory had all but melted away, and now the harsh reality of life after war was starting to bite. Servicemen had hung up their uniforms in closets all over the country, but very few had found new work clothes. She often despaired as she saw the men kicking up dust as they lined up for the morning work call. The lucky ones might get a day's labour, whereas the others were asked to come back and try again the next day. These men who had survived the horrors of war, lost their comrades and friends, and given everything in battle were being trampled underfoot by the lack of conscientious government. She felt the injustice of it all and knew that her boss did too and that that was why they did what they did.

Cohen and Mills had forged a working relationship built on respect for each other's professionalism. Neither would dream of making small talk, nor did they ever discuss their personal lives. There was nothing in Miss Mills's past life that she felt she needed to protect. She had lived a simple, almost Spartan existence free from any romantic entanglements and unencumbered by family. She often thought herself selfish for devoting all her energies towards her own purposes. Of course she felt for others, but she did nothing about it. Her mother had told her that if you allow your heart to be held, it will be dropped time and time again. So, she had kept her heart hidden away, and over time it had simply dropped of its own accord.

Mr Cohen, on the other hand, had chanced his arm in a romantic encounter. This she knew because she had once been tasked with making a copy of his personal record of service. She had felt like an interloper as his life ran through her head and down to her fingertips and onto paper. She tried to make sure none of it stuck, but like an embarrassing stain, it refused to go away. Dorothea Horowitz: The name had etched itself in her mind. She did not know the background surrounding their courtship; military files were harshly devoid of sensationalism. The words merely sat on the paper like a bird with a broken wing. "Became engaged to a Miss Dorothea Horowitz in March 1939. Marriage did not take place because of the unexpected death of his fiancée in July of the same year." After those words had settled into her heart, she always saw Elias Cohen in a different light, a man who did his upmost to hide his true self.

On this particular morning the reason for Cohen's foul temper soon became apparent. "How the devil am I supposed to make sense out of all this gibberish? They send me papers written in Chinese, Thai, and Japanese. I ask you. I need an army of interpreters here. Look at this one. It uses the English alphabet and yet is completely nonsensical. What the hell?" Mills knew better than to reply, because his rant as always was rhetorical. "Miss Mills, please get in touch with the linguistics department over there in that grand headquarters and see if they can extend us some assistance."

Mills knew Cohen felt marginalised by the executives over in the new Pentagon building. He failed to see the logic in their denying him office space in the new magnificent military edifice over in Arlington. The fact that Cohen was a civilian operative did little to appease his sense of exclusion. Many civilians were granted clearance to work close to the heart of the new military command centre. Deep down he harboured a suspicion that his efforts were considered meaningless by some of those in power. What real evidence was there to back up the claims that priceless artefacts had been stolen during the war? Was his work no more than a paper chase blowing about in the wind? Elias Cohen believed not. He knew men had enriched themselves through the war because that is what men do. Victorious armies loot their vanquished foes. That is how it has always been, and Cohen knew that had happened across the Pacific battlefields. Treasures that screamed out to be returned to their rightful place must have been scattered around the world by now, but that did not deter Cohen. In truth he was not really interested in the treasures themselves; he wanted to nail the thieves. This was his crusade, his mission, the start of his personal war. The sign on his door gave only the merest hint of his real agenda. "Mr Elias Cohen (Civilian), Department of Research and Investigations into the Conduct of Enemy Combatants." A grand title indeed and one that made him proud and equally determined to prove his worthiness.

Later that afternoon, after Miss Mills had tried and failed to secure the services of the linguistics department, the telephone rang, startling her and causing her to make an error on the page she was typing. She sighed because she knew she would have to start her work over. Submitting papers with corrections for

Cohen's approval was unthinkable. So it was with a slight irritation that she answered the call. Of course she had no idea at the time that it would change her working world and, more to the point, Elias Cohen's life. She made a note of the caller and diplomatically covered the mouthpiece as she asked Cohen if he was available to receive a Mr Robert Rushton. Cohen made a play of checking his schedule and said he would be available at ten the following morning. After she had relayed this to Mr Rushton, she listened for a moment or two before getting Cohen's attention once more. "The gentleman is most insistent that he meet with you this afternoon. He says it concerns a matter that is central to your work."

Elias Cohen felt the warmth of good fortune seep into his day, but his face betrayed little emotion. After looking through his empty appointment book, he glanced up and told Miss Mills that four o'clock appeared to be available and that he could offer Mr Rushton some time then. She gave the message to Rushton and replaced the receiver before returning to her business; however, Cohen could not contain his eagerness for long. "Miss Mills, this Rushton fellow, did he give any indication of who he was?" She said he had offered nothing other than his name and his intention. "How did he sound?" Cohen asked. "I mean, was he an officer type or more—well, you know—street level?"

She thought for a moment and replied, "Educated—I think he sounded educated."

Cohen shook his head from side to side. "How the devil would you deduce such a thing from a telephone call?" Then he went back to shuffling his indecipherable papers.

To his great annoyance Elias Cohen found himself unable to concentrate on even the simplest of tasks, because the impending visit of this Mr Rushton had set his imagination racing off into the distance. He harboured a wild hope that his visitor would be the bearer of irrefutable evidence that wartime larceny was indeed rife. He spent the afternoon dreaming of the possibility that the foundation to one of the great investigations of modern times was about to be laid and that he, Elias Cohen, was about to take his first steps towards something far grander than the small box of an office he shared with Miss Mills. Once he had some hard evidence in his hands, the brass over at the Pentagon would have to set up a team and could no longer merely play lip service to rumours that had refused to die.

At the stroke of three Miss Mills's typewriter fell silent and she stood to make the afternoon's coffee. It was a ritual they could both set their clocks by. She placed a cup and two small ginger cookies by Cohen's pen stand. He nodded his thanks, and without looking up opened the desk drawer and removed a dime, which he placed on the edge of his desk. Such was his manner that he would neither eat nor drink until his dues were paid. Miss Mills picked up the coin, added one of her own, and dropped them into the small tin marked "Refreshments." On the last Friday of each month after work Miss Mills would empty the tin and record its contents before going out to replenish their supply of tea and coffee. Elias Cohen had told her that the simplest of routines build order and calm. She had never seen it as her place to question his devotion to simple principles, but sometimes she wished she could find the courage to tell him that she did not care for ginger cookies all that much. Coffee break was officially ten minutes, but neither she nor Cohen felt it appropriate to sit back and take the time to just drink coffee. It was a time to pay a visit to the bathroom down the hall or water the few plants that sat on the window ledge. Miss Mills would from time to time apply her duster to the blinds or check the mousetraps that were loaded with pieces of her ginger cookies. Coffee time over, Miss Mills collected the cups and saucers and to her surprise noted that her boss had barely touched his drink. It was obvious that Mr Rushton had stirred up something in Cohen's mind that she could not begin to fathom.

The clock on the wall behind Miss Mills's desk showed four. However, of Mr Rushton there was no sign, and as the minutes ticked by, Cohen's annoyance at his visitor's shoddy sense of punctuality was beginning to show through. The telephone remained reproachfully silent. Mr Rushton had not seen fit to offer a reason for his tardiness. Cohen was a fastidious man. and this trait did not sit well with his vanity, for he often saw the failings of others as a sign of personal disrespect for his standing and authority.

A full fifteen uncomfortable minutes passed before a sudden rapping on the door caused both Cohen and Miss Mills to jump. The door was pushed open before Miss Mills could get to her feet, and in strode the lankiest gentleman she had ever seen. In an instant she registered him as a dashing young man—young being a relative term and certainly applicable in comparison with herself. His pencil moustache put her in mind of Errol Flynn, and his smile confirmed her opinion. "Good afternoon. My name is Robert Rushton; I do believe you are expecting me." He removed his trilby respectfully towards Miss Mills, who stepped forward to take it from his hands and, for want of a better place, set it down on her own desk.

Rushton looked over to Cohen, who had remained seated at his desk. His irritation at being kept waiting was still weighing on his mind, and he was making a show of exerting his authority. Without looking up from his papers he said, "Indeed, Mr Rushton, I was expecting you a full fifteen minutes ago, and as my time is precious, I would appreciate it if you would be seated and explain your business." Miss Mills felt a surge of embarrassment creep into her. This was a side of her boss she had never seen, as very few visitors had come through their door and they had always been punctual. Rushton took a moment to look over the office before striding over, pulling out the chair, and sitting before Cohen. He offered neither excuse nor apology for his lateness, merely shrugging as he settled down on the hard wooden chair that was set aside for rare visitations.

Miss Mills went back to her desk and found some papers that could benefit from some needless filing. However, she could not stop herself from peering up at the back of Rushton's head. Cohen's voice carried loud across the room. "So, Mr Rushton, state your business and feel free to speak in front of my assistant. She has full security classification." Cohen leaned back in his chair and clasped his hands together, staring at Rushton in an attempt to get a measure of the man before him.

"Mr Cohen. As you know, my name is Robert Rushton and I work for the Office of Strategic Services, the OSS. I thought it time to introduce myself, and as your superior officer, felt it only appropriate to brief you in person about the forthcoming changes that are about to be implemented." Miss Mills saw Cohen shrink into his chair, his self-importance deflating as fast as a punctured balloon. Rushton went on. "I have been monitoring your work and have been impressed with your commitment, but I feel the task before us requires a somewhat more direct approach, and I have been ordered to build a task force that will get results. Our area of investigation is deemed too sensitive for civilian operative involvement, and it has been decided that your office will be closed effective immediately. I have your termination papers here for you both to sign." Rushton leaned down and opened his small tan attaché case. He removed a slim sheaf of papers and took out a pen from his inside pocket. Miss Mills watched the colour drain from

Cohen's face as he was rendered speechless. In the space of only two minutes he had gone from being somebody to nobody, and that was a cruelty she wished on no man. There was a brief silence as Rushton sorted out his papers. "There, if you would be so kind as to sign here and here." Rushton swivelled around. "Miss Mills, if I could ask you to come here and do the same."

Rushton watched as the papers were signed, and then leaned back. Cohen could no longer bring himself to look his visitor in the eye. His face had reddened, and only his confusion stopped him from channelling his anger directly at Rushton. Rushton went on. "I wish to thank you for all your efforts. Your department will be in touch shortly with details of your severance." His words seemed like the final indictment as Cohen's pride was kicked from one end of the state of Virginia to the other. "Now, as you are both officially unemployed, I feel it appropriate to offer you both your positions back."

Confusion and disbelief reigned at that moment, and it all became a little too much for Elias Cohen. "Are you here to mock us, Mr Rushton? Because I feel that is exactly what you are doing."

Rushton shook his head in an attempt to quell Cohen's frustration. "Mr Cohen, if you would please give me a minute to explain. As a civilian you lack sufficient security clearance to be informed of certain matters pertaining to ongoing investigations. Therefore it has been decided to bring you both into the OSS. To do that, your current employment status needed to be dissolved. Please accept my apologies if my approach caused distress. I find it better for all parties if we get to the heart of the matter."

Cohen held up his hand to interrupt. "Are you saying that we are to join the OSS?"

Rushton gave him his best Errol Flynn smile and said, "That is exactly what I am saying, Mr Cohen. Both your good self and

Miss Mills are to join my task team. I need the best people around me, and there is a role for you both. That is, if you are willing, of course." Cohen managed to fluster out some words, but the general gist was that he most certainly was. Rushton looked over at Miss Mills, who nodded politely, an act of acquiescence that spoke of loyalty. Rushton took out another set of papers, which they both eagerly signed, and Rushton too added his signature as a witness. After the formalities had been completed, an air of calm descended upon the tiny space. Rushton looked around the office. "You had better start to say farewell to this place, because we're on the move. These are exciting times indeed. There is talk of a new dawn for the OSS; I have even heard we are to get a new name. Some say we are to be called the Central Intelligence Agency, or CIA for short. Personally I prefer the OSS, but time will tell. I will have someone call later this week to help you with your packing and inform you of your formal swearing-in. You will receive all the assistance you need to relocate to the new offices. In the meantime, I need not stress that confidentiality remains paramount." Rushton stood and strode over to Miss Mills's desk, retrieved his hat, bowed, and exited, leaving Cohen and Miss Mills gaping in his wake.

In truth Elias Cohen had mixed feelings about his new station in life. Six weeks had passed since the day Robert Rushton had walked into his life and overturned his orderly existence, and, with each day gone, the realisation that he was nothing more than a cog in the machine had firmly sunk in. He was not a man given to fond reminiscence; his life so far held few sweet memories, but at times he longed for his old office where he was the king of his own castle. Now, he found himself doing much more repetitive work. His primary duties concerned the collation of documents and witness statements in the hope of establishing some kind of time-line that would tell them what treasures and artefacts had gone missing, when, and from where. It was a devil of a task too, what with at least half a dozen different languages that needed translating, but he did have at his disposal a pool of linguists over whom he could at least exercise his authority, given that they were generally a pay scale or two below him. It seemed that the newly recruited once civilian staff were yet to be assigned ranks, so one's remuneration was as good a point as any at determining where you stood in the whole scheme of things. To add to Cohen's growing frustration, Miss Mills had been removed from his side and was now at the general service of all. They still worked under the same roof, along with a dozen others, but she had very little contact with her old boss. He would regularly look up from his desk to see her being handed papers marked "Highly Classified" and then watch as she arranged privacy screens around her desk before going about her business.

Elias Cohen was not a team player. In his world he was a team leader, and he was determined to shine through and let his talents guide him to the top. All he needed was a break, and despite his inner doubts he felt that something in the pile of papers that graced his desk each morning would turn out to be his beacon in the storm.

Robert Rushton occupied his own office. The sign that adorned his door was sufficiently ambiguous yet exerted the requisite amount of authority: "Director of Operations." What exactly he was directing Cohen was unsure, as he had seldom seen Rushton since that day six weeks ago. He caught glimpses of him as he swept through the main office looking flustered, seemingly rushing to attend to some urgent matter. Cohen reluctantly accepted that Rushton was indeed an important man and that he had failed miserably to get the measure of him at their first meeting.

In those rare moments of self-doubt he wondered if Rushton had formed a grudge against him because of his slightly bellicose manner, although he reasoned that if that were the case, then why take him under his command. So, it was a great surprise when he was handed a memo informing him that he was to attend a meeting in Rushton's office the following morning. He noted that the memorandum had also been copied to some of the most senior figures in the Office of Strategic Services. He felt that old swell of pride running through his veins, but it was quickly countered by a feeling of uncertainty. He feared he might have been summoned only to record the minutes of the meeting. He shook his head at such a thought, but that afternoon he found himself unable to concentrate on the work at hand. It was a repeat of that day when Rushton had breezed into his old office as if he owned the place, only this time Cohen was determined not to make the same mistakes, and he prayed for all he was worth to be given his chance.

The following morning Cohen rose especially early, which was not difficult, because he felt he had not slept at all. Refreshing sleep was a luxury that had deserted him long ago; even when he did find rest, he dreamt he was awake. For him there was no respite from his weary toil, a burden that grew heavier by the day.

He had once read that repressed grief could have tragic consequences for the sufferer and those around him. Well, if that was to be the case, then so be it. Somebody needed to pay for his loss, and the image of his own innocent Dorothea, lying cold on a mortician's marble table, drove him forward each day. They were to have been married in a matter of months. His world had been cut down by an immigrant who had not even been in the country a month, a man who knew nothing of the American way and yet was allowed to drive a truck that was offensively out of proportion to his ability. He said he was not able to see the rearview mirror before he struck Dorothea, who was waiting innocently to cross the road. The man had been prohibited from driving for three months and was given a community service order. That was what Dorothea's life had been worth in the eyes of the law. Cohen saw deeper into the mire—so deep, his soul became enraged in floods of racial hatred. The driver had been a young boy, only sixteen years of age, unable to speak any English and cheap labour for the owner of a local fruit-and-vegetable store. Fujisaki: The name was etched so deeply on Cohen's heart that his irrational hatred of all things Japanese was something he would carry until his dying breath. The dastardly attack on Pearl Harbour only served to confirm his belief that they were all felons and deserved what was coming their way. He revelled in the internment of Japanese Americans and even went to the camp where the boy was held in the hope of seeing Fujisaki himself suffering some laborious toil. He saw it as divine justice and celebrated as his "fellow Americans" descended on the deserted properties and businesses of the unfortunate Japanese American citizens, dividing their assets at a fraction of the real value. Even the final wrath of war, delivered in the form of two atomic explosions, did little to abate his hatred of a people he now saw as less than human. His vendetta was personal, and only he himself could find peace for his torment. He knew deep down that his thought process was warped, but somewhere amidst his crazed demons he believed he was on the side of justice.

Cohen made the daily commute to his new workplace by bus each morning. The monthly fare was more than the twelve-dollar pay raise he had received, but he was happy to make sacrifices for his career. His old office was close to his apartment, and he had walked to work each morning. Now, six weeks later, the fact that he'd gotten so little exercise had started to tell on his waistline. He came from a family that was inclined to gain more than their fair share of weight in middle age, and he silently cursed his sloth as he sat down in Rushton's office that morning. His trousers were no longer the ideal fit, to say the least, and he feared his buttons might pop open at any moment, but his suit carried such a sentimental burden for him that he was loath to forgo its discomfort. It was the suit in which he was supposed to have married, chosen for him by his own beloved Dorothea. Cohen truly believed she was looking down from on high and smiling with approval at his loyal diligence.

There were two other officers waiting for Rushton to finally put in an appearance. Cohen did not know their names, but he had seen them around the office from time to time. The three of them sat in silence, looking down at their blank reporters' notepads and doing their best to look as if they were pondering some great conundrum. One feature of being in the employ of the Office of Strategic Services was the total absence of small talk. Everyone worked in their own little world as if too afraid to speak for fear of letting some delicate information loose. This style of operating suited Cohen very well, for he had never been prone to speaking up, professionally or otherwise.

Ten minutes later than the time stressed in the memorandum, Rushton finally arrived for the meeting he himself had called. He was carrying a heavy-looking box file, which he dropped onto his desk with a sigh of relief. The two other men were about to stand out of respect, but Rushton motioned for them to remain seated. Cohen felt the discomfort of being caught off guard, as he was unfamiliar with office etiquette. Rushton sat behind his large desk and rummaged through his desk drawers, finally extracting his spectacles case. He opened the case and silently cleaned the lenses whilst looking intently at the three men sitting before him.

It was almost as if he were trying to finally convince himself that he was taking the correct course of action before it was too late. Rushton inspected his eyeglasses and, finally satisfied, gave out a sigh as if he were relieving himself of a great burden.

"Gentlemen, thank you for attending this fine morning. Now, let's get down to business, shall we? Introductions, if you please. Mr Cohen, you first." Cohen managed to bluster some form of personal introduction together—nothing too personal, of course. There was little he could say other than that he had been employed in the private sector before the war and was engaged as a civilian during the war at Fort Lee army base. After he had finished his introduction, he felt an inescapable sense of shame. He had avoided the draft because of his chronic asthma, a condition that had worsened after Dorothea's death. Whatever the reason for his lack of military service, he knew that other men always measured him against the war years.

Rushton nodded, and the first of the other two spoke. "My name is Walter Myers, retired army captain. Saw service in Europe and finally fought the Germans hand to hand in the streets of Paris before taking a hit that took away the best part of my right thigh. I was recruited into the OSS after my application for a civilian posting at army headquarters was turned down. Gentlemen, I look forward to working alongside you in whatever tasks we are assigned." Myers's confident tone was a marked contrast to Cohen's own carefully pondered delivery.

The third man now spoke. He looked down at his notes as if he needed reminding of the pertinent details of his life, which turned out to be rather amazing. "Good morning to you. My name is Adrian Harvey. I was a lecturer in mathematics at Yale University before the war put paid to that career. I was drafted into the OSS quite soon after the attack on Pearl Harbour. I spent most of my wartime service involved in breaking Japanese ciphers for the US Navy. After the war had concluded, I was given the option of returning to my old life or continuing my work at the OSS. My decision is obvious to you all. I too look forward to working with you." Myers and Harvey shook hands as if it were the most natural thing to do. Then almost as an afterthought they extended their hands in Cohen's direction. Rushton let his eyes linger on the three of them, and Cohen caught the sense that he was trying to get a measure of the dynamic forming between the men he had chosen.

Rushton was in the habit of letting uncomfortable silences hang in the air, and Cohen guessed it was deliberate, perhaps a habit he had carried over from his days as an interrogator. A tap on the door was enough to make all heads swivel, and Cohen was especially caught off guard when he saw Miss Mills step into the room. Rushton smiled for the first time that morning. "Gentlemen, I do believe you are acquainted with Miss Mills here. She will be acting as my personal assistant and confidential secretary. Please do not hesitate to use her services as a conduit between ourselves. She has the highest of security clearances, so rest assured." Cohen avoided looking directly at Mills; he pretended to be studying his notes in an effort to hide his frustration. He was incredulous that a woman who once took orders from him was now closer to the seat of power than he was. He then gave his own self-esteem a lashing as he questioned whether he had been selected for the team only to get Miss Mills alongside Rushton—a notion he tried his best to dismiss but that refused to go away. Uncomfortable formalities finally concluded, Rushton set about explaining why he had brought the three of them together.

"It is time to move our investigations along. Now we are to concentrate on the specific as opposed to the general areas that concern us. I have here in this box the sum total of an investigation into the wartime activities of certain individuals. They have been identified as the leading suspects in a criminal conspiracy of alarming proportions—wartime larceny carried out on a scale that is staggering beyond belief and has the potential to have a destabilising effect on the economies of several nations. It is our duty to make sure that our vanquished enemies do not profit or prosper from the ill-gotten gains of war. It is also our sworn duty to bring wartime criminals to justice. After all, we won the war, but it was a victory that came at a heavy cost. There is barely a family in this great nation of ours that has not been hurt by the tragedy of war. We owe it to each and all to make sure our foes do not take advantage of their crimes. Gentlemen, we won the war, but now it is time to make sure we go on to win the peace.

"That is why I am about to tell you about a certain individual named Tetsuyo Hamazaki. I have identified this man as the orchestrator of a plot so wicked, it beggars belief. It is my belief that he was assisted in his crimes by a high-ranking Japanese Kempeitai officer named Nishii and a certain Major Kojima, whom I personally interrogated in Manila at the end of the fighting. Most of my investigations centred on Kojima and Nishii. However, they are not the only players. Other names come up, such as Lieutenants Tanaka and Ogawa and most certainly a rat of a man named Santa Romana of the Philippine national intelligence service. It's a devil of a mess, but we need to sort it out and fast, before events get ahead of us.

"That is where you three come in. You are now my team, and you will devote every minute of your working days to solving this mess. So I suggest you all go off and lock yourselves in a quiet room for a week or two so you can get your heads around these documents and make a case that is credible enough to take to the chief of staff. Remember, gentlemen, that we are dealing with some of the most dangerous and despicable men on the planet, so do not take anything for granted." Rushton pushed the box across his desk. "Cohen, take the picture off the top and show the others." Cohen stood and took out a large black-and-white photograph. Rushton looked grave. "That picture shows what they did to their own men after they had used their labour to hide stolen war loot somewhere in the Philippine jungle. To preserve their dirty secrets they gassed and decapitated their own. That is what we are up against." Rushton paused dramatically and looked each of his team in the eye. "Gentlemen, may God be with you."

For the next ten days Cohen, Myers, and Harvey shared a closed office. That was about all they shared; conversation was kept to a functional level as they sifted through the mountain of papers, documents, and witness statements that Rushton had dumped on them. No matter how arduous the task, Cohen truly believed that God was indeed with them. He had found a target for his vitriol. This Hamazaki looked like a good fit for all that was wrong, and Cohen, driven by his well-hidden sense of burning personal vengeance, was determined to nail his man.

He was thankful for the organisation that Harvey brought to the team, but quietly despised the mathematician's natural sense of being. It was obvious that Harvey had assumed the role of team leader; Myers too easily succumbed to a higher intellect. The days dragged on, and the three of them, fuelled by bottomless cups of bitter coffee, finally began to make sense of what that box contained. As a picture began to emerge, Harvey, whose cynicism matched his organisational skills, voiced his own opinions as to what the agenda here really was. "Is what we are doing all about justice or is there something else at stake here?" This sudden declaration caught both Myers and Cohen off guard, for neither had the nuance to question their work.

Myers looked at Harvey as if he had just sneezed in his face. "What do you mean? Someone has to pay for the crimes amongst all this," he said, waving a hand over the piles of papers on the desk to emphasise his point. Cohen noticed he also touched his wounded leg as he spoke. Myers was a man of action who had been reduced to a paper shuffler, but in his chest still beat the heart of a lion. Cohen often found himself in awe of the man's bravery, and he desperately wanted to know how many men he had personally despatched on the streets of Paris. Harvey looked at Myers and Cohen and shook his head as if any further explanation would be wasted on their shallow minds, but Myers was in no mood to let it go. "Come on, Harvey, tell us what you mean."

Harvey looked down at some papers and collected his thoughts. "Justice is a subtext, a mere by-product of the process. We are the OSS, are we not? We are concerned with intelligence, something that can be used to our advantage. It is my belief that we are in search of information that will in turn become intelligence that will give us the power of leverage. Think about it. Why don't the Chinese or Thais search for their own missing treasures? It is obvious: because they don't have the resources to do so, right? So, if we do recover some of their national pride, then what can we, as a country, expect in return? Perhaps a little extra consideration towards our own diplomatic ends. After all, we are now living in a very different world. The bombs over Hiroshima and Nagasaki have seen to that. Our eyes are shifting towards the Commies and their intentions. We need as many friends as we can get, and that means money and lots of it." Harvey tapped the papers in front of him.

Cohen surprised himself as his voice seemed to find a life of its own. "What about the Japanese? They have to pay for their crimes. Surely that is about justice."

Harvey looked at him as if he were a dumb pupil unable to grasp the basic theory behind a simple solution. "The Japanese were, until two years ago, our sworn blood enemies. Now they are quickly becoming our new best friends. Their land is for the time being our land, our jurisdiction, but things will change, and fast. They are a hardworking and industrious nation. It will take a hell of an iron hand to keep them down, so it is in our interest to work with them and take some benefit from their present situation."

Cohen and Myers looked at Harvey as if he had uttered treacherous statements against their own precious country. Yet, despite the swell of contempt they were feeling, neither man was able to muster any rational counter to Harvey's intellectual reasoning. Sensing their unease Harvey tried to back up his opinions with a little simplistic reasoning. He opened the confidential file marked "Hamazaki" and leaned back in his chair. Pushing his spectacles high into his bushy hair, he began to give his own thoughts on the man they had all come to know as suspect number one. "Look, guys, let's use a bit of logic here. This Hamazaki fellow, well, I am not saying he is innocent. Oh no, far from that. What I am saying is that he is more than likely a man who got caught up in the crazy wrath of war. Tetsuyo Hamazaki was one of the wealthiest industrialists in prewar Japan. He came from an extremely wealthy background full of privilege and social standing. The kind of man who would be invited to take tea with the Emperor himself. Hamazaki Electricals was one of the biggest names in the country. The war must have been a major distraction for him. His company was requisitioned by the Tojo government and forced to divert most of its production toward the war effort. In return he was given a position in the cabinet, as armaments minister, I believe. For men like Hamazaki the end of the war spelt personal disaster. His company was dismantled, his wealth confiscated, and his liberty curtailed. It says here he was given an eighteen-month prison sentence by a United States military tribunal for 'the exercising of financial irregularities.' Now, if that is not as vague a crime as any, then I do not know what is. The question we need to ask ourselves is, Why would he want to go off and pillage half of Asia?"

Harvey's stare at the two men seated before him invited some kind of response, but when neither seemed about to offer anything constructive, he decided to put forward his own recommendation. "If you gentlemen don't harbour any objections, I think we should put it to Rushton that Hamazaki be brought here to the States and let him speak for himself. Such a move will lessen the chances of other parties being forewarned and sent scurrying away to cover their tracks. We must get the man out of his comfort zone, away from all that is familiar to him, which will stack the odds of success more in our favour. Yes, I do believe that Tetsuyo Hamazaki was involved in some kind of conspiracy, but as far as how deep his own criminal responsibility goes, we can only surmise. We need to apply a bit of pressure on the man and see what comes out."

Cohen and Myers certainly held no objections. In fact Cohen thought it a splendid idea that might result in some kind of real progress finally being made. Despite his misgivings about Harvey's slightly unpatriotic views, he was ready to put his name to anything that would get Tetsuyo Hamazaki in the same room as true God-fearing human beings. However, five long frustrating months would elapse before Cohen finally got his wish, and by that time the investigation had certainly grown teeth. The only question remaining was, Who would bear the bite marks?

"Time heals all wounds" or so they say, but for Elias Cohen nothing could have been further from the truth. With the passing of each day the vendetta he passionately harboured deep in his soul festered as it fed on the vitriol of his self-righteousness. He managed to control his hatred, or at least disguise it, having found effective ways to channel his emotions. His work became everything, and despite garnering a reputation as a bit of a zealot in the office, he was by and large taken for what he was: a hardworking and uncomplaining man who could be relied on to put in those extra unpaid hours without making a fuss. For Cohen, the daily grind of compiling the evidence against wartime crooks was not just a job, but a personal obsession, one he would have undertaken for no remuneration. Almost five months to the day had passed since he had heard the name Tetsuyo Hamazaki, a name he had come to regard as the epitome of evil, a man who in Cohen's eyes represented all there was to hate about a nation that he believed had escaped due justice.

His hatred of Hamazaki grew to an almost pathological degree as he investigated the man and the circumstances of his life. There was very little he did not know. The Tokyo office of the OSS had forwarded reams of documents pertaining to Hamazaki Electricals and to Hamazaki himself. The more he read, the more convinced of the man's guilt he became. The very fact that he had sworn witnesses' statements that placed Hamazaki in the midst of the fighting in Luzon in the final days of the battle was in itself rock-solid evidence. Cohen must have read Major Kojima's final statement a thousand times. He knew it by heart, and in his mind could picture the major broken by defeat and shame, pouring out his sickening tale of wartime looting and death, pointing the finger at Tetsuyo Hamazaki, the orchestrator of it all. It was a statement of guilt, a confession in its purest and simplest of forms.

A part of Cohen regretted the demise of Kojima, because it would have been useful to push that crooked bastard even harder and see what bile spewed from his mouth. Kojima had met a pre-dictable end. He had been serving time in a hard-labour penal camp when one morning an enlightened fellow inmate had taken it upon himself to bring Kojima's existence to a premature conclusion. Cohen was certain that Kojima had taken evil secrets to his grave, and for that sin he hoped the major had died squealing like a stuck pig as the knife that finished him was twisted between his ribs, skewering his black heart.

Cohen had tried his upmost to push Rushton's pragmatism aside, but his boss was surprisingly formidable in his approach. Rushton insisted on working with the facts and facts alone. He had no use for speculation and was not open to wild theorising, which seemed to marginalise his team of "crack" investigators. Myers was especially prone to speculation and was forever pushing various theories on Cohen and Harvey, but his rashness was almost always reasoned down. It soon became apparent that Myers the war hero was not blessed with an intellect to match his courage. At times Cohen thought Rushton was almost putting off bringing Hamazaki over to the States for interrogation, and although careful attention to detail was something to be proud of, Cohen felt the need for something a little more direct. He believed they had enough evidence in their dossier to make Hamazaki sweat, and he longed for the day he would see the man break under pressure.

Rushton had ordered Harvey and Myers to concentrate on this missing Lieutenant Colonel Nishii, who seemed to have evaporated off the face of the planet. It was Cohen's guess that Hamazaki had somehow granted him safe harbour and that the best way to find Nishii was to shake down Hamazaki himself.

Another figure who was central to their investigation was Santa Romana, a Philippine national who was now a high-ranking officer in that country's intelligence service. As he was a wartime colleague of Rushton, Romana was treated as a material witness for the purpose of the investigation into Hamazaki and Nishii. This did not wear well with Harvey, who believed that Romana should be treated with equal suspicion and that he too should be brought to Virginia to account for certain actions—particularly to explain the whereabouts of the initial cache of recovered gold and other treasures that had been located through Kojima's interrogation. Rushton insisted that Romana was an asset to the United States and as such was subject to monitoring by a different section. If their own investigation was to come across incriminating information that related to Romana in particular, then it was to be passed directly to Rushton, who would personally coordinate and make an executive decision about how to proceed. The investigations into wartime atrocities were moving ahead, but achingly slowly. It had taken the best part of two years to finally reach the point where nothing more could feasibly be deduced without face-to-face contact with their main suspects, but still Rushton pontificated to the point of inaction. It seemed to Cohen that Rushton was more interested in playing the long-term power game as all the major players and heads of departments in the newly formed Central Intelligence Agency jostled for the attention of the new director, Roscoe Hillenkoetter. To a certain extent this was understandable, as the new organisation needed a certain amount of time to "bed in," but the shiny new offices and an increased sense of self-importance could do only so much to quell Cohen's frustrations.

They were constantly told that results were all that mattered, but to Cohen that sounded more and more like a hollow mantra. Cohen knew he had much to thank Rushton for; his very position in the new CIA was down to Rushton, and he would never go against the man. He only wished for some kind of direct action, for he was sure they would break Hamazaki if only they got the chance. After all, when all was said and done, Hamazaki was nothing but a weak man who hid behind social conventions and inherited protocol. The short spell he had served in the Tokyo Detention Centre was only a taste of what lay in store for him. With God's iron hand firmly on the side of American justice, Hamazaki would barely last two minutes, of that Cohen had no doubt. If only Rushton would unleash the wrath of the investigation and bring the man to account.

It was no different from any other Thursday. Cohen had taken the bus to work as normal and had gone through his usual mental routine of staring at his fellow passengers' footwear in an effort to ascertain as much as he could about them before checking their faces to see if he were close to his ideas about their circumstances. Over the years he had convinced himself that he had become an expert at judging his fellow travellers' backgrounds. Of course there was no real way to determine the accuracy of his judgements, but for Cohen that mattered little; he was the final arbitrator in his own little fantasy world. As the bus passed the fringes of McLean, Cohen looked out at the grand homes of the power brokers who had adopted the area as their own. The neatly manicured lawns and high fences shouted conformity and order, far removed from his own domestic arrangements. His salary severely limited his options, and he was fixed in the "bedroom" area of Langley, which was convenient for work but inconvenient for life. His neighbour in the next apartment was a Puerto Rican man who worked in the sanitation department and would often park his truck on the sidewalk, sometimes blocking the entrance. Cohen had often willed himself to challenge such behaviour but had not been able to find the courage to do so. After all, the man was a hulk of a fellow who had an unpleasant smell about him and a livid scar down his left cheek.

Eventually the bus completed its horseshoe route and pulled up on the high street, disgorging passengers who battled with umbrellas and held coat collars against the wet and windy Virginia morning. Cohen had a short walk to his offices on Fairfax Avenue, and as he shook off the rain from his umbrella, about to enter, Alfred the security officer stepped out from behind his desk. "Mr Cohen, sir, I have been instructed to inform you to go immediately to the conference room on the sixth floor. You will need a temporary pass to clear security up there." Alfred handed over a pass with Cohen's photograph affixed and a green diagonal stripe embossed over the front. It was common knowledge that the higher the floor, the more important and powerful things became. Rushton occupied an office on the fifth, so he was going one up from his boss. So unexpected was this disruption to his usual routine that Cohen was caught completely off guard. His first and natural reaction was a sense of doom and gloom. He was being summoned to be terminated, and he quickly ran through any recent events that might have caused his seniors to be displeased.

Cohen nearly asked Alfred if he was the only one to be given a pass this morning, but he quickly remembered his place. Operatives did not talk with underlings other than to exchange civil greetings. He accepted his pass and walked through the main lobby to the elevators. The sudden onset of a migraine only added to his nagging self-doubt as he got onto an empty elevator. It was the first time he had ever had cause to press the sixth-floor button. In fact he had never even been to Rushton's office on the fifth. The doors opened, and he was surprised to find it almost identical to his own second-floor workplace. No security guards were present, and a sign on the wall pointed the way to the conference room. He walked along the short corridor, which was lined with pictures of eminent OSS men from days gone by, and stopped for a moment in front of Rushton's own picture, which had obviously been taken several years earlier. Cohen wondered what Rushton had done to be given the honour of a place on the wall. As he approached the conference room, two suited men appeared as if by magic and stood before him. One took Cohen's pass and looked it over, and when finally satisfied, told Cohen to go on through.

Cohen pushed the doors open to find his colleagues Myers and Harvey already seated along with Miss Mills, who was seated to one side with a recording steno machine at the ready. Rushton stood looking down at the street below, his back to them. "Mr Cohen, please take a seat. We are waiting on one more person." No sooner had he spoken than the door opened and in came the deputy director himself, Edmund Norris. Such a high-level presence caught the operatives off guard, and so did Norris's no-nonsense attitude. The deputy director was a short, rotund man who appeared to be in a constant sweat, forever wiping his brow. He spoke in a tone that matched his appearance, his words like bullets spat out from a carbine. "Men, today is action day. Our number one suspect is here in this very building. I have just taken him from his hotel. He is sitting in interrogation room five. He came willingly and declined to be accompanied. We have him for two hours only. That's two hours to nail him down, but let me warn you, he is no soft touch. Rushton, you and you alone will question him. You three have the next hour to prepare any pertinent points you feel should be put to Hamazaki."

Cohen, Myers, and Harvey sat in silence. The man they had spent the past five months focusing on was actually here, in the building. It was unbelievable, surely some kind of vivid dream or nightmare. Rushton nodded at his team. "You heard the DD. Now go and put some thoughts down on paper, but remember, I know everything there is to know about Hamazaki, so keep it on the button." He then apparently thought that a little more in the way of explanation was required. "Look, I appreciate all your efforts, and I know this must be something of a shock to you all, but believe me, it was necessary. Security is of the essence here. Even I did not know until last evening that Hamazaki was to be brought in. He is here in the country as part of an American-Japanese business forum. Hamazaki confirmed his participation only at the last minute. His delegation has been told he is attending a private meeting with the US secretary of commerce, and until thirty minutes ago, that is what he believed. We don't have much time, so we need to get in there with as much as we can. I will put the questions, and you three will observe through the screening glass. Pass me your notes after I have had an hour with him. See you downstairs."

Rushton nodded at the deputy director, who had taken a seat and was sweating over a file, and in an instant he was gone, leaving his team alone with Norris. The deputy director looked over at the three of them and made a vague attempt to ease their tension. "Guys, don't worry. I've seen Bobby Rushton in action, and if there is anything to be had from Hamazaki, then Bobby is the man to get it out of him. Now, let's get our butts down to the other side of that glass and watch Hamazaki's skinny ass squirm." His overt prejudice might have offended Harvey, but Cohen was already warming to this man. Apparently sensing he may have overstepped a line, Norris looked over at Miss Mills and said, "Ma'am, I apologise for my frankness and rely on you to strike my last comment from your record. Are we clear?" It was obviously an order dressed up as a question. Norris led the way out, followed by three men doing their best to mentally organise six months' worth of investigations.

Cohen could barely bring himself to look at the face of the man seated alone in the adjacent room. The one-way glass, which made up a whole wall, was very unsettling, and despite assurances that Hamazaki could neither see nor hear them, conversation seemed entirely out of the question. Even as much as a whisper seemed to bounce clumsily off the walls. The scene was utterly surreal. There sat Hamazaki, his chair unmovable, bolted into the concrete floor, a plain wooden table separating him from the vacant chair opposite that would be soon occupied by Rushton. Cohen, Harvey, and Myers looked at Tetsuyo Hamazaki as if he were a wild animal in a zoo. Here was the very man they had chased down on paper over so many late nights that had melted into early mornings. Now he was before them at last. Cohen was rather shaken by Hamazaki's apparent confidence as he drummed his fingers on the table and made a play of checking his elegant gold watch fob as if all this were a minor irritation in an otherwise normal day. Hamazaki's homburg had been laid in front of him like a barrier set up against whoever was to take the empty chair.

There was no escaping the fact that Hamazaki in the flesh was not the Hamazaki they had expected. He was far taller than his file suggested—five feet four gave way to nearly six feet—and attired in expensive and slightly dapper clothes. A flash of wine-red silk on the inside of his jacket showed as he swivelled in his chair, and he looked in fine shape for a man of sixty-two years. His grey hair was still thick and worn quite long, swept back behind his ears and held in place with a generous lathering of pomade. Considering he had recently spent eighteen months in detention, he was looking very sturdy, and this rattled something deep in Cohen's psyche.

Cohen, Myers, and Harvey took up seats close to the glass, notebooks on their laps, and waited for the proceedings to begin. Norris sat to the side of the room, making a show at being kept waiting. It was obvious that the deputy director was a man of little patience. "Where the hell has Rushton got to? The man should be in there by now. Jesus, we don't have all the time in the world." His voice seemed to carry tenfold in that almost reverential atmosphere. Cohen did not take his eyes off Hamazaki and was relieved to note that Norris's little outburst did not provoke even the slightest reaction from the man on the other side of the glass. Without fanfare the door to the interview room was pushed open and in strode Rushton. He was carrying a heavy file, which he dropped onto the table, the noise sounding thin and shallow as it was picked up by the concealed microphones. Surprisingly, Miss Mills followed Rushton into the room. She was pushing a small file cart, which she left by Rushton's side. Without so much as a glance in Hamazaki's direction, she turned and smartly left the two of them to the business at hand.

Rushton looked at Hamazaki for what seemed like a discourteous amount of time, as if weighing up the man, trying to unsettle him before a word was spoken. If that was Rushton's intention, it did not appear to work. Hamazaki stared back into his interrogator's eyes, stony faced and unflinching. It was almost comical, like two schoolboys trying to outstare each other before a playground fight. Rushton suddenly broke the silence. "Mr Hamazaki, you are in the custody of the Central Intelligence Agency and have been brought here today to assist with investigations into specific criminal acts, namely grand larceny and theft on an unprecedented scale. These acts were committed against various sovereign states, private institutions, and citizens during the illegal occupations by Japanese forces between the years 1931 and 1945, such acts being directly contrary to the Geneva Convention of 1929." Landsdale sounded stiff and overly formal.

Hamazaki did not flinch, but merely gave a brief nod to acknowledge Rushton's opening gambit. "Sir, you have me at a disadvantage. You obviously know my name, and yet you fail to introduce yourself."

Rushton looked down at his file as he spoke. "My name is Robert Rushton, and I am the chief investigative officer into these many cases of heinous acts purportedly committed by your forces in the final years of the war." Rushton tapped the stacks of files to emphasise his point.

Hamazaki gazed at Rushton as if he were deranged. "My forces?" He let his question hang in the air for a few moments. "Mr Rushton, I am not a military man, and I have never been in the service of any branch of my country's armed forces, past or present, so how can anything be 'my' forces?"

Rushton stared into Hamazaki's face and gave a sarcastic smile. "Mr Hamazaki, I was not seeking to imply that you were a soldier, heaven forbid. I am quite aware of your background, and when I say 'your forces,' that is exactly what I mean. You served in Tojo's wartime cabinet. You were the armaments minister, were you not?" Without waiting for a reply, Rushton pressed on. "So, because you were a member of the inner elite circle of decision makers, I think it is more than appropriate to describe them as 'your forces.' Whether you were a civilian in military guise or vice versa is entirely irrelevant and in any case not central to this investigation."

Hamazaki's face flushed a little. Was it anger or frustration? Whatever it was, it was clear he was not accustomed to being talked down to, and he crossed his legs, brushing something off his trousers and trying very hard to look nonplussed by Rushton's verbal aggression. "Yes, it is true. I served in that capacity. I had no choice but to do so, just as I had no choice but to turn my business over to the war effort. Refusal would have been tantamount to suicide. Those were different times, and many a good man lost all control over his actions and destiny." Hamazaki appeared to have regained his composure and to be trying to gauge the man before him.

Rushton took a file from the top of the pile, opened it, and sighed. He allowed the uncomfortable silence between them to unfold and surprise Hamazaki, a tactic that did not seem to have the desired effect, as it was obvious Hamazaki possessed enough mettle to stand his ground. Just as Rushton was about to speak, Hamazaki got his words out first, leaving the investigator open-mouthed like a carp sucking for air. "Mr Rushton, am I under formal arrest? More to the point, I question the legality of being brought here under false pretences."

On the other side of the glass, Norris gave a low whistle and muttered an expletive under his breath. Cohen got a sense that the interview was not going as smoothly as hoped. Rushton was not exactly the dominant force in the room, and it was plain as day that they had all underestimated Hamazaki.

Rushton cut in. "Mr Hamazaki, you are not under formal arrest, and we thought it best that you be brought here under these circumstances in order to prevent speculation within your own delegation."

Hamazaki gave a sarcastic smile before icing down Rushton's words. "So, you are dressing up my presence here in a veil of discretion. I do not know if I should be grateful or offended. If it is to be the latter, then I think I should request the attendance of my lawyer Mr Weinstein of New York."

Rushton shook his head. "I do hope that will not be necessary for the moment. We have only a few points that need to be cleared up, and then you should be on your way back to your delegation."

Hamazaki leaned back in his chair and took out a silver cigarette case. "Very well. I am a reasonable man, Mr Rushton, and I will offer you help in your investigations, but I have to say from the off that as armaments minister I was not privy to some of the more regrettable decisions our leaders made. Do you mind if I smoke? I find it helps me concentrate."

Rushton shook his head. "Be my guest." As an ironic statement it fell flat.

Hamazaki offered the cigarette case to Rushton. "May I tempt you? They really are made of the sweetest tobacco, all the way from Indonesia. Rare and expensive, like the best things in life."

Rushton was losing the interview. Norris knew it, and so did the team. It was like watching ice slowly melt. The fear factor had never come into it, and now they could only hope that Hamazaki would be shocked into letting something slip.

"Mr Hamazaki, I want to ask you about a specific event that occurred close to the end of the fighting in Luzon. You were sent to meet with General Yamashita at his staff headquarters, were you not? We have documented proof that places you there. We also have sworn statements that your intention was to make arrangements for the concealment of hoards of stolen war loot and to lay plans for such loot to be subsequently repatriated to your homeland. Do you wish to say anything?"

Cohen felt the tension in his chest rise as he and his colleagues hung on for Hamazaki's reply. One would have thought such an accusation would demand great thought on the part of the accused, would register shock or even fear, but Hamazaki's face betrayed none of these emotions. He took a deep drag of his cigarette, blew out the smoke upwards, and smiled through the fug. "I was in Luzon, as you say, and I did meet with Yamashita. It was a mission I was all too happy to undertake, perhaps the only decent thing I did as a minister. What strikes me as surprising is that all your files do not tell you the real reason why I was sent there." Rushton looked a little puzzled by the path Hamazaki was taking. Hamazaki sensed Rushton's confusion and pushed home his advantage. "I was sent there by my own government, as it was at the time, to order Yamashita to stand down his army and surrender his arms to the Americans. It was a mercy mission aimed at saving thousands of lives on both sides. Communications were desperate at the time, and Yamashita would not listen to the Tokyo War Command. He needed to be told face-to-face. The man was an obstinate so-and-so, but he was brave. The damn fool was even making plans for guerrilla warfare after arms down. So, I was sent out to talk him down. As for all this treasure nonsense, I do not have the slightest idea on earth what you are talking about. Neither I nor Yamashita, for that matter, would ever taint our hands with something as base as stolen property. Good heavens, man, I mean, I may have lost a lot to the war, but I am hardly destitute. It's absurd and offensive that my name should be caught up in some sordid fantasy. I am not a thief, nor would I ever lower myself to consort with such."

Rushton studied Hamazaki, looking for any telltale signs of nerves or weariness. "Mr Hamazaki, tell me why I should believe what you say when in my experience all criminals lie."

Hamazaki pointed to the files. "If the answer is not in there, then it is you, Mr Rushton, who is being duped. I was sent to that hellhole in Luzon with the complicity of the American command at the time. Use your common sense, man. How do you think such a mission could ever have been undertaken without help from your side? It would have been impossible otherwise, sheer suicide. Your high command were open to the suggestion of bringing the fighting to an end as soon as possible. They gave us a thirty-six-hour window and a relatively safe corridor to access Yamashita's headquarters. If that is not in your files, then someone has been overly censorious in their accounts. If you find it difficult to accept, then I am only happy to furnish you with documentation from my own side. I have always made it a personal rule to record all things relevant to one's life." Hamazaki's sense of indignation was there for all to see, and after he had finished his verbal tirade, he leaned back again and took out another of his exotic cigarettes. Not bothering to ask permission this time, he lit up, never for a second taking his eyes off Rushton.

"Why you?" Rushton asked. "Were you ordered to go into the thick of battle, or did you volunteer? I mean, either way it couldn't have been easy for a man of your age."

Rushton's attempt at belittling seemed to catch Hamazaki unawares for a moment, but he soon regained his composure. "I am not a vain man, Mr Rushton, but I consider myself fit enough for my age, and in answer to your question, of course I was ordered. Despite being the only capable man in that cabinet of fools, I was also the only one who could harbour any hope of getting Yamashita to understand the dire nature of the situation."

Rushton pondered this for a moment before countering with the obvious. "So, why did Yamashita ignore you and continue fighting what was clearly a lost battle?"

Hamazaki seemed to be tiring of this line of questioning, and he sighed. "That is something that can be understood only by the Japanese themselves. You may call it loyalty or something like that, but in Yamashita's eyes it would have been a betrayal of all he believed in. Surrendering his sword in the thick of battle was tantamount to cowardice, and he would not listen to me. He talked of all his brave soldiers who had died under his command; it was his duty to honour their spirits by following them to the grave."

Rushton shook his head as if dismissing Hamazaki's explanation as some absurd heroic fantasy. "All so noble, and yet Yamashita did indeed surrender, did he not? What happened to his will to follow his brave men?"

Hamazaki leaned forward in his chair and brought his face up close to Rushton. "'Fat Man' and 'Little Boy' is what happened. Two of our precious cities burnt, gone in seconds along with all their people. One great nation's supreme act of inhumanity carried out against another, and you, Mr Rushton, have the audacity to talk to me about the Geneva Convention."

Rushton appeared to consider his position as the moral high ground shifted beneath him, and then he went on to another line of questioning. "Does the name Santa Romana mean anything to you?"

Hamazaki drummed his fingers on the tabletop. "No, I have never heard of the man."

Rushton turned over the pages of the file in front of him. "Lieutenant Colonel Nishii?" Rushton looked long into Hamazaki's eyes as if he could will a positive answer out of him.

"I have met many military men in my time, but I cannot recall anyone by that name. Besides, a man of that rank is hardly going to consort with those in my own professional or social circle, is he?" Hamazaki let his last words hang in the air as if to emphasise his own high standing.

"So, I suppose you would not consider even looking at lowly men such as Lieutenants Ogawa and Tanaka." There was a flash of concern in Hamazaki's eyes, a moment of uncertainty, but it was gone in an instant. Cohen saw it, and so did Rushton. "Did you order those men to carry out special duties?"

"How absurd this all is," Hamazaki said. "I never did anything of the kind. Men like me do not speak with underlings. It is a ridiculous suggestion. What kind of 'special duties'?"

Rushton attempted to drive this momentary advantage home. "I have a sworn statement that you conspired with those officers to make preparations for the concealment of stolen treasures."

Hamazaki shook his head in disbelief. "Madness, sheer madness. Who has poisoned my family's good name?"

"Your so-called 'good name' was mentioned by a Major Kojima," Rushton sneered. "In fact he broke down right in front of me and confessed to his involvement in a conspiracy of your making." Just as Hamazaki was about to voice his outrage, Rushton cut him short, raising his tone a pitch. "I was the officer in charge of Kojima's interrogation back in Manila during the months of September and October in 1945." Hamazaki looked as though he were at a loss for words, and for the first time during the session appeared to be unsure of himself. Cohen felt certain Hamazaki would now cry out for his lawyer, but he remained impassive in his chair, slowly shaking his head. "As I said, I was heavily involved in Kojima's interrogation," Rushton went on. "He was a strong man, of that there was no doubt. I even found it within myself to sympathise with him, as he was obviously just a pawn in your scheme. He resisted the temptation to unburden his soul, and he came quite close to convincing me of his innocence. Close but not close enough. Inevitably he buckled under the intense guilt and shame he carried. I think it was when he was finally confronted with these photographic images." Rushton took some enlarged prints from the folder in front of him and pushed them across the table for Hamazaki to study. "These show what became of the forced labour that was used to go about your wretched business. If you look closely, Mr Hamazaki, you will notice that the faces on those corpses are contorted in agony and they are still wearing the uniforms of your once proud army. I have it on the finest of authority that their tongues were so swollen, they filled their entire mouths. The eyeballs were almost squeezed out of their skulls, and their lips were so purple, you would not find such horrors even in your worst nightmares. These were your men, your loyal soldiers, gassed with sarin or the like after they had toiled to conceal your filthy secrets. Gassed on your orders, Mr Hamazaki?"

Rushton let the silence between them stretch on for what seemed like an age. Hamazaki looked down at the pictures, studying each one with a morbid curiosity that verged on the obscene. After a few moments he spoke. "Mr Rushton, I know not why this Kojima sought to place me in connection with these terrible images. I do not know this Kojima at all. I have never met the man. The only thing I can surmise is that he was offering you a tale in return for some sort of clemency. Perhaps he was telling you something that you wanted to hear. I think you should go back to this man and subject him to further questioning, because if I were you, I would open myself up to the possibility that Kojima was working for someone far more fearful than I could ever be."

Rushton slammed his fist on the table and stood. He leaned over, bringing his face closer to his adversary, and shouted down at the shocked Hamazaki. "Do not ever patronise me or my investigation, or presume to tell me how to go about my business. We are thorough in our methods, and by Christ, all our roads lead to you, and as God almighty is my witness, I will not sleep soundly until you have been brought to account for your crimes. I will see you and your kind rotting in a cell before I breathe my last. So, Hamazaki, spare us all the pantomime and show some honour of your own."

There was no doubt Hamazaki was rattled. He looked anxious, and his left foot had started tapping out a fast rhythm. As he reached for his cigarette case, Rushton swiped it off the table. "I would prefer that you not smoke that filth in here." Cohen, Harvey, and Myers were gripped by the drama unfolding in front of them. Norris was leaning back in his chair, a wry smile fixed across his piggy face. Cohen started to feel a whole new level of respect for his boss.

Hamazaki was obviously unaccustomed to being spoken down to and finding it very difficult to keep his sense of order, but it was plain to all who were watching that the man was nobody's fool. Despite being subjected to Rushton's vicious accusations, he still had not let his mask slip. Cohen was willing Rushton to continue whilst he had the upper hand, but instead of haranguing Hamazaki further, he seemed content to let the uncomfortable silence between the two of them stretch. Hamazaki finally looked up from those torturous images and locked eyes with Rushton. "These are very serious accusations you seek to lay at my door, and I will contest them to my dying breath. Now, Mr Rushton, I suggest you formally place me under arrest or I will have no alternative but to instruct my attorneys to pursue a case of false detention against you, your organisation, and, as you represent your flag, your country itself."

Rushton shook his head in a show of mock disbelief. "You will not be arrested today, but believe me, your days as a free man are numbered. You will no longer sleep soundly in your bed for fear of the knock on the door that will take your liberty away for the rest of your days, and have no doubt, that knock is not far away."

Hamazaki allowed a wry smile to crack his steely demeanour. "As you wish, Mr Rushton, but as an innocent man I find your words more contemptible than frightening. Now, I believe I have nothing further to say to you or to your men who are sitting behind that glass watching and listening to this charade." Hamazaki pointed an accusatory finger at the pane of smoked grey glass, and to Cohen it seemed as if he were pointing directly at him.

Rushton slammed his palms down on the table in an obvious attempt to rein in Hamazaki's attention, but his distraction did not work, and to everyone's amazement Hamazaki stood, walked over to the dividing glass, and pressed his face so close that all those seated on the other side involuntarily leaned back in their chairs.

Rushton's raised voice hung in the air like a lost banshee's squeal. "Hamazaki, you owe my patience a great debt. Now sit down."

Hamazaki slowly turned and removed his pocket handkerchief, and before sitting made a great play of wiping down his seat. It was a defiant act of symbolism that was not lost on all those who observed. He brushed out the creases of his trousers and once more took his seat in front of Rushton. "I feel I have nothing further to say to you, Mr Rushton. It is obvious to me that you have me set as a blackened man; therefore any attempt on my part to assert otherwise would be futile. Now if you please, I demand that my lawyer be present before these ridiculous claims descend into absolute defamation. Please excuse my poor use of your language, but I am sure you fully understand what I mean."

Before Rushton had the opportunity to counter, and as if stage managed, the side door to the interview room opened and in stepped Miss Mills, closely followed by a stout fellow whose booming voice added a whole new dimension to the scene. "My name is Harold Weinstein, attorney at law, and I represent the man you have here before you." His words were thrown into Rushton's face as if each were a weapon in its own right. "Mr Hamazaki is my client, and I suspect he is being held illegally and against his will for the purpose of questioning that is, I believe, contrary to your own codes of conduct in addition to unconstitutional behaviour. Now, if Mr Hamazaki has no further business with you—and that is for him to decide—I will accompany my client out of this building, but not before issuing you this warning: Any further, illegal harassment of my client will result in the full weight of this country's judicial system bearing down on you all." Weinstein puffed up his chest, as if daring any challenge to come forth.

Cohen looked at his colleagues, who could do nothing but sit helplessly in the face of Weinstein's verbal bullying. Deputy Director Norris made no move to help his chief investigator, apparently preferring to let Rushton take the flak alone. Hamazaki stood and gave Weinstein a grave nod of approval. He looked at Rushton and then over to his hat, cigarette case, and lighter, which were still on the floor. His eyes returned to Rushton, and he stared at him. "Before I take my leave, I would like Mr Rushton to retrieve my property, which he so carelessly discarded across the floor." Rushton's face reddened, and it was plain that he was straining to keep control. Both parties stood awkwardly as if in a Mexican standoff. To spare her boss any further embarrassment Miss Mills picked up Hamazaki's items and nervously put them into his outstretched palm. "Thank you, madam. It is good to see that not all manners are lost in this tiny corner of your great country." He gave a little bow to Miss Mills and then faced Weinstein. "I think it is time we took our leave; I believe there is much we need to discuss." Hamazaki once more faced the glass and, raising his hat in mock salutation, said, "Good day, gentlemen." They left the room, leaving Rushton staring vacantly at the blank wall opposite.

"How the hell did Weinstein get wind of what was happening here?" Norris was working himself up into a stir that had flushed his face and shortened his breath. Nobody ventured a reply, figuring the question was purely rhetorical. Cohen, Harvey, and Myers sat in glum silence. The institutionalised grey walls of the debriefing room captured the collective mood perfectly. They were all waiting for Rushton to join them and to make sense of the pantomime they had just witnessed. It was obvious to all that Norris was, first and foremost, worried about how any negative fallout would affect his own personal position. It had been rumoured that he might be in the running for the director's chair, and he was ruthless enough to shift blame without so much as a second thought.

Norris looked at his dejected bunch of operatives. "Where are we now? We showed our hand, and it got us nowhere; my God, what a shambles."

The door creaked open and in stepped Rushton, who had obviously overheard Norris's little rant. "On the contrary, I think we have stirred up the hornet's nest sufficiently. Now let's see what happens." Everyone stared at Rushton as if he were high on some narcotic. He was unmoved by their lack of enthusiasm and pressed on. "Think this through. Hamazaki will now need to take some kind of action to make sure no dirt sticks to him. He will take it as a personal affront that we have managed to tie him to this grand criminal enterprise, and it would not be to his favour should his associates and social circle get wind of any scandals. Back in Tokyo rumours tend to follow you around like a bad smell. I think we have pushed him into a corner. He may be snarling and sneering, but for all his front, he will be a worried man, and worried men make mistakes, which is why I will be one step ahead of him. This evening I will leave for Tokyo, to oversee the second part of our investigations into the illicit dealings of Tetsuyo Hamazaki."

Deputy Director Norris appeared as surprised as the rest of the team. Rushton had never mentioned any second part of the investigation before, and they all looked like a bunch of lost souls desperate for a guiding light. Norris quickly covered up his ignorance of the situation by demanding that Rushton follow him to his office for a personal one-to-one, leaving the rest of the team killing time and waiting on further orders.

It was already late in the working day when Rushton finally reappeared in the main office. He called the team around to give them a rushed update of events, explaining that it had to be brief because he was heading out for his flight to Tokyo. Brief it was, but lacking in sensationalism it most certainly wasn't. Rushton told his men to relax and smoke if they wished. Only Harvey took up the offer. "Now, what you witnessed this morning was exactly what I wanted you to see—that is, Hamazaki acting out his false innocence in a display of bluff, bravado, and arrogance. I wanted to rattle him and let him know we are close to his dirty secrets. I wanted to provoke a reaction, and I think we will get it." Rushton could sense that his team were not entirely convinced, so he pressed on. "Hamazaki and his delegation are due back in Tokyo later this week; I will already be in place to monitor the next stage of investigations, which will centre on his reaction to our allegations. I have assembled a team of our best covert operatives, who will conduct round-the-clock surveillance and monitoring. Some Dutch engineers have developed a system whereby we can monitor all conversations that take place in a certain room. It's going to be a game changer, and we are to be one of the first to deploy it in the field."

There was an audible intake of breath as everyone tried to come to grips with this new information. Rushton carried on. "For some months now I have been exploiting one of Hamazaki's weaknesses, that being his blind devotion to his two children, Toshio and Ayumi. Now, Toshio, the son and heir, on the face of it appears most undeserving of his father's affections. He is a drinker and a blaggard to boot, which all plays nicely into our hands. His weaknesses are chinks in the armour that we will exploit. It seems that Toshio, apple of his father's eye, has fallen in love with a young man who goes by the name of Kawabata." There was a gasp of astonishment as Toshio Hamazaki's sexuality was laid bare as if it were an item on a dinner menu. "Yes, you heard me right," Rushton said. "Young Hamazaki is in love with a man. I know it is hard to grasp, but you have to remember, they kind of look on these things a bit differently over there in wildest Tokyo. Anyway, that's all by the way. What is important is that unbeknownst to Toshio, Kawabata is our man, and what's more, he is our man inside the Hamazaki residence. Kawabata will plant the listening receptor in Hamazaki's office, and the sweet little boyfriend will provide us with all the information we need to bring Hamazaki crashing down to his knees. Now, gentlemen, if you will excuse me, I have a plane to catch. Harvey will act as team leader in my absence, and he will receive updates as and when things happen. You will all take direction from him."

Without so much as a goodbye, Rushton was out of the door, his coat draped over his arm, leaving his team disconnected and lost for words. It was Harvey who broke the silence. "Clever folks, those Dutch. Obviously not all windmills and cheese."

Chapter 3
Hideo Tanaka
Tokyo
1949

It is the autumn of 1949, and Tokyo is starting to come alive again after years of suffering and deprivation. I can feel it all around me. The air is crackling with hope and anticipation. Almost fourteen years of continual wars have sucked the soul out of our country. The war-ravaged areas of our beloved Tokyo are no longer piled with the mountains of debris that bore testament to our failure. The streets are clear, and new houses, shops, and offices seem to appear daily, almost of their own accord.

The American forces announced a large scaling down of their presence. I see fewer GIs and other servicemen on the streets these days. The occupation was difficult for many of our tradition-alists to accept. However, a great many people have come to real-ise the value of peace and stability that MacArthur's administration has given them. At the war's end, we were a demoralised and bro-ken nation trying to come to terms with the horrors of Hiroshima and Nagasaki. The people had been betrayed by their leaders and political elite, and were bankrupted and beyond all hope. After so much hardship and sacrifice, anything that offered a brighter future was to be welcomed with open arms.

As an ex-combatant I experienced mixed emotions. Of course I welcomed the peace, but it was sometimes hard to accept that the men walking our streets holding hands with our girls, drinking and laughing in cafés and bars, were the very same men I had been trying so desperately to kill or avoid being killed by only a few short years ago. My personal feelings aside, it was impossible to deny the sense of optimism being generated by our American occupiers.

The plans put in place for the rebuilding of the economy are starting to pay dividends. The administration has played on our strengths to great effect. Our single-minded militaristic psyche, which was once the driving force of nationalist ambition, has been redirected into practical production. Our collective strength and determination to rebuild the country knows no limits. We were a defeated nation, bowed and broken. Now, four years on, our drive toward prosperity and full recovery is relentless. It is American money that is paving the way for us, and for that, we have to excuse the irony and be forever grateful to our American "guests."

If I were to try to explain why the country was able to find its feet after the devastation of the past, I would point to the spirit of co-operation between communities and business as our main strength. Our single-mindedness and our desire to become a proud country again is what drives us on. We work with the same fervour as the Communists do in the Soviet Union, except our collectivism is not centralized. We work to make things better, and to try to erase the bitter memories of the past. It still feels indecent to be alive when so many have died. We work in the shadow of their memory, so their sacrifice will never be in vain. I often wonder if it will ever be possible to smile once more without feeling a sense of guilt. Everybody lost somebody to the war, and it's the unspoken servitude of common suffering that binds us together. Work drives us all to put aside the grieving that has haunted all our nights for so many years.

The new politicians are already talking about a so-called economic surge that will propel us back into the light. Japan reborn, desperately trying to shed the shackles of guilt, willing to do anything that gives hope.

As for my own role in this new Japanese economic revolution, well, I spend all my days in a tiny room in the middle of a crowded noisy side street in Shinjuku. I make my living and manage to feed myself by repairing broken radio sets. Tube radios and some of the newer valve radios are the things of my life. I go out into the streets looking like a vagrant, pushing my cart along and shouting out my presence, asking for old, broken, and unwanted radio sets. For these I pay a few yen and then salvage any working parts, from which I put together "brand-new used" radios that I can sell for a small profit. This has been my life for the past three years. It's the only thing I can do and the only thing that stops me from going insane.

I hadn't planned to become a radio repairman; it was just something that happened. It came about because I needed a radio of my own. I went out and scoured the local dumps until I found something fixable. It was easy to repair, and I happened to mention it to one of my neighbours, who then brought me his set to fix. From then on I was the man to see if you were having radio problems. The radio is the focal point of most households and the source of news and entertainment for families nationwide.

It didn't take long before I was getting regular work. I can repair most sets without difficulty. If it is beyond repair, then, if the customer can afford it, I sell them one of my own remade sets with the promise of free repair if it ever breaks down.

Three years have passed since I came to my small room to set up my little workshop, the same room where I sleep and eat. I spend nearly all of my time in my small room, bent over the minute pieces that go together to produce the miracle of radio. Despite my long, hard days of work there are still times when I go hungry. If work dries up for a few days, I won't eat well. It is still a hand-to-mouth existence. I'm a whole lot better off than some, but a lot worse off than many. I have never eaten outside this room in three years. I possess only one pair of much repaired shoes. I wash my clothes once a month in a nearby stream. I never buy anything except radio parts and basic food. I pay for electricity by meter, sometimes waiting hours for daylight to come because I don't have any coins. My working hours are decided by the amount of work I get, but I seldom work less than twelve hours a day. I never have a day off. When I am not at my bench working, I'm out looking for scraps, anything that might come in useful. I read old newspapers that are left at bus stops or thrown into bins by people with money to waste.

Of course I don't have a bank account or an army pension. I badly need new spectacles, as the constant squinting at small parts that my work requires has taken its toll on my eyes. I can't afford a visit to the dentist to fix my rapidly decaying teeth. I never buy fresh fruit, and I don't have any running water in my room. I use the communal washroom and toilet down the street. We have a neighbourhood roster for cleaning duties, and I take my turn to throw out the shit and piss.

So, that is my life now. Here I am, former Second Lieutenant Tanaka Hideo of the former Imperial Japanese Army, living alone in filthy poverty and holder of the Heart of Japan.

If all this were not enough to make a man question life itself, then I will shamelessly add to my misery. My wife, daughter, mother, father, grandmother, and grandfather were all killed on the same night, March 10, 1945. An American bombing raid obliterated our entire neighbourhood, and the incendiary explosives and firestorm that followed killed all that I held dear in this world. My family was removed from this earth that evening. I do not mention this to garner any pity, as I know my situation is not uncommon. It is merely the madness of the gods and the angels who do not have a tear left to shed. Yes, I am alive, but I died inside a long time ago. Those years broke something inside of me that can never be fixed. My existence is a mocking insult to my own self, and the only thing I can do is lose myself in the mechanics of repair. The irony isn't lost.

I was told by a neighbour that the old war office, which had a new name that nobody could remember, had placed a notice in the *Yomiuri* newspaper asking war veterans to come forward and make a claim for a pension. It seemed that they had finally been embarrassed into taking some kind of action. Hundreds if not thousands of returnees across the country had found themselves homeless and destitute. These men had been forced to live rough on the streets, causing a debate about how to handle the problem, offending and shaming the administration in equal measures. On the one hand the Diet was pleading poverty to avoid war reparations, and yet they had a moral duty to help starving veterans. It had taken more than four years to get to this point where real help could at last be on offer. If our leaders were serious about building a new Japan, then something had to be done about the constant reminder that the old Japan still cast its dark shadow into places that people would rather forget about. The lost and hungry survivors on the streets were the starkest reminder of the failure to deal with our moral debt.

I decided to go to the local civic centre and try to find out if there was any truth to the rumour about pensions. I needed the money for sure. In any case, the war office held copies of my record of service, so I hoped that any claim I made would be treated favourably. I had also registered my details with the reception committee at Yokohama port office on the day of my repatriation. I had given my name, rank, unit, place of capture, and place of detention. I had been wary about giving up this information, but after weeks of soul searching I decided that subterfuge was unnecessary. I hadn't been warned against revealing my identity, and considered myself to be safe after reaching my homeland. If anyone wanted to find me, then they needed a place to look. The civilian clerk on the quayside, a young and pretty woman, wrote down my details that day. She was unable to hide her surprise when I told her I was a lieutenant. Not many commissioned officers had made it back.

That was more than three years ago. As the months turned into years, I gave up hope of fulfilling my final act of duty. No contact or approach of any kind had been made. I had expected to be sought out as soon as I got back, but I came to accept that I was a forgotten man.

My own war did not end in the Luzon jungle. It still rages in my heart and constantly deprives me of sleep. I scream myself awake, my sweat-soaked delirium now a common part of the fabric of my life. It is only my imagination that keeps me sane. I allow myself the sentimentality to live in the past, by which I mean happier days long gone. It is only this reverie that stops me from sinking into the foul pit of despair. I have become so wanting that I can almost make myself believe that I am back and living once more the life of an innocent young man free from the wicked madness that haunts him. It is often the case that when I am woken by my demons and find myself way beyond sleep, I give up to the night, brew stale tea leaves, and just sit in my room listening to the quiet of the new day coming.

I can't help but go over, time and time again, the events that have put me here, in this room, and I cannot for the life of me understand why I was not given a soldier's death like all my officer comrades. My blood and bones should be in the Luzon jungle, helping to feed the earth by giving something back after the destruction we sowed. I've heard that more than two hundred thousand of our troops perished there. I pray that the trees grow lush on their sacrifice. Fate, however, deemed that I was not to meet my end there and then. It was in the midst of a particularly brutal exchange with the enemy that I received notice to report back to command headquarters immediately. I could not look my sergeant in the eye as I handed over command of what was left of our unit. I knew I would never see him again, just as he knew that somehow I had been given another roll of the dice. Well, this absurd order seemed to come with the highest authority, and I was escorted farther behind our own lines than I thought possible. Two special operations troopers had been tasked to deliver me safely back to General Yamashita's command headquarters. We moved swiftly down our own supply lines, covering the ground easily, as it had been cleared for the heavy supply trucks earlier in the campaign. American mortar fire had taken a grisly toll. Whole encampments had taken direct hits, and sadly, the corpses of my fellow fighters were such a common sight that I accepted death as the new normal.

As we made our way through the ever thickening jungle, I began to worry about the reason for my recall. I concluded that whatever it was did not look good for me. I convinced myself that I was to be charged with some kind of dereliction of duty. I had no idea what that might be, but the mere fact that I was still alive may have caused them to question my commitment to death. Nearly all my fellow commissioned officers had died in battle. I guessed that my continued survival against the odds had stirred suspicion. My guides proved agile and knew the lines well. The fierce battle we had left was fading away behind us, but now and again there would be the odd almighty explosion and we would turn back to look at the glow against the night sky that one of our ammunition dumps left when directly hit. We all knew that with such a hit came a devastating loss of life and another big step towards our inevitable defeat.

It took the best part of four hours before we finally found ourselves at the heavily fortified outer cordon that ringed General Yamashita's headquarters. The special troopers were well trained in the established military protocol, and with the aid of torchlight signals and direct radio contact, we were soon within the heart of what stood for command headquarters of the Imperial Japanese Army. In better times it would have been a shameful sight, but these were desperate days, and the shambolic end that awaited our army had obviously permeated the ramshackle clearing of Nissen huts and timber frames thatched with banana leaves. My two escorts, duty done, snapped to attention, saluted, and doubled off, leaving me standing alone in what I took to be a small parade square.

A voice cut through the night air. "Lieutenant Tanaka, step forward." I walked towards the call and realised that the man before me was none other than Lieutenant General Muto, second in command to General Yamashita himself. I saluted and gave a gracious bow, which he did not even acknowledge. "Tanaka, follow me. Your orders are waiting." We walked into one of the Nissen huts and then down a long gloomy stairway. The earth had been hollowed out below to reveal a tunnel system of rooms and anterooms, dimly lit by very low-wattage lighting. Lieutenant General Muto stood before one of the doors. As I was about to enter, he held his hand in front of my face. "I will say this to you now. I do not know why you are here, nor do I care. That is by the way, but there is something I want to say. Whatever it is you are to do, I want you to understand that it is not at the behest of General Yamashita. An order was received from the Military High Command in Tokyo. It is of a highly classified nature and entirely irrelevant to our cause. The general confided in me that he found this distasteful and wanted no part in the matter. However, being an honourable man, he has agreed to allow you to follow that order, which was delivered in a sealed box and has remained untouched by the general and myself. So, whatever it contains concerns you alone." Muto pushed open the door and, unable to hide the disgust and contempt in his voice any longer, turned away. I stepped into the room, and as if this day could not get any stranger, standing there waiting was my oldest friend, Ogawa.

After we got over the shock of being suddenly thrown together in the wildest of imaginings, we made a little small talk. I remember Ogawa asking about my family back home. I told him I hadn't heard anything for more than a year, but was sure they were fine and well. Ogawa seemed to sense that my belief in their well-being was based on nothing more than hope and prayers. He placed his hand on my shoulder in a gesture of understanding. There was so much to talk about. I asked after his father, but like me, he hadn't heard anything for months on end. We talked of mutual friends, comrades in arms, those who, sadly, are no longer with us.

We could have talked for hours, but there was no getting away from the reason we were there. A large wooden strong box sat on a table in the centre of the room. I looked to Ogawa to take the lead as he had so often during our time at officer cadet school. Those days now seemed like a faded old photograph. Two young men filled with romantic ideas and foolhardy bravado. It would be impossible to place us now as the same people. I knew Ogawa had been selected for special duties straight after basic training, and by the look of him, he seemed to have had a rough time of it. His eyes were sunken, and his tunic still bore the smell of cordite. He caught me looking at a dark bloodstain on his shoulder. "Don't fret. It isn't mine," he said with the same sly smile I remembered so well. We both looked at the box and knew that we could no longer delay the inevitable. It was time to find out what fate the gods had in store for us.

My thoughts then drifted back to that day when our ship finally docked at Yokohama quayside. I had stood on the deck for hours watching and waiting to take that first step back onto the land of my birth. We had been repatriated on a merchant ship, the *Maru Nobu*. It had once been a fine vessel but now bore the signs of war damage, having been hit by an airstrike when part of a supply convoy. The repairs had been makeshift, as the need to get ships back into the supply chain as soon as possible was all that mattered. Our route back from the Philippines was slow, as we had to circumnavigate certain heavily mined sea channels. The ship was carrying more than seven hundred returnees and crew. We slept anywhere we could find a space. I slept on the open deck each night of our five-day voyage. I kept to myself, seldom speaking to anyone. Those who had the energy volunteered for work details—cooking, cleaning, even slopping out the toilet pails. It was easy to avoid any work, as there were so many of us, and losing yourself in the crowd was simple.

I would listen as the men talked of their excitement about going home. They talked of the things they had missed: their families, workmates, favourite drinking places, and, of course, the girls. It had been years since many of us had even seen a Japanese woman, and pent-up feelings were finally coming to the surface. We all knew deep down that the place we had left so many years ago was gone, but nobody wanted to face that harsh reality until it was an inescapable fact. In truth, none of us knew what to expect. Each one of us was desperately trying to find a thread from the past that would help us recover and pull us into the present and away from the hell we had been put through.

As the ship pulled alongside the dock, we were told to line up in columns for an orderly disembarkation. We were each given a small card with a number and the ship's name, which we were to hand to the clerks at quayside for processing. We filed down the gangways. A drab grey sight we must have been, hollow eyed, carrying what few possessions we had. The disabled, sick, or infirm were left on deck to be stretchered ashore later. Hundreds of people lined our path, anxiously scanning the ravaged faces of all the bewildered men thrust back into the land they called home. So much desperation etched into the faces of those looking for a long-lost loved one. Hoping against all hope that their father, son, or husband would be among the returning few. They scrutinised our faces, shouting out names, holding up pieces of cardboard with names painted on them. I saw several women throw themselves to the ground, desperately wailing out names in the hope that they could conjure up a miracle.

I didn't see any joyful reunions that day. People change as the years move on, but war changes people in ways you would never believe. The chances of finding that loved one they had bade farewell to years earlier were slipping away in front of their eyes. When I look in a mirror these days, I can hardly believe it is me looking back. The people waiting to greet the boats looked as worn and tired as we did. We had all changed; none of us would ever be the same.

As I passed through those pressing crowds of desperate, tearful people, I too was praying with all my heart—that my beautiful Fumiyo would be waiting for me, standing there holding the hand of our daughter, Sachiyo. The little girl I had never seen. How could I have known that they had been removed from the earth in a hellish way so long ago? Now as I spend day after day in my own little world, I close my eyes and see Fumiyo in her best kimono, standing by the roadside, white faced and beautiful, babe in womb, bowing politely and seeing me off to war. It is hard to believe that all this began with a simple bus ride, a journey that went to hell and beyond. Her last words to me will always ring in my ears: "Keep safe, and come back to us quickly." She patted her stomach and gave a shy smile, looked down, and willed her tears to freeze before they had a chance to streak her porcelain beauty. My own tears come easily, and I say to myself, *If this is life, then I welcome the day when I will join Fumiyo and Sachiyo somewhere in a place free from this madness we were all born into.*

October was fast approaching. The relentless summer heat had finally given way to a more bearable air. It wouldn't be long before we were in the depths of winter and faced with the challenge of keeping warm. As I was labouring at my workbench one evening, I noticed that someone had pushed a small brown envelope under my door. I left my bench and bent down to pick it up. I lifted the doormat to check for more and found a letter there. This was a rare occurrence. I could go for months without receiving correspondence of any kind, and two pieces in a day was unheard of. The first was a note from my landlord informing me that, with much regret, he had to increase my monthly rent by two hundred yen per month. It was the second time that year my rent had increased. Rents were going up all over the city, and our area, Shinjuku, though once poor, was becoming more desirable. My landlord was getting greedier, and I wondered how long I would be able to afford to live and work in this tiny little room. I looked over to the radio I had been working on. It had taken me the best part of a day to fix, and I would bill my customer seventy-five yen. In real terms it meant three days of work would be needed to cover the rise in rent.

The second envelope was from the Social Ministry of Work and Pensions Office. At last, after two months of waiting I had finally got my reply to the claim I had made nearly two months earlier. After the landlord's letter, I hoped this would bring better news. I was becoming desperate and badly needed a change in fortune. The address was elegantly written. I opened it carefully and took out the thin, white, typed notepaper and read it through slowly, hardly able to believe the words before my eyes. They read, "We have searched our archive for details of your service and cannot find any records that match the details you provided on your application for an ex-serviceman's pension. In addition your repatriation details are not on record. A further enquiry to the officer training school resulted in no record that matches your details. Your application is returned for you to review your details. However, based on your initial submission, your application is categorically rejected. Please be aware that making fraudulent claims is punishable by a fine and/or a prison sentence." I was dumbstruck. How could this possibly be? I felt hurt and anger in equal measure. I needed some time to think it through.

I gave up any idea of continuing with work for the day and decided to go out for some air. A strong wind was getting up, and it felt like we were on the edge of a typhoon. The weather matched my feelings perfectly. It seemed as if somebody were trying to erase my very existence. I didn't doubt the integrity of the Pensions Office; I was sure they had investigated my claim to the best of their ability. The more I pondered the letter and its implications, the more distracted I became. If my service records had been deliberately erased, what had been the motive for doing so? I had tried to make myself as visible as possible so I could complete my duty, yet someone was trying to push me back into the shadows, perhaps to conceal my involvement in the mission that has been dogging me all these years. It was impossible to make any sense of it. I only hoped that whoever was behind it all would come out of the dark and put an end to the whole sordid saga.

I had come to accept struggle as just a part of everyday life, and in truth I suppose it is nothing more than just another hardship that must be borne. The injustice of the matter was not the issue. I felt as if I had been reduced to irrelevance, a nonperson. Yet despite all my frustrations, nothing compared with the deprivations which my dear old comrade, Ogawa, must have faced. I had no idea whether he had survived the final days of our surrender. The last time I saw him was back in Luzon. Our mission finally completed, all that remained was for me to surrender into American custody and for Ogawa to slip back into the jungle and remain there for reasons known only to himself. As I walked into enemy custody, my hands on my head, I could feel the tears welling in my eyes. I could not bear the thought of abandoning my dear friend, and yet, that is what I did. Another stain on my heart that is excused in the name of duty. Even though four years have passed, it is impossible to make sense of what really happened to us during those awful days.

After we pulled ourselves together from the shock of being reunited in General Yamashita's headquarters, it soon became clear that our destinies were to be entirely different—that is, if we survived long enough to see the madness before us through to its end.

Ogawa broke the seal on the wooden box and slid the bolts this way and that before slowly lifting the lid. We both peered in as if it might contain the secrets of the universe itself, although unless those mysteries were contained within a hessian sack, we were sure to be disappointed. Ogawa bent down and heaved the object, shorter than a carbine rifle but, we discovered, a great deal heavier, out of the box. The weight took him by surprise, and he passed it to me. I remember mentioning that it weighed like a full box of rifle ammunition. We put it on the floor, both of us at a loss for words. Perhaps it was the fatigue or, more likely, the confusion at finding ourselves caught in such a surreal moment. There was a brown document file on the base of the box, fastened with a Japanese Imperial Army wax seal the likes of which neither of us had seen before. It was as impersonal as it was impressive. Obviously, no man had wanted his name affixed to it. The file was addressed to the attention of Lieutenant Ogawa. The seal had been untouched, which we took to mean it had come directly from Tokyo. Upon seeing his name, Ogawa took the file off into a corner, slumped down the wall, and ripped it open. I stared at him from across the room and saw the colour drain from his face.

The room was deathly silent. Not even the madness of the raging war we had left behind could intrude on this moment. Ogawa read the papers over and over again. Then he looked over to me. "Hideo, my friend, it seems we have been both blessed and cursed in equal measure." He tossed the papers across the floor in a fit of anger. I picked up the sheets and quickly reorganised them. Ogawa sat in the far corner of the room, his head bowed, rocking backwards and forwards on his haunches. I read the top page. "Operation Golden Lily." My eyes skimmed over the order contained within. I looked over at Ogawa, who seemed to have pulled himself together. I read through the orders and then stared at him. For the first time we were told that defeat was an inevitability and yet there were still ways in which the Imperial Empire could be served. This had nothing to do with honour. It was obvious that we were both thinking the same thing: sheer and utter, total lunacy.

We had been ordered to deliver the hessian bundle to a specific location and were given the map reference. Upon arrival at that location we were to conceal the bundle, go deep underground, and evade capture until the cessation of hostilities. I was ordered to place myself in American custody—literally give up the fight and walk out of my hiding hole, waving a piece of white cloth, straight into enemy hands. For sure, I would be shot down on the spot. It seemed I was to be given a coward's way out. I could not believe my eyes: a disgraceful end to my war. I thought of all my comrades who had bravely laid down their lives without even the slightest wavering. Surely, this could not be a legal order.

I read further and found that I was to be the bearer of what was known as the Heart of Japan, which turned out to be a small piece of rice paper, no bigger than a postage stamp, upon which was scrawled a series of numbers which looked like map references. It seemed that this was to be my saviour, the reason I was to be denied a soldier's death. I had been ordered to deliver this to the homeland. The paper was contained within a small hardwood tube that was easy to hide somewhere on your person. I slipped it into the hem of my tunic.

Ogawa's own orders were even more outrageous than my own. He had the responsibility of concealing the mysterious bundle and also keeping me alive at all costs. That was only half of it. It seemed that his own war was to go on. After I had been safely despatched into the loving arms of the Americans, he was to remain in Luzon on active duty regardless of any ceasefire he may hear of. Ogawa had been given a contact reference, which he had torn off and concealed on his person. I was beyond caring about such futile subterfuge. He was told that he would receive further orders at a later date. It was all too vague, too desperate. This smacked of stupid old men back in Tokyo, playing ridiculous war games without a clue about the consequences of their warped fantasies.

Ogawa asked me how long I believed our army was capable of holding off the American victory. To speak of defeat felt treacherous in itself, and yet I knew I could be honest with Ogawa. "We may have suffered defeat as we stand here talking."

Ogawa took a moment to digest my grim forecast before adding, "I would give it at least seven more days. Heavy rain is looming, and in this war that means the Americans will have to wait for their prize. Also, that gives us time to get about our own business." Ogawa had completely snapped out of his despondency and was now back in the moment. He had been given orders by the high command, and he was, sure as hell is hot, going to see to his duty.

We both turned our attention to the hessian bundle. Words were unnecessary. Ogawa took out his side knife and cut the bindings, freeing the sacking. We both knelt and unwrapped the coverings, revealing what was contained within.

I will never, in a million lifetimes, see another object as beautiful as that which lay before us then. A goddess crafted out of the finest gold, inlaid with thousands of precious glittering emeralds. Her beauty was beyond a normal man's understanding. We were both transfixed, speechless. Somehow, for reasons I could not begin to understand, this whole madness now seemed to make a little sense. I believed that we had been given a mission of far greater importance than either of us would ever understand. It was about the preservation of a serene beauty. Ogawa carefully placed her upright, and we marvelled at how the light seemed to alter her features. For the first time in months I smiled, and I noticed that Ogawa had relaxed a little also. We called her the Emerald Buddha, and I said a silent prayer that she would help us both through the trials of the days ahead.

Ogawa placed a hand on my shoulder and said it was time to go. He struck a match and set fire to our orders, and we watched as the flames consumed the madness from Tokyo. I saw the fire dancing in the face of the Emerald Buddha, her divine beauty unfazed by the wicked games men play. We both took time to say a prayer before we wrapped our precious goddess once more in her sad shroud and went about making preparations for our journey into the unknown.

The rain had started to whip its way down between the narrow Shinjuku alleys and buildings, being driven this way and that by swirling gusts that were getting stronger by the minute. I decided to head back to my workshop. As I got closer, I saw two men standing outside my door. The taller of the two was rapping against my door with a cane; the other was holding a large brown box. Naturally I assumed they were customers, and I silently cursed myself for being too tardy and possibly losing much-needed work. I picked up my pace and was slightly out of breath as I reached my shop just in time to catch them. "Excuse me. My name is Tanaka. I apologise for not being here when you first called. Is there something I can help you with?"

The taller man looked down at me with a stern and hard, calculating look. He seemed to be studying my face, cocking his head this way and that to check my profile from different angles.

He was making me feel very uncomfortable, and for a moment I thought I had misread the situation and these gentlemen were police officers who had come to question me about possible fraudulent claims. The tall man removed his hat and gave me a polite nod and then broke into a huge smile that completely transformed him from a man to be wary of to everybody's favourite uncle in the space of a few seconds. He bowed once more and introduced himself. "My name is Toshio Hamazaki, and this is my associate Mr Kawabata. Tanaka san, a dear friend recommended your services to me, and I do hope you can help us."

"Of course I will do my best to be of service. Excuse my manners. Please do come inside." I pushed the door open and held it for them enter. The room seemed to shrink in on itself with the three of us standing awkwardly in the tiny space. I asked Mr Kawabata if he would like to put his box down. Kawabata looked to Hamazaki for approval, and Hamazaki gave him a nod. Kawabata removed his hat, and I noticed he was no more than a youth. Hamazaki, on the other hand, was around my age, though it was hard to tell for sure, standing there so tall and dressed in such fine clothes. He had a habit of running his fingers through his thick, shiny black hair. His elegance was undeniable, and he was most certainly not my usual class of customer. I was beginning to feel ashamed of my own shabby appearance and of the odour that seemed to permanently hang about me. I was thrown by the moment and had to check myself from staring at Mr Hamazaki. His mere presence exuded authority, and his confidence was such that you felt as if you could reach out and take a little for yourself. He was well spoken and showed me the kindest of considerations, never once paying any heed to the scruffiness of my surroundings.

"Tanaka san, I have here in this box two radio receivers, both unable to receive broadcasts for reasons I cannot fathom. I was hoping you would use your expertise and check them over for me."

"Of course, sir. May I look in the box?" He nodded, and I removed the two sets and placed them side by side on my workbench. These weren't the kind of radios I usually repaired. They were fine, expensive models, both imported from overseas. I was curious about their workings but not confident that I would be able to repair them, especially if they required spare parts.

Hamazaki looked at me with pleading in his eyes. "Tanaka san, I was hoping that you would make this request a priority, as these sets belong to some very dear friends of mine and they feel lost without their daily broadcasts."

"Of course, sir. Shall we say next week at this very same time?"

Hamazaki looked over to Kawabata and then replied, "I was rather hoping for tomorrow at the same time." His tone, though not menacing, was hard to deny.

"That may be a little too soon," I said. "I don't know how much repair each of them might need."

Hamazaki nodded thoughtfully. "Nonetheless, Tanaka san, I shall call on you tomorrow at the same time and you will at least be able to apprise me of your progress."

As I said, the man was hard to deny. "Of course, sir." I was feeling belittled in his presence, yet on closer inspection he may very well have been younger than me.

"My thanks to you, Tanaka san. Until tomorrow." He gave a polite bow, which I returned, and stepped backwards out of my shop, followed by the young Mr Kawabata, who hadn't spoken a word during our encounter.

It was turning out to be a very strange day. First I was asked for more rent. Then I was denied a pension, because apparently I didn't exist. Lastly, a fine gentleman had brought me the most expensive radios I had ever seen to fix. I had no doubt, no doubt at all, that the elegant Mr Hamazaki was somebody more than just a man who wanted radios repairing. I was sure I knew what he wanted. I instinctively opened the small drawer below my workbench and with relief found Daisuke's pen. I turned it over in my hand as I have done every single day since I concealed the tiny piece of rice paper in its body. I held it tightly in my fist and prayed that whatever was to become of all this, the gods would grant me forgiveness.

I picked up each radio and inspected them closely. They were both made by Philco, an American manufacturer. One of them was from 1940, the other, a later model made in 1948. The newer model had an FM receiver and automatic tuning, two things that our home-produced radios had yet to incorporate. It was another example of the power and progress of America. Our politicians may well talk of a new Japan, but we are a long way from being able to put out products such as these. I pushed aside the JRC520 I had been working on; it looked cheap and ugly next to the Philcos. The 1940 set was a thing of beauty, housed in a sloping, polished wooden cabinet. The 1948 model was Bakelite with a strange shape I hadn't seen before but far more attractive than any I had previously worked on.

I found it hard to concentrate on the task in hand. Nevertheless, I was a radio repairman, and that is what Hamazaki had engaged me to do. Then it struck me. The name, Hamazaki, was familiar. I had heard it before, and now it came back to me. Hamazaki was a minister in the Tojo war cabinet. I couldn't recall exactly what his title was, but I was sure he was high ranking. Had he been minister for war or something? I tried to think, but nothing else came to mind. The elegant man bearing radios was obviously too young to be the same person. Or was he? I had never seen any photographs of our wartime leaders; I guessed it may have been possible, but it was highly unlikely. Maybe he was a relative of some kind.

Hamazaki . . . The name itself fired my imagination and fuelled my suspicions. This was no ordinary repair job. I was losing myself in a fog of paranoia and needed to clear my head. I tend to think better when I can shut out the outside world, so I decided to give these urgent requests my full attention. I opened the door and flipped the "Open" sign to "Closed" and went about my work. I moved the dials and checked the switches; both were dead. Nothing—no signal could be found at all. I started on the 1940 model, removing the back panel. I shone my torch into its workings. It looked pretty ordinary. What had I expected? A note or something? A tube had burnt out, and some soldering had melted away. Simple enough to repair if only I had a spare tube, which I didn't.

Sighing and cursing my lack of spare parts, I moved on to the second set. The problem was easy to find. The On/Off button spring had come loose. This I knew I could fix, and if that was the only problem, it should be easy to restore the radio to full working order. I removed the back to check for other problems and found none. To my great surprise this model came with a spare tube, which I removed and fixed into the first set. I resoldered the loose wire and after only twenty minutes of work had the radio receiving a clear signal.

I turned my attention to the other one. I needed to make a new spring from scratch. I was confident that I would have this one working in next to no time at all. It was far easier than I thought and took no more than thirty minutes. Both sets were now repaired and waiting for Mr Hamazaki to collect. I was satisfied with my work and decided to go out for a walk and take in some fresh air. The deluge of rain had abated, and the air was cool and crisp. It felt good to breathe. I was sure this was an omen of better things to come.

I locked the door behind me, something I seldom do. I didn't want to risk losing the radios to a sneak thief. Such occurrences are almost unheard of. In our neighbourhood we respect each other's poverty. I guess there is extra shame in stealing from people who have next to nothing to begin with. I found myself taking a familiar route, one I had come to know well since my return from the war. I headed along the narrow streets, dodging the bicycles, which always seem to be going faster than the cars. I stopped to buy a single flower, a small carnation, from a vendor for a few yen. I often walk these streets, soaking in the atmosphere and losing myself in memories of happier times now gone forever.

As I passed the street where my family were sent to the gods by American firebombs, I felt my chest tightening and tension gripping me. I found it nearly impossible to fill my lungs. For the life of me, I can't allow myself to imagine the fear and pain they must have suffered. It is to my eternal shame that I could do nothing to save them. I sped up my pace and stared at the ground before me.

I can't bring myself to even glance at the space where I lived with my parents and later with Fumiyo for those heavenly five months after our wedding. We lived in the shadow of Shinjuku station, a place now almost unrecognisable after being bombed and razed to the ground by constant air raids. Now it is a different place—rebuilt, remodelled, and regarded by many as a testament to the rise of the new Japan. For me it will always be a cemetery.

I paused for a moment at the place where the bus stand used to be, the very same place where my parents saw me off to Officer Training School all those years ago. I fought back tears as I recalled my mother with her own tears rolling down her red cheeks, waving her handkerchief, and my father trying his best to be strong for my mother's sake. It was also at this place that Fumiyo waved me off to war. I tried to take a great gasp of air, as if I were trying to capture the very souls of my loved ones. This small square of pavement has come to represent the most sacred place on earth. It is the final resting place of my family. I put the flower into the brick wall that sides the pavement, lowered my head, and said a silent prayer for the souls of my family. I said a special prayer for my little Sachiyo. I told her I was so sorry I couldn't protect her as a father should, and begged her forgiveness.

With a heavy heart I slowly moved along the street and paused outside the Sun Palace Theatre, where I enjoyed watching movies with Fumiyo during those halcyon days of hope, love, and endless sunshine. The theatre has been completely rebuilt but is still under the same name. I looked up to see what was showing. A new American movie, *Tokyo Joe*, starring Humphrey Bogart was advertised with a huge poster showing Bogart looking tough. I noticed that Sessue Hayakawa was also in the movie. He was an idol of mine when I was a youth. Every young man in Japan envied him, and it was said that all the girls were secretly in love with him. I hadn't heard his name for years, but I felt happy for him. He had got through the war and was now in a movie with the great Bogart. I hoped *Tokyo Joe* had a happier ending than that given out to most of us from the legacy of war. Movies don't have any part in my life anymore. I have enough difficulty accepting reality without losing myself in the fantasy of fiction.

Pasted onto a telegraph pole was a poster asking families to go to Ueno Zoo; a great day out was promised, and the animals were waiting to greet you and invite you to share in their fun and frolics. My father loved taking me to the zoo. It was one of my earliest memories. He would hold my hand as we made our way around the animals' enclosures, telling me which countries they came from, what they liked to eat, and so on. We loved those trips together, but even those precious memories have been turned bitter by the plague of war. When Tokyo came under attack from American air raids, the zoo's director expressed concern for the animals and told of the dangers to the public if wild beasts were to escape. The army agreed and sent a marksman team to shoot dead all the lions and tigers and so on. Poisonous snakes had their heads chopped off, and other smaller animals were gassed. Three elephants, a polar bear, and two lions that called the zoo home. They were all left to starve to death in slow, agonising circumstances. Even the innocent animals of Ueno Zoo were not spared the insanity that took hold of their human counterparts during those sick times. I hoped my father hadn't been aware of the fate of the animals that had given us so much joy in happier distant times. The long arm of war reaches into your precious memories and squeezes the joy out of all the things you hold so dear in your heart. I vowed to never set foot in a zoo ever again in my lifetime.

It was time to head back. Walking these streets was draining my soul away. I made my way back to my workshop, dodging the waves of office workers who descend on Shinjuku station at this time of day. It had started to rain heavily again. Another typhoon was approaching. The sixth of the season. I made good progress and was soon walking down my road. One of my neighbours, Mrs Yoshida, called to me from her doorway. "Tanaka san. You had a caller, a young man by the name of Kawabata. He waited for a while but left in his car. He asked if I would give you this." She rummaged through her apron pocket and found a letter, which she handed over to me. I had lived next door to Yoshida for more than three years and barely spoken to her other than the usual daily greetings and small talk about the weather and so on. She had the shop next to mine and sold candies and shaved ice for kids. Many a time I had silently cursed her little shop, as the local kids would gather outside and make endless noise that distracted me from my work. I knew in my heart that it wasn't the noise that irritated me, but the constant reminder that my own daughter would have been about their age. My little Sachiyo should be there, playing, laughing, and eating shaved ice.

I thanked Yoshida, took the letter, and fumbled with my keys to open the door. I sat down at my workbench and studied the plain white envelope, my name on the front in beautiful handwritten script. Before I opened it, I instinctively opened the drawer to check that the pen was still there. It was, as it had been every day. I had considered hiding it in a more secure place, but somehow it seemed safer to leave it in plain sight. I read the inscription. "To Daisuke. Do your best at university. From Father. October 1940." Daisuke was long gone. I had helped load his body onto a corpse cart but not before I had rummaged through his pockets and taken his simple fountain pen. I had watched as he and thousands like him were sent to the gods in a mass pyre. When was that? More than four years ago. I often wondered about his father. Was he one of those waiting at Yokohama quayside hoping to find his boy returning from war? Praying and hoping with all his heart that his boy might one day walk into the house and life would be sweet again? Ignorance affords the desperate souls hope, and yet every day Daisuke's poor father will be living his son's fate over and over in his tortured mind. Perhaps the father is now with his son in heaven. Who knows? Maybe one day, if I get the chance, I will try to seek him out and put his vigil to rest.

I opened the letter. It was from Hamazaki. So, Kawabata was merely the messenger boy. My eyes were drawn to the beautiful waxed family seal at the bottom of the letter. "Hamazaki." In various bold shades of red. It was handwritten in gorgeous script. I read it through. "My dear Tanaka San. It is with sincere regret that I am unable to visit your shop tomorrow as we had agreed. I am hoping that you will be able to deliver the radios to my address in person. Whatever state of repair you have managed to achieve will be sufficient. Please expect Mr Kawabata to arrive at your shop tomorrow at two o'clock. I hope this will be convenient for you. I apologise for the inconvenience this may cause you and look forward to seeing you tomorrow. Toshio Hamazaki."

I looked at the address, which was written at the side of the seal. Ginza, the most prestigious area of Tokyo. This only served to confirm in my mind that Hamazaki had used the radios as a ruse. Ginza was worlds apart from my area. I doubted that anyone in their right mind would travel across the city just to have two radios fixed. So, tomorrow I would no doubt find out Mr Hamazaki's true intentions. My mind cast back to Ogawa's warning. Was this the time to be cautious? I told myself that if anyone intended to do me harm, they would hardly ask me to their home by means of a written request and even leave that letter with a third party. I was still holding the pen as I tried to make sense of this charade. If Hamazaki wanted something from me, then why not ask outright?

It struck me that I didn't have any decent clothes to wear. I felt ashamed to go to Ginza dressed like a shabby beggar; my clothes were all dirty. The oil stains and polish from my work had become part of the fabric. Perhaps I should try to find a clean shirt from somewhere. But then again perhaps not. I was just a radio repairman delivering his work. What more could be expected of me? I rolled out my thin rattan mat and lay down to sleep. The air was fuggy. I had become accustomed to the smells of repair and grease. It was comforting. This is my life now, and I should be grateful for what it gives me. After all, I am one of the lucky ones. Every day is time borrowed, and I know that one day it will have to be paid back. Fate will decide.

My mind was racing at all speeds, and sleep didn't come easily. Even when I slept, I dreamt that I was awake. I was finally shaken to my senses by the community announcement which blared from the loudspeaker down the street and woke the neighbourhood as it did every morning at six o'clock. A call to rise and a warning to take care with wood-fired stoves when making breakfast and to make sure all cigarettes were extinguished completely. Fire was the greatest fear. One act of carelessness could result in the whole street being razed to the ground. The tinder-dry houses and shops would go down well before the fire services had time to respond. We maintain a local volunteer firefighting group which is basic, to say the least. A line of men passing buckets of water would be no match for an inferno.

I grabbed my washing and shaving kit and set off to the communal bath at the end of the street. It was basically a large wooden shack with a thin partition down the middle dividing men and women. Three water pumps were set up on our side. Usually we had to wait in line, each of us taking two or three minutes to wash. I never used soap or shampoo. Although we bathed together, we were all in our own worlds. We seldom spoke other than the usual morning greetings. So I was surprised when Kudo, the noodle stall vendor from a few doors away, struck up a conversation with me. "Tanaka! Going up in the world, eh?" I asked him what he meant, and he said he had seen the car that had stopped outside my shop the day before. It must have been Kawabata. "Rich customers, driving a car like that. Never seen a car like that before. What was it? Rolls-Royce?" I made light of his remarks and said that maybe I should charge a bit more. Kudo laughed and went back to his washing. I too got on with trying to clean myself up.

I listened to the women, their voices drifting over the partition, talkative as ever. I would catch snippets of local gossip, hear names that were familiar and yet impossible to put faces to. Listening to the women there was as close as I ever got to any kind of contact with the opposite sex. I hadn't given it much concern. I still desperately missed my Fumiyo. Her face, her tenderness, smile, and beauty still played wicked tricks with my memory and imagination. Some days she was so close by my side, I could almost touch her. Other days I found myself straining to find her in the clouds of time past. Our life together had been ever so short, a wartime marriage. We had both just graduated, Fumiyo from high school and me from the army officer academy. We were introduced by our parents, who were mutual friends from their own school days. We had five dates, were seldom left alone together, and were chaperoned diligently by Fumiyo's mother. My father asked Fumiyo's father on my behalf if he would consent to giving his daughter's hand in marriage. Reluctantly, he agreed, and we were married on Fumiyo's eighteenth birthday, November 26, 1941. It was an informal affair, just a few of the closest family members and some of my army colleagues. Wartime marriages were common, but circumstances dictated that happiness be constrained. My army deployment had yet to be decided, so we were able to spend our first few months of married life together. We lived with Fumiyo's parents at their spacious house in Shinjuku. It was the happiest time of my life. Our daughter Sachiyo was conceived there. My daughter, the little baby I had never held, never kissed, never seen. Gone after only four years of life on this earth.

I received my deployment orders in the spring of 1942. I was to be shipped out to join our forces in the Philippines. At the time we were all relieved at my deployment. The Americans had yet to engage us there, and our occupation had so far gone unchallenged. It was considered a safer place to be than some of the other areas of conflict. The image of Fumiyo waving me off to war will never leave me. It brings me to the edge of tears as I recall her standing there in her finest kimono, so brave. If I had known then that it was to be the last time I would ever see her, I like to think I would have found the courage to desert. To my shame I know that to be just a fanciful thought.

After my deployment I would write regularly to Fumiyo. As officers, we were allowed to send two letters a month. The rank and file were allowed only one. I in turn received only three letters from her during the first year of my deployment. Her letters were a joy to read. She would bring me up to date about life back home, never once hinting at any hardships. Her last letter told me of the joy of bringing Sachiyo into the world. I would read them over and over. Carrying them with me at all times, until they were unreadable after getting soaked in downpours of rain.

I waited month after month for another letter. None would come. We were told that communications from home had been suspended; the information ministry was worried about letters falling into enemy hands and being used for propaganda purposes. Later we all came to realise that the ministry was more likely worried that letters from home were becoming increasingly pessimistic and bad news was starting to have an effect on troop morale. Some faceless bureaucrat sitting at a desk in Tokyo had decided to cut us off from our dearest and most loved. Just another deprivation we had to bear without question.

I shook myself back into the present and realised that I had been holding up my neighbours as they waited patiently for their turn to wash. I dried myself and quickly put on my thin yukata and hurried back to my shop.

I spent the rest of the morning trying to do odd jobs to keep myself busy and stop thinking about my appointment with Hamazaki. I couldn't concentrate on anything at all. The work I had so valued only yesterday morning was now just an irritation. I gave up all pretence of trying to work and lay down on my mat and watched the clock tick. It was ten minutes to two when I was shaken to life by loud knocking on my door. I opened the door slightly to find Kawabata waiting for me. I asked him to wait a minute as I gathered the cardboard box containing the radios. I was going to take the pen with me but decided against it, although I wasn't sure why. Perhaps I was trying to hold on to some sense of security. It felt strange to be leaving the shop at that time of day. Still, I wasn't expecting any customers to call.

Kawabata was standing alongside the biggest car I had ever seen. He took the box from me as I was struggling to lock the shop door. I looked up the street and saw several of my neighbours, all of whom seemed to have found something very important to do that involved being out of their shops and houses. The local kids were not so tactful in their nosiness and just loitered about, staring at the car and also at Kawabata, who cut a fine figure in his dandy clothes. I took the box back, and Kawabata opened the rear door for me to get inside. I noticed we had a driver. I could see only the back of his head, but he looked like he was wearing a chauffeur's uniform. Kawabata got into the front passenger seat, and we drove away almost silently. For such a big car, the engine was almost muted. We seemed to glide, the outside world passing by in a haze. The car seemed almost as big as my room.

After we had been driving for a few minutes, Kawabata turned around and spoke to me. "I trust you are comfortable, Tanaka san." I said I was and thanked him for coming to collect me. "Please think nothing of it, nothing at all. You are most welcome." It struck me then that Kawabata's tone was condescending, or perhaps I was suffering from an attack of my usual paranoia. I tried to make small talk with him. The car was the obvious focal point of a conversation, and I said I had never seen the like before. He told me it was a Bentley Mark VI which Mr Hamazaki had imported new from England last year. It was the first of its kind in the country. I found myself lost for a suitable reply and settled for a knowing nod. Kawabata must have taken this as the end of our little chat, and we drove along in silence. The streets and shops seemed to get grander as we got closer to Ginza. We turned onto a wide tree-lined avenue. The buildings were all brick built and stood elegantly on either side of the road. There were pavements for people to walk along in safety. All this was a world apart from my own area. It didn't feel like we were even in the same country anymore.

The car pulled up outside an imposing four-storey building of red brick and granite construction. Kawabata got out first and opened the door for me. He took the box and ushered me up a small set of eight marble steps towards the front door. Two small, ornate Okinawan Shisa lion figures, sculpted from stone, sat on either side of the staircase. I knew that Okinawan people believed such symbols had the power to ward off evil spirits.

Kawabata opened the huge double doors and bade me enter. The entrance hall was majestic; it was like stepping into the foyer of a beautiful museum. I was completely in awe. There was a wide winding marble staircase opposite which a blood-red carpet ran up the centre. Above our heads a magnificent crystal chandelier touched by the gentle breeze from the open door was tinkling away. Imposing doors led off to other areas of the house, and exotic flowers were displayed in huge vases which stood on delicate-looking tables. I stood for a moment, taking in the surroundings. I must have looked like some kind of wretched misfit, standing there in my ragged work clothes.

Kawabata told me to remove my shoes before stepping into the hall proper. I did so and felt my cheeks burn in shame as the holes in my socks told a story of their own. I was also conscious of my sweaty feet and was relieved when Kawabata gave me a pair of indoor slippers to wear. Kawabata told me to leave the box in the hallway and said he would ask one of the staff to collect it. His remark took me a little by surprise, as I had assumed that he himself was "one of the staff." He told me to follow him up the staircase, as Hamazaki san was expecting me. He led the way up past some imposing-looking portraits of men from eras gone by.

There was a wide landing at the top with doors leading off to grand rooms. Kawabata knocked on one of the doors and, without waiting for a reply, entered and ushered me inside. "Hamazaki san will be with you in a few moments. Please make yourself comfortable." Kawabata gave a slight bow and went, leaving me alone in the room. It was a study or maybe even a library of sorts. The walls were lined with tall bookshelves filled with hundreds if not thousands of leather-bound volumes. The wooden floor had been recently polished, and a strong smell of beeswax scented the air. There were three leather armchairs and two large, matching leather sofas. A grand mahogany desk was the focal point of the room. It was all executed in exquisite European style. On the ceiling a large, slowly spinning, polished brass fan attracted my attention. It was the first electric fan I had ever seen. In fact the day was providing many "firsts."

I didn't sit down, choosing to stand while I waited for Hamazaki. I felt into my pocket for the invoice I had written earlier that morning. I had decided to charge a total of one hundred yen for the repairs. After all, the work had taken me only about four hours to complete. I had also prepared a receipt, should Hamazaki feel inclined to settle his account now. The door opened, and I automatically lowered my head and gave a formal bow. But instead of Hamazaki, I was face-to-face with a beautiful and elegant young woman who looked as startled as I was. She certainly hadn't expected to find a tatty workman in her gracious room. "Oh!" That was the very first word she said to me.

"Excuse me," I said. "I was told to wait here for Hamazaki san. My name is Tanaka; I am the radio repairman."

She gave me a deep bow. "Tanaka san? I shall go and find my brother and inform him of your presence. It is poor manners to keep you waiting. Please excuse us." She bowed again and left the room. My first thoughts had been that she was Hamazaki's wife. For some reason known only to the mystery of the heart I felt gladdened to hear she was his sister. I stood waiting, lost in my thoughts.

Without warning, Hamazaki burst into the room. His voice was booming with vigour and confidence. "Tanaka san. Thank you so much for delivering the radios in person. I am so sorry to have inconvenienced you with such a tiresome journey. I trust Kawabata san took care of you." I said he had and that he had shown me great courtesy. Hamazaki nodded thoughtfully. There was a knock on the door, Hamazaki called for whomever it was to enter, and an old gent came in carrying the box containing the two radios. Hamazaki told him to put the box on the desk. "Thank you, Ogawa san, that will be all for now." Ogawa? It was a common enough name, yet there was a hint of something in Hamazaki's tone as he said it. Hamazaki looked at me. "Ogawa is employed as my chauffeur and valet. I trust his driving here today was without incident. He is advancing in years, and I worry about his judgement when driving." I said the drive here had been perfectly smooth. Hamazaki clapped his hands together and let out a laugh, which startled me. I felt like a mouse being toyed with by a cat. "Let's have a look at your work. I apologise for giving you so little time for your repairs. Have you managed to make any headway?"

"Yes sir, I am pleased to say that I have. I can return both radios to you in full working order."

Hamazaki's face lit up with childlike glee. His wide smile and pleasure seemed genuine enough, and he slapped his palms against his thighs. "Wonderful—I knew you could do it. Please explain to me what the problems were." I went on to tell him about the repairs, and as I was doing so, he took the sets out of the box and set them up to receive some broadcast. We waited for a few moments for them to warm up and then, with beautiful clarity, piano music was filling the room. Hamazaki closed his eyes and gave a smile of satisfaction. "Tanaka san, you have done well. Now, please let me offer you some refreshment. If you would be so kind as to follow me."

We left the study by a side door and entered an adjoining room. This room, too, was breathtaking in an understated, elegant way. An enormous long table was positioned down the middle with at least twenty chairs along each side. More portraits graced the walls, and there was a huge marble fireplace on one side. I guessed the room was used for meetings or formal gatherings. Hamazaki had gone over to a small side table and was busying himself preparing drinks. He was talking, but his voice seemed to be miles away. I had the sensation of being in a different place, as if I were not there in person, just looking in through a misted window. Something in the room was taking me to another place, something that was screaming for my attention. I felt my blood run cold. I turned my head to face Hamazaki. He caught my stare, and his gaze followed mine. "Beautiful, is it not? I feel so honoured to have it in our family. It was commissioned by one of the royal princes, the Emperor's cousin Prince Chichibu. It is a painting of intense beauty and depth, and one that has so many meanings. Don't you think so, Tanaka san?" I could not stop looking, the focus of my stare being a huge painting in traditional style. It dominated the wall at the far end of the table. The artist had indeed done a fine job. A gorgeous pale green porcelain vase, decorated with orange-and-white koi playfully swimming around its base, held twelve lilies positioned with deft elegance. Eleven were ghostly white, and in contrast a single lily shouted out its presence in brilliant gold. If ever there was to be a confirmation, then there it was, right before my eyes. *Golden Lily.*

Hamazaki handed me a glass of whiskey, and we both stood in silence, looking at the painting. Hamazaki spoke, his voice no longer full of the pretence of friendship, his tone hard. "I see from your expression that you find my painting meaningful."

I nodded. "Yes, sir. I believe I do."

Hamazaki slugged back his drink in one quick motion. He gave me a firm pat on the shoulder. "Good. Now that there is no need for any further pretence, let's be open with each other. Tanaka, I believe you have something for me."

"Yes sir, I do." I had thought of this moment for years and dreamt of a thousand and one different scenarios. My fate, my destiny was now in the hands of the gods. Somehow, though, I had never dreamt that it would be like this.

"Tanaka. From this moment on, do not call me 'sir' ever again. It is I who owes you respect. You have performed a great service, and I will forever be in your debt. We have so much to discuss. But first I propose a toast." He poured himself a measure of whiskey, raised his glass towards the painting, and bade me to do the same. "To new beginnings, to new friendships, and to the new Japan." I repeated his words, and we both threw back our drinks in one draught. The whiskey burnt my throat and made my eyes water. It was my first taste of alcohol in more than five years. As I said, that day was one of many firsts. Hamazaki took a seat at the head of the table and asked me to sit at his side. "Hideo, you have something in your possession of the highest importance, and I thank you for keeping it safe all these years. Yet I have to ask you to keep it safe a little while longer. Now is not the time to go back over old ground. Opportunity will, in time, present itself in a more fortuitous manner, of that I am certain." Hamazaki had called me by my first name as if we were old friends. He was looking intensely at my face as he had done in my shop only yesterday. Again I felt the same sense of unease. My mind was in utter confusion. It was impossible to organise my thoughts. As if having the power to read me like a book, Hamazaki went on. "Hideo, I know you must have many questions, and in due course you will have your answers." He put his hand on mine in a gesture of reassurance that shocked me in its intimacy. "Please, I beg your forgiveness for leaving you in a state of abandonment for so long. Your identity was revealed to me only a few months ago, and I had to be sure we had the 'real' Tanaka. There are so many Tanakas in the outside world, eh? In fact I didn't even know of your existence until that time.

"My father died two months ago. His death was very sudden, and we still haven't come to terms with his absence." Hamazaki looked to his right side and pointed out the large portrait of an important-looking man dressed in a fine, dark kimono. His voice had slightly lost that air of confidence. He looked me straight in the eyes. His sadness was undeniable. "I have to ask you. Did you ever have the opportunity to meet with my father?" I said I had not. Hamazaki spent a few moments considering my answer, which seemed to disappoint him in some way. He shook his head and composed himself. "My father died in unusual circumstances. I still find it extremely painful to speak of the manner of his death. It is my belief and conviction that he was murdered."

He let a short silence hang in the air. When he spoke again, his voice was trembling with emotion, but he carried on, no longer looking at me but at the portrait of his father, who looked uncannily like him. "My father must have feared for his safety for a long time. He had become involved in something that required him to carry the darkest of secrets in his heart. You too played your part in this secret. It was my father who requested you, along with your good friend Ogawa, for your special duty. He had a very personal reason for doing so, and in time I will explain all. Father lived in a state of perpetual fear and stress for years. Fearing for his survival and sanity, he took me into his confidence a few years back. He hoped I would be able to achieve a positive outcome to what had become a tangled mess of falsehood and greed. His decision to involve me broke his heart, for he believed that I too would suffer the same uncertainties as him. Please excuse my somewhat meandering attempt at an explanation. I am still coming to terms with many things that I too don't fully understand. It was two months ago, almost to the very day, that I found my father's body. He was slumped across the writing desk in his study. My first thought was that he had fallen asleep whilst going through the mountains of paperwork that our business seems to accumulate.

Then I saw the revolver in his hand and the dark stain pooling out over the desk and the shocking crimson against the paper blotter. I went over to him and touched his cheek, but he was already cold.

"I called for help. My sister, Ayumi, and Ogawa were here first. My sister took one look at her father and collapsed into silent sobs. Like her, I couldn't face the shocking reality, and I left for my private quarters, leaving Ogawa to call the police and other services. The authorities arrived and, after some routine questioning, allowed the body to be removed. It was obvious that they were convinced it was a suicide. To all the authorities concerned there seemed to be no need for any further investigation. My father still had friends high up in political circles. He was once the armaments minister and served in several wartime cabinets. These friends came to offer comfort and sympathy in time of our deepest sorrow. They closed circles and used their power and influence to ensure that the circumstances of his death were recorded as natural, rather than by his own hand, therefore avoiding any unpleasant speculation. We were also spared the stigma that goes with death in those circumstances.

"Hideo, believe me when I say I know my father did not die by his own hand. He would never do that. He knew what it would do to his family, and I know he wouldn't put us through such hell. I am convinced without reservation that he was murdered and that it was staged to appear as a suicide. In the weeks before his passing he had become extra careful, emphasising security and safety at all costs. He ordered additional security personnel to be deployed at our factory outlets in Yokohama and Shinbashi, and it will always be my deepest regret that we failed to secure our home here with the same diligence. Fearing his demise, he left a final goodbye to me in the form of a letter that he had secured in his safe. He had trusted me with the safe's combination months earlier. The letter was a revelation, and it was the first time that I became aware of your existence and involvement in an affair that we have both been destined to see to its conclusion."

Hamazaki paused to give me time to reflect on his tale. I had barely been in his house more than thirty minutes, but he was taking me into his confidence as if I were an old friend. I was at a loss for a suitable response, unable to understand why I, of all people would be "destined" to join Hamazaki. He looked at me, again in that calculating manner of his, as if he were trying to see into my soul. "I understand that all this is very confusing for you, and I ask for your patience. As I said, I will tell all in due course, but first I have a question for you, Hideo. Do you trust me?" His question caught me completely off guard. I managed to find a reply along the lines of not having any reason to feel mistrust. Hamazaki smiled and said he liked my caution. He reached into his inside jacket pocket and took out a folded sheet of paper. "Hideo Tanaka, I want to make you an offer. I am about to form a new company. One that I envision will have a great impact on the lives of many. I want you to be a part of this new venture from its very beginning. I know a little of your background. I know that your studies in electrical research were interrupted by the war, and I also know that you are a fine and diligent person and that any organisation would be proud to have you as part of its staff. I am offering you a position in my new company. It's a position that will interest you. We are in the business of manufacturing and aim to produce a range of appliances that will revolutionise the lives of ordinary people. I want you alongside me as my chief engineer, responsible for the development of our product line." Hamazaki looked intently into my eyes. "Hideo, the next word to leave your mouth will shape the rest of your life."

I felt like a child being asked to stand in front of the whole school. I nodded and said the only word that I could think of. "Yes."

Hamazaki lit up, a smile of delight spreading across his face. He smoothed out the paper, passed me a pen, and asked me to sign in three places. He separated three extra sheets and gave them to me. "This is a copy of your contract of employment with Hamazaki Electricals. You can tear it up at midnight tonight." He smiled at my look of confusion. "Hamazaki Electricals will cease to exist at midnight. It will be replaced by a new company with a greater vision. We will be the most progressive business in the country, and you and I will be at the heart of it from this day forward." I was speechless and becoming more confused by the minute. Things had moved so fast, I hadn't had time to think about what anything meant.

Over the years I would come to realise that Hamazaki was one of the most impulsive men I had ever met. It was his way. He would make decisions almost on the spot, picking ideas out of thin air. He had a gift, and if I were to explain what that gift was, I would say that he could see into the future as no other mortal man could possibly imagine. Whether there are people with telepathic talents or it was simply a matter of luck and strategy, I do not know. What I came to realise was that Hamazaki was blessed with a unique vision. I would realise this in many ways over the years to come. He stood and offered his hand for me to shake. "Welcome to my world." It seemed a strange thing to say, but later I would understand.

"Tonight, in this very room I will host a dinner party," he continued. "It will be a gathering of friends and business associates—the perfect occasion to announce the launch of our new venture—and because you are my new chief engineer, I require your attendance." I began to offer protest about why I couldn't possibly attend. My clothes and downright dishevelment served as obvious testament. Hamazaki would have none of it. He pulled on the thick velvet cord that hung by the window side to summon some help. "Tonight you are my guest. It would delight me if you would agree to spend the night here. Well, not here, exactly, but at the nearby Empire Hotel, which is a mere few minutes' drive away. I have a personal suite at the Empire where I used to reside. Upon my father's death I returned here, to the family residence. However, out of sentimentality I have continued to maintain the suite of rooms, and it would give me pleasure if you would accept my offer and be my guest for the evening. You will find everything you require for this evening's function there waiting for you."

It seemed pointless to protest any further. Hamazaki had already made preparations for my stay. I said I would be honoured to accept. "Splendid," he said. "I will have Ogawa escort you to the hotel. One thing I must explain to you—that is, if you hadn't already guessed as much. Ogawa, my valet, is the father of your friend Lieutenant Ogawa, who I believe is still on active duty. I engaged his father as a member of my staff at the war's end. It was a way of ensuring that Lieutenant Ogawa's family were provided for in those hard times. He knows nothing of his son's ongoing duty and involvement in our Philippine business. He believes his son to be lost in action. He is at peace with his loss; however, I truly hope with all my heart that the day will come when he will be reunited with his boy. Until that day I will keep Ogawa's family in my thoughts and do my upmost to make their lives as bearable as I can." Hamazaki registered the look of shock on my face. He put his hand on my shoulder. "Hideo, we are like one family here; we look out for each other and stay loyal to each other. I hope, in time, that you will feel part of this family and that I can rely on your unswerving loyalty."

The double doors at the far end of the room were opened, and Ogawa Senior stood there keeping a discreet distance, awaiting his master's instructions. "Ah, Ogawa san, would you be so kind as to show Tanaka san to the Empire and assist him in any way necessary?" Ogawa gave a polite bow and took his leave. Hamazaki walked with me to the front door, his hand on my shoulder. "This is a great day, the first of many great days to come. It gladdens my heart to have you by my side." Hamazaki's intimacy made me feel uneasy. I was not accustomed to displays of affection. Perhaps time and events had hardened my heart and I had become distant. Whatever, it was impossible for me to reciprocate his enthusiasm. My own little world had been turned upside down by this man, someone I barely knew, someone who only one hour ago was merely my customer and was now my boss. So much had changed in the last hour, yet I was still Tanaka the radio repairman, dressed in his old clothes with holes in the soles of his shoes. Surely this could not be happening to me. I would wake up soon and find myself back in my shop, worrying about where the next meal was coming from. I tried to talk Hamazaki out of his offer of hospitality, saying it would be too much trouble, but he dismissed my reluctance with such amity, it was impossible to resist him.

We reached the front entrance where Ogawa was already waiting, standing beside the Bentley's open rear door. I climbed in, and Ogawa closed the door after me. I felt like a small man in the back of that huge car. It was nonsensical. I wanted to scream to Ogawa to stop the car and let me out here and now, but of course I did not. I sat there like the dumb fool that I was, a man who had lost control of his life, accepting what fate was to throw at his feet.

I thought of the animals at Ueno Zoo that had been cruelly betrayed by their war-crazed human masters. Was my situation any different? My life was now in the hands of Toshio Hamazaki. Was he sane? Here I sat, being driven to Tokyo's best hotel by my friend's father, Ogawa Senior. I was burning with desire to tell him about his son. It was a painful secret, and it truly hurt my heart.

The drive took only a few minutes, and we soon drew up in front of the Empire Hotel. A uniformed doorman opened my door for me. If he'd been expecting some grander guest to emerge from the Bentley, then he managed to hide his surprise well. Ogawa came around the side of the car and gave a courteous bow to the senior concierge. They seemed to be on familiar terms. I felt totally overwhelmed. I was in the wrong place, it was plain for all to see. As we proceeded through the beautiful, ornate lobby with its overhanging floors cascading with fine greenery, I could feel the stares of the other guests burning into my back. It was a walk of shame, and I will never forget that feeling. A reflective pool set in the centre of the lobby mirrored the decorative ceiling work.

Despite my feelings of insecurity and inadequacy, I could only marvel at this incredible place. What kind of people stayed in such a place? It was a joy to behold. I let Ogawa lead me; we didn't bother with any formalities such as registration. We walked up the stairs to the third floor and along a short corridor to a set of double doors, which Ogawa unlocked with a key he had produced from his pocket. He opened the doors and stood back respectfully, allowing me to enter first. I removed my shoes and stepped into a room fit for a king. It was stunning: a grand room decorated with a mix of Oriental and Western touches that complemented each other to perfection. There were leather sofas and armchairs similar to those in Hamazaki's study. The lounge room led into the bedroom where the biggest bed I had ever seen dominated the space.

Another door revealed a bathroom that was twice as big as my own room and workshop. A large, shining white porcelain bathtub stood on gleaming brass crafted lion's paws near a basin with similarly designed brass taps and a huge onyx-framed mirror. I caught sight of my shabby state in the mirror, and a wave of distress and depression swept over me. I stood there like Chaplin when he stumbled into a scene by accident, lost in my own thoughts.

Ogawa's voice shook me to my senses. "Sir, my master has provided you with a wardrobe of clothing that you may find in the closet in your bedroom. Should you require any assistance, the hotel valet is available at all times. Tonight's function is formal evening dress. You will find that all you require has been prepared. With sir's permission I will take my leave and allow you to rest before dinner. I shall return at seven o'clock to accompany sir back to the residence." I thanked Ogawa for his help, and he left me alone to take in my new surroundings.

I sat on the bed, which was bigger than my workshop. The large golden carriage clock on the bedside table told me that it was a little after four. In the space of two hours my life had changed to the point where it now began to feel like surreal mockery. I felt an incredible urge to escape this madness that seemed to have taken over my life. As I looked around the palatial room, all I could think of was the elegant Hamazaki. It was his place, and not for the likes of folk like me. I felt like a complete fraud. I went over to the wardrobe and opened it to find an evening suit and dress shirt along with two business suits and at least six fine white shirts, each draped with a silk necktie in various patterns. There were also three pairs of shoes next to a wicker basket that contained socks, underwear, and a selection of belts and suspenders. I held up one of the jackets for size. It seemed Hamazaki had gauged me to perfection.

I had about three hours to ready myself before Ogawa came back to escort me to dinner. I hadn't really given the function much consideration, but now the reality was beginning to hit me. I would be expected to engage in conversation with total strangers, a skill I had long since forgotten. I felt myself shrink within, and started to have serious doubts about whether I could manage. I did not have any idea what was expected of me. It dawned on me that I didn't even know the name of the company I was supposed to be in the employ of. I prayed to God that nobody would ask me questions of a technical or engineering nature. I had visions of being exposed as a fraud, or at best a half-wit.

A chime sounded from somewhere, and I was shaken out of my reverie by a finely dressed man who had allowed himself access to the rooms. He was pushing a cart not dissimilar to a dinner server. He introduced himself as Wada, personal butler to the suite. He had noticed that my service light was on and wondered how he could be of assistance. I replied that I thought I could manage by myself and that I wouldn't be requiring any help. He stood there with an obvious look of doubt written across his face. "If sir would permit me to make a few suggestions?" I nodded reluctantly. "I would strongly recommend the services of our gentlemen's grooming department. I could arrange for one of our personal valets to attend to you here in your rooms." Again, I said that would not be necessary, as I would be able to take care of myself. "But sir, Hamazaki san was quite insistent that I make every service available to you to make your preparations as easy as possible."

It was then that I realised that it was not an offer of assistance but more of a direct hint that my appearance needed more attention than I could possibly undertake myself. "I see. In that case, I would be most obliged if you would call for someone to assist me."

"Very well, sir." Wada left the room and was almost instantly replaced by an elderly gentleman who obviously had been waiting in the corridor outside. He took over Wada's cart and pushed it into the bathroom, where he made a few adjustments. It was easily transformed into a small chair that he positioned in front of the mirror. He asked me to sit and proceeded to give me my first ever civilian shampoo and haircut. The shampoo burnt into my scalp as the valet massaged it into my hair. I noticed the water ran dark when he rinsed out the dirty suds. Was my hair so filthy? I asked him where he had gotten the shampoo, as I had never seen any for sale. He told me in a rather pompous tone that Hamazaki san imported this particular brand directly from Schwarzkopf's of Berlin, and it was unlikely to be found on the shelves of any store. He told me it was called Schauma Crème Shampoo and that it was the most expensive of all hair products. I asked him if he had groomed Hamazaki's hair. He replied proudly that he used to attend to him regularly when he was living here, in the suite. However, Mr Kawabata handled all of Mr Hamazaki's personal arrangements now that he had moved back to his family's residence in Ginza. The last fact was stated a little too stiffly, and I found his answer to be a little odd but didn't press him further. I still didn't know what role the mysterious Kawabata played in Hamazaki's life, but I took him to be some kind of personal assistant.

The valet towelled my wet hair and then produced some scissors and with deft skill soon had me looking something like the person I once was many years ago. He couldn't do anything for the weariness that had etched itself into my face, but he had restored me to a semblance of my old self. He finished off with another shampoo and filled the bath with warm water. He advised me to soak for fifteen minutes before scrubbing away the grime of the last five years. I thanked him, and he took his leave.

I relaxed in the water, feeling guilty, enjoying the pleasure of allowing my body to soak in the calming warmth. I had bathed daily, but this was something different. I was shocked to see the water turn dark from the grime I had been wearing like a second skin. I stood and scrubbed myself with strong-smelling soap until I was pink all over. For the first time in many years I was truly clean again.

Wada the butler appeared again and offered his help in dressing me. I felt it pointless to refuse, and allowed him to lay out my clothes for the evening. He went about his business in an efficient manner, as if he were dressing a tailor's dummy. He finished off by expertly tying my black bow tie and brushing my shoulders with a horsehair brush. Wada seemed satisfied with his work. I went to the full mirror in the hallway to check the results. I stood looking. It couldn't be me. The image staring back was not the face I had grown accustomed to seeing but was merely someone who vaguely looked like the man I had been. This new me, dressed in elegant finery with slicked-back, short, pomaded hair was surely an imposter, yet he had my face if not my clothes. Tanaka the radio repairman had disappeared. Who was this new Tanaka? Even I had no idea who, or what, I was anymore.

The clock showed six fifty. With admirable timing there was a knock on the door, and I opened it to find Ogawa waiting to take me back to Hamazaki's house for the dinner. He startled visibly, such was his surprise upon seeing my transformation from vagrant to make-believe gentleman in only a few hours. However, Ogawa was a cool character and swiftly regained his deportment. "Sir, the car is waiting when you are ready. I shall wait here to escort you." He was so formal and efficient. I desperately wished I could tell him about his son. His boy, my best friend, left behind in that hellhole of a place. Four years have gone by since that day. I shook myself back into the present and followed Ogawa. We walked the short distance to the car, the same route but in reverse I had so self-consciously taken a few hours before. This time I was greeted with friendly smiles, and one guest even tipped his hat to me. The staff of the Empire gave me deep bows. They were all seeing a different man. My thoughts went out to Fumiyo, and I wished she too could see me right now, walking through the finest hotel in Japan like a true man of standing. I felt my confidence grow a little, but it was still with nervous apprehension that I climbed into the back of the Bentley, to be driven away by Ogawa, back to Hamazaki's grand house. We arrived in a matter of minutes, and as the car drew up outside, the place looked even more impressive, swathed in fine yellow lighting.

Ogawa was swiftly out of the car to open the door for me. He seemed quite agile for a man of his age. The huge front doors were open, and I climbed the steps and entered the hall to find Hamazaki there waiting to greet his guests. It seemed I was the first one to arrive, and he could not conceal his delight at my new appearance. "Well, well. Who is this?" He clapped his hands in a gesture of feigned surprise and then put them on my cheeks. For one moment I thought he was going to kiss me. "Is this the same Hideo? My word, what a transformation. It is wonderful to see you looking so refreshed." That was the first time I realised that there was a fair element of effeminacy to Hamazaki's gestures. In fact, he was very "gentle" for such a tall and imposing character. Hamazaki called to one of his staff of whom there were six waiting in a line to attend to the arrival of his guests. "Please show Tanaka san to the drawing room." He leaned over and whispered conspiratorially in my ear, "Tonight will be a night we will remember for the rest of our lives. It is the start of a great journey, and like all journeys, it begins with one step. Tonight we will take that first step." As usual, I was at a loss to find a suitable reply. Everything Hamazaki said to me seemed to be coming from a different place. He never spoke directly; everything he said was shrouded in an air of intrigue or needed further explanation. He would offer a promise of something, or give you a glimpse into his thoughts, but it didn't seem to be his style to just speak plainly.

I was escorted to the drawing room, which served as an anteroom for the guests to gather and share drinks before being called for dinner. I found myself standing in another wonderful room, one that was illuminated by a magnificent crystal chandelier. The ceiling had been decorated with vibrant images of colourful carp swimming around in a pond with Monet-style water lilies. It had a calming effect on the room. It was a truly stunning work of art. The walls were wooden panelled and adorned with even more portraits of fine-looking men from bygone ages. One of the staff approached bearing a tray of glasses filled with champagne. I took one and gulped it down. I needed to steady my nerves. I was beginning to dread what the evening might bring. It occurred to me that I might be called upon to make a speech of self-introduction. I felt my knees go weak at the very thought of such a thing.

As I was going through my fears, staring up at the gorgeous scene, I heard a familiar female voice behind me. "Oh, I'm so sorry to disturb you. Please excuse me. I just wanted to put this vase here." She was carrying a large heavy-looking vase, filled with those exotic flowers that Hamazaki seemed so fond of.

"Please allow me to help you," I said. I took the vase from her and placed it on the high table in the centre of the room. It was the finishing touch to an already perfect room, if such a thing were possible. "These flowers are beautiful."

I looked into her eyes, and she seemed a little lost for words. It was obvious she was trying to recall me. "Ah, yes, they are rather attractive. My brother has a liking for orchids. Excuse me, but have we met before?"

"Forgive me. I am Tanaka. We met briefly this afternoon in your brother's study. I was . . ."

She interrupted me with an expression of recognition. "Of course, Tanaka san. Please forgive me, for it is the second time today I have interrupted your solitude. I am pleased that you are able to join us for dinner this evening. You are a most welcome guest." She gave me a slow deep bow and took her leave. Being a woman of high manners, she didn't refer to my dramatic change in appearance at all. I had met her only twice, both times by chance. Yet for reasons I couldn't understand, I felt an attraction to her. Hamazaki had told me her name when he had confided in me his suspicions surrounding his father's death. Ayumi. I repeated it over and over in my mind, for she had touched a part of me that I had believed long dead. I told myself such thoughts were entirely irrational and tried to will them away as if shooing off a housefly. She could never be interested in a man like me. I resolved not to think of her in that way ever again. Besides, I had no idea what her status was. Was she married?

As I was drifting off into one of my fantasies, I heard Hamazaki's voice. He had silently entered the room. "I love this room. It is my favourite room in the whole house. Everyone refers to it as a drawing room. I like to think of it as a harmony room. It is a place I come to when I need to think through matters which are troubling my mind. I commissioned the talented wartime painter Ryohei Koiso to do the ceiling for me. I think he found it therapeutic to be engaged in the creation of something so beautiful after depicting the horrors of war for so long." We both stood for a few minutes, admiring the intricate artwork above our heads. Before I had a chance to pay my compliments, Hamazaki went on.

"The pool represents civilization. The koi, swimming freely without care or prejudice, symbolise an ideal world, one I'm afraid we may never experience. There are those amongst us who are only too willing to add a drop of poison to the pool."

I agreed with him even though I didn't have a clue what he was talking about. Luckily, I was saved from any impending embarrassment by the sound of voices coming from the hallway. Hamazaki excused himself and went down to greet his guests. I could hear the friendly commotion of several people, all of whom seemed to have arrived together. I couldn't catch any names, because they were speaking over each other in an excited and joyous manner. I felt the waves of insecurity crash over me and for the hundredth time that day wondered what in heaven's name I was doing here.

In a matter of minutes Hamazaki's "harmony" room was filling up with guests. Their confidence and bonhomie seemed to come naturally, in marked contrast to me. The horrors of our national suffering had apparently done nothing to reduce their sense of entitlement. I felt small and diminished, like an imposter in another man's clothes. I was a third-rate fraud and felt it proper to retreat to the far corner of the room, trying to make myself as inconspicuous as possible. I had shaken a few hands and exchanged a few bows—nothing more than simple greetings and pleasantries. I got the impression that they were trying to place me, naturally thinking that if I were a guest here, I must be significant in some form or other. They all looked like important men. I say "men," as there wasn't a single woman amongst us. Everybody seemed to know each other. It was a gathering that had obviously "gathered" many times before.

There was no sign of Hamazaki. I assumed he was still in the hall greeting late arrivals. I was standing alone with my back to the far corner of the room, a glass of champagne in my hand, wishing I smoked, as most of the guests seemed to be doing so and it would at least give me something to do. A portly gentleman of advancing years approached me. "Good evening, sir. My name is Kawakami." He handed me a name card which grandly informed that he was the president of a company that made pianos. I introduced myself and apologised for not having a card to present, as I had only recently been appointed to the company.

I realised that I must have sounded like I was speaking in riddles, for Kawakami asked me which company I was employed by. Not wishing to appear as witless as I sounded, I replied, "I am Hamazaki san's new chief engineer."

Kawakami patted me on the arm. "Splendid, splendid indeed. Tanaka, have you met Sasaki san?" He gestured to Sasaki to join us, and made the introductions. There was something very familiar about Sasaki, and it was an effort not to stare at his fine features and jutting cheekbones that appeared to have been accentuated by cosmetics. He was the only guest not wearing formal Western-style evening dress, choosing instead a brilliantly coloured red kimono.

Sasaki bowed. "I am most pleased to make your acquaintance, Tanaka san. I hope we have the opportunity to speak later." Sasaki left us and went back to mingle amongst a select circle of guests. Kawakami turned to me. "Those theatrical types, in a world of their own, eh?" I asked what Sasaki did in the theatre. Kawakami looked a little taken aback. "Tanaka san, where have you been these last few years? Sasaki is a national treasure, one of our greatest and most loved singers of *enka*. Ah, you must know him by his stage name, Oka Haruo." Kawakami looked at me in a quizzical way, as if I were having a little joke at his expense. I had indeed heard the name and the voice many times, filling my workshop with his ballads as I went about my work. I said I had heard of him and his work. Kawakami was about to say something when a gong sounded which took the words out of his mouth and we were called to be seated for dinner.

A large seating plan was displayed by the entrance to the dining room. Most guests had checked their name, and proceeded straight to their place. I stood staring at the list, not quite believing that my name would be there. However, there I was. "Tanaka Hideo, Chief Engineer, Hamazaki Electricals." I was seated alongside Kawakami, at the far end of the table and across from a young man by the name of Hosokawa from the Diplomatic Office. The room I had been in earlier in the day with Hamazaki had been transformed into an elegant dining room. The long table was shining like a jewellery box. Gleaming crystal stood alongside rows of dazzling silver cutlery. Candelabras were placed down the centre, and the twinkling lights gave a magical effect. My eyes were instantly drawn to the provocative painting of the *Golden Lily*. I looked around at the faces of my fellow guests, none of whom seemed to be the least bit interested in the picture. Most of them were concerned with finding their seat and who they had been seated with. I assumed there was some merit to where you were placed. Maybe the closer you were to the head of the table and Hamazaki himself, the more important you were. Hamazaki would no doubt take his place at the head of the table beneath the *Golden Lily*.

I was pleased to be sitting next to Kawakami, who proved to be an entertaining and amusing conversationalist. He had been a great friend of Hamazaki's father and became tearful when speaking of his dear friend and the sorrow he felt at his passing. He told me how they had "grown up" together in business and survived the hardships of war and the stress of running such a business, only for his dear friend to succumb to the failings of his heart. I looked puzzled, and Kawakami told me that nobody could predict their demise. When the heart switches off, it is time to go, without even so much as a farewell to those left behind. He dabbed his eyes with his napkin and took a few moments to regain his composure. So it was apparent that even Hamazaki's closest friends were not aware of the true events surrounding his father's death.

We continued making small talk until the room fell into a deferential hush and Hamazaki entered with the last two guests, one of them a tall, stern-looking Western man. The other, in contrast, was an elderly stooped and very slow-moving Japanese man. I could not recognise either, but Hosokawa leaned over and whispered conspiratorially and with a flash of mischief in his eyes. "There is a sight you don't see every day: our finance minister, Ikeda Hayato, with the next supreme allied commander." Kawakami asked who he was. Hosokawa said he was General Matthew Ridgway. Hosokawa went on. "It is an open secret that he is in line to take over from MacArthur early next year. Gentlemen, General Ridgway will be the most powerful man in the country. It is no wonder Prime Minister Yoshida deems it fit to allow Ikeda here tonight. It's on nights like this the real diplomacy gets done, eh, Kawakami?"

"I wouldn't know. I am just a simple man of music. On the other hand if Mr Ridgway would like to purchase a piano, I would be most happy to open negotiations." We all forced a little laugh at Kawakami's attempt at light humour.

Hosokawa studied the menu cards that had been placed at each guest's place setting. "It seems Hamazaki san has outdone himself yet again. A rare gourmet feast awaits us all." We all studied our cards, which were dated September 29, 1949, and embossed with fine gold ink and written in three languages: first French, and then English followed by a Japanese translation. The menu could have been written in any language, for the foods were so alien to me that I had no idea what to expect. We were informed that the menu had been specially created by the renowned French chef Fernand Point. Foie gras en brioche followed by gratin of crayfish tails accompanied by a selection of the finest vintage wines. Despite my wariness, I was hungry, having last eaten in my workshop many hours ago and another world away. My head was spinning a little from the glass of champagne I had drunk earlier. My nerves were settling, and to my surprise I found myself relaxing. The wine waiters were moving up and down the table, filling glasses with red wine.

The first plates of food were served, and without ceremony, we started dinner. I was careful not to eat too ravenously and studied the other guests, taking my lead from them, as I was unfamiliar with Western table manners. I had attended officers' nights during my army days but very few and nothing as grand as what was before me now. I looked up the table and saw Hamazaki, flanked on either side by Ridgway and Ikeda. He looked very much at ease, smiling one moment and looking serious and thoughtful the next. The food was delicious, and even though it wasn't quite voluminous enough to satisfy a very hungry man, it certainly took the edge off my appetite.

The wine was beginning to take effect, and the guests' voices were growing louder and the laughter was a little more raucous. It suddenly struck me how un-Japanese the whole evening was. Everything was far removed from what we thought of as typically Japanese. The food, the drinks, the clothes we were wearing, the room we were sitting in—all of it was taken from a different culture. It all suddenly seemed like a bizarre charade. We could have been sitting in Monsieur Point's own restaurant in Paris. Had the world gone crazy and me with it? The crayfish were despatched and followed by a sweet crème brûlée. I had avoided the wine and settled for water. The same could not be said of my dining companions, some of whom seemed to be getting more carried away by the minute. Coffee and port was served along with cheese and slices of apple and melon.

Suddenly, a rapping sound of knife against wineglass cut through the chatter. Hamazaki was calling the gathering to order. He had risen to his feet and was readying himself to speak. "Gentlemen, I thank you all for gracing us with your presence this evening. I am honoured and humbled to be amongst you all." He gave a small bow to his left and right to indicate that his words had extra significance for his guests of honour. "The last decade has been the most turbulent and trying era in the history of our country. We have all experienced the wretched devastation that war inevitably brings. We have seen our country undergo transformations that would have been unthinkable in the not too distant past. Yet the past is past, and though it is not forgotten, it is the future that we must embrace. The future is designed in the present, and we all have our part to play. Yes, each and every single one of us— every man, woman, and child. The reconstruction of Japan is underway, and it gathers momentum each day. For that we will be forever grateful for the benevolence and support given to us by our American friends, without whom we would never have been able to achieve so much in so short a time. We thank you." Hamazaki lifted his glass and nodded in Ridgway's direction. Everybody followed his lead, and murmurings of appreciation rippled around the room.

Hamazaki had the complete attention of his guests. His confidence and bearing demanded your admiration. He was speaking entirely off the cuff, yet he never faltered once in his delivery. "The rebirth of our nation is underway, but we must always be aware of complacency. We must strive to achieve more for the sake of all who are to come after us. It is not my place to speak of how this or that should or should not be done. That is why we have politicians." The guests murmured their agreement, a few of them tapping the table to emphasise their feelings. There had been a great deal of debate in the newspapers lately about the relationships between business and the political parties. Hamazaki was playing to his guests. "Like my father before me, I am merely a simple manufacturer, yet I see it as my obligation to make a contribution to the collective efforts towards progress. Our collective spirit is our strength, and it must be directed to achieve positive changes for the greater good of society as a whole." This, I suspected, was for the ears of Hamazaki's American guest, a reiteration of peaceful intentions. "Yet the past cannot be erased from the collective memory. It is what shapes us and defines us; it has put us where we are now. It is with this in mind that I want to take this opportunity to announce some major changes that I intend to make within my own company."

I felt my heart quicken, and a rush of nerves hit me like a charging stallion. I prayed to God that Hamazaki was not going to single me out to speak. I need not have been concerned; he was a driven man and would not allow for the spotlight to be taken away now. "Hamazaki Electricals is going to redirect its core base of production from heavy industry to the consumer sector. This will not be an easy task, but I have complete confidence in my staff, and I believe we will meet this challenge with the spirit that was shown by the company's founders so many years ago.

"Why are we changing our focus? It is a question that begs to be answered. As the nation grows, there will be a demand for products that can make life more comfortable for the ordinary household. We will devote our efforts and craftsmanship to satisfying those demands. Every household will have a dream of the three *s*'s: *senpuki*, *suihanki*, and *sentakki*." Hamazaki took a sip of water and allowed time for his guests to appreciate his visions. He spread his hands wide as though he were some messiah. "Gentlemen, I give you the future: fans, rice cookers, and washing machines." The English version was delivered for the benefit of Mr Ridgway. "It is my challenge to put these in every home across the country, to make them desirable, affordable, and accessible to the population."

Hamazaki was on a roll, and there was no stopping him now. He had the curious attention of his audience. I too was captivated. Rice cookers and washing machines? I had never even heard of such things. What could be more peaceful than improving daily lives by producing these magical products?

Hamazaki went on. "As we are to change our production emphasis, it seems fitting that our company should adopt a new name—a makeover, if you wish. I propose that from this day onwards our company be known as Mabuhay Portable Electricals."

Mabuhay. The name sent my mind flying back to the Philippines. I had heard it so many times: *mabuhay*, a Tagalog word meaning "long life," as close to our own *banzai* as you could imagine. Why would Hamazaki risk exposing any shady connections with the past? The war was still a sensitive topic and one best avoided, but Hamazaki had purposely opened the door to it. I looked around the table. From the blank expressions on the faces, it was safe to assume that most if not all of the guests had never heard the word before.

Hamazaki continued, looking more like a Shakespearean actor than a businessman. "Some of you here tonight may be familiar with the word *mabuhay*; it comes from the Tagalog meaning 'long life.' I think we owe it to the future to atone for the mistakes of the past. I want my company to be a symbol of enlightenment. Mabuhay will offer its outstretched hand in friendship and co-operation to those who find themselves in less fortunate circumstances. These are not hollow words that will be forgotten tomorrow. I will ensure that the new articles of incorporation and the company constitution contain the following promise: Ten per cent of our gross profit is to be donated to aid projects, and to welfare and regeneration programmes in the war-affected countries of Asia. Mabuhay will stand as a beacon of hope. We are living in exciting times, and opportunities are aplenty. These are the days that will define our nation and our humanity. We can look forward to the future with optimism, and yet it saddens me to say this is not true for our near neighbours. Once more the spectre of armed conflict hangs over us."

The room listened with rapt attention. War talk was frowned upon and one best avoided if at all possible. Our nationalistic fervour had all but been eroded. The Americans had insisted on various policies and safeguards to avoid the mistakes of the past. Economic recovery and making money was the new battleground, and some of the hardened financial warriors seated around the table must have been wondering where Hamazaki was going with his talk of possible trouble. "I fear that the outbreak of hostilities on the Korean Peninsula is inevitable. Whilst we pray for a peaceful solution, and hope diplomacy prevails, we have a moral responsibility to support our American allies, and if we are called upon, I would like to think our leaders will find the moral fibre to grant any requests for assistance." There was a subdued muttering of consent and a few people murmured "Here, here," but I think Hamazaki was playing a little theatre for General Ridgway.

When I think back and recall Hamazaki's speech, as I often do, I view it as a mastery of smoke and mirrors. I do not doubt for one moment that Hamazaki wanted to make a genuine attempt at goodness. His sense of philanthropy was real enough. However, the unspoken words had the greatest meanings. Mabuhay was born that evening and, like all newborns, needed constant attention to survive. Ten per cent seemed a small price to pay for what we were to get in return. It was time for him to conclude his speech. "Gentlemen, this evening we have dined on a menu specially created by one of the most outstanding chefs in the world, Monsieur Point of France. He is a man who understands his customers and gives them what they want. He is also a man who likes his fine wines, and he is a most perceptive thinker—a dangerous combination. I am reminded of one of his favourite sayings: 'One of the most important things that distinguishes man from other animals is that man can get pleasure from drinking without being thirsty.' We should take Monsieur Point's words to heart and drink a toast. Please stand and raise your glasses. To the future, and to happier days to come."

We echoed Hamazaki's simple toast and were settling back into our chairs when Hamazaki sprang one final surprise. "Gentlemen, may I suggest we adjourn to the adjacent room, where Oka Haruo san has kindly agreed to sing us one of his songs." Hamazaki looked to the centre of the table where Oka, seated in his bright red kimono, stood out like a splash of red paint against a background of black and white. "My dear friend, on behalf of everyone, I thank you so much for this rare privilege." Oka gave a slow bow and held his hands to his heart in a show of his own appreciation. The large double doors were opened, and Hamazaki stood to accompany Ridgway and Ikeda. That was the cue for the rest of us to vacate our seats and go listen to Oka.

We were led into a beautifully appointed music room that housed the most magnificent grand piano I had ever seen. As with the rest of the rooms I had been in, describing it as exquisite may be doing it a disservice. However, all the artistic pieces on show paled into insignificance in comparison with one outstanding beauty: Ayumi sat at the piano. She was wearing a long, pale pink silk dress which cascaded over the piano stool and gave the impression that she was floating on air. Her hair was done in traditional Japanese fashion and tied up with ornate hairpins. Her face was as smooth as fine china. I had never seen such beauty. Immediately I felt guilt and shame for thinking such thoughts, and said a silent prayer of apology to Fumiyo. But no matter how much I tried to will my thoughts away, I could not bring myself to take my eyes from Ayumi. She sat there, so close and yet worlds apart, a living testament to my loneliness.

Kawakami shook me out of my fantasy by sneaking up behind me and whispering into my ear, "She is a beauty, is she not?" Startled, I thought for a moment he had been able to read my thoughts. Then I realised he was referring to the piano itself. Years later I would come to understand that Kawakami liked his fun and that perhaps he'd been having a little at my expense. Oka strode into the centre of the room and spoke in a surprisingly high-pitched voice. "It is an honour to be invited to sing for you all this evening. I have chosen one of my favourite songs to perform for you—'Tokyo no Hanauri Musume'—and am delighted to be accompanied on the piano by Hamazaki Ayumi." My heart skipped a beat. So she was a Hamazaki. I felt an irrational joy in the fact that she was possibly unattached.

Oka took a deep breath and composed himself, and Ayumi teased the piano into life. We all stood, shoulder to shoulder, drinks in hand, allowing ourselves to be lost in the moment. Oka's graceful tones sweeping around the room had a magical effect. Ayumi's stunning mastery of the piano and beauty made for a sublime rendition that passed by all too quickly. The abrupt ending of the song and the accompanying applause brought me out of my reverie. It was as if the song had cast a spell on me and I had become lost in its very soul. That morning I had been just a simple nobody, and now here I was, perhaps still a simple nobody but one who had fallen in love. I watched the object of my affections take a graceful bow and leave the room, allowing Oka to enjoy his applause. The waiters were busy, deftly weaving in and out of the crowded room bearing trays on which champagne flutes were precariously balanced. Hands nonchalantly reached out to help themselves without a second thought. The air filled with the sweet smell of cigar smoke. Guests huddled into various groups. Laughter and camaraderie seemed to come naturally to these people.

I was left standing by myself and trying to look at ease, which was taking all of my efforts. Tiredness was giving way to exhaustion. I wanted to get out of the party and back to the Empire. The thought of that luxurious bed waiting for me only increased my agitation. It had been a long and stressful day, and although I had got through it somehow, I was still on edge. Raucous laughter almost made me jump out of my skin.

Hosokawa came up to me with two glasses of champagne and held one out for me. "Come on, Tanaka san, cheer up. You look like a man with the weight of the world on his shoulders."

I thanked him for the champagne. "Just a little tired, I guess." Hosokawa looked over to the far side of the room where Hamazaki was deep in conversation with Ridgway and Ikeda. "Looks like they have a lot to talk about, eh? And as for you, Tanaka san, seems like you will have your work cut out, eh?" Hosokawa was waiting for a suitable response, only to be faced with my blank expression.

He went on to emphasise his point. "As chief engineer, surely you will be leading the charge, so to speak. You are in a race, and your rivals may have a head start."

"I'm sorry, I don't quite understand your meaning."

"Tanaka san, were you sleeping during Hamazaki's speech? The three *s*'s: sentakki, senpuki, suihanki. You will have to develop them for production, will you not?" Hosokawa was right. I had sat through Hamazaki's speech in a state of nervous tension. Now the realisation of what might be expected of me was finally sinking in. Hosokawa seemed friendly enough, and I had warmed to him as the evening went on. He handed me his name card, and again I had to explain why I couldn't reciprocate the gesture, being new in the job. "Tanaka san, your rivals may have a head start, but Hamazaki is no fool. His father was a shrewd businessman, and Toshio has continued in the same vein. Mitsubishi and Sanyo will provide stiff competition for you, but my money is on Mabuhay Portable Electricals to win." I nodded my agreement, but kept my thoughts to myself. I felt it wise to wait and see exactly what Hamazaki had in store for me before making any pronouncements. However, Hosokawa was in a talkative mood. Perhaps the drink had loosened his tongue a little. "What about this ten per cent donation thing?" he asked. "Is your boss really serious?"

That was the first time anyone referred to Hamazaki as my boss, and naturally it seemed a little strange, as I had met the man only yesterday. I said I did not know about the details but it seemed like a genuine commitment. Hosokawa looked thoughtful for a moment. "I hope Toshio has judged the current political climate well. Donating large sums to overseas projects when many of our own people are still struggling to get by may prove unpopular and play into the hands of his competitors." Hosokawa was bringing his diplomatic thinking to the fore. In later years I would often seek out his advice when I was unsure which way to turn, but right now he was just a person I barely knew in a crowd of strangers. Still, I had cause to be thankful to him and also to Kawakami, as they were the only guests who had paid me any attention tonight.

Hamazaki and his guests of honour were preparing to leave. Ikeda had started to say his goodbyes to some of the other guests. Ridgway was already making for the door, accompanied by Hamazaki. They passed right by me without so much as a nod of recognition. I was hoping this would be a sign for the party to disperse; surely others here wanted to retire as much as I did. I was unsure what the etiquette was, but I hoped someone would lead the way soon. I was bone tired, and stopping myself from yawning was a major effort. Sure enough, some brave souls led the way, and I decided to tag along. Descending the grand staircase I saw Hamazaki standing by the door bidding good night to his departing guests. Their cars had been called, and chauffeurs were standing on the pavement next to open doors, waiting to transport their masters. I wasn't sure what I was supposed to do. It was an awkward moment. I wouldn't have minded walking; it would have taken only a few minutes to get to the Empire, and the air would have done me good.

Hamazaki spotted me and called me over. He took my hand and shook it. "Now, that wasn't too bad, was it? Thank you for coming this evening." I thanked him again for all he had done for me, but he waved away my thanks. "Think nothing of it, my dear fellow. You look done in. Go and sleep well, for tomorrow we have plenty to discuss. You and I will have a working lunch at the Empire. Shall we say twelve sharp? I shall call on you then. You will find Ogawa waiting to take you back. Good night, Hideo. I will see you tomorrow." Hamazaki gave me a firm pat on the back and then went back to his farewells. He had his own way of telling you what to do without it sounding like an order. Saying no was never an option.

It was with a great sense of relief that I stepped out into the cool, breezy air. The wind was rustling the branches of the trees that flanked Ginza Avenue, where a parade of grand cars, engines running, waited for the final guests to emerge. I spotted Ogawa waiting on the other side of the avenue and dodged between two parked cars and thanked him for his services once more. He nodded in his polite but reserved manner and opened the rear door for me. I took one last look at the house. A light was on in one of the first-floor rooms, and I could see somebody standing at the window, looking out. It was Kawabata. He was staring directly at me. I held his stare for a few moments and nodded in his direction, only to be met with his cold, unmoving gaze. He made me feel uncomfortable.

I got into the car and allowed Ogawa to take me once more to the Empire Hotel. I asked him to let me out by the Empire's ornamental pool. He bade me good evening and left me to find my own way back to the suite. A bellboy appeared as if by magic. He was wearing a name tag which told me he went by the name of Noguchi. "Good evening, Tanaka san. May I escort you to your suite, sir?" I thanked him and said I would be most obliged. We walked through the serene and tranquil lobby and up the stairs to the suite. There was an awkward moment when I realised that I didn't have any coins with which to tip him. I felt bad about that and resolved to seek him out the next day and make good. I took off my shoes and lay on the bed for a few minutes' rest before washing. A few minutes turned into ten hours. I slept the sleep of a man who had had all his energy drained from him.

I did not know it then, but that was the day I was reborn. It was a day I will never forget for as long as I live. I had met the man who would shape my destiny. That man had formed a company which would go on to become the wealthiest and most powerful privately owned enterprise in the world. Hamazaki and Mabuhay: names that would become synonymous with wealth and corporate power. In my vainer moments I allow a third name to be included, and that name is Tanaka.

Chapter 4
Toshio Hamazaki
Tokyo
1950

Finally, after month upon month of disappointment and frustrating setbacks, the day I had been waiting for had arrived. It had taken six months for us to reach the stage where my designers and engineers were able to present me with the three prototypes of the products that were going to change the way every home in the country went about its routine domestic chores. Mabuhay was about to go into production.

I tasked Tanaka with overseeing three small teams, each made up of some of the best electrical engineers in the country, and assigned them to produce our first rice cooker, fan, and washing machine. I set strict parameters for their tasks: Not only were they to develop working prototypes that could quickly be put into production, but these models had to come in at 25 per cent cheaper than any rival product on the market. The build quality and dependability had to be superior to anything our competitors offered. Each item also had to be as aesthetically pleasing as possible, because beauty sells. I knew that my demands bordered on the impossible, but it seemed that they had "pulled it off," and this morning there was to be a presentation of our first products, at my home, at the very table where I had set out my vision six months earlier.

Tanaka had been an absolute marvel; my father was so right about him. I praised the day I found him. He had proved himself, beyond all doubt, to be a genius, and I knew we owed this day to him. He not only foresaw any problems but already had the solutions worked out. Listening to him explain the technicalities of our endeavours was sweet music to my ears.

For some, our business may have appeared a little tedious. However, there is glory to be found in the mundane, and we were now so close, I could almost reach out and touch it.

I had gotten into the habit of sleeping late into the mornings, but my nocturnal routine was beginning to take its toll, and too many late nights were starting to show. I made a promise to myself to behave more responsibly. After all, I needed to stay sharp once Mabuhay hit full production. Normally, I love the luxury of lying in bed—that's when I do my best thinking—but there would be no such self-indulgence today. The meeting was scheduled for eleven, and knowing my staff, they would be ready and waiting fifteen minutes before the appointed time.

With an unusual spring in my step I got out of bed and made my way to the bathroom. I checked myself closely in the mirror and was satisfied that last night's debauchery was not too evident for all to see. The dark rings under my eyes were the only telltale signs of a series of increasingly late nights. My sister, Ayumi, often told me I was looking strained and implored me to slow down a little, but I am blessed with a strong constitution. I'm one of those rare folk who can drink their fill and next morning suffer little more than a bout of tiredness. Some of my drinking companions are not so lucky and cannot even look at a drink after a night on the town with the legendary

Hamazaki. Another reason I found myself dizzy with distraction was, quite simply, love. I believed I had found my soul mate, and the joy we shared knew no bounds.

I shaved slowly and dressed quickly, selecting a subdued wine-red shirt to complement my charcoal three-piece. I fussed over which necktie would make the best match. My father always said that the wrong choice of necktie ruins your whole ensemble. The look, like everything in life, is in the details. I settled on a solid cream with fine diagonal grey stripes, the perfect finishing touch. All that was left was to slick back my hair with a little pomade and I would be ready to host the first Mabuhay meeting of any true importance. Eventually satisfied that I was up to my usual standards, I turned, only to be met by my love, who was leaning against the bathroom door. "Hammy, kiss me."

I tried to resist, playfully protesting that I was a busy businessman this morning, but I knew my resistance would fall on stony ground. "I have a meeting downstairs in a few minutes."

Kawabata gave me a mischievous smile. "Hmm, so do I." I closed my eyes and submitted myself totally. I felt my belt being undone and my trousers fall to my ankles. I was aroused so quickly, the pure pleasure of that lovely mouth working its magic was too much to bear, and Kawabata sent me to heaven. I tried to keep my rapture under control, but anyone passing my door would have been under no illusion about the ecstatic groans. I tousled Kawabata's hair, and he slowly rose to his feet and put his face close to mine. He swallowed hard and said with a boyish, playful gleam in his eyes, "Breakfast was delicious."

That same look had caught my attention many months earlier at the Club Flamingo, where he was working as a host. On that unforgettable night, I paid for his "services," but now, he was mine, and mine alone. I could not bear to think of him with another man. We had to keep our relationship hidden; our kind of love was not accepted amongst the circles I frequented. I was sure my sister knew; it is hard to keep secrets from women, especially when they live under the same roof. Ogawa, my valet, certainly knew, having, to my horror, had the misfortune of intruding upon our lovemaking one rainy afternoon a few months earlier. I was concerned about his reaction, but he maintained his cool and, much to Kawabata's amusement, even asked if we required any refreshments.

At that time I resided at the Empire; I moved back to the family residence after my father's death. It was an opportune moment, as keeping Kawabata a secret in a hotel was proving increasingly difficult. I offered my suite to Tanaka as his permanent residence, which irked Kawabata and sent him into a petulant sulk. He loved spending his days at the Empire, idly passing his time, ordering fine wines and exotic drinks in the lobby lounge. Kawabata had taken an irrational dislike to Tanaka, one I dismissed as mere jealousy, a sign of his immaturity. After all, he was twelve years my junior.

There was a knock on my bedroom door. I knew it must be Ogawa, coming to see if I required any assistance with the morning's preparations. Kawabata scuttled off back to bed, where he made a great play of hiding under the bedclothes. I bade Ogawa entry, and he waited patiently in the hallway, my bedroom safely concealed from view. I checked my look once more in the mirror, to make sure there were no visible signs of the last few moments' shenanigans. "Ogawa san. Good morning to you."

"Good morning, sir. I trust you slept well?" Was there a hint of something verging on sarcasm in that cool monotone delivery of his?

"Perfectly well, thank you for asking, Ogawa."

"Sir, Tanaka san has arrived at the house earlier than expected. He has asked to meet with you in private before the meeting. He apologises in advance for arriving unannounced, but insists he needs an audience with you." I thought about this for a few moments. My first thoughts were that some last-minute problem might have surfaced that threatened to put back our products' launch, but then I realised what must have brought him to my door at such an early time. There could be only one explanation for Tanaka's arriving in such circumstances, which was out of character for him, and if I was correct, I would allow myself a little celebratory pat on the back.

I gave Ogawa my warmest smile and said, "Of course, my doors are always open for my chief engineer. Please show him into the dining room and prepare morning refreshments. I shall join him in fifteen minutes." Ogawa bowed and left, closing the door silently behind him.

I went back to the bedroom where Kawabata was lying on the bed, covered only by a thin silk sheet. He had overheard my exchange with Ogawa and said in a rather mocking tone, "So it's morning tea with Hideo, is it?" I started to explain, as I had so many times, that it was business and what I did, but he gave me a dismissive look and then pulled the sheets back to reveal himself. He was hard, and I felt myself stirring again. "Hammy, I need you. Come on; finish me off before you go." I was about to protest about the lack of time, but without thinking, I found myself on the bed, my head between his legs, repaying the compliment. It seemed to take him longer than usual to come, but we got there in the end. I rolled off the bed and went to the bathroom, rinsed out my mouth, and checked myself for the third time that morning. Good God, how many times must a man make himself presentable?

Kawabata came up behind me and gave me a hug. "Hammy, I'm bored. You have your big business to do, and I'm left alone all day. I want to go shopping." This meant he wanted some money. His spending had started to reach levels of concern, but I had so far not drawn attention to it, and today of all days, I did not want a scene that would distract me from the business at hand. I went over to my writing bureau and unlocked the drawer with a key I kept on my waist chain. I took out ten new crisp, hundred-yen notes and handed them over to him. It was the equivalent of three weeks salary for most of my employees. I kissed him on the cheek and told him to buy something nice to wear for tonight, because I thought we would have marvellous news that would require a fitting celebration. I left Kawabata in the bathroom looking rather pleased with himself, and at the third time of trying, emerged from my room to face the day.

Before my hastily arranged meeting with Tanaka I stopped by my "harmony room," as was my habit every morning, to allow myself a few quiet moments alone to reflect on the business of the day. I looked up at the gorgeous and intricate painting on the ceiling and tried to find something I had previously been unaware of. The serenity of the koi swimming playfully always managed to bring the world around me into some kind of focus. This morning, my mind had been filled only with business matters and company concerns. Now, Tanaka's early arrival had shifted my focus. I told myself that this could be about only one thing: my sister, Ayumi. If I was correct in my assumption, Tanaka was here because he intended to propose marriage to my sister and needed my consent. As Ayumi's only living relative and as Tanaka's employer, seeking out my approval before proposing would, in Tanaka's eyes, be the correct way to proceed. If they had reached this stage, I could only presume that Ayumi had indicated to

Tanaka that she would be receptive to such a proposal. Perhaps it was her idea for Tanaka to approach me at this time, right before the unveiling of our prototypes.

My sister and Tanaka: Such a union would have been unthinkable six months earlier. When I had finally located him and brought him into the fold, he was in the most dire of straits. But he was a special man and one chosen for greater things, a man who had been known to my father since the day of his birth, and one who had been watched over in a benevolent manner from afar. Tanaka did not know who he truly was, but soon the time would come when I would have to sit down with him and have our special little talk. Marriage to my sister would ensure that he was "sympathetic" to my cause and provide the necessary leverage should he find my agenda distasteful.

Our destinies were on course to collide from the day we were born. I had to be certain he would stand by me all the way. A union of Hideo and Ayumi would make the bond between us unbreakable. I had staged several "chance" encounters between Tanaka and Ayumi, acting as an unofficial matchmaker from the very first day Tanaka had stepped into my house and I had asked Ayumi if she would check on the arrangements for that evening's dinner party. She had thus happened upon Tanaka waiting alone in his dishevelled state, and later that same day marvelled when she chanced upon him for a second time whilst placing orchids in the harmony room at my request. I had gauged her reaction to his newly transformed appearance and found it favourable. In the days and weeks that followed I set up small dinner parties, inviting Tanaka to the house under the pretence of discussing his work and progress. Invariably I found a reason to excuse myself, leaving Tanaka and Ayumi alone to get acquainted. It was obvious from the start that Tanaka was love-struck. He would constantly snatch surreptitious glances in Ayumi's direction. His admiration and devotion to her was plain for all to see, especially for a man like myself, one who prides himself on understanding the sensitivities of the heart. Tanaka and Ayumi were two lonely souls drifting in a misty sea, before finally colliding and forever sailing the same path.

Ayumi, like Tanaka, had been married before. She had been a wartime bride and, sadly, became a wartime widow within six months. Her husband, Captain Ryosuke Kano, had been killed in the Marianas Islands six years earlier. His death had left her in a permanent state of devastation. She bore her bereavement for years; it seemed like a black cloud followed her wherever she went. Our father's death and the tragic circumstances surrounding it had only served to push Ayumi further into the depths of despair and misery. There were days when I thought she would never smile again.

Shortly after her husband's passing, our father urged her to revert to using the family name. He was convinced that Ayumi would once more find happiness through matrimony and that appropriate suitors would be more amenable to the Hamazaki name. He yearned for a grandchild to continue his bloodline, and Ayumi was his only hope. He had long given up on any dream of me fulfilling his wish, having reluctantly accepted my predilections long ago. In the months before his death, my father had often expressed his concern about Ayumi's welfare and made me vow to seek out a path that would lead to her happiness. I had been at a loss as to how to proceed after she had icily rejected a long list of suitors of my choosing. It was with great relief that she seemed to be at one with Tanaka.

Yes, it was a mystery that only the heart could answer, but as they say, the heart must have what the heart wants. Perhaps she had found someone who, like herself, carried their heart forever wrapped in a black shroud. Now the time had come to cast away that shroud and tie ribbons as bright as a rainbow in its place. Such happy endings were the things of fairy tales but not real life. But was that about to change today?

I went into the meeting room to find Tanaka waiting for me. He was sitting in front of a tray of morning foods: rice balls, soup, and crackers. There was hot green tea, but I doubt whether Tanaka had taken as much as a sip. He was not that kind of person, preferring to wait until his host joined him. So, there we sat, facing each other. It was an effort to stop myself from smiling, and I desperately wished I could ease his obvious discomfort. He was always so serious, which was his nature. When something weighed heavily on his mind, he became as rigid as a board. "Tanaka san, it is so good to see you this fine morning. I trust everything is well and you are not here as the bearer of bad tidings." I gave him a cheeky smile to show I was jesting a little.

He returned a feeble smile and replied, "Please forgive me for intruding on you at such an early hour. The prototypes are ready for your final approval. I believe they are the best that exist anywhere in the world today. I don't want to take away any of the limelight that deservedly belongs to the team leaders. Each of them has prepared a short explanation and demonstration for your benefit. Also, I took the liberty of informing the production manager, Araki, to prepare a manufacturing update. He is concerned with the tooling of the lines."

I decided to cut Tanaka off there and then before he got too technical, which he tended to do. I hated it when the boffin types started to rattle on about nuts and bolts. "That seems fine. I look forward to the meeting where all will be revealed." I made a theatrical gesture with arms wide open. It was obvious that Tanaka required some prompting, so I made to leave. "If that is all, there are one or two things I need to attend to before the meeting, if you would excuse me." I stood to leave.

"Hamazaki san, there is one more thing." I sat again, a look of contrived concern on my face. "It is of a personal nature and concerns your sister, Ayumi." I felt the blood quicken in my veins, and a tingling sensation swept over me.

"Yes, what about my sister?"

I tried to keep my face as straight as possible. I could see this was not easy for him. His shyness was battling with his desire, and his voice was a little higher than usual. "As you may be aware, Ayumi san and I have been spending time together, and we have grown fond of each other's company. Toshio san, I have come here this morning to seek your approval so I may ask for Ayumi's hand in marriage."

He had managed to get his words out and now lowered his head and avoided eye contact. He must have rehearsed this moment a hundred times in his mind, like a dumbstruck teenager in love, and now he was going through inner turmoil. The devil in me was tempted to have a little fun at his expense, but I dismissed the idea. "You have talked this over with Ayumi, have you not? Is she aware that you are here seeking my consent to your union?"

He raised his head and looked at me with imploring eyes that begged for a release from his emotional prison. "Yes, she knows. It is important to her that your approval be sought. Convention dictates that as her only family…"

I cut him off with a wave of my hand. My gesture must have taken him by surprise, for he lowered his head once more in a dejected manner. "Hideo, to hell with convention. In life there are so few things that a man may gain pleasure from. A companion who shares in the love you feel is so rare a thing. We have lived through bloody times, and now it is time for life to repay our sufferings with a little happiness. Of course you have my consent. You have made me a happy man, and I know our father is smiling down from heaven right now. My sister is a lucky woman."

Hideo raised his head and looked me straight in the eye. "Thank you, Toshio, thank you." Tears were rolling down his cheeks, which he hurriedly dried in a fit of embarrassment.

I stood up and opened my arms wide. "This is turning into a great day, and like all great days, it should be rounded off with a celebration. Tonight we will mark this day in our family's history, and your future union will be a sign of the good fortune that Mabuhay will enjoy forever."

Tanaka was at a loss for words. He stood and again thanked me. "Toshio san, there is one more thing." He reached into his pocket and took out a black pen and placed it into my hand. "Please take it. I have carried it for so long, I would feel easier if you secured it."

I looked at the pen, which had some kind of inscription written on it. I had let Tanaka have safekeeping of this for a long time. It was a sign, or perhaps a measure of my trust and faith in him, and now, he was giving it to me of his own will. Did he know the secret he had been securing all these years? I doubted it, but the time was fast approaching when his faith in me and Mabuhay would be tested to the full. I felt it necessary to express my gratitude, and hoped my words did not sound too hollow. "Hideo, I thank you on behalf of all who fell and all who suffered so that this would finally be delivered. We have here in our hands the means to make a difference in a world that has lost its way. Mabuhay will be a light that I hope others will follow." I walked around the table and drew Tanaka close to me in an awkward embrace. "Welcome to my family. There is one more thing. I have to ask a favour of you."

Hideo looked a little surprised. "Of course, yes, anything, anything at all." I reached into my waistcoat pocket and took out a shining pink diamond ring. "This was my mother's engagement ring. My father proposed with this ring thirty years ago and kept it close by his side until the day of his death. I know it would make him happy if you would present this ring to Ayumi." Tanaka was speechless. At first I thought he was going to refuse, but he saw the emotion in my eyes and humbly agreed, saying what an honour it was. I doubted he would have agreed with such readiness if he had known that the ring was taken off my dead mother's finger two minutes after Ayumi's birth. Tanaka looked at me, realisation spread across his face, and he allowed himself a rare genuine smile. I know he wanted to ask me how I had come to be carrying an engagement ring at this opportune time. Some things are best left unsaid. We looked at each other with mutual understanding and went about our preparations for the morning meeting which was nearly upon us.

It seemed fitting to hold the gathering in the harmony room. After all, it was in this very place that my own dreams of the future had come to me. The first steps towards that vision were now on the table before me in the form of two finished prototypes: a rice cooker with built-in thermostatic control and timer, exciting innovations that our rivals had yet to develop, and a free-standing floor fan with a fine copper finish, again outsmarting rival products with the introduction of a twin speed setting. My engineers had done me proud; they had exceeded my expectations.

Our third product had proved to be the most difficult to develop. The combination of water and electricity had been a challenge, but one that had been met head-on. At the far end of the room some technicians were tinkering about with what I hoped would be Japan's first mass-produced domestic washing machine. Oh yes, it was certainly shaping up to be one of the greatest days ever. Every household would have cause to thank Mabuhay Portable Electricals for giving them these labour-saving appliances.

Each of Tanaka's team leaders explained the development and cost forecasts of their particular projects. There was cause for optimism all round, engineers and technicians were enthusiastic, and we all knew that we were on the brink of something grand. Tanaka sat at the far end of the table, nodding encouragingly as each of his boffins went through their reports. He stayed silent, preferring to remain in the background, allowing his colleagues to take much of the credit. Yet I was not fooled for one minute. We wouldn't have been at this stage if it hadn't been for the brilliance of my future brother-in-law. I had not spoken at all, allowing the teams to go through their projects whilst I sat back enjoying their childlike enthusiasm. However, I felt the moment had arrived to show my gratitude for the magnificent efforts of my staff. I rose to my feet.

"Gentlemen, you have done me proud, and in the future we will look back on this day as the moment that Mabuhay finally came alive. These products will be the foundations for our company, and I say 'foundations' because we have a great structure yet to build. Today marks an important step on the path to glory. Time is now of the most crucial importance. We must start production at the earliest opportunity. Araki san, our production manager at the Yokohama facility, informs me that the first products may roll off the line as early as the end of next month."

There was a spontaneous burst of applause, and I felt a swell of emotion that I quickly reined in before continuing with my address. "I have arranged for the patents officer to visit me here this afternoon and receive our product descriptions. We must ensure that your innovations are well protected from corporate thievery. There will be many challenges ahead of us. Some we will meet with spectacular success, and with others we may fall short. However, we will always strive to move forward.

"My goal is to make Mabuhay the market leader in small domestic appliances within two years. Yes, gentlemen, two years. It may seem like a great and impossible goal to achieve, and yet as I look around this table, I know we have the talent to succeed. Our rivals, and you all know who they are, will give us stiff competition, but they will find that the newcomer has teeth and bites hard.

"Gentlemen, if this were the evening, I would propose a toast. However, it is the dry part of the day, so please indulge me a little further. Please be upstanding and repeat after me in your most spirited voices. Mabuhay, Mabuhay, Mabuhay." The technicians and engineers repeated the chant, and their voices filled the room with optimism and pride. I looked up to the ceiling, the koi more spellbinding than ever. I hoped the whole of Ginza could hear us, for we had arrived. "There is just one more thing I would like to add. I think we all owe a great deal of thanks to our chief engineer, Hideo Tanaka. I know his modesty does not allow him to be self-congratulatory, so it falls upon me to offer thanks on behalf of all of us here today. His inspiration and vision has not gone unnoticed, and in recognition of his fine qualities I propose that our products be named in honour of his achievements. From this day onwards all Mabuhay products will be prefixed with the letters *MHT*: Mabuhay, Hideo, Tanaka."

For the second time the room broke out into spontaneous applause. I looked down the table at Hideo, who was flushed with embarrassment. I thought of calling him up to make a speech, but knowing his shyness, I knew it would be the last thing he would want to do. "Gentlemen, I think this is an opportune moment to take a break. Refreshments are served in the next room. Thank you." I caught Hideo's attention and signalled for him to wait behind for a moment.

When the room had cleared, leaving only the two of us, I asked him if he would sit in on the meeting I had scheduled for later in the afternoon with the patents officer, in case there were any technical points that required clarification. He said he would be happy to do so. "Toshio, I thank you for all you have done for me," he said. "You have changed my life, given me purpose when I had only despair. I owe everything to you. I believe I am the most fortunate man in the world. I promise you that I will care for Ayumi until my dying day." He was holding my hand in a tight grip, barely able to hide his emotion. We stood face-to-face for a few seconds, the silence between us speaking volumes.

From that moment, I knew that Hideo was going to be, without doubt, my man. I watched him leave to join his fellow workers, who were still buoyed with excitement, their chatter carrying through the open doors. I envied Hideo in that respect. To be part of a team, to have the respect of your workmates, was indeed a treasured thing. I, by the very nature of my position, operated in a more solitary world. I had a certain amount of deferential respect, but there were times I needed more.

I decided to go back to my room, where I would take luncheon alone. Kawabata had left, surreptitiously letting himself out via the rear domestics' door. This seedy arrangement always left me feeling dejected. I cursed the world for its petty protocols. Why should we live by the standards of others? I fell onto the bed. Kawabata's presence was everywhere. His disorderly habits, such a contrast to my own neatness, were annoying, and yet I could never find it in me to berate him. A wet towel was left draped over my writing bureau, a hairbrush on the pillow, the closet doors left wide open. I would do a bit of basic tidying before calling Ogawa to arrange the maid to enter for my daily cleaning.

I decided a whiskey was called for, poured myself an extra-generous measure, and lay back on the bed to enjoy a moment's solitary peace. The meeting had gone well. It now fell upon me to do my part. I was mentally going through the scenarios concerning the next phases of our development when my mind was cast back to a year earlier, when all this had really started. My father had joined a group of business leaders and economists on a monthlong visit to the United States. Their trip had to be sanctioned by the American government. It was a sensitive time, and there was still a mood of anti-Japanese feeling throughout the United States. I have no idea what happened during that time, but my father returned from that sojourn a changed man. He started to involve me more in the day-to-day running of the business. I was given more responsibility and encouraged to make major decisions. It was almost as if he had given up and decided to hand over the mantle to me, his only son.

Hamazaki Electricals had profited from the misery of war. We had made a fortune from government armaments contracts. The basic electrical components of the Japanese war machine had been manufactured at our production facilities across the nation. My father had become a leading light in successive war cabinets, finally holding the joint portfolio of minister for armaments and minister of war. He had resisted his appointment with as much courage as he could muster, but to no avail. Those were hard times, and to refuse outright would have been tantamount to personal and professional ruin.

The war ended with disastrous consequences for men like my father. Their businesses were dismantled by the American occupation government, broken up and sold at pitiful prices. Many people were charged and put on trial, receiving lengthy prison terms or in some cases death sentences. My father was taken away and imprisoned for more than a month. Those were awful times. We feared the worst, and waited daily for news of his fate. Then without notice he returned home, a free man. He had been spared a trial, but what price he had paid for his freedom, I do not know. However, his company was no more. It was taken without any recompense and mercilessly carved up. We were powerless to do anything and could only stand by and watch as it was divided amongst our rival companies. There was no course of appeal; all we were left with was a sense of injustice. However, we were given permission to keep and operate one manufacturing outlet at Yokohama. We concentrated on the production of electrical cables and copper wires, supplying the ever increasing demand from manufacturers further up the supply chain. In the space of four years Hamazaki Electricals had once more grown into a market force. The rehabilitation of the business had been remarkable, and in recognition of his success my father was invited to join that business delegation to America.

I often wondered what deal my father had made to ensure his immunity from prosecution by the wartime tribunals. It must have been a deal of great significance, one that allowed him to walk into the country of his onetime nemesis a free and unhindered man, but as I said, that trip changed him. It seemed as if he had lost the will to continue with his effort to build on his success. He also became prone to bouts of depression and despair, locking himself away for days at a time in his room, this very same room where I now found myself, trying to make sense of what had come to pass.

He confided in me that from a business point of view, we were twenty years behind the Americans. The average income of the salaried middle class in our country was the equivalent of six hundred dollars per year. In America women factory workers could earn nearly three hundred dollars in a single month, more than most of our company presidents were earning. It was this disparity and the different attitudes toward consumer spending that had to be tackled if we were to ever make real headway and narrow the divide. My father had visited a television production facility in the States and realised that no matter how efficient we became in our production methods, fundamental changes needed to be made to the economy. In America a television set could be bought with a month's salary. In our country it would take most people a year to earn the price of a new television. In any case, that observation remained academic, as the luxury of television was to be put on hold for the time being. The Yoshida government had decided that the introduction of television at this stage in our economic development would be divisive, causing friction between sectors of society.

War and crushing defeat left the populace with an ingrained mentality of frugality and suffering. This obstacle had to be overcome if we were to ever achieve real and meaningful progress. Father's opinions and views on our plight weighed heavily on my mind. The American trip had been an epiphany for him, and he had decided to take the biggest business gamble of his life. He handed complete stewardship of Hamazaki Electricals over to me with two conditions attached. The first was that I change the direction of the business, and the second was to vow to forever strive for a greater good. I was a little confused about his reasoning, but later I came to understand the logic behind his thinking.

His behaviour in the months before his death was driven by paranoia. He had an irrational fear for his own safety and even hired security guards to drive him to and from work. He implored me to do the same, but when I asked what was behind his fear, he would not say. I pressed him time and again for more information, but all he would say was that there were evil forces against us that I could never begin to understand. Ayumi was convinced that Father was in the early stages of dementia and that he required special medical attention. I was not of the same conviction. I knew he was lucid enough, and was beginning to believe his fears were genuine. His death served to convince me that there were indeed evil forces rallied against us.

I intended to engage private professional help to investigate the circumstances of his death, but that was not a viable option, as I was about to come into possession of facts that could never be known to outsiders. My father had left a sealed letter addressed to me in his safe, along with a heavy, large brown manila envelope that contained a bulging file of papers with the words *Golden Lily* written in his script on the cover. The contents of that letter left me in such deep shock that I could barely function for days. In it he had made a confession but handed me the burden of his guilt. I locked myself away in grief and confusion whilst I tried to make sense of it all. My emotions were out of control, yet even in the chaos I managed to see the possibilities it offered. It was during this lowest point of my life that I decided to do what I believed Father had intended all along, which was to form Mabuhay and make it a benevolent enterprise. This I could well afford to do, as I was now the custodian of one of the largest hoards of gold and gemstones in the history of modern mankind.

I had become quite maudlin, lying there on the bed, allowing the past to sweep me up. The whiskey had taken the edge off any appetite I had, so I abandoned the idea of lunch and decided to concentrate on more pressing matters. It had become obvious that I needed a confidential assistant, someone who would be able to take some of my burden. Recently my workload had become mountainous, and I had found myself ground down by the most mundane of tasks. I needed someone, a very special person in whom I could place my unquestioned trust. That person would, by the nature of my business, find themselves compromised. Their own morality would be called into question, just as mine had been when I had been made fully aware of the extent of my father's involvement in a wartime conspiracy of mind-boggling proportions.

I had decided who to approach. In fact, my father's confidential letter had pointed me in the direction of an old school friend of mine. Makoto Hosokawa was my first and only choice, and I was determined to get him on my side, the sooner the better. I had been keeping a close eye on Hosokawa for a few months now. I had invited him to my dinner party on the evening Mabuhay had been launched, deliberately seating him close to Tanaka. After all, if my plans came to fruition, we would all be one happy team, so to speak. It would be no easy task to persuade him to "jump ship" and retire from the profession that he was born to be a part of. He was already making quite a name for himself in the Foreign Ministry, and despite being the son of a former minister for foreign affairs, this had not hindered his climb up the greasy pole. Past associations tended to be viewed with distaste by our new generation of autocrats and politicians. However, Hosokawa was one of the rare breed who had managed to shake off the past and embrace the present—very much like me. He seemed popular with the MacArthur boys and equally so with our new brand of politicos—no small feat for a fellow who was supposed to be above the dog-eat-dog world of what was passing for democracy in our country.

Despite his fine career and family connections Hosokawa had a chink in his armour, one that I was prepared to exploit. His father, like mine, was involved in the initial plan to embezzle and conceal the stolen war loot. Hosokawa Senior had sat with a close circle of influential men and helped to formulate the plan that would eventually see billions of dollars of stolen loot concealed in secret sites in the Philippines. The Hosokawa family had been outspoken advocates of Japan's nationalistic agenda, allowing their rhetoric to be toned down only when defeat was inevitable. He would have been the ideal choice to join men of a similar persuasion, who could not accept that defeat was final. They had devised a plan that would help to finance the rearmament of the country. Stolen loot was to be repatriated and directed towards a resurgence of a new Japan. These desperate and ruthless men, cornered by fate and their own prejudices, were blinded by their nationalistic fervour and failed to take into account the shifting mood of the populace. Their aims were despicable and their methods even more so.

My father had kept a detailed account of his own involvement in Operation Golden Lily and spared no details of the identities of others. I thought my good friend Hosokawa might be more amenable to my offer of alternative employment when he heard the extent of his own father's involvement in that scandalous conspiracy. Should rumours start, then inevitably his ambitions would be checked and he would forever find himself in the draughty corridor of hopelessness.

Acting on impulse as usual, I rang for Ogawa and asked him to bring the Bentley round and ready himself for a drive to the Ministry of Foreign Affairs. I had decided to drop in on Hosokawa in person on the off chance that he would have a moment to spare for an old friend. Time was of the essence, as I had a meeting scheduled with the patents officer at three o'clock. I quickly changed my shirt to a more formal white high-tipped collar and chose a subtle grey necktie which would make me more at home with the fashions of our pen pushers. I opened my dresser drawer and took out my favourite Willson Tay, round-lens tea shades. They had been a present from an old lover and always reminded me of a time when life was simpler and seemed to be just a succession of parties, late nights, and even later mornings. Reminiscing had become something of a habit recently and one I was determined to stamp out. If I wasn't careful, I would end up like those old rakes down at the American Club, who chattered on endlessly about how glorious life was before the war.

I went downstairs to find Ogawa, dependable as ever, waiting in the hall. We strode out into dazzling sunshine and the baking heat of early summer. I took my place in the rear seat of the Bentley and instructed Ogawa to take the shortest route to Chiyoda-ku, where Hosokawa's workplace was, and despite Ogawa's overly careful driving, we were in Chiyoda in a matter of minutes. I could see the imposing Germanic-style Diet building perched up on the hill, a place that held bittersweet memories for me. I had served out the war in the relative safety of that symbolic edifice. My father had acknowledged that the army was no place for such a sensitive soul as me. He had used his contacts to ensure I was given a special dispensation which excused me from conscription into the army. I was assigned as a confidential secretary to various public figures, a position for which I was ill suited. I hated being told what to do by those hypocritical self-serving liars.

Merely looking back on those days was enough to give me the shivers. I often accompanied my father when he had business to attend to during his wartime cabinet service. Quite often he would leave "closed door" meetings in a foul mood which seemed to follow him for days on end. I wondered if Golden Lily was conceived in the rooms and corridors of that bastion of power.

We drove up to the ministry, where a uniformed guard opened the barrier and gave us access without so much as a name check. Perhaps it was the impressive power of the Bentley; after all, it did seem to exude an authority of its own. Ogawa stopped at the main entrance and I told him to stand by for me, as I did not think my meeting would take much time. I approached the young lady at the reception desk, removing my sunglasses as I spoke. "Would you be so kind as to direct me to Hosokawa san's office?"

She looked a little unsure of herself but eventually managed to find her words. "Do you have an appointment, sir?"

I shook my head in a thoughtful way. "I am afraid I do not. However, I am sure Hosokawa san will be able to spare me a few minutes. We are old friends. My name is Hamazaki, and he is forever asking me to drop by."

"Just a moment, sir." She stood up and walked over to a large door which she unlocked with a key that she produced from her person as if by magic. After a few moments she returned and asked me to follow her. We went around a maze of winding corridors and up one flight of stairs, finally arriving at our destination, as the underwhelming plastic name sign affixed to the door announced: "Makoto Hosokawa, Foreign Bureau." The clerk knocked and opened the door slightly. "Sir, Hamazaki san is here to meet with you."

I strode into the room, which was surprisingly small. I must confess I had expected something a little grander, but then again, Hosokawa had at this point made it only as far as the first floor. No doubt our taxes allowed for grander accommodations upstairs. Hosokawa was surprised to see me, but he hid it well. I noticed his eyes flitting over to his wall clock, no doubt mentally calculating how much time he could allow from his precious schedule. I offered my outstretched hand and best smile. "My dear Makoto," I said, deliberately using the friendly form of address. How the devil are you? My word, you are looking a little worn. Working you hard at the diplomatic, are they?"

"Hamazaki san, a pleasure to see you as always. You should have told me you were planning a visit. I could have arranged refreshments."

I gave him a friendly smile. "Please, no need for such fuss on my account. I do not intend to take much of your time." I settled into the leather chair in front of his desk and waited for him to pick up the conversation.

"So, what brings you over to the dull and dusty place we unfortunates call work?"

I nodded thoughtfully. "Not so dull, and certainly not dusty, Makoto. You do yourself an injustice. I am sure you are cooking up some big adventure right here, eh? In this very room."

Hosokawa looked a bit perplexed. "Not really. It is rather dull at the moment." He leaned a little closer and lowered his voice as if he were bringing me into his confidence. "Perhaps I shouldn't say this, but we are working on the agenda for a meeting that will take place next year in San Francisco. We are finally to be trusted to be the masters of our own destiny once more."

"Be careful there, Makoto. For a moment you were beginning to sound a little like your father."

He looked a little shocked and quickly replied, "No, no, I did not mean free to—"

I interrupted him with laughter to show I was teasing him a little. "Actually, it is your father who brings me to your door. I will get straight to the point, as we are both busy men. You see, Makoto, I need help with my business, and I need people I can trust, people who will give me their unerring loyalty. In short, I need you. I am here to offer you a place at Mabuhay. I want you to work alongside me. We have known each other since we were children; there is no other person who could do what I require of them. You are special. I need you."

He looked at me as if I had lost my mind, words for once failing to trip off his tongue. "Toshio, are you serious? What makes you think for one moment that I would walk out on a job I love and a future in which I have placed all of my efforts to make my own?"

"As I said, it was your father who led me here, your father along with mine—old friends both now sadly gone forever, but dearly missed. Well, it seems they shared a few secrets of, well, let's be diplomatic and say a 'sensitive' nature, although 'criminal' would be a more appropriate word."

Hosokawa's face was ashen, and he sank back into his chair. Then he looked at me with a contempt that was, in my view uncalled for. "So are you here to blackmail me or something?" he asked, his tone challenging. "To threaten me by using my family's past against me?"

"My dear Makoto, of course not. I am offended you would even think such a thing. I would never allow myself to stoop so low. As I said, I am here to make you an offer of alternative employment—one that I hope you will find attractive enough to make the bold decision to resign your post here and join me in an enterprise that will shape the future in ways you may not have even dreamed of. Mabuhay is no ordinary business; it is a channel for a greater good. I need your help to realise a dream. I want to offer you a partnership in Mabuhay. If you agree, I will give you a thirty per cent share in my company. Acceptance would immediately make you one of the wealthiest men in this building. I am offering you a future that promises to give you all your heart's desires. If you refuse my offer, I still hope our friendship will continue forever, and we shall never speak of this meeting again. I leave the decision with you. You have my word that I will never make it known that your father, like my own, was a thief of the highest order."

He looked even more dumbfounded, as if he didn't know whether to be flattered or outraged before settling somewhere between the two. "What is this great crime my father is supposed to have perpetrated? How do I know it is not some illusion that you have dreamt?"

I stood up to signal my intention to leave. "Makoto, it is as real as the sun that shines. Do not doubt that, ever. I cannot tell you more, but should you make the wise decision to join me, then all will be explained. However, I do believe you are not as ignorant of this affair as you would wish me to believe. Maybe your father took you into his confidence and told you all about his shady past. I don't know. But I could not help but notice that you took an extra-special interest in a certain painting that hangs in my dining room."

Hosokawa looked down at his desk and massaged his temples as he considered his response. "Toshio, I am nobody's fool, and please do not take me for one. I would be grateful if you would give me time to think over your proposal. I do have considerations of my own to take into account. You also have my word that what has passed between us today will remain ours and ours alone."

I had the feeling that Hosokawa was coming around to my proposal. His pride would not allow him to submit so easily; he had to give the impression that he was in control of his own destiny. It was time to take my leave. "Makoto, I am planning a little soirée this evening at one of my favourite ryotei, and I would be honoured if you would grace us with your presence. We dine at eight. I believe you know the place—Ishikawa in Kagurazaka." He stood and gave me a graceful bow which I returned, both of us fully aware of what my invitation truly meant. If Hosokawa chose to take his place at the table that evening, Mabuhay would have gained a person of immense value.

I made my own way out of the building, passing the clerk with a wave of my hand. I found Ogawa where I had left him and sank into the rear seat of the Bentley for the drive back home and my meeting with the patents officer. It was turning into a day of engagements; each one had been to my advantage so far, a fine run of form for sure.

It was approaching three o'clock as we pulled up outside the front door. I let myself out of the car and strode purposefully up the front steps to the music room, where I had arranged for our new products to be displayed, each with its technical description attached. The patents officer could be a problem if he insisted on following his rule book to the letter. If we were to begin production without the protection of patents, we would be exposed to commercial thievery. Our rivals would be able to steal our innovations, and legally, there would be little we could do about it. I walked into the music room at three o'clock sharp to find Tanaka and one of his team in discussion with a young man who was holding a clipboard and looked to be checking off items on some kind of list. "Gentlemen, I see you have started without me."

Tanaka looked a little flustered. "Hamazaki san. May I introduce Sato san from the patents office. He was just checking the basic points of the descriptions before going through the technical details. I have asked Nojiri san to assist him with any queries that may arise." I was grateful to Tanaka for taking this in hand. I was not the most eloquent of people when it came to explaining the finer workings of our future products.

Nojiri was in deep discussion with Sato, so I took Tanaka aside for a little chat. "Hideo, it is vital that Sato leaves here today and directly files our applications. We need the patents to be granted without delay. I have started planning the gala to mark the launch of Mabuhay's entry into the market. That is fixed for one month from today, and I do not intend to delay a single day. I need those patents. If Sato proves to be unwilling, bring him to my office, where I will speak with him personally."

Hideo looked over to Sato, who was on the floor examining the underside of the washing machine. "I do not foresee any problems. The descriptions are accurate and do not contravene any of the requirements, so we should not have any problems." I thanked him and said I would be in my study if I was needed. I left them to it and with relief sat down at my desk. I opened my red ledger to record my meeting with Hosokawa and what had passed between us. It was for my own purposes only, a habit I had picked up from my father, who had always said the day would come when the memory started to fail and you needed to recall a meeting or an event. A record of what has passed is like an old friend reminding you of forgotten memories, he said.

I had left Hosokawa's office in a positive frame of mind, but now I was not so sure. Had I allowed my optimism to carry me away? I knew Hosokawa was stubborn by nature, and cunning to boot. I wondered what he was up to at this very moment. Was he looking for some way to tender his resignation without causing too much suspicion about his motives, or was he looking for a way to outmanoeuvre me? Approaching Hosokawa in such a direct manner was a calculated gamble, and I was well aware of the risks I had taken. I decided a whiskey was called for and went over to the drinks cabinet and poured a large measure for the second time that day.

Just as I was about to write up my ledger, there was a knock on the door. I thought, *Dear God, is there nothing that can be done without my being involved?* The door opened slightly, and I was surprised to see Ayumi there. "Brother, I am so sorry to disturb you; I know you are extremely busy." Her gaze found its way to the whiskey glass in my hand. She resisted the urge to comment, as she had obviously dropped by on another matter and did not want to be distracted by my little vices. "I was passing by your door and took the opportunity to enquire about your dinner plans for this evening." Before I could tell her I had already made arrangements, she continued quickly in a nervy kind of way. "I was hoping we could dine together along with Tanaka san, here at home." For my sister to be so direct I could only assume that she and Hideo were about to make their engagement official. My eyes checked the finger of her left hand. No ring yet, but I wagered it would not be long before Mother's engagement ring found its way back onto a finger after spending the last thirty-three years in a drawer. I felt a little caddish about dashing her plans, but I had already made arrangements for my "dinner of destiny" with Hosokawa. I also intended to invite Hideo. After all, he and Hosokawa were already acquainted, and if my visions proved to be true, then the three of us would be working together like brothers.

"Ayumi, my dear sister, I must apologise, but I have already made arrangements for this evening, and I am to further disappoint you, as I require Tanaka san to accompany me. We have important business to discuss ahead of our gala launch. Perhaps we could have dinner another evening. Maybe tomorrow?"

She looked a little crestfallen but handled her disappointment well. "Of course. It was inconsiderate of me to impose upon you at such short notice." She left me to myself, and I felt slightly uneasy. When had our relationship become so formal? Our exchanges were becoming quite "stuffy." At one time we had been totally relaxed in each other's company, but now we always seemed to be overly considerate of each other's feelings. Father's death had left a void that neither of us had come to terms with. I hoped her marriage to Hideo would bring us all closer together and be the start of happier days to come.

Just as I was about to recharge my glass, there was a knock on my door. "Do come in." Hideo opened the door and ushered Sato into my study. Hideo quickly brought me up to speed with the patent applications in a tone of deference that he tended to use when addressing me in front of others. "Sato san has finished recording our applications for the patents and is satisfied that all legal requirements have been met. He will return to the Ministry for Trade and file our applications. If approved, our patents are to be assigned in three months' time in accordance with statutory procedure." Hideo emphasised the last part for my benefit, fully aware that I would find this totally unacceptable. We needed the patents to be effective immediately. I had a date set for the gala launch, and it could not be delayed by a petty bureaucrat and his overly officious regulations.

I kept calm and asked Hideo to leave Sato and me alone for a moment. Sato suddenly seemed a little nervous, sitting before me like a naughty pupil brought up in front of his headmaster. "Sato san, let me be plain and to the point. I need these patents to be assigned within the week. The future of our company depends on it."

Sato rummaged in his briefcase and finally extracted a sheet of paper. "Sir, these are the rules set out by the minister for trade, and the process for the granting of patents is clearly stated. It takes a minimum of three months from application to issue. I am sorry, sir, but there is nothing I can do. I am merely following the directives."

I opened my bureau drawer where I had placed some paperwork regarding our gala launch. "Sato san, we here at Mabuhay

Portable Electricals have a gala event planned for the first day of next month. It will be a grand affair at the Empire Hotel, to celebrate the start of production. I would be honoured if you would be one of our guests; I have prepared a personal invitation for you. I would be obliged if you would accept." I pushed a white envelope with the name Sato Eisuke written in gold script across the desk.

"Hamazaki san, it would be most inappropriate for me to accept such an invitation. Please understand my position." Sato was looking very uncomfortable. I could see the sweat beading down his forehead.

"Of course, Sato san, but before you decline my invitation outright, please do me the courtesy of opening the envelope." I stood and walked over to the window and looked down at the street below, giving Sato a moment to fully comprehend what a thousand dollars in United States currency looks and feels like. When he spoke, his voice was trembling with confusion. Of course he wanted the money. What sane man would not? But would he allow himself to be bought? "Sir, I am speechless. I am in an impossible position. There is nothing I can do to change the regulations. Please understand."

I turned to face him and said, "Would it not be possible to backdate our applications by three months?"

He sat there, mentally going through the possibilities. "That may be possible, but there is the registrar to consider. I could not do that without his noticing."

"I see. Do you think the registrar would also like to attend our gala event?"

Sato looked sheepishly at the green bills in front of him. "I do believe he would, sir."

I reached into my drawer again and took out another envelope containing a thousand dollars, and put it on top of Sato's invitation. "I think we are finished here today, Sato san. I expect the patents to be on my desk by the week's end. I look forward to seeing you at our gala launch. Good day."

Sato hurriedly scooped the cash into his briefcase and left my study with as much dignity as a newly corrupted man could muster.

The meeting with Sato left me with a feeling of distaste, so I decided to call it a day as far as the afternoon's business was concerned. I resisted the temptation to have a reviving shot, and instead went back to my room to see if Kawabata had returned from his shopping or whatever it was that he did with his days. His life outside my home was still a mystery to me, and it irked me that I did not know what he got up to once he was out of my sight.

We had been almost inseparable for the last eight months, but there were still days when I felt I knew very little about him. I knew he had grown up in Kumamoto; his country accent was easy to place, and much to his annoyance I took delight in his amusing verbalisms. Being far too young to be conscripted, he had grasped the opportunity to flee from his unhappy home at the earliest chance. His alcoholic father was unable to accept his son's sexual inclinations, and Kawabata was subjected to regular beatings. After one drunken, enraged thrashing too many, Kawabata left Kumamoto for good and headed up to Tokyo, where he did the only thing he could to survive: sell his body. He told me he had lived rough on the streets for a few months before finally being taken in by the Club Flamingo. He was, like most of the boys at the club, treated like a slave. The owner was a bent, crooked old coot who went by the nickname of Tojo. He made them cook and clean by day, and by night, service as many customers as physically possible.

I had chanced upon the Flamingo almost by accident, after a heavily fuelled night when I felt the urge to escape the stuffiness of my companions and tread on the "wild side." I ventured into the area of town where gentlemen prefer not to be seen. That evening, all of eight months ago, has etched itself into my mind, and I know every vivid detail will stay with me until the day I die. The devil himself was dancing by my side that evening, and I willingly gave myself over to his every whim. I headed over the "akasen," the metaphorical red line where I knew I would find something to entertain me for a few hours. I did not know that love was waiting and about to spring an ambush.

The Flamingo was a new establishment, one that I had paid little attention to on my previous visits to the area. However, the young man working the door stepped into my path and asked if I would like to "chat" over a drink. Given the state I was in, his striking good looks were just too tempting to resist. I let him take my arm and lead me down a ridiculously steep flight of stairs into a gloomy basement. He settled me into a booth well away from prying eyes, where the only illumination came from a tiny candle. He told me his name was Kawabata and he would love to be my friend.

I cannot remember much of the Club Flamingo, except that it was dark and rather depressing, and the unpleasant odour emanating from the toilet room was making me feel sick. I said I wished to leave, but Kawabata begged me stay a little longer. Only the copious amounts of sake I had taken on board could explain my rash decision to invite Kawabata to join me. A disgusting toothless old hag of a man with advanced halitosis introduced himself as Tajiri, the owner, and demanded two hundred yen to allow Kawabata out for the night. He seemed mightily surprised when I paid without argument. After Kawabata got a few of his things together, we left that revolting place behind. Kawabata had to support me up the steps while Tajiri Tojo stood at the bottom, shouting a reminder for Kawabata to be back before ten the next morning. That was the last Tojo would ever see of "his" boy. That evening we stayed at a local hotel, the kind of place where they have hourly rates. I did not think the Empire would be so welcoming, given the state I was in.

That night nothing happened between us. I passed out in a state of inebriation, only to wake the next morning to find I had spent the evening with the most divine-looking person I had ever seen. I found myself lost in time as I propped myself up and stared at this beautiful person sleeping like an angel. Upon waking, and despite the early hour, Kawabata was agitated and fearful that if he did not make it back to the club on time, he would be punished by that dreadful Tojo creature. I made one of my impulsive decisions there and then. I decided that this was going to be something special. I told him he need never go back there ever again, and if he wished, we could stay friends. He looked totally confused, and I tried to reassure him that I would care for him from that day on. Such was the hopelessness of his life up to that point that he agreed without the need for any further cajoling.

I told him to write a note to Tojo saying he would not be coming back, ever. He wrote it in a childlike script. It was just a simple note that looked as if it had been written by a six-year-old. We made a little small talk, like two nervous people on a first date. He told me about where he had come from and how he had fled from his violent, drunken father. I felt a swell of protectiveness towards him and could sense he was warming to me. We soon found ourselves in each other's arms and inevitably in each other's bodies.

Later that morning we retraced our path to the Flamingo. I told Kawabata to wait on the corner while I walked down the street to the Flamingo to hand over his note. I knocked on the door and could hear curses bawled from within, getting louder as someone came up the steps from the dank club below. A voice shouted the most vile threats and abuse. "You little, bitchy whore, what time do you call this? I will have you sucking off GIs for a month, you little bastard." The inside bolts were thrust to the side, and the door was flung wide open. Tojo stood there, wheezing and out of breath. He looked totally shocked to see me, towering over him. His short stature and my own height made it appear he was talking to my crotch. Now, I am not a violent man, but I do have my limits. I was beginning to explain to this vile man that Kawabata would no longer be returning here and was about to take out the letter, in which I had placed one hundred United States dollars. Tojo looked at me with his greedy, bloodshot eyes. "So, you want the little cocksucker all for yourself, do you, sir? Well, in that case we need to negotiate, do we not?"

What happened next remains something of a blur. Seemingly of their own free will my arms shot out and gave Tojo a quick, violent shove down the stairs. He tumbled down head over feet into the darkness below. There was no scream, and I could not make out whether his crumpled body was moving. I took a step back and heard voices from below. The sound of Tojo bouncing down the stairs had awoken the Flamingo boys from their slumber. "It's the master; he has fallen down the stairs," someone said.

I listened carefully as the commotion from below began to build into a kind of panic. There must have been at least six different voices all talking at once. I heard someone say, "Is he dead?" I prayed to God that was the case. I took my leave as quickly as possible, checking the street to see if anyone was about. To my great relief, the streets were still deserted, as most of the inhabitants work at night and sleep through the days.

I found Kawabata waiting. He was a nervous wreck, biting his nails to the quick. "Did you see Tojo? What did he say? Am I free to leave?" He was full of questions. I took him by the arm and we walked away as fast as we could from that cursed place. I told Kawabata not to be concerned and that nobody had answered the door and I would try again later. I tried to ease his fears, which wasn't easy, as I too was in a state of semi-shock. Had I just killed a man? My God! What if he was not dead? He would come looking for me for sure.

I took Kawabata back to my suite at the Empire. This only served to further confuse him. Until then he'd had no idea who I really was, and he spent the rest of the day looking at me like some kind of frightened animal. He kept asking me questions that I did not really want to answer. I reassured him that I would find him a place to live and make sure he was looked after. That day I had been between heaven and hell, a journey that had taken me from someone's lover to possible murderer in a blink of an eye.

My nerves were fraught to the point where I could barely talk. I had to know if Tojo had survived the fall. I left Kawabata to wait for me in the suite for an hour, saying I had an important errand to undertake. I asked Ogawa to bring the car round and instructed him to drive me over to my tailor, which was a ruse to allow us to drive through Shinjuku and past the Flamingo without raising suspicions. To my blessed relief I saw that the Flamingo was already draped in the black funeral wreaths that mark the passing of someone resident. I told Ogawa to slow down, and looked at some of the floral tributes from the car window. "Nobuyuki Tajiri," they said. I had never been so joyous to have the death of someone confirmed. I sank back into my seat and made a play of forgetting an appointment and told Ogawa that I was giving up on the tailors and to return to the Empire.

I still had to cover myself from any possible connections to the demise of the foul Tojo. If Kawabata suddenly disappeared from the club, the police might get suspicious. I decided that it would be best if he took the letter and money to Tojo himself. He was reluctant, and fearful about showing his face back at the club, but he had come to trust me, and eventually the lure of an alternative lifestyle was enough to see him set out in all innocence to deliver his "resignation." I told him that my name must never be mentioned, as Tojo would be able to find us and make life difficult for the two of us. He returned an hour or so later in a state of nervous excitement. "Tojo is dead! Can you believe it? It's unbelievable, a sign from the gods. I am free, free!" he said, dancing around my room. His youthful joy was a delight to behold, and I could feel my emotions running away with me.

I asked him what had happened. "The old drunken fool fell down the stairs and broke his neck." I had never seen anyone rejoice in the death of another. Free from his slave owner, he clapped his hands and celebrated the deceased's passing with so much obscene happiness, it was difficult not to share in his pleasure.

That night I allowed him to stay with me in my suite and made promises to care for him forever. The following morning I gave him some money and told him to go and find a place to live and buy some new clothes. He came back later looking sweeter than ever and told me he had found a small place in Ebisu. I have yet to visit his place; in fact I'm not even sure where it is.

Our relationship was born out of an evening of madness that led to someone's death but also led me along the path to happiness. I was not sorry that Tojo had died at my hands, and his death had little lasting effect on me. In truth, I had surprised myself by how easily I had coped with that traumatic event. I seemed to gain strength from it. The gods were truly on my side.

It was fast approaching seven, and I had tired of waiting for Kawabata to return. I had intended to arrive at the ryotei, Ishikawa, thirty minutes earlier than Hosokawa. This would give me time to settle in and adjust to the mood. I also liked to take a few solitary moments and compose my thoughts over a few cups of the finest sake. Ishikawa was one of our city's most delightful and exclusive ryotei. Their discretion was impeccable. Reservations were accepted only from an exclusive list of patrons. It was a veritable fortress of secrecy, a place where politicians and business folk alike made the real decisions and deals of the day. Its exclusivity was legendary, as were its geishas, who could read a situation like a child's picture book. The geishas would come from the best okiya in Tokyo. I loved the geishas. Their humour and flattery was always a welcome escape from the reality of the outside world. They indulged the whims of their patrons with a skill that demanded respect. I seldom took pleasure from the company of women, but I found a special joy amongst the white-faced courte-sans. But men seldom came to Ishikawa just for the pure pleasure of it all. The true purpose was to find agreement, secure that elu-sive deal, and shake hands on that sensitive matter. The business of the day done, this was the time to let loose and enjoy the finer aspects of the evening's entertainment.

I had asked Hideo to join me at the club at eight o'clock. I did not leave him any chance to refuse; after all, this was to be one of those evenings that would change a person's life. His romantic plans with my sister would have to be put on hold for a short while. Maybe he would have second thoughts after what his future brother-in law had to tell him, but I thought not. I believed it might only strengthen his resolve. Hideo was not my concern. I was confident he would bend to my desires. No, my real worry was Hosokawa. He was an independent and strong-willed character, and I hoped his obstinacy would not be at the fore this evening.

I dressed quite formally in a light grey suit. The jacket was in the latest style: short and box shaped. I chose a dandy silk waistcoat of dark gold with small ruby-coloured diamond shapes woven into its threads. It was an appropriate choice, given what we were about to discuss. I finished off my look with a Western-style bootlace tie held together by a fine gold clasp. Satisfied with my look, I rang for Ogawa to drive me over to Ishikawa. I had a sense that this evening would be the start of something grand for the three of us.

The Bentley crawled up the narrow streets of Kagurazaka. It had suddenly started to rain, and shopkeepers were busy bringing in the wares they had displayed outside their shops. Ogawa had to take extra care to steer clear of man and goods alike. The Bentley was like some kind of elegant mechanical monster crawling along streets that were originally designed for rickshaws. Several times we had to stop and wait whilst an obstruction was cleared from our path, wicker baskets, straw mats, and carts of dried corn ears being the main hindrances.

Eventually, a little later than I considered ideal, we pulled up outside Ishikawa. The entrance was so unimposing, you would be forgiven for passing it by without a second thought. A plain, simple wooden door had the characters "Ishikawa," meaning "Stone River," branded upon it. The door opened, and old Mrs Ishikawa and a young man carrying a parasol stood by the car in a bowing position. Ogawa opened the door and I stepped out. Mrs Ishikawa said "Welcome," the only word I would hear from her until we left later that evening.

I was shown through to the hall, where I sat on a wooden bench and allowed the young man to remove my shoes, which he placed in an ornate shoebox. I followed Mrs Ishikawa down a sho-ji-screened corridor to our dining room, which was simplicity and understated elegance itself. The floor was covered with tatami mats, and a large low table in the centre held several small examples of beautiful ikebana. These decorative flower arrangements were the only splashes of colour against the subdued hues that dominated the room. The table was set for three guests as I had indicated. I took my place opposite those reserved for my guests. A young girl dressed in a kimono appeared bearing a tray of sake and some seasonal delicacies for me to enjoy whilst I waited for them. She bowed and poured with a skill that must have taken hours of practice. In places such as these, words between staff and patrons are not necessary. Needs are anticipated and appreciation is observed with natural good grace. As soon as she had taken her leave, I threw back my sake and poured another cup. I wished I could quaff the whole bottle, but I remembered my manners and settled down to enjoy the soothing sounds of a koto drifting along from a nearby room. Such was the exclusivity of Ishikawa that we were afforded the privilege of being the only patrons that evening. What passed between the three of us would be totally sacrosanct.

Surprisingly it was Hosokawa who arrived first. I would have wagered a tidy sum that Hideo would make it to the table first, but nonetheless I was relieved to greet Hosokawa. He was shown to the table and settled down by our young server girl, who poured his first cup with practiced grace. Hosokawa, like me, was born into this life, and he made himself completely at ease, unruffled by the social niceties that seem to trouble others who were not as fortunate as we were. We were left alone together; there was a stony silence between us. Had I completely misjudged Makoto? Was he here to throw my offer back into my face? His expression gave nothing away. I suppose such a quality may be useful in the heat of a diplomatic debate, but now, it had an unsettling effect on me.

It had been a long day, and I had not realised how tired I was. The urge to yawn was difficult to suppress, especially as I was wearing my own best poker face. The sake had relaxed me a little too much, making me dreamy. Just as I was about to raise my cup, Makoto was ahead of me. "To the future." The most simple of toasts, and yet its meaning touched my soul and released me from so much pent-up agitation that I could barely contain my joy.

"To the future," I echoed, and we both threw back our drinks. I had gained a new confidant, a man who would help me in the liberation of millions upon millions in secreted bullion. His skills were essential to the success of Mabuhay, and now my relief was almost seeping out of my pores. I felt the need to mark the occasion, my tiredness of a few moments ago now completely forgotten. I told Makoto that we were waiting on Tanaka's arrival. He was a little surprised that we were to dine with my chief engineer. I told him that all would be explained later. The usual practice at gatherings such as these was to make the small talk during the meal and then, as we lay back with our stomachs satisfied, get down to the real agenda.

Tanaka arrived a little after eight and apologised profusely for his tardiness. He looked a little flustered and uncomfortable. I tried to put him at ease. "Hideo, you remember Makoto?"

"Of course I do. How are you? It is so good to see you again."

"Likewise, my dear Tanaka san."

The formality of Makoto's reply told me more sake was called for, and I charged all our cups, hoping that a little drink would go a long way towards loosening up these two beacons who would light the path to Mabuhay's destiny. Seeing the two of them facing me, seated side by side, brought to mind the American comedy players Laurel and Hardy, with Tanaka the thin, bemused-looking Japanese Laurel and Hosokawa the podgy, round-faced Japanese Hardy. The urge to laugh out loud was uncontrollable, and my mirth emerged as a kind of snort. Makoto asked me what was so amusing. I said it was nothing, just the feeling of happiness taking over me. He and Hideo looked a little unsure of how to react. Perhaps they thought I was already half-cut.

I raised my cup again, and the others followed my lead. "Mabuhay." It felt good to be among friends with whom I would now be able to share the secrets that I had carried alone for so long. However, those secrets would have to wait a little while longer, as the first of many culinary delicacies was about to be served. Three serving girls silently entered, each bearing identical lacquer trays which they set down before us. I was relieved to notice that each serving was accompanied by bottles of sake. I was ravenous. I had eaten very little during the day, and all the lovemaking, bribery, and cajoling had left me feeling like a starving lion.

The first course consisted of several seasonal delicacies. Bamboo shoots with slices of mushroom lightly brushed with miso paste, and baby octopi marinated in pickled seaweed were just a couple of the outstanding delights served for our pleasure. In keeping with tradition, each dish was an art form in itself, both visually appealing and delicious in equal measure.

Our conversation bounced from one topic to another, all very light. Even Tanaka was relaxing, and he and Makoto were once more finding the rapport they had enjoyed at their previous meeting more than six months earlier. I asked them if they had seen the new movie *All About Eve*. Neither of them had even heard of it. However, such was my enthusiasm for Bette Davis and George Sanders that they were easily persuaded to promise to go along to the theatre with me to see it. I immediately felt a pang of guilt, as I had earlier promised to take Kawabata with me. I would not mind seeing it twice, as George Sanders was a personal favourite of mine; I loved his effortless style and his screen persona, my idea of the perfect man.

I observed my dining companions closely. Despite being the same age or thereabouts, the three of us were entirely different people. I loved the arts, movies, and modern music, whereas Makoto and Hideo were of a more traditional disposition. In fact I had known Hideo more than six months, and still I did not know what consumed his private moments. Surely my sister did not demand his complete attention. I could not believe that they had not even heard of Frank Sinatra. It was clear I had a lot of work to do to bring them round to the fast-moving ways of the new world. This was the start of an era, one in which it was perfectly acceptable to take enjoyment and be seen doing so.

We progressed through the courses at a leisurely pace. A delightful char-grilled monkfish was especially well received. The sake was also flowing with carefree abandon; Hideo's face was turning a shade of red, a sure sign that he was reaching his limit. Makoto was made of sterner stuff as far as the rice wine was concerned. Like me, he enjoyed a drink, and I enjoyed drinking with people who tried to keep pace with me. We poured each other's drinks in accordance with etiquette, and it became a cycle of endless cups of sake. Any inhibitions we may have had were totally forgotten, and our talk was taking on a more risqué tone. We were all single and relatively young men, after all. Makoto lived with his aged mother. I did not know if he had anyone special in his life, and made a mental note to myself to find out a little more about his personal affairs—in the friendliest of ways, of course.

Perhaps it was the effects of the sake or my uncontrollable urge to know, but without thinking, my mouth was ahead of my mind. "Hideo, have you had the opportunity to speak with my sister?" Makoto looked puzzled and shot me a quizzical look. I was just about to explain when Hideo took the words out of my mouth.

"As a matter of fact, I have. That is why I was a little late this evening." We both looked at him as he lowered his head and started to take special interest in his stewed vegetables.

"Well?" I said in a mock exasperated tone. He raised his head, and the cheeky, shy smile beaming across his face gave me the answer. Makoto was still all at sea as to what we were talking about.

"She said yes. She has agreed to become my wife." I thought he was going to allow his joy free rein, the sake having brought his emotions to the fore. Makoto was lost for words, eventually managing to find his tongue and offer his congratulations. I just felt pure happiness for the two of them. We raised a glass to the happy moment, and I asked Madame Ishikawa for a bottle of the finest champagne.

The final dishes of rice, pickles, and soup were warmly accepted. The champagne arrived perfectly chilled. I excused our server girl and did the honours myself. When our glasses had settled, I toasted to the happiness of the future Mr and Mrs Tanaka. It was quite an emotional moment, and I felt myself welling up before quickly pulling myself together. I changed tack and proposed another toast. "To my dear friend Makoto Hosokawa, my new partner in business. Mabuhay welcomes you with open arms."

Now it was Hideo's turn to look all at sea. I explained to him that Makoto had agreed to an offer I had made him earlier. He was to join us at Mabuhay, bringing his special talents to the team. Hideo congratulated Makoto on his new position and said the Foreign Office's loss was Mabuhay's gain. Setting aside Hideo's clichéd remark, I looked at the two of them. "My friends, you have brought the best news I have ever heard. It has been a wonderful evening and one I hope will only get better, for I think it is time for me to tell you a few things I think you have a right to know. But before I do, I am going to ask you to please reserve your judgements until you have heard me out." I needed to tell them about the dark secrets that had weighed so heavily on my heart and soul ever since I had taken on the burden of Golden Lily.

The soothing notes of the koto could still be heard floating through the air from the adjacent room. The simplicity and innocence of the music was in stark contrast to the tale I was about to tell. I was unsure how much Makoto actually knew. He had intimated that he knew something of our dark secret, but I was certain his knowledge was sparse, to say the least. As for Hideo, well, he had actually played a part, albeit a cameo role. He would be shocked to learn the truth about his little adventure in the Philippines. For his own sake I would wait until the right moment to tell Hideo all about himself, for the revelations would shock him to his core. How he would react, I could only guess, but one thing was beyond question: The old Hideo Tanaka would be gone forever.

"My dear friends, it has been more than half a year since my father passed away, and yet it seems as if it were only yesterday, and I suppose it always will. He was the dearest father a boy and man could ever wish for. I grew up without the love of a mother, and I think he always tried to over-compensate for the void left by his wife's premature departure from our lives. My father had an indulgent nature, and both Ayumi and I were given everything we ever wanted. You may think we were spoiled, and yes, that may have been the case, but we were always taught to be thankful for the privileges life had bestowed on us.

"The Hamazaki family goes back into the misty annals of time, each generation striving to make its mark and secure its legacy. Without doubt my father left his mark and will continue to do so for many years to come. It is to him that we owe our own futures, for we have been presented with an opportunity that will allow us to make a difference in a world that only a decade ago was hell-bent on death and destruction. I often wonder what life would have been like if it were not for the war. Where would we be? What would we be doing? One thing is certain: We would not be here at this table together, about to make our own little piece of history.

"Yes, it was because of the war and our failure as a nation to achieve a positive outcome that the seeds of the greatest criminal conspiracy in the history of Japan were sown. Those were dark times indeed, and my father found himself an unwilling partici-pant in the planning and execution of a highly classified operation, code-named Golden Lily. However unwilling he may have been and however distasteful he may have found his role, he managed to find the resolve to undertake his obligations with admirable effi-ciency. Quite simply, my father conspired with a close circle made up of the highest echelons of society to conceal vast amounts of stolen war loot at secret locations in the Philippines.

"My father acted as the supreme coordinator of Golden Lily and was the only man involved in all stages of its execution. Upon his death he left me a binder containing hundreds of papers relat-ing to this most secret of operations. He was a fastidious man; he recorded every detail, however small or seemingly unimportant. You could say he was like a curator. In fact that would be an appropriate description. He left no detail unrecorded. It seems he memorised meetings and then later wrote up the minutes of those meetings for his own records. Absolutely everything is docu-mented and is now in my possession."

Hideo and Makoto were spellbound, hanging on every word, and listened like two children whose father was reading them a bedtime story. I was sure they would have many questions, but they let me carry on, and I was warming to my narration.

"The first my father ever heard of Golden Lily was in August 1944. The Americans launched their offensive against our forces in the Philippines in December of that year. Between August 1944 and December 1945, loot from all over Japanese Imperial Asia was shipped to the Philippines, because it had been decided that that country offered the best terrain in which to conceal this bounty. At the turn of 1945 the Americans had control of the seas and it was virtually impossible to get through the blockades. Repatriation of the treasure to Japan was impossible, and rather than risk valuable treasures falling into the enemy's hands, the plan to conceal the stolen loot was put into action. We are speaking of vast sums accumulated from our Imperial Army's rampage through Asia. One particular site holds bullion and gems valued at nine hundred million United States dollars. Multiply that by sixteen and you have an idea of the sums we are talking about."

I noticed the visible shock on Hideo's face as the full implications of what he was hearing took shape. Makoto kept his own counsel and nodded thoughtfully at appropriate moments. "There were sixteen different burial sites containing this loot. Now fourteen sites remain. One site was located and liberated by the Philippine intelligence service shortly after the surrender. I will tell you more about that little episode later. Shortly before his death my father made arrangements for the successful liberation of one of the sites. I am the only man alive who knows the exact location and contents of each of the remaining fourteen sites, and it is my intention over time to liberate each and every one of them. I intend, with your assistance, to put the proceeds towards building the greatest company on earth, a company that will become one of the most important single entities on the face of the planet. A generous slice of our profits will go towards a greater good. That is nonnegotiable, a promise I made to my father some months before his death.

"If we are to do this, it shall not be for the sole purpose of enriching ourselves, but also to improve the lives of others who are born into circumstances far less fortunate than ours. To this end I intend to keep this matter out of the control of corrupt and wasteful governments who would only divide it between their cronies and squander the rest building a war machine, as they are so obviously blind to the lessons of the past. We need only look across the ocean to our neighbour's plight in Korea, where politics has pitted brother against brother, to have that depressing scenario confirmed for us."

I paused to let them have a chance to digest what I had said so far. Also, I needed time to gather my own thoughts. We all lapsed into a reflective silence. No doubt, Makoto and Hideo were addressing their own morality issues and making their personal risk assessments. What I was proposing was a continuation of a grand theft that had once had the sanction of an immoral government but if now exposed would leave us all open to criminal charges that could result in our spending the rest of our days in some foul prison. It was a dilemma that screamed for your attention and rapped your brain, one that demanded clear thought when the capacity to think had deserted you. I knew what they must be thinking, because I had faced the very same moral quandary.

Hosokawa was the first to break the silence and voice his concerns. He must have had a thousand questions, for I had barely scratched the surface. "Toshio, are you seriously suggesting that we would be able to excavate all this loot and bring it back to Japan, invest it in Mabuhay, reap the rewards, and manage to do all this free from detection? Surely we would be exposed, and then what? It is without doubt the wildest fantasy I have ever heard." He leaned back and took a long draught of sake. I realised that I still had distance to cover if I was to win them over. No doubt Hideo felt the same. He was not as forthcoming as Hosokawa, but I could see the objection written across his face.

I gave Hosokawa my most defiant of looks. "Yes, that is exactly what I am proposing, although with a few adjustments."

Makoto shook his head in exasperation. "Toshio, it is not just a question of getting your hands on the stuff. Those countries left devoid of their wealth will be searching high and low for their own lost treasures. We will never get away with it. The more I think of it, the more ludicrous it becomes. It's madness, pure madness. Even the company name, Mabuhay, stands out like a flashing beacon demanding attention. My word, we would come under so much scrutiny, we would be bound to buckle under the strain."

Was Hosokawa playing devil's advocate or was he going to turn his back on me and my company? I did not have that option. I had to follow this through. It was my destiny, what I was born to do.

"You must believe me when I say it is possible," I said. "It has been done once before. Three months before his death my father put into place an operation to open up one of the sites. He made arrangements with a Philippine government official, a man who carries immense power and even has a small private militia at his command. The deal came with a heavy price—five hundred thousand dollars in cash, to be exact, and a price well worth paying when all you have to do is forward your Swiss bankers deposit codes and the map coordinates. My father's Philippine contact put into place a clandestine operation of his own. The loot was excavated, transported across land in the original sealed crates, and shipped to Belgium, where arrangements were already in place for it to be collected by our bankers. Eventually it was deposited in the vaults of our Swiss bank. Our representatives in Switzerland then divided the loot into two categories: first, artefacts and treasures that best remain stored in order to avoid suspicion, and second, liquid assets, such as gold, loose gems, and untraceable currency. These are traded to our advantage and obviously the source of our profit.

"The process was all very civil and business-like. Later, my father was able to borrow a large amount from our Swiss friends in the form of an unsecured loan. The bank agreed to allow us special privileges, as we had such a large amount of security on deposit. Sixty-five million dollars, to be exact, and every dollar came from the hidden depths of the Philippine jungle. A loan such as this attracts far less official attention than a great dollop of hard cash, and is easily explained, especially when you have millions to start with. Also, of late I have developed a very special relationship with our Swiss bankers. Let's say they are sympathetic to our needs, and that gives us a lot of room to manoeuvre."

This gave Hosokawa plenty to think about, and I could see he was formulating his next objection. Was this how they worked in the diplomatic service? An endless round of verbal attrition was taking place, and I was becoming a little frustrated with the way our exchanges were developing. As a natural manipulator and a man who prides himself on decisive action, I was feeling the irritation of having my judgements questioned, which only increased as Makoto prepared his next attack on my scheme.

"I understand that you may have devised a way to handle the money," he said. "That side of things is not my main concern. I know the Swiss are practical and we could rely on their banking ethics to ensure total secrecy. What concerns me is the Philippine side of the operation. How can we place our faith in such a lawless, almost anarchic country? We would be turned over at the first opportunity. I would find it impossible to place my trust in anyone who would kill their own grandmother for a few dollars."

Hosokawa was becoming a little excited; perhaps the sake had begun to chip away at his ability to think rationally. His last comment seemed to bring Hideo to life, and he spoke as if he were the referee settling a dispute between two rival players. "Yes, that country has its problems and we are responsible for much that ails them. But it is wrong to dismiss the people as a bad lot. They are a fine, proud, brave, and loyal folk in whom I would place my trust. It seems to me that the lawlessness we have spoken about is to our favour. It would be impossible to even think of mounting a recovery operation in a country that was secured. My experience of that place is that anything can be done and any man can be bought. We are operating from a position of strength. We hold all the aces. Of course there are risks, there always will be, but it is up to us to assess whether those risks are worth the rewards, and I believe they are."

His bluntness seemed to take the barb out of Makoto's negativity, for which I was thankful. Was he acquiescing so easily out of loyalty, or did he truly believe in me and my enterprise? Whatever lay behind his reasoning, I had cause to be thankful, for it was at this point that Makoto started to look at the problem from a more positive point of view.

We talked late into the night. Old Mrs Ishikawa must have been pulling her hair out. I had requested six of the finest geisha and presumed they were all in an adjacent room waiting to be summoned to ply their magic and ease us into a state of divine relaxation. But however much my mind started to wander towards more pleasant activities, I was brought back to earth by Hideo or Hosokawa demanding more details about Golden Lily. I could see in their eyes that they were well and truly hooked, and the more we talked, the more positive and ambitious our scheming became. I had decided to take Hosokawa into Mabuhay because he was a superb negotiator and his planning and logistical talents were second to none. He would certainly have much to do. Hideo would be more involved in the day-to-day business of running the company. His mandate would be more practical, turning loot into products that would make Mabuhay into the market leader, leaving all our rivals gasping in our wake. I saw myself, perhaps because of my vanity, as the figurehead steering Mabuhay through the many challenges that lay ahead. I had not covered all the details; it would have been impossible to do so. The coming months and years would see us learn from our experiences.

Makoto asked if he would be able to read my father's Golden Lily binder. I felt a strange sense of disloyalty as I agreed to his request; however, I would not let any of the papers leave my residence. I said it was a good idea for both he and Hideo to come to my place the next day and go through the papers together. I knew they would come across many potential problems and drawbacks, and I was all too aware that my plan had one fundamental weakness that they were not yet aware of. I would deal with their concerns the next day.

I had been thinking for some time about how best to deal with the man who was at the centre of my problem. Santa Romana was the only man in the Philippines with the power and connections to make it all work. He was without doubt an evil man whose greed knew no bounds, but he was a man of vital importance. I hoped he would become my ally and not my nemesis.

It was fast approaching midnight, and any notion of further entertainment here at Ishikawa was becoming less fanciful by the minute. We did not want to outstay our welcome, so I suggested we take our leave. Mrs Ishikawa escorted us along the white paper–screened corridor to the hallway where all the ryotei staff had gathered to bid us farewell. Few words were spoken; the elegant minimalism of the place also extended to verbal exchanges. I thanked Mrs Ishikawa for the excellent food and service. Makoto and Hideo echoed my praise. I asked her to convey my regrets to the geishas, explaining that our talk had taken a little longer than expected. She slyly suggested we all return when we had the time to set business aside and lighten our hearts a little. I promised we would do so and said that next time, our companions' talents would not be wasted. She gave a deep bow and said we were always welcome.

Mrs Ishikawa was a fine lady of at least eighty years of age. I wondered how many times she had hosted parties where the great and good of the day had shaped policies, sealed deals, and made promises that touched the soul of our nation. My own father had been a guest here so many times that he often referred to Ishikawa as his second office. Hosokawa's father was also no stranger to this place. No doubt they would have found cause to dine together, discussing the business of the day. Maybe their minds had been occupied with an agenda similar to the one that had taken up much of our own evening.

Perhaps it was the calming effects of the sake, for we had all taken a lot on board, but an image as clear as day formed before my eyes. I could see my father sitting at the low table, waving his Turkish cigarette around as he tried to make his point to Makoto's father. Had history just repeated itself? Had we followed in their footsteps? Their problem would have been the concealment of the loot. Ours was the reverse side of the dilemma: how to get it out. I sat on the low wooden bench in the hallway and allowed one of the staff to lace my shoes for me. The vision in my mind refused to go away, and I saw a third man in the room. He turned to face my father, and his profile sent chills racing through my body. I dismissed the ghosts of the past, shook myself into the present, and looked over at Hideo. I studied his features closely and decided there and then that it was time for us to have our little "chat."

Ogawa had been summoned by a forward-thinking member of the staff and was waiting by the open rear door of the Bentley. He had his chauffeur's cap tucked neatly under his arm and stood formally, as if he were on parade. His dignity was in total contrast to the three of us as we made our clumsy exit, voices a little raised because of the drink. I insisted on giving Makoto a ride home, but he was bent on walking, muttering something about clearing his head. He thanked me for my hospitality and strode off purposefully into the night. I called after him, but he was away with a friendly wave. In any case there is little purpose in trying to dissuade someone who is half-cut. I was having no such protestations from Hideo, and before he could say no, I ushered him into the back seat and slid in alongside him.

Ishikawa's full retinue was still in attendance as we pulled slowly away. They would not leave their positions until we were fully out of sight, when Mrs Ishikawa would go straight to her office and put her abacus to good use to calculate my fees and, after a respectable day or two and with a certain amount of glee, forward it to me for my attention. I instructed Ogawa to drive straight to the Empire, and we made the short journey in no time at all, although our rather tedious small talk made it seem a little longer. Hideo was still quite reserved in my presence and perhaps not totally comfortable. The sake he had drunk had little effect on his naturally taciturn and cautious nature, admirable qualities for sure but qualities that would be put to the test when he heard what I had to tell him.

Ogawa steered the Bentley with practiced ease around the Empire's ornamental pool and up the ramp to the front entrance. I invited myself in for a nightcap, and Hideo was too gracious to refuse me. I let Ogawa retire for the evening and return to the residence. I would follow Hosokawa's example and take the short walk to my home later and enjoy the sobering air. I felt a pang of nostalgia, for I had loved living here at the Empire. I enjoyed the free and easy style that living in such a place affords, although towards the end of my days here I had become a little tired of the top brass American servicemen who had made the bar one of their favourite watering holes. Now, six months after my departure, I was a little dismayed to find their type still very much in evidence this evening, their presence marked by raucous laughter and thick cigar smoke.

We strode into the lobby, where a bellhop who appeared to be on friendly terms with Hideo offered us assistance. Despite the lateness of the hour the place was still quite crowded. Hideo looked to me for guidance, and not wishing to intrude on his private space, I indicated a quiet table in the corner of the lobby far away from the rowdy crowd at the bar. I wondered if my sister was keeping his bed warm for him—an unlikely scenario, but not beyond the realm of possibility, given their recent betrothal. We settled into our chairs and a waiter hovered nearby, eager to take our orders. I asked Hideo what he fancied and was somewhat taken aback when he told me that he had never taken a drink in this bar before and was unfamiliar with the choices on offer. He had lived here for all of six months and had never been in the bar. My word, what kind of a man could resist a bar on his own door-step? I thought of my sister and her future happiness. Would Hideo's dullness eventually wear her down? She was not the most adventurous of women, but compared with her future spouse she was virtually swinging. I shrugged off those rather uncharitable thoughts and ordered two gimlets. The waiter scuttled off to the bar with our order and left us to pick up our conversation.

Our grand surroundings befitted what I was about to tell Hideo. I looked around the tables at the clientele and recognized very few people. At one time I would have known nearly everyone in the bar. I looked over to a table where a young couple were seated, him a handsome-looking chap and his companion trying her best to look cool in a tight-fitting pencil dress. They sat at the table that Kawabata and I preferred when we were in the mood for a cocktail or two. I felt guilty abandoning him for the evening, but promised myself I would make it up to him the next day, perhaps with lunch and some champagne at one of the new restaurants in Shibuya that seemed to spring up as if by magic. I wondered what he had done with his time today and hoped he was now waiting for me back at home, but that had to wait, for the night would not be over until I had unburdened my soul to Hideo and told him what he had a natural right to know.

I began by asking how he was finding life at the Empire. He told me that every day was like a dream and he could still not believe that this was his life. He thanked me again for giving over my rooms for his use. I waved his gratitude away; it was a conversation we had danced around many times. I told him a little of the history of the hotel. No doubt he already knew more than I did, but being a gracious fellow, he listened like a good little pupil. "About seventy years ago the first Empire was built at the request of the Emperor, who thought Western visitors would feel more at home in familiar surroundings. Land was even given up from the Imperial estate for the project, and Tokyo's first attempt at East-West harmony was finally completed in 1890. It served its purpose for a time, but such were the whims of the times, it was decided that it looked rather outdated and had become a slightly embarrassing edifice. As fortune would have it, the first Empire Hotel was completely destroyed by a 'mysterious' fire."

The drinks arrived, and I broke off from my scholarly lecture to take a much needed reviving sip. Before the waiter had the chance to take his leave, I asked him to put a bottle of Dom Perignon on ice. Hideo gave me a look which, if I read it correctly, said he would love to decline that particular offering if at all possible. I soldiered on with my lecture. "In 1915 the great American architect William Lionel Francis was commissioned to build a new Empire, and here we are, in his vision of what an Empire hotel should actually be. Grand, don't you think? My father was a little sceptical of the Mayan concept of design, but I think he was eventually won over, as he decided to become an investor in the project and like the Meiji Emperor before him realised he needed a place to accommodate his own foreign visitors. He bought the suite you now call home and gave the hotel much needed patronage by holding and hosting all kinds of grand events here—just as Mabuhay will do with our gala products launch, a tradition that I hope will continue for many years to come. Francis's hotel opened in 1923, the year of the Great Kanto earthquake. The hotel famously survived, but at a cost. Have you noticed the door-jambs and sagging ceilings? Also, the floors tend to slope in strange places. Quite disconcerting, especially when drinks have been consumed aplenty."

I was boring Hideo with my ramblings. He had managed to stifle a couple of yawns; after all, it had been a momentous day for him, too—one that might just get a little more memorable.

I decided to liven things up a little by getting to the purpose of our little tête-à-tête. "Hideo, do you mind if I ask you something?"

"Of course not—ask me anything," he replied. He looked sleepy and worn out. The long hours he had spent on the projects must have meant many a sleepless night.

I threw back what was left of my gimlet and got to the heart of the matter. "You did not tell Hosokawa that you were one of the officers ordered to take part in Golden Lily. Why did you keep silent?"

This complete shift of focus unsettled Hideo so much that he seemed to squirm in his seat. Then he found his words. "I did not speak of my involvement because I was not sure if it was appropriate. I thought you would enlighten Hosokawa if and when it was necessary." I nodded thoughtfully and studied him for a few moments whist contemplating his answer. He looked increasingly uncomfortable. "Toshio, if I have done something that displeases you, tell me."

I gave him one of my best smiles and the reassurance he needed. "Not at all, my dear Hideo. I ask only because, well, I have to tell you something, and it concerns your special duty in the Philippines."

With ill timing the waiter began to fuss around our table, setting up the ice bucket stand, and made a great play of showing off the bottle. I waited until he had finished his task and then, with a fresh glass of champagne in my hand, continued my tale.

"Hideo, it is one of my great regrets that you never had a chance to meet my father. I believe you would have found much common ground for discussion. He was a far more methodical man than I am, and like you, enjoyed the technical challenges that business presented. When he died, he left me the Golden Lily binder detailing his own involvement in that complex and rather sordid scheme. Along with the binder was a letter. The contents of that letter were what first brought you to my attention.

"Thirty years ago my father was summoned to the Imperial household. At that time he was a relatively young man himself, a widower with two small children to care for. He had inherited the family fortune and was well placed in the upper echelons of society. The Hamazaki name was one that went back generations, and as such, my father, and his father before him, had enjoyed a great deal of royal patronage. Being almost a neighbour, he was a regular visitor to the household and often told us he had played together with the royal princes when they were all children.

"My father held the trust of the Imperial close circle, and when a favour was needed, he must have seemed like the ideal man to call upon. On this particular day he was summoned to the household, He must have assumed that it was some matter concerning the social calendar or perhaps his advice was being sought regarding a sensitive business issue. It was none of those things. He arrived at the gates and was immediately shown into an anteroom where he was greeted by the protocol officer, an elderly man by the name of Aizawa who explained to my father what was required of him. The need for the utmost secrecy and discretion was called for, and Aizawa stressed that the Imperial household had placed complete trust in my father. A young woman was ushered into the room along with a stern-faced old maid. The young woman was quite distressed and had been crying. She was holding an infant in her arms. She sank to her knees and bowed at my father's feet, then held her infant out for him to take. As he took the child, the woman broke down into sobs and was roughly taken from the room by the old maid. Hideo, that infant was you."

I let those words hang in the air for a few moments. I felt the need for a drink and threw back my glass and, without waiting to be served, poured myself another. Hideo was speechless, and the colour drained from his face. I carried on with my revelations, surprised to find myself filling with tension. "My father was told to take you to the Tanaka home, where you were to be raised by the people you have always believed were your true birth parents. My father was also told that he was now your unofficial guardian and to keep a watchful eye over your growth and life. He may have used his influence on several occasions to ensure a certain passage in life was afforded you.

"Your 'parents,' the Tanakas, were considered good, solid, and dependable people, and as your adoptive parents they received an annual stipend in return for giving you a home where you could grow up a normal and well-adjusted person. They had only one promise to keep, that they would take you to the local portrait studio each year on your birth date and have two pictures taken: one they could keep, and the other to be passed to my father, who in turn delivered it to the Imperial household. It seems they like to keep track of their royal bastards."

The second my last words were uttered, I regretted my choice of phrase. Hideo looked totally dejected, and I felt his sadness. He slumped back into his chair, rubbing his temples. For a moment I thought he was going to break down in tears. I waited for him to speak, and after an uncomfortable silence, he looked up and said, "My parents will always be my parents. I have no other mother or father." I was about to say that did not appear to be the case but held my tongue and said nothing, giving him time to come to terms with what he had just heard. In another era, not that very long ago, his birth would have been celebrated and his birth-right acknowledged. Regardless of whether his mother was an official concubine, Hideo Tanaka would have taken his place in the line of succession. But times had changed, and now Hideo and the other "accidents of Imperial birth" were farmed out to take their place in life's struggle. I poured myself another glass of champagne, waving the waiter away as he tried to apologise for his tardy service skills. I handed a glass to Hideo, who took it and looked down at it as if expecting it to reveal the key to his dilemma. Then he looked at me with an expression of sadness from the depths of his soul.

I felt wretched for being the bearer of such shattering news and waited for him to break the silence. His first question caught me a little off guard. "Toshio, does Ayumi know about this?" I assured him she did not and said I would leave it to him to decide if he should tell her. He looked totally lost. "Do you think I should tell her?"

I made a play of thinking for a moment, but I already knew my answer. "I think you should tell her everything about your origins but nothing of your wartime duty. However, it is your decision, and I will respect whatever course you take." It was his turn to nod thoughtfully; he took a small sip of champagne and then the rest in one draught. Was he searching for Dutch courage?

I leaned over the table and gave him a brotherly pat on the shoulder. "That's the spirit, Hideo, my prince." Judging by his expression, he seemed to find my levity a little off-putting. Perhaps I was being too direct. The drink along with the tiredness was starting to make its mark. We both sank into a weary silence, allowing the ambient sounds of the Empire to fill the void.

Our contemplation was interrupted by a couple of uniformed American officers who paused by our table, unsteady on their feet. Their voices could be heard across the lobby. It seemed they were bent on having a bit of sport at our expense. "Look, Jake, my boy. Who's drinking champagne? Makes you think, eh? Goddamn, who won the fucking war?" Jake looked at us, unable to disguise his contempt. His bright red hair made him seem all the more threatening. We ignored them and they moved on, their attention diverted by two girls who seemed to appear out of nowhere. Was the Empire allowing streetwalkers in these days? I knew standards were slipping, but a line had to be drawn somewhere. At least they had saved us from a potentially distasteful scene. Then to my shame, I realised they were staff girls, dressed in the new and rather daring Empire uniforms that showed a flash of thigh. No doubt the management was trying to keep up with the tastes of their bawdier clientele.

Hideo looked all in, and I was about to suggest we call it a day. But it seemed the champagne had given him a burst of energy, and he found his tongue. "So, this letter that your father left. Did it say who my father and mother were?"

I shook my head. "Please believe me when I say I do not know and neither did my father, for he would have said for sure. However, because of the continued interest in your welfare, we can only assume your birth touched the higher echelons of the household." I studied his face closely as I had done so many times before. His features gave little away about his natural paternity. Other than a slightly hooked nose there were few clues, and yet in a certain light you could be forgiven for thinking…! I shrugged off the thought.

Hideo must have guessed what was going through my mind, but he too decided to let it rest for the time being. "Toshio, forgive me, but I have many questions. But if you wish, perhaps we could speak tomorrow." I was becoming desperate to go home, and was barely able to stifle a monstrous yawn. Before I could say what a great idea that was, Hideo was off again. "You mentioned something about my special duty in the Philippines. I am eager to hear how that is connected to anything."

I pulled my best narrative powers out of the box for one final airing that evening and told him what that little episode was actually all about. "As you know, my father was the chief coordinator of Golden Lily and as such was able to use his powers to influence various outcomes. He made two trips to the Philippines. The first was about a year before hostilities ceased. It was an executive mission accompanied by a high-level delegation. They met with Yamashita and ironed out some logistical problems. The trip was undertaken in total secrecy. The risks were immense, but it was thought that a face-to-face meeting would ensure the mission was given the highest level of devotion it required.

"That's slightly by the way, and I apologise for deviating a little. The point is, my father made the first trip to the Philippines as Golden Lily coordinator. However, he made a second visit only months before the end of the war in his capacity as your guardian. The sole purpose of the second trip was to save your life. My father had used his influence to ensure you were commissioned into the army and would serve as an officer rather than a regular listing. At the time he thought it would be safer for you. However, when it was time for your posting to be decided, all he could do was ensure you were assigned to the Philippines, where fighting had yet to start. He hoped that the Tojo cabinet would see that any attempt at defending the islands would be futile and that some form of retreat would be organised, thus ensuring you would stay out of harm's way. As usual, insanity prevailed and, well, you know better than I do what kind of hell that place turned out to be.

Fearing you would be lost in action in the final battle, my father decided to use Golden Lily as a subterfuge to try to save your life. He assembled an elite troop of the finest marines and set out on a hellish trip by plane and submarine and finally on foot through enemy lines back to the heart of Yamashita's army. Such a trip was madness in itself, but as an honourable man who had promised to do all he could as a guardian, he felt there was no alternative. Against the odds he made it to Yamashita's headquarters to find a demoralised, defeated, and scattered army. They were unable to immediately establish whether you were alive or dead. With regret my father had to leave without you, as the window for extraction was closing in.

"Being a resourceful man he had made a contingency plan. He had brought along a priceless treasure, a thing of immense beauty and historical significance: an Emerald Buddha, said to be more than two thousand years old. It was looted from a Burmese temple in 1942 by British forces and captured by our own army shortly afterwards. It was said that this divine goddess held special powers and would protect all who placed faith in her. My father came across the figurine when he was inspecting batches of loot on his first trip. He had been ordered to return to Tokyo with the Buddha, which he did, but he conspired to keep it out of the hands of certain, let's say, undeserving types. It was his intention to have the Buddha returned to Burma as soon as safety would allow.

"When he made that second trip to the battle zone, he took the Buddha with him. He prayed for protection, and his faith was rewarded: He managed to undertake his mission without harm. He left the Buddha in the trusted custody of Yamashita, who alone was to pass along the final orders to you and your good friend Ogawa. Yes, it was the Emerald Buddha that you and Ogawa secreted that night in the Luzon jungle."

The mere mention of Ogawa was enough to bring Hideo to the verge of tears. He was finding all this a little too much to process. "I still don't know why we were taken out of the battle to hide a Buddha," he said, shaking his head in disbelief.

"Hideo, leaving you in the battle would have been as good as a death sentence for you. Nearly two hundred thousand of our men died in the battle of Luzon. Only nine thousand men managed to return home alive. Out of those nine thousand, only twenty were commissioned officers. So, an alternative mission had to be given to you. In a way, you were the treasure. Ogawa was selected for his skills in the field; his bravery and loyalty were unquestioned. He was the perfect choice to ensure your safety. To this day he keeps watch over the site where you placed the Buddha. He has become her guardian, and I believe she bestows her protective powers upon him."

He looked down into his drink, which must have turned warm by then, and then slowly looked up. "The paper I brought back, in the pen, was meaningless?"

I shook my head sadly. "Hideo, I did not plan this. All I can say is that the madness of war took over and rational thinking went out the window. Yes, of course your Emerald Buddha site was always known, and yet maybe it was thought that should anything happen to my father, then there was at least a backup, and that was held with you."

The pleading in his eyes was moving. "Toshio, we have to rescue Ogawa from his vigil. The immorality of it all weighs heavily on me. I cannot sit around drinking champagne whilst my dear friend is living like an animal in God knows what conditions. We must do something. We must!" He was losing himself, and I tried to calm him down. I promised him that Ogawa would be our priority and we would talk it over with Hosokawa the next day. I could not bring myself to tell him that Ogawa's situation was more complicated than he knew. Better to leave that little problem alone until we had cleared our heads. Anyway, this seemed to settle him down a little, but the agitation was still written all over his face, and who could blame him?

I put the drinks on Hideo's charges and made ready to take my leave. What a day it had been! I felt weary to my bones and now regretted letting Ogawa off duty early. It would be too churlish to hail a taxi for a two-minute ride, so I summoned what was left of my strength and heaved myself out of the chair to start the short walk back to my residence and, I hoped, my lovely Kawabata waiting for me. The thought of him seemed to rekindle my fire, and suddenly the walk did not seem the worst of things. Hideo accompanied me through the lobby and we said our good nights by the side of the ornamental pool, which was nicely illuminated by the moonlight. The calming sounds of frogs croaking filled the air. I looked down into the water to see the moon in all its glory reflected among the water lilies. There were discarded cigar butts and tobacco ends aplenty floating on the still water—a depressing sight and one Mr William Lionel Francis had not accounted for when he built his harmony pool. The foibles of human nature were a mystery to us all.

I left Hideo to himself and set out. It was a little before three in the morning, and the air had cooled considerably. I felt invigorated as I strode out, although a little unsteady on my feet. I heard footsteps behind me, quickening in pace. I stood to one side to allow whomever it was to pass, and without warning I was struck by an almighty punch to my jaw which sent me reeling to the ground. Shiny black shoes delivered three or four heavy kicks to my rib cage, and I found myself curled into a ball. The violence that was being rained upon me passed quickly. My assailants seemed satisfied with their work and left me on the side of the road, gasping for air. I dared to look up and saw my attackers walking briskly away. Maybe they were laughing, I was not sure, but the moonlight caught the flame-red hair, and I was sure of one thing: They would not be laughing come this time tomorrow.

I staggered to my feet and slowly covered the last two hundred yards to the house, clutching my aching sides and holding a handkerchief to my bloodied nose. I let myself in at the front door and, not wishing to cause a fuss, went straight to my room to find my bed untouched, cold, and empty. Of Kawabata there was no sign. I sat on my dressing-table stool and looked into the mirror. Blood had ruined my shirt and jacket. My ribs were tender to the touch. I looked at the lonely bed and then back to the mirror and my swollen nose and cheek. There were lessons to be learned here, and perhaps an increase in personal security was called for. Yes, it had been an inglorious end to one of the most momentous days of my life, one I would never forget. Despite the throbbing pain building in my head and the frustration of not knowing where my lover was, I was able to say a silent prayer of thanks, for now I had my ambassador and my prince right by my side.

I awoke the next morning fully clothed, lying on top of my bed. The heavens had opened, and the rain was beating so hard against the windowpanes, I feared they might break. My head hurt like the devil. It wasn't from the drink—I never suffered from the cursed hangovers that seem to blight others of a weaker disposition—but from the violence I had suffered on my way home. Not yet ready to face the day I threw back the sheets and crawled under, fully clothed. The odours from the previous evening—Turkish tobacco, whiskey, and witch hazel—still lingered about me and only served to further remind me of what had played out. I gave a groan and cursed my loose tongue, for now in the cold sober light of day, everything did not seem well at all. *In vino veritas*: In wine there is truth. I could not agree more, but in my case, *in vino fatuitas* would have been more appropriate: In wine there is foolishness.

Staring at the ceiling, enjoying a little respite from the rain, which seemed to have abated a little, I went through the events that weighed heavily on me. I thought of Tanaka and the feelings he must be waking to this morning. Had he already told Ayumi? I doubted it somehow; he was not a man to rush head-on. He would need time to come to terms with his new origins in life. I had always believed that once the truth was out, he would find the emotional shackles of the Hamazaki family too hard to shake loose. Last night he had given me no indication that I should be worried, other than one small concern. When I had told him of the background concerning his "ghost mission," he failed to mention that Yamashita had not given him his orders in person, but had delegated that task to Muto, his chief of staff. I knew this to be the case, as Yamashita had refused outright to be a part of my father's plans and had waited until my father was back in Tokyo before informing him through a communique that Muto had been given the responsibility. There was little that could be done. Yamashita's obstinacy was legendary. The man had principles, but his lofty ideals had not spared him from the rope. Muto too was long gone, also despatched to the gallows. There was little to be gained from fretting over minor things, but still, the question remained. Why had Tanaka held back such a small detail? Loyalty to his general, perhaps, a soldier's code, heaven knows. More than likely, his thoughts were lost in the confusion I had heaped upon him.

I dragged my weary self out of bed and into the bathroom. Normally I loved the mirror, but today, the brutal, honest reflection staring back shocked me. There was an ugly welt under my right eye, and I had rough scrapes down the side of my face. I lifted my bloodied shirt and saw dark crimson bruises decorating my rib cage and lower back. I ached like hell. The blood from my nose had oozed over my shirt and dried to a dark colour. I thanked God that my nose didn't appear to be broken and I still had all my teeth firmly in place. It would be unbearable to carry a constant reminder of that foul beating.

I went back into my bedroom and pressed the bell push to summon Ogawa, who knocked on my door within moments. If he was shocked at my dishevelled appearance, he hid it quite well. "Ogawa san, seems I took a tumble on the way home last night," I said. "Nothing to worry about. Would you be so kind as to call the maid to prepare me a bath?"

Ogawa bowed and went off to do my bidding. After a moment or two he came back into the room. "Would sir require any more assistance?"

I thought for a moment. "Yes, I have a luncheon appointment with Tanaka san and Hosokawa san at the Empire at one o'clock. Please stand by."

"Of course, sir." Ogawa bowed and left me to get ready for my meeting. I knew he would be wondering if in some way I blamed him for my unfortunate "accident," as I had let him leave me to walk home alone. Those were nonsense thoughts, of course, but it doesn't hurt to keep the servants on their toes.

Before I bathed, I had to make a few calls. The first was to Tanaka, who, luckily, was still in his suite. He sounded perfectly normal, not allowing any trace of what had passed between us the previous evening to intrude on his emotions. I took it as a given that he hadn't told Ayumi. He thanked me for the lunch invitation and said he was looking forward to seeing me later. Next, I called Hosokawa at the ministry. I hung on to the line for an age before eventually being connected to his secretary. "Hosokawa san will be with you in a few moments."

I waited a good few minutes more before Hosokawa finally came on the line. "Toshio, sorry to keep you waiting. Just clearing my desk. They have cut my private phone line, so I'm having to use the secretary's, which suits me fine, as these lines are out of the reach of unwanted third parties. Well, it seems after my resignation I am persona non grata around here. I've been given the week to clear out." I let the silence hang in the air, not being in a sympathetic mood to listen to any moaning. "Toshio, are you still there? My God, you aren't having second thoughts, are you? I've put my papers in."

The temptation to have a little fun at his expense was almost too much to resist, but to my credit I managed to get to the point in hand. He told me he would be delighted to meet for lunch and would be at the Empire at one. Suddenly, a thought came to me. "Makoto, I think we may need some extra security around us. I was wondering if you might know of anyone who would fit the bill, so to speak."

There was silence for a moment or two, and I could hear muffled voices in the background and then the sound of a door closing. Hosokawa came back on the line. "Sorry, just sent my secretary out on an errand. Now we can talk. Toshio, I think you have a gift for reading minds. It was only this morning that I was signing off on some paperwork—extradition orders, in fact, which are usually a formality, providing we have a reciprocal agreement with the country concerned." My head hurt too much to listen to Hosokawa's diplomatic spiel, and I rather rudely told him to get to the point. "Well, there is a chap—goes by the name of Daigo Hamma—currently residing in Chiba jail and waiting to be extradited to France to face various charges. I think a man such as him would be very sympathetic to our cause, especially if we were to rescue him from a lifetime of misery."

Any other day I would have been very impressed with Hosokawa's efficiency, but today I was not myself, and plaudits were hard to come by. "This Daigo Hamma sounds like a good candidate. Can you get him out of the system without leaving a trail?"

There was a snort on the other end of the line. "Consider it done. After all, this is what I am now paid so handsomely to do." That was Hosokawa through and through, a thinly veiled reminder that he would want to see his 20 per cent share contract as soon as possible. I told him that we would discuss it further over lunch and hung up. Suddenly I was reminded of an image from the not-too-distant past, a silhouette of a man speaking on the telephone and a caption below that read "Loose Tongues Cost Lives." Chills ran down my spine, and I cursed my lack of discretion and vowed that confidential matters would, from now on, be handled only face-to-face. I would insist that Hosokawa also learn to follow this simple rule.

It was just after eleven, and I decided that a shot of Scotland's finest would do wonders for my mood. With an overly generous measure in hand, I opened the small writing bureau kept by my bed for convenience and wrote the name Daigo Hamma in my ledger. I left the page blank and wondered what words Hamma would cause me to write.

My head aching, I eased myself into the bath, the warm water stinging my battered body. I added a spoonful of witch hazel crystals, which stung like the devil. However, after a few moments I was relaxed and felt my mind clearing. Life had become one long whirl of irritations, and I was determined to rid myself of petty distractions. Constant drama, and endless scheming, conniving, and manipulating was taking its toll. I desperately wanted to simplify my life.

Where had Kawabata got to? It irked me that I didn't know his whereabouts, which forced my jealous mind to conjure up all kinds of sordid scenarios. There was no doubt, I had to be stricter with him and lay down some solid rules. The time had come for him to realise who the master was in this relationship. I slunk under the water and held my breath for a full twenty seconds, shutting out the world. I repeated this ten times until my lungs hurt like hell and I was gasping for dear life. I closed my eyes and thought about how best to bring Hosokawa and Tanaka into the full picture. Last night we had talked a lot about the possibilities of our enterprise, but I had deliberately avoided any mention of the danger posed by one man, Lieutenant Colonel Nishii. My colleagues were about to hear his name for the first time, and one thing was for sure: Lunch would be a lively affair. I allowed myself the luxury of shaving in the bath, feeling my bristles through fingertips and guiding the cutthroat blade by instinct.

The bath along with the whiskey had put the spring back into my step, and I was now ready to face the day head-on. Because it was a Saturday, formality could take a back seat where dress was concerned, and I chose a short tan calfskin jacket paired with a thick white cotton open-necked shirt and a pair of black trousers from one of my favourite Lanvin suits. As I checked myself in the mirror, I thought of my father, who would not have been caught dead wearing anything less than a two-piece and necktie, however casual the occasion may be. Well, times were changing, and for that I was eternally grateful.

I ran some scented pomade through my hair and checked my injuries, which now appeared less shocking. In fact I didn't mind this temporary distraction; it made me look a tad like a beaten Joseph Cotton. I put on a pair of Bausch and Lomb aviators, the same kind favoured by MacArthur. *Now, there lies an irony!* I thought. I clasped tight my silver Patek Philippe wristwatch, and my look was now complete. As an afterthought I opened one of the small drawers on my writing bureau and took out the pearl-handled switchblade I kept there. It felt reassuringly comfortable in my palm. Without a second thought I dropped it into my jacket pocket. Resisting the temptation to have another "reviving" shot of Mortlach, I made my way down to the hallway where I knew Ogawa would be waiting to drive me over to the Empire.

The heavy rain and balmy air caused condensation to form on the windows of the Bentley. I was surprised Ogawa could make out the road before him. I spent the short journey massaging my temples and running the meeting through my mind. In no time at all the Bentley was drawing to a halt outside the grand foyer of the Empire. The hotel manager, who must have been alerted of my arrival, was waiting to greet me. I stepped out of the car and felt like a Hollywood actor. I loved a grand entrance and enjoyed the attention of all those around me. As I strode purposefully through the lobby towards the stairs, I noticed that the afternoon patrons were far removed from those who frequented the hotel during the evenings. American women, the wives of servicemen and officials whose coffee morning had spilled over into lunch, were seated in groups, their unrestrained laughter and loud, gossipy voices piercing the Empire's usual serenity. There were a few children weaving in and out of the tables, arms spread wide as they chased each other, pretending to be fighter planes, their boisterous behaviour drawing disapproving stares from some old-fashioned types. I, for one, found this casual atmosphere quite refreshing, for as a child, I had suffered many a dull day in this very lobby, reproached for even daring to speak. No doubt I gave the chattering women and their little ankle biters something to talk about as I breezed past them, boldly wearing my sunglasses indoors, as much of a social faux pas as forgetting to remove one's hat.

The manager and one of his underlings escorted me up the winding stairs to one of the smaller private function rooms that I had reserved for our lunch meeting. He told me that Hosokawa and Tanaka were already here and waiting for me. I thanked him for his courteous service and said I could make my own way. After all, I probably knew the ins and outs of this place better than anyone.

I opened the double mahogany doors to find my colleagues standing by the far window, which looked out over towards the Imperial grounds. I wondered what was going through Tanaka's mind as he gazed down on the place of his conception. I very much doubted he was entertaining Hosokawa with an amusing tale about his stately beginnings. They were both dressed as if it were a Monday morning, and I made a mental note to have a word with them about their stuffiness. Hosokawa, never being the type to stand on ceremony, already had a glass in his hand; Tanaka, predictably, did not. Hosokawa strode across the room, hand outstretched to greet me. "Toshio, my dear friend, how are you feeling this morning? You sounded a little on the heavy side this…" His greeting trailed off into shock when I removed my sunglasses and revealed my battered face. "Good heavens, what has happened?"

I nonchalantly brushed aside their concerns. "It is nothing to worry about. On the way home last night, I crossed the road to avoid a group of roughs, lost my footing, and slipped down a nullah. I got a few cuts and bruises—looks worse than it feels." I looked at Hideo, who didn't look as if he doubted my feeble explanation at all and hadn't connected any bad feelings from the American servicemen to my mishap. After voicing his own concern, Hideo, ever the practical one, offered to call the hotel doctor to check me over. I told him that would be unnecessary, but thanked him all the same. Hosokawa, reading my thoughts, poured me a large whiskey from a decanter that had been set out for our convenience. I gratefully accepted and suggested we be seated and get about our business, for we had a lot to get through.

Not wishing to be distracted by the palaver of choosing from a menu, I had instructed the hotel to ask the chef to prepare us lunch per his recommendations, and the table was already set to receive his offering. I suggested we delay the food service for an hour or so and make headway, as we had a lot to get through. Tanaka nodded enthusiastically, whilst Hosokawa acquiesced reluctantly. He always enjoyed his food, so perhaps he was a little disappointed to have lunch put on hold.

Once seated, they both looked at me to get matters started, and although I had gone through this in my head many times, it was still difficult to put across, as I did not wish to shock them into turning their backs on Mabuhay. I hoped we had come too far for that ever to happen, but all the same it was a real concern. However, I could no longer hold back the Nishii problem.

"Well, there is a matter that demands our immediate attention," I said. "There is no easy way to tell you this, but now that we are working in Mabuhay together, it is your right to know all the details. Last night, we talked about the possibilities, practicalities, and potential glory of our business. Much of our talk was drink-fuelled bravado. Now, in the cold light of day, we must address certain issues that we cannot ignore." Hosokawa and Tanaka were nodding thoughtfully, not aware of the shock I was about to impart upon them. I guessed Tanaka was hoping to talk about Ogawa and how we might liberate him from his loyal duty. If that were so, he was about to be gravely disappointed. "Last night, I told you that two of our sites had already been unearthed. The first was excavated by the Philippine intelligence service, shortly after the cease-fire. I told you this organisation is led by a man called Santa Romana, perhaps the most powerful individual in that country. He is a greedy, murderous snake of a man who will stop at nothing to get his hands on our loot. To my blessed relief, Romana does not know where the sites are. I know he has been through hell and high water turning over the jungle looking, but his searches have led nowhere, and he realised he needed help from within our ranks. So, at the end of the war he made a deal with a man, Lieutenant Colonel Nishii."

I saw the surprise on their faces, and they shifted uncomfortably in their seats as they realised our enterprise was possibly compromised. Before they started to hit me with questions, I carried on.

"Nishii had been selected to oversee the initial phase of Golden Lily and was tasked with going to Luzon to carry out his orders. If my father's papers are correct—and I have no reason to doubt their truth—then Nishii was responsible for overseeing three of the fourteen sites, which means he is in possession of valuable information. To fulfill his duty Nishii enlisted the help of a Major Kojima, who at the time was on Yamashita's staff. It seems they went about their duty in a clinical manner and all was going as planned. Nishii's loyalty was never questioned, and he seemed the ideal man for the job. After the cease-fire Kojima was taken into custody by Romana, and although details are hard to come by, it seems that under duress he turned traitor and informed on Nishii, who by then had gone to ground and evaded capture.

"Kojima, out of operational necessity, knew only of the location of the first site and tried to strike a bargain with Romana. He was led along until he was of no further use, eventually meeting his end in a penal camp, stabbed to death, perhaps on the orders of Romana himself. The big fish was Nishii. If Romana could get to him, the ground would open up and spew forth immense riches."

Hosokawa was about to speak, but I waved him down, as I was not going to lose the thread of my distasteful narration. "It appears Romana did not have to look far. Nishii, no doubt concerned about his safety, broke his cover and made a treacherous deal with Romana. Now, I suspect Nishii, being no man's fool, realised that the knowledge he possessed could lead to his salvation. I have no idea what the actual terms of their deal were, but my father interceded and offered Romana a far more lucrative alternative in the form of a long-standing agreement. This deal was made on the understanding that Romana would agree to kill Nishii and provide proof of his death. The bounty on Nishii's head was set at two hundred thousand dollars."

This shocking revelation did not seem to disturb either of my companions. Perhaps the whole thing had descended into such a sordid low that neither could quite believe what they were hearing.

"At this point my father put into place the operation to excavate the second site. It was mainly undertaken as a show of faith and to reassure Romana that Nishii was now worthless to him. If all had gone as planned, there would be no need to talk of this matter. However, as you may have guessed, the road to riches is seldom smooth. Romana reported back that Nishii had become suspicious and escaped. My father recorded his own doubts, believing Romana had allowed Nishii free passage out of the country, as he could still be of use to him should the deal with my father founder. Romana still demanded his 'blood' money, insisting Nishii was a dead man walking. My father was faced with no option other than to pay the man. I believe they settled on half the original amount.

"The second site was eventually excavated under the terms we discussed last night, and my friends, that's where we now find ourselves. Nishii remains at large, a threat to our ambitions, our agenda, and even our liberty."

Hosokawa and Tanaka stared at me, both rendered speechless. I knew they would have lots of concerns, and I silently prayed that I would have the answers to ease the burden I had placed upon them. Hosokawa was the first to speak. "Do we have any idea where this Nishii may be?" I shook my head. Tanaka asked if Nishii had any family through which we could make enquiries, but again I replied in the negative. Hosokawa leaned back in his chair. "There must be some way of tracing him. I mean, he has to survive, and for that he would need money. I say concentrate on the money and you will find the man." I didn't see how this was at all helpful, but nodded encouragingly all the same.

After they had exhausted all reasonable suggestions and several ridiculous ones, I thought it time to tell them of the steps my father had put in place. I charged Hosokawa's glass with a generous shot of whiskey, then my own. Tanaka helped himself to a cup of jasmine tea. They had sunk into deep thought and looked all at sea. They needed something to cling to.

Tapping my pen against my glass to catch their full attention I carried on. "If there was one thing my father hated, it was gambling, which on the face of it seems strange, as he loved winning. It strikes me that his whole life was a struggle to load the odds in his favour, and to this end he was obsessed with the gathering and recording of information. He was driven by his desire to create an advantage and exploit any opportunity that would give him the edge to stay ahead of the game. He was represented in the States by his attorney Mr Harold Weinstein, who thought it wise to have eyes and ears inside the system."

Hosokawa immediately interrupted, a habit of his that was especially annoying when it broke my chain of thought. "Do we have total faith in this Weinstein's loyalty to our cause?"

His directness was quite challenging, and I thought perhaps he needed a little reminder of who was in charge here. I tried my level best not to sound irritated. "Absolutely, the man is way beyond doubt. He was my father's trusted aide, and his loyalty has naturally transferred to me. Weinstein has done all that has ever been asked of him and more. He has worked tirelessly to find a way into the system."

Hosokawa seemed satisfied and did not seem to take my answer as any kind of rebuke. I carried on. "It took many months before they found their man. As always, money rose above morality, and Weinstein was approached by a high-ranking official who said he could offer classified information for the right financial inducement. On the face of it, it seemed too good to be true and my father was sceptical, fearing it to be some kind of trap. He decided to put some distance between himself and this official, but not before instructing Weinstein to look further into the matter.

"To cut to the heart of the episode, an agreement was eventually struck, and the official received a tidy sum as a retainer for his services. The money was paid through various channels, impossible to trace back to its source.

"Only Weinstein and I know the identity of our source, and that is how it will remain. He has proved his worth and come through with valuable information from time to time. For instance, he was the first to make me aware that the federal government had established a task force to look into missing war loot." This worrying development had weighed on my mind for days, but after a great deal of research and probing for further information, Weinstein had assured me that it was nothing more than political posturing and existed only to appease the new liberal left. I explained all of this to Hosokawa and Tanaka, and told them I had issued instructions for Weinstein to contact our source and make the Nishii matter a priority.

Hosokawa looked as if he were readying himself to challenge me. "Toshio, this is all very well, but how does it really help us to find Nishii?"

"Well, if I found myself in Nishii's position, caught between the devil and the deep blue sea, I would try to make a deal, hand myself into American custody, and request political asylum in return for my knowledge."

Tanaka spoke up. "Why would the Americans be willing to make a deal with a wanted criminal?"

I made a point of praising his reasoning, but it was obvious that he was still a little "green" where the unsavoury side of human nature was concerned. "Think about it carefully," I said. "It is not beyond the realm of possibility that the Americans, too, have their eyes on the prize, and it does not take a great leap of imagination to figure out why. Access to millions of dollars of undocumented assets would enable rogue elements within their government to fund all kinds of illicit activities. Americans believe Communism to be the gravest threat to their way of life. They have an irrational fear of the collective and, I believe, will stop at nothing to wipe out the Reds, whatever the cost. So, Nishii would be a prize catch. The possibilities for the Americans are obvious, but also for a treacherous lowlife like Nishii, who would want the highest level of safety."

Now it was a matter of waiting to see if my reasoning was proved correct. There was no escaping the fact that should Nishii be found, he would need to be dealt with. Hosokawa and Tanaka looked suitably impressed, and they nodded thoughtfully. They seemed to understand perfectly well that they would be complicit in his demise. I found their relaxed attitude toward corruption and murder very reassuring.

We went on to debate many things during that long lunch. The food, delicious though it was, served only as a distraction as we talked ourselves deeper and deeper into the tangled mire that was Mabuhay. I asked Hosokawa to speed up the release of Daigo Hamma from the Chiba jail, as we could be in need of his services very soon. He had some positive news on that front. Reaching into his battered leather briefcase, he removed a slim document wallet. He passed it across the table. "Some background reading on Hamma. I think you will find it makes for an extraordinary tale." As I read through the file, Hosokawa leaned back in his chair, hands clasped behind his head with a smugness that suggested he was waiting to be praised for finding this remarkable fellow.

I clasped my hands together in delight. "This is one colourful character. I hope he will be thankful for the lifeline we are throwing his way. Makoto, excellent work."

I slid the file over to Tanaka, who soon became captivated with its contents. Hosokawa then went on to explain how we were to "spring" Hamma from his incarceration and avoid unwanted attention. One of his friends in the diplomatic office had been assigned Hamma's case and, being a lazy type, offered no objection to Hosokawa's recommendation that Hamma's extradition to France be refused on the grounds that the request failed to fulfill dual criminality, a legal point whereby the alleged crime had to be recognised by both countries. He was wanted for desertion from the French Foreign Legion. Because Japan no longer had an army as such, the offence was not recognised under Japanese law and therefore did not fully satisfy the Japanese government's condition that Hamma be granted an unbiased trial. Flimsy objections for sure, but enough smoke to allow Hamma to walk.

Hosokawa, being no fool, had kept his name well out of the matter, leaving his friend to sign the release documents. He proudly told us he would be making a personal visit to the Chiba jail in the next few days, just to make sure that Hamma fully understood the terms of his release. I had a good feeling about this Hamma character, and if my instincts were to prove correct, then perhaps I had found my general.

We talked well into the afternoon—in fact it was almost six when I suggested we call time on our little soiree. I had caught Hosokawa glancing at his watch at shorter and shorter intervals, a sure sign that he was restless to be somewhere else. After all, the man was used to keeping office hours. I clapped my hands, rose to my feet, and offered to stand them a few rounds of drinks down at the lobby bar. Hosokawa was onto it like a flash, gathering up his jacket and making ready for the door. Tanaka, I knew, was looking for the best way to decline without causing offence. I saved him the trouble by placing my hand on his shoulder and flashing my disarming smile. "Hideo, maybe you have other plans for this evening, eh? You wouldn't want to risk the wrath of Ayumi for a pair of old soaks such as Makoto and myself. Be off with you and enjoy your evening. I will see you tomorrow." Tanaka looked genuinely pleased to be spared from another evening of watching us get blotto, clumsily making his exit as he gave his thanks.

I put on my sunglasses and slung my jacket over my shoulder, and followed Hosokawa down to the bar. The lobby was bustling with an entirely different kind of clientele from those who were there when I arrived. The wives and children had been replaced by their menfolk, some in uniform, others dressed casually. I looked them over, hoping to pick up a few stateside fashion tips that may have made it over. I was disappointed, which was not surprising, really, as military types were a tad set in their ways where finery was concerned.

The air was thick with Cuban fug, and I felt myself gasping for a stogie. The lobby waiter appeared and showed us to a table set well apart from the merrymakers. Lowering his voice to almost a whisper he apologised for the noise. I strained to hear as he explained that there was an informal party for an officer who had been called back to the States. We placed our orders—two large gin and tonics—and I asked for a Clear Havana.

Hosokawa was eyeing up the floor waitress as she skilfully negotiated her way around groups of jiggering men, not spilling a drop from the delicately balanced glasses on her tray. It was obvious that the daring new uniforms for the female staff were proving popular. I scanned the bar, and every other man seemed to looking at some waitress or other, or more particularly the figure-hugging cheongsam dress they wore, which was proving to be a major distraction to normal conversation. After a few minutes our waitress appeared and set down our drinks. I noticed Hosokawa tilt his head a little to get a glimpse of thigh.

It goes without saying that this was all mere comedy to me. I was just about to make some witty observation when, through the crowd, I spotted a young fellow, his flame-red hair making him stand out like a beacon amongst a crowd of dullards. It was Jake. The sheer damn cheek of the man, only last evening striking me down not a stone's throw from this very place, and now here he was, laughing and joking amongst friends as if he didn't have a care in the world. It was obvious that he didn't give a fig about what he had done, the arrogant bastard. I let myself spiral down into an almighty dark pit, my anger bubbling under the surface.

"Toshio, are you feeling all right? You have come over all quiet, which is not like you at all."

Hosokawa's words seemed to hit me like an echo coming from a great distance. I drained my glass. "I'm fine, no problem. Let's have another and then call it a day, shall we?" Hosokawa looked a little crestfallen to have his evening pulled from under him, but he agreed all the same. I got the feeling that he was hoping to talk about his partnership and the terms of his 20 per cent. I was in no mood at all to go through any of that. My mind was filled with one thing and one thing only: revenge.

Hosokawa tried to tempt me into having another drink, but I was already on my feet and ready to head off. I laid the drinks charges on Hosokawa, and before he had time to protest, I was on my heels and heading for the door. I thought about summoning Ogawa to drive me, but the air had cooled and the walk would do me good.

Looking back over my shoulder, I saw Jake laughing amongst his friends. There was a lot of backslapping and handshaking going on, and it seemed their party was breaking up. I knew this was my chance, as if some divine power were offering me the opportunity to satisfy my need to make things even. I made my way out of the Empire and past the beautiful reflection pool, as yet unspoilt by discarded cigar butts. It was an unusually dark evening. The earlier downpour had left a blanket of thick clouds swirling ominously above. I walked a few minutes, stopping to take shelter in a doorway, as the rain had started to fall once more.

The street was deserted except for one man, head down, collar turned up against the rain. He was walking fast, no doubt heading for the Ginza tram terminus up ahead. I quickly turned my jacket inside out—the black lining offered more protection—looked up and down the deserted street, and, once satisfied I was safe from unwanted eyes, made my way back along the path I had just trodden. I stared straight ahead, my hands shaking, not from fear but from the exhilaration that revenge was now at hand.

Jake was walking at a pace, his red hair now sodden, plastered down by the rain, which was turning into a deluge. I reached into my pocket and took out the switchblade, pressed the clasp, and held it tightly in my palm. As we were about to pass each other, I sank the blade into his stomach, in and out, frenzied, repeatedly. He reeled back in shock, not quite understanding what had happened. He tried to take a swing at me, but the blade had altered his senses, and life was oozing away. He sank to his knees. I wiped the blade on his jacket and pushed him into the storm drain, where he would spend his last minutes on this earth.

Breathing like a mare after a race, I quickly crossed the street and made a circuitous path back to my house, all the while checking over my shoulder. The risk I had taken was enormous, but it had been well worth it. I felt euphoric, unstoppable. I had nothing to fear except fear itself. Deep down I knew I had committed a despicable act, and I briefly thought of a mother somewhere in the States crying over a son who had lost his life on a Tokyo backstreet. For a second I could not help but feel sympathy. Unwanted sentimentality aside, I had satisfied a primeval urge and proved myself worthy of the challenges that lay ahead, for when you have conquered the darkest corners of your mind, all other matters seem trivial in comparison.

I slept surprisingly well that night and awoke feeling remarkably invigorated. My sodden clothes were in a pile, where I had discarded them next to my bed. I closed my eyes and tried to focus on the sounds of the new day; the faint hum of traffic from the Ginza intersection and the rattle of the plumbing as the hot water jangled through the pipes seemed to confirm that this day was as normal as any other. I felt I had earned a few extra hours in bed, but as I lay there, going over the events that dominated my thoughts, paranoia started to creep up, and I knew I still needed to attend to vital matters of importance.

Throwing back the sheets, I swung my legs out of bed and stared at my clothes. I picked up my jacket, holding it between thumb and forefinger. On close inspection I couldn't see any bloodstains, but that didn't mean none were there. The same could not be said for my trousers. A dark stain on the right leg immediately set panic bells ringing. I had left my suede boots in the hall, and now, a vision of blood-soaked footwear decorating the shoe rack flew before my eyes. I threw on my dressing gown and bounded down the stairs to retrieve the incriminating items. Upon hearing the commotion Ogawa was quickly on the scene, no doubt thinking I was in need of his services. He was a little taken aback to see I was not yet dressed. The trace of a knowing smirk crept across his face, as he no doubt believed I had been up to morning frolics with Kawabata. How wrong could he be?

"May I be of any assistance, sir?" It was an effort to keep the irritation out of my voice as I told him I was fine, just checking the post, as I was expecting an important letter. He informed me that nothing had arrived, but he would keep an eye on the delivery. There was a bit of a standoff as we both waited for the other to leave. Eventually I asked Ogawa to go down to the kitchens and tell them I would like tea sent to my room. He bowed and left. I knew he didn't like being treated as a dogsbody. After all, who does? I quickly grabbed my boots off the rack and charged upstairs. Once safely back in my bedroom I checked them over. There were a few dark smears, but it was hard to tell if they were blood or common dirt. I opened the wardrobe and took out an old Boston bag, gathered up all the clothes off the floor, and stuffed them in along with the boots. I checked the jacket pocket, just to make sure the switchblade was still there. Satisfied that all the dastardly items were present, I secured the fasteners together with a small padlock taken from an attaché case. Not knowing what to do next, I placed the bag well out of sight at the back of the wardrobe, where it would have to stay until I worked out a disposal plan.

A knock on the door made me jump. I was getting jittery. The bravado I had felt earlier was all but gone. This would not do at all. I needed to get a grip of myself or the unthinkable consequences of my actions would bear down on me. I had forgotten that I had asked for tea to be sent up. I let the maid set down the tray, and once she had gone, went to the drinks cabinet and poured myself a large brandy, which I slugged back.

Nervous sweat had left an unpleasant odour about me. I needed a bath. Whilst the water was running, I slumped into an easy chair, massaged my temples, and frantically went over the events of the previous night. Had I overlooked anything? Could anybody have seen me? I kept telling myself to calm down, there was nothing to fear, to behave normally.

Minutes later, relaxing in the hot water, everything seemed to come into focus, and I had a flash of inspiration. I was out of the bath in a shot and got dressed quickly, selecting a casual camel-coloured two-piece suit and chestnut roll-neck sweater. I checked my face in the mirror. The bruises had started to take on a yellowish tone, and suddenly, like a bolt out of the blue, it hit me: my sunglasses. I searched frantically through the contents of the Boston bag, my heart leaping out of my chest, hoping against hope. It was no use: They were not to be found. I was having palpitations. Had they fallen out of my pocket as I went about my business? It was too risky to go back and search. There was nothing for it but to stand firm and bluff it out. I cursed my stupidity, threw the clothes back into the bag, and in the foulest of moods went downstairs to look for Ogawa.

The March air was crisp and chilly; spring had yet to show its face. I told Ogawa to drive me over to the Yokohama factory. This was an unusual request, as I seldom involve myself with the practical matters of production. However, with the product launch only a matter of weeks away, it seemed appropriate to drop in and keep them on their toes, so to speak. Ogawa must have picked up on my mood, as he kept a respectable silence. We covered the journey in no time at all. The roads were very quiet, and I spent most of the time lost in thought, desperately trying to place my blasted Bausch and Lomb sunglasses. We pulled up at the gatehouse. The guard on the barrier walked round to Ogawa's side of the Bentley, and they exchanged a few words before he smartly raised the bar to allow us through. No doubt he would be straight on the phone to alert those ahead that the boss was on his way.

We pulled up outside the main entrance. I let Ogawa go off to find his own refreshments but told him to stand by, as I did not know how long my visit would take. He asked if he could carry my bag, but I waved him away and went into the reception. I hadn't been here for an age, yet it was all so familiar. The sounds, the smells immediately brought back many childhood memories. I had spent many long days here, as my father used to insist on dragging me along and then inevitably abandoned me in the company of the office ladies. This place was the flagship production facility of Hamazaki Electricals. It was from here that we produced most of the country's steel cables. The business was still in operation, but would be gradually scaled back as Mabuhay Portable Electrics took hold.

I was slightly at a loss where to begin my surprise visit, but Nojiri, the line manager, appeared, confirming my earlier notion of advance warnings. He looked a little flustered to have his day interrupted and did not know what to make of my surprise visit. Why do people always fear the worst when they see me? "Sir, I am sorry, I was not informed of your visit. Is there any way I may be of assistance?"

I looked around as if considering his offer. "Is Tanaka on site?"

"I'm afraid not, sir, though I do believe he is expected later this afternoon."

I feigned disappointment. "Well, in that case, Nojiri, you will have to be my guide."

He visibly puffed up in a swell of self-importance on being given this honour. "It would be my pleasure, sir. Shall I take your bag?" I declined his offer, which he must have taken as strange; nonetheless he didn't press the matter. "Where would sir like to start?"

I thought for a moment or two, then pointed directly ahead. "For old times' sake, I would like to take a look at the smelting plant." Nojiri bowed, and we walked towards a building which was set way apart from the main body of the factory. At the entrance a foreman gave us both a thick protective apron, eye goggles, gloves, a helmet, and a mouth guard to wear. After the rigmarole of putting on those coarse items, we made our way into the plant. When I was a child, this process had always held a strange fascination for me. The sheer mind-numbing fact that iron ore was melted down at 1400 degrees was magical to my young ears. Small cars would be loaded with ore and ascend the conveyor. Upon reaching the summit, some forty feet up, they would tip their load sideways, feeding the blast furnace, a process that was repeated continuously around the clock, day after day. The furnace would run for five or six years before finally being cooled down in order to change the earth bricks that lined the kiln.

Nojiri and I stared at the little cars for a moment or two. I distracted his attention, pointing over at something in the far corner. "What is that pipe? It seems to be leaking." We walked over to have a closer look. By now the Boston bag was halfway up the belt, and in seconds its contents were incinerated, removed forever from the face of the earth. I glanced over my shoulder just in time to see the bag drop down into the molten hell. A whiff of black smoke curled out of the furnace, and in the blink of an eye, my problem was solved.

Nojiri didn't seem to notice that I had "misplaced" my bag, as he was too busy berating one of the maintenance men about the importance of regular checks of the plant. The leaky pipe, which now appeared perfectly normal, was attracting a fair bit of attention, and I decided to move on. I asked Nojiri about the production lines. He fairly glowed as he informed me we would be able to start rolling out products within the next two weeks. I declined his offer to show me over the assembly lines. My purpose for being here had been fulfilled, and I was eager to get going. Nojiri tried to press some tea on me, but I told him I had to make my way back, as I had an important meeting to prepare for.

We walked through the heart of the factory, where my workers were hard at their tasks. I stopped to look around and in that moment realised that the vision I had had some six months earlier was to become reality: Mabuhay was almost ready. I told Nojiri to go back to his work, as I could make my own way. He seemed a little hesitant to leave me, but bowed and went about his business.

I found Ogawa waiting for me in the lobby. He was a little surprised to be summoned for the drive back to Ginza so soon after our arrival and scuttled off to bring the Bentley round to the front door. The receptionist appeared bearing a tea tray, which she almost dropped when she saw that it was me and not Ogawa now waiting. I accepted a cup from her and tried to think of something to say, only to find my mind a complete blank. I was drained of energy, and the thought of a long afternoon nap was very inviting.

The Bentley ate up the miles of the return journey like an insatiable beast, but as we got closer to the city, the traffic thickened, and in the last mile or so, we slowed to walking pace. I noticed several police officers standing on the street corners, some holding clipboards and stopping pedestrians to question them. This was obviously the start of the investigation into Jake's death. My senses were immediately heightened. I stared out the rear window, curious, all the while trying to appear as nonchalant as my nerves would allow. "Ogawa, what is going on?"

He shook his head. "I'm not quite sure, sir. I believe there was some kind of altercation last night and a man was taken to hospital." I felt my face drain of colour. If anyone had been studying me at the moment I do believe they would have seen the guilt written across my face as plain as day. Hospital! I could not believe it. Surely not. No man could have survived my attack. I had lashed the blade into him many times. My hands were trembling as we pulled up outside the house. I let Ogawa open the door for me, stepped out, and took a big gasp of the crisp Ginza air.

An ugly, squat grey car was parked ahead of the Bentley, looking out of place amongst the finer vehicles of the area. It was one of the new domestically produced cars. The Americans had only recently allowed us to start making our own vehicles once more, and this was the disappointing result, a Toyota SA. Having such a car parked outside my home could mean only one thing: The police had come to call. I had to be on my mettle. I gave the shisha lion a pat on the head for luck and went inside. It was important to appear as normal as possible, so I made as if to head up to my rooms. Ayumi appeared in the hallway and, upon seeing my bruised face, held her hand to her mouth in shock. Before she could speak, I told her it was nothing to worry about and I was perfectly fine.

I was heading for the stairs when she called me. "Brother, there are two men here to see you—police officers." So, there it was. I took a deep breath, gave her a reassuring smile, and followed her into the drawing room. With hand outstretched and all the bravado I could muster, I greeted the men before me. "Officers, so sorry to keep you waiting. My sister tells me you wish to speak with me."

The older of the two stepped forward. "I'm Senior Investigator Hirai, and this is Investigator Ishida. We are from the Tokyo Metropolitan Police." We shook hands, and I prayed that he did not pick up on my jitters. I asked them to be seated and called for the maid to bring us some tea. The officers said that would not be necessary, but I insisted all the same. Ayumi had taken a seat, and I was glad she was there. Her presence seemed to give me a bit of extra courage.

Hirai was looking at my face. I knew he was desperate to ask me how I had come of my injuries, but he held back for the time being. "Sir, an innocent young man was viciously attacked last night in this very neighbourhood. We are making enquiries into whether any of the residents saw or heard anything out of the ordinary." The younger officer, Ishida, took out his notebook ready to make a record of my reply.

"My word, this is awful, but I don't see how I may be of any help to your investigation," I said. I hesitated for a moment and touched my battered face—a moment of pure theatre. "Where did this unfortunate incident take place?"

Hirai leaned forward and told me what of course I already knew. I had to be damn careful not to let anything slip. I leaned back in my chair, shaking my head in feigned shock. Looking Hirai straight in the eye, I spun my tale. "Two nights ago I took that very path. I had been drinking with some colleagues over at the Empire and had rather overdone it, so I decided to take the short walk home, get some air, and clear my head for the next day. On the way back, up ahead of me, I saw a group of roughs. I decided to cross to the other side to avoid them, lost my balance, and ended up taking a tumble into the nullah. My face took the brunt of it, as you can see." I looked at Ayumi, who was visibly shocked.

Hirai leaned forward, sensing some kind of breakthrough here. "Sir, did you manage to get a good look at this group of 'roughs'?"

I strained my brow in mock thought. "I'm sorry, officer, I did not. In fact, I could not even say how many of them there were. I'm afraid I can't help much, other than to say they had scarpered by the time I had got back to my feet."

Hirai seemed to be in deep thought, and the silence was quite unsettling. "Sir, I have to tell you that you may have had a very lucky escape. Last night at around nine o'clock an American serviceman was attacked very close to that place. He was not as fortunate as your good self. It could very well be that those roughs got a little desperate and went too far. This being an affluent neighbourhood and all, they must have been on the lookout for easy pickings."

I let the mock shock show on my face. "This poor fellow who was attacked, I mean, is he seriously hurt?"

Hirai shook his head from side to side. "I'm sorry to say, he did not survive his injuries. He had been stabbed several times and was left by his assailant to die in a storm drain."

Ayumi let out a shocked cry. "How dreadful to think something so awful could happen so close to here. It is unthinkable. I do not know what has become of the streets today." She looked at Hirai. "Officer, do we need to be worried? Is it safe to walk our streets without fear?" Hirai assured her that he believed this was just an unfortunate incident and certainly not the normal way of things.

Ishida, who had been quiet until now, was tapping his pencil against his notebook as he looked at me. "Sir, may I ask where you were last night?" Hirai shot him a look which I could not read.

"I was over at the Empire on business all day, had a few sundowners in the bar, and left around seven."

Ishida wrote down my reply and without looking up, continued. "How did you make your way home last night?"

Without missing a beat, I haughtily replied, "I walked."

Ishida sensed something was not quite right. "After what had happened the previous evening and given that it was raining would it not have been prudent to arrange some transport for yourself?" This Ishida chap was starting to get my back up.

"My driver is quite elderly, and I had let him stand down for the day. Besides, I had no reason to think anything untoward would befall me."

Ishida nodded. "Of course, sir. Just one more thing. Our victim was also in the Empire last night. He had attended a function there. It may prove that the attackers were lurking in the vicinity with the intent of 'rolling' a wealthy customer."

I considered his line of thought. "That sounds possible."

Hirai, not wishing to be upstaged by his underling, chipped in. "The victim's wallet was untouched, which leads us to think the attackers may have panicked and run off. Did you see anything untoward on the way home last night?"

I tried for a look that conveyed deep concern. "I'm sorry, officers, I neither saw nor heard anything, and it was just a normal night as far as my own walk home was concerned. I really wish there was something I could say to help you with your enquiry."

I was hoping this would be enough to end the matter, but Ishida was a persistent officer. "The victim was a young American serviceman of quite distinctive appearance. He had red hair, which made him stand out in a crowd. Do you remember seeing him in the Empire last night?"

I shook my head. "I'm sorry, I can't help you further. If anything comes to mind, I will, of course be in touch."

Hirai was on his feet ready to make his way out. "Thank you, sir, your help is greatly appreciated. I will have an officer stop by to take a full statement, at a time which is convenient to you, of course."

Ishida looked a little unconvinced. The man was beginning to make me nervous. "Just one more question: Last night, in the bar, did you notice anyone out of place?" I spread my arms to show I had nothing to add. Ishida went on. "Our victim managed to speak a little before he bled out completely." Ayumi took a deep breath, shocked by Ishida's bluntness. Hirai apologised for any distress, but Ishida carried on. "He was delirious by the time the medical team attended him, and his speech was garbled. Nobody could make out what he was saying. One medical officer, however, swears that the victim was repeating the same words, *champagne man*, over and over. Does that alert you to anything? What I mean to say is, does it bring back anything that might help the enquiry?"

Again I shook my head. "It means nothing at all. I only wish I could help more, I really do."

I walked the officers to the door, relieved that the interview was finally over. But I counted my blessings too soon. Ishida turned to face me. "Would it be possible to have a quick word with your driver?"

Without missing a beat, I smiled. "Of course." I asked the maid to go and find Ogawa, excused myself, and left the officers waiting in the hallway. No doubt they wanted to confirm a few things with Ogawa—about that I had no worries. I went up to my room and looked out on the street below, and after a few minutes the officers appeared on the footpath and got into their little car. As they drove away, they left a cloud of dirty black smoke hanging in the air.

Chapter 5
Ayumi Tanaka
Tokyo
1955

As the black limousine slowly drew to a halt alongside where we were all gathered, I could almost feel the tension rising from Hideo. He had been in a strange mood ever since we'd been invited to be amongst the privileged few at today's commemoration ceremony. The past month had seen him behaving entirely out of character, and at times I felt like I was sharing my life with a complete stranger. He resisted the invitation with as much rational argument as he could muster, but I stood firm and demanded that he stand by our side on this most auspicious of days.

His attitude towards the day's ceremony had taken me completely by surprise. I had naturally assumed that he wanted to pay his respects and would be grateful to have the opportunity to do so. After all, he had served our country and seen his comrades in arms fall before his very eyes, an experience that must have touched him in ways most of us would never be able to fully understand. As his wife I had hoped he would let me into the troubled depths of his soul, but Hideo was adept at controlling his emotions, and I never pressed him. He was a good husband, caring, and thoughtful, and he had given me a lot to be thankful for, yet there were times when I felt like pieces were missing from our marriage.

Perhaps we could never be complete; both of us carried so much hurt from the past. We had been blessed with a child: Tatsuya, my joy and the light in my life, the little boy who had brought me the happiness that I believed I had lost forever.

Today I would say a prayer of thanks to the gods for gifting me my little angel, and would also pray for all those dear brave men who laid down their lives for some cause they barely understood. I planned to pray for all the mothers who lost their boys and who now had to sit out their days with hearts weeping. I hoped my prayers would reach all the tortured souls who were still grieving for their loved ones, for it was the ones left behind who had to carry their suffering with them like a dead weight. I also planned to say a special prayer for my dear lost first husband, Ryosuke, my love for so short a time but the precious memories of whom would never leave my heart. My love forever, my Ryo, is your spirit here? Can you see me now? Here I stand, as another man's wife, but you will never be forgotten. You were my first love, and my heart will always belong to you. I beg your forgiveness. Yes, I will pray with all my heart, for that is all I can do.

We were lined up with the regimented formality that the occasion demanded, my brother Toshio and Makoto Hosokawa standing to my left, the two of them showing uncharacteristic patience. Toshio had whispered in my ear earlier, "I know he is the Emperor, but I wish he would get a move on!" Typical of my brother—always ready to take the heat out of the rigid pomposity of such a sombre occasion. However, his attempts at humour were not welcome on this day, for this was a sacred place, and even he should have given it the respect it deserved. This was Yasukuni, the place where the spirits of the fallen are enshrined for eternity. We had gathered to honour the memory of all those who gave the ultimate sacrifice, for this day marked ten years since the end of the war.

We all bowed our heads slightly and lowered our collective gaze as His Excellency passed us as if we didn't exist. When the last of his entourage had gone by, the Lord Chamberlain gave a slight bow in our direction and we all followed, keeping a respectful distance. The clouds in the sky had deserted and left us all at the mercy of the morning sun. Despite the early hour, the heat was stifling, and all the men in their formal morning suits had perspiration rolling down their faces. I considered myself fortunate to have a little shade from my parasol, but the August sun was not to be thwarted, and I felt my body burning inside the thick folds of my kimono.

There was an almost deafening and hypnotic noise coming from the trees as the cicadas went through their own morning ritual. For a moment I felt quite faint, and the remaining short distance to the "Tori" gates suddenly seemed much longer. We were obliged to pause whilst His Excellency and his party went through the rituals of paying their respects. I wondered what must be going through the mind of the Emperor. Ten years and a day earlier, he was a living god amongst his subjects, and now he was a mere mortal amongst us. After the surrender, the Emperor had been "obliged" to renounce his status by the Americans, and in return he was allowed to remain as a symbol of national unity. Did he still believe he was a divine being? His courtiers obviously maintained the pretence as they went about their duties in reverential fashion.

I lowered my parasol and handed it to one of the attendants standing nearby. My husband was bearing the heat with admirable dignity, his military bearing in marked contrast to my brother, who was fidgeting around with his collar and grumbling under his breath. Hosokawa was, as always, on social alert, allowing himself surreptitious glances at those around him. He was a man who never forgot a name or a face and was constantly making connections. He did not believe in coincidence and saw life as a grand design. Who was talking with whom and the order in which the guests were to be called forward were the kinds of details he looked for and that he filed away in that memory of his for future reference. His powers of recollection were staggering, and he never ceased to amaze me as he instantaneously plucked out faces from our childhood and pointed them out to me, people we had all forgotten long ago but were never forgotten by Makoto Hosokawa.

His role in Mabuhay was still unclear to me. He was often out of the country on business, and when pressed, Hideo merely dismissed his responsibilities as overseas negotiations. Whatever Hosokawa was doing, it was obvious that the business was prospering. The newspapers often featured articles on Mabuhay's amazing rise. It had been recently reported that Mabuhay was now the country's second-largest manufacturer and supplier of consumer products, which was why we found ourselves in the first wave of invited guests to be called forward to pay our respects—a position I was most grateful to be in, as I felt I could bear the stifling heat no longer. We watched in silence as the members of the royal party were led by a sombre monk back to their waiting motorcade.

We were called forward and climbed the few creaking wooden steps. Solemnly we bowed our heads, and each of us said our silent prayers. I found myself lost in the moment, unable to focus on my prayers. My mind had taken me back in time, twelve years before, when I stood in my white wedding kimono, my face painted white and my Ryosuke beside me. That was the happiest day my heart had ever known. My prayers were forgotten, lost to the wind, and I stood numbly, head bowed, and allowed the tears to roll down my cheeks. Hosokawa and Toshio, having finished their own silent rituals, turned to the left and led us to one side to allow the next guests to pay their respects. I fumbled with my obi and found a handkerchief and dabbed at my cheeks. Toshio glanced at me and gave me an understanding look that spoke more than words. Hideo had been stoic throughout and did not even care to look at my face at all. I wondered if he prayed for his own lost family. Surely today of all days, they must be in his thoughts. He had often said that a common place of worship and remembrance was needed for all the souls who had lost their lives and not just a place to remember brave soldiers.

We made our way back along the side of the path to our waiting cars. Ogawa san was waiting by the Bentley and upon our approach opened the rear door for Hideo and me to slide into the back seat. Toshio and Hosokawa travelled separately in the new Rolls-Royce that my brother had recently had shipped from England. They were driven by my brother's personal assistant and aide Ken Miyazaki, who had been a member of my brother's personal staff for nearly five years and throughout that time had maintained an aura of mystery and menace. I had always felt uneasy in his presence, but Toshio had insisted that Miyazaki was an invaluable member of his team and always performed his duties with uncompromising loyalty. I had complained to Hideo that having a person constantly lurking in the background would give people the wrong impression. Hideo dismissed my concerns, saying that high-profile figures were easy targets for the deranged and Toshio was merely taking sensible precautions.

Hideo reminded me of the incident that had led to Miyazaki's appointment. It was five years earlier and the same day Hideo had proposed marriage, and he and Makoto had joined my brother to celebrate our engagement. After their little party, Toshio had seen Hideo back to the Empire and then decided to walk back to our house alone to clear his head. On the short walk home he was attacked by a gang of youths who demanded money and his gold watch fob. Toshio rather foolishly refused to hand them anything, and a scuffle ensued that left Toshio with a severely bruised cheek and painful sides. The next morning when he came down to breakfast and reluctantly told me of his misadventure, I urged him to visit a physician and report it to the authorities. His pride would not extend that far, and he dismissed my concerns. The very next day a young American serviceman was also attacked in the same vicinity, only this time the victim was not so fortunate. He was repeatedly stabbed and left to die by the side of the road. The police made routine enquiries around our neighbourhood, and after much prompting from me, Toshio finally told them about his own encounter. The police were grateful for his assistance and told him they believed it was the work of the same gang and he was lucky to escape with his life. After this incident Toshio felt the need to increase his personal security; hence the appearance of Ken Miyazaki.

Our cars pulled away, leaving the Imperial Shrine of Yasukuni behind us but always in our thoughts. I asked Hideo if he had snatched a glance at the Emperor. It was the closest either of us had ever been to His Excellency, and perhaps most people would have let their natural curiosity take over for a few moments. Hideo shook his head and smiled for the first time in days. "No, I could not bring myself to look at him. Old habits die hard." Hideo had told me that when he was a child, he was taken to a royal procession by his schoolmasters and that as the regal coach passed them, all the children were ordered to avert their gaze and look at their shoes. A teacher wielding a cane made sure there were no dissenters. He turned to me and said, "Did you sneak a peep at His Divine Excellency?"

There was the merest hint of sarcasm in his tone, which I chose to ignore. "No, I managed to resist the temptation too, but I did manage a glimpse of his little brother." Hideo muttered something that I could not catch. He stared out the window, smiling away to himself, but did not seem to want me to share in his mirth, so I did not press.

We were heading back to the Empire, where we were to host a luncheon to mark the day's occasion. It was not to be a celebratory affair but one in keeping with the solemn nature of remembrance. Toshio and Makoto were to join us later at the Empire. I had warned my brother to show restraint where sake was concerned, a warning I feared would not be taken too seriously. Hideo leaned forward and asked Ogawa to take a detour and drive by Shinjuku station. I gave him a curious look, but he was lost in thought. We travelled in silence for a few minutes, and then as we approached the station, Hideo asked Ogawa to stop the car by the side of the road. He asked us to wait for a few moments, and got out of the car. I watched him in the rearview mirror as he went into a nearby flower shop. He emerged a minute or two later with a few red flowers in his hand. He stopped on the pavement and bowed his head. At first I thought he was studying the bus timetable that was fixed to the lamppost. It suddenly dawned on me that he was praying. He stayed for a few moments and then placed a flower into the drainage wall, bent down and touched the ground, and then put his fingers to his lips. He climbed back into the car and told Ogawa to drive home.

I looked at him and he must have felt my curiosity, for he turned to me and said, "That place is my personal Yasukuni." He did not need to explain any further, for I knew exactly what he meant. I put my hand on his knee to show my support. He gave me the remaining flower, a small red rose, and said, "This is for all of our sufferings." Had he noticed my tears back at the shrine? I could not tell, for Hideo was a complex character and a man who usually kept his emotions firmly to himself. This was a rare display of affection and one I hoped would signal the start of more shared feelings between us.

We arrived back at the Empire a little after ten in the morning. The head bellboy, Noguchi, was the first to our door, and as he opened it, he greeted us with his usual refrain, "Welcome home, Mr and Mrs Tanaka," as opposed to "Welcome to the Empire," which he must have said more than a hundred times a day. As much as I disliked it, the Empire was our home. Hideo had become so attached to the place that he downright refused to even consider moving somewhere more befitting a married couple with a young child. I had suggested to him many times that we give up residence there, but the man was obstinate. I had even asked Toshio to use his influence, but his half-hearted attempts at persuasion were to no avail, and for the time being we were the Empire's longest-staying "guests," for I could never bring myself to consider it my home.

I knew I should not complain too bitterly, for life there was more than comfortable. All our needs were well catered for, and we were pampered like spoilt poodles. I was not required to perform even the simplest household chores. All our catering, cleaning, and laundry was done for us, and the closest I got to being a housewife was choosing the menu for the evening meal and arranging the gorgeous flowers that were delivered daily. During the early years of our married life my daily routine was quite similar to the one I had enjoyed at the family residence over in Ginza, but when Tatsuya came along, our suite suddenly seemed a little inadequate. I had hoped that Hideo would now see the sense behind my reasoning and finally accept that a move was the only solution. You may imagine my displeasure when I found out that Hideo had entered discussions with the Empire to extend our accommodation to include the two large rooms on either side of our own suite. To my further annoyance, I was not even consulted and was expected to accept it without question. I saw it as a sign that Hideo was finally exerting his power.

Toshio had taken Hideo into the company under circumstances that appeared rather bizarre. Hideo was down on his luck at the time, but my brother had spotted his potential and taken him under his wing as his protégé. Toshio often told me that Hideo was the heartbeat of Mabuhay, the man who turned his visions into reality. It was to Hideo that Mabuhay owed the most thanks, and because of his inspirational genius, Mabuhay was producing the products that were revolutionising life in homes across the country. My brother had the talent for spotting talent. That was why he surrounded himself with the best and brightest and rewarded them with riches beyond their wildest dreams, snaring their unquestioning loyalty.

As we walked through the lobby, which was bustling with guests eager to check out, an experience that I might never have, I was reminded of the reward Toshio bestowed upon Hideo on the day of our wedding. During the banquet Toshio rose to give one of his speeches. I smiled like a good sister should, but I was dreading what he might have to say, for he was sufficiently inebriated and quite emotional. I need not have been concerned; he kept his speech short, sweet, and to the point. He said he had gained a brother and wished us all the happiness in the world, and when we were all standing, he proposed a toast to our health and a golden future together. After we had all settled down, a waiter approached

Hideo bearing a silver tray upon which was a sealed envelope. Naturally I recognised the ruby-red Hamazaki seal and looked over at my brother, who was pretending not to notice and busying himself talking to Hosokawa. Hideo took the envelope and, out of the view of the other guests, discreetly opened it. He read the enclosed letter, and the growing look of shock and surprise on his face was a picture to behold. Luckily everyone was too busy enjoying dinner, and I doubt anyone noticed. Hideo handed me the letter to read. Toshio had written that this glorious day should be marked with a gift befitting the occasion. He had presented Hideo with a twenty per cent share in Mabuhay, which put him on equal terms with Hosokawa—a gift that instantaneously made him the third-wealthiest man in the room. We both looked over to Toshio. He and Makoto raised their glasses in unison and mouthed "Congratulations." I too was dumbfounded. My brother's generosity was legendary, but this surpassed anything we could have imagined.

We let Noguchi escort us as far as the staircase and then made our own way up to our suite. There was still little more than an hour to go before the first of our guests were expected to arrive for the luncheon. I still had to bathe, change, and inspect the function room to ensure the place settings were all in order. However, I could do none of those things without checking on Tatsuya first. I left Hideo to himself and went to the end room where my handmaiden, Araki san, was caring for my boy. When I opened the door, I surprised Araki san, who was standing by the window cradling Tatsuya. She bowed to me and held my little joy out for me to take. I held him close to my breast, burying my face close to his and breathing in his sweet scent.

This was what gave my life meaning. I wished Hideo felt the same. I was sure he loved the boy as much as I did; he just never demonstrated his affection. Toshio, on the other hand, was completely the opposite: the love-struck, besotted uncle who couldn't leave Tatsuya alone. He was forever enquiring about his health and whether I had done this or that. It was my hope that one day some of Toshio's love would find its way into Hideo's heart and he would allow himself to experience the true joy of fatherhood. My brother would make an ideal father, and I prayed that one day he would be blessed with a child of his own.

But I liked to consider myself a woman with a realistic view of what surrounded her. I was no fool, for I knew my brother's heart was drawn elsewhere and he was never to be a father. I prayed that his predilection would not lead him into a life of perpetual loneliness. There was a time not too long ago when he genuinely seemed ecstatically happy. He had tried to hide the reason for his joy but had failed to deceive anyone. A young man had befriended Toshio, and the two of them had become quite intimate. I knew he had often stayed the night here in this very suite when my brother had called this place his home. Their relationship had obviously deepened, as Toshio was constantly allowing him to sleep over in his rooms even after he moved back to the Ginza house upon Father's death. I would watch from my bedroom window and often see my brother's special friend taking his early morning leave, exiting from the rear of the house. It would have been funny if it hadn't been so sad.

I felt for Toshio. It must be awful to have to hide your true feelings behind a mask of deceit. Toshio was in a state of shock after Father's death, and his friend was obviously helping him through that difficult and emotional time. I would never have dreamed of talking it over with him—it was just something that would remain unspeakable between us—but there was a time when I wished I could help him.

Shortly after Hideo and I announced our engagement, Toshio informed us that some urgent company business required immediate attention. An opportunity to invest in a company in Hong Kong that supplied electrical parts had arisen, and Toshio was determined not to let the chance pass him by. He said he needed Hideo's technical expertise to review the company. It was decided that the two of them would make the journey to Hong Kong, and the travel arrangements were made. I was worried about it and begged them to rethink the trip. The war had left a legacy of anti-Japanese feeling in Hong Kong, and I feared for their safety. My brother told me not to worry, that everything would be fine. It was about this time that Ken Miyazaki was appointed to my brother's staff, and he was to make the trip as well.

Anyway, the trip was undertaken, and I gathered it was not the success that Toshio had hoped it would be. Contracts were not exchanged, and Hideo and Toshio returned in the dourest of spirits. My brother fell into the darkest of depressions, unable to leave his room for days. His drinking had become heavier, and he was not eating at all well. I asked Hideo what had happened on the trip, but he just shrugged it off and said negotiations had failed to produce the desired outcome. I had wanted to seek help for Toshio, but Hideo said my brother was stronger than us all and to just give him time to rest. We had cause to be thankful to Hosokawa, for he stepped up to fill the void and provided the business with the day-to-day leadership it desperately needed.

My brother's descent into despair was compounded by the absence of his special friend, who never visited again. I wanted to enquire about his whereabouts, for I was sure Toshio was pining desperately for his company. Had they had some kind of tiff that neither of them could get over? I would never know, but I knew

Toshio was in the depths of despair and needed all the help he could get.

That was five years ago, and now he was a different man. I still saw glimpses of his old, depressed self—the long, forlorn stares out of windows and the moments of insecurity were still there—but on the whole, Toshio was mostly restored as the force we all knew him to be. It was that force that was driving our little luncheon today. Although we, Mr and Mrs Tanaka, were to host the function, it had, as always, an underlying purpose, which of course was Mabuhay business. I feared the men around me would at some point find the opportunity to put their heads together and "talk shop," if only for the briefest of moments, and do whatever it was they did. Time was of the essence, so I kissed Tatsuya goodbye for the second time that day, although it was not even eleven in the morning. I handed him back to Araki san and went to our suite next door to make myself ready for the luncheon.

I found Hideo, still in his morning attire, sitting in the lounge. He beckoned me over to watch the television that he had recently installed in the corner of the room. He was looking in wonder at the grainy pictures; I knew he was more fascinated by the science of television than by the dull broadcasts on offer. Today, however, it was a news report that held his attention. The item featured His Excellency's visit to Yasukuni, which had taken place only a few hours ago. Hideo drew my attention to this fact and was going on about the possibilities that television would be able to offer. He was talking about "real-time" broadcasts or something like that; I was only half listening, as time was against me.

I went into the bathroom and left him to his thoughts. Why is it that men seem to be able to work time around their needs, whilst we women are constantly trying to accommodate many tasks in a short time? I quickly bathed and changed into a simple, formal, one-piece black dress. I did not have the time to have my hair redone, so I had to settle for changing the long coloured hair-pins. I decided to wear the pearls that Hideo had presented me as a wedding gift. I looked myself over in the mirror, closely examin-ing my hair. I had recently noticed that the few grey hairs were starting to multiply. Since Tatsuya's birth I felt as though I had aged in one great leap. The stress of childbirth had left its marks on my body and lined my face. My physician had cautioned me to take care during the pregnancy, and on his advice, I had spent the latter part in my room resting. Bearing a child at thirty-eight comes with numerous risks, all of which passed me by without concern. Unlike my brother I was not a vain person, but it was still a little disturbing to see myself aged in so short a time.

Hideo had never commented on my appearance and had diplomatically avoided mentioning my inability to lose weight after the birth. I often wondered whether he was still physically attracted to me. He had not touched me at all since we found out about the pregnancy. The last time we'd made love was the night Tatsuya was conceived. I did not particularly miss his passion, which was always more dutiful than sensual, but I did worry that we may have moved into a marriage of companionship. I was nearly four years older than Hideo, and I believed thirty-five was too young to turn his back on carnal desire. I had only ever known two men intimately—Ryosuke, my late husband, and Hideo. I knew it was wicked and immoral to make comparisons, but inev-itably I found myself unable to avoid doing so. I had made love with Hideo many times with eyes closed, guiltily wishing it was Ryosuke on top of me. Did that make me a disloyal and wanton wife? Sometimes I shamed myself.

Much to my annoyance Hideo did not appear to have made much progress in his preparations, so I left him to get ready alone and made my way downstairs through the lobby to the function room where our luncheon party was to be held. With dismay I noticed that I had only about thirty minutes to ensure all the preparations had been undertaken and our special instructions fulfilled. We had hosted so many functions, meetings, and events at the Empire that the management are fully aware of our standards and requirements. In fact, the Hamazaki family had patronised the Empire for decades. I could remember attending weddings, wakes, and countless other gatherings there as a little girl. I had even attended the grand opening in 1923 as a mischievous six-year-old—an event remembered more for the great earthquake that hit Tokyo on the very same day. The mere fact that the hotel survived was, to my father, confirmation that this was indeed a blessed place.

The Empire also survived the war but not without some bomb damage to the south wing. Ten years ago the war had left this place virtually uninhabitable. It was said that the vermin that infested the hotel's foundations made more noise than the guests. During the occupation someone deemed the hotel a suitable place to billet the top American officers and their families, so at great expense, a huge cleanup and refurbishment was undertaken. The hotel was commandeered by the occupation forces, and for a time our living arrangements came under scrutiny. Despite this we were able to maintain our suite, albeit at considerable inconvenience, as we lived through most of the major refurbishments and the disruption they caused.

In time the Empire was quickly restored to something resembling its grand past. The hotel had served as a backdrop to our lives; it had been a second home, and now, I thought with a heavy heart, it was my only home. However, on days like this there were many reasons to feel grateful for the organisation and the devoted efforts of the hotel's employees. I had complete confidence in the staff; nonetheless, it did not pay to leave anything to chance.

For today's event we had chosen the Sakura Lounge, which was a relatively small room but tasteful and perfectly understated. We had used this room as a reception area at my wedding, where guests were received before being shown into the Peacock Hall. As I entered the room, I found that one "guest" had already arrived. Toshio was moving around the low tables, which were set out in a large rectangle. He had his back to me and with drink in hand was inspecting the name cards at each setting. The air was pungent with the odour from his Turkish cigarette, a foul habit he had recently picked up, mimicking our father, who had smoked the wretched things all his adult life. "Toshio, dear brother, you are so early. Is everything in order?"

He turned in surprise. "Dear sister, I did not know you were there. You move like a mouse. I was just making a final check to see who will be sitting with whom." He seemed a little uneasy, as if something was weighing on his mind. I checked the flower arrangements and inspected the gift table, which was concealed behind an ornate mother-of-pearl screen. On the table were twenty-two gift boxes tied with red silk ribbons and "Tanaka" written across the gold wrappings in beautiful calligraphy. We would present each guest with a gift as they departed. Toshio came over to my side and remarked that we had done a splendid job and all seemed to be ready for our guests. He called over one of the staff and asked them to fetch him another large gin and tonic from the bar.

"Sister, may I ask you something?" He had a quizzical look on his face.

"Of course, anything."

"It may be a little indelicate of me, and perhaps I should seek out Hideo's thoughts first, but I was wondering if you would be interested in heading the Mabuhay Foundation. It would not be too demanding. In fact, I believe the committee convenes only once a month. We are looking for a director to oversee the running of the foundation, and I would feel comfortable having someone close to me fill the role. Someone I can trust implicitly. I see you as the perfect choice."

I was flattered to be offered the position, even if it came with a heavy dose of nepotism. "Toshio, I do not know what to say. Of course I am interested. The foundation is dear to my heart, and I take great pride in the good works it performs. I feel honoured that you are even considering me, but I would have to talk to Hideo first." A waiter appeared bearing Toshio's drink, which he took with a nod of appreciation.

"Ayumi, I think it best if I sound out Hideo. All I need to know now is whether you are inclined to take on the role. If you feel it would intrude too much on your personal time—after all, you are now also a busy mother—then we need not trouble Hideo at all."

I knew there and then that I wanted to be involved in the foundation. It was an opportunity too good to let pass by. My interest must have been written all over my face, for Toshio did not wait for my affirmation. "Very well, I will bring it up with Hideo when we have an opportune moment. I am sure he will be as enthusiastic as I am, but do remember to look surprised when he asks you." He raised his glass in a mock toast and finished his drink in one quick, easy motion. "Now I must go upstairs and visit my nephew."

I could not stop myself from smiling. I was so blessed to have the kindest and most considerate of all men for a brother. I walked around the tables, doing a final check. I noticed that Mr Ichimanda, the minister for finance, had been moved and was now no longer to be seated alongside Mr Jean Meursault. It seemed that Toshio had made one or two last-minute adjustments to the seating plan.

Hideo finally put in an appearance with only minutes to spare as the first of our guests arrived. I gave him a reproving look but nothing more; I had come to accept his dislike of formality. He hated what he called "being on show." However, he seemed to have found release from the agitation that had taken ahold of him earlier; in fact he appeared to be in quite good spirits. Mr Samara, the hotel manager, would greet the guests at the main entrance and welcome them to the Empire and then escort them through the lobby to the Sakura Lounge, where Hideo and I would take over as hosts for the afternoon. Mr Jean Meursault, a banker from Switzerland, was the first to arrive, and there were a few uncomfortable moments as he struggled with his poor command of Japanese. I wished Toshio was on hand, as Mr Meursault was "his" guest and as such I saw it as his responsibility to keep him at ease. However, we did not have much time to consider the conversational predicament of poor Mr Meursault, as the other guests were starting to arrive en masse.

Hosokawa arrived with his latest female companion, who was dressed in a most exquisite gold-embroidered kimono. Perhaps her choice of colour was a little too extravagant for the occasion, or maybe I was feeling a little envious as I greeted them in my simple black attire. Hideo and I both bowed and thanked them for gracing us with their presence and bade them entry to the lounge, where drinks were being served. I whispered to Hideo, "Who is the girl?" He said he could not remember her name but not to worry too much, as she would no doubt be replaced with the advent of the new moon. Hosokawa's womanising was becoming something of an embarrassment; however, it was surprisingly out of character for Hideo to talk in such a manner.

We stood by the double doors, dutifully greeting each of our guests. We were still waiting on Toshio, Minister Ichimanda, and also our guest of honour, for we were to be honoured with the presence of the great entertainer Hibari Misora. Hideo, Hosokawa, and Toshio were all great admirers, and I hoped they would manage to keep their enthusiasm under control. My hopes were slightly dashed when I spotted Misora san being escorted by both Toshio and Ichimanda. It seemed that the minister was as much in awe of the talented actress as the rest of the male population. Hideo was gaping like a juvenile, but managed to keep his dignity intact as we welcomed them all to our luncheon. All the invited were now in attendance and taking their places at the tables. Waiters and serving girls were busying themselves making sure the guests were settled. When all the guests were seated, Hideo and I took our places at the head table, a gong was sounded and we bowed in unison to the gathering, and without further formality we began to take lunch.

We ate in relative silence; conversations were kept short and were mainly in praise of the numerous foods, which were served individually, kaiseki-style. I noticed Hosokawa snatching jealous glances at Toshio, who seemed to be engrossed with the divine Misora san. As with most of our functions the guests were from diverse backgrounds. Some were Mabuhay people, and others like Mr Meursault were in one way or another connected with the business. Government figures and well-known names from the arts and entertainment were always in attendance. We called them all "friends," but as usual I felt sadness when I looked around the tables and realised that I did not have one true friend of my own amongst the invited guests. My life was very ordered. I was a dutiful wife and this was how things were.

I thought of the Mabuhay Foundation and the purpose it would give to my life. There were few opportunities for women like myself to make their mark on the world, and I needed the challenge to feel alive again. The foundation was born out of a promise Toshio had made when he had set up Mabuhay five years earlier. At that time he had pledged that ten per cent of all the company's profits would be donated to aid people in less fortunate circumstances. Being a kind and considerate soul, he was particularly concerned with the plight of the people in war-affected countries and wanted to make an effort towards righting the wrongs of the past. Our father had made a huge fortune from the misery of war. Hamazaki Electricals was closely tied with supplying the military and, as such, had benefited from lucrative government contracts. Toshio wanted to distance himself from the tainted past, so he had dissolved Hamazaki Electricals and formed Mabuhay with a true spirit of benevolence. Even the name Mabuhay was chosen because it brought to mind a feeling of optimism and hope for the future.

The donations were written into the company constitution and were the talk of the business community at the time. Many cast doubt on the legitimacy of such a promise; others merely dismissed it as a sensational act. Those doubters had been proved wrong, and Mabuhay's generosity was the envy of all, for that ten per cent alone was a vast amount of money. Last year it was agreed that a foundation was needed to oversee the use of the funds and ensure the donations were distributed to causes where the most good would be truly felt. I had a great respect for the foundation, and now I had a chance to be part of it. I felt a swell of determination like I had seldom known. I was not prepared to let anybody stand in my way. If Hideo was to oppose me, then he would find his wife to be a formidable opponent.

We had been seated for over two hours, and if I were to be honest, it seemed that most of us accepted the final dish of sweet red beans and fresh lychees with relief. The Sakura Lounge was beginning to feel uncomfortable as the heat from the midday sun was proving too fierce for the slowly rotating ceiling fans. The food had been excellent and had been presented with all the beauty and grace one would expect from the Empire. I made a mental note to myself to personally thank the head chef. We were served hot barley tea, which no one seemed inclined to drink. Our guests were politely making small talk but no doubt waiting for some kind of signal to be finally dismissed.

To my amazement Hideo rose to his feet and cleared his throat. My husband loathed speaking in public and avoided speech making at all costs. His natural shyness and modesty meant that Toshio had done most of the speaking on our behalf. I suddenly had a strange sense of foreboding. Hideo's voice seemed a little shaky as he began. "To all our dear guests. My wife and I wish to express our sincerest thanks for gracing us with your presence here on this most solemn day of remembrance. I think it appropriate that we bow our heads and take a minute to reflect and remember all those poor souls who lost their lives, and to count our blessings for all the extra sunrises that the gods have blessed us with." The room fell into complete silence as everyone obediently lowered their heads. Hideo's voice seemed especially loud as he broke the silence a few minutes later. "We thank you for your kindness and patience. If you require any assistance, please do not hesitate to ask." It seemed an abrupt way to end the party, but one that seemed to have the desired effect, as all our guests started to rise to their feet and prepare to leave. Hideo and I made our way to the table where the gift boxes were laid out, ready for us to present to each of our departing guests. A member of the hotel staff, a smart young man wearing pristine white gloves, passed a box to Hideo. He in turn passed it to me, and finally, with a bow, I presented it to the guest. "We would be honoured if you would accept this small gift as a token of our thanks." I uttered the same words to each person, who in turn expressed their deepest thanks. Toshio was still firmly attached to Misora san. I would tease him a little later for monopolising her company.

Hosokawa and his young companion were looking relaxed in each other's company. At close quarters she looked much younger than I had first thought. She bowed graciously and kept her eyes lowered. Hosokawa, with a mischievous glint in his eyes, spoke on her behalf. "Miss Tanezawa and I would like to thank you for your gracious hospitality and esteemed generosity." There was an element of playfulness in his tone that was best ignored. I wondered where they would be heading later.

The last guest to leave was Mr Meursault, who was accompanied by Ken Miyazaki. Meursault gave a deep but clumsy bow, his face a little flushed from the sake he had taken. He made a little comment which seemed to amuse him but left Hideo and me confused.

Then to my astonishment Ken Miyazaki stepped forward and translated his words. "He said, 'First to arrive and last to leave. As a rule we Swiss are great timekeepers but not, it seems, on this occasion. Please forgive me.'" Hideo asked Miyazaki to tell Mr Meursault that it was a pleasure to see him, as always. Miyazaki translated, and Meursault accepted his box with thanks and took his leave. I handed Miyazaki his own gift box and complimented him on his language skills. He graciously nodded; his eyes were burning into mine as if he were looking for something that was buried in my soul. He made me feel uneasy, and I was relieved to see him turn and leave the room.

I watched him as he quickened his pace to catch up with Meursault. Then I turned to Hideo and said, "Miyazaki seems to be a man of many talents."

"Of course," Hideo agreed. "Why do you think your brother hired him?" With that mysterious aside I suggested we go back to our suite and take a well-earned rest. Hideo said he wanted to take some time to thank the manager and his staff in person. He asked me to go on ahead and said he would join me later.

Tiredness was sweeping over me like crashing waves, and the events of the day were beginning to catch up with me, coupled with a feeling of relief that the stuffy luncheon party was finally over. As I walked through the lobby, I noticed Hosokawa's young companion sitting alone at one of the tables. I went over to ask if she required any help. "Tanezawa san? Hosokawa san has not left you alone, I trust. Would you like me to call for assistance, perhaps arrange for some transportation?"

Beneath her heavy white makeup was a natural shyness that shone through. "Thank you for your concern, Tanaka san. Hosokawa san has asked me to wait here for a moment whilst he attends to some urgent matter. He said he would not be long." She looked very vulnerable, and I admired her stoicism. Not many young women her age would have been able to conduct them-selves with such decorum. I sat next to her to keep her company for a few moments. I was at a loss as to what to talk about and was just about to make some trifling small talk when she spoke. "Tanaka san, thank you so much for allowing me to attend your luncheon party. It was a great honour for me and one I will never forget."

I felt myself warming to her. She had an easy way about her, a confidence that belied her years. "Are you and Hosokawa good friends?" I regretted my question the moment it left my mouth, for it could be open to misinterpretation.

She did not seem to find any double meanings and answered with refreshing honesty. "I like to believe we are good friends. I hope so." They seemed an unlikely couple, and perhaps it was that notion that drove my curiosity a little further. "So how did you two meet?"

She looked at me, and I thought I saw a little doubt creep into her mind. Nonetheless she answered directly. "Actually we have only recently become acquainted. About two months ago Hosokawa san came to call at my home. I say 'my home,' but it is in fact an orphanage. Nonetheless, it's home to many children who, like me, were left alone after the war. I was soon to become sixteen years of age, and the time had come for me to consider my place in the outside world—a prospect I had come to fear, as the Hibari Orphanage was the only world I knew. Anyway, my sensei called me to one side and said I had a visitor, and that was Hosokawa san. He told me that I had been chosen to receive a sponsorship from his company because I had shown great promise in my studies and attitude. My sensei was delighted for me and urged me to accept, which I gratefully did.

"I did not meet Hosokawa san again until this very morning, when he called once more to escort me to today's luncheon. He presented me with this fine kimono as a graduation gift." She ran her hand down her sleeve and looked a little uncomfortable, gazing down as she spoke. "I so wanted to refuse his invitation because I knew I had no right to be here, but Hosokawa san insisted I attend. He told me it would be a useful addition to my education. He said that it was important for young people like myself to stay in touch with the past. I hope I have not offended you by being here today. Please forgive my intrusion."

She had started to weep, and I offered her my handkerchief, which she reluctantly accepted. I felt awkward, for I had always considered myself a good judge of character, but it seemed I had failed markedly in the case of Tanezawa san. Why had Hosokawa not said anything about Tanezawa san? Did Toshio know about her? I was certain Hideo was in the dark, as his earlier flippant remark demonstrated. I reassured her and said all was perfectly fine and it was a delight to meet her. I said I would go along and find what was keeping Hosokawa san, and then, as an afterthought, invited her to accompany me.

We walked together through the lobby, making small talk about the unbearable heat and the various ways in which we attempted to stay cool. I saw the hotel manager, Samara san, and caught his eye. He came over to enquire if he could be of any assistance. I asked if he was aware of Hosokawa san's whereabouts, and he said he had last seen him heading towards our suite accompanied by my brother. I thought this a little odd, as neither Hideo nor I were at home to receive them. I thanked Samara san for his help, and Tanezawa and I climbed the stairs that led to the upper floor and our rooms.

Tanezawa was in awe of the hotel and its décor. She kept remarking on its beautiful features. The chandeliers and carpets seemed to hold a special fascination for her. I doubted there were such things in the orphanage where she had grown up. Of course there weren't—I checked myself for even letting such a thought into my mind. She was wide eyed with wonder and exuded innocence, a quality that made me feel quite protective towards her. I was certainly warming to Tanezawa san.

We arrived at the double doors of our suite. There was still a discolouring of the wood where the "Hamazaki Suite" nameplate had been removed and its replacement had yet to be decided, let alone fixed. The door was slightly ajar, and I could clearly hear the unmistakable voice of my brother. He seemed to be in high spirits—the man was incapable of speaking in hushed tones. I indicated to Tanezawa to wait a moment, as I did not want us to disturb their talk. Eavesdropping is wicked and you will seldom hear anything in your favour, but there are moments when you find yourself in a position where you simply cannot avoid hearing things that you perhaps should not. This was one of those moments. As Tanezawa and I hesitated outside the door, I heard Toshio say, "So it is agreed. Great work, my friend. We can finally say good riddance to those two dinosaurs that masquerade as parties. What is it they are calling it?"

Hosokawa replied, "The Liberal Democratic Party, and our money is on Hatoyama to lead it."

Toshio said enthusiastically, "So there is no room for doubt—Ichimanda knows our support is conditional on the reform bill going through?"

Hosokawa's voice carried on. "Clear as crystal. The Installments and Finance Reform Bill will face little or no opposition. We are home and dry."

Then, to my absolute astonishment, Hideo joined the conversation. "Makoto, you are a genius. All that time spent in the diplomatic corps has served you well. Two birds with one stone, eh? Nip the Red Menace in the bud and open up the purchasing power of the nation at the same time. I take my hat off to you, genius that you are." Hideo must have made swift work of thanking the staff for him to be here ahead of me. Inevitably, at this point, Toshio decided this was all worthy of a toast, and asked Hideo if he had anything on hand to drink.

I took this as a reasonable opportunity to make our entrance. I gave a polite knock on the door and entered with feigned surprise at seeing the three of them standing there. They, in turn, looked a little sheepish, but managed to appear as if they had just been discussing the weather. Toshio did not miss a beat as he said, his face beaming, "Sister, Makoto and I were just saying to Hideo what a fabulous luncheon that was. You both did a splendid job. Our thanks go out to you." Makoto nodded to show he was in agreement, but looked puzzled as he glanced from Tanezawa to me, clearly wondering why I should have her in tow.

"You are both so welcome," I said. "The pleasure is all ours. Is it not, Hideo?"

My husband looked a little awkward, as he was becoming adept at identifying my tones.

"Yes, of course," he mumbled.

I turned to Tanezawa san and said, "May I introduce my husband, Hideo Tanaka, and my brother, Toshio Hamazaki." She gave a deep and courteous bow and respectfully held her silence.

Toshio said he was delighted to finally make her acquaintance, and Hideo agreed: "Likewise, my dear." I turned to Makoto and said in a teasing manner that I had found Tanezawa san looking lost in the lobby, we had decided to take a little walk together, and now here we were. He looked a tad flustered and turned to Toshio for inspiration.

My brother, never at a loss for words, then pulled the rabbit out of the hat, so to speak, and said, "Well, sister, fate seems to have presented us with a moment that cannot be missed. I think it an opportune time to make our little announcement. What do you think, Hideo?"

All eyes turned on Hideo, who looked like a trapped animal. "Yes, yes, it seems so." He suddenly came over all formal, as if he were talking to a regular employee rather than to his own wife. He cleared his throat. "Ayumi san, as you may be aware, the Mabuhay

Foundation is to appoint a new director. Well, in fact its first-ever director. I have discussed this matter with Makoto and Toshio, and we are all in agreement. We would like you to take up that position. Now, before you make a decision, you must think carefully. It is a position that will take on a greater significance in time, and as head of the foundation you are likely to become a high-profile figure. All this would come with certain disadvantages, and I think you may need time to consider."

I could feel all eyes on me as they tried to gauge my reaction. Tanezawa looked like she had mistakenly walked into the wrong scene of a stage play. My brother was nodding expectantly. I looked at the four of them and said, "Yes, I accept." There were hoots of delight as Hosokawa and Toshio stepped forward and congratulated me on my new role. Hideo held his ground. It was hard to judge his expression, but I would err on the side of proud acceptance. I was happy to finally have something real and meaningful with which to occupy myself. It would give me great pleasure to tender my notice with the flower arrangement circle and the tea mornings that had been a part of my life for more months than I cared to remember.

Tanezawa san stayed respectfully in the background, but Hosokawa called her forward. "I have just had a flash of inspiration. Ayumi will certainly have her work cut out for her in the coming months and will require all the help she can get. If she is in agreement, I propose that Miss Tanezawa be engaged as her personal assistant."

I could not believe my ears. My surprise must have shown, but before I could say anything, Toshio said, "What a splendid idea, Makoto. What do you say, Hideo?"

Hideo had a slight grin on his face; he seemed to be enjoying my confusion. "Anything that would ease the burden on my wife has my full support."

"So it is decided then," Toshio said. "All that needs to be said is welcome to the Mabuhay Foundation, my dears. Now, where are those drinks?"

Tanezawa san seemed as confused as I was. I was not unhappy to have her work alongside me. In fact, deep down I was quite grateful for all the help that would be offered me, and I was sure she would prove to be quite capable in her role. But despite all the positives, I could not stop myself from thinking that both Tanezawa and I had somehow been played like two pieces in a game of chess.

The following morning, after a fitful night, I finally gave up on sleep altogether and lay idly in bed, staring at the cracks in the ceiling. After an hour or so, I finally summoned the willpower to rise. I put on my morning robe and went through the connecting room to our main suite. It was still early, but I was not surprised to find that Hideo had beaten me to the breakfast table. Despite it being a little after six, he was already fully dressed and engrossed in the morning newspapers. We exchanged morning pleasantries as if we were neighbours who happened to have walked into the same restaurant rather than husband and wife. Lately I had taken to sleeping alone in the room next to the suite. Tatsuya slept with Araki san in the room on the other side, and Hideo had the suite all to himself. I had come to accept our unconventional sleeping arrangements without question; we had started to sleep apart quite early in our marriage. Hideo was an especially light sleeper, and the slightest disturbance would cause him to wake. He was under constant pressure at work, and his day's toil would exhaust him. I too was drained by pregnancy and the state it left me in. What had started as a night or two sleeping alone had turned into a solitary routine.

This particular morning Hideo was not to be distracted by my presence; he was engrossed in his morning newspaper. We took two newspapers each day, the Asahi Shimbun and the Daily Yomiuri. I did not care for newspapers at the morning table, but I had come to accept that my protestations were falling on deaf ears. Hideo would always pore over the papers, scouring the columns for news titbits that might prove of some value. He said that in his line of work it was important to keep abreast of events and happenings, and this was the only time of day that he could find the time to do so. It appeared petty to protest any further, so as a consequence I usually took breakfast with a newspaper furled in front of my face.

It was impossible not to notice the lead news item, which proclaimed "New Party Born." I twisted my head and read a little of the subhead, which went on to announce that the liberal party and the social democrats had agreed to merge and form a single new unified political party that was to be called the Liberal Democratic Party. They had apparently come to the conclusion that a single unified party was the best option for opposing the increasingly popular socialist party. I was trying to read farther down the column when Hideo must have felt my curiosity, for he lowered his paper and asked me if anything was wrong. He must have had a feeling that I had overheard Toshio's remarks from the previous evening. I did not see any reason why I should act to the contrary. After all, I was to head the country's largest private aid organization, so perhaps the time was right for a little more sharing and common understanding of all that was going on around me.

Words escaped my mouth before I had time to consider their full meaning. "I could not help but overhear Toshio referring to this political merger. He said something about supporting it. What did he mean?"

Hideo put the paper down and removed his glasses. He looked at me, and our unblinking stares locked together for a few moments in a kind of standoff. I half expected him to dismiss my interest, but to my surprise he seemed to welcome it. "Ayumi, my dear. Your brother is an extremely influential figure in the business community, and his patronage is highly sought after. Toshio has decided to give his full backing to this new political venture. He believes it is the correct and best way forward for the country as a whole."

Hideo was about to return to his newspaper, but I was not going to let this rare chance to gain a little business knowledge slip away. "Why does Toshio believe it to be the best option for the country? Hideo, I have been around businesspeople all my life. I know that everything comes with conditions. If Toshio is to give his support to this new party, then he will expect something in return, will he not?"

Hideo put down the newspaper with an exaggerated "Hmm." I was ready for him to dismiss my curiosity; after all, he was quite adept at speaking volumes and saying very little. I had sat through hours upon hours of listening to him excitedly explain some kind of technical innovation and the science behind it, dutifully giving my encouragement to topics that were entirely beyond my comprehension. Now at least we could talk about something that held interest for us both. I was waiting for him to explain, but he was merely looking at me, his finger tapping at the newspaper in front of him. He was drawing my attention to a small story that had made the front page but was dwarfed by the major news headlines. I read the header "Financial Reform Bill to Become Law."

Hideo was looking at me with an expectant smile across his face. Obviously it was something that pleased him, but I was not quite making the connections. After all, it was still very early in the morning. "I take it this is something of significance to Mabuhay?"

Hideo put his hands behind his head, leaned back in his chair, and gave a nod that seemed to confirm his satisfaction. "Ayumi, this piece of legislation will prove to be the single most important factor in Mabuhay's future growth. Consider this: Mabuhay manufactures the most desirable products in the land. We are constantly adding to our range, and update our existing products almost weekly. Our research and development budget is way in excess of our competitors', which guarantees our company is the leading innovator in its field. Our quality and range of product is second to none.

"We will be the leading electrical products manufacturer in the country before the year's end, and yet there is still one problem. It is estimated that only ten per cent of the population can afford to purchase our items outright. Only those with hard cash in their pockets can achieve the dream of owning their very own washing machine, vacuum cleaner, or whatever. When this becomes law"—he tapped the paper to emphasise his point—"every household in the country will, overnight, become a potential customer. This legislation will give purchasing power to the masses like they have never enjoyed before. Potentially, ninety per cent of households will join the customer base. It will allow families to buy on installments at low rates of interest. It works in America, and it will work here. Toshio believes we could see a fifty per cent increase in sales within six months. Of course our rivals also stand to benefit, but we have the product range and also the edge where retail prices are concerned. In fact this could not have come at a better time, as we are ready to launch our new range of televisions.

These will be the single most coveted items in the country. Mabuhay stands on the threshold of economic glory. I cannot emphasise how important this is to the future of our business."

I sat and listened to Hideo as he explained what it all meant and how it would affect the business. It was hard not to be swept away by his enthusiasm, but I had a feeling that I was being told only about the positives. I know there are two sides to every coin. I had to ask the price at which this position had been brought about.

"Hideo, I'll be honest. Yesterday I overheard Toshio remark that support for the new party depended on this reform bill being passed. What has Toshio promised in return?"

Hideo looked a little uncomfortable, his enthusiasm now subdued. "I believe it was a promise to become a benefactor for the new party."

I had guessed as much, for it always comes down to money. "How much did he agree to contribute?"

Hideo raised his hands dismissively. "That is for Toshio to explain. In fact I am not privy to the final agreement. It was something negotiated between Hosokawa and the representatives of the politicos involved."

I did not believe it for a moment. Hideo was in the middle of it all, along with Toshio and Hosokawa. It was inconceivable that a 20 per cent shareholder would be kept in the dark for something as major as this. "Hideo, promise me one thing."

He looked at me, relieved that the conversation was returning to "safer" ground. "Yes, my dear, anything."

"You must swear that none of this is illegal. No laws must ever be broken. I could not live with the shame should anything foul and corrupt befall this family." I looked deep into his eyes for any telltale signs of untruthfulness and to my relief could detect none.

"Ayumi, how could you think such a thing? With my hand on my heart I may say that there is nothing for you to be concerned about. It is standard practice amongst the business community to patronise certain parties or give support to those individuals whom we believe may be sympathetic to our own agenda. On the surface it may appear to be an unethical practice, but it is part of the way that business is done.

"If such practices should ever become outlawed in the future, then of course we would desist. I am sure Toshio would never step over the line. He is an honourable man, and I know he carries all our best interests at heart. If we do not actively promote our own cause by any means possible, then we may as well sit around and allow our rivals to steal a march on us. Believe me, it is a dog-eat-dog world out there, and we can be thankful that Mabuhay is no puppy." However reassuring his words were, I could not help thinking that Hideo was sounding more and more like my brother with each passing day.

Hideo left for work at ten minutes before seven. He was a stickler for punctuality and did not like to keep his driver waiting. Each Monday he would make the journey to the Yokohama production facility, where he would inspect the lines and go through any technical problems that might have arisen during the previous week. I knew this was the day when he felt most at home with his work. He was a meticulous, methodical man. Hosokawa once referred to him as a "mad scientist," a comment that drew a withering look from me. But it was true; Hideo was a creator by nature and a businessman by accident.

The opposite could be said of my brother, whose day-to-day activities were somewhat of a mystery to me. Toshio would often disappear for days at a time and then suddenly reappear and seem to be everywhere for days on end before vanishing once more. I knew he still preferred to work from home, in Ginza. In fact he had turned the house into a kind of head office for Mabuhay.

Makoto also had a set of rooms there where he worked and held meetings. What kind of meetings, one could only guess. I knew he was heavily involved in the endless cycle of negotiations that large businesses find themselves engaged in. He was often out of the country attending to business matters. I envied his trips, for I had never been out of the country and longed for the adventure of visiting faraway places. I had come across an illustrated timetable for Pan American Airways' China Clipper that he had once left behind after visiting us at our suite. The pictures looked so appealing. Important people flying through the skies on their way to wonderful places, speeded along with exotic-looking cocktails in their hands and the happiest faces I had ever seen.

I had kept the timetable in the drawer of my bureau. Somehow I could not bring myself to return it, and anyhow, Makoto did not seem to notice its absence. I saw that he had made a few notes in the columns and circled several routes. It seemed his business had taken him to the Philippines at some time or other. He had written "SR" in the margin several times. No doubt some kind of liaison, a romantic encounter. In my mind Makoto was Rick Blaine straight out of Casablanca. I allowed myself to get carried away and enjoy a dreamy moment where I was Ilsa Lund being swept away without a care in the world.

Perhaps my dreams were one step closer to becoming reality. As the new director of the Mabuhay Foundation, I might insist on personally visiting the countries that received donations. In fact, I thought, that should be an essential aspect of my involvement. As director I believe it to be my duty to ensure the funds are not being misused and that they are being put to work in the manner for which they are intended. That will be my role; I will absolutely insist that my involvement encompass all aspects of the foundation's work. Hosokawa had scheduled an informal meeting for later that afternoon to bring me up to date on the latest workings of the foundation. I would put forward my desire to visit the actual projects, and see how much enthusiasm I received in return. The meeting was set for three o'clock at the house in Ginza, which gave me plenty of time to go about my daily business.

I returned to my room to find the morning maid finishing up her work. I asked her to arrange for some tea and freshly cut fruit to be brought to my room; I never had much of an appetite in the mornings and joined Hideo for breakfast only from a sense of marital loyalty.

I opened the closet and selected a light summer dress for day wear. I would change into something a little more formal for the meeting later. I discarded my morning robe and underwear and stood naked before the full-length mirror. Examining my body and its imperfections had become something of an obsession. Perhaps I was looking for clues to why my husband no longer seemed to find me physically attractive. My breasts had lost the fullness that childbirth had inevitably bestowed, and my hips were narrow once more. I twisted to one side to look at my behind, which was still plump—or was I being too self-critical?

There was a quiet knock on the door, and I called the maid in to deliver my morning tray. I held my robe over my lower body in a modest gesture but left my breasts exposed. The maid set down the tray and kept her eyes lowered to the ground; she nodded demurely and took her leave. I had heard it said that we Japanese were used to seeing the naked form but seldom looked at nakedness. A subtle distinction but one I believed to be true. I had sadly resigned myself to the fact that my husband neither saw nor looked at my naked form at all. With a heavy heart I quickly dressed and sat at the small table to take my tea and fruit. The morning routine would soon begin. Araki san would bring Tatsuya to me at nine, and I would spend an hour or so with him before going about my daily business.

I took a moment or two to ponder my future routine. I had no idea how much work would be involved once the foundation started to demand my time; no doubt this afternoon's meeting would enlighten me a little. As I was about to settle down with my tea, the house telephone chimed. This happened so rarely at this time of the morning that it startled me, and I upset tea all over the tray. I picked up the heavy ornate receiver and tried to hide the annoyance in my tone. "Good morning, Ayumi Tanaka speaking."

"Tanaka san, this is Wada from the front desk. So sorry to disturb you at such an early hour, but you have a visitor waiting here in the lobby: Tanezawa san. She informs me that she has been instructed to report to you at eight o'clock. Shall I ask her to wait here in the lobby, or should I arrange for her to be escorted to your rooms?"

I was momentarily lost for words. I did not wish Wada san to know that I was uninformed about Tanezawa's visit, so I asked him to have her brought to the room straight away. As I waited for the imminent knock on the door, my irritation was building to a point where I feared I would no longer be able to hide my feelings. Who had asked Tanezawa to report to me, and what else had I not been informed about? I was determined that this would not happen a second time.

After a few moments there was a louder-than-expected knock on my door and I called for them to enter. The head bell-boy, Noguchi, opened the door and announced Tanezawa san, who entered the room looking fresh and bright. She gave a deep bow, and there was a slightly awkward moment while she was obviously waiting for my instructions. It was apparent that she didn't know I hadn't been expecting her that morning. I looked over her shoulder, thanked Noguchi for his assistance, and dismissed him. He looked confused as he hesitated in the doorway.

Tanezawa broke the silence. "Tanaka san, Noguchi san has offered me assistance in carrying the boxes here. Where would you like him to put them?"

This caught me off guard, but I managed to pull my thoughts together. "Noguchi san, please bring them into the room and unload them here." He nodded and went out into the corridor for a moment, only to reappear pushing a luggage trolley laden with four heavy-looking cardboard boxes. He placed them on the floor beside my breakfast table and quickly took his leave.

Tanezawa san remained standing by the door. She was obviously nervous and waiting for me to instruct her. She looked completely different in her two-piece suit; her clothes were very elegant and expensive looking. Could a girl from an orphanage afford such attire? The day before, she had told me she was sixteen, but seeing her before me now, I realised that if I hadn't known better, I'd have guessed her to be about twenty-five. She was strikingly beautiful, and her youthful elegance made me feel a little dowdy. "Tanezawa san, please come and sit down alongside me. Would you care for some tea?"

She bowed and sat demurely at the table. I poured her a cup of tea, which she accepted with thanks. "Who instructed you to deliver the boxes this morning?"

A look of surprise crossed her face as she undoubtedly realised I had known nothing of her visit. Then her surprise quickly turned to embarrassment. "Tanaka san, I apologise if my early arrival has caught you unawares. Yesterday evening, as I was being driven back to Hibari, Hosokawa san said it would be a good idea for me to deliver these boxes to you this morning. He told me they contain all the documentation relating to the Mabuhay Foundation and that you would want to go through some of them before the meeting this afternoon. Hosokawa san arranged for me to be collected this morning and driven here by Miyazaki san."

She was becoming a little distraught. It was apparent that she had come here in all innocence. I sought to put her at ease and she soon composed herself, but I was determined that I would not be usurped again. "Tanezawa san, please understand that you are my assistant, and as such from this day on, you are to take instructions from me and me alone. Should you have any doubts about how you should conduct yourself in the course of your work, I hope you will look to me for guidance. Do we understand each other?"

She looked a little shaken. My words may have seemed a bit harsh, but I had to make sure we both knew where we stood. I would deliver the same message, albeit a little less curtly, to Hosokawa when we met later that afternoon. Tanezawa looked downcast, and I felt a wave of guilt. She was an innocent in this misunderstanding, but it was important that she understand her position. She nodded her assent, and I felt any further reproach was unnecessary. I found a positive tone and stood up and said encouragingly, "Right. I think it is time for the director and her assistant to find out what is in these boxes that is so important, it could not wait until this afternoon."

I called Araki san to bring Tatsuya to me at once. From experience I knew that I would be unable to concentrate on even the simplest of tasks without seeing my baby first. It saddened me to think that Hideo could go for days without setting eyes on his son and it never seemed to trouble him in the least. I comforted myself with the thought that at least one of Tatsuya's parents had a loving disposition. Tanezawa san was opening the boxes when Araki arrived, cradling Tatsuya in her arms. He was in a deep sleep and smelt of soap and warm milk.

I cradled him for a few moments, walking over to the window and looking out over the green parkland that bordered the royal estate. Hideo had once said it was this very view that kept him here at the Empire. At the time I had been desperate to move and selfishly prayed that some development would be erected outside our window, forcing us to find a new abode. I could feel Tanezawa watching me. Was she thinking of her own long-lost mother and father? The parents she never knew? I had many questions to ask her, and I hoped that as we became closer, she would open up to me and treat me more as a friend than as her employer. I turned to Tanezawa san and said, "Meet my son, Tatsuya, my precious little boy, all of eight months old."

She came over to me and smiled down at my little angel. "He's so adorable."

I held him out for her to take into her arms, which she did with a natural ease that surprised me. "You seem so comfortable with him." She smiled and told me that at the orphanage the older girls were expected to take care of the little ones. She had a confidence that belied her years. I did not doubt that she had the strength to match.

I felt a twinge of guilt as I handed Tatsuya back into the care of Araki san. Spending only ten minutes with my son was not the way for a loving mother to be. Hideo had tried to caution me, albeit half-heartedly, about the demands of my new role. Was this what he was referring to?

I looked at Tanezawa, who was sitting on the floor and struggling with the bindings on one of the boxes. Each box was numbered and labelled. Box number one was said to contain documentation relating to the Philippines and dated 1951 to 1954. The Mabuhay Foundation had started to grant donations four years earlier, so this box must have contained all there was to know regarding the foundation's work in that area. The other boxes were similarly labelled and covered Burma, Malaya, and Indonesia.

Tanezawa had finally managed to free the bindings, and we both stared down at the sheaves of documents. A dark red file on top appeared to contain some kind of a memorandum. I picked it up and went over to my desk to study it in more detail. I asked Tanezawa to open the other boxes and see if they too contained the same kind of memoranda. As she got on with her task, I sat down and studied the Philippine memorandum. There were several documents, each relating to a specific project. My eyes scanned the top page, which was headed "School Project—Tuguegarao." A summary included a brief discussion of the amount of financial support to be offered for the establishment of a school that would take on three hundred children annually from the poorest areas of Tuguegarao. It seemed the proposal had been well received. A section titled "Conclusion" seemed to be an agreement to give full support to the project. I turned the page to find the document had been signed by Toshio, Makoto, and Hideo. This gave me an inkling that I would not have full autonomy in my new role. However, I was determined that I would be involved as much as possible and equally determined that I would not be seen as a mere figurehead.

I flicked through some of the other papers and found that the Mabuhay Foundation was funding three other projects in the Philippines: one, a mobile field hospital that served people living in large tracts of wilderness, another the construction of an irrigation system, and one that appeared to be a little bizarre—the development of a new airfield in northern Luzon. All the projects required long-term commitment and financing, and it seemed the foundation had pledged ongoing support.

Tanezawa had opened the other boxes and extracted the same style of documentation. We placed the boxes to one side and shifted our attention to the dark red files. For the moment they seemed to contain all I needed to know. The format was simple, for which I secretly gave thanks, and after a few hours I was able to ascertain that the foundation was actively involved in funding eight projects in total: four in the Philippines, two in Burma, and one each in Malaya and Indonesia.

What was blindingly obvious to anyone studying these documents was the complete lack of financial information. Where funding was mentioned and amounts should have been recorded, the spaces were bracketed, and rather confusingly, "Details held by Foundation Treasury Committee" had been inserted in their place. Did this mean the foundation had a committee that handled all the finances? It seemed a cumbersome way to operate, but no doubt there was a reason for it. I was about to make a note in my personal paper file when I remembered I had an assistant who looked a little lost. Passing the file to her, I said, "Tanezawa san, please make a note that I require an explanation about the financial workings of the foundation."

She wrote on the paper and then looked up expectantly, waiting for her next instruction. We had been looking at papers for most of the morning. I felt an early luncheon was called for, since we had the meeting scheduled for three. I told Tanezawa we would stop and go downstairs to take a break in the lobby restaurant.

We walked along the winding corridors towards the grand staircase in silence. I wanted to engage Tanezawa in conversation, but my mind was still back in the room going over the files. It seemed the more I found out, the more questions I had. I was looking forward to the opportunity to gain a clearer understanding later that afternoon. As we walked through the lobby, I realized that because of the distraction of the morning's work, I had forgotten to freshen my hair and makeup. Once more I had the strange feeling that I was being overshadowed by the elegant Tanezawa.

Wada san, the head concierge, came over and offered to escort us to my preferred table. Luckily, it was still quite early and the restaurant was quiet. In the past I had avoided the Empire's public areas, as they were usually frequented by the resident wives of American servicemen who were given rooms here when the hotel was under the control of the occupying forces. I did not resent their presence; quite the contrary. I envied their free spirit and the way they could enjoy themselves without being concerned with social niceties. I wished I could be part of their fun, but an unwritten rule ensured that we never fraternised, and respectfully kept our distance. However, those days were in the past, and the howls of laughter and excited English chatter were long gone.

Upon entering the dining room I immediately spotted Ken Miyazaki sitting with Mr Meursault at the far end of the room. Both men half stood to show their greetings to us and then sat to continue their discussion. From where we were seated, I could see them clearly. I was struck by Miyazaki's use of hand and arm gestures, which looked slightly amusing from a distance. I had never seen a Japanese man be so demonstrative in his conversation. Mr Meursault responded in kind; perhaps that is the way with Europeans. I had of course met and talked with many Americans over the years and on the whole, despite their being a little loud, found them to be most agreeable. But the Europeans were still a mystery to me, as was Miyazaki san.

Toshio had told me that Jean Meursault had first been employed by our father, and that was the highest reference a man could receive. I had never been able to find out much about Ken Miyazaki. My curiosity had always been met with some kind of a collective indifference from those around me. Why I was so interested in his life I could not explain, but he held a certain fascination for me. He was unlike any other man I had ever met. He had a certain menacing aura about him that left me feeling repulsed and excited at the same time. I had to check myself from staring across the room. I did not want to give the wrong impression to Tanezawa, who was busy studying the menu and looking a little puzzled. Perhaps she was unused to Western cuisine.

I let her peruse the menu for a few moments before offering my suggestions. "The lobster bisque is highly recommended, and the filet mignon is usually done to perfection. Would you care to join me in the same?" She smiled and thanked me for helping her, seeming mightily relieved that she need not make her own choices. Everything must have felt overwhelming to a young girl, finding herself here in such unfamiliar surroundings.

This was as good a chance as any to get to know Tanezawa better; I hoped she would feel relaxed enough to let me into her world a little. "First, I think it friendlier to call you by your given name," I said. "Would that be all right with you?"

Her smile told me that she agreed. "Tanaka san, thank you so much for all your kindness. I would feel happy for you to call me Sakura." I smiled too, for I was beginning to feel very protective towards her. She had an air of independence, yet there was a vulnerability that made her quite fragile. I got the feeling that she wanted to ask many questions but was afraid to do so. We were both still hovering on the sidelines as far as meaningful conversations were concerned.

A waiter came and took our order, and we sat in uneasy silence for a moment or two. I was curious about her plans for living after she had left the orphanage. "Sakura chan, have you thought about where you are to live after you leave Hibari Orphanage?" Perhaps it was my use of her name for the first time that caused her to hesitate—or was I being insensitive? I guessed it must be difficult for her to be forced to leave the place she had called home for most of her life.

She was not at a loss for words. "Yesterday evening as I was being driven home, Hosokawa san mentioned the very same thing. He said he would arrange for some accommodation for me. I am so grateful to him for all his kindness, for I could never have dreamed such a wonderful thing. I am truly blessed."

I looked for any signs that she might be holding something back but saw none. I could not help but think, Yes, you are blessed, but what makes you so special that Makoto is personally seeing to your needs? "It seems Hosokawa san has all your best interests at heart."

She blushed a little and replied, "Everybody has been so kind to me. It is like a dream come true." I asked her if the question of her salary had been decided. Again she looked embarrassed as she replied, "Hosokawa san mentioned that I was to receive eight thousand yen per month. I protested that it was too high a figure for someone as inexperienced as me, but he said it would be appropriate, as I would have a lot of personal expenses to meet."

I was surprised to hear that she was to receive such a high salary. Hosokawa was certainly being overly generous. Tanezawa, only sixteen years of age, was to receive the same salary as a middle-income salaried worker! This only strengthened my curiosity. Of course, I would not receive any formal payments for my own work. I had no need to be concerned with income. We had more money than we could possibly ever need, which put me in the privileged position of being able to disregard financial rewards for my efforts. I had grown up around wealth, which perhaps was why I had always found it distasteful that some people were motivated only by money. Even during the darkest days of the war and its disastrous effect on Father's business we never seemed to be in any difficulty and managed to live in the usual comfort. The only restraints were the ones that we imposed upon ourselves.

A server arrived pushing a trolley upon which was a large tureen containing our soup. We sat in silence whilst he ladled the soup into fine bone china bowls, placed them in front of us, bowed, and took his leave. Tanezawa san was most impressed, watching wide eyed and taking in all the details. I noticed that she hesitated in her actions, always waiting to follow my lead. I took this as a mark of her good manners and common sense. She tentatively tasted her soup. "Sakura chan, is the taste to your liking?"

She placed her spoon down and dabbed her mouth with the linen napkin before replying. The way she conducted herself and her impeccable table manners aroused my suspicion that this was not the first time she had sat down to take fine French cuisine. "It is sublime. I have never tasted such a wonderful soup. Thank you so much for your kindness."

I held my hand up ever so slightly. "Sakura chan, please do not feel the need to constantly thank me. I hope you feel comfortable in my presence and that over time we will develop a fine working relationship based on trust and respect. This is a business lunch, like those our male counterparts seem to find the time for as part of their daily routine." As the last words left my mouth, I gazed in the direction of Ken Miyazaki's table. This caused Sakura to look that way too, and I am sure I caught the hint of a mischievous smile.

Our soup bowls were cleared, and the table was laid with gleaming silver cutlery in preparation for our main course. During the respite between courses a waiter approached our table; he was bearing a small wooden message tray upon which was an envelope with my name written on the front. I thanked the waiter and took the note, which, surprisingly, was written in Japanese but was from Jean Meursault. "Ladies, please forgive this intrusion on your private time. However, if time allows, I am hoping that you both will be able to join us for coffee in the lounge after luncheon. Yours, J Meursault." I looked over to Mr Meursault's table and saw that he was looking our way with an expectant expression. I nodded to signal my acceptance of his invitation and was rewarded with a cheery salute and a raised glass in return. Despite the early hour it was clear that Mr Meursault had decided wine was to be his drink of choice. Toshio had told me that the French take wine at every luncheon. I had teased him at the time, saying that if that were true, then he must be half French, as he himself seemed to adopting the habit. In any case Mr Meursault was Swiss; perhaps it was a European thing. Ken Miyazaki seemed to be forgoing the wine; in fact I could not recall ever seeing him drinking alcohol at all.

I turned to Sakura and said, "It appears that we have been asked to join those two for coffee later. Perhaps we can spare a few moments, but I must have enough time to prepare myself for the meeting."

She looked over to their table and smiled to herself and then said, "Miyazaki san was so kind to drive me here this morning. He is so dashing, and the way he speaks such fluent French with Mr Meursault is to be admired." Indeed, it was rare to be able to speak a foreign language, and Ken Miyazaki seemed an unlikely type to have acquired such a skill. Perhaps I would take this opportunity to ask him how he had managed to become so accomplished in linguistics.

I turned to Sakura and said, "How did you know Miyazaki san could speak French?"

Perhaps my question came out sounding sharper than I had intended, for she looked a little surprised. "Oh, this morning when Miyazaki san was helping me with the boxes, we met Mr Meursault in the hotel lobby. They talked, and Miyazaki san explained that Mr Meursault knows little Japanese so he had to speak in French. I was so impressed—a true person of manners."

Before I had a chance to reply, the waiter arrived once more, pushing his serving trolley. He set out the warmed china plates and began the rigmarole of serving our filet mignon with practiced dexterity. We both watched him in silence as he went about his business of setting down the side plates and vegetables. He bowed and left us to enjoy our meal. I noticed that Mr Meursault and Ken Miyazaki had left the dining room and assumed they were settling down in the lounge. We ate in relative silence, passing the occasional compliment on the food. Sakura persisted in thanking me and kept telling me that she had never eaten such fine fare before. She was becoming a little repetitive with her platitudes, and I found myself hurrying through the meal, which was not my usual manner. To be truly honest, I was eager to finish the luncheon and move on to coffee.

The meal came to its speedy conclusion, and the waiter appeared to enquire if we would like dessert, which I declined on behalf of us both. We took our leave and made our way to the lounge, leaving the headwaiter bowing in our wake. The charges for all our hotel expenditures were calculated and settled monthly, so I never had cause to fuss with cash or even sign a charge slip. Hideo was far more thorough in his checking of all charges. He often said that to truly appreciate wealth, you had to come from nothing. His statements, though no doubt intended to be profound, often left me cold, as I had been brought up to believe that money talk was vulgar.

We entered the lounge and were greeted by the headwaiter, who seemed to be expecting us, for he escorted us straight to Mr Meursault and Miyazaki san seated at the far end of the room at a corner table in the alcove. Both men stood to greet us, Miyazaki san bowing respectfully and Mr Meursault clasping both our hands in a quite clumsy fashion. I could smell the wine resting heavily on his breath. We took our seats, and Miyazaki san called the waiter over and ordered coffee and mints for us all. Mr Meursault also ordered some kind of liqueur, which, he said with the help of Miyazaki san's translation, was to aid the digestion. We all declined his offer to test the theory. After our orders were placed, Mr Meursault went into a rather long-winded and serious address. Despite the fact that we were completely uncomprehending, we bowed and nodded at seemingly appropriate moments. Miyazaki san offered his words up in Japanese. "He wishes to thank you once more for the wonderful luncheon party yesterday and for your generosity. He feels humbled to be presented with such a wonderful gift." Each of our guests had received wristwatches from the Swiss maker Rolex. I hoped Mr Meursault saw the presentation of a gift from his own country as a mere coincidence and nothing more. Miyazaki san continued. "He would also like to offer his congratulations on your new appointment as director of the Mabuhay Foundation, and as Mabuhay's chief overseas banker, he looks forward to working with you." This took me by surprise, but I did not wish to show it. I thanked him for his kind words and asked how long he would be staying in Tokyo. Another long-winded reply followed, which, fortunately, Miyazaki abbreviated to a few sentences. "He will be in Tokyo for another week and then, given the successful completion of his business, he will head back to Switzerland. He remains at your service and available for any assistance you may require."

I smiled at Mr Meursault, thanked him, and said I wished him a safe journey and that I was sure his other clients in Switzerland were waiting on his safe return.

There seemed to be a little confusion as Miyazaki san spoke my words, and after a moment to digest Mr Meursault's reply, he said. "Tanaka san, Mr Meursault does not have any other clients. Mabuhay is his sole client, and he is devoted and committed to the service of our business." I got the feeling that I had made some kind of blunder, perhaps offended Mr Meursault in some way, for he seemed to have become a little subdued. I asked Miyazaki san to tell him that I was still unsure about the financial side of the business and asked for his patience and understanding. There was an exchange of words and a little hand gesturing which seemed to bring Mr Meursault back to more cheery ways; he was further buoyed by the arrival of his ghastly looking green digestive drink.

I complimented Miyazaki san on his linguistic talent and asked him how he had managed to learn to speak such a difficult language. I could sense that Tanezawa was also eager to hear his reply. Miyazaki san looked at us both and replied, "It is down to my adventurous spirit and the necessity to survive. Besides, like most things, it really is not so difficult if you practice a little each day."

It wasn't really the answer I was hoping for, so I pressed him a little more. "That sounds so mysterious. Did your adventurous spirit lead you to distant lands? I am sure you have an interesting tale or two to tell."

He looked a bit uncomfortable with my probing, and I could almost sense his mind working on his reply. "Tanaka san, you are most perceptive. Yes indeed, I travelled a little in my youth, but my adventures were not as exciting as you might imagine. In any case they were brought to an abrupt end by the war, and my life, like so many others', changed for the worse." It did not seem fitting to press him for more details, as he had moved the conversation to a more personal level.

Our coffee arrived and was served by a young waiter who seemed very nervous; he spilt a little as he poured it into the cups. I noticed Miyazaki san's face take on a granite-like look as he coldly dismissed the waiter and chastised him to take more care next time. A moment of uncomfortable silence followed, and after a few sips of bitter coffee, I decided that we should leave the men alone to their talk. Besides, I had to make myself presentable for the meeting, which was in a little over an hour's time. I thanked Mr Meursault for his hospitality and said I hoped we would have the opportunity to meet again before he left for Switzerland. He said the pleasure was all his and that he remained at my service should I need his advice. Miyazaki san translated these final words and then added that Hosokawa had instructed him to transport us to Ginza, where the meeting was to be held. I expressed my thanks and told him to expect us shortly.

I was considering letting Tanezawa have a little break time to herself, but I was sure that she too would appreciate the opportunity to freshen up a little before our meeting, so I asked her to accompany me back to our rooms. We walked smartly through the lobby, which was unusually quiet; perhaps the summer heat was preventing people from travelling. Whatever the cause, I was thankful, for I did not care much for the throngs of onlookers who came daily to gawp and take photographs of Mr William Lionel

Francis's overrated edifice. I had always thought it rather over-
stated and its Mayan style of architecture out of place. Hideo, on
the other hand, held quite the opposite view. He thought it a masterpiece of design, something that could be created only from the
mind of a genius. My brother also would hear little said against the
place. He loved it so much, he often called it his spiritual home. In
fact he had tried to persuade Mr Francis to make a return visit to
Tokyo as his personal guest. Unfortunately, ill health had prevented the great architect from doing so. Tanezawa was obviously
also an admirer, as she was still gaping in awe at the place like a
love-struck teenager.

It seemed that I was the only one who took umbrage with
the Empire. I did not care much for the way the doors never
seemed to perfectly close, and the constantly creaking floors
underfoot. The walls were forever being repainted to cover the
cracks, which spread out like cobwebs. The plumbing was basic
and noisy. All those defects could be traced to the great earthquake
that had struck on the very same day the hotel had opened more
than thirty years earlier. Toshio said they were not defects, merely
charm points. I failed to see his reasoning and one day soon would
step up the pressure on Hideo for a move to more conventional
living arrangements. That was most certainly at the top of my
personal agenda for the future.

We climbed the winding staircase to our rooms, and I wearily fumbled in my clutch bag for the key. As I was doing so, I
heard Tatsuya crying from the room he shared with Araki san. I
was torn between going straight to his room and getting ready for
the meeting. With guilty feelings I asked Tanezawa to go and
check for me and to tell Araki san that I would be along shortly,
after I had changed. She told me not to worry, and off she went
with a spring in her step. I watched her as she walked down the

corridor. At thirty-nine years of age I was plenty old enough to be her mother, and with that depressing thought, I let myself into my room to change.

I was determined not to be outshone by my assistant at our first meeting, so I rang the concierge to arrange to have a hairdresser sent to my room. I told them I had little time and required something to be done urgently. I quickly stripped off my clothes and went to the closet to select an outfit, something formal and elegantly understated. I hated the current fashion of wearing tight-fitting pencil skirts that seemed to have made inroads into the attire of most office ladies. I looked through the racks and decided on a Chanel two-piece suit in dark navy and one of the new Chanel quilted leather handbags to match—perhaps the most expensive items amongst the racks of Western clothing I had acquired over the years. I laid them out on the bed along with a white silk blouse and went for a rushed shower.

As I was washing, the hairdresser arrived with the tray of her trade. I told her to wait a moment. I was so short of time, I barely managed to get wet. I wrapped myself in a towel and told the hairdresser she had only fifteen minutes to make me look presentable. She set about her task with admirable efficiency and soon had me feeling pleased with my appearance. I dismissed her with thanks and made a mental note to request her by name next time, such was her skill. Sato. I jotted it down on a piece of paper.

After I had applied a little makeup, I was feeling satisfied with my look, which I checked from all angles in the mirror. I often thought to myself that I had two images: my traditional self and my Western self. Today I was a thoroughly modern "European" woman dressed in the finest haute couture, director of the Mabuhay Foundation. I had arrived. I checked the time, which seemed to have evaporated into the air itself. I had left Tanezawa with little or no time to get ready; however, needs must. I placed the red Mabuhay project folders into a large carrying bag and left them by the door for Tanezawa to pick up. I went down the corridor to Tatsuya's room and gave a courtesy knock on the door before entering. My little angel was fast asleep in his crib, and Tanezawa was sitting in a chair having her hair brushed by Araki san. Both girls stood and bowed respectfully. Araki san looked particularly uncomfortable, as if she were waiting for a scolding for stepping out of her job description. Tanezawa had also changed clothes. She was now wearing the type of tight-fitting black pencil skirt that I found so vulgar and a tight white blouse that emphasised her ample breasts. Tanezawa explained that as she was cuddling Tatsuya, he had been sick all over her clothes and Araki san, luckily being the same size, had offered her a change of clothing. I could not find any reason to reproach either of them, so I merely said we had only a few minutes before we were expected in the lobby.

Tanezawa stood and said she was ready to leave at any time. I could not help looking over her figure. However much I disliked her fashion, it seemed to have been made with her body in mind. An irrational rush of jealousy swept over me as I realised that I had been upstaged by my assistant, who had been clothed by my maid. I did not have the time to let such feelings settle over me, so I rather curtly said we had to leave. I turned on my heel and headed out of the room down the corridor with Tanezawa a few paces behind. I told her to pick up the files and hasten her pace. Then it struck me that I had forgotten to ask about Tatsuya. My God, was I turning into a mirror image of my husband? Just for my peace of mind I would ask Tanezawa about Tatsuya later, perhaps in the car on the way over to Ginza.

We came down the winding staircase to find that the lobby had become more crowded because of the number of guests waiting to be assigned rooms. I spotted Miyazaki waiting by the main door. We made our way through the throng of people and outside into the scorching heat of the day. The Rolls-Royce was parked directly in front of the main door for our convenience. A small crowd of onlookers had gathered, attracted by the car and no doubt hoping to catch a glimpse of some matinee idol. I could almost feel their disappointment when we emerged to be driven away. Miyazaki san slid into the driver's seat, and we crawled away on the short ride over to Ginza. I was trying to put myself into the correct frame of mind for the meeting, mentally preparing myself and going over the questions I wanted to ask. I wondered who else would be in attendance besides Hosokawa san. I turned to Tanezawa and asked her if she was prepared for the meeting. She nodded and said of course, but I had a strange feeling that her mind was elsewhere. I decided to try to put her at ease a little. "Sakura chan, I apologise for rushing you along, but I felt we were a little short of time. Also, thank you for seeing to Tatsuya for me. I trust everything is fine. I mean, Araki san does not have cause to worry about his health, does she?"

She smiled and said, "He is fine—perhaps a little wind, that's all." I was grateful to hear it and felt more relaxed. We arrived outside the Ginza residence, where Miyazaki san quickly got out of the car and opened the rear door for us. Since my marriage I had had less cause to visit the Ginza house. Occasionally Toshio would invite Hideo and me to one of his so-called business functions, and I always found myself looking forward to the place rather than the event itself. I had grown up here and spent the happiest days of my life in this house as well as some of the most terrible. If buildings were artworks that portrayed a person's life, then this house would be a montage of joy, happiness, comedy, and tragedy. I had had my first experience of real passion with Ryo on my wedding night here, all of twelve years ago—a night that is scorched into my memory and will remain so until the day I depart this earth. The release of so much sexual frustration had brought me the sweetest sense of being myself that I had ever had. It was here—in fact, in the very same room, my bedroom—where my father informed me of Ryo's death. Life has a cruel way of reversing your happiness, and misfortune has no respect for time or place. I fell into despair and wished myself dead, so much so that my father employed a nurse to keep vigil over me for months. My dear father—it was now more than five years since he too had passed away in this house. Had I been so self-absorbed, wallowing in my own pity, that I did not see the signs? I knew Toshio believed foul play was at the heart of his death, but as time passed, I had come to believe that Father made the decision to end his own life and that Toshio's failure to accept it was his way of dealing with a tragedy that I believed he felt was, in some absurd way, his own responsibility. Yes, this house was full of bittersweet memories, and yet I felt I belonged here. It had a grip on my soul.

Ogawa san greeted us on the pavement side, and we climbed the few steps leading to the grand main door. I touched one of the ornamental shisa lions for luck, as was my habit each time I entered the house. The Okinawans believe such images ward off evil and protect homes and families. Where was the protection when we needed it most? I am not superstitious, but I don't believe in disregarding things we don't understand. Hideo, being a man of science, would find such a notion completely nonsensical.

Miyazaki handed Ogawa the file bag and bowed to us and said he would be available to transport us back to the Empire when needed. Ogawa san looked very frail. The last few months had been especially telling, as if his spirit were draining away in front of our very eyes. He was a proud and stoic servant whose loyalty to Toshio was profound, and I was dismayed to see him in so fragile a state. He still managed the occasional driving duties, but I feared he would be permanently housebound within weeks.

He bowed to me and said, "Mrs Tanaka, welcome home. Hosokawa san is expecting you. He is waiting in the drawing room." I smiled, and he led the way up the shining marble staircase. He always said "Welcome home" whenever I had cause to visit here, which gladdened my heart. Tanezawa followed, keeping a respectful distance. I could not see her face, but it must have been a picture of amazement. She had found the Empire a place of wonder, so she must have believed this house to be a palace. No expense was ever spared here, and it showed. It was a stunning residence, one of the finest in Tokyo. Toshio loved to indulge the feminine side of his character and was forever investing in the upkeep, and I would notice minor changes here and there in the décor and furnishings.

As we climbed the staircase, I wondered why Hosokawa san had chosen the drawing room as our meeting place. It was certainly the most impressive room in the house. Toshio loved it and called it his "harmony room." He had had the ceiling specially painted with intricate koi that gave the place a sense of tranquillity and peace. But as a place for a meeting? Surely a smaller office would have been more appropriate. We walked along the silk carpeted corridor to the huge white double doors that led into the drawing room, and Ogawa knocked to announce our presence. The doors slowly opened and we were greeted by a loud round of spontaneous applause. There, gathered before us in a semicircle, were at least thirty people, all smiling and clapping. I was left speechless and stood rooted to the spot. The applause seemed to go on for a long time, and I was feeling awfully self-conscious and slightly vulnerable standing there.

Finally, Toshio stepped out of the crowd, took my hand, and led me into the centre of the room. I looked around and saw Hideo standing there alongside Hosokawa. My eyes were darting along the faces of those lined up. I noticed Mr Meursault and the finance minister Mr Ichimanda. Ken Miyazaki had managed to join in and was smiling along with the rest. There were many unfamiliar faces and many familiar ones I could not put a name to. It was all too much to take in, and I struggled to control my emotions. I feared I was about to break down in tears of frustration—or was it happiness? I could not account for my own feelings, such was my surprise.

Toshio raised his hands to quell the applause and cleared his throat to speak. "Ladies and gentlemen and any other types that may be present." There was a smattering of laughter in reward for his attempt at humour. I knew it was Toshio's way of saying this was a lighthearted occasion, and that he was trying to be easy with his audience. "First, I hope my sister finds it in her kind heart to forgive the liberty we have taken by surprising her with this fine gathering. But events like this do not come around with so much regularity that we can afford to ignore them. They deserve to be marked with an occasion befitting the grand scheme of things." I looked at the assembled and noticed they were muttering their agreements. Hideo looked stern, and it was difficult to read his mood. Waiters were busy moving along the lines of people, bearing silver trays laden with champagne flutes, which the guests accepted gratefully.

Toshio continued his speech. "Today is such an occasion. A day when we welcome my sister, Ayumi Tanaka, to her new role as director of the Mabuhay Foundation." There was a brief round of applause, which Toshio spoke over. "It is a proud moment for me, as I can now see that the future works of the foundation are in the safest possible hands, for such a benevolent enterprise deserves the qualities that Ayumi will bring. I am confident that the greatest good will be achieved under her leadership, and she has the complete trust and confidence of all of us at Mabuhay."

At that moment I knew what this was all about. Toshio was publicly giving me his endorsement. In a society dominated by men this was a grand gesture and the finest statement of intent one could receive. I was moved by his sentiment, for I had become expert at reading his intentions. "The Mabuhay Foundation is making great improvements to the lives of those born under less fortunate circumstances than ourselves; as I speak, the foundation is funding several life-changing projects across developing Asian countries. Everyone involved in these works can take great pride in their achievements. Although the foundation is nonpartisan, I do believe that as Japanese citizens, we can allow ourselves a little satisfaction as we work towards healing the divisions of the past.

"I do not intend to speak at length, though I am sorely tempted to do so, and it would be a little too much to ask Ayumi to speak, given the surprise we have just sprung on her. So, if you would all raise your glasses, I would like to propose a toast. 'To the Mabuhay Foundation and its great works.'"

There was an echoing of the salute, and I felt all eyes turn on me. It would have been easy to bow and smile politely and blend into the crowd, but I felt that I could at least offer my appreciation for the gathering. I handed my glass to a nearby waiter in preparation for my very first public speech. "I thank you all for gathering here today, and most of all I thank you for all your good wishes. The Mabuhay Foundation is close to my heart, and I will endeavour to continue its work and strive to achieve the greatest good. I intend to be involved to the greatest extent. It is my desire to visit the projects personally and make myself fully aware of the needs and hopes of the very people the foundation aims to help. Your help and support will always be a source of great encouragement for me. I thank you all." There was a brief silence and then hearty applause, which sent floods of relief coursing through my veins. I had not felt so nervous since I had accompanied Oka Haruo san on the piano as he treated us to a rendition of one of his famous songs in this very room and on the very same night Hideo and I had met for the first time. When was that? All of five years ago now.

I looked around at all the faces, trying to avoid direct eye contact but at the same time trying to place as many as possible. Toshio came forward and pressed a drink into my hand. My mind was still a whirl of confusion, and I wasn't sure whether I should be joyous or downright annoyed. I settled on something in between. My brother, on the other hand, was positively beaming with satis-faction. "Sister, everyone is so delighted with your appointment. You can see it in their eyes. They adore you." I ignored his over-exuberance and instead asked him when I could get down to some real work with the foundation.

"Real work? This is real work for the likes of you and me. This is a part of what we do, and now I suggest we lose ourselves in the crowd and become acquainted with our guests." I followed Toshio across the floor like a sullen schoolgirl trailing after her master. I caught sight of Hideo, who was in conversation with Tanezawa. He had a beaming smile across his face and looked happier than I had seen him in months. Tanezawa was smiling and, I must say, looking a little too relaxed for someone who pur-ported to be a novice in this company. Was that a glass of cham-pagne in her hand? I made a mental note to have words with her later.

Ken Miyazaki was talking with Hosokawa, and they broke off their conversation as we approached and Makoto bowed to me. "Tanaka san, please forgive me for the slight deception. I hope you were not too taken by surprise. We wanted this day to be one that would stay with you for years to come. Besides, I had little choice in the matter. You know your brother: When he gets a notion, it seems to find a will of its own." He gave Toshio a mischievous grin and was rewarded with a friendly pat on the shoulder from my brother, the man for all parties.

I looked back over my shoulder to locate my husband and Tanezawa, but they had disappeared into the crowd. I felt a creeping sense of agitation that I could not quite place; something was just not quite in order. I could not shake the feeling that I was taking part in some kind of elaborate masquerade. Perhaps I was allowing my paranoia to run free, for I did not care for surprises, and I vowed to be my own woman from that day forward, free from the interference of petty-minded businessmen who seemed to revel in their own self-importance and petty little games.

Was I being too harsh? After all, I had been gifted a wonderful opportunity by the very same men who seemed to be the cause of all my frustrations. Toshio was full of joy, his arm around Hosokawa's shoulder, laughing away as if he did not have a care in the world. In that instant I realised that I was the luckiest woman in the entire world, for I was surrounded by the kindest and most caring people anyone could ever imagine. My worries had been for nothing. These men did not have the heart for wrongdoing, and I truly believed they were working towards the greater good on behalf of their fellow men.

Chapter 6
Elias Cohen
Virginia
1956

The newspaper was spread open over the low coffee table like a shroud. The small picture tucked away at the bottom of page seven was testament to the failure of their effort to deliver any kind of justice. The four men huddled together and stared down at the indecipherable newsprint, their grimaces matched only by the sourness of their thoughts. Despite being involved in the sensitive areas of investigations that required at least a working knowledge of the Japanese language, none of those faced with the previous day's edition of the Daily Yomiuri could make head or tail of what was printed before their eyes. Words were one thing, easily manipulated and buffeted about with reckless abandon, strung together by skilled manipulators. Meanings could be forged to serve any purpose one might choose. However, pictures never lied, and there he was, almost out of sight at the bottom of the page, beaming at the camera whilst shaking the hand of some nameless civil servant. Toshio Hamazaki, the son and heir. The new "evil emperor."

It was supposed to have been so easy—spook the father into making some kind of rash move that would open him up and expose a weakness they could ruthlessly exploit—but nobody had taken into account Tetsuyo Hamazaki's resolve. Many years had passed, yet they all carried the shame of underestimating the old man's strength and determination. If anything, they had made the mistake of treating him like a common criminal, when in fact the truth was far more complex. Of Tetsuyo Hamazaki's culpability in crimes against humanity they were, as one, convinced of his guilt. The grey area descended when they were forced to examine the old man's motives, which was where they might find the answer to why Tetsuyo Hamazaki had put a revolver to his own head and ended his life.

Elias Cohen was convinced that impending shame had forced his trigger finger into action. All the talk about honour and the Code of Bushido was pure nonsense to his ears. Harvey, prone to a more romantic view of the world, was open to anything that could explain Hamazaki's ultimate and desperate act. Myers tended to align himself with the view that Hamazaki was ordered to take his life by men higher up to preserve their filthy secrets. Conspiracy theories bounced back and forth with so much abandon, they became "cheap talk." The one thing they all knew but never morally acknowledged was that their own actions had forced a man to take his own life. Nobody actually shed any tears for Tetsuyo Hamazaki; they were all far too blinded by the conviction that the world was better off with one less war criminal. However, they all felt that their job had been sidetracked by Hamazaki's final selfish action.

It had taken some time to refocus the investigation. Toshio Hamazaki had stepped into his father's shoes with such consummate ease, they might have been one and the same person. In the eyes of the team that is exactly what they were. Robert Rushton had managed to wrangle more funds out of the central budget to pursue investigations into Toshio Hamazaki's activities. When he heard about Tetsuyo's suicide, Rushton's first words were, "Then the son will have to pay for the sins of the father."

Eight long, impotent years had passed, each unfolding with an increasing sense of doom and failure.

Toshio Hamazaki had shown himself to be a dangerous and formidable opponent, beyond the reach of justice—a far cry from Rushton's initial assessment, which had dismissed him as weak, a sexual hedonist, prone to importunity, and enslaved by greed. Toshio Hamazaki had flaunted his newfound status as the leader of the new breed of Japanese aggressor. This time around, the battle-field was the boardroom, and the weapons were balance sheets boasting returns that showed Japan chipping away at the rock of American economic dominance.

They were all too aware of Hamazaki's audacity. Upon his father's demise and after a respectable period of mourning, he had dismantled the bedrock of the family business. Hamazaki Electricals was no more. That once proud company was now a mere foot-note in the annals of Japanese corporate history. A new company had been born, and Hamazaki in a fit of brilliance or stupidity had decided upon Mabuhay as the masthead for his new venture. Upon hearing this news, Rushton was apoplectic with rage; he had taken it as a direct afront to those who sought justice for the poor people of the Philippines. To use a word so synonymous with that coun-try's goodness was, in his eyes, despicable.

Hamazaki had said in an interview shortly after the forma-tion of his new enterprise that he was offering the hand of recon-ciliation and that his choice of business name was a statement of his intent, especially fairness in business. He had gone on to stress that he believed business was not all about profit at any cost. He wanted to forge a new business model, one that he hoped would be the inspiration for many other entrepreneurs around the globe. He had smugly said that he believed the "American model" of capitalism had alienated itself from the very people it should be serving. He went on to say that American workers were by and large an unhappy collective, toiling merely for their weekly pay without any feeling of loyalty to their companies. The customer base was treated with an attitude that verged on contempt; products were put out that were hugely overpriced and often shoddy, forcing consumers to spend most of their disposable income just to get by. Americans were unable to save; therefore a feeling of uncertainty was brewing amongst the lowest paid.

Mabuhay was to fly in the face of such behaviour, and as an example Hamazaki insisted that a sum not less than 10 per cent of his company's profits would be distributed to the countries of South and East Asia in the form of benevolent aid. The recipients were to be those who had suffered from the aggressive acts of Japan's misguided wartime governments. Hamazaki had established the Mabuhay Foundation to oversee the work of his corporate philanthropy. All this was public knowledge, and it sat very uneasily with Rushton, who was utterly disgusted by the whole thing. He was convinced Hamazaki had been handed his father's criminal legacy. He was equally convinced that Mabuhay was founded on stolen war loot from the battlegrounds of Asia and that Hamazaki was flaunting this in the face of all who stood to challenge him.

The failures of the past weighed heavily around the office. Rushton carried more than his fair share of the burden. He had taken responsibility for missing out on Tetsuyo Hamazaki, but had skilfully protected his team from the subsequent fallout that had come crashing down on all their heads. Five years ago Rushton had managed to place a young man in the Ginza household of the Hamazaki family. By means foul he had turned Toshio Hamazaki's lover into a common traitorous spy. The situation had been far from ideal and was fraught with danger. The youth in question was a rent boy called Kawabata who was working out of some despicable companion bar that was frequented by homosexual men from all sections of society. It was said that some of the clientele were even American servicemen, but Cohen could not bring himself to believe such downright slander. As it happened, Toshio Hamazaki had found himself a customer of the young Kawabata and had seemingly fallen for his charms, taking him on as his lover and, in his eyes, rescuing the lad from the lowlife existence that had been his lot up to that point.

It was common knowledge that Toshio Hamazaki would sneak his lover into the Ginza house under cover of night and that after a night of lovemaking, Kawabata could be seen sneaking back to his hovel somewhere in the pits of Tokyo. It was after one of his love-ins with Hamazaki and making his way home the following morning that Kawabata was confronted by an American intelligence operative who gave him little alternative but to cooperate. Apparently Kawabata had wet himself in that alley. He was not difficult to break, and his superficial bravado had fallen away in an instant. A sweetener had been thrown into the deal: two thousand dollars upon completion of the operation. Kawabata could hardly believe his luck. He had Toshio Hamazaki in the palm of his hand, he was treated like a prince, lavished with gifts and money in return for his fidelity and love, and now the Americans wanted to give him money to put some things in Toshio's father's office. It was all too good to be true. What was the problem? After all, it was Toshio he loved, not the stuck-up old bastard of a father.

Kawabata suddenly disappeared off the face of the earth six months after Tetsuyo Hamazaki's suicide. That was more than five years ago, and Kawabata had never been seen again. All efforts to find him had been in vain. Some of his "old colleagues" in the bar had speculated that he had returned to Kyushu, gone straight, and married. Nonsense, as the team knew. He had been made and was now dead—as dead as their investigation seemed to have been at the time. Rushton believed Kawabata had been murdered and his body dumped out at sea. If this were true, then they all knew they were dealing with a man who had an extra menace to his already growing reputation. Nothing could be proved; if Toshio Hamazaki had any involvement in Kawabata's disappearance, then he had skilfully covered his tracks.

As the years unfolded, the team had largely been involved with gathering intelligence on the business activities of Mabuhay and its associates. They painstakingly sought a weakness in the organisation, one they could exploit. It was almost as if a colourful canvas had been drawn before their very eyes. The major players were all too familiar, especially the addition of the reclusive Hideo Tanaka, for here was further proof, if needed, that a conspiracy was being played out. The very same Tanaka, the Lieutenant Tanaka who had been named by Major Kojima in his confession all those years ago, was now working alongside Hamazaki as his chief engineer. It was a gut-wrenching confirmation that Mabuhay was deeply involved in the darkness of the past, and Rushton's team members were as dedicated as ever to bringing the past out into the light and shaking it out for all to see.

It was still thought that the best possible way to secure evidence against Hamazaki was to get on the inside of his business. It was a near impossibility to place one of their own, so efforts were made to turn someone already close, and that someone was to be Makoto Hosokawa. Of all the men close to Hamazaki, Hosokawa was seen as the easiest target to compromise. Reports showed a man born into high society who was arrogant and believed himself untouchable by authority. He was a drinker and womaniser, two qualities that made the team members rub their hands together in expectation, but in truth they all knew it was a long shot. Desperation had forced their hand, and not a man amongst them failed to question his own value as an investigator.

Cohen had come to see himself as a collator of intelligence, all of which fed his sense of vitriol but did little to satisfy his appetite for retribution. He had long since managed to control his frustrations about the number of blind alleys his job had led him floundering down. Despite all the disappointments, his belief that one day justice would win was all the sustenance he needed. He assuaged his frustrations by making anonymous contributions to right-wing publications and gained satisfaction from the feedback that like-minded folk cared to leave. He was a man sinking in a sea of delusion but nonetheless one utterly convinced of his own righteousness.

Rushton would often disappear for weeks and sometimes months at a time, leaving the team to pursue paper chases and shadows. During these periods of absence he unofficially handed the day-to-day authority over to Harvey, who was all too content to polish the seat of power with his backside. Little was made in the way of progress. Rushton would return and offer no hint about the reasons for his absence. It was generally accepted that he was engaged in other duties besides the Mabuhay investigation, but Cohen often wondered what could be more important, and on this stormy October morning of 1956 he was about to find out. Rushton had arrived back in his office the previous day and called a meeting of his team, including the loyal and tight-lipped Miss Mills, at the ungodly hour of five in the morning.

Harvey, Myers, and Cohen were seated around the conference table that was usually reserved only for high-end business. Miss Mills had taken up a place against the far wall, her trusty notepad at the ready. Despite the early hour there was a certain frisson in the air. Perhaps it was because moments like this were so rare, but Cohen knew something was about to unfold. Rushton, true to form, arrived late, unburdened by the usual mountain of papers and files. He was accompanied by two austere-looking elderly gentlemen. "Team, thank you for your punctuality at such an early hour; however, as needs must." Rushton seemed stressed and more than a little uncomfortable, and yet he pressed on. "I guess you are all wondering who these men are, and although I wish I could introduce you, professional protocol precludes me from doing so. All I can say is they are here to monitor our meeting."

This was not going as Cohen had expected. He had attended enough meetings to know when a sting in the tail was about to be given. Rushton looked at his team in an effort to convey some kind of sincerity. "There is no easy way to say this, but our investigation is to be concluded and the team reassigned to other duties. I thank you for your efforts. It has been an honour to work alongside you all." Cohen felt his blood run cold, and a numbness spread through his body that he could not contain. He started to physically shake, and gripped the sides of his chair in the effort to conceal his emotions. Rushton was silent for a moment and seemed to be mulling over his next words. "I am not the kind of man to walk away from blatant crimes against humanity, and it is my conviction that one day all the guilty perpetrators will be held to account. I believe that is God's will. But the investigation into Mabuhay and its illegality has taken on a direction far beyond that of a criminal investigation. Its scope has broadened into the diplomatic, economic, and political arena to such an extent that we are simply deemed to be out of our depth. The Treaty of San Francisco signed only four years ago and now in full play has changed everything before us. Japan is no longer an enemy of our fine country, but is now seen as an ally in a region of volatility. The Korean War should be enough to satisfy any doubters in that respect. It is the opinion of higher-placed men than I that we will see conflict once more in Southeast Asia, and I for one also believe this to be inevitable. The Treaty of San Francisco made provisions for repatriations to former Japanese-occupied countries. The sovereign government of Japan has now requested that a line be drawn under the mistakes of the past, and someone in our present administration has seen fit to agree."

Rushton looked down at the bare tabletop as if he were reading a paper that only he could see. The two men shifted uncomfortably in their chairs; it was obvious they were there to monitor what Rushton had to say. Harvey and Myers were impassive, staring at their boss as if he were an apparition and all this was just a dream. Cohen had whitened with anger and for a moment thought he might actually weep tears of rage. Rushton once more looked up, and his voice quivered with emotion. "They call us the 'shadow chasers' back at headquarters. It hurts me, but I had nothing to offer them. Maybe they are right—"

"No, it is not so," Cohen broke in, his voice unusually high. "We have so much evidence, it is a damning indictment."

Rushton nodded at him. "We all know that, but the truth is, the world has changed, and we all must change with it. Armies have looted since time immemorial; men have enriched themselves through war. Why should we expect anything less of our own era? The animals of war once more seem to have ceded against virtue. It hurts, but we have to take it. History tells us so."

Harvey was quick to the fore. "Hamazaki gets to walk away scot-free? With the stolen riches of nations at his disposal? My God, is that what we have come to?"

Despondency hung heavy in the air. Even Rushton was at a loss for any words to counter the taut emotions of the men before him. He raised his hands in an apologetic show of defeat. "We are in the midst of a paranoia that has spread like a fever across our own establishment. The cleansing of certain government departments, high seats of learning, and sections of the entertainment industry of so-called 'Communist sympathisers' has, I believe, contributed to our own closure. Men of rank have failed to offer us the support we need to carry on our work. They have been too preoccupied with preserving their own status rather than doing their jobs. The fact that we have been unable to achieve any tangible results despite a decade's worth of effort has, I believe, gone against us. It is an ironic fact, but one that has gone against the grain of patriotism all the same."

Just as Rushton was about to continue, one of the two men, who until then had kept silent, brought his palm down on the table, shaking everyone out of their stupefied frustration. "Mr Rushton, I think your team has gotten the message." He looked around at them, and for the first time Cohen could tell that he was not a man to be reasoned with. Toughness was etched into his features, and his southern drawl cracked with unsettling determination. "My assistant here will hand you each a paper, which you all will sign before you leave this room. This paper is an affidavit, a legal document that absolutely prohibits the disclosure of information, facts, or activities of your employment. In addition, once you leave this room, you are prohibited from communicating with each other in regard to any aspects whatsoever of your previous work. Now, believe me when I say that this document has teeth, and should you be foolish enough to contravene its intentions in any way, then it will come and bite you in the ass. Do you fully understand?" Such was the power of this man that they all nodded as one, without question.

Cohen found himself on the streets that midmorning. Unable or unwilling to take the bus back to his apartment, he drifted aimlessly, mulling over the shock of losing his job. The full impact had yet to settle into his mind. He had experienced deep lows in his life before; losing his beloved Dorothea had left a permanent scar on his heart, and now there was to be another one etched alongside. The morning streets seemed unfamiliar to him. He usually dashed from bus stop to office with little regard for anything around him, but now he looked around as if seeing things for the first time. The newsstand where he bought his morning paper seemed smaller, the vendor older, the streets grubbier, and the townsfolk shabbier. He noticed the trash cans were overflowing, and there seemed to be an abundance of feral cats rooting through the leftovers. On every other bench, occupants sipped something from bottles hidden in brown paper bags. He sucked in the air, which smelled like a mixture of cinnamon from the bakery and gasoline fumes that spurted from the exhausts of each and every truck.

A giant billboard pictured someone named Elvis, who sat in a rocking chair with a guitar at the ready. Cohen wondered what chance the young man might have in today's America—especially with a name like that. Better to have a real all-American name like good old Roy Rogers, a man with unlimited talent and a true patriot to boot. Cohen stared at the Elvis board for a moment before shaking his head and moving on. In his mind he knew America would forget Elvis just like it had forgotten him and all he stood for and believed in.

Chapter 7
Makoto Hosokawa
Tokyo
1960

I made my excuses months ago, as I did not have any desire to play any part in the celebrations that Toshio had so meticulously planned. A long quiet weekend in the country would suit me just fine, as far away from all the fuss and shenanigans as possible. Some people would no doubt see my decision not to attend Mabuhay's tenth anniversary as a deliberate snub. Nothing could be further from the truth, and both Toshio and Hideo accepted my decision with good grace. But now, on the eve of what the newspapers had been describing as the biggest and most glamorous social event of the year, I felt a strange sense of envy. It was always nice to have plaudits and praise heaped upon you, especially when they came from the mouths of those who really mattered. Toshio had been at his grandest for weeks. I had never seen him so excited. In all truth, this was really his event. It marked his arrival as the country's wealthiest and most influential businessperson.

Mabuhay was ten years old and now the country's most important privately owned business. It was the most powerful enterprise in the country by far and looking to expand even further as we developed our export division. As I sat on my bed packing my weekend items for the trip to my lodge in Karuizawa, I could only shake my head in disbelief at the amazing rise of Mabuhay and also that of its little sibling, the Mabuhay Foundation. We had built an economic powerhouse. Toshio's vision combined with Hideo's genius and my cunning had proved to be the driving force behind our great company. Yet, strangely, I felt little pride in my own contribution. I was devoted to the business, as were my two partners, yet of the three of us, it was I who had to broker the deals that set us on our way. Some of those "deals" made me proud; others had left me with a sense of shame. But I am nothing if not tenacious, and I considered it a fine quality that I always achieved my objective. Perhaps that was the reasoning behind Toshio's decision to rescue me from a lifetime of servitude in the Diplomatic Office. Ten years had passed since he'd knocked on my door at the Foreign Ministry and, with all the cheek and bravado that comes so naturally to him, made me a proposition that was too tempting to ignore. Any sane man would have done just that and chosen the easy option, which would be to dismiss his wild scheming as the ideas of a deluded man losing all sense of reality. But Toshio Hamazaki was not deluded. He was a man driven by powerful forces, and his charisma and charm would take hold of your rationale like a giant boa constrictor, squeeze out any opposition, and leave you at his whim.

The master manipulator himself needed my help, and I suppose I was flattered to be asked. In all truth my career as a diplomat had started to flounder. I had been overlooked for several key promotions and had been sitting at the same desk for months at a time. I suppose it was an inevitable consequence of having a father who had been tainted by his wartime associations. The ministry had changed; it was no longer the open passport to prestige and respectability for the privileged few, amongst whose number I count myself. Distancing oneself from the past and the blatant interferences of petty politicians was the new order, and this had made Hamazaki's offer of alternative employment seem heaven sent. In truth I would have accepted his offer without further inducement, but when he crowned it with a partnership in Mabuhay, my soul was already wrapped, sealed, and delivered.

I went over to the window and looked out over Ginza. I could spend hours just staring down at the happenings that make up the daily toil of ordinary people. I sometimes fooled myself into believing that I was one of them, that I too was just a small part in the grand scheme of things. In my heart I knew it could not be further from the truth. The words and deeds I had been responsible for would never be considered ordinary. It was almost as if I had managed to divorce good and evil and stay on friendly terms with both. Perhaps that was a by-product of working with Toshio. Some of his "finer" qualities would inevitably find their way into my soul. As I looked down at the street scene below and tried to find the rhythms which would go some way toward explaining why folk settle for such a mundane existence, I felt delicate arms embracing me from behind, sweet kisses on my neck, and soft breasts pressed against my back. Her nakedness aroused me, but I let her vie for my attentions a little longer. This was a girl I liked, not loved, for I believed I was not capable of that emotion or perhaps had not met the one who would ignite that within me.

For now, Azusa would keep me from being lonely. She had been my bedmate for the last month, ever since we met at a fundraising event for the foundation here at the Ginza house. She was attending with her father, a high-ranking bureaucrat in the welfare ministry. Our relationship had been kept a secret to preserve her honour, as her family had matrimonial designs for her and the merest hint of sexual impropriety would see their hopes come tumbling down. I often wonder what kind of man is deluded into thinking their new sweet, pure wife is so innocent when, in the throes of first-night lovemaking, their new brides let their passion run with abandon.

Azusa was no innocent, but that did not concern me, for she had no place in my future, only my present. She pulled me away from the window, and we fell onto the bed in a clumsy heap. She had just bathed and smelt of rosewater, and her skin was paper white, almost translucent. When she was hot, you could see the blue veins in her large breasts, and her hair was so black, it almost shocked me. She lay on the bed and spread her legs, running her fingers over her breasts and between her legs, moaning in pleasure and urging me to take her. I took my time undressing. Her self-pleasuring was a joy to see. She loved this ritual as much as I did, and ever since I'd told her that I liked to watch, she had always put on a show. I removed my trousers and lay on top of her. She took me in her hands and guided me in, and in a few short strokes I felt myself coming. I could feel a palpable sense of disappointment from her, as she always wanted more. She had a voracious sexual appetite for an eighteen-year-old, one which left me at forty-two clinging on for dear life. I rolled off her and cursed my irresponsibility. The last thing I needed was a little Hosokawa in my life. The very thought of children sent me cold. I had seen Hideo and Ayumi fawning over their little pampered brat and for the life of me could not see the attraction.

I went off to the bathroom to wash and change for the drive to Karuizawa, telling Azusa to hurry up, as time was short. She had told her parents she was visiting a school chum and staying overnight. In any case they too would be too preoccupied with raising glasses and joining the party across the way at the Empire Hotel to question their daughter's whereabouts. The thought made me smile; their little angel would be getting more than her fair share of Mabuhay hospitality.

I hurriedly washed and cleaned myself up and went back into the bedroom to find Azusa still half naked. Although she had not washed, she had put on her underwear. I was about to tell her to clean herself up a little but refrained, as her washing tended to take an age. There was a newspaper on the bed, and a headline caught my eye. It was a feature on the Greek shipping magnate Aristotle Onassis. Apparently his wife was divorcing him because she had caught him in flagrante delicto with the opera singer Maria Callas. It made you wonder what the world was coming to when one of the world's wealthiest men could not control his own wife. I could not imagine such a thing happening here. Onassis was something of a hero of mine. I loved his style and the way he was able to enjoy his wealth without any second thoughts. To me he was the epitome of what it meant to be rich. I wished we had the same freedom here, but being Japanese meant showing restraint in nearly all you did. Toshio, Hideo, and I had millions and millions on deposit, we were among the richest men in the country, and yet we did not swan around on yachts bedding opera singers and playing the gaming tables. That kind of lifestyle was not for us; we lived in conservative luxury and took our pleasures in a more discreet manner. Occasionally there would be an ostentatious display of our spending power such as tomorrow's celebratory party, or perhaps my new Ferrari 250, which was parked and ready for the drive over to the lodge. I doubted if even Onassis had one of those. The thought brought to mind one of the great man's quotes. "If women did not exist, all the money in the world would have no meaning." I believe you got that one wrong, Ari, but I respected the sentiment.

Azusa pulled on a bright yellow summer dress over her tight white underwear. She was sitting at my dressing table piling her hair up into some kind of arrangement. She had an amazing figure; I could not help but admire her, and looked forward to speeding along in the Ferrari with her at my side. Two things of beauty for sure, but it would be a cold day in hell before a woman took my name and an even colder one before she took my car. I stood behind Azusa and watched as she put on some lipstick. I put my hands on her waist and slowly moved them up, pushing the straps of her dress off her shoulders and cupping her breasts. She closed her eyes and started to get in the mood again. I forced her tight-fitting brassiere down and played with her gorgeous breasts. She moved her hand between my legs and maybe noticed that I was not aroused. She slipped out of her panties and pulled her dress up around her hips. She spread her legs and watched me as I watched her in the mirror while she played with herself. In those few minutes I would perhaps have been more inclined to agree with Onassis, but although all good things must come to a close, money goes on and on. Azusa finished her erotic pantomime with exaggerated screams of ecstasy. This time I told her to clean herself up; I did not want any stains on my car seats. I whispered into her ear that all passengers had to give up their underwear. She giggled and went off to the bathroom, leaving me a few minutes to finish my preparations for the trip.

I took a moment to look myself over in the mirror. I had been putting the weight on recently, and it was sitting heavily around my waist. My face was looking a bit heavy jowled, and my hair, although thick, was greying at an alarming rate. Still, no point worrying about the things we have little control over. A long weekend away enjoying the clean air at the lodge might well put the sparkle back in my eyes.

I told Azusa to leave via the rear door for modesty's sake and said I would pick her up on the corner of Ginza Street by the clock building. She left, cheekily hitching up her dress to reveal her bare backside. Oh my, this girl was certainly as game as they come. I quickly checked over my rooms, locking all the doors and double-checking the safe, which was housed at the rear of the wardrobe. Satisfied that all was in order, I locked the main door and made my way down the grand staircase. On the way out I heard Toshio briefing the staff behind closed doors. I lingered long enough to hear the words "champagne perfectly chilled and cigars to be smoked only in the smoking room." There seemed to be some confusion about the wording of a sign that was to instruct the guests. That was typical of Toshio, the master of fine detail—hands on in all respects. I considered popping my head around the door and wishing him luck for tomorrow, but as time was pressing, it was probably best to leave him to his fussing. Besides, I did not want to be sidetracked into reconsidering my decision to be elsewhere this weekend.

I rang the bell in the hallway to summon some help with the loading of our bags, which I had left outside my rooms. Ogawa san appeared, and I instructed him to get one of the houseboys to bring the luggage down immediately. He bowed and shuffled off to see to his task. I had implored Toshio to let Ogawa drift off into retirement, but Toshio could not find it in himself to let him go. We all had a moral debt to this man, and Toshio would never let us forget it. I put on my new aviator sunglasses and stepped out into the warm wintry sunshine. It was a perfect day for driving. A small crowd of people had gathered to admire the car. Even in Ginza such symbols were hard to ignore. I hesitated to get in the car, as my luggage had yet to be loaded, so I lingered on the steps for a moment or two. A young fellow recognised me and without warning was halfway up the stairs, followed by an even younger chap who had his notebook out. I recognised them immediately as cub reporters, nuisances at the best of times and downright troublesome at the worst.

We had been attracting quite a lot of attention from the press recently, especially with the company anniversary and its magnificent planned celebration. Hideo kept such a low profile that I doubted whether any reporters would even recognise him. Toshio, on the other hand, would, at times, chair press conferences. He was on good terms with the editors of the "big three" national newspapers and tended to revel in the spotlight a little too much for my liking. I took the view that the least said, the better. I hated any intrusion on my privacy and as a result had got myself a reputation for being brusque and obtrusive.

Now the cubs were almost face-to-face with me and ready to fire off their questions. Maybe it was the combination of the fine weather and my upbeat mood that made me surprise myself, for I did not push them aside but smiled amiably. This seemed to give them a little extra bravado, for they took little time crafting their questions. "Hosokawa san, congratulations on the tenth anniversary. Could you tell us if there is any truth in the rumour that His Excellency the Emperor will be attending tomorrow's celebrations?"

I smiled as if I found the question amusing, which in its naive way it was. "None whatsoever." The houseboy squeezed past us to load the car with my bags, and I looked over the reporters' shoulders to signal that further questions would be unwelcome.

Undeterred the young cub pressed on. "Who will be the guests of honour? Can you comment on the speculation that Mabuhay is to launch a takeover bid for the American company Sonic?"

The last question caught me completely off guard, but being so practiced at looking stony faced, I hoped it did not show. I pushed past them, leaving their questions hanging in the breeze. The houseboy was waiting by the car and opened the door for me. As I stepped into the car, a camera flash popped in my face, and with a growing sense of annoyance I fired up the Ferrari's throaty engine. I floored the accelerator a few times in an aggressive manner. The onlookers took a few steps back to avoid the smoky exhaust fumes. I drove away, checking the crowd in my rearview mirror. No doubt the press boys would stay, hoping to stop a member of the staff there at the kerb, someone with a loose tongue willing to spill a little tidbit for a few hundred yen.

I drove slowly down the street to the corner where I had arranged to pick up Azusa. I spotted her gazing into a shop window. I glanced into my rearview mirror once more to ensure the reporters' persistence did not extend as far as following me in the hope of chancing on some scoop. Satisfied that I was safe from preying eyes, I pulled over by the kerbside and gave the horn a little honk. Azusa turned around, smiled, and skipped over; I leaned over and opened the door for her. As I did so, I felt a sharp twinge in the small of my back, which I put down to a combination of too much romping and drinking. She carefully got into her seat, giggling like the adolescent she was and keeping her legs together, as she did not want to give any passersby a free peep.

I had figured the drive to Karuizawa would take the better part of two and a half hours and was looking forward to giving the Ferrari the freedom of the road. What I had not taken into account was the close confinement with Azusa. We were not a couple given to deep and meaningful conversations; in fact I could not recall having had any kind of meaningful discussion with her at all. She seemed quite content to pass the journey gazing out the window, and when that became a tad tedious, she would rummage through her bag to locate something or other. I noticed that she spent a great deal of time checking her face in her compact, tilting her head this way and that. If I gave a sideways glance in her direction, she would reward me with a mock pouty kiss or a pat on the knee. But mostly we travelled along in our own little worlds, each lost in our own thoughts.

I suppose the age difference between us was most telling when we lacked the welcome distractions that life provides. We were a generation apart, but it seldom preyed on my mind. I mean, I did not have any designs on her other than satisfying my carnal desires and of course the gratifying boost to the old ego. To fall in love with her would be to surrender to my inner weakness, and that just would not do. I thought about my dear old friend Satoshi san from my days in the diplomatic corps who had given his heart to a young thing half his age and the miserable wreck he had become when it all came crashing down. She had left him with a wardrobe full of attire that was too young for him, a half-empty bottle of hair dye, a depleted bank balance, and a broken heart. Oh no, that route is not for the fainthearted and one I would not be venturing down. When the time came to say our goodbyes, my pride would be fully intact.

We were making fine time. The roads were clear of traffic, and the weather was exceptionally mild for the time of year. The Ferrari, despite all its glory, was proving to be mighty uncomfortable, and the small of my back was beginning to ache like the devil. We had long left behind the urban sprawl and were going deeper into the lush greenery and beautiful pine forests as we wound our way up ever-increasing inclines. If you were to put a stranger in this very spot and ask him to guess his whereabouts, I am certain he would tell you he was in Norway or Sweden or the like. The outside air was also chilling, and I comforted myself with the thought of the raging log fire that awaited our arrival at the lodge. I had sent four of the domestic staff ahead to ensure all was in order and to tend to the cleaning and catering duties. Without doubt it would be a fine weekend. My company would be toasting its birthday and I would be tucked up with my little sweetie—well, at least most of the time.

I did have one little item on my agenda that required my attention, but I did not anticipate that it would take up much of my time. I was expecting a visit from my trusted colleague Miyazaki san, who I hoped would bring me some welcome news regarding a matter that had caused me a great deal of irritation and more than the odd sleepless night over the last few months. The last decade had been witness to Mabuhay's phenomenal rise in becoming the nation's most profitable privately owned business. Massive investment into research and development had given us the products that were proven world beaters. We were looking out to the world and the world was waiting with open arms. However, life was seldom simple. Our success had put us under the spotlight, and certain elements prayed for our demise on a daily basis. The frequency and the level of malevolent attacks on our company and against our own good reputations had left us with no option but to take countermeasures.

Today as I was driving along, I could picture the scenario at a certain residence not too far from here. It was about this time that Miyazaki should be paying a visit to the country residence of our leading detractor, a despicable man by the name of Ono. We believed him to be in the pay of our rivals, and that as chairman of the Monopolies Commission, he felt he had a God-given right to kick the corporate hornet's nest just to see what came flying out. We had gathered evidence that a campaign of rumour and innuendo had been launched from his office. The man himself had done little to hide his belief that he found our dealings to be, in his eyes, questionable.

This smear offensive had little effect on our business dealings, but recently the attacks had become more personal. Both Toshio's and my own character had been subjected to barbed attacks. We had been called cowards for avoiding the draft during wartime and had been the subject of satire, depicted in comic books as two rich pigs getting fat off the sacrifices of the dead. Posters had started to randomly appear, pasted on lampposts or disused buildings across the city—vile filth, in which we were depicted once more as fat pigs feasting on the corpses of slain soldiers in the aftermath of battle. Thanks to the vigilance of the police, the comics had disappeared from the streets where they had been left by unknowns for anyone to pick up for free, and the posters were almost gone from sight. The references to the war were particularly disturbing, and we believed that the instigator was sending a personal message, a thinly veiled threat that they knew something about our "funding arrangements" and would taunt us before no doubt stepping up pressure.

It was plain to us all that we had to put a stop to this disgusting filth before it attracted further attention, so I instructed Miyazaki san to conduct an investigation of our own, the result of which had led him to the door of Taku Ono. He was a former board member of one of our leading rivals, a company that had long since disappeared, unable to keep up with the vigorous pace set by Mabuhay. Perhaps that was his motivation for joining the Monopolies Commission; maybe he felt he could oppose us from there. However, the commission's review of our business practices failed to find any malpractice. We were confident that he would find little support amongst the commission's members for his scheming. We were equally confident that we had that base covered and in our pocket, literally. Toshio was the master at making friends in all the right places. Our true concerns were not related to the workings of the business itself or even the spiteful personal attacks on our good names. We dismissed those as petty jealousies and accepted that success would bring issues to the fore that required us to find the resolve to ignore them.

However, some things could not be ignored, and we had irrefutable evidence that Ono was in league with others and that together they were determined to do us harm. For some reason he had taken it upon himself to be the scourge of Mabuhay. He had gone looking for anything that could be used against us, and it seemed like his irrational actions had attracted support from similar deranged fools. Miyazaki san had placed Ono's Tokyo residence under twenty-four-hour surveillance and was rewarded when one of his operatives captured photographic images of a late-night caller. Ono's visitor, an elderly man, stayed for about twenty minutes and upon leaving was shadowed by Miyazaki's man all the way to Haneda, where he spent the night in a cheap hotel before boarding a commercial Japan Airlines flight to Hong Kong the next morning.

The mere words Hong Kong were enough to set the personal panic alarms ringing. The debacle of ten years ago still haunted us all, and it seemed that our failure to take care of the problem then and there was coming back to haunt us. I immediately called a confidential closed-door meeting with Toshio, Hideo, and Miyazaki. We all stared down at the grainy photographs, which had been taken only a few days before. Toshio was descending into a tailspin; he had been so high and full of the joys of celebration. He did not want to deal with the possibility that our nemesis had finally broken his cover and was on some kind of revenge crusade. The pictures were inconclusive, and we all looked to Hideo for some kind of confirmation. He was the only one amongst us who had been in close contact with the man, but it had been fifteen years since he had last set eyes on him and ten years since that fateful night in Hong Kong. He could not be sure, as time makes a comedy of all our faces, but we all agreed that a coincidence was unlikely and that we needed to take drastic and urgent action if we were to preserve the secret of Mabuhay's unprecedented success. It was solemnly agreed that Ono's time on earth was to come to an end. For a man of sixty-four who had led a stressful life, heart failure would not come as a surprise to any who knew him.

My loyal and trusted friend Miyazaki san should be delivering the fatal hypodermic at about this time. A meticulous search of Ono's personal belongings should bring us further reward about the whereabouts of our true enemy, Lieutenant Colonel Nishii, latterly known as Lung Cheuk Man. Only then could we finally put our demons to rest. So, it was with a certain amount of trepidation that I awaited Miyazaki's visit to the lodge.

Azusa was finding the journey a little tiresome and had even grown weary of checking her own face. She had fallen into a petulant silence, and I sensed she was more than a little anxious. Perhaps she was beginning to have second thoughts about the wisdom of spending a weekend away with a man older than her father. Was it the deception she wove to cover her absence from the family home that was finally dawning on her? Or was she overawed by the remoteness of our surroundings? We were now deep into Mother Nature herself, and I knew that city types felt naked without their creature comforts. Not that she needed to worry on that score, for I believed the lodge would surpass all her expectations. I decided it was best to leave her to sulk alone.

Besides, we were only a few miles away from the lodge, and I found myself too preoccupied with other thoughts.

No matter how hard I tried, I could not escape the mental image of Miyazaki going about his deadly business. Ono would put up little resistance, being asthmatic and frail. And Miyazaki would have the help of his most trusted aide, Kudo, who would hold the old man down whilst Miyazaki administered the fatal injection behind one of Ono's knees. The concentrated solution of pentobarbitone would be strong enough to see off a horse.

The very thought of what was going on over at Ono's residence was, in a perverse way, quite thrilling. I found myself excited by the notion and styled myself as some kind of commander in charge of a secret mission, which in a way I was. It had taken a great deal of planning, and we had left no trail. The pentobarbitone had actually been sourced at a horse facility in the north whose veterinary quarters had experienced a mysterious burglary where nothing seemed to have been taken. In actual fact, and unbeknownst to them, a few vials of the lethal liquid had been replaced by harmless water. The genius of it all washed over me, but I knew this was just the beginning. If the gods were on our side, Ono would leave some kind of trail that would lead us straight to Nishii. The hunt would commence. If that proved to be the case, we would have to be expedient and act without hesitation. Once Nishii became aware of Ono's demise, he would go deeper undercover. "One step at a time. Be precise and be meticulous, keep calm, and always look over your shoulder." The words of my father were never far from my thoughts, even though they had failed to serve him with the good intent he offered to others.

I leaned over and put my hand on Azusa's thigh, then slowly moved it up under her skirt. She closed her eyes and parted her legs a little; I ran my hand between her thighs gently, brushing her hair with the back of my fingers. We were driving along winding roads, and I had to interrupt my sensual exploration to change the gears, an operation that proved to be a passion killer as far as Azusa was concerned. She placed her hand on my crotch and whispered into my ear, "Be patient," then turned her attention back to the wild outside. A few moments later we were driving up the small road that led to the driveway of the lodge. I did not tell Azusa that we had finally arrived, as I wanted to gauge her reaction to the sight that would appear before her in a matter of minutes. I had played down the lodge, referring to it as "a little retreat in the country" when in fact it was as palatial a country house as one could imagine. The design drew heavily on the French chateau style, and I had insisted that authentic building materials be used throughout. We had imported thousands of tonnes of French limestone, Italianate marble, and English oak. The finest Japanese craftsmen along with their European counterparts had taken three years to complete the grandest country house in Japan. Although it was built at my insistence and basically for my own purposes, my colleagues still saw it as a Mabuhay property. Toshio would often spend weekends here. The isolation would suit his needs for privacy, as his romantic life was far from conventional. Hideo and Ayumi had visited less frequently, preferring to spend most of their time in that gin-soaked wreck of a hotel. The arrangements suited me fine, as I considered it my place and deep down hated the idea of others staying in my lodge. At times I had entertained business associates there, especially when we had difficult negotiations to complete. I had often found that if you take the city folk out of the city, their minds tend to relax and they become a little more pliable. The correct environment is essential, especially when you are seeking to impose your will on those who think obstinacy is a quality to be proud of.

Last year we were having some minor trouble with a Buildings and Land Department official who was opposing a planning application for one of our new production facilities in Sendai. I had invited the jobsworth in question down to the Mabuhay offices to review the application, only to change the venue to the lodge at the last moment. We had spent an afternoon of fruitless negotiations and, despite our countless concessions, made little headway. On this occasion the charms of the Karuizawa countryside and laid-back feeling of the accommodation had failed to work in our favour. To show we had no hard feelings, despite having our planning application turned down, we hosted a small dinner party that evening for a few city types. Toshio had seen to the guest list, which comprised "friends" of Mabuhay and some charming female company to lighten up the evening. For a man who to my knowledge had never enjoyed a woman's body, Toshio was mighty adept at finding sophisticated beauties who were inclined to walk on the wild side. The wine and champagne flowed, and inevitably our stubborn planning fellow succumbed to the charms of a young lady who had been massaging his ego all evening.

Well, as is often the case when too much alcohol is combined with a mind-blowing beauty, things went a little too far. They found themselves alone in bed, and after a rather athletic session between the sheets, she lured him into the bathroom, where she put her sweet mouth to work in the place I guess his wife rarely went. She was already on the train, Tokyo bound and a thousand dollars to the good, before our man from Sendai awoke the next morning to find an envelope that had been pushed under his door and contained several revealing pictures of his drunken frolic, together with a copy of our planning application ready for his signature. Being a respectable married chap, he saw reason and also swiftly came around to thinking that Sendai could not afford to pass up the opportunity to have a great new industrial facility and increased employment prospects for hundreds of men and women. As men of honour, we made sure all the evidence of his little erotic episode was destroyed and bade him on his way with the sincerest of thanks. Sometimes the simplest investments pay the highest dividends. I'd had my doubts about the installation of a two-way mirror in one of the guest suites, but it had more than served its purpose on that occasion and had also, on more than one occasion, provided me with a moment or two of illicit pleasure.

We finally crested the winding road which had taken us through some dramatic Nordic-style scenery, and there before us, as if by magic, was my pride and joy, my country retreat looking resplendent in the weak wintry sunshine. Azusa gave a squeal of surprise, and her face lit up as she took in the magnificent splendour before her. I had played down its grandeur to the point where she may well have expected to find a log cabin awaiting her. She was mightily impressed, as were all visitors to the lodge. I felt a swell of pride coming over me and with a sense of boyish excitement was looking forward to giving her the grand tour. I slowed the Ferrari down so we could appreciate the lodge in all its glory as it loomed up large before us. Her manner had completely changed; she put her hand on my knee and asked, "How many bedrooms does it have?"

"Only ten, not including the servants' quarters," I replied.

She gave me a sly and provocative look and said, "I want to do it in every bedroom."

"Absolutely, my sweet little angel," I said, though I had grave doubts regarding my stamina on that score. The Ferrari was making a wonderful sound as it crunched along the pebble-stoned driveway, and with great relief, I killed the engine outside the main door. Four domestics had taken up their places by the entrance to greet us and make themselves ready for any tasks I needed. I had an excellent staff here at the lodge. Four permanent domestics kept the place in order when I was away. I supplemented their number with an additional four from the Ginza residence when I had a visit planned. In addition to the in-house staff, I employed four groundsmen whose responsibilities included vigilance, maintenance, and the upkeep of the gardens. You might say that we were well looked after.

I exited the car like a man twice my age. Those Italians must be nimble fellows. The small of my back was almost crippling me. I would get Azusa to put her soothing fingers to work. I instructed one of the maids to go and prepare a herbal bath for me and have a bottle of champagne and delicacies made ready in my personal suite. Azusa let out a rather embarrassing childlike whoop of delight, which made me cringe slightly. I would have to have a word with her later about self-control in front of the staff.

The senior member of the household staff, a loyal chap by the name of Niwa, enquired if we had any special needs that required attention. I told him I was expecting a visit from a colleague sometime tomorrow and that I was to be informed the moment he arrived. I also told him to make dining arrangements for seven o'clock and to make sure that at least one staff member would be available at a moment's notice around the clock. I shuffled alongside Azusa, who was too busy taking in all the wonders of the lodge to notice that I was in severe discomfort. The air had become noticeably chillier; you could just about see your own breath. Azusa, being typically underclothed, was shivering in a comical fashion. One of the maids had the wits to offer her a shawl, which she gratefully accepted. We all trooped along and up the few marble steps that led into the hallway. The hall was splendid as usual and smelt of the beeswax polish that was used to keep the timbers in fine fettle.

I said we would go straight up to my suite for a short recuperation. I felt sure I had seen the beginnings of a cheeky smirk on the face of one of the houseboys. A glance in his direction was enough to put him straight. The staircase was a little steep, and as I did not want to display weakness in front of the staff, I sent them on their way and began the painful ascent up the forty-three steps to the upper floor—a step for each of my years plus one. Azusa, who had finally realised I was in a spot of pain, assisted me by placing her arm around my waist and cajoling me up the stairs one by one. "My poor Makoto, I will make you better." She kept whispering sensual promises into my ear in an attempt to take my mind off the searing pain that had now moved into my left hip. I was starting to fear that I had slipped a disc in my back and would require the attention of a physician. My God! How the hell had this happened? I cursed myself for not letting Ogawa drive us in the Rolls. It would have taken an age, but at least I would have arrived refreshed and ready for a spot of bed action as opposed to bed inaction.

I had my arm around Azusa's shoulder and noticed how muscular her shoulders were. She was not long out of school, so I guessed she was still benefiting from all those long and arduous physical pursuits that today's educationists believe to be good for mind and body. I was in no kind of shape myself, and despite the coolness of the air, beads of sweat were breaking out on my forehead. Eventually we made the landing and I directed her to my suite, which housed the grandest rooms in the lodge.

Toshio also had a suite of rooms reserved for his private use; I had offered him exclusive use in return for his generosity in allowing me the upper floor in the Ginza residence. The suite was open, and a maid was standing by the door awaiting any further instructions. I dismissed her and with a great deal of support from my foxy nursemaid made it to the bed, where I lay whilst Azusa agonizingly helped me out of my trousers. I desperately needed to get into the bath and ease my lower back muscles. I prayed to God that I would find relief. With considerable effort and cursing I was finally down to my undershorts. Azusa went to the bathroom to check that the bath was ready. I could smell the sandalwood and prayed to God for deliverance from the burning pain that seemed to be spreading down my leg. She came back singing of the joys of the bathroom, which was indeed magnificent—the finest Italianate marble and gold plate, so pleasing on the eye and body.

Azusa flicked my undershorts and asked if I was ready. She removed my shorts and gave me a pitying look, as my flaccid state was obviously disappointing for her. She tried to give me a bit of encouragement by rubbing her hand over my crotch, but the little lad was not for moving, so she settled for helping me to the bathroom. She wanted to call for assistance, but I firmly refused. It just would not do to lose your dignity in front of the help. After a few minutes I was eventually finding relief in the water. The pain had subsided a little but only if I remained motionless. If I moved, it came in a searing wave, as if a dog had sunk its teeth into my hip and refused to let go. My lovely, anticipated weekend was slowly coming apart in front of my very eyes. I lay back and cursed my rotten luck.

I was joined in the tub a few moments later by Azusa bearing two glasses of champagne in all her naked glory. The girl was game and trying her best to take my mind off the hellish pain. She sat on the edge of the bath, washing her body in the most erotic fashion, soaping her large firm breasts, and making an exhibition of cleansing her womanhood. She was watching me the whole time, waiting for a response, but although the mind was willing, I was as soft as the day I was born. My mind was totally focused on dealing with this wretched pain. Azusa helped me out of the bath and gently towelled me down. Gingerly I made my way back to the bed and with a great deal of suffering managed to get between the sheets. There was no relief to be had, so I resigned myself to summoning a physician. I told Azusa to ring for Niwa and ask him to seek out someone to come to my aid.

I spent the next three or four hours lying in bed, not daring to stir. The slightest movement was enough to send me into spasms of agony. The only physician on call was a chap by the name of Kato, and he had been called out on an emergency to Iruaza, which was more than an hour's drive away. My body might have been in the throes of agony, but my mind was still as bright as a button. Iruaza was the small village where Ono kept his country house. Was Dr. Kato attending to a scenario that I had been playing through my mind for days?

Azusa tried to distract me from my suffering by telling me all about her friends and what bores they were. She went on about how much she had hated school and what a relief it was to finally get out into the real world. Her monologue was grating on me, and finally I snapped at her and told her to be quiet. She started to sob, quietly at first, and then descended into great chest-heaving wails. To my surprise I felt more than a little sympathy for her. I mean, it could not be a lot of fun being shut up with a bad-tempered, middle-aged, immobile fellow, even though he was one of the wealthiest men in the country.

I reached out and stroked her hair and said I was sorry. I asked her to open the bedside drawer and remove a small black velvet pouch that I had discreetly managed to place there before being stripped of my clothes. She did so without paying much heed. I asked her to open it. Her curiosity was aroused, and her sobbing abated a little. There was a fine gold necklace with a beautiful ruby pendant set in black jade. It was a fabulous piece of jewellery, unique in its design and origin. Through the excruciating pain, which was now ripping me to shreds, I managed to soften my tone to something resembling affection. "Azusa, it is yours to keep for all time. Please accept it as a loving symbol of my affection for you."

She burst into floods of tears again—this time tears of happiness, I hoped. She was astounded and at a loss for words. Forgetting my condition she made a play to hug me, a move that nearly sent me to the ceiling and back in agony. She smiled and asked if she could go to the mirror to try it on, and disappeared into the bathroom, emerging a few moments later wearing nothing but the necklace. She looked absolutely stunning, and in that second I believe her beauty was unlike anything I had ever seen before. Perhaps it was the pain that was making me soft in the mind, but I do believe I was beginning to feel the stirrings of something deep in my emotional backwater that caught me off guard.

Is this how it starts? I mean, Azusa and me? Surely it was the pain playing tricks with my mind. The necklace had finally found a neck to grace, even though I had my doubts about presenting it to one so young and fickle. How would she explain how she had come about it to her parents? My reckless generosity could find a way of coming back to haunt me. But in that moment I did not care two hoots. The necklace had been in my possession for an eternity, and I had very nearly presented it to various other lovers over the years. Luckily for Azusa, I had managed to fend off my desire to make a grand romantic gesture and keep ahold of it. It may have been beyond value, I wasn't sure—it was crafted from pieces that once made up a splendid late Ming dynasty artefact, an ornamental Chinese lion. The ruby was its eye and the jade a part of its feet. I had resisted the temptation to indulge myself with any of the Mabuhay loot, but after I had successfully negotiated our second shipment, I thought a little reward was in order. I had asked Romana to check the inventory for a suitable item that could be rendered untraceable and at the same time personalised in an exquisite form. The necklace was the result. I believed his daughter, Ismarelda, owned the other "eye" and wore it set into a gold bracelet. I had never told Toshio—or anyone, for that matter—that I had "dipped" into the hoard to satisfy my own personal desires. I feared he would not approve at all, and I had no desire to find myself on the dark side of Toshio Hamazaki, for I, amongst all men, had been witness to his excesses and the brutal havoc he was capable of unleashing.

I had been lying in agony for hours. Azusa had been kindly pouring champagne down my throat in an attempt to lighten my suffering; alas, her efforts were in vain. The pain had now taken me over, and I felt a mix of relief and foreboding when Dr. Kato finally managed to put in an appearance. He was ushered into the room by Niwa, whose knock had sent Azusa scurrying off to put some clothes on. I doubted he could have seen anything that might have tickled his fancy, as his spectacles had the thickest lenses I had ever seen. They magnified his eyes to almost grotesque proportions, most unnerving for his patients, I was sure. Kato came over to my bedside and placed his hand on my forehead, then took my wrist in his hand to feel my pulse rate. "So, Hosokawa san, what ails you on this fine evening."

His voice seemed to boom around the room, or perhaps it was just normal in comparison to Azusa's sweet, gentle tones. I did not care much for his manner, which had an edge of sarcasm about it, but I was in no position to take a stand. I explained how only that very morning I was the picture of health and mobility, only to find myself now in agony and feeling as if I were being seared with white-hot pokers. Kato nodded and asked if I had recently carried anything heavy or engaged in any form of unusual physical activity. I so wished to shock him by telling of my bedroom sessions with Azusa, but good manners caught ahold of my tongue. Instead I said that nothing untoward had occurred, and then I remembered the discomfort I had suffered when I leaned over to open the car door for Azusa.

Upon my telling Kato this, he just nodded as if I had diagnosed myself. At this moment Azusa appeared from the bathroom wearing a fine cotton yukata. Kato looked her over. "Young lady, you are in fine time to give me a helping hand with your poor father here." My immediate indignation and Kato's verbal gaffe were enough to send her into hysterics. Kato ignored her amusement and told her to pull back the bedcovers, which they did in unison, revealing me in all my pained, naked glory. Kato shook his head slowly. "My word, most unfortunate. Avert your eyes, young lady." He placed a bedside towel over my less-than-impressive manhood and then proceeded to inflict the most painful thing ever experienced by a mortal. He gripped each of my ankles and pushed my legs, bending them at the knees. I thought I was going to pass out. I'm sure my screams echoed around the house. I was drenched in a cold sweat and uttering the vilest range of curses known to man, all of which seemed to wash over Kato like water off a duck's back. Azusa had made herself scarce and gone back into the bathroom.

Satisfied with his torturous endeavour Kato replaced the bedcovers and tutted to himself. "It seems that you are suffering from a slipped disc. I would say the nerve is pinched in the fifth or sixth vertebra. I will administer something for the pain and also leave some oral medication that should bring some relief." Those last words were like honey to a starving bear. Kato rummaged through his bag and eventually extracted a hypodermic, which he filled with colourless liquid. Now, the irony of this was not lost on me, but I was in no state to offer it any further contemplation. Kato rolled me over onto my side, ignoring my wails of agony and pleas for mercy. I did not feel the needle prick me, but the wave of relief that oozed through my body was the most welcome sensation I had ever experienced. Pure joy and lightness descended on me as if by magic. I immediately changed my opinion about Kato's skills, for I now rated him as the finest physician in the entire world.

He rolled me onto my back and proceeded to explain his treatment. He said he had administered a mild opiate that should bring relief for about four to five hours. When the pain returned, I was to take two tablets, which had a similar base of medication. He stressed that the medication was merely masking the pain and making it more manageable. My condition could improve only with prolonged bed rest, of which he prescribed ten days. I was so light-headed and drowsy, everything was looming in and out of my vision. I had the feeling that I could see his words as well as hear them. I muttered my thanks as he packed his bag to leave. Then I remembered the reason for his lateness and through my drug-induced haze managed to find my words, which I slurred out like some barroom drunkard. "Doctor, I only wish you had brought me this relief sooner. I take it you were delayed on some mission of mercy?"

He looked down at me, his big, magnified eyes like billiard balls in my increasingly hallucinogenic state. I thought he was just going to let my query hang in the air, but he must have thought I deserved some explanation for his tardiness. He shook his head. "Yes indeed, an emergency and a most distressing one at that.

Some poor fellow over in Iruaza suffered a cardiac arrest the likes of which I have never seen. Looked like he had seen the devil himself. Such blueness about his features, his poor heart must have literally exploded inside of him. Tragic case. Anyway, Hosokawa san, I will leave you now. Take plenty of rest whilst you have the relief. You may want to get that daughter of yours to apply a hot poultice to your lower back. I will call on you tomorrow to assess your condition. Good night."

I am sure he winked at me—or was it a nervous twitch? I found I could not contain my laughter and started smiling away like some simple village idiot. Kato looked down at me, shook his head understandingly, and left. Perhaps he put my giggling down to the medication, which was partly accurate, but in my chemically induced state I had a vision of Ono's blue head exploding. It was somehow shockingly comforting.

Azusa had shown a bit of uncharacteristic initiative by asking the staff to make up a futon for her so she could spend the night by my bedside. The medication was playing merry hell with my mind, and I was unsure if I was awake or in a deep sleep. Perhaps I was somewhere in between. I felt a cool towel placed on my forehead and looked up to see my long-gone mother standing there, tears streaming down her cheeks. It was so real, I reached out to touch her, but as my hand found hers, she drew it away and in one sudden motion gave me a violent slap on the cheek. I pleaded with her to go away and leave me in peace, muttering apologies for past misdeeds. "Mother, Mother, it was all for the best."

An icy cold towel placed gently on my forehead brought me back into the real world. Azusa sat on the bed, all kindness and sweet smiles, whispering in my ear. "Only I am here, my sweetest. No other. I will care for you." I looked up through teary eyes and reached for her. She took my hand and kissed it gently and started to sing a lullaby. Cute baby Chinese dragons danced around her throat in a hypnotic fashion.

I drifted off into the recesses of my mind. I was flying the Pan American China Clipper to Manila. We were floating on cotton wool clouds, and all of my fellow passengers were convulsed with hysterical laughter as if they were all privy to some private joke. I was seated next to Azusa, whose bosom seemed to have trebled in size, and she too was laughing manically. Toshio was dressed in a stewardess uniform, replete with tight skirt and high heels, moving about the cabin pouring everyone "Mabuhay cocktails" and regaling all with tales of his foulest deeds. Tanezawa was coupled with Miyazaki, and they were enjoying the most violent sexual encounter I had ever witnessed. Not a single soul was paying them any heed at all. Hideo was going up and down the aisle, demonstrating a new vacuum cleaner, weaving in and out of the mayhem. Ayumi was soundly beating him about the head with a large portfolio and shouting, "Clean up your own mess!" repeatedly. It was a madcap sojourn into hell. The doors to the pilots' cabin burst open, and there, looking back over his shoulder, flying our plane was Romana. He had a devilishly blue face and jet-black teeth. He was smiling directly at me. No words passed his lips, but I could read his thoughts as if they were on a billboard. "I have your life in my hands. You are mine."

I let out a violent, high, wailing scream which immediately put a stop to the madcap laughter. Everyone turned their stares on me. Their merriment had turned into anger, and abusive threats started to rain down on me like confetti. Romana was the only one still smiling. We locked eyes, and for a brief second he looked almost human. Then he slammed the cabin door shut with such force that the plane started to descend into a tailspin, and we were all flung from our seats, screaming and bouncing around in blind panic. We were all being smothered in foul-smelling excrement as we descended towards our doom. The screaming reached ear-splitting proportions. Then everything went black.

The ice water brought me around. Azusa was standing there with a towel that she had soaked in the champagne ice bucket. "Makoto, you scared the life out of me. You must have had some kind of foul nightmare. Your screams and shouts were the strangest things I have ever heard. Who is Romana?"

I shook my head. "I have no idea," I said, praying that my drugged self had not caused my tongue to slip. "It was just the medication playing tricks on my mind. How long have I been out?" She thought I had slept for about two hours or so. I tried to move, but my back seemed to have seized into some kind of spasm. Although the pain was not back to the epic proportions of before, I asked Azusa for some water and two of Kato's pills. Little did I know that I had taken my first steps into a spiralling cycle of dependency that would blight my life forever.

The oral medication combined with the harder stuff that was still cruising around my system sent me into a deep sleep—so deep I believe I was almost comatose. I came round late the following afternoon, completely disoriented. It took a few moments for me to find my wits, and much to my relief I was able to lean over and pull on the velvet rope to summon assistance. Azusa was nowhere to be seen. I looked over at the clock on the mantel; it told me it was one o'clock. Surely I had not been out for over twelve hours. With a growing sense of irritation I yanked on the rope again. Within seconds there was a knock on the door, and I shouted for them to enter.

Niwa appeared, bearing a decanter of ice water and some sliced apple and pear. I asked him to prepare a bath for me and arrange to have the bedsheets changed, as I had been sweating like a horse in the night and the dampness was grossly uncomfortable. I asked him if he had seen my "companion." He replied, "Yes, sir, I do believe she is having tea in the library with Miyazaki san. Shall I summon her for you?"

This took me by surprise and instantly unleashed a swell of emotions. I was not too concerned about Miyazaki knowing about my private life. I mean, it is hellishly difficult to conceal the everyday tidbits of one's own daily life when you work so closely with somebody like Miyazaki—especially in our particular line of work. I was quite sure he already knew of my relationship with Azusa. Surprisingly, though I hate to admit it, I found myself in a jealous haze. I was all too aware of Azusa's flirty nature, and that combined with Miyazaki's lustful personality was enough to set my emotional alarm bells ringing. I had seen women almost throw themselves at Miyazaki. Begrudgingly I had to admit the man had a certain "animalistic" charm which sat easily alongside his wildness. He was at least a decade older than me, yet carried his age well. In fact he looked almost youthful. Perhaps all that punishing physical exercise carried some merit after all. He was in fine shape for a man in his fifties, but surely Azusa would not open her romantic parameters that far.

However irrational my thoughts, I could not get them out of my head. Perhaps my hallucinogenic nightmare was still playing. Tanezawa and Miyazaki had copulated in my dream, and I could not rid myself of the image. I closed my eyes for a moment, but now Azusa had taken over where Tanezawa had left off and was being ridden by Miyazaki in brutal fashion. The cold sweating was gathering momentum. I took a long drink of ice cold water and told Niwa to send Azusa to me immediately and inform Miyazaki that I would see him in ten minutes. He bowed and left the room. I could feel my pain creeping back up on me. The medicine bottle was within reach, and I took two pills for good measure. Only six pills remained. I would ask Kato for more when he called on me later.

There was a knock on the door and I prepared myself to greet Azusa, only to find it was the maid bearing an armful of freshly laundered bedclothes. I told her to leave them by the bed and come back later. Maybe the medicine was once again "kicking in," but she looked divine in a cute sort of way, and it was all I could do to restrain myself from reaching out and giving her a friendly pat on the backside. My thoughts were lustful, but my body was not in tandem.

As I was admiring the maid's shapely figure, Azusa, having silently entered the room, caught me completely unawares. "It's so good to see you have recovered a bit of your old self," she said, a comment which was too close to the truth for comfort, and wickedly insightful for one so young.

"Where have you been?" I asked. "Leaving me to suffer alone in the depths of this wretched state."

She looked nonplussed; maybe my reliance on her nursing skills had given her confidence a boost. "I have been keeping your friend company whilst you were in a deep sleep. I thought it a courtesy to do so, especially as the poor man has been waiting all of two hours to see you." She was looking at me, trying to muster up a bit of defiance whilst at the same time trying to gauge my reaction.

"How did you explain your presence here to him?" I asked. "I mean, it may have been damned awkward."

She picked up on my tone. "Don't you remember? You introduced me to Miyazaki san on the night of our own first acquaintance. You were a little far gone, as I recall. It was Miyazaki san who drove me home later that evening after I had spent a little time with you alone in your rooms." She looked intently into my eyes for some kind of affirmation, which I could not muster. Her hand had roamed under the bedclothes, and she was gently tickling my stomach. Her teasing was having no effect, as the medication had once more dulled my senses. Had I asked Miyazaki to take her home? I had a vague recollection of something along those lines but for the life of me could not recall the details. As she said, I was far gone at the time and possibly in a much worse condition now. I considered it one of my finer talents that I never forgot a face or a connection, so how had I let something so close to me pass me by? I did not have the energy or inclination to work through the implications of this, and in any case I was eager to hear what Miyazaki had to report about his murderous mission.

Azusa was becoming adept at reading my mood and could see that I was not in a companionable frame of mind. Not wishing to be in the firing line of a verbal backlash, she offered to go and find Miyazaki. She was already halfway out of the room before I realised she had left my bedside. My eyes were feeling as heavy as two Fuji apples and my mouth was bone dry, but I could not muster the effort to drink anything at all. I had the strange sensation of looking down at myself from above, as if I had become two beings.

Miyazaki's sombre tones brought me back to earth, and a small sense of reality crept back into my drug-addled self. I had not even realised that he had entered my room, and now here he was, standing by my bedside looking like a dashing version of the Grim Reaper. He was dressed mostly in black as usual, but had a fine burgundy silk scarf tied around his neck. His hair as always was swept back, immaculate, the few strands of grey giving him an added sense of authority. "Hosokawa san, can I get you anything? You look all in." I motioned towards the decanter of iced lemon water and he poured me a glass, pausing to examine my medicine bottle. He shook his head slightly in an almost disdainful manner, as if my medication had offended him. I tried to manoeuvre my body upright, but the pain in my back was still too much, even though it was a different kind of pain. I now felt like I was weighted down at the hips, a kind of grinding agony.

Without so much as a hint of warning Miyazaki hoisted me up and propped two pillows behind my back. The pain was heavy and dull but I managed to bear it whilst he held the glass of icy water to my lips. I took a few gulps, most of which dribbled down my front. Miyazaki's care skills did not extend to wiping me down, so I dried myself off with the bedsheet. "I was speaking with Ito san just now, and she told me all about your pain," he said. "She said the doctor prescribes ten days bed rest. Are you going to be laid up for so long?"

Ito san? It took a moment for me to realise that he was referring to Azusa. It seemed as if he were speaking from far away. I wanted to reply, but I was having trouble getting my words out. It was almost as if it was not worth the effort. I motioned with my hand for him to come closer. He bent down and I said in a feeble tone, "Ono—tell me about Ono." He straightened up and walked over to the door, opened it, and checked outside to make sure no stray ears were around. Ever so vigilant, that was Miyazaki san through and through. Satisfied with his precautions, he came back to my bedside and drew up an ottoman and sat down to regale me with his report.

Miyazaki was succinct and to the point. That was his style, and in my present condition it was something I had cause to be grateful for. He leaned closer and told me how he and Kudo had arrived at Ono's place in Iruaza around four in the afternoon. They spent two hours observing his house from a wooded area opposite.

Once satisfied that Ono was spending the weekend alone, they made their move. Leaving their car concealed, they approached his door on foot. They could hear the strains of a piano concerto coming from one of the rooms beyond the hall. Miyazaki tried Ono's front door and was relieved to find it unlocked—not uncommon in this part of the world but careless all the same. They crept through the house, following the source of the music, which could be heard coming from the lounge, the door of which was slightly ajar. They could see Ono working at his bureau with his back to them.

They paused for a moment whilst Miyazaki readied the hypodermic. Kudo pushed open the door, which creaked on its hinges. This startled Ono, who stood to confront his intruders. Miyazaki tried to calm the now frightened Ono and reassure him that they meant him no harm, a difficult play when concealing a hypodermic behind one's back. Miyazaki switched off the radio, which was, ironically a Mabuhay product and incidentally one of Hideo's finest. Ono must have sensed he was lying and his wits kicked in, because he tried to make a dash for it through an adjacent door. But he was no match for Kudo, whose agility coupled with his speed and strength soon had Ono under his control.

Kudo gripped Ono around the neck, manhandled him over to the couch, and forced him down, careful not to leave any signs of struggle on his person. Miyazaki asked Ono to be sensible and cooperate, something he flatly refused to do. The only thing he said was "Did Hamazaki send you to do his dirty work? Tell him from me I will not be threatened and I will not give up my duty to expose his dirty secrets." It seemed that Ono had not fully grasped the fact that he was in the final minutes of his mortal life. Miyazaki pressed him about his links to Nishii, possibly known as Leung Cheuk Man. Ono said nothing, but merely stared ahead stubbornly. Miyazaki told me that he admired Ono's fortitude and the fact that in the face of such a threat Ono had managed to keep a certain dignity about him. Aware that precious moments were ticking by, Miyazaki gave a nod to Kudo, who instantly grabbed Ono's left leg and forced it high into the air. This threw Ono off balance, and as he floundered, Miyazaki stuck him behind the kneecap with his deadly potion.

At this point in telling me the story, Miyazaki shook his head almost in disbelief. He said it was something that had to be witnessed with one's own eyes to be believed. It was obvious we had gotten the dosage wrong. Ono had been injected with about 25 per cent of the amount of pentobarbitone that would be given to an injured horse. The effects were instantaneous; Ono had gone into a wild convulsion, his head had filled with blood and literally swelled in size before their very eyes. Miyazaki was convinced that Ono's head was about to explode. Kudo and Miyazaki stood back whilst Ono was in his death throes, speechless but no doubt morbidly fascinated by the gruesome spectacle unfolding before them. It was over in a matter of seconds, though to Miyazaki, it seemed like minutes. With a final few spasms and twitches Ono was history. Kudo and Miyazaki carried his body back to the bureau, where they left him slumped over his papers, a position they hoped would look more natural to the first person to find him. Ono's face had settled down a little now that his "pump" had given up the ghost, but it was still grotesque, and his features were so contorted that anyone would believe that the man had died from pure terror.

Kudo was sent upstairs to search for any paper clues to the whereabouts of Nishii or for anything out of the ordinary. Miyazaki searched downstairs, but found little of interest. The house was modest in size and they thought they had covered it well, but as they were about to give up and make their retreat, Miyazaki found a sheaf of papers concealed below the bureau's writing surface in a crudely fashioned false bottom. There were copies of the disgusting posters that had plagued us a few months back as well as new designs that were intended to mock and taunt us further. This was the confirmation that we needed: Ono had been engaged in a vendetta against us and in league with others who were still at large. Nishii was the prey, but we still could not put him in our sights. Miyazaki put the posters back in the bureau. He carefully made sure that nothing look disturbed. It was vital that Ono's death be seen as free of suspicion. As he was putting them back into their exact place, he noticed a card had fallen onto the floor. It was a plain white card with "Hotel M Rm 617" written on it. Miyazaki placed it in his pocket, knowing it was unlikely to be missed.

Just as they finished their final checks, making sure all was in order, they heard a car approach and stop in the driveway to the house. From the lounge window they could see a young woman unfastening the barred gate to drive her car up to the entrance. Kudo and Miyazaki quickly moved to the kitchen, where they hid inside the walk-in pantry. From their lair they could hear her open the front door. There were a few tense moments when they thought she would come straight into the kitchen, but to their relief she went directly to the lounge, shouting, "Daddy, Daddy! Surprise!" The surprise was all hers, and Kudo and Miyazaki quickly slipped out of the house to the woods beyond, with Ono's daughter's frantic screams ringing in their ears.

I had listened serenely to Miyazaki recounting his story; his words were flowing all over me and giving me a marvellous sense of comfort. I could feel my heart tingling with satisfaction, a feeling that took me back to my childhood when my nanny would sit by my bed and read me a bedtime story. I opened my eyes and stared at the ceiling for a few moments, then turned my head to Miyazaki. "You did well. Thank you as always. You must go back to town and report to Toshio before tonight's celebrations. He will want to know. Convey my best wishes and tell him that I will be laid up for a while." The effort of speaking drained me of all energy, and all I wanted to do was close my eyes and sleep. But Miyazaki seemed reluctant to take his leave. I sensed that there was something on his mind. "Yes, what is it?"

Miyazaki cleared his throat and poured himself a glass of water. "It's Ito san. She has asked me to ask you if you would permit her to leave earlier than planned. She was hoping, with your permission, of course, to be able to ride with us back to town today."

This was something I had not figured on. Originally, we had planned to return to town together tomorrow at lunchtime; those plans had been well and truly scuppered. I had not given any thought to how she would get back now. I suppose Miyazaki was the obvious option, but there was this nagging sense of jealousy that I could not shake off. I so wanted to tell him to leave her be, but it was plain that I was not in any condition to exert my will. "That seems like the sensible thing to do. Ken, tell Azusa I want to see her now." He gave me a sympathetic smile that was laced in pity, as if he were the one indulging my last wishes, nodded, turned on his heels, and left without so much as a friendly wish for a speedy recovery.

My relationship with Miyazaki was complex. We needed each other to the point where the boundary between employer and underling had eroded so much, we were almost as one. Sure, Miyazaki worked for Mabuhay and more specifically for me directly. He was without portfolio, but I had come to regard him as my "man for all seasons." He owed me his life, for I had saved him from certain imprisonment or possibly worse. In return he had pledged his unswerving loyalty to me, and I had never had cause to question his professionalism or commitment to duty. The man was ruthless and cunning, and possessed the requisite amount of evil in his soul to be successful. His personal charm left a lot to be desired, but it never failed to amaze me how the ladies would melt in his presence. I often observed women giving him a sideways glance at parties or other functions and working their way into his circle, fashioning an introduction for themselves. I had the wealth, but he had everything else, and it would leave me cold when I found myself on the outside looking in whilst Miyazaki could sit back with a relaxed, natural ease and seem comfortable with any woman of his choosing. However, I was determined that he would not be so at ease with my Azusa.

I was born cursed with a vivid imagination, and once an image takes root in my mind, it grows into something that is impossible to separate from reality. Right now my imagination was working itself up into a jealous sexual fantasy. I pictured Miyazaki pulling his car over to the side of the road and Azusa smiling as he leaned over to kiss her. Her hands working frantically to unbuckle his belt, his left hand finding its way inside her blouse and pushing up her brassiere to cup her large breast. Her nipples hardening as they always do when touched.

My mind was racing through this sexual voyeuristic fantasy. I had just reached the point where she frees his manhood from his trousers and gasps in delight at his size as he pushes her head down to take him in her mouth when her voice startled me into the present. It was like being caught by matron back at school with your pants down and something naughty in your hands. "How are you feeling?" She was sitting by the bed, her hand on my brow, a look of concern on her face. I looked into her eyes, and at that moment

I knew she was something more precious to me than just another flighty bedroom partner. Perhaps the drugs had warped my brain, but I wanted this girl more than any other I had ever known. Was it love? Had I finally stumbled into love?

"Azusa, please marry me." The words were out before I knew what I was saying. I could not believe myself. What in the world was I thinking? She looked shocked and put her hand to her mouth in a gesture of surprise. She was speechless, but her eyes were smiling. I looked deep into those dark pools as if trying to find her soul. "Say something. Anything. Yes or no?"

She moved her mouth, but words would not come out. She turned her head to one side and bit down on her lip. When she looked back at me, a tear was rolling down her cheek. "Yes." She took my hand and brought it to her lips and gave me a gentle kiss. I could feel her true affection and my heart-warmed satisfaction. She was now my betrothed, and our relationship was bound on a promise. Her simple "yes" was all the reply I needed.

I closed my eyes in relief, and for the first time in what seemed like an age, I felt as if I had done something good, something that brought happiness into my life. Azusa found her voice and went on about how we would tell her father and other such things. Yes, the father would be a problem, especially since he was younger than his future son-in-law, but nothing that could not be overcome. His daughter was to marry into Mabuhay, and that alone would give her a lifestyle far above that of other people. How could the man object? His little girl was set to become one of the wealthiest teenagers in the country, not to mention the fact that she'd be able to make the lucrative connections that would no doubt help him climb the greasy pole of his own profession.

I pulled her closer to me, gave her a kiss on the cheek, and whispered that we would make it official after I had sought her father's consent, and to keep it between us until the formal announcement had been made. She smiled and nodded and stood up and wrapped her arms about herself in a self-hug of happiness. I so wanted to kiss her passionately to mark our new status, but I knew my breath was not at its sweetest, to say the least.

Azusa was almost dancing around the room in a fit of excitement. "Makoto, I have to go back to town, and Miyazaki san has kindly offered to drive me. I have so much to do and think about." She saw the look of disappointment on my face and came back to my bedside with a look of concern. "My poor Makoto. Please, please, please hurry back to Tokyo. I will be so lonely, and we have so much to plan and do. Oh my! I am so excited." She gave me a big wet kiss on the cheek and almost danced out of the room, pausing at the door to blow me another kiss and holding her hands over her heart in an affectionate gesture.

She closed the door gently behind her, leaving me to my solitude. In those first moments alone and feeling physically helpless, a heavy sense of insecurity descended on me. I was bedridden and feeble, old beyond my years, but I had the most beautiful fiancée any man could ever wish for and more money than I could ever spend. I tried to muster up the determination to remain positive and get back on my feet, but my mood was heavy. I reached for the medicine bottle and took the last of the pills—a double dose just to see me through this spell. When I awoke from the depths of unconsciousness, all would be well with me and the world.

★ ★ ★

"Hosokawa san! Can you hear me? Wake up!" The voice was miles away, familiar, and yet I could not put a face to it. Ice cold water which smelt of lemon brought me around a little, but I preferred to slumber in my own little world. I mumbled as such to whoever it was that was trying to disturb my bliss. There were a few voices and I could hear some comings and goings, but they were not real, and they faded away to nothing. I recalled smiling and trying to say farewell, but the light had been turned off, and it was just me in the darkness. I was left alone to myself, bathing in my own warm sweat and singing nonsense songs for my own amusement.

Then, without warning the blinding light came cascading and crashing into the core of my brain. I squeezed my eyes tight shut, but there was no escape. I had finally returned to the banality we call everyday life. With a great deal of difficulty I managed to squint through heavy, painful eyes. My eyeballs felt as though they were on fire. The effort to speak was too much. I had not noticed that someone was in the room with me; the curvaceous maid whose name I did not know was attending to me. She pressed a glass of water to my lips and I tried to take a drink but failed to get it down. I looked her over. My word, she was fine.

She explained how Dr. Kato had called on me yesterday evening and had become concerned when he could not wake me. The doctor had asked her to stay vigilant by my bedside and to call him when I had come around. My senses were slowly returning. I was light-headed, but my brain was still dulled. To my relief I found that I could move without too much pain in my back. I asked the maid what time it was and was astounded to hear that it was four in the afternoon. I had been out for nearly a day, which meant that the celebrations down in Tokyo were over. I felt a strange sense of detachment from my ordinary world. I asked the maid to prepare a bath and some food for me. I was ravenously hungry. I could not remember the last time I had eaten anything. Was it three days ago?

I lay in bed, listening to the sound of running water coming from the bathroom. The maid came back and placed a cool towel on my forehead. She asked me if I required any assistance to get to the bathroom. It was obvious I could not do anything for myself, and I just nodded. She said she would call for Niwa, and stood to move. I gripped her wrist and in a pitiful tone said, "Please don't." She looked a little frightened and lowered her head. I pulled back my dank bedclothes, forgetting that I was still totally naked. She gasped and looked away. I peered down at myself and much to my surprise found that I was standing proud and rock hard. Maybe it was the drugs or the injection or simply the pain, but I seemed to have lost the mental connection with my state of arousal. I locked eyes with the maid and gave her my most pained and pitiful look, and with a little coaxing she reluctantly began to help me to my feet. I was a heavy deadweight for such a delicate girl, and the task proved beyond her.

I sank back into the bed with an exaggerated groan. I was able to move without too much pain, although it was still there. The small burst of effort had brought me out into a sweat. The maid towelled my forehead once more. I stroked the back of her hand and felt a little emboldened when she did not resist. I coaxed her hand onto my chest. She was still holding the icy cold towel, and it felt good on my hot skin. I became more daring and guided her lower and lower. "Please," I whispered. She bit her lip and looked away towards the window. I had hold of her wrist and moved her hand down onto my engorged penis. She held it for a moment and then tried to withdraw, but I coaxed her to move her hand up and down. I closed my eyes as she went about the business of bringing me relief. I was not long in coming and let out a whoosh of breath as I did so. I felt totally relaxed for the first time in days.

My tranquillity was broken by the sound of gentle weeping. I opened my eyes and saw that the maid had tears rolling down her cheeks and her shoulders were heaving up and down as she tried to control herself. For a moment I experienced a sense of self-disgust, but I managed to chase that notion from my head. I looked at her and patted her on the arm. "There, there, my dear. It is nothing to cry about. Our little secret, eh?" Her sobbing continued. "Tell me, what is your name?"

"Murakami, Megumi Murakami," she managed to get out between breathy sobs.

I stroked her arm a little more. "Megumi, go over to my closet and bring me my briefcase." She looked across the room and then back to me. I gave her a nod of encouragement, and she walked slowly with her head held low. She found my case and carried it clutched to her chest back to my bedside. I asked her to open it and look for a brown envelope, which she did. She passed the envelope to me, and I rummaged around the contents, finally finding a money clip which held fifty thousand yen. I pressed it into her hand. "Megumi Chan, take this, it is yours." She looked astounded and began to cry some more. I closed her fingers around the money and whispered, "Our secret." She looked at me and nodded. The tears had stopped, and she had regained a little control over her emotions. She stood and bowed and left my bedside, walking backwards all the way to the door, giving little bows on her way. The door closed, leaving me to reflect on yet another sordid little incident, the latest in a long line of similar occurrences. Had I just corrupted a sweet little innocent thing or had she been coy all along? For my own conscience's sake, I decided to believe the latter.

After Megumi had left, I began to experience remorse. I thought of Azusa, and remorse suddenly turned into guilt. What kind of husband would I make? I knew myself all too well. My own failings were so much a part of me that I could not even recall any time when I had led a pure and simple life. In my heart I knew I could not become a different person no matter how hard I tried. If anyone had to change, it would have to be Azusa. She would have to learn to be an "accommodating" wife. I would do my best for appearances' sake, but she must learn to live under my rules.

As I was daydreaming about my future marital life, there was a knock on the door and, after waiting a respectable minute, Niwa opened it and enquired if he could deliver my meal tray. I bade him entry. He was pushing a small serving trolley which was laden with a large silver salver and teapot. He did not make any eye contact with me at all, preferring to go about his business in a rather brusque but efficient manner. Had he picked up that something had happened between the maid and me? I tried to deduce as much from his demeanour, but Niwa had a cool poker face which gave nothing away. Still, the nagging doubt preyed at the back of my mind. I cursed myself for being so rash and vowed not to go down that path again. Good domestics are hard to find, and there is little to be gained from upsetting the household just to satisfy a moment of weakness. My word! Was that common sense sneaking up on me?

Niwa lifted the lid to reveal a culinary delight that had my mouth watering like a hungry wolf. Poached salmon, mushroom rice, boiled spinach with sesame seeds, and a tray of salted pickles: Everything was presented and cooked to perfection. They had prepared hot barley tea and a glass of freshly squeezed tangerine juice. There was also a small dish of sliced persimmon. Niwa asked if I needed help to sit up in the bed. I nodded, and he held me under both arms and without warning hoisted me into some kind of a sitting position. The pain gripped me for a second or two before subsiding into something almost bearable. I had to bite my lip to prevent myself from hurling expletives in Niwa's direction. He then deftly placed the lap tray on my bed, and I set about my feast. I must admit my eating manners left a little to be desired, as I was so hungry I could have thrown the whole lot down my throat with my bare hands. Niwa enquired if there was anything else he could assist me with, and I told him to return shortly to help me into the bathroom. He bowed and left me to my gorging.

I soon cleared my tray and was thinking of calling for seconds when I noticed a newspaper on the lower shelf of the trolley. With a great deal of discomfort I reached over and managed to grab it. It was the latest edition of the Yomiuri, and as I had expected, the Mabuhay anniversary celebrations were featured on the front page. My eyes shot to the picture of Toshio smiling like a Cheshire cat. He was wearing some kind of fancy blue sash. At first I put this down to his flamboyant dress sense, but it took only a few seconds for it to trigger recognition in my mind. You don't spend a decade in the diplomatic corps without recognising honours regalia. With a swelling sense of invidiousness I read through the article. My eyes skimmed over the parts about the splendour and the guests and all the other contrite nonsense that seems to pass for news until they reached the point that sent my blood cold with resentment. "The event marked the extraordinary rise to prominence of Mabuhay, a company that has become a household name across the nation. Company founders Toshio Hamazaki and Hideo Tanaka were rewarded for their contributions towards the regeneration of the national economy. His Excellency the Emperor conferred the Grand Cordon of the Order of the Sacred Treasure, 1st Class upon the pair. Our picture shows Hamazaki san proudly wearing his sash, which was presented on behalf of His Excellency by the Lord Chamberlain, who made the surprise announcement at last evening's event."

I frantically worked my way through the article to see if any award for my own self was mentioned. I reread the piece to make sure I had not overlooked anything. With sinking despair matched by a flood of envy I tossed the newspaper to one side. The injustice of it was downright hard to stomach. I was just as much a part of Mabuhay's success as they were. Why had I been overlooked?

Then I began to get an inkling why. I had left the diplomatic service to pursue a life in private enterprise, something the high echelons of civil life find hard to accept, least of all understand. Was this their way of showing their spite? Toshio had been a business type from the beginning, and Hideo had dragged himself up from the sewer, so it would be considered fair and just etiquette to reward them. As for me, they could not bring themselves to overlook what they perceived as an act of disloyalty. I cursed the petty pen pushers and vowed to find out who was behind the decision to exclude me. Someone somewhere must have sat down and decided to award those two and leave me in the cold.

Tears of rage and self-pity swelled in my eyes. Damn the pain: I gripped the food tray with both hands and flung it into the wall opposite. The sound of breaking china and cutlery crashing around the room was enough to bring Niwa running to my door once more. This time he did not find a contrite master but one who was filled with enough venom and spite to send fear into even the coolest of souls.

Niwa diplomatically avoided any mention of the food tray and the scattered debris, merely asking if I was ready to bathe. I could barely conceal my anger, but swallowed my pride in practiced fashion and grumpily nodded. Before he left to summon assistance, I told him to get Kato back here at the double. I wanted a new bottle of his mind-numbing medication, just to see off the anxiety that now riddled my soul. Niwa was back in quick time. He had brought along a sturdy-looking lad to assist me. Together they had me on my feet, and slowly we negotiated our way through the broken crockery to the bathroom. I was shuffling along like an old rake twice my age.

The bath was a sunken type, made from fine, white grained marble. A fragrance of sandalwood drifted from the water. I had made it so far without too much drama, but the step into the tub was proving too much, as I could not lift my right leg without a sudden shock of pain. Niwa's burly assistant offered to help me in. He scooped me into his arms as if I were a child, which was no mean feat, for I was especially heavy around the midriff. He bent his strong back and gently lowered me into the water. My whole body was as taut as a piano wire; I was constantly anticipating the pain which would surely come. Slowly, I began to relax and enjoy the warm water. Niwa went to supervise the cleaning of my room, leaving the younger lad outside the door to assist me. After a good thirty minutes I called to him and he appeared bearing a large white bathrobe. With a little difficulty and some select cursing I managed to stand under my own steam and accepted his help only to step out of the bath. I thanked the lad and complimented him on his strength. He was a shy and silent type, and it took a bit of prob-ing to finally get him to speak. "Tell me, boy, what is your name?"

"Murakami, sir."

The name rang a bell. I had heard it recently, but my faculties were not quite up to speed. "Murakami. Sounds familiar. Have you been in service here at the lodge for any length of time?"

He shook his head. "No, sir, I am new in your employ, but my sister has been working here for a number of months now."

Then I remembered. "Your sister? Megumi Murakami—she is one of the maids here, is she not?"

"Yes, sir, she is."

I silently cursed my feckless actions once more, for I had no wish to be on the wrong side of this man mountain. I made a mental note to have the siblings dismissed from my employ as soon as an opportune moment presented itself. I was not one for sharing my failings, and a surreptitious web of domestic intrigue was hardly the best environment for a newlywed.

I decided I needed a change of setting. I had spent the last three days or so in my bedroom, and an eventful time it most certainly had been. When Niwa came to my door to inform me that the doctor had arrived, I told him I would see him in the sunroom and to tell Murakami I would require his assistance to tackle the stairs. I prayed that my descent would be a little less painful than its opposite of three days ago. I was light-headed, but the food seemed to have restored a little fight into my soul. The bath had soothed my aching back a little, but it was with a great deal of trepidation that I gingerly swung my legs out of the bed and allowed Murakami to help me on my way to the sunroom.

It took an inordinate amount of time for us to reach the top of the stairs. Young Murakami kindly supported me all the way and showed a great deal of courteous reverence towards his stricken master. Surprisingly, I managed to negotiate the stairs with far less difficulty than I had expected. Perhaps it was a reflection of my character that I feared pain more than actual pain itself. Was this somehow a reference to my cowardly true self? I managed to find my steps, and without too much drama we reached the foot of the grand staircase. The hallway of the lodge is the area most blessed by an abundance of natural light. There was a huge full-length mirror set to one side, a mirror that never lied and now spoke back at me with barbed truisms that shocked me to my very core. I could not believe the reflection looking back was really me. I looked as if I had stepped out of the grave. My eyes were black rimmed, and my face was sagging more than usual. My hair was wild and seemed much greyer than a week ago. There was a tiredness about me that I felt I could almost reach out and touch. My father had often said that we do not age gradually, but that our years tell in periods of great pain and stress. Now I could see the truth in his words. I looked ten years older than I had last week. The physical pain had wracked my face into a kind of permanent grimace; the emotional pain caused by being overlooked for my own contributions to economic regeneration was tearing me apart inside. The heavy doses of drugs had provided an escape for a while but had left me feeling confused and insecure.

I felt like crying. If Murakami had not been by my side, I fear I would have broken down right there on the spot. I allowed him to lead me on to the sunroom, where I found Kato waiting. He was sitting in an oversized rattan chair, leafing through some volume that had caught his eye. From a distance he reminded me of Mr Toad from the books Nanny used to read me as a child. His thick round glasses caught the sunlight as it danced around the room. The sunroom always felt a little humid, and several plants both exotic and native thrived in the warmth created by the vast glass roofing. I soon found myself perspiring profusely as I shuffled along the polished chessboard-style tiles, supported under one arm by Murakami. Kato stood and watched me from a distance; he looked like he was evaluating my performance.

A chaise longue sat in the corner, and I told Murakami to bring it over so I could recline. It also added a little more drama to my predicament. Kato seemed satisfied with my progress and kept nodding in short bursts as if someone were controlling him like a puppet. I sank into the chaise longue and, with a wave of my hand, dismissed Murakami. Kato sat opposite me and spoke in that booming voice of his, his words almost making me shrink within myself. "Hosokawa san, what remarkable progress you have made. A few more days and we shall see you almost righted."

I sullenly thanked him but saw little point in making any small talk. "Doctor, your medication has been a great relief to me, and I fear my path to full recovery will be hindered without medication to ease my way. I would be obliged if you would prescribe me some more of the same."

Kato nodded as if listening to an errant pupil's lame excuse for some roughhousing. "Hosokawa san, I feel that would not be the appropriate way to proceed at this time. Simple rest is all you require. Your body needs to recover naturally, and when you are well enough, I will recommend that you start some form of mild exercise to aid the blood flow."

I could feel a dark cloud descending on me. I wanted the medication, and I was determined to have it. "Doctor, I believe there is wisdom in what you say, but believe me, I cannot rest when I am in the throes of mind-numbing pain. I need some more."

My last words came out rather aggressively and betrayed my desperation, something Kato picked up on. He tried to placate me in a tone he might use when speaking to a little nipper with a snotty nose. "An additional supply of medication would perhaps create more problems than it would solve. Besides, I am governed by my profession's guidelines. This is exceptionally strong medication we are talking about, something to be used only in extreme cases."

I fixed him with my hardest stare. "I want the medication." The silence between us seemed to stretch miles. The doctor stood to leave, believing his continued presence to be of little benefit towards my recovery. "Doctor, I will pay a premium or make some kind of contribution to a cause of your choice. In return you furnish me with medication to see that I am completely free of pain."

Kato stopped in his tracks, his back to me. "Hosokawa san, you are a wealthy businessman, and I am fully aware of your importance. Your money and connections can certainly smooth the way to a better life for your good self and for others around you. I on the other hand am just a simple country doctor, going about his business, doing the job I have come to regard as a duty. I have the greatest respect for my profession, and I would not cheapen it for any kind of fiscal inducement. However, there is something you may be able to do for me."

I could feel the fish nibbling the bait, but would it bite down on the hook? "Tell me, what is on your mind, doctor?"

He continued standing with his back to me as he spoke. "The position of chief medical officer in your company was recently advertised. Should I apply for such a position, I hope my application would be treated with the favour it deserves."

The bite down onto the hook was swift. Here was a man who was on my wavelength. "Dear doctor, you may be assured it will be. I will see to it personally."

Keeping his back to me, Kato placed his bag on a nearby table, opened it, took out a brown bottle of medication, placed it on the table, and without even a glance over his shoulder took his leave. "Good day, Hosokawa san. I wish you a speedy recovery."

The distance from the chaise longue to the table suddenly seemed insurmountable. I wanted the medicine now but could not muster the effort to stand. My growing sense of anxiety was battling with my feelings of insecurity. It is not often in my life that I have felt vulnerable. My money and name have generally provided enough protection from any such displays of weakness, but right now I felt as if I was at the mercy of forces over which I had little control. I knew that I could ill afford to spend the next week closeted away, recuperating like some aged and feeble old man. I had important business to attend to.

There was the matter of my imminent trip to Manila, which was scheduled to take place in three weeks' time. Thinking of that trip was enough to send my mood spiralling down into the darker recesses of my mind. I had grown to hate my sojourns to the Philippines. Over the last ten years I had made six such trips, each one fraught with potential problems. I was dealing with volatile elements and knew that my own personal safety was at great risk. I thanked the heavens for gifting me Miyazaki, without whom I would not even consider setting foot in that wretched place. I thought of Romana and how much I despised the man. Soon I would be smiling to his face and shaking his hand whilst wishing that I could squeeze the very life out of his corrupt and filthy soul. It had been a major play act to disguise my contempt for him. In this regard I appeared to have been successful, as he always welcomed me as a friend, arms open to embrace me on my arrival. His hospitality was driven by his ruthless greed and ambition. I was under no illusion whatsoever; he needed me as much as I needed him. We were like two necessary evils, each feeding on the lifeblood of the other.

Romana saw himself as a kingmaker, and he had set his sights high. Very early on I had identified this as his weakness and decided to play the long game. Romana was the only man in the Philippines with the power and means to conduct our kind of business. He had control of a relatively well-disciplined private militia and had the connections to make the seemingly impossible happen, for which he was well rewarded with an amount that no doubt made him the wealthiest man in his country. That he needed us was certain, as his naked ambition was now to the fore. His daughter, Ismarelda, had recently wed a senator from Ilocos, a young man called Marios. It was this man that Romana was backing, and now he was funding the drive all the way to the Malacañan Palace. Romana saw himself as the man behind the future president, the iron father-in-law. For this he needed money, and lots and lots of it. He needed Mabuhay, and for the time being we would use his edacity for our own purposes.

I sat back in my chaise longue, closed my eyes, and looked forward to the time when Santa Romana became surplus to requirements, for his demise would bring me the sweetest of feelings. It had been agreed from the outset that Romana should believe there were far more sites than actually existed. As the business of liberating each site was conducted on an individual basis, Romana was always left waiting for the next piece. This arrangement afforded us a degree of extra security and safety for which I was mightily grateful. You see, nobody wants to kill the goose that lays the golden egg. For the last decade Mabuhay had come knocking on Romana's door, and he had no reason to believe our business would cease soon. To date we had completed six "transactions," with a further six outstanding. The consensus was that after our business had finally been concluded, Romana would be a liability. We feared that once the realisation had dawned that there would be no further payments, he could resort to some form of coercion. Hence, his time was marked. He was a dead man walking.

I was happily drifting off to sleep, comforted by the thought of a Romana-free world, when Niwa came into the sunroom and told me I had received a phone call from Hamazaki, who was waiting on the line. I was tempted to tell Niwa to inform him that

I was temporarily engaged, but I managed to push that trite notion aside. "Go and tell him I am on my way to the phone. It may take me a few minutes." We did not have a telephone extension in the sunroom, the nearest being in my office.

I managed to stand with great difficulty and began the slow, painful shuffle across the marble floor. I passed the small table where Kato had left the medication, pocketing it on my way. It took me two or three minutes to cover the distance to my office, and eventually, I slowly lowered myself into my deep leather desk chair. I let out a great sigh of relief, one which must have been audible all the way down the line to Ginza. "Hosokawa speaking," I said quite brusquely, aiming for a stern note in my voice but failing to disguise my pained discomfort.

"Makoto, how the devil are you?" Hamazaki asked. "My poor friend. Miyazaki san has told me about your unfortunate condition. How are you bearing up?" He sounded so full of the joys of life.

I would not allow myself to be pitied. "I do believe I am through the worst—in fact I am on my feet as we speak," I lied.

"That is marvellous news. When can we expect you back here? We have much to get through. I do not mean to rush you— please take all the time you need—but there are a few matters that we need to discuss."

I took a few moments to think, and without giving it too much consideration found myself saying, "I have a little work to get through here. Perhaps the day after next. Please tell Miyazaki san to drive up and collect me in the Rolls." I silently prayed that I would be able to make the journey.

"Splendid news. We all await your return to full recovery. By the way, you missed a blinder of an event, which was all the poorer because of your absence."

I shook my head. Toshio was the master of flattery, but I had gotten used to his style long ago, and any sweetness merely rippled over me. "So I believe, my dear friend, and also I hear congratulations are in order."

There was a short silence before Toshio regained his verbal footing. His unease was almost palpable. "Ah yes. I suppose you are referring to the award. A mere trinket, nothing more. It is of no significance, merely symbolic." The more he wittered on, the deeper the hole he dug. I listened in silence as he explained how it had completely come from out of the blue and both he and Hideo were taken completely unawares by the awards, which were a recognition of the company's success, and how he had little or no personal attachment to it.

We both uncomfortably avoided the matter of my omission, verbally dancing around it. However, Toshio, highly sensitive to all that went on around him, picked up on my tone when I said, "I am delighted for the both of you. You fully deserve to be recognised." My voice cracked and my eyes welled up. I thanked God nobody could see me now.

"My dear Makoto, your day will come, of that I am certain," Toshio said. "Please do not take this in a personal way. I know you are a character with a strong sense of fortitude, and one fine day your reward will be waiting. Now hurry back to health and back home. We have a business to run. We all await your return. In fact I propose we go out for dinner to Ishikawa on your return. The very same place where it all started for us ten years ago. What do you say?" I said that would be wonderful and I would look forward to it, and coolly replaced the receiver. As if without thinking I opened the bottom drawer of my desk and took out the small bottle of whisky that I kept there for moments such as these. I took the medicine bottle from my pocket and took two morphine pills washed down with a generous slug of Scotland's finest. Knowing that blissful oblivion was soon to descend on me, I shouted loudly for Niwa to come and help me back to my bed.

★ ★ ★

A raging thirst and a blinding headache were the first sensations that greeted my return to the world of normality. I did not know how long I had been out this time, but judging by the brightness of the hour, I knew I had managed to get through the night and well into the next day without waking at all. I lay motionless for a few moments, trying to gauge the level of agony that awaited me should I decide to move. To my great relief I found I was no longer a prisoner to spellbinding pain and could move my legs up and down without much trouble. I had got through the worst of it, and now it would be only a matter of days before I was restored to my normal self.

I was about to call for help when I noticed that my sheets were damp and pungent. The sudden realisation that I had wet the bed brought a sense of shame that enveloped me like a shroud. For a moment or two I was back in my school dorm, experiencing once more the humiliation of having rubber under sheets on my bed, something that marked you out as a bed wetter. I decided against calling for help, preferring to deal with my own sanitary issues. I was able to get out of bed without much difficulty. There was still a dull but bearable ache in my lower back, but I was confident that I could overcome the discomfort. I went to the bathroom and turned on the taps to fill the bath. I drank three large cups of cold water and noticed that my teeth had become sticky. I could even smell my own breath, which was not far away from putrid. I brushed my teeth and rinsed my mouth in an attempt to freshen up. I could not bring myself to look into the mirror. I had not shaved for days on end and no doubt would look like some wretched Robinson Crusoe.

I ambled back into the bedroom and managed to strip off the sheets, which I then bundled up and left on the floor. I was determined to restore my dignity and decided that personal hygiene was a good place to start. I took a leisurely bath and luxuriated in the warm water, after which I scrubbed myself almost pink. I shampooed my lank and greasy hair. I was starting to resemble the Hosokawa of old. The only thing left was to shave off this unflattering beard. I stood at the basin, cutthroat razor in hand, only to realise that I could not stop my hands from shaking. I tried to shave but nicked my skin at the first attempt. I decided to let Niwa or one of the staff shave me. I knew that I was suffering from the after-effects of the medication and made a promise to myself to take no more.

I went over to my closet and found some fine red silk pyjamas and my heavy bathrobe, and put them on. I called for help, and good old, trusty Niwa was not long in answering. I told him to prepare me some breakfast, which I would take in the dining room. He looked a little perplexed and, after a moment's uncertainty during which he no doubt assessed my sanity, went on to explain that it was six thirty in the evening and perhaps dinner would be more fitting, given the hour. I agreed, waving my hands to indicate that some kind of absentmindedness had gripped me. I told him I wanted to be shaved before dinner and to prepare my dress suit and shirt. It was time the master of the house started to act and look the part once more.

An hour or so later found me seated at the dining table, cradling a dry martini while awaiting dinner. I had eaten very little over the last few days, and yet I was not particularly hungry. I guess my stomach was becoming accustomed to deprivation. I ran my hand over my face, enjoying its freshly shaved smoothness. Murakami had been given the awkward task of shaving his master, and a fine job he had done, too. Maybe I should reconsider my earlier rash decision to terminate his employment, I thought. After all, I do believe his sister will keep her silence in regard to "our" little indiscretion. Indeed, with a spot of professional training I believe the young man would make a fine valet. I thought of Azusa and wondered what she was doing right now. Had my promise to her been a reaction to my suffering at the time? I began to question the wisdom of making such an impetuous proposal, but being of an analytical bent, I could see the benefits of such a union. From a practical point of view Azusa was young enough to see me out and to satisfy my carnal desires for years to come. Also, it would provide me with a channel through which to bequeath my estate. I had no living family, save for a couple of grand old aunts whom I never saw. If I were to remain a bachelor for life, who would benefit from my estate? Toshio? Hideo? Not over my dead body, literally! Also I would be damned if the department of revenue was going to see a penny of my hard-earned cash. Marriage seemed a sensible way forward, and who knows, in time maybe an heir would not be such a bad thing. After all, I would hardly have to do much beyond attending the events that mark one's offspring's progress through life.

I closed my eyes and allowed myself to drift off into a personal reverie, to a world where I felt secure and free from the paranoia that seemed to take hold of me with such voracity that it dug deep into my soul. A knock on the door startled me to my senses. Niwa entered the dining room, bearing a silver tray with a message card. He bowed and presented the tray with such exaggeration that his action begged me to think he was being facetious. I took the card from the tray and thanked him with a nod. It was a message from Toshio written no doubt as dictated. "Tatsuya's seventh birthday celebration. Tomorrow, Empire Hotel, two o'clock. Hideo and Ayumi are expecting you. Miyazaki san will pick you up at seven in the morning. Good health to you—Toshio." The audacity of it. Did they think I had little better to do than rush around to attend some spoilt brat's birthday party? As I was smouldering away, one of the houseboys appeared, bearing a tray upon which was the night's culinary offering. Various small dishes of assorted delicacies such as quail eggs in caviar, slices of raw venison, and squid marinated in a ginger sauce caught my eye but unfortunately failed to appeal to my appetite. In truth I did not feel at all hungry. I waited until the houseboy had left the room, then pushed the food around the plates for effort's sake and decided to retire for the evening.

I looked around the dining room, a place that reminded me of so many wonderful times, including evenings now long past when laughter and joy had been in abundance. This evening I was truly alone with only my memories for company. Sitting here at my vast dining table only seemed to emphasise my solitude and further sour my mood, so I gave up on dinner and started to make my way back to my bedroom. I was still feeling a little delicate but declined the offer of assistance that the houseboy felt was his duty to give. I began my slow ascent up the long winding staircase. My determination to exert my independence was waning with every painful step, and with a growing sense of self-pity I eventually managed to negotiate the stairs and shuffle along to my room, where I collapsed in a heap on the bed. I struggled out of my necktie and loosened my shirt button. My medicine bottle was within easy reach, and instinctively I leaned over and grabbed it. I swore under my breath as I unscrewed the top and vowed that this was to be my last dosage, ever. These little purple pills were destroying my sense of who I was, and yet they brought me joyous release from all that preyed on my mind. Tomorrow I would throw the remaining tablets away, but right now I saw no harm in taking two more little saviours.

* * *

I was being tossed around in some sudden, violent maelstrom. Frantically, with my arms flailing about, I tried to gain a hold on anything to save me from the perilous fall into the black void below. I cried out, but the shaking only intensified. I could hear voices, but they were too far away to be of any assistance. Then suddenly I was under freezing water, desperately fighting to make my way to the surface. The ice cold water penetrated my skull with mind-numbing ferocity.

I forced my eyes open to confront my fate, only to see Miyazaki staring wildly down at me. I was totally lost to the world, and it took a good few moments for any semblance of normality to be restored. I realised that I had taken hold of Miyazaki's arm, grasping it in my desperation, and only now did I reluctantly release my vise-like grip. There was an ice cold towel over my forehead, and my shirt was drenched in freezing water. Miyazaki was telling me how I had given him a scare when he failed to rouse me from my slumber. He had resorted to the ice water, for which he was now offering his apologies. "Hosokawa san, sorry for bringing you around with such a clumsy tactic, but you were giving me cause to worry," he said. "Are you feeling well enough to travel, or should I summon the doctor for you?" As I regained my bearings and came to my senses, I told him I would be fine. I just needed a moment or two to recover. He said he had been waiting for me since seven and time was pressing, as we were expected at the Empire for the birthday function. I wanted to tell him that I would not be attending, but Toshio himself had gone out of his way to make arrangements for me, and reluctantly I resolved to show my face for the sake of appearances.

I told Miyazaki to wait downstairs and take some refreshment while I readied myself for the journey back to Tokyo. He seemed reluctant to leave, no doubt suspecting I would slumber afresh. He pointed out the time once more, and I was astonished to see it had already turned ten. I swung my legs out of the bed with an agility that surprised me. If I carefully avoided certain positions, I was virtually pain-free. Suddenly I felt a surge of optimism for the day ahead. I had slept in my clothes, and Miyazaki gave my dishevelled state a disapproving look but said nothing. I told him I would be ready in a few minutes, and he left me to get ready.

I stripped off my clothes, and took the briskest of showers to freshen my skin and wash my hair. I checked the mirror. My eyes were a little bloodshot, and the dark rings seemed to scream out against my sallow skin, but overall I thought I did not look that bad for someone who had been to hell and back. I quickly dressed, choosing a pair of casual checked trousers, the kind recently favoured by fashionable golfers. A plain white shirt and black sports coat seemed to be the appropriate match. I selected a dark red cravat, which I fastened with a gold ring. Just one problem: I was unable to bend sufficiently to put on my own socks, so I pushed a pair into my jacket pocket for later. I slicked my hair with a little pomade and checked the mirror again. My one-day beard gave me a wild look that was strangely pleasing. Satisfied that I was now presentable, I made my way out of my bedroom suite, pocketing my magic medicine as I left.

Miyazaki had the Rolls on standby outside the main entrance. I spotted Kudo lurking around as if on guard duty. Niwa was waiting for me at the foot of the stairs. "Good morning, sir. So pleased to see you restored to health. Miyazaki san is taking coffee in the sunroom. Shall I summon him?" I told him I would join Miyazaki for a few moments and to prepare some soup and rice to fortify me for the journey ahead. "Very good sir." He bowed and went off to attend to his duties.

I went into the sunroom to find Miyazaki relaxing in my favourite chair, reading the newspaper, coffee cup to hand on the table beside him. Upon my entrance he put the newspaper down but did not stand. I ignored this lack of respect for his master, simply putting it down to low breeding. However, I knew the truth was more personal. We no longer observed the master and servant code of behaviour. Our relationship had become one of uneven equals, and any attempt to correct that now would cause us both unease. I needed this man more than he needed me, and at times I was astonished that he managed to put up with my petulance with such good grace.

I pulled up the smaller chair in front of him, and we sat in silence for a few moments. Miyazaki looked at me with an intensity that made me feel uncomfortable. Eventually he broke the silence. "Hosokawa san, morphine brings great relief to injured and dying soldiers in the field of battle. I have seen it and even had cause to use it myself, but that is where it belongs, and that is where it should stay. It has no place in everyday life. It leaves one witless, and that is a state in which nobody would wish to find themselves."

I felt like a chastised child. Miyazaki's words carried a degree of menace. He had a way of speaking that made you want to scurry away and hide in shame. I looked over his shoulder and out of the window behind him. There was a large black crow screeching in the tree beyond. An ominous portent of things to come? Niwa arrived with my refreshments, as welcome an interruption as I could have wished for. As Niwa fussed about, setting the tray before me, Miyazaki returned to his newspaper, another act of servile defiance for the benefit of the domestic help.

I quickly drank my soup and ate a little rice, which I washed down with green tea. I still felt quite weak and reluctantly made the gut-wrenching decision to allow Kudo to drive my car. I told Miyazaki to go tell Kudo he would be driving the Ferrari back to Ginza and warn him not to go tearing off, and to stay close behind the Rolls. He stood, nodded, and went off to attend to his preparations. I closed my eyes, and for a moment I was a child once more, jealously guarding his precious toys.

With a great deal of difficulty I struggled into my socks and gingerly made my way down to the hallway where, much to my surprise, I found that Niwa had assembled the staff to bid me farewell. They were lined up single file, and each gave a deep and gracious bow as I passed them by. I stopped in front of Murakami and thanked him for his help during my distress and told him that his assistance had not gone unnoticed. I passed by the ranks of domestics all dutifully bowing their heads. I ignored Murakami the maid, and she kept her head lowered as I expected. I slipped my feet into my leather loafers and then on the spur of the moment decided to address the assembled staff. "This visit has not seen me at my finest, but I thank you all for your help and understanding. As a token of my appreciation I propose to pay each of you an extra month's salary, which you will receive in your next pay. I bid you all good day." One thing I had learnt from Toshio was to always try to leave on a high. Make a grand gesture, one that will always be remembered.

As the staff mumbled their collective gratitude, I stepped out into the fresh air for the first time in five days and found that the crisp, cool air tickled my throat. The weak early winter sunshine played tricks with my eyes, and I wished I had my sunglasses on hand. Kudo was standing around by the Ferrari; he had a childish excitement about him, as he was no doubt thrilled by the prospect of driving my pride and joy back to town. I called him over and instructed him to be extra careful, as he was in custody of the only one of its kind in the country. I had my doubts about entrusting him with the car, but Miyazaki reassured me that he was more than capable of handling it. I told Kudo to go retrieve my sunglasses from the Ferrari. Suitably adorned, we then boarded our vehicles, and our intimate convoy set off on the ride back to Ginza.

Miyazaki handled the Rolls with admirable deftness. His gear changes were so smooth, you hardly noticed them, a welcome relief from the crunching efforts that often accompanied Ogawa's driving. I sat in the spacious back seat with little more to do than gaze out the window. It did not take long before I was feeling the tedium of the journey, and it struck me how Azusa must have experienced the same sense of monotony on the drive up. Miyazaki was not the talkative type, so we each retreated into the comfort of our own thoughts. It was in this manner that we passed the journey. I stared out the window, numbly allowing the changing scenery to wash over me. The landscape gradually metamorphosed from calm, green, rural tranquillity to concrete urban chaos, and in a matter of a few hours we were back in the thick of the metropolis.

Occasionally I locked eyes with Miyazaki as I caught his stare in the rearview mirror. I knew he was trying to assess my state. I could not blame him for harbouring doubts about my reliability; after all, we were involved in matters that required the deepest trust and confidence. My hand strayed to my coat pocket, where I felt for the medicine bottle. I was tempted to make some kind of grand exhibition by throwing the pills out the window, a dramatic gesture for Miyazaki's benefit, but my inner self prevented any such rashness. I glanced back out the rear window to make sure that oaf Kudo was keeping up with the pace. The traffic had thickened, and he had dropped back two or three vehicles. I could just make out a splash of brilliant red, which stood out against the predominant grey, black, and brown and the other various depressing colours favoured by our capital's motorists.

As we neared Ginza, I began to make my plans for the day. We had a little over an hour left in which to make our preparations for the birthday party. Then it occurred to me that I had yet to purchase a birthday gift. It would seem discourteous to arrive empty-handed. Without giving it too much thought I made one of my rash judgements. "Ken, as a great favour I was hoping you could stop by Ito's residence for a few moments. There is a matter I wish to attend to before going over to the Empire." The look of weariness Miyazaki gave me begged to be ignored, but he had little choice other than to indulge me.

Azusa resided quite close to Ginza, and her address was no more than five minutes out of our way. I had never had cause to call on her before and was quite surprised when Miyazaki drew the car to a halt outside a tidy and quite spacious low-built traditional residence. A small garden to the front was home to some tall cedars and pines which afforded a great deal of privacy from prying eyes. I wound the window down a little and told Miyazaki to call Azusa and inform her that I wished to have a quick word. He said nothing, but from his manner I could sense he was not particularly overjoyed with his task. I watched as he disappeared behind the trees. A few moments passed and I felt my anxiety build. I began to seriously regret my rash decision to come here. What if Azusa had changed her mind about our proposed union?

As I worked myself into a nervous state, Miyazaki loomed into view. He bent down and told me that Azusa was out but expected home at any moment. However, her father was at home and demanded to know what business I had coming to call unannounced. He insisted that I call into his home to state my purpose. I was tempted to tell Miyazaki to get in the car and beat the hell out of there, but I knew he would not go for that. He was a man who faced his demons head-on and expected others to be of a similar bent.

It was with a heavy sense of foreboding that I forced my inner cowardice aside, pushed open the heavy door, and cautiously stepped out of the Rolls. I slowly walked up the path to the door of my future wife's home. I vaguely recognised the man waiting to greet me; he had been a guest at several Mabuhay functions. His face betrayed his anxiety and puzzlement about why I should be making a surprise call. I decided there was little to be gained by beating about the bush, and when I came to a halt before him, I gave a small but courteous bow, which he returned in kind. He invited me into his home and I stepped into the hallway. "Ito san, may I introduce myself? My name is Hosokawa. I believe you know of my company, Mabuhay? Anyhow, that is by the way. I apologise for what you must perceive to be my lack of manners in calling on you unannounced, and I will not take much of your precious time. My visit concerns your daughter."

I sensed he was more than confused, but he was of high breeding, and his good manners dictated that he hear me out without interruption. Being a reasonable judge of a man's character, I put him in the meek category, which emboldened me a little as I steadied myself for delivering my life-changing words. "I find myself at your door this fine morning for one reason only, and that is to ask you for your consent and your daughter's hand in marriage." He looked at me as if he were being confronted by a madman, his mouth agape, speechless; he was at a total loss for words.

I pressed on. "I have taken the liberty of asking your daughter, and I believe she is amenable to my proposal."

His objections were now plainly apparent, but he was still in some kind of shock, and words were not easily forthcoming. I decided that it was best if I left him to his thoughts. Besides, Azusa would soon return, and that might cause too much domestic drama for one morning. Ito had sat down on a small wooden stool and was shaking his head from side to side. I doubted that he was struck by wonderment; more likely it was disbelief.

"Ito san, I would be most honoured if you and your good wife would accompany Azusa san to the Empire, where my company will be holding a small informal gathering at two this afternoon. Despite such short notice I anticipate your attendance. Good day to you, Ito san." I was talking to the top of his head, and he looked dejected as I took my leave. I went back down the path, quite pleased with myself, and back to the car where Miyazaki was waiting. He flicked his cigarette into Ito's garden and opened the door for me, and we left on the short drive to Ginza.

I felt weary as I arrived home and very leaden footed as I hauled myself up the stairs to my rooms. The house was near deserted and strangely quiet. I assumed some of the domestics had been seconded to assist with the party. Ogawa was hanging about the hallway, and his cadaverous presence did little to lighten my mood. He told me that Toshio had already left for the function at the Empire and that he would be on call to transport me when required. Miyazaki had taken the Rolls straight to the Empire to assist with the preparations. I had a little over ten minutes in which to get ready. I resigned myself to being late but forwent bathing, instead opting for a liberal splash of cologne. I selected one of my finest three-piece suits and white shirts, changing with a speed that would have been unthinkable a day ago. My recent trauma had seen a few inches fall from my waist, and I gleaned a bit of vain satisfaction in tugging my belt into a new notch. I tousled my hair into something that was acceptable, rinsed my mouth with antiseptic, and made a final check in the mirror. Satisfied that I did not look too much like a dog's dinner, I made my way out of my rooms, fixing my Rolex timepiece on my wrist as I walked down the stairs. I pocketed my morphine pills for reasons that I did not fully understand. It just felt comforting to have them close to hand.

Ogawa was waiting for me at the foot of the stairs and held the door open for me to step out once more into the late autumnal sunshine. Six days earlier I had stood on these very steps and answered questions from young reporters. The world had seemed a different place then, and now as I took a moment to reflect, I believed that I too had become a different man. Was it possible for someone to change in so short a time? In the past week life had dealt me some cruel blows, and I had dealt a few in return. The stigma of being ignored for the award still burnt bitter in my soul, but I would brave that out for now. Opportunity would present itself in its own time, and when it did, I would be waiting.

Ogawa held open the car door for me. He looked like an old tortoise, his wily frame absurdly small as he stood by the hulking Bentley. The street was unusually quiet for the time of day, and the relative calm was disturbed only by the wail of a police car making its way at speed with red lights flashing, an unusual occurrence in this part of town and one that made people stop for a second look. I climbed aboard the Bentley for the short hop over to the hotel and then suddenly realised that I had still not organised a birthday gift for dear little Tatsuya. I had intended to ask Azusa to take care of that, and in any case it was too late to do anything about it now. I would deliver a promise to make good on my empty-handedness at the first opportunity.

Ogawa swung the Bentley round the corner in such a clumsy motion that I was sent sliding along the shiny, well-worn leather seat. I resisted my desire to scold him, and instead concentrated on smoothing out the creases in my suit trousers. We slowly drew to a halt outside the main entrance of the Empire, and as Ogawa laboriously made his way round to my door, I was taken completely unawares by Miyazaki, who flung my door open and almost wrestled me out of my seat. "Hosokawa san, there is no time to be lost. Hurry, if you please." My first thought was to yell at him, to tell him that it was only a nipper's birthday party and what the blazes did he think he was playing at, but something in his tone and manner told me that things were not as they should be. I exited the Bentley with as much decorum as a man forced on could gather. Miyazaki was agitated and glanced wildly around the hotel lobby. We collided with a few stray onlookers as we urgently made our way through the Empire's lobby and its assembled bunch of guests and gawpers.

There was a small room adjacent to the reception area, which I presumed was set aside for use by the staff on their downtime. Without hesitation Miyazaki pushed the door open, and I was astonished to find myself face-to-face with Toshio and Hideo, who both stared at me for a few moments as if they could scarcely bring themselves to credit my appearance. Toshio looked unusually pale and was cradling a large brandy glass with a generous measure in his hand. He placed his drink on the ramshackle table, stepped over to me, and with a genuine display of affection embraced me. "My dear Makoto, thank God you are safe. For a good moment we all feared the worst. What a terrible business, absolutely awful. I was given only the patchiest of details by my man over at the Yomiuri. His cubs were on the scene in a flash, and in the confusion, the car, so distinctive, we all thought you were a goner."

I was just about to thank him for his concern, which I thought a little indulgent even by Toshio's own standards, when he went on. "Of course the police will want to talk to you at the earliest opportunity. In fact we are expecting them imminently."

It was at this moment that they all realised that I did not have the faintest idea what Toshio was talking about. Hideo stepped forward and in his dry tone began to tell me what had occurred. He used the tone he reserved for explaining the workings of a new product. "A terrible crime has been committed, a shocking act of violence that has resulted in the death of one of our own." I desperately wished he would get to the point without the dramatic buildup. Then my thoughts immediately turned to Azusa, and for a second I was afraid some awful catastrophe had befallen her. My mind went into overdrive, and I even thought perhaps her father had taken it upon himself to commit some foul deed upon her precious person.

I looked from face to face, trying to will the story out of them. It was with some perverse relief that I heard the words. "Kudo has been murdered, shot to death at the wheel of your Ferrari, in this very neighbourhood, as foul a cowardly act as one could imagine," Hideo said. "It seems an assassin waited for the opportunity at the long traffic signal at the junction before Ginza. He fired twice, fatally wounding our associate." They all stared at me with the gravest of looks, and the relief I had felt at Kudo's demise suddenly turned into horror as realisation finally hit me. I had been the intended victim. It was my car, and I was the one who was supposed to have died today. Toshio produced a brandy out of thin air, and I gratefully accepted it and knocked it back in one draught.

For a moment everyone was silent. It was Miyazaki who brought a feeling of control to the gathering. "I will deal with the police initially, but they are going to want to talk with each of us, especially you, Hosokawa san." I shifted uncomfortably from side to side. Miyazaki went on. "We need to keep tight but at the same time express our shock and sadness at this appalling act of violence. First they will try to ascertain if any of us had a motive for seeing off Kudo, a line of inquiry they will soon dismiss. It will not take long before they conclude that Kudo was not the intended victim, and I believe a thorough investigation may even lead them to make possible connections to the recent demise of our antagonist Ono."

Toshio shot him a look that could have silenced thunder. Miyazaki was not to be distracted. "The police may find Ono's slanderous posters and begin to look for links. I'm only saying that it is something we need to consider."

Toshio and Hideo both nodded thoughtfully, as if working out the problem from a scientific perspective. I studied their faces closely for any sign of panic but found none. It appeared I was the only one having a panic attack about the whole thing. Miyazaki continued his clinical assessment. "Remember, gentlemen, we are not party to any knowledge that may help in the investigation. Hosokawa san, you do not know of anyone who wished you grave harm. If you are asked to speculate, you will consider this heinous act to be the work of a deranged madman. I think under the circumstances we should offer the police as much respect as we can but of course nothing that can aid their enquiries."

We all nodded in grave unison. After a respectful moment of deliberation Toshio broke the ice and clapped his hands together. "Gentlemen, I do believe we have a party to attend, and furthermore, it may look a trifle suspicious if the long arm of the law finds us all closeted together in this small room. So I say let us go about our business as best we can and put on our bravest faces and go and celebrate my nephew's birthday." He clapped his hands once more to signal that that was all for now, and my word, I do believe the man smiled. He was made of stern stuff, Toshio Hamazaki, the man for all seasons. What the devil was there to be worried about when he was in your corner?

Toshio and Hideo went on ahead, leaving Miyazaki and me to follow on a minute or so later. Left alone with Miyazaki in that small staff room only seemed to intensify our dilemma. We both knew who was behind this outrage, and yet neither of us could bring ourselves to speak his name. There was an edge to Miyazaki that unnerved me, and as he leaned over to reach for the door handle, I caught a glimpse of what looked like a revolver holstered on his belt. Suddenly my world seemed a whole lot smaller. I desperately wished I could swallow a few of my little pills and sink into that sweet oblivion to escape this madness.

Miyazaki indicated that it was time for us to follow on and join the party. He pushed the door open, and we strode out into the crowded lobby. It was only then that I realised Miyazaki had taken it upon himself to act as my personal bodyguard. His tension was infecting me like a virus, and I noticed that my legs were shaking slightly. Miyazaki looked at the crowd, studying faces as if each were a potential danger. I, on the other hand, just about managed to stay on his shoulder as we reached the staircase that took us up to the function room on the second floor. The upper floor was off-limits to the general public, and we slowed our pace a little. I heard a piano beating out a jolly tune. It was a familiar children's favourite and accompanied by the loud, excited gaggle of children having a whale of a time. We followed the noise, which was coming from one of the rooms at the far end of the corridor. Two hotel staff, resplendent in their brilliant white tunics with shiny brass buttons, stood on either side of the tall mahogany doors. Before we made our entrance, Miyazaki gripped my arm and told me to be extra vigilant and stay close. His tone sent fear cascading into my soul. I nodded, and as we approached, the staff opened the grand double doors and we stepped into the party.

It was a large space, and several children ran about the room, wearing paper animal masks, screaming like banshees, and weaving in and out of the tables and around some of the adult guests, most of whom looked put out at the little brats' raucous behaviour. A waiter appeared bearing a tray of drinks. I helped myself to a glass of champagne, and Miyazaki took orange juice. He shot me a disbelieving glance, which I chose to ignore. Ayumi appeared out of the crowd, concern written all across her face. "Makoto, how are you? Hideo told me of your sudden ailment; we were so worried that you would not be able to make it, and yet here you are. It's so wonderful to see you restored to health—and looking a little trimmer, if I may say so. Those back problems can be a menace, you know. I had an aunt who was a total prisoner to her condition. Nothing could heal her."

It was obvious she knew nothing of the shooting, and I decided to keep my cards close to my chest. I was just about to proffer my apologies for not furnishing her little angel with a birthday gift when Ayumi looked over my shoulder to the doors, which had been opened. "Ito family? I cannot recall inviting them," she said under her breath.

Just as she was about to go over and greet Mr and Mrs Ito, I held my hand up in a conciliatory manner. "Ayumi, please forgive me, but it was I who took the liberty of asking them here. It was such short notice and I fully intended to seek your approval, but events seemed to have overtaken me today." She smiled and said she understood and they were most welcome. Ayumi had been around Mabuhay for far too long to believe events such as these did not cross the business and social divide. She naturally assumed that the Ito family invitation was part of some sub-agenda on my part. How far from the truth could she possibly be, or how near? Would she be more than a little "put out" when her little Tatsuya was upstaged by the announcement of my betrothal to Azusa?

Ever the consummate hostess, Ayumi went over to greet the Itos and with admirable graciousness invited them over to join a group of people, comfortably easing them into the conversation and helping them to feel at home. All those fundraising events for the foundation had sharpened her ability to smooth the edges out of any awkward situation. I admired Ayumi's style. She was a natural in these circumstances, the polar opposite to her husband's wooden demeanour. I often wondered what had attracted Ayumi to Hideo in the first place. The mysteries of the heart I doubt we will ever understand, and right now, I was about to complicate perceptions of love even further.

I looked over to Ito Senior, who seemed to be doing his upmost to avoid my stare. Azusa looked resplendent in a bright red dress that fell just below her knees; her casual youthfulness like a drop of sunlight in a dark forest, she stood out like a beacon amongst the dowdy crowd. Without doubt the women were thinking she was a flighty young thing as their menfolk wrestled with lusty thoughts. She was mine, and I felt a swell of pride as I anticipated telling the world about my prize. My near brush with death—or more specifically my association with death and its accompanying shock—had begun to wear off a little.

I grabbed another glass of champagne from a passing waiter and took a few steps closer to the Ito crowd. Azusa's father could no longer ignore my presence, and slowly we locked eyes. I raised my glass in his direction and waited for his affirmation. He gave me the slightest of nods, but it was all I needed. I went over to the group, excused myself for interrupting, took hold of Azusa's hand, and walked her into the centre of the room. The guests parted in a natural fashion to allow us space. The children buzzed about eagerly, expecting to be told what the next game was to be. We had caught most people's attention, and those who were still lost in their own little conversations were brought to order when I rapped a spoon against a waiter's silver tray.

The room fell completely silent, and I allowed myself a moment to compose myself. Azusa blushed and looked down at her feet. I locked eyes with Ayumi, who was full of puzzlement about why I was hijacking her little boy's party. Hideo was close to Tanezawa, as he always now seemed to be, and Toshio was nowhere to be seen. Azusa's father looked stoically ahead, not even affording me the slightest of glances, and her mother held a hand-kerchief to her face and appeared to be hiding her distress.

My voice was a little shaky as I stumbled to find the right words for my address. "Ladies and gentlemen and all you little ones." I ruffled a kid's hair in an attempt to lighten the mood. "Please forgive me and allow me a moment of your time. First, I would like to wish little Tatsuya a very happy birthday. My word, how the years roll by. Five years old already!

Congratulations to you, my little fellow. I would also like to thank Ayumi and Hideo for their kind hospitality."

There was a ripple of agreement amongst my fellow guests. I steeled myself for my big moment. "There is one more thing I would like to say. I have asked Miss Ito for her hand in marriage, and she has agreed to be my wife." There was a collective gasp of astonishment, which I chose to ignore. "Everybody, I present to you all my future wife, Azusa Ito. I thank you all for your patience."

Azusa and I both gave a deep bow to the assembled group. The silence was a little too prolonged for my liking, and I hoped it was not a reflection of their shock. Then there came the sound of one man's lone clapping. At first I feared it to be some kind of sarcastic salute, but when I looked up, I saw Toshio striding through the crowd. "Bravo, bravo, my dear friend—congratulations are in order to you both. This is a wonderful and joyous surprise. We are all so happy for the two of you. Waiters, more champagne! This calls for a toast of the highest order." His booming voice and expression of genuine happiness was enough to embolden people, and one by one they came forward to offer their felicitations. I looked through the crowd and spotted Azusa's parents standing alone with their backs to the wall. Her mother was still holding the handkerchief to her face and was visibly weeping. Tears of joy, I believe.

The party quickly came to life, hurried along by the children, who were eager for their next round of entertainment. I kept Azusa close by my side as we worked our way around the guests. It was not really my kind of crowd, and a lot of the faces were unfamiliar. I assumed most were the parents of some of the little mites charging about the place. People were friendly enough and some of the felicitations seemed genuine, others merely for appearances' sake. Perhaps I was being a little oversensitive, but I believed it was the women who showed the more judgemental sides of their character.

I accepted the well wishes from many folk that afternoon but could not escape the feeling that eyes were burning into my back like cold daggers. Perhaps it was mere petty jealousy that clouded their view. After all, Azusa would automatically rank higher on the financial pecking order than any of them, and their natural retort would be to put her down as a gold digger. The differences in our ages would also fuel their gossipy tongues, which would be let loose once we were out of sight and earshot.

Let them talk all they want; to me it was all nonsense. I had never been the conventional type, and I naturally loathed those who settled for a lifetime of mind-numbing drudgery, to be rewarded only with a trinket watch and an early death. I saw myself as an outsider, a kind of rebel. That was what Toshio had recognised in me when he had come and "rescued" me a decade earlier. My role in Mabuhay was a reflection of my character. I knew that neither Toshio nor Hideo could undertake the kind of negotiations I had to endure. I shuddered to think how they would handle being face-to-face with one of the most dangerous men in one of the most lawless places on earth. Matrimony would be a walk in the park compared with some of the difficulties I had had to deal with in the course of my life so far.

I lost count of how many glasses of champagne I had quaffed but figured one more would not be unwelcome. I grabbed one from a nearby waiter, but Azusa declined the offer. She was playing her part with all seriousness. Her beauty was undeniable and she was certainly a coy little one. I doubted a single person in the room had even the slightest inkling about her true character. She was totally unique among her peers. Her emancipation was profound, and I was the one to claim her as my own.

I spotted Tanezawa standing close to the doors; for once she was alone, and I excused myself and left Azusa in the company of a pair of dowdy old matrons for which she gave me a teasing look of reproach. "Tanezawa san, do you have a moment? I would like a quick word, if you please."

She looked a little flustered but quickly regained her composure, her eyes darting to and from the door. "Of course, Hosokawa san, I am always ready to be of assistance."

A waiter passed by, and another glass of cold champagne found its way into my hand. "Tanezawa san, I have a candidate in mind for the position of chief medical officer, which I understand was recently advertised. I wish to put forward a certain Doctor Kato, a skilled physician who recently treated me with great success. You may retrieve his contact details from Niwa, up at the lodge." She nodded thoughtfully as if considering my request. Before she could voice any form of reply, I left her in no doubt as to my will. "Tanezawa san, see to it that Kato gets the job. Also, there is a strapping fellow by the name of Murakami who is employed at the lodge as a houseboy. I want him transferred down to Ginza and to start training as my personal valet. Is all that understood?"

She gave me the briefest of nods, which I had come to know and trust. I knew she would see to my requests personally. Tanezawa was remarkably efficient, and I had come to realise that she was the driving force behind Ayumi's success as director of the Mabuhay Foundation. She also helped Hideo on various projects, and I always sought her assistance when faced with some tricky hurdle or company protocol. We walked together back into the centre of the room where Toshio was in deep conversation with Hideo and Ayumi. Once more Toshio placed the hand of friendship on my shoulder and said how happy he was for me. Ayumi and Hideo both seemed genuinely pleased as well. Ayumi asked me if I had any particular date in mind for the wedding, but I said I had not managed to think that far ahead.

Suddenly, I had the strangest feeling that everyone had become distracted for some reason. Conversations were trailing off into almost silence. Even the children had ceased their reckless charging about. The crowd of guests seemed to take a step back, as if in some kind of deferential respect.

Toshio looked over my shoulder and gave a nod. I turned around to see that two men had entered the room and were walking side by side towards us. One of them held his arms out, bearing a cushion. The other, a tall, elderly, grim-faced gent, had the demeanour of a funeral director. I turned to face them and with little ceremony, the grim, austere chap announced, "It is on His Excellency the Emperor's personal order that Hosokawa Makoto be awarded the Order of the Sacred Treasure in recognition for his efforts in the regeneration of the national economy."

It was as if the world had stopped and this dignified gentleman and I were all that existed. From the cushion he picked up the bright blue-and-yellow silk sash, which was resplendent with a shining white enamelled badge, and placed it over my head, draping it across my shoulder. I stood as if to attention on a parade ground. It was the deafening crackle of applause that brought me back to my senses. I nodded in thanks and found that I could no longer control the tears that rolled down my cheeks. I gibbered like a child trying to find appropriate words, but the shock had rendered me speechless. I took out my handkerchief and dabbed at my eyes.

Through my misty gaze I saw a group of men gathered just inside the entrance to the room. They were wearing long gabardine coats and seemed to be engaged in deep, animated conversation with Miyazaki. The law had finally arrived at our door, but I felt a surge of confidence, invigorated and untouchable, standing there with the Emperor's award around my neck.

Chapter 8
Elias Cohen
Washington
1963

Elias Cohen stared at the walls of his small, damp living space and shook his head in an effort to stop the nagging doubts that constantly chipped away at the foundations of his sanity. If any other living soul had stepped into his apartment, they would without question be forced to admit that the occupant was a manic obsessive in step with the deranged. The walls were covered entirely by a collage of newspaper cuttings, pictures, maps, and wartime photographs. Keener-eyed observers would pick out adverts for electrical products that sat uncomfortably amongst some of the more grisly decorative features. To a stranger it would look like the work of a madman, one whose mind had been possessed by war and all its attendant misery. There seemed to be no discernible logic to the kaleidoscope montage. The Japanese language screamed out from the chaos alongside snaps of bespectacled Japanese businessmen shaking hands over deals or other business.

All this was not for the eyes of any person other than its maker's. Besides, no other human being had ever had cause to cross the threshold into Elias Cohen's chaotic home. It was his sanctuary and his reason for carrying on. Elias Cohen knew the significance of each and every scrap of paper that covered his walls. They were all part of a deep personal quest, his odyssey. He lived through them, and they fed his impotent rage against the man who featured so heavily: Toshio Hamazaki.

This was Elias Cohen's way of keeping the crusade for justice alive. He spent hour upon hour each evening at his rickety kitchen table, battering away at his equally rickety typewriter, compiling reams of correspondence to almost anyone he could think of who might have an interest in the whereabouts of stolen war treasures. His endeavour had amassed a pile of letters from victims, but he struggled to make any kind of connection to Hamazaki. Since he had been "stepped down" from his official post in the Bureau, Cohen had refused to let his obsession die. He devoted nearly all of his free waking hours to the pursuit of his quarry. The madness fuelled his passion; the bitterness gave him the resolve.

He had managed to secure employment as a security supervisor working night shifts, which involved overseeing a staff of three watchmen, all of whom kept vigilance over a business complex on the outskirts of town. The pay wasn't much, but the work suited him, as it came with his own small office where he could hide away and secretly work on the more pressing matters that demanded his attention. He often wished he could allow himself the freedom to use some of the equipment that was in some of the offices he oversaw. He would make his nightly rounds checking on his men, who would invariably be skiving and smoking in the dark corners of the building. Cohen could hardly blame them. Their pay was pitiful, and there was no chance of improvement. He would halfheartedly cajole them into making an effort, but it was taken as given that nobody wanted to be hassled, so each and every night was an exercise in dealing with the heavy eyelids of boredom.

The dead of night is a fine time to think. There is a perverse satisfaction to be gained from being productive whilst the outside world sleeps. Cohen had found that he did some of his best thinking in the dead hours, and this particular night was no exception. He had been reading in the local paper about a successful campaign to clear the name of a convicted killer. It was not the result that grabbed Cohen's interest as much as the campaign to clear him and how the metamorphism of support had been conceived. It had started with one man, George Isaacs, a civil rights activist who took on cases of perceived miscarriages of justice. Isaacs used methods that built up a huge groundswell of support that became such a powerful force, it was impossible to ignore.

Cohen instinctively knew something was stirring in the recesses of his imagination, and he had walked the corridors in the dead of night, pondering how best to put his thoughts into some kind of action. He resolved to write to Isaacs and seek his advice about how best to construct support for his own crusade.

Now, Elias Cohen was well aware that if he were to come across as some kind of fanatic, his letter would be dropped into the nearest wastebasket. He agonised over his next move, asking himself the same question over and over again. What did he expect to achieve from Isaacs? From what he could gather, George Isaacs was a man who lived his life with a passionate sense of what justice actually meant. The newspaper article had gone on at great lengths, exalting his virtues, even alluding to the idea that he might one day divert his talents to aiding the Democratic Party. Whatever the future held in store for Mr Isaacs was of little concern to Cohen, who merely wanted his advice, here and now.

Night followed night, each indistinguishable from the last. Cohen sat in his windowless cubbyhole that was designated his office by someone who had either a vivid imagination or a wild sense of humour. He must have run through more than a hundred drafts of his letter to Isaacs. The wastepaper basket was a nightly testament to his efforts. Even after settling on a final version he was still not quite satisfied, and self-doubt ate away his confidence. He read through his letter for the hundredth time before finally agreeing with his desire to move this thing forward. He stared down at the paper in front of him as if reading it from a distance would somehow make it appear more appealing.

November 18, 1963

Dear Mr Isaacs,

It was with great interest and admiration that I read of your recent triumph in the quest for justice on behalf of the wrongly convicted and imprisoned Mr Marcus Gates. Your efforts deserve all our respect. I truly believe that our great nation is made stronger and more just in the light of such success.

I am writing to you today in the hope that you may be in a position to offer me a little guidance. I too am an activist of sorts, though I do not seek to highlight the plight of any single innocent individual. Indeed, I am more concerned with delivering justice for millions upon millions of people whose own countries were systematically looted and pillaged of their sovereign wealth over the course of the war that ravaged the Pacific states and many countries of Asia in the decade up to 1945.

I was employed by our own government at the highest levels in the investigation of this grand crime—that is, until my employment was suddenly and unexpectedly terminated at the very moment when all our efforts were about to be realised. I considered that the greatest affront to justice I could ever imagine. I am still bound by the secrecy of my agreement with the agency, which still plays a laudable role in the safety and security of the nation.

My correspondence with you may have its own repercussions, but desperation and desire have given me the strength to face the consequences of my actions.

Over the years I have compiled a detailed dossier on certain people who need to be called upon to account for their actions. The evidence is as strong an indictment as one may ever see, and therein lies my problem and my reason for seeking your help. I am bound by my agreement with the authorities to pursue this matter no further. Indeed, on the occasions that I have approached my former colleagues, I have been met only with threats of arrest and the restriction of my own liberty.

Mr Isaacs, I am not the kind of man to sit by and do nothing whilst evil is allowed to prosper. I fully appreciate that this kind of matter is not of your usual remit. However, it is a true campaign with justice at its heart. It is also a complex and equally beguiling investigation, one that is impossible to convey in simple correspondence. Nonetheless I hope it may have piqued your interest. I apologise if my meanderings have caused you any ill feelings, and it is with great hope and expectation that I await your communication.

Yours in expectation,

Elias Cohen

After satisfying himself that this was enough to at least prompt some kind of response from Isaacs, Cohen carefully tri-folded the letter and sealed it in its matching high-quality nonpersonalised envelope. He then agonised about whether to append the sender's details on the outside, finally deciding that anonymity was the better option. He attached a separate memorandum in which he carefully wrote out his home address and telephone number. He had once read that anything written in haste was best reviewed the following morning; if it still made decent reading, it was fit to serve its purpose. Cohen's letter had hardly been written in haste, but he was not an impulsive man, so he decided to sit on his actions, and resigned himself to one more sleepless night.

* * *

It was one of those moments when everybody in the country would remember where they were and what they were doing when they heard the news. Elias Cohen was lying in bed. It was past midday, and he had been unable to sleep after another night of grinding boredom walking the corridors that he was paid to protect. He was past tired and deep into exhaustion, but sleep never came easily. The demons in his mind would play tricks with his imagination and feed on his insecurities. His life had become one dark canvas without colour, joy, or any other form of happiness. He was the original sad case. It had been three days since he had dropped his letter into the mailbox on the corner of his street by the bank, and now he lived in the grip of paranoia and fear. He had somehow managed to convince himself that he was under surveillance and that his mail had been intercepted and would never reach Mr Isaacs. He was equally convinced that he would be dragged from his bed and taken away to some wretched detention centre, where he would be forced to confess to crimes he had never committed. It often took a few restless hours of sleep and a few strong cups of coffee to bring him back round to a more realistic view of his own circumstances.

If Cohen were truly honest, he'd admit that only one thing was worse than being the subject of investigation, and that was to be nobody, a nonperson, one whose existence was of no consequence to another living soul. Is that what he had become? Whatever was coursing through his mind this particular afternoon stopped dead in its tracks, and an ice-cold rush surged through his veins. He had switched on his radio to listen to some classical music, hoping it would soothe him to sleep, and was agitated to find that his usual station was not broadcasting music as usual but talking about something that had happened in Dallas. The voice of the newsreader sounded out of place, his words unreal and beyond belief as they filled Cohen's tiny, dank bedroom. "It is with deep and grave sadness that we report the president is dead. His death was officially confirmed a few minutes ago by his personal physician, Doctor George Burkley. The cause of death was a gunshot wound to the head which was inflicted by an assassin as the president rode in his open-car motorcade through the streets of Dallas approximately one hour ago. I repeat this sad news. President Kennedy has been assassinated. We will bring you more details as and when we receive them. Our thoughts and prayers are with the president's family. God bless America. Now we will play Mozart's Requiem in D Minor."

Cohen sat upright in his bed, unable to believe the shocking news. He closed his eyes tightly and put his hands over his ears. Mozart's sorrow was filling the room with black flowers. Cohen rocked back and forth, mouthing "No, no, no" over and over, but his emotion was not for the president. He was concerned that this momentous event would serve only to distract Mr George Isaacs and render his interest in Cohen's letter nil. With these selfish thoughts in mind he leaned over to his nightstand, picked up his radio, and hurled it at the far wall, screaming "Hamazaki!" at the top of his voice.

The room fell quiet, Mozart's beautiful, deathly masterpiece silenced. Cohen felt the tears of rage and pity welling up in his eyes. His hands began to tremble. It was only when he looked down beside his bed that he noticed the smashed photo frame which had been caught up in his rage. The face of his lovely

Dorothea smiled back at him, a young woman whose beauty would be forever frozen in time but was now distorted by shards of broken glass. Now the tears came all too easily. Elias Cohen pulled the bedcovers over his head and wished the world would swallow him up.

That very same afternoon at the very same time, some 230 miles away in his Lexington Avenue apartment in New York, another man was reacting in a similar manner to the awful news. George Isaacs slumped into his armchair by a crackling log fire, thankful to be alone, as he did not wish another to see his tears of sadness. He had always been an emotional man by nature. As a child he had cried in movie theatres and opened himself up to the taunts and bullying of his peers. Those were valuable life lessons, and as he grew, he managed to steel his emotions and put them aside in a place where only he knew they could be found. He had cultivated an icy demeanour, one that perfectly complemented his sense of determination. So it came as a shock to him to find his cheeks moistened this tragic afternoon.

Isaacs looked up at his mantelpiece, upon which was placed a large decorative envelope embossed with a gold eagle, underneath which was simply written "The White House, Washington." It contained an invitation to attend one of President Kennedy's dinner parties and had arrived only this very morning, delivered by personal courier. Opening that invitation had been one of the proudest moments of George Isaacs's life, for it told him that what he had managed to achieve was recognised and lauded by the highest in the land. Now only hours later, all had changed. Isaacs believed in Kennedy; he trusted him as any decent man would. He believed in Kennedy's vision of America and the noble values he espoused. Now he felt shattered. The tears were nothing other than a reminder that deep down he was still a child crying his eyes out in a movie theatre as his so-called friends circled and mercilessly taunted him.

Isaacs stood up and took the president's invitation in both hands and dropped it onto the burning logs. He took a step back and gave a clumsy salute. "The death of America, the death of the dream" he mouthed as he watched the gold eagle being consumed by flames.

Isaacs once more sagged his weary body back into his armchair and tried to organise his thoughts. Of course this did not particularly affect him on any personal level, though he had recently toyed with the notion of getting involved in the Democratic Party. Indeed, certain representatives had even sought out his views on matters of policy. He had always told himself that as a social reformer and campaigner for justice he would never allow his principles to be compromised. Stepping into the political arena would be a betrayal of what he held so dear. He was desperately trying to convince himself that he could make more of a difference from within the system than from outside.

Now the one man he held in such high esteem was gone, leaving a void that Isaacs was having difficulty understanding. He needed focus in his life. As he sat there, he recalled another letter that had arrived this same morning by regular delivery. Isaacs had given its contents only a cursory look-through before despatching it into his wastebasket. He received hundreds of letters a month and was unable to reply to each and all. The good majority of his correspondents were desperate people in desperate situations. He felt for their plight, but in reality there was little he could do for them.

In truth, George Isaacs was interested only in the battles he could win and as such was very careful about whom he took on.

But something started to nag his brain, and he wearily stood and began to sort through the morning's trash, muttering under his breath something about wars and treasures. Having found the crumpled envelope, he pulled out the letter once more, this time studying the neat handwriting and its strange message. He scanned down the page and read the signature, "Elias Cohen."

Isaacs tried to build a mental picture of Cohen. He had a certain pride in his often accurate assessment of a person's character, but he was having difficulty putting Cohen into any mould. Parts of his letter were quite disturbing and even hinted at a man with possible mental health issues, but other areas suggested the writer had a genuine point and a story to tell. Isaacs knew that this was not or anywhere near his area of expertise, but something told him to at least offer the man the chance to put his case forward in person. This is what Kennedy would have done. Why in heaven's name the awful news from Dallas had prompted him to go back to that strange letter, he would never know. Perhaps it was the voice of his dear lost brother, taken in battle on the Japanese island of Okinawa, eighteen years gone now. A half-blood waif of a brother, not even twenty years on this earth, whose blood, bone, and flesh would forever nourish that place so far away.

Isaacs was neither a superstitious man nor one who put much stock in coincidence, but he did believe in providence, and with this in mind he sat down and wrote to Elias Cohen.

Chapter 9
Ken Miyazaki
Manila
1965

I pulled the window blind to one side and squinted out at the barren airfield; the sunlight was blinding, and I cursed myself for forgetting my sunglasses. We had just touched down at Nichols Field, Manila, after flying for more than six hours, a feat that almost beggared belief. Over the years I had become accustomed to the long hauls in noisy, draughty, propeller-driven bone shakers that required countless stopovers for refuelling, but we had entered the age of the commercial jet, and flying was no more difficult than sitting in your own front room.

A mere six hours earlier we had boarded our flight at Haneda, where the temperature was a notch above freezing. The previous day had seen the first snowfall of the winter, which necessitated a last-minute inspection of the runway before the airport authorities considered it safe enough for us to take off. Our aircraft was one of the newer types of DC8 that Japan Airlines had recently brought into service, and despite the lingering whiff of cigar odour, I could smell its newness as we boarded and took our seats. The front section of the aircraft had been cordoned off for our exclusive use, in order to afford the privacy that wealth and status provide.

An hour or so before boarding and from the comfort of the Haneda Tower VIP lounge, I had watched our fellow passengers as they embarked ahead of us. I scanned each and every one for telltale signs that any of them might be shadowing our own journey. I was particularly concerned about overzealous press boys or government officials from certain departments who may have posed as regular businessmen. We could not be vigilant enough, for it was times like these that saw us at our most vulnerable, and this was when I had to show my mettle. I had taken all the usual preflight precautions such as requesting the flight manifest and running background checks on our fellow passengers. We had a cordial working relationship with the airline, and their cooperation was always forthcoming. Toshio treated his connections in high places extremely generously with all the gravitas befitting a high-ranking businessman.

I was satisfied that nothing was out of the ordinary, and there was no cause to believe that this "business trip" would be any different from others we had concluded. Yet I could not rid myself of the feeling that all was not as it should be. Perhaps it was because of Hosokawa's insistence that he make the trip, despite the fact that he was obviously unfit for anything other than signing papers. I looked over to where he sat, still wrapped in his large fur-lined coat, oblivious to the surge of tropical heat that would hit us once the cabin doors opened. He was wearing dark glasses to hide his equally dark and sunken eyes. It was not possible to tell if he was awake or slumbering. His physical state was now completely hostage to the morphine to which he was enslaved. Over the last five years I had come to despise his weakness, and I feared his drug dependency would be the downfall of us all. I had voiced my concerns to Toshio and Hideo, but neither one had seen fit to act on my worries. "Mabuhay stays loyal to its core" was the opaque response I had gotten from Toshio, admirable for sure but fool-hardy in the extreme.

Seated behind Hosokawa was Doctor Kato, who was still pestering the stewardess for another brandy to fortify himself against the blazing elements. Kato had been appointed as Mabuhay's chief medical officer some five years ago now. Although he was mainly concerned with the implementation of company health programmes for employees, he had somehow found himself amongst our group for this trip. Ayumi had insisted that he make the trip to give his expert medical opinion about the effectiveness of the food aid program that the foundation was sponsoring. As far as I was concerned, the man was a liability, and his mere presence here was enough to make me seethe with contempt, which I found increasingly difficult to conceal. Kato was well aware that I found him repugnant, and we kept a cool distance between us. I knew he was responsible for keeping Hosokawa fuelled with his vile "medication."

Seated in front of me were Ayumi and Tanezawa. The pair of them had spent the entire flight poring over papers that contained all the details about the foundation's current projects and financial arrangements. Their devotion to the Mabuhay Foundation was total and demanded respect. I doubted there was anything that would get past those two, a formidable team for sure. Ayumi had taken on the mantle of chief representative for this visit, because Hosokawa was certainly in no shape to give the details the attention they deserved.

Although it was not Ayumi's first trip to the Philippines, I had my reservations about letting her out of my sight. This was still a male-driven society, and on past trips we had come across more bigots than I cared to count. I resolved to keep her as close as I could without appearing overly protective. It would be folly to arouse the suspicions of my companions about the depth of my relationship with Ayumi. I doubted that we would get the opportunity to lie in bed together at the Manila Hotel on this trip. I closed my eyes and reminisced about an earlier trip when, in the dead of night, Ayumi had taken me unawares and slipped between my sheets. The Manila air had been heavy that night, and the open louvered windows had allowed a cacophony of noise to drift into my room from the insects that sang in the courtyard below. She had held me close, her embrace more needy than lusting. We lay together in contented silence, lost in a moment that seemed to last an eternity.

The storm that shook us to our senses came suddenly; the rain beat down, and the violent crashes of thunder provided a dramatic backdrop to our lovemaking. Ayumi had taken me by surprise, her enthusiasm for my body knew no bounds, and we both shelved our inhibitions for a time when they would be better suited. Our secret trysts had become more precious to me, as opportunities to be alone together were scarce. I found myself feeding off my memories. Ayumi's staged iciness towards me in public left me with a feeling of impotent frustration. I also had the problem of facing her husband on a near daily basis. Hideo was fast becoming the focus of all my spite. I cursed the man for being married to the woman I was in love with. He was the jailer who had lost his keys a long time ago and did not even give a hoot. Ayumi would never consider a separation; it had not even been mentioned. To all, she was the epitome of a true and loyal wife, everything an ungrateful husband could wish for.

I wondered how far I could push her loyalty. Would she be so steadfast if she knew that the woman now sitting next to her shared pillow talk with her husband? So many times I wished I could enlighten her, but I suppose I am a little old-fashioned in many respects, and in any case my silence was more in deference to Tanezawa than to Hideo Tanaka.

Our plane slowly made its way to the disembarkation point. From the window I could see that little progress had been made as far as the airport construction was concerned. You soon came to accept that life here seemed to exist in a different dimension. The slow pace of enterprise could be considered quaint if it were not equally infuriating. Three years had passed since my last visit to Manila, and I was convinced that I was looking at the same pile of masonry dumped at the runway's edge.

Hosokawa's valet, Murakami, was quickly out of his seat and tried to attend to his master, readying him for arrival. I did not envy him his task. Hosokawa was one of the most petulant people I knew, and very difficult to handle. Luckily, Murakami was blessed with the patience of a saint and the strength of an ox. I do believe he held genuine respect for Hosokawa, but I guessed he had to dig deep into his reserves to find the fortitude to continue with such mild-mannered acquiescence. Murakami had come into our close employ at a time when Hosokawa was at his most vulnerable and feared his life was under threat. One of our own had been brutally murdered, and Hosokawa believed that he himself was the intended target. Police protection had been offered but firmly refused. Murakami had stepped into the breach, and although he was employed as a personal valet, Hosokawa treated him as a glorified dogsbody. Hosokawa had become a little too reliant on Murakami for my liking, and I often wondered if Murakami was aware of the true nature of our business here in Manila.

In a few moments our plane would draw to a halt, and after the stairs had been fixed to the door, we would step out into the early December heat of a bright, humid Manila afternoon. I could see the convoy of limousines waiting to transport us directly to the Manila Hotel, a familiar place that would serve as our home for the next five nights. Our party was rounded out with the welcome presence of Jean Meursault and Luc Rinehart—a banker and a lawyer, but two of the most ruthlessly efficient professionals I had ever had the good fortune to work with.

Meursault worked out of Switzerland and was our exclusive banker; as far as the money was concerned, he was the man who made the magic happen. He had been a close confidant of Toshio's father, and the two had developed a mutually profitable relationship interrupted only by the onset of war. It was to Meursault that Toshio turned when the extraordinary venture that became Mabuhay was first conceived. Jean Meursault was the only man in such a position of power amongst the Geneva financial community who could turn dangerous fantasy into the reality we all enjoyed today. Meursault's unique skills were matched by his total lack of probity. The man was a crook, but he was our crook, and for that we had cause to be more than grateful.

Rinehart was cut from the same cloth; although he was a lawyer by profession, he acted as right-hand man and was heir apparent to Meursault, who was undoubtedly in the twilight of his years. The pair of them had slept for the entire journey at the rear of our section, still jaded from the long-haul continental flights they had just undertaken. Now that they were roused, the cabin was filled with mild expletives as they took advantage of their lingual anonymity and cursed everything in a light-hearted manner. I smiled at their humour. French was a joyous language and one I felt privileged to be a party to.

So there we were, that was our delegation, and officially we were there in Manila to pursue the business of the Mabuhay Foundation. Visits to various projects and rounds of endless meetings with people whose names we could barely pronounce had been scheduled. The evenings would be taken up with entertaining and being entertained. In the midst of all this whirl of philanthropic activity, Hosokawa, if he proved fit enough, and I, along with our European friends, would find the time to sit down face-to-face with Santa Romana and agree on terms for the next excavation and shipment of another hoard of priceless loot that had remained buried deep under the Luzon rain forest for over twenty years.

The aircraft drew to a halt, and the stewardess asked us to remain in our seats until the door had been opened. Her words went completely unheeded by our European companions, who fussed over the checking of their attaché cases and the folding away of bulky winter coats. Murakami was also going about his duty, trying without much success to coax Hosokawa out of his own great hulking bear of a coat. The women, on the other hand, were the true epitome of efficiency. Ayumi and Tanezawa sat patiently, ready to make their entry onto Philippine soil with all the dignity that would be more in keeping with the arrival of royalty.

I had decided that Hosokawa and Murakami should be the first to disembark and should travel in the first limousine. Kato could accompany them; perhaps he would take the opportunity to fortify Hosokawa with a shot of morphine topped off with some sleeping medications to be absolutely sure his charge wouldn't require much of his attention. Ayumi and Tanezawa would travel together in the second car, with Meursault, Rinehart, and me bringing up the rear.

There was a loud clunk as the portable stairs were fixed into place. The captain had taken up a position by the door and signalled for it to be opened. The stewardess, a nimble young woman, threw back the giant lever, and the door swung open and released a blast of hot, fetid air into the cabin. The heat was stifling, and through the window I could see the haze rising off the cars. Hosokawa staggered to his feet and, with Murakami's support, began his perilous descent down the steps to the waiting limousine. He was still wearing his Tokyo winter coat, which covered his emaciated frame, a tragic sight, pitiful and comical in equal measure. One by one we trooped off the plane, each of us thanking the captain for our pleasant journey. The heat was repressive, and from experience I knew we would find little respite once inside the vehicles.

The short distance to the downtown area would also take longer than necessary because of the chaos and reckless abandon of the streets. Our drivers were standing by their open doors, expressionless behind dark sunglasses. They offered no help with the loading of the luggage, leaving that menial task to the airport lackeys. It never failed to amaze me how official procedures were conveniently ignored in this country. There was no check of our travel documents, and everything was taken at face value.

I was the last of our group to leave the aircraft and, after confirming that all of my party were safely inside their respective limousines, made my way to the rear vehicle, where a familiar face waited to greet me. The hand was outstretched in welcome. Over the years I had come to think of this handshake as the "hard hand of welcome," a fitting euphemism for such a trip. I gripped the leather-gloved hand that Hector Ramirez proffered. The stone-hard prosthesis always disturbed me, but I hoped I managed to hide my discomfort well. "Welcome back to the Philippines, Mr Miyazaki." He leaned closer to my ear and said in a conspiratorial tone, like a ham actor, "Mr Romana sends his apologies; he is unable to greet you in person but is eager to meet soon." There was no surprise there; Romana had never once been out to the airfield to meet us on arrival. This was my eighth such trip, and I had come to understand the foibles of Hector's boss. However, things had changed drastically since my last trip. Romana was now at the heart of all power in the country. He was the father-in-law of the newly elected president; his daughter was the First Lady of the Philippines. Last month's dramatic national elections had seen Marios wrestle power from the long-term incumbent, Macapagal. Accusations of fraud and vote rigging were rife, but Marios had swept to power on promises of reform and redevelopment. I could only imagine the swell of pride that Romana must be feeling, but it remained to be seen how his newfound status would affect the dynamics of our working relationship. I had no doubt that he would use his increased influence as leverage and try for an increased share of the spoils. His gratitude for past offerings would have expired; perhaps he would need to be reminded that it was our generosity that had helped fund his son-in-law's run for office.

I sank into the rear seat of the limousine and settled down for the ride over to the hotel. I always found this part of the journey the most depressing, for it was at this time that the reality of our situation really hit home. I had often asked Hosokawa why we were still involved in this side of the business. Was it really worth risking everything when we were so far ahead of our field? Why not just hand the lot over to Romana and be done with it? Hosokawa also thought along similar lines; however, Toshio would have none of it. He said we had a moral obligation to see this side of the business through to its conclusion. He was adamant that somehow we were performing a service by keeping the loot out of the hands of financial predators. Toshio often spoke in clouded terms, and his statements were laced with self-irony. Hosokawa once told me that our "transactions" were part of a greater good and that in time, all items would be repatriated to their rightful owners. I was not privy to the more intricate details of our business and certainly had little influence over matters other than those I was presently engaged in. Because of Hosokawa's unreliable state of mind, I had been given more responsibility, and Toshio had taken a great leap of faith when he entrusted this delegation and assignment to me. Sure enough, it would be Hosokawa who would be expected to give the final agreement, but I was the one Toshio had turned to when the time came to hand over the extraction details of site number eleven. For the first time in my inglorious Mabuhay career, I had been entrusted with the exact location of a site, and that was a sure sign that I was the one in control of the agenda.

Our motorcade caught the attention of the street folk, and when we stopped or moved along at a snail's pace, faces pressed against the glass. I heard shouts and chants of "Marios, Marios" from the street kids, who deluded themselves into believing they had just seen the presidential motorcade. Meursault and Rinehart were for the most part tight lipped about what they thought of the new president. I had known Meursault for over fifteen years, ever since I had joined Mabuhay, and I knew he was not a reticent man—quite the opposite, in fact. He would often be overly generous with his praise. His silence did not bode well, and I took it as given that he was not an admirer of Romana's son-in-law.

As we drew closer to downtown Manila, I noticed a heavy military presence on the streets. Gangs of soldiers crowded on corners, and military trucks and jeeps were parked across the streets, forcing vehicles to slow down and giving the soldiers time to stare down the occupants. The soldiers were very young and full of bravado. Some of them wore ammunition belts across their shoulders, and nearly all wore dark glasses; they looked more like bandits than a disciplined force. Rinehart gazed out the window and said under his breath, "Marios is flexing his muscle already. He needs to make a stand, to show there is a new boss in town."

Our convoy was halted by a group of rough-looking gung-ho types. They rapped on the windows of our limousine, and I lowered the glass a fraction. The young soldier was full of macho posturing, but his eyes told a different story. He demanded to see our "papers." I told him that we did not have any papers and that we were a delegation on a trade mission from overseas. My English was not as good as my French, but I felt confident enough with my ability.

Before the young buck could reply, he was distracted by a voice shouting him down. Hector, who had been travelling in a smaller car at the rear of our motorcade, was now out on the dusty street, shouting at the military goons with a fury that was easy to comprehend in any language. He came alongside the limo and gave the soldier a violent push backwards. By now some of the other soldiers had gathered to see what the fuss was about, and I noticed that some of them had unholstered their pistols. I had been around violence long enough to realise that this was getting uglier by the second. Hector's own men were now also out of the car, all of them wearing brilliant white Barong shirts and sunglasses, and they quickly bore down on the military men.

Hector had worked himself up into a frenzy and delivered a hail of abuse at the hapless soldiers, who were having serious mis-givings about their decision to halt our convoy. Eventually a jeep drew up alongside our vehicle and out stepped a grand-looking chap in full camouflage dress, sporting a gold-braided peak cap and the standard-issue aviator sunglasses which seemed to be worn by every testosterone-fuelled male in the country. Hector soon marked himself out as a man who held little respect for rank and continued to harangue everyone before him. It did not take long for the officer to come round to Hector's point of view, and within a minute they both turned to us. Through our window the officer offered his apologies for any inconvenience we may have suffered. He even wished us a pleasant stay in his country.

Hector seemed satisfied with this outcome and, believing he had won this little showdown, waved the military lads away, but not before delivering a painful blow to the head of the young man who had asked for our papers. That heavy prosthesis of his was a fine weapon, and the young soldier was left standing in the road, clutching his bleeding scalp. As our convoy moved off, Rinehart repeated, "Marios flexing his muscle. That little show was as much for the benefit of the onlookers as it was for us. Gentlemen, welcome to the goon show."

Our motorcade glided smoothly along Roxas Boulevard, and I wound down the windows to enjoy the crisp breeze that blew in from across Manila Bay. The exotic trees that lined the road swayed and danced in hypnotic fashion, the coconut, mango, and acacia trees providing a dizzy contrast to some of the uglier features on view. The buildings looked as if they had been thrown together without much aesthetic appreciation; I suppose that is one of the legacies of war. At the turn of the century this city was to be an architect's dream. Daniel Burnham, the man who designed Union Station, had a grand vision of a planned city with vast boulevards, parks, and splendid buildings in keeping with the elegant sprawl. Somewhere, lost in the mists of time, his plans had floundered, and given that history had not been particularly kind to the city, we were left with what we could see today.

The Manila Hotel was part of the grand scheme, built to rival the presidential palace, the Malacañan, and at the time, no expense was spared. I had always found the hotel to be an oasis of calm in the middle of a confused and chaotic city. If ever one wanted to draw stark contrasts between the affluent and the desperately poor, one needed look no further than the Manila Hotel and the life that went on around its perimeter. Guests quaffed five-dollar cocktails in the vast lobby bar, while a mere stone's throw away on the streets outside, ragged, barefoot children begged for sustenance, their distended bellies bringing home the dire truth about this poverty-stricken nation.

It was a nation of contradictions and one I believed I would never understand, but I refused to let it get under my skin. I had seen what it had done to Ayumi. She had been reduced to tears of frustration as she could not, for the life of her, understand why all the good works of the foundation seemed to have very little effect on the lives of those we intended to help. The Mabuhay Foundation donated millions of dollars annually to a wide range of projects— health, education, and sanitary programmes aimed at improving the lives of children, to offer hope and the dream of a brighter future. In reality all we did was make the present a little more comfortable for kids who found themselves benefitting from a Mabuhay project. The real problem lay in the dearth of opportunities. In a society that lacked a working social infrastructure and failed to reward or recognise effort, there was, depressingly, no alternative other than to sink back into the black hole of poverty. The challenge of the country's new president was to build a fairer society and a healthy functioning middle class that ordinary folk would aspire to join.

Ayumi had prepared a speech along those lines, for she had come to realise that real change needed to come from the top. Toshio and Hideo had strictly forbidden any kind of criticism of the regime, as Mabuhay policy was to avoid political conflict, but knowing Ayumi and her headstrong nature, I believed her frustration had finally spilt over, and I feared she would take the opportunity to air her feelings in public. Her views might not sit well with the new Marios regime, and kicking the hornets' nest was probably not the wisest thing to do right now. What is that saying about "people in glass houses"? I felt as if I had one arm tied behind my back. Ayumi was totally and blissfully unaware of Mabuhay's dealings with Romana and all the nastiness that entailed.

Our party was greeted at the hotel's main entrance by the general manager, whose name I should have remembered by then but always escaped me. A train of bellboys were tasked with delivering our luggage to the accommodation. Ayumi's set of pristine Louis Vuitton trunks were treated with deferential respect, whilst the rest of our bags were piled onto carts in a haphazard fashion. We moved smartly through the impressive Doric-columned lobby, following the many hotel staff who were getting under our feet. Hosokawa shuffled along like a man twice his age, Murakami supporting him at the elbow. Ayumi and Tanezawa had been assigned the MacArthur suite, which was a three-bedroom palatial indulgence that smacked of hypocrisy, given her mission here. Hosokawa was accommodated in the presidential suite, though I doubted he would be in any state to appreciate its fine features and the splendid view across Manila Bay. I believed he would spend the trip mostly comatose in his huge bed, waking only to summon Kato for more "relief" or to shout for Murakami to aid his ablutions.

The rest of us were assigned regular rooms on the floor below, which were more than adequate for our purpose, and I felt a wave of relief as the bellboy finally delivered my luggage and closed the door, leaving me alone for the first time in hours. I stepped out onto the balcony and took a great deep breath of breezy, warm air. I often wished I could be here as a regular person without an agenda other than pure hedonism. From high up the city looked almost sensible, the madness below unable to breach the sanity that this grand edifice effortlessly provided. I went back into my room and poured myself a glass of iced lemon tea from the pitcher that had been left on the bedside table.

Stretching out on the gigantic bed, I closed my eyes and tried to will Ayumi into my room. I was desperate for her touch and wanted her between my sheets right now. Such fantasies were brought crashing down when, in stark contrast to that beautiful reverie, I unlocked my case and felt for my revolver. Its feel in my hand was both satisfying and disturbing in equal measure. I opened the chamber to check the rounds and, satisfied, clicked it shut. I lay back on the bed and took aim at the ornamental vase opposite. I conjured up a vision of Santa Romana and desperately wanted to pull the trigger. I prayed for the day when the real Romana would be in my sights.

A knock on the door made me jump. I quickly slipped the revolver under the pillow and called out to whoever it was. There was a faint, gentle reply, and for a second I thought my prayers had been answered and Ayumi had come to call. My ardour was soon dashed, as it was Tanezawa who had come to update me on the latest developments regarding our commitments. She declined to come into my room, preferring to hand me an envelope which had my name neatly written across the front. I recognised the handwriting immediately; it was from Ayumi. I thanked Tanezawa for bearing my message and watched as she walked down the corridor. She was a shapely beauty who had fine, rounded curves in all the right places. If circumstances had been a little different, I might have pursued Tanezawa all the way, but I was wise enough to keep our relationship on a professional level. In any case, I had witnessed Hosokawa's disastrous marriage to Azusa, where the age difference had proved to be too great a barrier for their mutual happiness. Although they were still married, they lived entirely separate lives, and I believed this caused Hosokawa great sadness, not to mention damaged his pride. Perhaps that was why he sought deliverance from his personal hell and lost himself in a perpetual narcotic haze day after day.

I stepped back into my room, lay back on the bed, and ripped the envelope open. There was a sheet of hotel notepaper upon which Ayumi had written a brief note. She informed me that we were all invited to a cocktail reception that evening here at the hotel, hosted by the Friendship Society of the Philippines, followed by dinner, also at the hotel. What caught my attention most was the word later, which she had underlined and emphasised with two bold question marks. My spirits soared as I took it as a sign that I would soon be welcoming my lover back to my bed.

I spent the next two hours keeping myself busy by unpacking and putting the shine back into my shoes. The room was equipped with quite a few luxuries, radio being one. I went about my chores whilst listening to the latest American hits and the enthusiastic Tagalog commentary that announced each song. I felt older than my fifty-six years, as I could not relate to the songs that were popular these days. I recognised some of the names—Elvis Presley, the Beatles—but for the most part I was two generations adrift. It was 1965, and the world had changed beyond all recognition. Exactly twenty years earlier, our army had fought one of the bloodiest battles of the war, right here in this city, on the very streets down below, and now here I was, listening to piped radio, relaxing in a hot tub, and about to attend a civilised cocktail party in the very spot where so many had lost their lives. It barely credited thinking about, the madness of the human condition. I only hoped the fallen could not see us now, for I believed that if they did, they would die all over again as the crushing futility of war bore down. I tried not to think about the absurdity of our presence here and went about my preparations. It did not take me long to get ready, unlike Toshio or the Hosokawa of old, both of whom dallied and fussed about like a pair of old dames. This evening we were informal—that is to say, in two-pieces and neckties.

I had fifteen minutes to spare, so I decided to call on Hosokawa. I doubted he would be in any fit condition to attend this evening's event, but he was still my boss, and protocol had to be respected. Murakami had relieved me of most of the daily tedium of catering to Hosokawa's whims, and for that I was eternally thankful. Hosokawa's current condition and the speed of his deterioration was alarming, and it would be heartless to say I had little sympathy for his self-inflicted state. For I, more than anyone alive, had cause to be grateful to the man. Fifteen years earlier he had saved me from deportation to France and a lengthy jail term, his last official act as a diplomat. He visited me as I languished in my Chiba prison cell, and offered me salvation in return for my unquestioned loyalty. He left me little alternative but to agree, but secretly I had been making plans to be rid of this man, who at the time I thought to be deranged. He caught my attention by telling a tale of a great scheme that he and his eminent colleagues were in the process of turning into reality. He was full of optimism and egotistical bluster, but possessed enough self-confidence to pique my interest.

He told me he was about to embark on a grand enterprise and needed a trusted personal lieutenant. He had gone through his files at the ministry in search of likely candidates, and mine had happened to be on his desk the very day he was to clear it and leave his post. He saw it as a divine sign and drove out to Chiba Prison, where documents were exchanged, financial inducement was settled upon, and finally I was released into the custody of Makoto

Hosokawa. My release had been determined by judicial proxy. Hosokawa filed papers with the authorities which said there was insufficient evidence for a deportation order. It was automatically "rubber-stamped," and I had walked out of Chiba Prison alongside Hosokawa.

To say that I had been impressed by the man would be a gross understatement, for I quickly came to realise that he was nobody's fool and that perhaps his "grand scheme" had just enough credence to be more than wild fantasy. That was the day Daigo Hamma died and Ken Miyazaki was born. He had chosen that name for me, as Miyazaki was the prefecture of my birth. Hosokawa told me that my past was now forgotten and my old self was dead and gone. From that day on I never had cause to look back. I had grown to like my new self, and I had repaid Hosokawa's trust in me many times over.

Now, many years later, I still felt a strong sense of loyalty to the man who had saved me from a Legion étrangère prison. If Hosokawa had not come into my life that day, I do not know what would have become of me. Some things are certain, and for sure I would not be in the Manila Hotel wearing a five-hundred-dollar suit and anticipating making love to the wealthiest Japanese woman alive.

I walked along the wide corridor, enjoying the relaxed feel of this wonderful hotel. This place managed to feel home-like without compromising its business sense. However, in contrast the place also had an air of the chaotic about it; perhaps that was an inevitable reflection of the country itself. Despite having twice as many staff in the hotel as appeared necessary, things seemed to take an age to get done. Perhaps we had just become accustomed to the frantic pace of our own lives and direct comparisons were unfair. Ayumi enjoyed her stays here. She would inevitably draw unfavourable comparisons with her own home back at the Empire, which she found stuffy and overbearing. On her return to Japan she would sink into a melancholy state as the reality of her surroundings came home to bear. Hideo stubbornly refused to consider even the very notion of moving out of the Empire. For the life of me I could not understand his logic at all, but then again the man was a tangled web of contradictions, his very marriage to Ayumi being the most obvious.

I climbed the lushly carpeted staircase to the floor above, where Hosokawa's suite was situated. The huge seashell chandelier above my head tinkled, and radiant shafts of light from the late afternoon sunset over Manila Bay danced through the huge windows on either side of the grand staircase. The whole effect was very soothing and relaxed my mind, and I felt my stress levels sail away. As I reached Hosokawa's suite, the door opened and out stepped Kato. He was dressed for the function but had his medicine case in hand. I knew what he had been summoned for. No doubt Hosokawa had sunk into an induced narcolepsy. I gripped Kato's arm tightly and stared into his face, bearing into those ridiculous big eyes of his. "Doctor, I think it is time you and I had a serious talk about the future treatment of my employer."

Kato looked shocked and tried to shake himself free of my grip. "Unhand me this instant; I will not be intimidated by you, Miyazaki. I am a medical physician going about his duties, simply administering to the needs of my patient." The man had a sense of bravado, but I could tell he was unnerved. I released my grip but kept my gaze locked into his eyes. He scuttled off down the corridor, steaming with indignation but not daring to glance back.

I waited until Kato had gone out of sight and then with a sense of increasing trepidation knocked lightly on the door. Within a matter of seconds I heard the safety chain being fixed into place, and the door opened slightly. Murakami peered out. "Yes, who is it?"

"It is I, Miyazaki. Open the door now." The door closed and the chain was rattled loose. Murakami opened the door and gave me a deep, deferential bow. The curtains were drawn together, and there was no illumination save for the dying natural light of day which managed to seep through them.

I told Murakami to wait in the sitting room, and closed the door so I could speak to Hosokawa in private. He hastily made himself scarce, and I went over to Hosokawa's grand bedroom, which was the largest in the entire hotel but completely wasted on the sad spectacle propped up on the pillows before me. The gloom made it difficult to determine if he was out to the world or completely awake. He was still wearing his sunglasses and had a silk cravat tied around his neck. I spoke softly. "Hosokawa san, it is I, Miyazaki. I have come to check on your well-being and to see if I may be of any assistance to you." There was no response; he remained motionless in front of me. I switched on the small table lamp by the bed and looked intently at his face. There was still no sign of movement. For a moment I feared the worst, and cursed Kato for overdosing a weak man. As I was about to reach for Hosokawa's wrist to find a pulse, his head lolled to one side, and a large bubble of spittle formed around his lips. It burst, and drool ran down his chin. I felt disgust for his weakness and cursed Toshio for allowing him to make the trip. I was about to stand and leave when I noticed he was trying to say something. I leaned towards him and put my ear closer to his mouth, recoiling slightly from his fetid halitosis. At first I thought he was saying, "Hear me," but after a moment I realised he was saying, "Help me, help me."

I didn't have the necessary disposition to deal with the sick and had always felt uncomfortable in their presence. The only words I could find seemed mightily inappropriate. "Hosokawa san, be strong." I stood to take my leave, grateful that I did not have to bear the sight of my master in such a pitiful state any longer. I went into the sitting room and found Murakami standing by the door, almost to attention; the lad was stoic and dependable. I told him to stay by Hosokawa's side and administer a cooling towel to his brow from time to time and that if he had any cause for concern, to not hesitate in summoning help. I asked him if he had eaten at all, to which he replied that he hadn't yet. It was typical of Murakami, uncomplaining and devoted, just like the young men who had thrown their lives down on the streets below some twenty years earlier. I do believe the lad would have gone all night without sustenance if left to his own devices. I said I would arrange for a tray to be delivered to him, wished him a good evening, and with relief stepped back out into the welcome brightness of the corridor.

As I made my way down to the function room, I found myself thinking about the events that had pushed Hosokawa to gamble so recklessly with his health. I was convinced that I might have played a small part in his decline. Five years earlier, Hosokawa had invited his young female friend Azusa, who later became his wife, to spend a weekend with him at his country home. Because of some kind of mishap, he became laid up in bed with a painful back injury. It was at this time that Kato first came into Hosokawa's life. He administered the first narcotic as a pain reliever and had continued to do so ever since.

Anyway, that was by and by. During this time, no doubt driven by pain and morphine, Hosokawa in a fit of paranoia and delusion proposed marriage to Azusa, which seemed like a delightfully novel notion to a lass just turned eighteen, and she had assented without so much as a second thought. Hosokawa, no doubt spurred on by her keenness, presented her with a symbol of his troth, a stunning and unique ruby and black jade necklace. It was quite an arresting piece, and even I, a man who remains largely unimpressed by material tokens of wealth, was taken with its beauty.

The next day Hosokawa asked me to drive Azusa back to town, as he was still in the throes of agony. That was the first day I set eyes on her new acquisition, which she wore proudly around her neck. She coolly told me how Hosokawa had surprised her with his offer of marriage and about his substantial generosity which she believed knew no bounds, as her new necklace seemed to confirm. I was mightily taken aback; it was the marriage proposal that shocked me most, as I had Hosokawa pegged as a life-long bachelor. I drove her back to Ginza that day not quite able to comprehend the new direction that my master seemed to have decided for himself. Azusa spent most of the journey either asleep or playing with her necklace, rolling the heavy gold chain between her fingers or checking the ruby, which nestled provocatively in her cleavage.

As we arrived in Ginza, I said I had to collect some things for Hosokawa at the house and, as we had undertaken such a long ride, enquired if she needed a comfort break. She readily agreed, and we parked outside the house just as Toshio was leaving with a small entourage, in typical style, making one of his last-minute dashes to be on time for some meeting about the ten-year Mabuhay anniversary function which was to be held that very same evening. Azusa stood alongside me as we stepped aside to let the "flying" Toshio Hamazaki by.

Now, Toshio Hamazaki is not the kind of man to stop in his tracks for any woman—in fact, I have seen him "look through" some of the most striking beauties as if they did not even exist—but that day he stopped dead in his stride. He appeared to be mesmerised by the presence of Azusa Ito. I was not sure if Hamazaki had ever formally been introduced to Azusa, but there was something rather odd about the moment. I felt our being together demanded some kind of an explanation, so I went about telling Toshio of Hosokawa's misfortune and how I had offered to see Azusa safely to her home. Hamazaki did not seem to be listening to a word I said, and it was at that moment that I realised it was the necklace that was holding his complete and undivided attention. He looked at Azusa and gave her one of the coldest smiles I have seen and said, "That is a rather fetching item you are wearing. May I?" He delicately took hold of the ruby and black jade, rolling it about in his hand in much the same fashion as Azusa herself had on the journey down.

He looked intently at the necklace as Azusa told him, "It was a gift from Makoto—I mean, Hosokawa san—and it is so beautiful, is it not?"

He looked her in the eyes and smiled. "It is a truly divine piece of epic beauty. You are so fortunate to be the custodian of such a sublime artefact." As he spoke, I sensed he was desperately trying to control some hidden rage, and behind his eyes burned a fire of pure anger. There was a moment when I thought he might even wrench the chain from her delicate neck. However, he regained his composure, placed the necklace delicately back on her bosom, and gave her one of his wild smiles. He said it was a pleasure to make her acquaintance, bade us good day, and with a quick turn of heel was off towards his waiting Bentley. Azusa was left smiling in his wake, completely oblivious to any menacing undertones. The encounter had disturbed me, for I knew that Hamazaki had seen something that I had not, and then after going over his words once more in my mind, I found myself repeating the word artefact. Suddenly I knew that Hamazaki had come to a conclusion regarding the provenance of Hosokawa's generosity. I resolved to put it out of my mind; after all, it was a matter between Hamazaki and Hosokawa and had nothing to do with me. The intensity of that encounter faded a little as the days wore on, and I believe I had convinced myself that I might have misread Hamazaki's mood.

A few days later I was back at Hosokawa's country lodge with my man, Kudo. Hosokawa had recovered sufficiently to make the journey back home to Ginza, and we were there to assist with the transportation. Hosokawa was to travel with me in the Rolls-Royce, and Kudo had been told to follow in Hosokawa's Ferrari. As we waited for Hosokawa to finally put in an appearance, I was called by the head butler, Niwa. He told me there was a caller on the telephone asking for me. I went into Hosokawa's study to take the call. It was Toshio Hamazaki on the line. "Miyazaki san, wonderful news—I mean Makoto making such a speedy recovery. Please give him our best regards and tell him we are all looking forward to seeing him in full spirits at my nephew's birthday celebration later today. Remind him not to be late; we can't keep the little nippers waiting, can we?" I said I would speed him along, and then Hamazaki continued. "Splendid, splendid. Tell me, is Makoto fit enough to drive that magnificent machine of his? I know how much he loathes letting it out of his sight, never mind giving it over to anyone else."

Call it my sixth sense, but at that moment a cold shiver ran through my body and I knew I had to be swift in my reply. "I do believe he will endure his pain a little longer rather than give up the keys to his pride and joy."

I heard Hamazaki laughing on the other end of the line. "That's the Makoto I know so well. We will see him in no time at all. Have a pleasant journey back to the realms of the civilised.

Good day to you." The line clicked dead and the receiver purred in my ear. I had told Hamazaki an untruth. Hosokawa was in no fit state to drive at all. Later, with a heavy heart, I handed the keys of the Ferrari to my loyal colleague Kudo. I sensed what was in store, and so it proved to be. At the Ginza crossing three hours later Kudo met his maker, shot to death whilst at the wheel of Hosokawa's Ferrari. The assassin had lain in wait to take advantage of the long stationary traffic signal. Quite rightly, Hosokawa believed he was the intended victim, which was a view shared by the police at the time, and the finger of suspicion pointed to various elements. Perhaps only I knew where the true menace lay. Of course I never uttered a word, but just stood by and let Hosokawa sink into a void so deep, I feared there would be only one way for him to find true solace.

The cocktail reception was being held on the second floor, and as I approached the grand function room, I noticed a couple of sinister-looking characters hanging about the corridor. From their demeanour and awkwardness it was not difficult to place them as bodyguards. Their ill-fitting attire was an obvious sign, for it is difficult to wear a suit with ease when you are weighted down with a heavy weapon on your belt. I walked nonchalantly past them and pretended not to notice their hard stares. For a moment I thought I was about to be stopped and questioned, but they allowed me to pass by without undue concern.

The large double doors to the reception room were wide open and flanked by a couple of hotel houseboys who looked resplendent in their brilliant whites. I entered the room and immediately spotted Meursault and Rinehart, both of whom seemed at ease and relaxed as they joked with an American guest, Joel Richardson. I had never met Richardson in person, but his reputation went before him. He was known as a hardnosed business type, ruthless in his dealings and reputed to go to great lengths to achieve what he wanted. In short he was a man who loved money and lived his entire life working out possible financial returns from life's opportunities. If he was of such ilk, then no doubt he had found his equal in Meursault. "From the depths of a man's misery, another may find joy," was one of the Swiss banker's favourite sayings, which tended to sum up his approach to life in general.

Richardson had been in competition with Mabuhay for the acquisition of the American electronics giant Sonic. Exactly whom he represented was unclear, and in the end his backers could not match the generous offer that Mabuhay put on the table. It took longer than expected, and the takeover was the subject of heated debate across the social and political arena, but inevitably Sonic became Mabuhay's American subsidiary in a deal that was reputed to be worth over seventy million dollars. Hamazaki had been impressed with Richardson's dogged tenacity and the way he had aggressively fought his corner. Perhaps Toshio could see some similarities with his own approach to conducting business.

After the deal for Sonic was sealed, Hamazaki had offered Richardson a directorship in the newly restructured American division, and now the loud American was here in Manila, although for what practical purpose I did not quite know. I suspected he had been invited here on some kind of fact-finding mission and to offer support to the Mabuhay Foundation, which, after all, received 10 per cent of all Mabuhay gross profits. That figure included overseas revenue too, so no doubt Richardson wanted to see where his cash actually went. The Mabuhay Foundation was now the world's largest private donor of financial aid, most of it centred on this corner of the world. That was the reason we were to be feted by the great and the good this evening. The Friends of the Philippines organisation brought together enterprise and investors who felt they had something to offer the country. As far as I could tell, it was cronyism disguised as benevolence. Aid projects were managed by its members, donations and budgets divided up by committees with impressive names but invariably chaired by the same few individuals.

It was an inescapable fact that business here involved far more people than you would like. It was a matter that Ayumi had so far failed to tackle. She was aware of the corruption, and it broke her heart to think that foundation funds were being diverted from the people who were most in need, but she could not find a way to resist the overwhelming tide of graft that was endemic in this culture.

I spotted the lady herself looking resplendent in a burgundy-coloured full-length dress. She stood out like a beacon, and I felt some kind of primeval urge to march across the crowded room and give her my protective support. I was politely making my way through the crowd when I stopped dead in my tracks. Ayumi was being introduced to the new First Lady of the Philippines, Ismarelda Marios, daughter of Santa Romana. So that was why we were surrounded by goonish bodyguards. From across the room I saw Ayumi and Ismarelda exchange pleasantries and polite smiles, no doubt each taking the measure of the other. I was only a mere four or five yards away, yet I could see that Ayumi found the young First Lady very captivating. Or perhaps it was the magnificent necklace she wore that had caught Ayumi's attention. I felt a heavy sense of déjà vu: Surely not again. I had no doubt Ayumi would recognise such a piece, for it was almost the twin of Azusa's own. I tried to think what conclusions she would draw from this and only hoped they would not be as damning as those her brother had drawn five years ago. Whatever they may be, I had a feeling that Hosokawa would have a bit of explaining to do—that is, if he ever found himself in a fit enough state to put a coherent sentence together.

I accepted a glass of champagne and stood back to get an overall view of the room and who was with whom. My stare was instantly drawn to one man, Romana himself. He had his back to me, but I would have recognised that figure in any crowd. He was holding a small court of his own: a group of aged men, dressed in their traditional shirts, laughing uproariously at some anecdote or other that Romana was regaling them with. The man obviously enjoyed the sycophancy that was piled at his feet; after all, he was the man who had put Marios in office. I only hoped he had not forgotten that it was Mabuhay money that had smoothed the path for his son-in-law to rest his head in the Malacañan Palace. As much as I would have welcomed Romana's appreciation of Mabuhay's overly generous commissions, I feared it would not be forthcoming and I would have to find the steel for the inevitable showdown. This evening, at least, we were to play the role of strangers. Our charade extended as far as not even looking at each other, but we both knew what the real business of this visit was all about, and very soon I would sit down with this despicable man and make an agreement to unearth a hoard of valuables that would make any king green with envy.

As far as I understood, these gatherings were for the purpose of making as many acquaintances as possible. Speeches were usually reserved for later, after dinner. So it came as something of a surprise when a small gong sounded and a voice called for order and quiet. The chairman of the Friends of the Philippines, a dashing old rake with sparkling gold fillings in his teeth, stepped forward to speak. The crowd parted to allow him some floor space; he seemed flushed with pride and full of himself, grinning like a greased black cat. "First Lady of the Philippines, esteemed guests from home and afar, on behalf of the Friends of the Philippines I would like to take this opportunity to thank you for gracing us with your presence here tonight. We are on the verge of a wonderful new dawn, for our country can now look forward to the bright future it deserves. At last we have the leader who will guide us into the light, and with the generous support of the Mabuhay Foundation, we are building solid futures for our less fortunate citizens. It is with the most profound sense of pride and optimism that we welcome you all here.

"I would like to propose a toast, if you would all be so kind as to raise your glasses. To President Marios and Mabuhay, may God always be with you." I looked across to Ayumi, who I knew was uncomfortable with this fellow's words. She had not repeated the toast or joined in the round of applause. I had become adept at reading her moods and knew something was amiss. I looked around the room and noticed that I was not the only one who had read the discomfort on Ayumi's face. Romana was staring directly at her; his contempt was dripping off in bundles. The applause rang out for much longer than was necessary, and it took me a few moments to realise that it was now directed at Ismarelda, who was making her exit. The guests were standing to one side and had unconsciously formed a guard of honour; they were enthusiastic in their show of gratitude. Romana stepped out of the crowd and took his daughter's arm in much the same fashion as any father would do when leading his girl down the aisle. A few daring souls verbalised their love for Ismarelda and offered their best wishes to her husband. It was all a little surreal, as if the entire gathering had, as one, become intoxicated.

As the pair passed before my eyes, I got the strange feeling that this country was on the verge of being duped by a cult of personality. Marios would shamelessly use his wife, exploiting her beauty and popularity, using them as a shield to distract from his own shortcomings, for the man was no more than a demagogue. I looked forward to the day when I no longer had to tolerate this hypocrisy. As I watched Romana and his daughter leave our little party, I felt someone slip something into my coat pocket. I was not concerned, for I knew what to expect, and I did not even bother to turn my head to see who the messenger was. It would be a note from a certain person telling me when and where our little assignation would take place.

I would read that later, but right now my attention flew through the throng of guests as I heard someone shout, "Give her some air, and make space." There was a bit of commotion, and I spotted Ayumi sitting on a chair, her head lolled forward. Kato was quickly on the scene, holding her wrist to check her pulse. Tanezawa appeared bearing a large shawl which she wrapped around her mistress's shoulders. Between them they helped Ayumi to her feet and escorted her from the room—an exit all the more humbling in the wake of the grand one we had witnessed just a few minutes before. The guests proved to be a ductile bunch and were now showing sympathy for the departing Ayumi. As she passed me, I swore she gave me a little mischievous wink, but in my emotionally confused state I could not be certain.

I waited in the function room while the other guests drifted off to dinner, which was being served in the grand dining hall next door. I thought it proper to hang back before going to check on Ayumi's condition. Having waited longer than my patience could stand, I was just about to excuse myself when Kato appeared, sweating from his unexpected exertion. I called him over. "How is Tanaka san? Has she taken ill?" I tried to keep my concern on a professional footing, not wishing to betray anything that gave away my true feelings for Ayumi.

"Tanaka san is resting in her room," Kato said. "I believe she was suffering from mild exhaustion—not surprising, given the flight over and her hectic schedule. I expect her to feel a little stronger after a good night's rest. Now if you would excuse me." He brushed past me in a manner which suggested that our earlier encounter still weighed on his mind. I let him by; dinner for me was out of the question. I had to drop by on Ayumi. I waited until the last of the guests had gone through to the banquet room and then made a quick departure before anyone got the chance to distract me. I walked through the hotel at a fair pace, barely acknowledging the endless greetings proffered by the countless staff I passed on my way. Within a few minutes I was outside Ayumi's suite, slightly breathless from tackling the stairs two at a time. I rang the bell and could hear the lush chimes from deep within the rooms beyond the splendid mahogany door. Tanezawa opened the door and bade me entry without so much as a moment's hesitation. She avoided looking directly at me, and I could tell she felt uncomfortable being alone in my presence. I could understand her feelings, as she must have suspected that I knew of her trysts with Hideo. If knowledge is power and ignorance is bliss, then Tanezawa seemed hopelessly lost between the two. I wondered if she in turn knew of my own romantic entanglement with Ayumi. We were both trespassers in the same marriage, neither of us able to find the contentment to be at peace with our own conscience.

Tanezawa led me through to Ayumi's bedroom, gave a polite knock on the door, and announced my presence. I heard Ayumi's voice, which sounded quite muffled. Tanezawa held the door wide open for me to enter. Surprisingly, Ayumi was not in bed resting as I had expected but sitting at her desk going through some papers. She looked at me over her half-moon spectacles and then glanced over my shoulder at the lingering Tanezawa. "Sakura,

I insist that you attend the dinner. I have called for Doctor Kato to come and escort you down. He should be here any moment now. Please go, and remember you are my eyes and ears. I expect a full account later." Although Ayumi's tone was light, there was no mistaking that it was an order. She gave a friendly wave to Tanezawa which indicated she had no further need for her. The door chime rang out, and Tanezawa went to answer. We could hear Kato's voice, no doubt more than a little irritated to be called away from his dinner. Tanezawa kept him waiting in the corridor as she collected her purse and shawl. I admired her discretion; she had a natural ability to read most situations and instinctively knew that neither I nor Ayumi would like Kato to see the two of us alone together. After a few moments we heard the door close, and at last we were alone.

Ayumi removed her glasses and rubbed her eyes. She looked a little worn out, but otherwise as fine as could be expected. She bade me into the room and asked me to pour drinks for the both of us. There was a drinks cabinet with a fine selection of decanted spirits, and I settled on a cognac, two small measures. I handed a glass to Ayumi, and she swirled the liquid around, staring at it like a fortune-teller would, trying to find the correct words.

I asked how she was feeling, and she said she was fine. She had feigned her distress to get out of the reception. Her words gave me an indication of what was to come. "I could no longer find the fortitude to remain in the presence of those hypocritical sycophants for a moment longer." I could tell there was something serious eating away at her, and had a notion what it might be. She looked up and said almost pleadingly, "Ken, did you know? I want to know what has been going on." I looked at her and shook my head. I did not know where her concerns lay, as there were so many paths where the truth had become entangled with deceit.

I sank into a leather armchair and loosened my necktie, took a sip of the hard cognac, and tried to feign a look of concerned surprise. "Ayumi, what is troubling you?"

She shook her head from side to side, a gesture which I feared showed her disbelief. "That necklace that Ismarelda Marios was wearing this evening, it is the exact duplicate of the one Makoto gave to his wife five years ago. What does that tell you?"

I shook my head, not knowing what to say. I knew that Ayumi was blissfully unaware of Mabuhay's secret agenda here in the Philippines, but I was not certain where her thoughts were leading her. She stood up and walked to the window. She looked down on the scene below, where the lights twinkled like fireflies. With her back to me, she broke the silence that hung between us. "Ken, I do not like being played as a fool, and right now I would appreciate the truth." There was added steel in her voice which reminded me that she was the sister of Toshio Hamazaki. I did not know where to start, and floundered for words. She turned and stared straight at me. "It is obvious that some kind of dealings have been going on between Hosokawa and Romana. Something so special, they both feel the need to reward their women with identical gifts. You have been here with Hosokawa so many times; you must know what it is. Ken, tell me the truth. Has Hosokawa been playing politics with my foundation?"

Ayumi had come to the wrong conclusion, and perversely I gave a sigh of thanks, though for what I was blindly unaware. "Ayumi, believe me, in the early days I was little more than a bag carrier on those trips. I do not know what passed, if anything at all, between Hosokawa and Romana. I do not know where Azusa's necklace came from nor do I know anything about Romana. I have never spoken to the man." I hoped my untruth would pass without any further probing from Ayumi.

She shook her head—whether in disbelief or just from plain confusion, it was difficult to tell. She slumped into her chair; suddenly she seemed weary and tired. "I feel that my efforts and the work of the foundation are being undermined by something or someone. There is another agenda here, one that I am not a party to. It is plain to anyone with even the basic sense of business that we are not making progress here. The funding is sufficient to make real changes for the good, and yet we seem no further down the road than where we were fifteen years ago. Someone is using my foundation for their own good, and I want it to stop. If Hosokawa is involved, I want to know. Ken, I want to trust you. Believe me when I say that I pray with my heart that you will help me. I want the truth."

There was nothing I could say. I looked at her and nodded. My mind was working through the connotations of what she had said. She still trusted me, and for that small mercy I was grateful. I was tempted to go over and put my arms around her, but I knew her too well, and my affection would not be welcome at this moment. I stood to leave. "Ayumi, I will do my upmost to ease your mind, but I fear Hosokawa san is in no fit condition to provide any answers at the moment."

She looked up and said coolly, "Perhaps the answers can be found closer to home, in Ginza." Her words were closer to the truth than she realised, but nonetheless they were shocking, as they were delivered with such clarity. I knew her suspicions were built on real foundations. I told her I would be in my room if she needed me and to not hesitate to call, whatever the hour. I hoped she would realise that my words were cloaked with an open invitation to join me later, but I very much doubted it, given her mood. As I was leaving, Ayumi spoke once more. "Ken, there is something you should know. If I do not get the answers I seek, I intend to suspend all funding here in the Philippines whilst a review of the foundation's finances is conducted."

I nodded, but in my mind I was already thinking about what Toshio would have to say to that. I went back to my room, heavy-hearted and downcast. Damn Hosokawa and his stupidity and naivety. The man was a downright liability, and God only knew what had been in Toshio's mind when he had allowed him to make this trip.

It was still quite early, but I decided to call time on my day. I freshened up a little and brewed some tea, which I decided to drink in bed. I took the revolver from my case and placed it under my pillow; I suppose old habits die hard. I undressed and slipped between the fine cotton sheets, enjoying the smooth, crisp, luxurious feel against my skin. I had come to appreciate the finer things in life, but I never took them for granted. When you come from nothing, your greatest fear is going back there, and that tends to temper your enjoyment a little. Sleep did not come easily, and I found myself unable to adjust to the heat. I had the windows wide open to catch what little breeze there was, but even the mosquito netting hardly swayed. I lay in bed and listened to the hypnotic buzz of the night sounds which drifted into my room from the streets below. I knew that sleep would not come easily. An unfamiliar environment always put me on my guard, and I resigned myself to merely dozing away the hours. After a couple of hours I heard Rinehart and Meursault return to their rooms, their voices bouncing off the walls of the corridor in inebriated joy. Perhaps I should have attended the dinner. With Hosokawa and Ayumi absent I was the next senior Mabuhay figure. Then I realised my absence had handed that particular honour to Kato, a notion that left a bitter taste in my mouth.

My insomniatic irritation finally got the better of me, and I got up and stepped out onto the balcony to take a little of the sweet, aromatic night air. I thought of Ayumi. Was she still working on her papers? The clock told me it was just after twelve. A new day was upon us, but I had the feeling it would not be all joy and light. I remembered the note which had been slipped into my pocket at the cocktail party. I had given it only the briefest of glances, but now I took it out and studied it more closely. The message was as plain as could be, giving me only the time, "7.00." I already knew the place, and it was taken as understood that it meant the next day. I would have to work my absence into the schedule, but that was the least of my concerns. I felt as if the world had suddenly laid its entire burden on my shoulders.

Weariness set into my soul, and I lay back on the bed once more, resigned to a sleepless night. As I was half drifting in and out of sleep, I dreamt I heard a tapping at my door. It took me a moment to realise it was no dream. I thought about the revolver but decided any potential malice was hardly going to come announced. I went over to the door, and the sight through the spyhole sent my spirits soaring. Ayumi looked anxious as she glanced left and right. I dashed back to the bed, quickly removed the revolver from under the pillow, and locked it safely away in my case.

I threw back the door chain, and she smartly stepped inside. She was wearing a hotel bathrobe, which she clutched to her body as if she were freezing. I stood to one side to let her past me and into the bedroom. As I followed, she let the robe slip to the floor. She was naked and sank onto my bed. I fell into her arms and we kissed passionately. I could feel her pulling down my shorts, and she took me in her hands. I did not need any coaxing, and she guided me inside. Our lovemaking was frenzied and intense, the frustrations of the last months, weeks, and days driven away by a few minutes of unrestrained passion. We were careful to keep our voices low, which only seemed to add to the clandestine thrill of the moment. I was spent, and rolled off her and lay by her side, perspiring from the humidity, slightly breathless. Not a word had been spoken between us, and yet we both felt like we had said all there was to be said. It was a magical moment and one I hoped we would enjoy again when I had recovered.

Ayumi was now in her late forties and still carried the looks and figure of a woman much younger. She was one of the few women I knew who actually took exercise to keep her vitality levels high, and at this moment I had cause to be thankful for her diligence. At fifty-six I too took a certain vain pride in maintaining myself. I undertook a daily regimen of calisthenics, and controlled my alcohol, unlike my peers who seemed dedicated to self-destruction.

Ayumi was slowly caressing me, willing me into action again. She seemed more vulnerable than usual. Her need was almost touchable, and for a moment I thought she was weeping. The sparse moonlight that had managed to seep into the room was not sufficient for me to see. She whispered into my ear. "Ken, tell me about yourself. Where did you come from?" Her question caught me off guard; she had never probed me for personal details before. Perhaps she was feeling insecure and her curiosity was getting the better of her. It was plain that we were at a point where she had to feel she could trust me. I, too, felt I had to give her some kind of reassurance. I had heard it said that pillow talk between lovers is usually regretted in the morning; nevertheless I cast my usual prudence aside and gave Ayumi an abridged version of my early life, one that I hoped would bring her closer to me.

I told her that I was born in Kyushu, the youngest of three boys, to poor parents. My father worked as a salt trader and my mother was a seamstress. I grew up with a sense of freedom, spending the summers swimming in the local river and the winters scouring for firewood. I told her how the early wars with China saw my two brothers drafted into the army and that I had never seen them since. In 1936 the draft officers came for me, but my father, having already given the army two sons, told them I was away at sea fishing and he would send me when I returned. I was upstairs hiding, listening to their words. I guessed my father must have thought that giving them his youngest to slaughter would be more than any family could stand.

The next morning I came downstairs to find my mother weeping at the kitchen table, clutching a crumpled letter. It seemed that my father, being such a proud man, had decided that his deception was too much to bear and had "gone away." At the time I did not understand what she meant, but soon I came to realise that he had decided to take the honourable way out. It did not take long before the neighbourhood began whispering. Draft dodging was seen as a despicable and cowardly act, and my mother urged me to leave for good. I did not have any notion where I should go, but in the dead of night I stowed away, hidden in a railway carriage full of pigs bound for Yokohama. How I managed to avoid detection I will never know. Guards inspected the carriage at every stop. I hunkered down with the pigs and prayed for divine help. That journey took the best part of two days. I drank the water that was meant for swine and even ate the foul slops that were passed into the carriage through the feeding hatches. I did not chance sleep, for I feared the brutes would eat me alive. As the train pulled into the sidings near Yokohama station, I slipped out. Luckily it was the dead of night, and I managed to slink into the shadows easily enough. I was wretched and smelt foul, but I had always lived on my wits. It did not take me long to find a washing line with some clothes that suited me. I bathed in a community bath, neglecting to leave the coins, of course. I stole food from the open back door of a noodle shop.

I lived like that for a week or so, drifting around until I came upon Yokohama port, where a fine French vessel was moored and readying to set sail. Men were carrying sacks of rice up a gang-plank. Without so much as a second thought, I joined the chain and, concealing my face with a huge sack of rice, soon found myself on the ship unchallenged. I blended into the shadows and hid in a cleaning room. I stayed there until I heard the ship's horn blaring away, signalling our departure for France.

On a ship it is impossible to hide forever. You need food, and it is kept in only one place. After three days I was caught by some deckhands as I tried to steal sustenance from the galley. I was dragged in front of the captain and shouted at in a language that meant nothing to me. In exasperation the captain ordered me to be shackled and confined to a small dark room below the waterline. The only positive was that humanity dictated I got some food from time to time and a bucket for my ablutions. It was the lowest point of my life. After a few days I was let out onto the deck, a brush was thrown at my feet, and I was told to sweep for my life. I went about my work with as much energy as my tired and sea-sick body could muster. I lost track of time. It seemed like weeks had passed, but one morning the crew became joyous and started singing songs in their language. We could see land. A burly fellow grabbed me and pointed to the shore. "Japanoise, Marseille, vive la Marseille."

I was placed in irons again, as the captain did not want to risk me making a break for it once land was within reach. We docked, and the crew ran around, looking forward to all the joys of a homecoming and the shedding of their deprivations with as much wild abandon as they could muster. From the deck I watched them, my ankle shackled, fearful that I would be given a heinous punishment for my crime. I was right to be fearful. The captain came up to me, accompanied by a uniformed guard. Of course I could not understand what was being said, but I remember their words. "Emprisonnement, Legion étrangère?" They shouted into my face. It seemed they were offering me some kind of a choice, but of what I did not know. In the end they made the choice for me. I found myself in the local jail waiting to be transferred to the French Foreign Legion training camp. I was the only Japanese in the corps and one of only a few Asians. There were times when I wished I had died, but other times, I found myself falling in with my new family. I got my head down and concentrated on survival and thoughts of better days ahead. I had fallen into a life that was brutal and absurd in equal measure.

Ayumi held me tightly as I told her my tale. She listened in silence for the most part, breaking my flow only with exclamations of shock or sympathy. To my own surprise I found that recounting my life's miserable beginning had a cathartic effect. I enjoyed the liberating sense of freedom that it gave me, and I had to catch myself a few times from letting slip a little too much detail. Ayumi prompted me further, no doubt feeling that this was the opportunity to find out all there was to know. Of course she was keen to know how I had gone from some strange foreign army boot camp to working for Mabuhay. This was the most dangerous kind of talk, and I knew I had to be at my most censorial in my account.

I told her that I had accepted my lot in life up to that point. I kept my head down and got on with the daily business of survival.

I found that I had an aptitude for French and learnt the rudiments of the language without much difficulty. Over the next three years I learnt a whole lot more about myself and swore to dedicate myself to my foreign army. But something was lost inside of me, and no matter how hard I tried, I could not feel a complete person. In short, I was homesick and found myself constantly thinking of my motherland. I knew that I had to get back somehow, and the start of full-blown war in Europe forced my hand to the point where I had to act. Once I had finally decided to desert, the actual act of doing so came easily; it was the moral dilemma that caught me floundering. I convinced myself that what I was doing was for the greater good and that I was returning to help my own country in its greatest hour of need.

I had saved a small amount of money from my pitiful Legionnaires allowance—enough, I hoped, to pay for my passage. One afternoon, whilst on a work detail, I slipped away from my group and never looked back. I made my way to the harbour and gave all my money to a Chinese ship's steward who smuggled me aboard his vessel. We sailed for Hong Kong that evening, and my money bought me a bunk and the basics to keep me alive for the voyage. There was a steely tension aboard that ship that made everyone jumpy. There was talk of the sea lanes being closed or mined, and rumour had taken hold that ships were being blown out of the water by German mini-submarines.

It was a perilous trip but one that eventually found me fetching up in Hong Kong. Hostilities on that front had yet to break out, and from there it was easy to find a Japanese-registered ship to take me back to my homeland. I enlisted in the Imperial Japanese Army and after some basic training was shipped off to Malaysia, where I saw out the war.

Ayumi listened in awe, shock, or disbelief—it was hard to tell. I knew that she had lost her first husband in the war, and the very mention of it must have triggered awful memories for her.

I asked her if she would like me to continue. She said yes, so I picked up my account, conveniently omitting certain key details. I told her how I was repatriated at the war's end, only to find, like so many others, that total and utter devastation awaited us. Defeat on the battlefield had been a humiliation that was hard to accept, but I and many other returnees felt a profound shame that we had somehow failed our country and that the sufferings of our people were caused by our own failings.

I spent the next five years or so back at my parents' house. My mother had died of tuberculosis some four years earlier, and what had once been a happy family home was now inhabited by my family's ghosts and me. I survived by growing vegetables in the small garden and hunting rabbits in the mountains. I shut the outside world away and resigned myself to seeing out my days in squalor.

A friend of mine told me there was plenty of work to be had in Tokyo and that we should give ourselves the chance to put our lives back in order. I was tired of talking to ghosts every night, so reluctantly I let him talk me round, and we made the long journey up to the capital. It took us two weeks to make the trip; we cadged rides when and wherever we could. On arrival the opportunities we had dreamed of were no more than a figment of my friend's imagination. We were worse off than ever, homeless and hungry, like so many of the ex-servicemen who slept rough all over the capital. One day after wandering the streets looking for any prospects of work, I chanced on a line of lads queuing to apply for the newly formed police force. I joined them, duly filled out my forms, and was told to return the next morning to see if I had been chosen for the interview stage.

Return I did, only to find myself apprehended and thrown into a police cell. It seemed that my past had caught up with me. The French government had in a routine course of action filed my details with the Japanese authorities; I was wanted by the French to answer a charge of deserting my post whilst on active duty. I denied that the person in question was me, and said it must be a case of mistaken identity. The chances of this happening must have been a million to one. I knew that the Legion never gave up in their attempt to apprehend all deserters, but this was ridiculous. I was kept in the cell whilst my case was investigated. This was at a time when the American occupation government was doing its best to connect with the world. Anything to please seemed to be the order of the day. I stuck to my tale of mistaken identity, knowing that the authorities would not have the resources to pursue their investigations. I was sent to Chiba jail whilst the slow arm of the law went about its business. I had a deportation order hanging over me, and it was my good fortune that one man eventually saw through all the nonsense and got that order thrown to one side. That man was Makoto Hosokawa. He attended to my case personally, visited me at the jail, and arranged my release. He not only gave me back my freedom but must have seen something in me that piqued his interest, for he gave me a new chance in life and offered me employment as an aide in a new business that he was involved in. That was how I had come to Mabuhay.

Ayumi listened in silence as I concluded my story. I felt her hand on my brow as she smoothed my face, gently caressing my cheek. "Ken, I had no idea. I am sorry for your sufferings. It must have been a hell for you." She was right, it was a hell, but one of my own making. I had not told her of the man whose neck I had broken in a barroom fight and how that "unfortunate" incident had forced me onto a train full of pigs, nor had I told her of the fellow Legionnaire I had knifed to death after I had caught him stealing money from my safety box. A Chinese ship was far more preferable to a life spent in jail—or worse, a firing squad. Those details were better left unspoken. Besides, "Ken Miyazaki" was not responsible. They were the evil deeds of Daigo Hamma, and he had died so long ago, I could barely remember what that man looked like, let alone being him.

My woeful tale had drawn an emotional response from Ayumi, who held my head to her breast and stroked my hair whilst cooing sympathetic sentiments into my ear. She told me how, when I first came to work for Hosokawa and Toshio, I had made her feel uneasy and that she always thought of me as the dark, broody, and mysterious Miyazaki. I told her that I was no more than a simple soul who had little bearing on his own destiny. We talked a little more into the night, both of us staving off the exhaustion that was settling upon us. Ayumi, being the ever so conscientious type—work was never far from her mind—tried to elicit my views on how she should proceed with her anti-graft statement. I took the opportunity to steady her notion of suspending funding. I advised her to "keep her powder dry" at least until we were all safely back on home ground. It would be unwise to ignite an already volatile country that was still coming to terms with its new leader. She thought about it for a moment, and judging by her silence I do believe she came round to my way of thinking.

She kissed me on the cheek and said jokingly, "For a country boy you have a wise head on your shoulders, my dear not-so-mysterious Miyazaki san." I felt her hand straying down my chest, and she started teasing me back to life. We made love once more, and I smothered her with affectionate kisses, which she lapped up like a woman who was not accustomed to being loved. There was always a sadness about Ayumi. It was as if she were shadowed by a constant hurt, and her vulnerability would sometimes be let loose at inappropriate times. As we were making love and about to reach our climax, she suddenly burst into a fit of sobbing which I first mistook for pleasure. She was gripped by a crisis of conscience, and it took an incredible amount of convincing to reassure her. I had to fight back my desire to tell her about Tanezawa and Hideo, but as life's lessons dictate, nobody appreciates the "messenger." Ayumi left my room in the real dead of night, that being a little after three. I had offered to see her to her door, but she strongly declined my gallant advance on the grounds of keeping her virtue intact. She said if anyone was to meet her on the corridor, she would say she was unable to sleep and felt like stretching her legs a little. Unlikely, I know, but slightly more credible than walking alongside the dark and mysterious Miyazaki.

After she had left me alone, I felt the familiar feelings of insecurity and hopelessness descend upon me. A few stolen moments of sublime passion comes with a heavy price, but one I knew I was more than willing to keep paying.

I awoke after a few hours of feverish sleep. My sheets were soaked in sweat, but I felt well enough to give up on further rest. The city was coming to life, and the noise that filled my room became a cascade of sounds, a myriad of the comings and goings from the streets below. I filled the bathtub with lukewarm water and washed my hair using the large water pitcher provided for that purpose. Only the suite rooms were blessed with showers, which were still a rarity in most hostelries. I used the bell push to summon up some breakfast, which I would take in my room. I was absolutely ravenous, having missed out on dinner, and despite feeling a bit on the weak side, I started my morning routine of physical exercise. The stretches came easily, and I found I could still lock my body into some poses that even an accomplished contortionist would find satisfying.

I performed my routine for about twenty minutes, after which the door chimed to signal the arrival of breakfast. I threw a towel around my waist and called out for them to enter. A moment passed, and, annoyed, I went to open the door. To my astonishment Tanezawa stood there, looking mighty sheepish and more than a little hesitant. I asked her into the room. Reluctantly, she stepped inside but not before looking up and down the corridor. My first reaction was to assume that my tryst with Ayumi had brought her to my door; however, I soon dismissed that notion, as she was hardly the person to bear any misgivings. She looked a little ashen, and when she spoke, her voice cracked, betraying her nervousness. "Miyazaki san, I have come to seek your guidance on a matter that is troubling me greatly." I had always kept my relationship with Tanezawa on a purely professional level, and despite her tender years did my level best to treat her as an equal. She rarely sought out my advice, as she had a direct line to Ayumi and of course Hideo. Whatever had brought her to my room must have been of grave importance.

I asked her to take a seat and offered to brew some tea. She declined and gave me the impression that she wanted to say her piece and get out as soon as she could. "Tell me, Tanezawa san, what brings you to my door at such an early hour?"

She looked up and into my eyes; I could see that she was riddled with confusion. "It concerns Hosokawa san." My heart immediately sank, and my first instinct naturally led me to think he might have passed in the night. My concern quickly changed to annoyance as she went on to tell me what had really passed in the night. It was a little after one when she heard a knock on the suite door. Her bedchamber was closest, and she quickly answered, not wishing any disturbance to interrupt her mistress's slumber. That wasn't very likely, given that her mistress was cuckolded with me at the time. Murakami had called, sent by Hosokawa, who was in the grip of some feverish delirium and had called for Tanezawa. She went up to Hosokawa's suite accompanied by Murakami to find him sweating and shaking, mouthing incomprehensible words laced with the foulest of obscenities.

She asked Murakami to send for Kato, but at the mention of the doctor's name, Hosokawa shouted, "No, no, no more!" Murakami told her that Hosokawa was trying to fight his weakness and was determined to resist the needle. Tanezawa said that Hosokawa acted like a man possessed and at first did not even realise she was there. Then, as she mopped his feverish brow with a cool towel, he gripped her arm and pulled her close to his face. She shook and wrapped her arms around herself as she repeated his words. "'We are all living a lie. Everything is lies. Kojima, you are Kojima. Romana killed him, it was Romana, always remember you are Kojima, Romana killed Kojima, Romana killed Kojima, your father Kojima.'" She repeated his words verbatim, as if they had imprinted themselves on her mind. "Miyazaki san, what does it mean?" she asked me. "Who is Kojima?"

I pretended to think for a moment, giving the impression that I was searching my mind for some lost piece of knowledge. I told her I had no idea what had gone through Hosokawa's mind, but I would visit him later to try to find out what had troubled him. I could tell she was still quite disturbed by her encounter with the wretched Hosokawa. Tanezawa was a tenacious character, and I knew she would not let this rest until she had peace of mind. I did my upmost to send her on her way with a lesser load than she had borne minutes earlier, but alas, it seemed that I failed.

I ushered her out of my room, and once the door had closed behind her, I bit down on my lip and cursed Hosokawa once more. It seemed my damnation of the man had become a habit that I could not shake off. I knew a little about Tanezawa's life, because Hosokawa, in an uncharacteristic fit of indiscretion, had told me a little of her background. Those more trusting days, sadly, now seemed gone forever. He told me how, on the orders of Hamazaki, he had been sent to "rescue" her from an orphanage. She had spent most of her life there after being "orphaned" in the war. She believed her parents had fallen along with so many others.

Hamazaki had told Hosokawa the true tale of Tanezawa's loss. Her father was indeed Kojima, Major Kojima, who was an aide to General Yamashita during the last days of the battle right here in the Philippines. When fighting ended, Kojima was taken into captivity along with the general. The Americans believed Kojima was a party to or had knowledge of secret treasure sites. He was separated from his fellow captives and tortured mercilessly, but to no avail. The Americans finally gave up and handed him over to the Philippine secret service, headed at the time by no other than our dear friend Santa Romana, who subjected Kojima to a brutal series of interrogations. What passed between them is a little unclear, but Kojima eventually found himself sentenced to twenty years in a penal work camp. He managed to survive only three months, after which it was decided that isolation was not in his best interest. He was put amongst the most hardened murderers in the country, and being Japanese and the "enemy," he lasted only a day before some scum stuck a knife into his ribs and twisted the dying breath from his body.

In the three months of his isolation, Kojima had managed to write a journal of sorts and smuggled it to a fellow sufferer with hope and prayer that it would be passed to Hamazaki's father,

Tetsuyo. It was these writings, which were mostly written in innuendo and veiled intent, that brought the first shafts of truth to shine on a tale that would haunt Hamazaki's father until his dying days. Kojima had been handpicked by Hamazaki Senior, and at the time it was believed that the major had betrayed him and his scheme. The journal told a different tale, and the suspicion fell on another, Colonel Nishii, but not before Hamazaki's partners in the conspiracy had, in a fit of misguided vengeance, extracted a terrible revenge on the family of Major Kojima. His innocent wife, who had survived the war, was taken by a mysterious house fire, which on closer examination looked more suspicious, as her five-year-old daughter was found the next morning on the steps of an orphanage with a letter tied around her neck giving instructions that she be taken in without question.

When Kojima's journal eventually found its way back to the hands of Hamazaki Senior, the old man sank into a sea of remorse and self-recrimination. He did his best for the girl—even had her transferred up to Tokyo to the Hibari Orphanage—but his best was not good enough to stop his ever spiralling mood of self-hatred. Upon his death, he left instructions to his son, Toshio, that the newly named Sakura Tanezawa was to be given all the opportunities in life that unfortunate circumstances had so far denied her. In short he was to treat her as a "lost sister."

I needed time to think all this through. Hosokawa had opened up a new avenue which could lead to all kinds of problems. There is an old adage which says, "The past is a foreign country." How true, and how wonderful it would be if we could all leave it there forever. The irony of Tanezawa's predicament was not lost on me. As I was telling of my own past, she was learning about hers at the very same time. I was opening up out of love and the need to feel closer to the woman I loved, but why had Hosokawa chosen this moment to open up his own little box of filthy secrets? Was it the drugs talking, or had he been lucid enough to understand what this might lead to? He had brought Romana's name into the fray, and all it would take was a word here and there before some ingenious soul started to make the connections. Something needed to be done about it, and the only man who knew what was back in Tokyo.

The sun had barely crested the bay, and already the day had a bad feel to it. I knew it would be a long day, too, as I had an appointment to keep with a man who kept many a secret himself. Breakfast arrived, and the smiling room boy was reduced to nervous fumbling as I let my irritation boil over. My hunger had been replaced by something bitter that now ate away at my emotions. I was beginning to feel like this whole "mission" was falling apart at the seams.

The casual elegance of the Manila Hotel never failed to impress, and this morning was no exception. The staff were busying about the lobby like a colony of worker ants, eager to please and always on hand. Faced with so many brilliant white smiles, my own dour mood must have made me seem more surly than usual. Even Meursault picked up on my demeanour quite quickly, his morning greeting laced with a bit of mocking humour that left me groping for hidden nuances. "Miyazaki, you look like you have been busy through the night. A fine, diligent chap you are for sure." Paranoia sits uncomfortably in the domain of the guilty, and even the most innocent of comments is taken as an indictment of past indiscretions or deeds. I had lived with such feelings for so long that they had become part of the very fabric of my soul, and I was quite expert at brushing them aside. I rewarded Meursault with a simple nod as a greeting in return and turned my attention to the business of the morning.

Genuine Mabuhay Foundation business was the order of the day, and we were scheduled to make a short drive to inspect one of our school projects. Education was Ayumi's pet love, and of all the foundation's endeavours, the one that remained closest to her heart. The foundation funded a total of twenty-six schools across the country, and nearly a thousand children were being educated at no cost to their families or the nation itself. The schools' programme was entirely funded by the Mabuhay Foundation, and I knew that Ayumi favoured even more expenditure in this area. She had a vision of coupling the healthcare programme together with the educational, the two operating out of the same campuses. Before her visions could become reality, somewhere had to be found where these places could be built. Land purchase in this country was a financial minefield and a complex issue, one that was guaranteed to raise tensions on all sides. She made a strong case for such reforms, but it was a step too close to interference in the murky world of Philippine politics, even though there would be little audience for her views and it would be hard to resist her drive. It remained to be seen what the new respective ministers had to say about that. I feared they would be more than a little reluctant, as they would not want to see their opportunities to skim off the top diminish.

Before this trip Ayumi's thinking was quite positive, but who knew what must be going through her mind now. I believed if she had her way, she would abandon many of the so-called "infrastructure" projects in favour of more schools. She thought such projects were too exposed to the graft that she had no control over and often failed to understand where the funding had ended up. At least with the educational projects the balance sheets were a little easier to comprehend.

I waited in the lobby for Ayumi. The rest of our group were already assembled. Even Kato had been "asked" to make the trip, and I spotted him sitting on a lounge sofa, shielding his bulging eyes behind sunglasses, which he comically wore over his usual bifocals. He was no doubt suffering from the alcoholic excesses of the previous night. Never a wallflower as far as partying was concerned, he had no doubt downed quite a lot of the local brew, tupay, a rice wine similar to our own sake. I silently prayed that he was suffering to hell. The man repulsed me to the heavens, and if it were not out of respect for Hosokawa, I truly believed I would not be able to restrain my hatred.

Reinhardt arrived accompanied by Joel Richardson; they looked quite chummy together and seemed to have found something that amused them both. I knew little about Richardson, except he was fast becoming Mabuhay's figurehead stateside. Toshio had thought it more politically acceptable for the business to be headed up by one of their own. The buyout of Sonic had been more than acrimonious and the press coverage vitriolic. One headline in a popular daily broadsheet read, "The Japanese Invasion has Begun." What Toshio's long-term plans for Sonic were, nobody could guess, but Richardson was here and staying close to the money. His cosiness with Rinehart was duly noted, and I would make sure to keep an extra-close eye on their developing dynamic.

Ayumi finally arrived looking remarkably fresh and relaxed, given her supposedly "bad turn" the previous evening. She was dressed in a rather fetching feminine safari suit which effortlessly managed to combine the erotic and exotic to great effect; I felt a longing to be at her side. Of course it was Tanezawa who occupied that position, and the pair of them walked past me with only the barest of acknowledgement and out towards the waiting limousines. Kato dragged his rotund self to his feet and followed them. Meursault linked up with Rinehart and Richardson. I followed from the rear, where I could get an overall view of what was going on. I doubt any of them had noticed the pair of mean, thuggish-looking men who had tried to blend into the background by hiding their faces behind newspapers. Certainly not Richardson, who seemed transfixed by Tanezawa's backside as they made their way out of the grand lobby doors. Our two "shadows" threw their newspapers to one side and clumsily tagged on behind.

Our convoy was made up of the same vehicles we had used for our journey the day before. It was impossible to say whether we were being driven by the same drivers, as they all were inconspicuously similar in their dark glasses, black peak caps, and white patterned shirts. I found myself travelling alone in the third car, feeling a little sidelined as Meursault, and Rinehart had palled off with Richardson, and Kato had wormed his way into travelling alongside Ayumi and Tanezawa. Hosokawa should have been alongside me at this moment and not ailing in his luxurious bed. My thoughts went back to earlier trips and the excitement I had felt, thriving off the nervous energy that fuelled my ambition. In those times Hosokawa was a force to be reckoned with, and any self-doubts about our enterprise were pushed well and truly to the back of our minds. With a sigh of remorse I reflected how times had changed.

We were headed toward Mabuhay South Manila Primary School, which had been chosen as a representative example of the current state of the foundation's work. I tried to make a little small talk with my driver, but he shook his head and merely replied, "Sorry, sir, no English." I spent the whole fifteen minutes of the journey gazing out the window, occasionally looking back to check on the small black sedan that shadowed our progress.

We turned into a dusty drive. The school's name, written in rainbow lettering on an arch over the driveway, told us we had arrived. If we needed any further confirmation, it was provided by the hundreds of children who had lined the driveway and were enthusiastically waving small Philippine and Japanese flags and shouting "Mabuhay" in wild unison. Their crisp white shirts stood out against the lush tropical trees that swayed in the mild breeze and doused the air with a sweetness that was almost intoxicating. Their smiles and joy were truly heartwarming, even if, as I suspected, they were motivated more by a morning away from their studies than genuine affection. Our convoy slowed down to a walking pace and drew up outside the main school building. A reception committee had been put together comprising the district education official, a government minister, the school headmaster and all his staff, including gardeners and cleaners, and, bizarrely, the local police chief. They were falling over themselves to greet Ayumi, and the welcome descended into friendly farce as social protocol struggled to keep in line with individual enthusiasm.

I decided to stay in the background, as schools were not my thing, given that my own personal experience was hardly worth revisiting. I left them to it and stayed by the car for a moment or two and watched the children being marshalled back into the school where no doubt they would be put back at their desks to regurgitate some lesson they had been drilled to repeat for our benefit. My reluctance to follow the party through the doors seemed to have been noticed by one of the school staff, a strikingly beautiful young woman who approached me. "Excuse me, sir, may I assist you into the school to join your party?" I told her I was fine and preferred to remain outside; I lightheartedly said speeches were not really my thing. She smiled and said she understood what I meant. I asked her name, and she told me she was called Gloria and was a junior teacher at the school. Her smile and warmth were infectious, but as she looked over my shoulder and noted the ominous figure lurking behind me, her whole demeanour changed in an instant, almost as if she had suddenly seen Lucifer himself. She apologised for interrupting me, turned on her heel, and headed to the main building.

I called after her, "Gloria, I hope we get the chance to talk a little more." She pretended she could not hear me and smartened her pace back towards the school.

Feeling more than just a little irritated, I turned to face the man who now was showing his unprofessionalism by feigning an interest in a dying mango tree. His partner must have followed the group inside, and I was flattered to think that my lone presence commanded such close scrutiny. As I walked towards him, I could see him tense up in preparation for a confrontation. He stood his ground, staring at me from behind his dark glasses, not once dropping his gaze as I got closer. I put my hand inside my jacket pocket for the reassurance that only a revolver can give. My words came out more aggressively than I had intended. "You! What is your business here? Why are you following us?"

He was chewing some kind of liquorice root, as was the custom amongst some of the local folk. It had blackened his teeth, and gave an air of comedy to his words. "We are here merely for your safety, Mr Miyazaki. You have nothing to fear from our presence. We are your guardian angels." He laughed as if he had found something incredibly amusing in his own words.

I stared at him for a moment as if challenging his intentions. Just as I was about to turn away, he said, "Mr Miyazaki, how is Mrs Tanaka? She looks well, especially after your close affections. I am sure her husband will be very grateful that you pay such kind attention to her well-being." I turned to face him, but he had already turned his back on me, although not before a snide farewell. "By the way, Mr Romana sends his regards." His words hung in the air like a deadweight. I stood root still and watched him as he nonchalantly walked away, disappearing around the bend in the driveway. The force of his words had fully hit home. In this place there was no such thing as privacy. Romana had eyes and ears all over the place. He was a Hydra, and it would take a beast slayer of epic strength to lay him low. He knew of my affair with Ayumi and would be more than willing to use it as leverage to secure a greater share of the spoils for himself. Could I risk calling his bluff?

As I made my way back up the drive, I could hear the children singing some kind of folk song. Their sweet voices drifted out the open windows and filled the air with fresh innocence. It struck me that I really was caught on the path between the decent and the damnable. It was now a question of which direction I would follow.

I passed the time leaning against the car door, deep and dark thoughts spinning around in my head. The drivers sat under a shady banyan tree, smoking and muttering to each other. They never took their eyes off me for a moment. It was plain to me they were also Romana's men, and if their posturing was supposed to intimidate, they failed miserably.

The noise coming from the school had reached a crescendo, and it seemed events had finally reached a conclusion. The drivers must have received some kind of signal, as they threw their cigarettes down and ground them into the dust and, with much exaggerated macho posturing, went to stand by their cars. The main doors of the school suddenly burst open and the children poured out, screaming like excited banshees as they ran down the drive to take up their places to wave off their visitors. Ayumi and Tanezawa were the first to leave; they both cradled huge bouquets of exotic-looking flowers and were holding hands with a small girl. They were accompanied by the same folk who had greeted them, except the uniformed officials now seemed to have pushed themselves closer to Ayumi than the school staff themselves.

I caught sight of Gloria, who brought up the rear. We locked eyes for a moment, and she gave me a warm smile and a little wave, perhaps in apology for hurrying away earlier. I smiled back and tried in vain to hold her attention for a moment longer, but she was soon lost in the crowd. I said my mental goodbye to Gloria, but kept her image in my mind. She was truly a beautiful woman, and I would have liked to have spent a sweet moment or two with her if circumstances had been more fortuitous.

I watched as everyone got into their cars for the return to the hotel. Kato was sweating like the devil, and his shirt looked to have plastered itself onto his back. Meursault and Reinhardt carried heavy bundles that looked like a sheaths of documents. Richardson shared a joke with the police chief; they looked too intimate for my liking. Perhaps I was too suspicious of friendship. A loner by nature I found it hard to understand why people felt the need to be liked and wanted. Many people were milling around, but thanks to good fortune, more than skill, the drivers managed to negotiate the chaos without injuring anyone.

We returned to the hotel in good time for lunch. There was no schedule for the rest of the day, but I knew Ayumi would want to go through the morning's events with Meursault and Reinhardt. She would require an initial appraisal of the financial direction of the foundation's endeavours. Perhaps the visit had ignited some kind of new initiatives in her mind. She was never the kind to tread slowly. Perhaps impetuosity was a family trait. Toshio was renowned for his lightning-fast decision making. It was a shame that none of it seemed to have rubbed off on Hideo's character. The man was very cautious, but it was said that he provided the perfect balance to Toshio's firebrand style. Hosokawa had long since slipped from the reckoning and had been a passenger in the business sense for many a long year.

With a sinking sense of irritation I decided to pay a visit to his suite. After all, it was my duty to keep him informed about events so far. I had no idea what kind of state he would be in; perhaps he had truly found the fortitude to resist his addiction. I did not hold any strong hope, though. I knew Hosokawa was not made of stern stuff and resigned myself to facing the usual withering wreck of a man. There was also the Tanezawa problem to deal with, and I needed to talk to Hosokawa to find out if he harboured any shrouded motive for spilling that little story.

As I walked through the lobby, I could not rid myself of the feeling that the hotel itself had somehow betrayed me. I no longer thought of the place as an old friend, and the tinkling of the seashell chandeliers would in my mind now forever be associated with betrayal. I looked around the lobby but could not see any of Romana's goons. Perhaps they had decided to leave us alone for the time being, satisfied that their hateful message had been delivered, though I very much doubted that was the case. Ayumi was still in the lobby, talking with Meursault, no doubt making plans for some kind of working luncheon. She caught my attention and waved me over. I waited until Meursault had left before approaching. She gave me a wan smile and asked me why I had not joined the rest of the party inside the school. I told her that I preferred the air outside.

She shook her head in disbelief. "Ken, is there something I should know? I am getting the strangest sensation that I am missing something. Sakura has been acting like a scolded kitten all morning, and you are doing your level best to stay out of sight." I shook my head and said I had no idea what she was talking about. She leaned closer to me and said, "I don't believe you for one minute. You look worried, and I have never, in all the years I've known you, seen you like this. If there is something going on, you have to tell me."

For an instant I was tempted to tell her that our midnight liaison had not gone unnoticed, but I quickly shook away such thoughts. She stared at me, almost willing some kind of confession out of me. When she realised nothing of the kind was likely to be forthcoming, she shrugged and turned away. But then, as an afterthought, she turned back and said, "Who is Romana? Sakura asked me if I knew of anyone here called Romana."

I shook my head, playing as dumb as I possibly could. Tanezawa had been asking questions. Was it all unravelling? "I have heard the name here and there," I said. "Why do you ask?"

"Sakura wanted to know, for some reason or other. I told her to read the background notes on the new First Lady. She was a Romana, was she not? Ismarelda Romana before marriage?"

I nodded. "Yes, I do believe she was, but what has that got to do with anything?"

She was already walking away when she said, "I don't know. See if you can get any information out of Sakura and let me know when you find out. That is, if you don't already know."

I had no desire to build walls between Ayumi and myself. I wanted her to trust me and thought we were closer than ever, especially after our little bedroom tête-à-tête, which was still so fresh in my mind.

It seemed that I had been excluded from any luncheon arrangements; this caused my irritation to build even more. I did not particularly wish to dine with anyone, but an invitation would have been welcome, if only to give me the satisfaction of refusing.

With Ayumi's thinly veiled rebuke still ringing in my ears I quickened my pace towards Hosokawa's suite. I was all too aware that my determination to find out what was going through his feeble mind might be thwarted by whatever state of awareness he was in at the moment. I did not hold any realistic hope of finding him in a fit condition to answer my questions, so it came as something of a shock when Murakami opened the door and I saw Hosokawa fully dressed, sitting out on the balcony in an easy chair and looking out over the bay. He was still wearing his dark glasses and despite the heat had a blanket draped over his shoulders. He seemed to be shivering slightly, and I noticed his hands were shaking uncontrollably.

Murakami stood in the background not knowing where to put himself. I felt for the poor lad. It must have been hell caring for Hosokawa around the clock, and the dark shadows that ringed his eyes bore testament to his daily toil. I doubted he had managed more than a few hours' sleep since we had left Tokyo. Despite all its glory, this suite must have seemed like some sort of luxurious confinement to a strong and clever lad like Murakami. Anyway, my little talk with Hosokawa was not for his ears, so I sent him on his way for an hour's respite. He hesitated at first, unwilling to leave his master, but I could sense he was grateful for small mercies, and he disappeared to enjoy his short liberty and left me alone with Hosokawa.

I drew up a chair and sat alongside him, taking in the fine view of the bay that was before us—and what a sight it was. The water shimmered beautiful hues of yellow and orange as it reflected the intense sunlight. An aircraft carrier of colossal size was moored far out, and we could see tiny crafts, servicing its needs as they ferried back and forth. "A fine sight, is it not, Hosokawa san? Almost as refreshing as finding you up and about. Are you well?"

For a moment I thought he could not hear me and had fallen asleep. Then he raised his shaky hand and waved it in front of himself as if he were brushing away a cobweb. His voice was croaky and weak; I had to strain my ears to make any sense of his words. "Miyazaki san, I have to thank you for standing by me through these hard times." He took hold of my arm in an awkward display of affection and slowly turned his head towards me, his voice lowered even more and barely audible against the babble of sounds that drifted up from below. "Ken, my dear, loyal friend, there is great sadness in my heart, for I fear I have failed you. I have failed you all. Please forgive my weakness." His head lowered, and drool spilled from the corner of his mouth. It was difficult to feel anything but pity for the man, and I felt my desire to push him for answers slipping away. However, fearing that I may not find him so lucid again, I decided to press on.

Bearing in mind that he was still my boss of sorts, I phrased my questions as respectfully as I could. "Hosokawa san, it seems that Tanezawa has become a little disturbed by your words last evening. Is there any special reason why she should know of this matter at this time?"

Hosokawa rolled his eyes and attempted to speak, but it seemed his thoughts were hard for him to verbalise. Eventually, when the words did come, they were not what I expected. I had to lean in closely to hear his croaky voice. "Tanezawa is the only innocent among us; she deserved to know the truth. That is her birthright. This place is haunted by the souls of the fallen. I feel them, and they speak to me. They tell me things, terrible stories. I heard her father's voice. It came to me in the night. He said he had a message for her and she had to know before it was too late."

I looked at him, but his eyes had closed. I had seen this many times and knew his comatose state would last for hours. I realised he must have taken something moments before I came into the room. In annoyance I shook him a little and raised my voice aggressively. "What do you mean, 'before it is too late'? Too late for what?" But it was no good. He had slipped into his cowardly retreat from reality and left me feeling more confused than ever. Hosokawa's fragile grip on normality had finally been prised loose, undone by the vile concoctions he had fed daily into his blood over the last five years. The drugs had altered his mind to such an extent that he truly believed he was in some other world. Paranoid delusion was a dangerous state of mind, especially in our line of work.

There was little point in wasting any more time, so I stood to leave. I thought about carrying Hosokawa over to his bed but decided to leave him where he was. I was past caring for him. Besides, Murakami would be back soon, and he would know better what should be done with the pathetic husk of a once fine man. As I was leaving the suite, I saw that Hosokawa had left his attaché case unlocked, and without hesitation I naturally took it as an open invitation to have a look at what was inside.

Amongst the grubby papers from meetings gone by I found his travel papers. I looked at the black-and-white photograph that was attached and then back out to the sleeping figure on the balcony. It was hard to believe they were one and the same person. There were stacks of sweet candy bars made from Japanese treacle. Murakami had once told me that Hosokawa liked only sweet foods, another side effect of his addiction, no doubt. There was a large portrait photograph of his wife, Azusa. She was smiling and looked blissfully happy, an indication that the photo was from times gone by. I knew the couple rarely spoke these days, and

Hosokawa barely mentioned her existence, but he must have missed her more than he cared to admit; carrying her picture everywhere seemed to bear that out.

At the bottom of his attaché case my hand felt a small brown paper package, which I took out and unwrapped. It contained six hypodermics, loaded and ready for use. It sickened me to my stomach, and without giving it a second thought I went to the bathroom and emptied each one into the basin. As I did so, my anger turned on Kato, but even I realised that the doctor would not be so foolish as to give an addict an unlimited amount for him to self-medicate. It was plainly obvious that Hosokawa was in no fit state, mentally or physically, to procure a supply like this.

It did not take long for realisation to dawn upon me: Murakami must be the source. It was no wonder the lad looked jumpy whenever I called. He must have been ordered to keep Hosokawa supplied, a depressing situation for sure and one that I vowed to stop. It was apparent that Hosokawa's decline was gathering a dangerous momentum. He had sunk into the black hole of no return, and none of us could afford the risks of being exposed because of his weakness. He had become a liability to us all. I looked at him silhouetted against the blazing sun and paused for a few moments. Time seemed to stop dead in its tracks. I had an ominous feeling that there was to be no return passage for the man who had saved my life and made me what I was today. We had reached the crossroads, and I believed he too must have seen that his fate hung in the balance. Perhaps the ghosts had told him so.

I wearily dragged myself down the stairs to my room. The maid had been about her business and the place was immaculate. Even the apples in the fruit bowl had been polished. My meeting with Hosokawa weighed heavily on my mind. His paranoia was infectious and had seeped into my soul, his rambling disturbing me more than I cared to admit. I looked around the room for anything out of place or any unusual oddities. My sixth sense had served me well in the past, and I had no reason to doubt it now; it told me the place was somehow compromised. I checked the walls for any tiny spy holes; I even removed the large ornate mirror from its holding but could not find anything out of the ordinary. A similar sweep of the bathroom failed to turn up any signs of encroachment.

Frustration and fatigue finally beat me down, and I decided to catch up on some of the sleep I had missed. I stretched out on the bed fully clothed, intending to take only a few hours before my "meeting" that evening. It seemed I had misjudged the extent of my exhaustion, though, for I awoke a good four hours later. The sun was sinking and dusk was upon us, a breeze billowed about, and the curtains danced against the window frame. It was unusually dark, and it looked as if we could anticipate the arrival of a storm. It was the perfect setting for my mood and my impending rendezvous. I had barely an hour in which to prepare for the meeting and had the added problem of making sure my absence went unnoticed not only amongst my own party, but also from the prying eyes of others.

I dressed in a style that spoke of inconspicuousness. It was important to blend into the background, to become the grey man, just another somebody of no significance. I chose a pair of tan linen trousers and a white barong shirt, worn untucked. It was a couple of sizes too big, but that was the style the locals seemed to prefer. I brushed my hair straight and then combed in enough pomade to slick it back close to my scalp and behind my ears. Finally, satisfied that my greased-back hair bore little resemblance to my usual style, I made ready to leave. As an afterthought I donned a pair of plain-lens spectacles to complete my look. The thick black frames made me feel a little self-conscious, as I now felt I had slipped into a different persona. When I looked into the mirror, the man staring back at me was a gawky-looking version of myself. Certainly not a disguise per se, but I hoped the few subtle alterations here and there would give me enough anonymity to go about my business. Time was of the essence, and I could little afford to spend any more precious moments fine-tuning my appearance. As I was about to leave my room, an almighty rumble of thunder shook even the windowpanes. I secured the balcony shutters to protect against the deluge which would surely come. The rainstorms here could turn a dusty street into a flowing river in a matter of minutes, and I hoped I would be able to make my destination before getting caught in the mayhem that usually accompanied such a violent change in the weather.

I knew the Manila Hotel well; it was a home away from home, as they say, but obviously not as private as I had thought. Still, previous trips had taught me how to get out of the place unchallenged via numerous exits. This evening I thought it appropriate to leave from the rear staff doors, which were to be found by passing through the laundry area next to the staff restrooms. I took a circuitous route: Up a floor and then doubling back on myself, I found the doors to a large function room unlocked and walked through, out the opposite doors, down the emergency staircase, and finally into the back corridor, which I knew connected to the staff areas. I never once looked back and carried myself with confidence at all times. Faced with a set of double doors which accessed the laundry area, I stood to one side to allow an elderly woman pushing a cart laden with bedsheets to pass me by. I caught the doors as they flapped closed in her wake and strode down the corridor.

The heat was stupefying; the industrial-sized dryers seemed to have taken up most of the breathable air. This area was staffed mostly by washerwomen, and nobody paid me the slightest attention as I walked through. I could see the door which gave access to the rear of the hotel and out onto the back streets. I prayed to the gods that it would be open as it had been on every other occasion, and the gods answered my prayers. I pushed the handle down and stepped out into the rear compound. The smell of rotten food dumped on either side of the walkway waiting for collection was overpowering. I quickened my steps and held my breath. A huge brown rat was enjoying the hospitality of Manila's finest hotel and did not even flinch as I walked by. The compound was ringed by a tall chicken wire fence, the last obstacle before reaching the street proper.

A guard at the gate would be in his small sentry box, maybe snoozing. I walked up to the gate and rattled it as loudly as I could, which brought the expected response. The geriatric guard emerged yawning, fumbling with his key chain, not even bothering to make eye contact with me as he opened up the last obstacle. It was his brief to keep thieves and ruffians out, not to keep respectable, well-dressed gents in, so it was with a great deal of relief that I found myself walking down the street with enough time to spare to keep my appointment.

The narrow streets were unusually busy as vendors brought their wares in out of the rain which was now falling in great drenching drops. I did not have far to walk. My destination was well known to me and a mere five minutes away. I stuck to the walkway as much as possible, taking advantage of the blue plastic awnings that the shops seemed to universally favour. Every minute or so I checked back over my shoulder to satisfy myself that my progress was going unobserved. As I approached my destination, I felt my heart lurch as it always did at this time. The Puwerto Café looked like any other, it had no special redeeming features, and the clientele were the simple folk of the neighbourhood. However, today there would be one customer who was far from simple, sitting at his usual table, sipping his bitter black coffee and looking far more relaxed than he had any given right to be.

I took a few moments to watch the café from the opposite side of the street. Nothing seemed out of the ordinary; the street was almost deserted, as the rain had driven most people indoors. It now beat down and bounced back off the street, creating a ferocious rhythm. To my right a group of old men squatted on their haunches under the awning next to me, smoking and talking. Not wanting to draw their attention I decided to dash across the street to the café, just an ordinary fellow caught up in the storm who sought shelter and a fortifying drink. The place was almost empty, save for a couple of old women so deep in gossipy chatter, they did not even raise their eyes to look at me. The owner, a large greasy-looking fellow who I knew went by the name of Jessie, sat behind the counter reading his newspaper, a cigarette dangling from the corner of his mouth. He looked up at me, gave me a casual nod of welcome, and went back to his reading. The man I had come to meet was sitting at the far table, the same man I had met in this very place many times. But this time was different. In the past I had been with Hosokawa, acting as his aide, but now it was all down to me and me alone.

I approached the table, and we locked eyes for a few seconds. He stood to greet me and embraced me in a customary display of affection. His smile was warm and genuine; he took my hand and held it firmly for a good ten seconds, a sign that all was well and one that I accepted with relief. He motioned for me to sit and called out to Jessie for another pot of coffee. His Tagalog was excellent, and to all who knew him he was just another regular Filipino. Yet nothing could have been further from the truth. Before me was a man I had nothing but the upmost admiration for, the bravest and most resourceful of all men and one who had made our fantastic venture the thing of wonder that it had become. Lieutenant Ogawa looked remarkably well for a man supposedly lost in action for over twenty years.

We waited in silence for a few minutes whilst Jessie served our coffee, neither of us wanting to break into our native tongue until satisfied that we were out of earshot. I knew what Ogawa's first sentence would be. It was always the same, and he never disappointed. "Miyazaki san, tell me. How is my father? Is he well?" Toshio had warned me before the trip not to be too graphic when recounting Ogawa Senior's health, which had declined rapidly over the last six months. The old man was now bedridden and confined to a nursing home, details that might cause undue distress to his son and only living relative. I told him that his father had slowed down a little but could still handle a Bentley better than any other old man on the planet. Ogawa smiled at my attempt at light humour, but there was sadness behind his eyes, and who could really deny him his moment of anguish? The man had made a great sacrifice. Even his own father believed him to be dead and long gone. His best friend, Hideo, believed him to be living in some kind of hideout, a wild jungle man who kept vigil over hoards of loot. Necessary deceits, engineered by the master of cunning strategy, Toshio Hamazaki. To my knowledge, Ogawa and Hamazaki had never met face-to-face. It was Hamazaki's father who first gave Ogawa his task, and Toshio merely redefined that task to great effect.

Twenty years ago, after the cessation of hostilities, Ogawa was ordered to go to ground, stay close to the treasure sites, and await further orders. In the beginning, communication was sparse if not nonexistent, and Ogawa suffered a frustrating few years. However, his role took on a new dimension when Santa Romana entered the picture. Romana was a necessary evil, the only man capable of meeting Hamazaki's demands. Hamazaki needed a way into Romana's circle of confidantes, and that was provided by his closest aide, Hector. It was an opportunity spurred on by a feeling of betrayal and unrequited love. Hector had fallen madly in love with Ismarelda and they had had a passionate love affair, which resulted in Hector asking his boss for his daughter's hand in marriage. Romana, no doubt suppressing his shock, had far grander designs for his daughter's future and politely explained that he could not consent to his daughter marrying a one-handed man. He forbade the couple to meet and forced them apart, and Ismarelda was moved out to the country to stay with her aunt. Romana tried to make amends with Hector and gave him a little extra share of the spoils and arranged a steady stream of women for him, but Hector was a heartbroken man. He did his best to hide his hurt, but it ate away like a cancer.

When Romana announced his daughter's engagement to Marios, Hector was still riddled with hate, and although he may not have realised it at the time, he was open to suggestion. It did not take much persuasion for him to sell his soul and loyalty to Toshio Hamazaki. Every man has his price, but I do believe Hector's was too low. He was now in a bad place, torn between the devil and the deep blue sea. Failing either of his masters would be tantamount to a death sentence. Hector reported to Ogawa, and they had their own special communications of which I knew little. Ogawa, in turn, consulted directly with Toshio, and that was how we kept up with Romana's thinking and stayed one move ahead of him at all times. It allowed us to call his bluff or bend a little to his demands if they were intractable. I looked at Ogawa wincing at the bitterness of the coffee as it burnt his throat and hoped he had some good news for me on this storm-drenched evening.

I did not ask any questions. Ogawa was a man who liked to deliver his information in quick, precise bursts, and I knew he would tell me all I needed to know. Despite our numerous meetings over the years he looked at me as if he were still not convinced of my credibility. Perhaps it was Hosokawa's absence that had somehow disturbed the dynamic, but I was sure he had something on his mind that troubled him. Ogawa leaned in close and said, "Romana will ask for more. He wants to double his price. He is desperate for extra funds. The campaign to put Marios in office has all but bled him dry, and now he has an army of sycophants to satisfy. Marios already had his dirty hands on the state budget, but it would take months before he could prise substantial funds away from the exchequer. The word from Hector was that Romana would push for more, but would settle for a ten per cent increase, as his options were limited. So, that is to be Mabuhay's stance: ten per cent and no more. I wish you good luck when you tell the thieving bastard to his face." Ogawa leaned back in his chair and studied my face. I kept my silence, waiting for him to pass me the details. He shrugged and took out a tiny piece of paper from his shirt pocket on which would be written the grid reference for site eleven. Without a word I took the paper and stuffed it into the waistband of my trousers, where I had stitched a special pocket just for the purpose of keeping this most valuable of papers. Usually at this point, Hosokawa would stand and pat Ogawa on the shoulder and leave him to his coffee, but this evening was different. Hosokawa was not here, and it was obvious that Ogawa had some other business on his mind.

He poured me another cup of foul-tasting coffee and told me, with an ominous look in his eye, that he wanted a few more minutes of my time. Not many men made me feel uneasy—in fact, I took great pride in my steely demeanour—but some special quality about Ogawa made you feel belittled in his presence. He had a natural sense of authority that commanded respect, and even though he was at least a decade younger than me, I found myself willingly falling into the role of a servile accomplice. "Miyazaki san," he said. "Something has come to my attention. My friend reported to me that you have been a little indiscreet with the wife of a close friend of mine."

He stared at me, waiting for my reply. I knew it was pointless to try to deny my affair, and I also knew it would gain me little credence should I try to justify my actions. I stared at Ogawa, and for a moment we had a slight standoff, which Ogawa broke with cold, cutting, detached words. "Although the morality of this sordid scenario concerns me greatly, I am more inclined to focus my misgivings on how Romana will use this information for his own ends. Miyazaki, your rash actions have exposed us and may prove more costly than you could ever imagine."

Still I held my silence, merely staring back at Ogawa as he considered how to proceed. After what seemed like an eternity of icy silence, he spoke, choosing his words with the upmost care, as if he were a pious judge presiding over the trial of a miscreant. "I presume that neither Hideo nor Toshio know of your dalliance?"

I told him that I believed that to be the case.

He nodded and then went on with chilling, clinical clarity. "It seems that fate has thrown us a wild card, and we will use it to bluff our way out of this little mess. That card comes courtesy of Hosokawa, or more precisely the wretched state he currently finds himself in. We will transfer your immoral transgression onto

Hosokawa and lead Romana to believe that you were in fact only covering for Hosokawa, by allowing him to use your room for his secret assignations."

It took a few moments for me to understand what he was proposing, and I had a feeling where this was heading. Ogawa went on to explain further. "Your job is to make the story believable, keep as close to the truth as possible, and pray for deliverance from your sins." I nodded to show I understood.

Ogawa looked down at his lap. I knew it was difficult for him to look me in the eye and say the inevitable, but he somehow found the resolve and went on. "It is with the heaviest of hearts, and what I have to tell you brings me enormous sorrow." He took a moment to compose himself before pronouncing the inevitable. "When opportunity is in your favour, you will release Hosokawa from his personal hell. It will be a mercy for him, and you have all our blessings. It has been sanctioned by Tokyo for reasons that have become clear to all who are close to Hosokawa. I believe you are in possession of a vial of coronary-inducing medication, are you not?" I nodded, and he went on. "Use it wisely and make sure it appears natural, and let us pray that your affair goes the same way as Hosokawa himself."

I could barely bring myself to believe what I had heard: Hamazaki had passed a death sentence on Hosokawa, and I was to be his instrument. I looked at Ogawa and said, "Hosokawa has shown me great kindness and considerations over the years. I owe him a great deal. It will not be easy for me to do as you ask, but I will not fail in my duty, of that you can be sure."

Ogawa looked deep into my eyes as if he were trying to find any signs of weakness in my soul. "Our friend has been living on borrowed time, as you well know. He broke an edict that was sacrosanct when he helped himself to a little of the sacred treasure.

He failed to understand that we are merely the custodians of those artefacts and that we have a moral responsibility to return each and every piece when time and events dictate it is fortuitous to do so."

Ogawa's personal view of Mabuhay and the way we went about business was not one that I recognised, and I wondered how detached from reality this man had become. The years spent removed from his homeland and his devotion to duty seemed to have taken a toll on his ability to grasp the fallible nature of our work. Ogawa leaned over and reached for a newspaper which had been left behind. He pushed it across the table and tapped at a picture on the front page. It had been taken at the previous evening's reception and captured Ismarelda and Ayumi in conversation together, both women looking relaxed and elegant. Ogawa shook his head in a pitying way. "This picture bears testament to a connection between Mabuhay and our 'other business.' Hosokawa's wife was seen wearing an identical piece of vulgarity at the company's tenth anniversary celebrations. All it would take would be some bright-witted investigator seeing both pictures and making connections. Do you understand where our concerns lie?"

There seemed to be little more to say. Hosokawa had done himself to death. It was not solely the drugs, but I do not doubt his abuse made it easier to condemn him. I made to stand, but Ogawa bade me to remain seated. "Miyazaki, you will never speak of what has passed between us this evening, and you will never lie with my friend's wife ever again. Should word of your immorality reach certain ears, then I can only say that you will find yourself reunited with Hosokawa far sooner than you ever imagined." His words sent my blood boiling and I knew my face had reddened in anger, but I also knew he occupied the moral high ground and I had to take his searing rebuke as best I could.

I stood and nodded to him. Words were unnecessary. He remained seated, and when I left, there was no friendly pat on the shoulder. Ogawa took another sip of his bitter coffee and waved me on my way. I felt belittled and chastised. As I left the café, I turned to take one more look at the man who had lived like a ghost for over twenty years, but he had already gone.

The rain had eased and the storm had passed. It seemed more than fitting that my own life had suddenly been thrust into the maelstrom of emotional tumult. My love for Ayumi was exposed, and now I had become the designated executioner to the man who had saved me from such a similar fate. Two burdens had been laid down at my feet which I now carried, heavy in my heart. It felt like a virulent cancer was eating away at my soul. I looked up into the black sky; I could see the dark clouds passing by the moon. The air had cleared and tomorrow Manila would awaken to another grand day, but it would be no grand day for me. I prayed to the gods to help me find the fortitude to see it through.

I am not a man of letters; in fact I doubt you could find anyone further away from such a thing as me. It is to my shame that I have only ever read one book in my life, but that one book has stayed close to my heart. It was given to me by my captain as he lay dying in the Malaysian jungle. He had been shot through the lungs and died in my arms; his final mortal act was to press Laozi's Tao Te Ching into my hands. He tried to explain something to me, but the bubbling blood foaming from his mouth was all the explanation I needed. He was a good man and deserved more from life than to die in a steamy foreign hellhole. I had kept that book with me ever since, and the bloodstained pages only served to further exalt the wisdom it contained.

As I walked back to the hotel, I constantly repeated one of Laozi's quotes: "Being loved by someone gives you strength, while loving someone gives you courage." Repeating this mantra some-what calmed my nerves and seemed to fortify my convictions. Whatever fate held in store for me, I was more than ready to face it head-on. I had no fear. Far greater men than me had passed through this world, and my own passing would not be missed by many. I did not have any living family, had no sons to carry my name. In truth I did not even have a real name. When a man truly has nothing left to live for, he becomes a dangerous, wild creature full of abandon, driven by primeval instinct. He is capable of almost anything, even the killing of his benefactor, but not capable of denying his heart of the love it so craves.

I did not attempt to conceal my arrival at the hotel. To do so would only bring unwanted attention upon me, and in any case a man had a right to go for an evening stroll should he so wish. I was soaked from the aftermath of the storm, which had combined with the heat to create a stifling humidity. Sweat poured from me, and I needed to bathe. I prayed that nobody would impede me as I stepped into the lobby. I did catch a few stares, as my appearance naturally drew attention. I left a dripping trail along the marble floor through the lobby towards the staircase.

As I was about to climb the stairs, I heard a voice. "Mr Miyazaki, sir." I turned to see a suited chap approaching with a silver tray, upon which was a small sealed envelope. He gave a deep bow and proffered his message. I took it, thanked him, and carried on to my room. Once safely inside my room, I went into the bathroom and removed all my clothes, taking great care to extract the small paper from my waistband. I took it into the bed-room, and for no apparent reason other than sentiment, placed it inside my Laozi book. I left the sealed envelope by my shaving mirror. I knew it was a message from Romana, and I would deal with it after I had refreshed myself a little. It was a personal thing but a small triumph nonetheless that I gave my own hygiene needs a higher priority than the demands of the president's father-in-law.

I filled the bathtub with cool water and rinsed away the grease from my hair. As I lay in the water, I felt exhaustion settle down on me. For the second time in my life I felt an almost irresistible urge to desert from my duty—after all, I had pledged my loyalty to Hosokawa and not to Mabuhay—and yet in my heart I knew there was to be no escape for me. At some point I would have to confront my own demons, but I had an ominous feeling someone was holding court with them, on my behalf, at this very moment. Whatever Toshio Hamazaki had in store for me, I would accept it with the grace of one who deserved his due, as my time here on earth had been mostly stolen from the hands of the Moirai, the three goddesses of fate.

I towelled my hands dry and reached over for the envelope; it had been sealed with a nondescript circular black wax stamp and hand couriered to the hotel for personal delivery. After inspecting it closely for any signs of tampering, I ripped it open and took out the small piece of paper. It simply read, "Drinks and midnight poker, Jasmine Room." I had not expected the meeting with Romana to take place so soon and would have liked to have put a night's rest between the depressing events that had blighted the day and having to face down Romana.

Midnight would bear down upon me sooner than I liked. I dried and dressed myself hurriedly. Casual and comfortable would be appropriate. White open-neck shirt and black trousers, no jacket: The simplest of outfits would suffice for our secret charade. Having dressed, I poured myself a good measure of Philippine rum and threw it back in one gulp, letting the burning liquid course through my body. I was tempted to take a brief rest, but I knew sleep would be impossible as nervous agitation drove me forward. I opened my case and took out the small ebony-coloured box that I kept with me on trips such as these—my little box, which contained some of the less fanciful items of my profession. Two vials of medication along with two hypodermics were packaged in the standard medical format and labelled "IPV," but these vials were not polio vaccines. Rather, they were deadly equine euthanasia drugs which, when administered to humans in the correct dosage, could induce almost instantaneous cardiac arrest. I had had cause to use this fatal concoction once before, and unfortunately the dosage was miscalculated with alarming effects, but I believed that problem had been resolved. A heart attack was as good a way to pass in a natural sense as any other, especially if the victim was a frail drug abuser.

The irony of this situation was apparent, as it was Hosokawa who had first devised this method for the purpose of bringing about the demise of one of his bitterest opponents. I was the reaper's messenger on that day, and I would be so again. I checked my watch: a little over an hour to go before my "poker game." I pocketed the vial and syringe and set out for Hosokawa's suite.

I had to fight the urge to give up on my deathly mission, as I could not rid my mind of images of happier times spent with Hosokawa. Drinking together in shochu bars and teasing the hostesses, driving along dangerous roads at terrifying speeds and laughing together in the face of danger. So many memories flashed before my eyes, bittersweet memories that I was about to poison forever.

As I reached the top of the stairs, I heard the click of Hosokawa's door being opened and saw Murakami almost running along the corridor. I pressed myself into an alcove and waited a moment until he had disappeared and then without hesitation approached the suite. Murakami had left the door unlatched, and I slipped inside like a thief in the night. The room was only semi-lit, and I heard Hosokawa moaning from his bedroom beyond. His words were barely comprehensible, but I could make out "Kato" every now and again. I took it that Murakami had been sent off to get the doctor to come and administer some relief. If I were to be proven correct, then the opportunistic hand of fate had just dealt me a royal flush.

I went into Hosokawa's room to find him writhing around the bed, shaking and mouthing vile obscenities. My intrusion went completely unnoticed; I opened the door of the huge dressing chamber and secreted myself behind a large bedclothes box, silently pulling the door closed behind me. It did not take long before Murakami returned with Kato in tow. I could just about make out part of the scenario before me. Kato was wearing his hotel bathrobe and had obviously been disturbed from his slumber, further confirmed by the irritation in his voice. He was only a few feet away from me. My own breathing seemed amplified beyond reason, and I was sure I would be detected. If so, I would bluster my way out of it by claiming to be exercising vigilance for Hosokawa's well-being. I need not have worried, for Kato was all too keen to hasten his medical attention and get back to his bed. I could hear his booming voice as if it were next to my ear. "Hosokawa san, you disappoint me. I thought you were going to see this through and clean your system. As your doctor I must advise you to resist your urges. Can you do that?"

There was a shout that sounded like it was coming from a wounded dog, a shocking cry from a man who had hit the floor of hell. It was plain that Hosokawa was missing his "secret" supply that I had disposed of earlier and now had to rely on Kato's weaker methadone substitute. There was some fumbling about as Kato opened his bag, and through the gap in the slatted door I watched as he filled the hypodermic and injected Hosokawa in the forearm.

I heard the doctor say, "That will see you through the night. If you have any pain, send your boy for me at once." He turned to Murakami and said, "Got that, boy?"

They both left the bedroom, but I could still hear Kato's voice drifting in from the sitting room beyond. "Murakami, give me those two bottles of Scotch whisky, if you please, and give me a hand to carry them down to my room." The doctor was pilfering Hosokawa's drinks cabinet. I did not mind in the slightest, as it opened up the perfect window of opportunity for me to go about my own business. I knew I would have about three minutes to get everything done before Murakami was back to check on his master.

I waited until all was silent and then filled my own hypodermic. Silently I pushed open the door and stepped out into Hosokawa's room. His eyes were closed, but his breathing was alarmingly shallow, and he was making a kind of grunting noise as he filled his lungs. I looked down at him, and for a moment I tried to make myself believe that what I was about to do was truly for the best. But I could not find enough conviction to deceive myself, and through tear-filled eyes I grabbed his arm and inserted the deadly drug.

Hosokawa's eyes shot wide open, and he made a lunge for my own arm, gripping it tightly. He looked at me, his bloodshot eyes pleading, but it was too late. His last words shocked me to my core. "Ken, I thank you and never blame you. Tell Azusa I love her and always will." His voice was wheezy and weak. His eyes flickered, and he was gone. I looked closely at the man who had saved my life, serene in death. I wished I too could find a peace that would last an eternity.

With the morbid efficiency of an experienced killer I arranged his body into a sleeping position and pulled his bedclothes up tight. Ideally Murakami would not notice his master had passed away until morning had set in, when no doubt he would run once more to the doctor's door, bearing his fateful message. I took one last look at Hosokawa, silently prayed for his forgiveness, and sneaked out of the room.

Once back out on the corridor I took the opposite route in order to avoid Murakami. To my relief I did not pass any staff or fellow guests as I made my way to the Jasmine Room. I was a few minutes early for our meeting, but experience had taught me that punctuality tended to pay dividends. The room Romana had chosen for our "discussion" was at the far end of a long, deep carpeted corridor that was lined with vases of orchids and, of course, jasmine flowers. The air was filled with a sweet fragrance, almost intoxicating in its freshness. As I approached the doors of the room, another scent hit me, one which instantly brought home memories of meetings gone by, times I had sat alongside Hosokawa as he took the lead. I had always felt at ease with Hosokawa's style of upper-crust bluff and bluster, but now it was down to me and me alone. I felt fortified with a renewed sense of determination to see this through, if only in honour of my dear recently departed associate.

The heavy, acrid smell of cigar smoke told me Romana was already there, a fact confirmed by the sudden appearance of two thickly set chaps who took up positions on either side of the door. They pushed the doors open, and I stepped into the room. The air was fuggy from the sickly cigar smoke. A small card table was set up in the centre where Romana sat, staring directly at me. He did not stand to greet me, and motioned toward the empty seat opposite. Hector Ramirez sat behind Romana and stood to pour some drinks from the bottles that were set out on the large hospitality table.

Romana stared at me for a few moments as if he were weighing up his approach. Then he broke out into a wide grin, flashing his gold tooth that always seemed to catch whatever light was bouncing about. "Come and sit, my friend. It is my pleasure to welcome you; I only wish our business would permit me to be more hospitable. Please forgive the strained circumstances that always seem to limit our time together." I nodded to him and sat opposite. Hector placed two glasses of drink on the table. Romana lifted his glass. "Scotland's gift to the world." He took a small sip and closed his eyes in a sign of appreciation. "I wish I could take more of this stuff, but all men slow down. Do they not, Mr Miyazaki?"

I told him that it was the natural way of things and that maybe things around us had started to go faster. He smiled at my attempt to lighten the mood, but as always his smile could turn into a look of pure contempt. I knew the legacy of war still filled him with an intense hatred for my nation, one he managed to put aside only to satisfy his insatiable avarice. It was said he had lost a son in the fighting and had never managed to find peace. However, I believed men like Romana were born evil and that whatever fate chose to place in their path only served to add fuel to an already raging dark soul.

I took a sip of my drink and waited for Romana to get to the point. We both knew the agenda, and there was little to be gained from small talk. I also knew from experience that Romana was a man who liked to feel he was in control, so my approach would be to respond rather than instigate. "Tell me, how is Hosokawa? I hear he finds himself in poor health. I hope our fine climate will see him back on the road to recovery. Please convey my best regards when you next see him." I thanked him and said Hosokawa would be most heartened to hear of his concern, a comment that seemed to draw a contemptuous look of reproach from Romana. "So, we find ourselves face-to-face once more. I take it you have been vested with the full authority to finalise an agreement?" I said that was the case. Romana nodded and looked down at the deck of cards. "Miyazaki, are you a gambling man?"

I looked at him and said, "I believe there are better ways to satisfy your desires than risking what you already have."

Romana smiled. "Very wise approach, and yet one that lacks a spirit of adventure. I only wish life were so simple. I will be straightforward with you. My continued assistance may be secured only by a substantial improvement of your terms; I believe the time has come to renegotiate our agreement." He stared at me, looking for any hint of surprise or weakness.

I steeled myself and calmly took another sip of the whisky. "What figure do you have in mind?"

Romana stretched back in his chair and casually announced he was doubling his fee. "Two million dollars: half paid in advance, the other half within one week of the shipment's arrival."

I smiled and looked down, then raised my eyes to meet his. "Mr Romana, such terms are not acceptable. I am instructed to offer you an increase of ten per cent on the standing arrangement. Should you refuse, then I am afraid we have no further business to discuss."

Romana brought his fist down hard on the table. "You insolent piece of shit, I do not work for you, and you will not tell me what my effort is worth." His anger was virulent and even now, in his advancing years, a force to be reckoned with. I thought of Tanezawa's father and the hell he must have gone through when faced with a younger Romana, officially sanctioned to torture information out of his captives.

Hector felt his boss's anger and stood to add more menace to the already deteriorating atmosphere. I stood to take my leave. "Our offer to you is entirely nonnegotiable. Should you decide it is not sufficient, then there is little point in taking up any more of your precious time. I wish you good night, Mr Romana." I bowed in his direction and turned my back on him and walked to the door, silently counting out the paces before he called me back. It took seven strides.

"Miyazaki, sit down." I turned back and saw that Romana was now standing, gripping the edge of the table in an effort to calm himself. I walked back and sank into the chair once more.

Romana looked exasperated as he tried to stare me down. "Perhaps I should talk with Tanaka; maybe I could get her to raise the price a little. After all, I hear she spreads her services quite thick on the ground these days."

I wanted to stretch across the table and strangle the life out of him, an urge I just managed to keep at bay. "Please explain what you mean by such a remark."

He sneered and looked me up and down. "Miyazaki, your dirty secret is out. We all know where Tanaka goes for her bedtime fuck, and it is not to her husband."

His expletive shocked me, but jolted my mind into action. "Romana, it seems you are under some illusion. Where you get your fanciful notions from is your business, but do not try to blemish the good name of a decent, charitable woman." Romana laughed as if it were the most amusing thing he had ever heard. "The good lady was seen going to your room in the dead of night wearing her bathrobe. She left sometime later wearing the look of a satisfied woman."

Now it was my turn to laugh. I threw my head back and smiled. "You seem to have been misinformed. I do not deny Mrs Tanaka visited my room last evening, but not for the purpose you are insinuating. She had important and urgent business to discuss with Hosokawa. My room was chosen for added security. We felt the suite was too indiscreet for such sensitive discussions. Hosokawa and I traded rooms for the evening."

Romana smiled. He had the look of a totally unbelieving parent who had been told a yarn by an errant son. "Do not take me for a fool. If that is all the feeble explanation you have, I hope Mr Tanaka is more believing of such nonsense."

I was just about to reinforce my fallacy when I got support from an unexpected ally. Hector added his voice to the matter. "Boss, Mr Hosokawa was reported to have been helped to Miyazaki's room earlier that evening." Romana looked at Hector as if he had just been stabbed in the back. His face turned puce, filled with anger, and I felt for Hector. He was paying back part of the price for selling his soul; I said a silent thank-you to Ogawa for giving my story a little more credibility than it deserved.

Romana turned his anger back towards me. "You take a message back to Tokyo. Tell your putik-assed boss that if he ever wants my help again, he had better pay me what my services are worth.

Tell him this will be the last time he gets my cooperation unless he pays what I ask. I want six hundred thousand dollars in cash before your delegation leaves my country, and the remainder as agreed."

I nodded, satisfied that the deal was secured. "Mr Romana, please rest assured that I will convey your sentiments." There was a flash of anxiety in Romana's eyes. It was there only a second, but there it was. Romana may have questioned the wisdom of

496

insulting a man who commanded more wealth than his own entire country could muster. With a rush of sangfroid I slowly unfolded the small piece of paper and pushed it across the table. "Here is the location of site eleven. On the reverse you will find a list of the countermeasures that need to be taken when excavating the site. There are six boxes in total. All have to be delivered with their seals intact, and any tampering will be taken as a breach of our agreement. We expect secured delivery within four months of this day. I thank you for your time. Good night, Mr Romana."

I stood to take my leave. Romana sat stone still, staring down at the stack of playing cards. I turned my back and made for the doors, not daring to risk a look in Hector's direction. I walked to the doors and tapped, the guards let me out, and I set off down the corridor. From the Jasmine Room I heard Romana's deranged anger bounce off the walls as his savagery was unleashed upon the hapless Hector.

I was not the kind of man who found sleep easy to come by, but I slept better than any man deserved to under such trying circumstances. No doubt the stress of being unmasked as a party to adultery, followed by the murder of my own boss, and finally, having to face down one of this country's worst criminals had left me totally void of energy. After I returned from my meeting with Romana, I collapsed onto my bed fully clothed and fell into a sleep so deep, it seemed my soul was attempting to deny the heinous events of the past day.

So it was with some confusion that the new dawn announced itself as a distant banging in my head. It took a few moments for me to realise that the noise was in fact real and someone was desperately rapping away at my door. My first thought was that the law had finally caught up with me, but then with a sinking sense of realisation I knew that it meant the news of Hosokawa's demise had finally broken. I threw my bathrobe on over my crumpled clothes to hide the fact that I had slept in such a haphazard manner. I opened my door a little way and peeped out.

To my surprise—and further adding to my guilt—it was Ayumi who had taken it as her duty to come and inform me of the tragic news. I opened my door wider and she fell into my arms, crying great heaving sobs, which prevented her from getting her words out. I tried to soothe her with doses of concern and care. After a minute or two she finally found the fortitude to deliver her shocking words. "Ken, it is Makoto. He has died in his sleep."

I managed to feign the look of complete surprise at this "bombshell" news and forced myself to playact in a display of shock and sadness. "How?"

She looked at me, and there was no question that her emotion was raw and genuine. I felt for her, a feeling that was only compounded by the fact that I was directly responsible for her grief. "It seems his heart gave out. Kato is up there now. We are waiting on a local doctor to come and sign a death certificate." Her last words were barely audible as they snivelled out in a fit of sobbing.

"Ayumi, I have to go up to his suite to see if there is anything to be done. Please stay here if you wish." She shook her head determinedly, and I knew there would be little point in trying to dissuade her from following me. I grabbed a clean shirt from the wardrobe and went into the bathroom to change. Ayumi stood in exactly the same spot, waiting for me, her arms wrapped about her body. She was shivering slightly, a sure sign she was in a state of shock. I would ask Kato to give her something, perhaps a mild sleeping tonic.

We walked in grim silence along the luxurious corridor towards Hosokawa's suite. On approach I noticed that quite a crowd had gathered outside the door. The hotel general manager was trying his best to politely coordinate matters and seemed to have appointed himself as a kind of liaison between the local authorities and his establishment. There were a couple of uniformed officers, perhaps police, but in this country it was difficult to say with any degree of certainty.

I pushed my way through the crowd with a comforting hand on Ayumi's shoulder and we made to enter the suite, only to find our access denied by a scruffy-looking fellow who wore the grubbiest of white shirts. He held out his hand. "Nobody enters this room without first entering their details into the crime scene register."

I looked at him coldly. "Our dear friend and colleague has passed away, and you are calling it a crime? On what basis do you presume foul play has occurred?"

He looked at me as if I had landed from another world. "It is the regulations. We treat all deaths as suspicious until two doctors have been satisfied that death is the result of natural or nonsuspicious causes." He seemed smug as he stated his operating protocol, and I knew there would be little point in trying to make a stand in the face of such narrow-minded stonewall bureaucracy. I entered our details into a shabby and frayed book. I hesitated at the section where it said "title" and "position." I had never been officially given a title in the company, so without further ado I decided there and then to appoint myself one. "Mabuhay. Senior Delegation Official." I mouthed the words as I inked them on paper. I offered to complete Ayumi's details, but she was made of sterner stuff and, albeit with a shaky hand, made the necessary entry in the book.

The scruffy officer, who I now took to be some kind of crime scene detective, seemed satisfied and pushed the door open to allow us inside. It seemed that the Manila Police Department was rather flush with personnel, as there were several uniformed officers lazing around the lounge. Quite what their purpose was I did not know.

We entered Hosokawa's bedroom, which looked like it had been turned over by thieves. The bedclothes were heaped on the floor, and there was an upturned ice bucket by the bed. In one corner sat the distraught Murakami, his knees drawn up to his chest. He was rocking rhythmically back and forth, tears rolling down his cheeks. Ayumi went over to him and placed a comforting arm around his shoulders. Kato sat at the bedside table, filling in some forms and documents; our eyes met, and he shrank into himself. He steadied himself to receive my anger and literally drew his hands to his face as I approached. The body of Hosokawa lay on the bed covered by a thin white bedsheet. The smell of human excrement hung heavily in the air.

"Kato, what happened here?" I asked.

The doctor seemed relieved that I had taken a civil tone with him and not pointed an accusing finger in his direction. He shook his head from side to side, and kept his voice low for my ears only. "Without doubt the cause of death is cardiac arrest, but there is something suspiciously premeditated about this whole sorry affair."

I gave him a hard look that demanded further explanation. Kato drew back the bedsheet, and I looked down at Hosokawa's husk of a corpse. I had often heard it said that the recently deceased took on an almost childlike or angelic repose, but for Hosokawa there was no such parting glory. He was blanched, save for the blue tinge around his eyes and lips. His mouth was agape, and his yellowed teeth stood out in shocking contrast. I noticed his fingers and toes were also blue.

Kato looked at me with an expression I found difficult to read. "I saw something similar to this once before—five years ago, to be precise, a poor fellow by the name of Ono whose heart gave up in the same fashion."

I looked at the doctor with contempt and hissed aggressively. "Really, and was this Ono fellow also a patient of yours? Did you give him free access to your needles, too?" Kato's anger quickly rose, but he knew better than to let it surface here, especially as he must have harboured an element of doubt about whether his own injection had hastened Hosokawa on his way. Any further sparring between us was halted by the arrival of the local doctors, who asked us to step aside whilst they went about examining Hosokawa's body. It was all too impersonal for decent taste, so I went over to Ayumi and Murakami and firmly suggested we withdraw to the lounge and join the loafing police officers. We did not have long to wait—no more than ten minutes—before the two doctors emerged and declared they were both satisfied that death was the result of a cardiac arrest and not suspicious in itself.

The information was received with relief by the scruffy police officer, who now thought it safe to identify himself as Captain Hernandez and was no doubt thankful that he had been spared the stress of a difficult investigation. The captain ordered his men to stand down and said that we were free to make arrangements for the repatriation of our recently deceased colleague.

I took Ayumi to one side and said we ought to make those arrangements as soon as possible. She agreed, and it was decided that we would leave for home at the earliest opportunity. I would work with Tanezawa and the airport authorities to arrange a private charter, perhaps as early as that afternoon. The hotel manager, relieved that nothing untoward had blemished the reputation of his fine hostelry, was more than willing to assist with the formalities, such as casketing up poor Makoto for his final journey and seeing to the transport arrangements. I also instructed him to immediately send messages to Tokyo to inform them of the sad turn of events. In my own mind I knew such a message was unnecessary, as it would be received only as mere confirmation of an order obeyed.

I did not hold much conviction that we would be able to depart as early as midafternoon, but I must admit I was pleasantly surprised by the speed and efficiency with which our arrangements were undertaken. Tanezawa went about her business with almost ice-cold efficiency. I believed she buried herself in her task in an effort to deny her grief. After all, she was particularly fond of Hosokawa and kept a special place in her heart for him, as she had come to believe that he was some kind of kindly benefactor who had "rescued" her from the strained circumstances of her previous life.

I decided to retire to my room, but ordered Tanezawa to clear any arrangements with me first. The undertakers were given a free hand to prepare Hosokawa for his heavenly departure, as none of us had the will to get too involved with that side of things. It proved difficult to procure a privately chartered aircraft at such short notice. It was Joel Richardson who came to the fore and drew on one of his connections at Civil Air Transport. I was assured that an aircraft would be waiting for us to depart at four in the afternoon.

There was one piece of outstanding business that needed to be resolved before we could depart. Romana would be waiting on his advance, and I did not doubt that our leaving would in some way be stalled if we failed to hold up our end of the agreement. Meursault was told to put the payment provisions in place and had spent the afternoon dealing with the intricacies of illegal untraceable finance.

Ayumi had also withdrawn to her room. She had refused the offer of some calming medication, preferring to confront her grief with all the stoicism and resolve she could muster. Bad situations never failed to bring out the best in humanity, and people did tend to show their mettle under adversity. If this were not the case, then how could wars ever be fought?

There was little left for me to occupy myself. My case was packed, and I had long since changed into my black mourning suit. I lay back on my bed, fighting the waves of fatigue that crashed around inside my head. The events of the last three days had finally caught up with me, but I refused to succumb to sleep, which would have been tantamount to weakness. Nevertheless, I closed my eyes and tried to make sense of all that had happened. I asked myself if I had missed some kind of vital connection. The question that most deserved an answer was obvious. Why did Hosokawa have to die here, in this city far from home? Why not wait until circumstances were completely within our remit?

The knock on my door rattled my nerves and brought me back to harsh reality. It was Tanezawa. She had come to inform me that Hosokawa was prepared and all arrangements were in place for our transfer to the airport. She also asked me if I would like to view the body before the casket was sealed for the journey. Her manner was brusque, and her eyes seemed colder than usual. I felt a shiver run through my veins. Unwilling though I was, I acquiesced and followed Tanezawa along the corridor. We walked together in silence; any words would have been inappropriate and unnecessary.

The open casket was in a room that looked like it was normally used for storage—quite appropriate under the circumstances. It was not far from the laundry room and the rear exit where I had snuck out the previous evening. The hotel had arranged for most of the clutter to be removed, and some impressive flower displays had been stacked against the wall. The casket was heavy looking and a grand affair, made from dark wood and decorated with intricate carvings of trees, flowers, and mountains along its side. It was supported on a wheeled trestle, and the lid was underneath. Two undertakers stood solemnly against the rear wall, their heads lowered in deferential respect. The pair of them bowed and left us alone to pay our final respects.

Tanezawa bade me to step forward, and cautiously I obliged. The body before my eyes bore little resemblance to the one I had seen earlier that morning. Hosokawa's face had been shaved clean and was heavily made up. Some kind of flesh-colored compound had been carefully blended with rouge and applied to his cheekbones, his eyes looked like they had been lined with ladies' eyeliner, and even his lips had a sheen of red about them. His hair had been greased back and his mouth fastened shut. He was laid out, dressed in a black suit, white shirt, and fine silk floral-patterned necktie that seemed to hint of his once renowned flamboyance. His arms were crossed across his body in an angelic repose. Hosokawa certainly looked finer in death than he had in the latter stages of life.

Truth be told, I could now say I felt little or no remorse for my part in his demise. I was merely the instrument of death, not the cause. If blame were to be assigned, then others had a greater need to look at themselves than I did.

Tanezawa stood alongside me and looked down for one final glimpse of the man she had once idolised. Then, rather shockingly and in an act that seemed to lack all respect, she placed her handbag on Hosokawa's chest and took out a small wooden box about the size of a book. She opened the box and showed me what it contained: Ismarelda's necklace, glittering against the photograph of Azusa. It was a stunning and shocking indictment, one that said more than any words could do justice. Toshio Hamazaki had made a statement. He had sought and found retribution. Hosokawa's death had not been enough; somehow he had to take a piece of Romana's pride too. Quite how he had forced the necklace to be returned I do not know. As I have said many times, I was merely a small player in a grander game. Tanezawa placed the box into the folds of Hosokawa's jacket and then called in the undertakers to seal the coffin. Once the lid was bolted down, it was locked by means of an ornately inscribed locking device which required a long key to free it. Tanezawa then placed that into the care of her bag.

I had many questions to ask of Tanezawa, but I knew they could wait. This was not the time or place, but I knew our own working relationship had moved into new and unfamiliar ground. She told the undertakers to load the coffin into the hearse, and with the help of a few hotel porters they carefully carried it out to the rear of the building while we watched. They used the staff corridors to avoid offending the delicate sensibilities of the hotel's regular clientele. Any staff we passed along the way turned their backs to us in a traditional mark of respect for the dead. Tanezawa explained to me that they had to be extremely careful not to let the casket touch any of the walls or fittings, as local custom held that any collision would mean the building would be forever haunted by the spirit of the deceased.

Our convoy made its way solemnly out to Nichols Field airstrip. We drove at a respectful pace, and I noticed that many of the local folk still followed the custom of turning their backs on the approaching hearse. The motorcade drove straight to the steps of the waiting aircraft—which to my dismay was an old-style propeller-driven DC-4. I knew we would be in for a longer journey than we would have liked, but my disappointment was dwarfed by the joy of finally leaving this place. The cars drew to a halt, and we were told to board the aircraft first and then the coffin would be loaded into the hold.

A farewell party had gathered at the steps of the aircraft. I noticed that the hotel manager, along with some of his staff, had taken the time to come say their final farewells. A small number from the Japanese mission in the Philippines along with some members of the Mabuhay Foundation's regular staff had also gathered. Ayumi and Tanezawa were to be the first to board, but as they were about to climb the steps, amongst the crowd Ayumi spotted the headmaster from the school we had visited the previous day. He seemed to be in an inordinate state of distress, and naturally she approached to console him. I walked over to her side as she was telling the others to go ahead and board. The headmaster, whose name had entirely escaped my memory, was in the throes of genuine grief. Ayumi calmed him with soothing platitudes as he expressed his sorrow for our loss. Then he told us that that very morning he had suffered a loss of his own and was overcome with sorrow for all our sakes. Ayumi sensitively asked him about his own loss, and through his tears he told her that one of his teachers had been attacked and murdered by bandits.

My blood ran ice cold, for I knew he need not say her name. It would be Gloria, the girl with the beautiful smile whose only mistake in this world was to ask me if I was lost. My fears were confirmed as he did indeed say her name, his voice becoming smaller as the plane started cranking up its engines. Ayumi placed a consoling hand on his shoulder and said that the foundation would look after her family and she would personally make arrangements for such provision once back in Tokyo.

Time did not permit us to linger any longer. Ayumi made her way up the aircraft steps, stopped at the top, and gave a final wave to the assembled folk. I waited until she was safely aboard and then turned to the headmaster and asked if the police had apprehended anyone for this heinous crime. He said no, but it was early days yet. He shook his head in tearful disbelief. "Such a lovely, innocent girl. They took her eyes, they took her eyes." He clutched at my sleeve as he repeated his sad words, which were confirmation if ever it were needed that Romana had extracted a price for his humiliation. An eye for an eye, and it had been aimed at me personally. There was nothing to be done now, but I swore I would have my revenge and prayed for the day when Hamazaki finally decided that Romana had outlived his purpose. I expressed my condolences and climbed the stairs.

Just as they were about to remove the wheel jams, I took one last look out across the runway, and through the heat haze, swore I saw Romana looking on from the rear of a limousine. Or was it just the heat playing tricks with my emotions?

Chapter 10
Sakura Tanezawa
United States of America
1970

Why in heaven's name we had agreed to do this, I did not know. Six months earlier it had all seemed like a fine notion, but even then I'd had serious reservations about the wisdom of Toshio's appearing on a television show that would be seen by millions, coast to coast. But now, as the nerves and reality started to hit home, six months felt like a lifetime ago. The invitation to be a guest on Small World had appealed to Toshio's vanity like a siren blaring in a storm. I hoped he would dismiss it out of hand, but to everyone's amazement, he embraced it and said it would be the perfect stage from which to announce his arrival to the American public at large. After all, it was here that success was celebrated and praise was heaped on the deserving, and in Toshio's mind, no one was more deserving than he was. It was hard to deny his logic. In the land where the dollar was king, Toshio Hamazaki must therefore be God—the wealthiest man in the world, a man whose riches were beyond calculation, a man whose company was known the world over and whose products touched the lives of nearly every person on the planet. Indeed, America wanted to hear from Toshio Hamazaki.

It was six months ago when Toshio and Hideo decided that an "inspection" tour of Mabuhay facilities across the United States would be a sound public relations move and two months were blocked out for an extensive cross-country sojourn that would take in all aspects of Mabuhay and Sonic's research, development, manufacturing, and commercial retail interests. The tour was organised to coincide with the twentieth anniversary of Mabuhay's founding. When the intention to visit the United States had been made public knowledge, a plethora of invitations had arrived at the Mabuhay offices in Tokyo. From the White House to flea circuses and everything in between, it seemed everyone wanted to share time with Toshio Hamazaki. Of course we were selective about who would be graced with our presence, and given the constraints of time, I believed we had managed to take in a broad spectrum of American life.

Right now, Toshio was about to spend the next ten minutes beamed out to television screens in millions of homes across the nation. We had agonised together for hours about whether his English was sufficient for the challenge, but Toshio dismissed all concerns with a wave of his hand. It took an inordinate amount of persuasion to get him finally to agree to be flanked by an interpreter, in order to avoid any uncomfortable pauses in the chat. Because he was flamboyant and extroverted by nature, I honestly believed he saw himself as some kind of idol who deserved to be feted and adored, just like the movie stars he spent hours watching on his private screen in Ginza. So here we found ourselves, in the makeup room of a television studio in New York.

The show was already underway, and the host, Darren Allen, was getting great audience response from his first guest of the evening, the popular comedian Pete Silver. We could hear the continual rumble of hysterical laughter drifting backstage. I looked at

Toshio sitting there in the makeup chair, and for a moment I believed I saw a flash of self-doubt as he seemed to question the wisdom of mixing entertainment with business. The raucous crowd only seemed to play on his nerves. The makeup girl applied a creamy foundation to Toshio's long, angular face and gave him a slight touch of dark rouge to accentuate his cheekbones. His shoulder-length hair, now laced with streaks of grey, was oiled back behind his ears. He gave a little smile into the mirror and tilted his head this way and that, checking his angles. For his appearance he had chosen a gaily patterned floral wine-red waist-coat to strike a contrast with his sober charcoal lounge suit. At fifty-two years of age Toshio was still an imposing figure, striking and graceful and handsome in a gothic sense. He had told me that he wanted to break the mould of how the average American thought of a typical Japanese businessman, and now the American public was about to find out he was most certainly not the arche-typal Japanese businessman.

A young man put his face around the door and announced that we had ten minutes to stage time. Toshio swivelled around in his chair and spread his arms out wide and looked at me. "Tanezawa, how do I look? Is America ready for me?"

I smiled, faked my best American accent, and said, "Go knock 'em dead, boss."

A stagehand appeared and led Toshio away, ready for his entrance. I decided to forfeit my seat in the audience for a place in the wings and waited as preparations were made for Toshio's introduction. At this very moment in homes across the country, televisions were broadcasting commercials and messages from sponsors. Perhaps some viewers had switched their sets off, believing a Japanese businessman would not be able to provide the kind of entertainment they were accustomed to. I peered out at the audience; I could make out only the first three rows, but spotted our party on the front row, centre section. Azusa Hosokawa, despite being a widow for the past five years, looked stunning and relaxed, obviously enjoying being so close to the glamour of the small screen. Sitting alongside her was Joel Richardson, chairman of Sonic and Mabuhay's man in America. Ken Miyazaki was talking with Ayumi Tanaka and pointing out something or other. Ayumi's son, Tatsuya, was straining to hear what they were saying, but they did not seem to want to share their comments. Tatsuya was now a young man of fifteen, and nature had not dealt him a particularly good hand.

He was rather overweight, and this was compounded by a lack of height. Still, he was jolly enough, and seemed to be enjoying himself on this, his first visit overseas. I looked at him and Ayumi and sighed: the two obstacles to my own complete happiness. Hideo had chosen to remain in Tokyo to keep an eye on things on that end. In truth I believed he could not bear to be in such close proximity to his family with me in tow. Wife, son, and lover—too many complexities for a man like Hideo Tanaka.

The footlights dimmed, and a red light started flashing to indicate the countdown to live broadcast time. The stage lights were raised, and the theme music to Small World struck up. Darren Allen stepped out of the opposite wing into centre stage; he looked every bit the model host, relaxed and unflappable. I wondered how Toshio was feeling at this time. "Ladies and gentlemen, boys and girls across the country, welcome back to Small World." There was an appreciative round of applause, and Allen continued. "My next guest this evening does not come from the world of show business or the arts, oh no. His domain is a world where you have to be tough to survive, and to get to the top and manage to stay there takes a lot of—what's that word? Well, why don't we ask him? Please welcome the chairman and owner of the Mabuhay Company, Mr Toshio Hamazaki."

Toshio stepped out onto the stage, and the theme music played whilst he settled into his chair opposite Allen. The audience gave an audible gasp of surprise. Obviously he was not what they had been expecting; a dandy tycoon might not prove to be so dull after all. Allen opened the exchange, aiming to put Toshio at ease. "Mr Hamazaki, welcome to the United States—and may I say, I like your vest." Laughter rippled around the room.

"Thank you so much, Mr Allen. I will give you the name of my tailor later." This drew an even bigger laugh, which brought a wide smile to Toshio's face.

Allen went on. "Mr Hamazaki, if you would allow me a moment and let me expand a little on your introduction for the benefit of viewers who may not be familiar with your achievements." Allen spun in his chair to face another camera and began his prepared delivery. "Mr Toshio Hamazaki is the founder and chairman of Mabuhay, the world's leading electronics company, a company that accounts for over fifty per cent of all global domestic sales. Perhaps you are even watching this show on one of his TV sets right now. He is regarded as an industry pioneer and innovator, and has been credited with changing the very way we live our lives. Every household across the country has cause to be thankful for his time-saving appliances. He has been awarded honours and distinctions from governments around the world, and if all that is not enough, he is widely regarded as the richest man in the world."

The audience broke into a round of applause at this last statement, for everyone in this country understood money. On receiving such a glowing welcome Toshio smiled and bowed his head slightly in acknowledgement. He turned to Allen and said, "You make it sound as if I have done all that by myself. I have to say, much of the credit is owing to my business partner, Hideo Tanaka, who unfortunately could not make the trip this time, and our team of amazing experts."

Allen nodded his understanding and then pursued with his light touch—that is to say, giving the interview a semblance of entertainment. "Mr Hamazaki, what does it feel like to be the richest man in the world?" There were a few whoops of delight from the audience as they took on board Allen's daring question.

Toshio moved around a little in his seat and looked Allen straight in the eye. "It feels no different from any other time in my life. I am still the same person I have always been. My life is relatively simple, and I do not have any great desires. I never strived to become a wealthy man. It is just a by-product of good, honest endeavour mixed with a fair helping of luck."

Allen stroked his chin, leaned closer to Toshio, and said in a conspiratorial tone, "Yet it must be great to be able to do anything you want, or buy anything at all. I hear the Empire State Building is up for sale. Are you interested in that?" Allen's joke fell a little flat, and I noticed he was trying to bait Toshio out of his cautionary stance, but from experience I knew Toshio would only get more confident as the interview progressed.

"Maybe," Toshio said. "How much is it? We could all do with a landmark or two in the portfolio. King Kong is one of my favourite movies, after all." Toshio's rather facetious comment seemed to go over the heads of most of the audience, but they laughed politely.

Allen pressed on. "Is there anything you are particularly looking forward to seeing or doing during your stay here in this great country of ours?"

"I am looking forward to so many things; every day will be like a new adventure. It does not have to be special to have meaning. We can all learn from the ordinary as well as the extraordinary."

My word, Toshio Hamazaki had turned into a philosopher. He was trying to impart some words of wisdom, but sensing he was starting to lose his audience, he moved on to lighter areas. "I am also looking forward to a glass or two of your excellent bourbon. Also, our party has been invited to the opening night of the Elvis Presley show in Las Vegas, an evening we are truly looking forward to with great excitement."

Allen turned to the crowd and said, "Bourbon and Presley in Vegas—doesn't get more American than that." The crowd applauded—in appreciation of what exactly, I was not sure, but Toshio seemed pleased with the response.

Allen raised his hand, and the crowd hushed a little. "Mr Hamazaki, don't forget your little date at the White House too."

Toshio moved his hands from side to side to indicate that it was of no significance. I knew he wanted to avoid any talk of politics, especially because Richard Nixon was not the most popular president the country had ever had, and the nation's military was mired in the struggle over Vietnam. "Yes, it is an honour to be invited to the White House. I wonder what presidents serve for dinner."

Some wag from the audience shouted, "Humble pie," which drew the biggest laugh of the evening.

Allen, not wishing to be upstaged, said his audience was on form and maybe a few questions from selected members would be in order. He asked Toshio if he was willing to field a question or two. "Of course, please go ahead," Toshio said.

This was not part of the running order, and I noticed Toshio tense up a little. Nonetheless, I did not have too many concerns, because it was a live broadcast, and I doubted the network would allow any controversy to hijack their show.

Allen asked for questions, and about half the audience shot their hands up. He chose a young fellow wearing a bright red pullover who stood, and a mike was lowered from the ceiling to pick up his voice. "Mr Hamazaki, welcome to America. My question is this: Has your company in any way, shape, or form profited from the war in Vietnam, and do you think it is morally acceptable to make money out of people's sufferings?"

Allen looked at Hamazaki. "That is a very heavy question, and I apologise for putting you on the spot, but at this time in our nation's history, maybe it is a question that deserves a response."

Toshio's interpreter leaned close and whispered something in his ear, and then Toshio cleared his throat and spoke. "It is my view that all wars are the scourge of humanity and a blight on our civilization, and yet we fail to learn from history. Given that I hold such a view, it would be reprehensible for my company to profit from the sufferings of others. However, I will not try to conceal the fact that some of our technology has been used for military purposes. With a company as large as ours, it is an inevitability, but I will make this promise to you all: Whatever profits have been made, I will personally ensure they are unconditionally turned into projects that aid those afflicted by the war. That is my promise." It was a conciliatory answer and one well received for its honesty, but it was unlikely to appease the antiwar lobby, who had the mega-capitalists in their sights.

Allen looked all serious and scanned the audience for another question. He picked out a sombre-looking women in a kind of pinafore dress. "Mr Hamazaki, my question is a little personal, and I apologise in advance if it causes you offence, but are you a practicing homosexual?" There was a great rumble amongst the audience as they collectively took a giant intake of breath.

Allen raised his hands and said, "Now, that is far too personal, and on behalf of the station I would like to apologise to Mr Hamazaki and move on to the next question."

Toshio raised his hand and stared at the woman, who was still standing and now looked more than a little nervous. "Madam, why do you ask such a question of me?"

She looked down and then found her voice. "Like many others in this fine country of ours, I believe homosexuality to be a sin in the eyes of our Lord, and as so many of our good citizens are employed by you here in America, I think they have a right to know what kind of man they work for."

There was the odd cry of "Hear, hear," but for the most part, the audience fell silent. Even Allen's eyes were fixed on Toshio.

"Very well," Toshio said. "In that case I will give you an answer. If I were a practicing homosexual—and having reached the age of fifty-two, I would hope to consider myself more than accomplished, thank you very much—and anyone felt compelled to withdraw their labour from my employ for whatever reason, then I would, with regret, accept their resignation tomorrow or at any time. I hope that has made things clear for you."

His brutal honesty was shocking in the extreme, and the audience did not know whether to applaud or heckle him. I looked out, trying to gauge their feelings, but their faces were swathed in the darkness of the studio. There was a ripple of applause, and then it grew into something else until the majority were on their feet applauding. It seemed that we had the most liberal-minded audience ever assembled, but I knew there would be repercussions. Allen stood to shake the hand of Toshio, who was on his feet, milking the limelight. For a man who had just nailed his sexuality to a post, he looked mighty calm, but I could not stop myself from asking whether 1970 America was ready for such a bold move.

Allen turned side-on to the camera and made his closing remarks. "A great big thank-you to our guests this evening, Mr Pete Silver and Mr Toshio Hamazaki. Thank you for tuning in to Small World, and we look forward to seeing you next week at the same time. Until then, stay safe and happy. Good night." The applause seemed genuine enough, but as the house lights came up and the magic of television disappeared, I knew it would be only a matter of time before we felt the fallout.

I hurried backstage to the small reception area where drinks and canapés had been set out on a large table. Toshio was already there, and I saw he had already been served with a drink. He was talking to the young stagehand and looked very relaxed, as he always did when there were drinks to hand. Pete Silver was also there; he was surrounded by a group of his friends and had them rolling in laughter, although I could not for the life of me think what could be so funny. Perhaps we Japanese were not accustomed to loud, raucous laughter or other ostentatious displays of public emotion. Silver kept his entourage entertained, and his mirth was unrelenting. I joined Toshio just in time to hear him explain to the young stagehand something about the time difference between Tokyo and New York and how he felt fortunate to have been granted an extra fourteen hours, a debt of time that would have to be wearily paid back on his return to Tokyo. Toshio introduced me to his new friend. "Sakura, this is Geoffrey; he works here at the studio. Geoffrey, this is my personal assistant for the duration of this visit, Sakura Tanezawa. Actually, I have 'borrowed' her from my sister, as her skills are second to none. She's a gem amongst our staff."

I greeted Geoffrey politely whilst wondering how many drinks Toshio had taken on board; his introduction was far too gushing with praise, even for Toshio. I had not seen him take a drink before going on set, but there had been ample opportunity to imbibe whilst being prepared. Was it the drink that had loosened his tongue and caused him to slap Mother America in the face? We were soon joined by the rest of our party, and from the morose looks on their faces, I gathered that Toshio's little performance had not played well.

Ayumi looked most distraught, and for a moment I thought she might actually break down in tears. Without doubt she, like the rest of us, must have known about Toshio's sexual predilections. Perhaps it was the shock of having him brazenly air them in front of the world that had hit her so hard. Ken Miyazaki was his usual laid-back self, acting as if nothing out of the ordinary had occurred. If anything, he was more concerned with Ayumi's increasing level of distress. Joel Richardson looked downright angry and no doubt would have loved to spit his venom in Toshio's direction had he sufficient mettle to do so. I had seen Richardson unleash his anger on countless occasions, bullying underlings with the foulest language and threats of beatings, but he knew it was in his best interests to hold his tongue where Toshio Hamazaki was concerned.

We all stood around awkwardly. Nobody quite knew what to say, and each of us politely skirted around the subject. Toshio called over a server and ordered a round of drinks for us all. I checked my watch and silently prayed that this was not going to turn into a long-winded drinking session. Surprisingly it was Tatsuya who ventured to be a little conversationally daring. "Uncle Toshio, that stuff you said in the interview—I mean, you were only joking, right? Having a little fun?"

Toshio beamed at him and said, "Tatsuya, I was most certainly having fun, and I guess there was a little joking, too, but I do have a serious side." He slugged his drink back in one gulp, and before the waiter had time to leave, asked him for another of the same.

Ayumi could no longer contain her frustration and edged up to Toshio. Her voice trembling and barely audible, she said, "Brother, my word, I am speechless. What were you thinking? Why would you wish to share your private life with the world? Have you given even a moment's thought to what this will mean back home?"

Toshio looked from one glum face to another. Perhaps for the first time his eyes showed a hint of regret, but it was there only for a second or two before he snapped, "Listen, all of you. I have lived my life in fear of being exposed and I have taken great measures to protect my privacy, but I did not have the will to continue in such a fashion. This evening the perfect opportunity presented itself, and I took advantage of it. Now I feel as if a weight has been removed from my shoulders, and furthermore, I do not care one fig for the thoughts of anyone else. As Allen said, I am the richest man in the world and can do anything I damn well like, and that includes living my life as I please. If any of you do not like that, then slip your resignation letters under my hotel door at your convenience. Now, I believe there is no more to be said on the matter. Is that perfectly clear?" His face was boiling with raw emotion, his frustration barely under control. We all nodded like chastised children.

The waiter appeared with Toshio's drink, which he grabbed and slung back before banging the glass down on the tray. He called over to Geoffrey. "We are leaving now. Please arrange for our cars to line up." Geoffrey turned on his heels, dashing out to see to his task.

As we all started to follow him out, Silver's voice carried across the room. "Hamazaki, leaving already? One word of warning, my friend. Be careful down in the Bible Belt. Down there they are not as friendly as we sophisticated New Yorkers appear to be."

Hamazaki turned to him and said, "Thank you for the advice, Mr Silver. It was an honour to meet you, and I wish you continued good fortune in your comedy career." Hamazaki's tone held a hint of sarcasm, as if he had intentionally belittled Silver in front of his friends. I noticed that Silver picked up on it too and for a moment lost his bravado. We left him to his lapdog friends and made our way out of the studios.

There was no sign of Allen to bid us farewell, and it was down to Geoffrey himself to lead us out to our waiting limousines. It was raining heavily, but several pressmen had braved the elements to get shots of Toshio as he departed. The rain thundered down as Toshio and I dashed into the first limousine. Before the door slammed shut behind us, I heard one of the pressmen shout out, "Mr Hamazaki, are you a Communist sympathiser?"

Toshio missed the remark, and I did not want to risk his ire by repeating it. We sat in silence for most of the journey, but as we pulled into the Plaza Hotel forecourt, Toshio turned to me and said, "Sakura, do you think I have made a great mistake?"

I shook my head. "I believe you are one of the bravest men I know. What you said took courage, and it's never a mistake to stand alongside your convictions."

He smiled and said, "Thank you, Sakura. You are a good woman." He winked at me and said, "Maybe we should get married. That would confuse the hell out of them." He was still laughing at his own humour as he got out of the car and stepped into a barrage of blinding light while camera flashbulbs popped from all directions.

With a little help from the doormen, a path through the melee of eager newsmen was cleared, and Toshio cut a dignified figure as he made his way into the hotel, ignoring the shouts from a desperate press pack. He was still wearing his stage makeup, and it was difficult to escape the feeling that he was an unwitting actor who had stumbled into the wrong scene. It was a whirl of confusion, and I was shocked at the aggressive furore Toshio seemed to have caused. Once safely inside the lobby, we looked back at the small crowd, which was being kept at bay by a crew made up of bellhops and security staff. A police siren could be heard, and flashing red and white lights heralded the arrival of a more competent form of crowd control. We waited for the other members of our party, and once they too had been safely escorted into the hotel, we started to make our way to our rooms. The hotel manager came over and apologised for the unruly scene outside the lobby. Toshio merely smiled and told him it was nothing to be alarmed about, and then in typical Hamazaki style, he in turn apologised for being the cause of the problem.

Just as we were about to take the elevator, I heard a voice calling from across the lobby. It was Harold Weinstein, looking all flustered and windswept. He was carrying a battered old brown leather briefcase, and his overcoat looked drenched from the downpour that he had obviously been caught in. "Toshio, I am relieved to catch up with you. I think we need to have a quick talk. Can you spare me a moment or two?" Weinstein was Mabuhay's corporate lawyer stateside and one of the sharpest legal minds in the country. He was also Toshio's personal lawyer and handled all kinds of legal issues, the majority of which I was not privy to.

Toshio looked Weinstein up and down, and for a moment I thought he was going to refuse him an audience. I was mistaken, of course. Nobody—not even Toshio—could afford to ignore Harold Weinstein, especially with the evening's commotion still whirling about the place. Hamazaki and Weinstein had been thrown together, both great men who took over from where their fathers had left off. Weinstein Senior, who was still alive but quite senile, was Hamazaki's father's representative and took care of the old man's business interests in the States before the war put paid to any further cooperation between the two. It was only natural that Toshio should turn once more to the Weinstein family to take care of Mabuhay's legal interests. Toshio spun on his heels, calling out to the following Weinstein, "Lobby bar. I need a drink, and I do believe there may be a secluded table to be found. Sakura, feel free to join us if you please." I had been around long enough to realise that it was not a request but an order. I trailed after the two men into the Oak Room bar.

Because it was quite late in the evening and the clientele was rather thin on the ground, Toshio had his pick of any table. He indicated a small table in the corner and told the bar maître d' that we required privacy, a bottle of the finest Kentucky bourbon, and three glasses. We settled into our chairs and made small talk whilst the waiter served up the drink and a pitcher of icy water. Toshio expressed concern about Weinstein Senior's health, and sadness when told the old man's days were marked. He shook his head and poured three generous measures of bourbon. He drank his own in one and poured himself a second measure, then leaned back in his chair, hands behind his head, and stared at Weinstein. "So Harold, what drags you out of your warm abode on a night like this?" Before Weinstein could respond, Toshio with a sly smile tried to guess his reply. "I think you must have been watching your television and something sent you to my door."

Weinstein smiled playfully as he indulged Toshio a little. "Of course I was watching, and may I say that for the most part you came across quite well. In fact I was impressed. However, not everyone is of the same feeling."

Toshio groaned theatrically, but he was still smiling. "Well, let me have the bad news. I presume that is why you are here?" Weinstein looked at me and then back to Toshio, who gave him a withering look. "Harold, say what you want. Sakura is discretion personified. I asked her to sit in with us because I hoped to spare you any unnecessary embarrassment. I mean, just the two of us having a drink together, people might reach the wrong conclusions."

Hamazaki laughed out loud at his own humour, but I noticed Weinstein blushed a little before regaining his authoritative composure. "I received a call from the White House press office this evening. Nixon has withdrawn your invitation to dinner. No specific reason was given, but I think we can safely assume it has much to do with this evening's events." To me this was a bombshell of an insult. I feared Toshio's reaction, but he was calm and nodded thoughtfully. He looked at me and said, "Well, Sakura, it seems I now have a free evening tomorrow. What do you suggest?" He laughed and slapped his thigh in a show of high-spirited humour. Weinstein looked even more uncomfortable as he spoke again. "There is one more point. The New York Times also called. It seems they have you pegged as some sort of Communist sympathiser. They picked up on a comment you made about helping all victims of war. The war in Vietnam may be very unpopular, but patriotism still runs high. I think it may have been wiser to have shown a little more tact, perhaps coming down on the side of Uncle Sam a little more."

This time Hamazaki did not smile, and his eyes reflected an anger coursing through his veins. With a coolness that belied his emotion he turned to me and told me to go and call Meursault in Geneva and arrange for him to get the next flight to New York. I stood and left them to their talk. In all truth I was grateful to escape, as I feared things might get a little fractious. I knew that Toshio was planning his next move and it would involve some kind of financial counteraction; that is why I had been ordered to contact Meursault, the man who made the money go round and round. I left the Oak Room, glancing over my shoulder to see Weinstein heave his briefcase onto the table. It seemed like the two men had some business to get through that evening, and I knew it would include things that were not meant for my ears.

I thought it best to make the call to Meursault from a direct line, so I went straight to the front desk and told the clerk that I needed to place an international call to Europe and would appreciate the use of a secured line. He was all too happy to assist, and within minutes I found myself alone in the assistant manager's office, dialling the number for the international exchange. The efficiency of American communications services was far more advanced than that of our own, and I had no trouble placing my call through to the Zurich office of Meursault Reinhardt and Company. I was connected to the bank's switchboard operator who handled calls outside of normal working hours. I looked at the clock on the wall and calculated it to be a little after five in the morning over in Zurich. I allowed myself a wry smile as I pictured grumpy old Meursault woken early from his sleep and plunged into even greater depths of confusion as he realised that he must get himself across the Atlantic without hesitation. The voice that boomed down the phone line was French, a language I knew little of. I answered in English and gave our client code, a number Hamazaki had forced me to memorise. There was a moment's hesitation, and then a different voice came down the line. It was a man's voice, rather pompous but efficient and to the point. No doubt Mabuhay's billions had caught their undivided attention. "How may we be of assistance to you today?"

In return, I too was brief and to the point. "We require the presence of Monsieur Meursault in New York. He is requested to take the earliest flight possible, and we are to greet him at the Plaza Hotel. It is a matter of the upmost urgency."

There was a pause and then the man said, "I will make sure Monsieur Meursault receives your message without delay and he is in touch with you as soon as time allows. Would that be all?" I concluded with thanks and hung up. Dealing with Meursault's bank never failed to impress me, and I was always in awe of how business could be conducted without even exchanging names. I guess the code number said all there was to say. I left the office and thanked the staff for allowing me the use of their facilities, and went back into the lobby. It had certainly quieted down since our hectic arrival a little over an hour ago. I thought about returning to the Oak Room to see if I was needed for any further tasks before retiring for the night, but considered that to be a little overly zealous. Besides, I did not want to interrupt any confidential matters, and in truth, I felt Hamazaki was better left to his own problems. Over the years I had witnessed many a foul temper and mood swing, and it appeared the events of this evening were sufficient to trigger the most extreme reactions. Fatigue was setting in, and I was looking forward to my sleep.

As I walked across the lobby towards the elevators, I suddenly had the strangest feeling that I was being observed. Looking around the lobby I noticed that most of the patrons were men and that several were seated on sofas reading newspapers. Well, I believed it to be slightly odd that at eleven at night, anybody would find a day-old newspaper so compelling. I resisted the urge to stare and kept on walking straight. The lure of a night's rest was more compelling than falling prey to my sense of paranoia.

I rode the elevator up to the eighteenth floor. My room was just to the left of the elevator doors, and as I stepped out onto the corridor, I suddenly realised that I had forgotten to collect my door key from the front desk. The irritation I felt was compounded by the tiredness sweeping over me. I banged the call button and waited a few minutes for the elevator to return. As the doors opened, a heavy aroma of Turkish cigar smoke wafted out. I knew of only one man who smoked those foul things. Toshio must have called time on his day and retired up to his penthouse suite.

I braved the confines of the smoky elevator and within seconds was back walking across the lobby. Three men were sitting together on one of the sofas, seemingly in deep conversation, which was odd, as I remembered them sitting separately only minutes earlier. My presence caught them unawares, and it was almost comical as they tried to feign nonchalance, as if nothing were untoward. I walked past them and noticed the strange earpiece one of them had left dangling on his shoulder. That was all the confirmation I needed. It was obvious that some kind of government agency had us under observation—more than likely the Federal Bureau of Investigation. Without giving them a second glance I breezed past, retrieved my key from the front desk, and retraced my steps to my room.

When I opened my door, I noticed that someone had slid a note under it. It was from Ken Miyazaki and simply said, "Breakfast tomorrow morning at eight o'clock in the Palm Court." Tiredness prevented me from giving too much thought to why we were to have breakfast together, though it was no doubt tied into the enforced changes in our itinerary. Perhaps it would be an opportune moment to bring my suspicions that we were being kept under observation to someone's attention.

I went into the bathroom and filled the large marble tub with hot water, adding some mineral crystals which were kept in an ornate glass jar by the basin. As the bath was taking time to fill, I went into the bedroom to undress. I turned on the television as a background distraction, and distracted I most certainly was. There staring back at me from the screen was a still picture of Toshio. It seemed his appearance on Small World was now the cause of serious consternation. Two presenters, both quite sombre and serious, were discussing the evening's events. I heard one say, "Did Hamazaki actually admit to being a homosexual on live TV, or was he just fooling and making a play on words? Let's go to our current-affairs reporter, Max Jones, for his take on the matter."

Jones appeared on the screen. It looked as if his report had been captured on film earlier, right outside the main entrance of the Plaza Hotel. "I am standing outside the Plaza Hotel where Toshio Hamazaki and his party are staying, but there has not been any further comment from Mr Hamazaki himself. He arrived back here around ten, but dodged all the questions fired at him from the waiting press mob. What is still unclear is whether Mr Hamazaki was aware of what he was saying or got himself into difficulties with the English language. He is well known for his extroverted nature, and maybe he was merely trying to be entertaining in his own way."

There was a voice-over, presumably from the studio. "Max, could you tell us a little of what you know about Toshio Hamazaki?

I mean, apart from being the wealthiest man in the world, what is he really like?"

Jones looked drenched, as the rain had set in for the night, but he stoically faced the camera and continued to deliver his report. "Toshio Hamazaki is fifty-two years old and from a wealthy entrepreneurial family. He founded Mabuhay on the ruins of his father's business, Hamazaki Electricals, a company devastated by the effects of World War Two. From the very outset of his entrepreneurial career, Hamazaki has displayed a generous and benevolent attitude towards countries in Asia that suffered, and he pledged unconditional aid for humanitarian projects. He founded the Mabuhay Foundation, which is headed by his sister, Ayumi Tanaka, and is now the largest single donor of aid in the world. So we could say the man has an impeccable record as a philanthropist. However, there have from time to time been dissenting voices. Critics often say Hamazaki has used his wealth to gain advantages in developing markets, and others have said he has had too much political influence. He is often seen with senior government officials and even heads of state. Here in the States his business interests are served mainly through Mabuhay's subsidiary company, Sonic Enterprises, which is headed by Joel Richardson. Richardson is president of Sonic and also sits on the board of Mabuhay. I am pleased to say we have secured an exclusive interview with Mr Richardson, who has kindly agreed to give us a few minutes of his time."

The camera panned a little to the left, and there stood Richardson, being sheltered from the rain by a hotel employee holding a large umbrella, replete with Plaza Hotel logo, over his head. I could not believe my eyes. I was certain Richardson would not agree to an interview without Toshio's consent, but I could not recall an instance when they had talked. I wondered if Toshio was watching this up in his suite. Of course he must be, and I had the feeling that I was watching some kind of game unfold. This must have been agreed to beforehand.

"Mr Richardson, thank you for your time tonight," Jones said. "I understand you were actually quite close to the confusion of this evening's events. Can you shed any light on the matter?"

Richardson looked straight into the camera, determined to enjoy his few minutes of fame. "Well, I believe the whole thing has been blown up all out of proportion. Mr Hamazaki was having a little fun with us all. Perhaps his comments did not come across as he may have wished. He is truly bewildered by the furore he seems to have caused."

Jones came back at Richardson. "So are you saying there is no substance to Mr Hamazaki's comments, that they were merely flippant, off-the-cuff misinterpretations?"

Richardson was not the type of character to be pushed into a corner, and he retorted rather curtly, "To my knowledge, none whatsoever. Mr Hamazaki is here on a tour to inspect Sonic and Mabuhay business interests and facilities nationwide, and although he accepts that there will be a certain amount of media interest in his visit, he hopes he will be afforded a degree of privacy to go about his business and stick to his stated agenda."

Richardson looked pleased with himself, but Jones was a dogged reporter who obviously had sources of his own. He came back with a bombshell of a question. "Is it true that Mr Hamazaki's invitation to the White House has been withdrawn?"

This would be a hard corner to fight, and Richardson could not fall back on bluff alone. "Absolutely not. Mr Hamazaki will be one of the guests attending tomorrow evening's function at the White House." Jones's jaw literally dropped. It was obvious that he had heard that Toshio had been deleted from the guest list and that he was more than a little put out that his "exclusive" had fallen flat, as he could not reasonably follow up without compromising his source. I too was confused; I had heard Weinstein tell Toshio to his face that he had been uninvited. So, what had happened during the last hour, I did not know. Some grander game was afoot, but for the life of me, I could not fathom what it was. Jones concluded his interview by thanking Richardson, and then we were back to the studio, where the presenters turned their attention to the day's depressing events over in Vietnam.

I stripped off my clothes and went into the bathroom, where I soaked myself in a luxurious warm bath, but despite the overpowering tiredness that had me in its viselike grip, relaxation was now near impossible.

After a fitful night's rest where I seemed to be constantly woken by bouts of either hot or cold shivers, I eventually gave up on any further hope of refreshing sleep. It was seven in the morning and New York was coming back to life, ready to take on another day. I went over to the window and looked down at Fifth Avenue, which was already bustling with yellow cabs and folk on foot making their way to offices, shops, or morning diners. America appeared to be a mighty and industrious nation, complex and compelling and yet at times almost simplistic in its outlook. Our countries had once been bitter enemies, but as the years unfolded, we had moved closer together in a friendship that could only be described as awkward, a novice couple practicing unfamiliar dance steps. If we were as truthful as our hearts allowed, I believed, both countries would admit to harbouring a certain amount of suspicion and mistrust of the other. That is the inevitable consequence of a bitter conflict, one that has indelibly marked the conscience of two generations and at times rises to the surface and reveals itself in the form of moral indignation at some perceived wrongdoing or moral digression. It was evident that Toshio had triggered this emotion in many people, a public easily outraged and quick to condemn. His wealth did not sit comfortably with some who saw it as an indicator that times had changed and with it a shift in the economic balance of power. The power brokers of this fine nation were being forced to take notice.

Toshio Hamazaki was a master manipulator, and whatever game he was playing, it was obvious that even I was not to be brought into his confidence. Perhaps it had to do with my relationship with Hideo. I had been playing with fire for over six years. An illicit affair with Ayumi's husband had left me drained of moral fortitude, and yet I could not give him up. Though I had willed myself to find the strength to do so, it had proved to be beyond my emotional capability. I often wondered how much Toshio knew of the situation. Hideo and I had never spoken of this matter, and yet there were times when Toshio looked at me as if he could read my thoughts like a book. I was sure the man possessed a demonic magic that allowed him to undress your emotions and leave your thoughts naked before his eyes. At times I felt it was too much to bear and the temptation to throw in my lot became almost a pleasurable wanting, but I knew such notions were nothing but mere fantasy. I was a part of this life forever; Mabuhay, Hamazaki, Hideo, and everything that went along with it was my destiny.

The course of my life had been dictated by a fateful legacy, one that became known to me only when my supposed "benefactor," Makoto Hosokawa, in the final days of his life, told me some shocking truths. What had motivated him to finally speak out I could only guess. Perhaps he was confronting his own demons in preparation for the afterlife, but more likely, he was overcome by an overwhelming desire to create mischief, as befit his character. His mind was certainly disturbed in those final days; drug dependency had removed all notions of judgement and perhaps even his loyalties. I might never know the reasons he chose to tell me, but his words changed everything I had come to believe about myself.

Even my name was a lie. Fifteen years earlier I had been taken from my orphanage home by Hosokawa and given employment as an assistant to Ayumi Tanaka. It was only later that I came to realise that this was not merely a fortunate step in my life, but one that had been planned all along. I was part of a moral obligation to repay some of the emotional damage of the past. Hamazaki's father had forged my destiny, and I was to be taken into Mabuhay. Toshio had ensured that his father's wish was carried out.

It was only after Hosokawa's talk that I found the resolve to confront Toshio about the truth of my past. He told me everything I needed to know, and yet no doubt many things remained unspoken. Toshio had said it came as a great relief for him to finally be able to speak to me without hiding behind a false representation of the past. It was his hope that the truth would help me find some kind of harmony and understanding of the events that had shaped my life. He also gave me the choice to leave or stay without prejudice. That was five years ago and here I still was, looking down at Fifth Avenue, as far away from finding inner peace as any living soul could be, a prisoner of my fears and a loyal servant to the man whose father had killed my mother, or at the very least had done little to prevent her death.

I did my upmost to make myself appear presentable, but lack of sleep was showing all over my face. I seemed to have recently lost my sparkle. Perhaps it was the weight of the past that was finally bearing down. The more trust placed in me, the more I found myself sinking into a quagmire of guilt and deceit. I suppose I was flattered to be taken into Hamazaki's confidence, but it was a leap into the unknown for me, and at times I questioned my own strength of conviction. But now there was no turning back. That option had expired long ago. The only escape now would be to follow the path taken by Hosokawa, and I knew for sure I was not ready for that journey just yet.

As I was putting the finishing touches to my face, there was a light, jolly rap on my door. I knew who it was, and sure enough, I was correct. As I opened the door, Azusa brushed past me and flopped onto the bed. She looked fresh and full of life, and even though I was only four years her senior, I felt like a dowdy old maid by comparison. Widowhood had not dampened her ardour one bit; in fact she seemed to revel in her glorious status. Child bride of Hosokawa, married at seventeen and single again four years later, and, as the heiress to Hosokawa's fortune, well placed in certain people's eyes and untouchable in others. She was not to everyone's liking, if the truth were to be spoken—she was flirtatious and loose—and yet I had seen a different Azusa of late. She was a little more guarded when passing comments about others and perhaps more selective about whom she took to her bed. This morning she seemed put out about being summoned to the Palm Court for breakfast.

Azusa was not a morning person and could be quite grumpy if the mood took her, but today she was quite chatty in an offhand way. She was going on about Richardson and how he would not take no for an answer. It seemed the pair of them had visited some bar or other the evening before and Richardson had got a little overly frisky, allowing his drunken hands to lose control. She laughed as she told me how she had rendered him a blow with her handbag. It was obvious she enjoyed the attention and Richardson had pursued her for years. Maybe he had already tasted the prize— who knew? She was giggling and telling me how she had told him that she was saving herself for Elvis, which had sent him into a bout of jealous sulking. I wondered when Richardson had found the time to pursue his ardour, before or after his exclusive interview.

I left Azusa to entertain herself for a moment whilst I went into the bathroom to put the finishing touches to my face. I left the door slightly ajar and could hear her humming the melody of "Takeda Lullaby." She was gifted with the voice of an angel, and I truly believed she would have made a fine singer had she been inclined to follow such a vocation. It was her morbid habit to drift back in time, and the lullaby had seared itself into her consciousness. I looked into the bathroom mirror, and my eyes welled up uncontrollably as Azusa's sad lament brought back sad, haunting memories. We had all sung "Takeda Lullaby" at her husband's funeral, and every time I heard it, the door to the past opened and I stepped into a world of sorrow and solitude. I felt for her loss, though my raw emotion was personal and would be forever associated with that time in my life.

Five years had passed since she had lost her husband and I had learnt the truth about who I really was. I had found a part of myself, but the revelation had come with a great burden. My parents had been taken from this life under violent circumstances, murdered by evil men who had been motivated by greed and revenge. My poor sweet, innocent mother, a victim only of circumstance, was chosen to die in an inferno that was meant as a warning to others. Hamazaki had told me as much as he could, but much more was left unsaid. I knew I had been given a censored version of the truth. Toshio himself had adopted a sanitized version of the past, one that allowed him the freedom to still hold his own father in affectionate regard. He was at pains to put some distance between his father's involvement in my parents' demise, and emphasised the overbearing malice of others. I took pride in being no man's fool and I was not naïve. I knew there was more to be told, but to my shame I had neither the strength nor the fortitude to chase the ghosts that hid in my past.

Shortly after Hosokawa's funeral, Hamazaki had escorted me to Osaka to my mother's graveside, where we both prayed over her final resting place. The small patch of earth had long since become overgrown by weeds and brambles. I moved the wild foliage to one side and read the inscription on the mossy granite. "Mieko Kojima. Died January 13, 1946. Wife and mother." That was all that remained of my mother's memory, a stone that had been paid for by community donations and said nothing of the love she had given or received. As I stood by her graveside, I tried in earnest to will myself to remember her face, her touch, her smile, but it had all gone. Everything had turned grey years ago; my memories had been worn away by years of institutionalisation. I had been placed into an orphanage at six years old and given a new name, deprived of natural love. My circumstances had forced me to be constantly grateful for life's small mercies and had left me more damaged than I had realised. Perhaps all this would go some way towards explaining why I was naturally drawn to strong and powerful men. Hosokawa, Hamazaki, Miyazaki, and Tanaka—even Weinstein and Richardson, whose company I found loathsome but still preferable to those of my own sex. The only woman I truly respected was Ayumi, and I had been going behind her back for years. I had no choice in shaping my destiny. I was fated at birth, and I would be fated in the face of death. Should my affair with Hideo ever be made public, I had vowed to end my days here in the mortal life and lie next to my mother in that unkempt graveyard in Osaka.

I heard Azusa call me. "Sakura, hurry up. We can't keep the big man waiting." I looked into the mirror; I was Tanezawa and forever would be. This was my life now. There was so much I had to be grateful for, and yet I felt an important part of me had gone missing. I prayed that my corrupted soul would one day be redeemed and I would be able to find peace amongst the debris of my hypocritical existence.

Azusa and I were the last to arrive for breakfast, and although we were a good ten minutes early, it seemed the others had already started without us. Toshio was sitting at the head of a long, elegantly laid table. The cutlery and crystal caught the light from the chandeliers overhead and glistened splendidly. We had the table in the corner, and adjacent diners were kept at a distance to afford us a little extra privacy. The men wore open-necked shirts, an attempt at being casual but one that did not quite come off, as they were all so accustomed to the rigid formality of the business suit.

I noticed that despite the early hour, Toshio had ordered champagne and was raising his glass as we joined the table. "Ah, ladies, perfect timing as always. Please raise your glasses to welcome the new day—and a most auspicious day at that, for today marks an important milestone in the history of our business with this fine country that is hosting us. This morning we are all invited to attend an auction where all monies raised will be donated to good causes. Various items of differing values will be put up, and bidders will offer outrageously inflated bids in the name of various worthy charities. It will be an opportunity for us at Mabuhay to once more show our benevolent spirit and also to have a little release from the hectic demands of business that will bear down upon us in the coming days. The auction will take place at the Waldorf Astoria Hotel at ten thirty this morning, which doesn't leave us much time, but I expect you all to be in supportive attendance."

He beamed at each and every one of us like an expectant child waiting for praise. Somewhat confusingly, Toshio finished his little address with "To the glory of others." We all clumsily repeated his words and nodded as if we understood his meaning. Azusa broke out in delighted applause. Such an event would appeal to her flamboyant nature, and I knew she would revel in the occasion. The others merely smiled and nodded their acquiescence. It was obvious that this had been hastily arranged and no further explanation was needed: It was a publicity-seeking exercise aimed at garnering some much-needed positive press after the previous evening's TV show.

Hamazaki was not yet through. He had one more announcement to make, and for this he lowered his voice slightly. "As you are all aware, I have been honoured with an invitation to dine at the White House this evening—the first businessman from our country to receive this honour in over forty years—and I am humbled to be in such a position. Sakura, I would be obliged if you would accompany me this evening."

It took a few moments for the enormity of his words to strike home. I was lost for words and must have looked a sight, my mouth agape. I managed to finally say what an honour it would be and was about to go on with further platitudes of thanks, but Toshio waved me quiet as if this were just a normal dinner appointment. I caught sight of Ayumi, who was sitting to Hamazaki's left. She was biting down hard on her lip, and her cheeks had blushed. It was obvious she was distraught at having been overlooked as her brother's escort, and she could barely control her emotions. We had worked together for years and I could read her like a book. I hoped and prayed that this was not a prelude to some confrontation. Without a doubt the others had noticed, too, for we were all caught up in an uncomfortable moment of pure silence where everything seemed to stop dead in its tracks.

Azusa took hold of my arm, and her grip brought me back to my senses. She squealed with simple delight. "Sakura, this means you are going to meet the president. Do you have a dinner dress?" I said I thought I did, but she looked doubtful and whispered that she wanted to give me a presidential fashion check later. Breakfast was served, and as we ate our fine American eggs and ham, I had the strangest of feelings—as if I had been given a promotion right there in front of the rest of our party. My own personal stock had risen, and my newfound importance was noted by all.

After breakfast we were given the next couple of hours to prepare for the day's events. I had quite an agenda to work through, mostly making contact with site representatives for the forthcoming week's engagements. My tasks were a welcome distraction from everything going on around me, and as usual, I was at my best when I had a steady workload. One of my duties as Toshio's personal assistant was to handle all queries from the press and other interested parties who wanted interviews. This morning as I passed through the lobby on my way to my room, I was handed a large envelope full of messages that had been scrawled out on cards by the front desk staff, who had been busy fielding telephone enquiries and taking messages throughout the night. It was obvious Toshio's visit was now the focal point of the business community. My brief from the man himself was to go through each request and ensure there was nothing out of the ordinary, then politely decline them all with a standard response along the lines of being pre-engaged and the limits of time. Toshio trusted my judgement, and I did not feel the need to consult with anyone else. After all, I had been working in a similar capacity for fifteen years as Ayumi's assistant in matters concerning the Mabuhay Foundation. Judging by the number of cards, messages, and letters in the envelope, I would, undoubtedly, be occupied all morning.

Azusa caught up with me as I was about to ride the elevator up to my room. "Sakura, come on. Let's go shopping on Fifth Avenue and get your dress for this evening." I said I could not possibly spare the time, a comment which brought a pouty response from Azusa, who said, "Very well, but you must trust me to choose your gown, and you must promise to accept my choice. Agreed?" I told her to go ahead, but not to get anything too daring, as I was going merely as an aide to Toshio, not as his "date." She laughed and said not to worry. I must admit, she did have a good eye for fashion, and as we were nearly the same size, I guessed she would be able to find something that would suit me. She left me to my tasks and skipped over to the concierge, where she would no doubt engage a chauffeur and bag carrier for the morning.

Just as the elevator doors were closing, I caught sight of Ken Miyazaki, who was making his way to the front desk, and on impulse I hit the Open button and stepped back out. Ken would be the man to talk to regarding my concern about our being kept under observation by the authorities. Miyazaki was like a rock, solid and dependable, and I knew he had the complete trust of both Toshio and Hideo. After the death of Hosokawa he had stepped up his workload and been given wider responsibilities to fill the void left by his late boss. Miyazaki was always seen as Hosokawa's man, but now he was undoubtedly Mabuhay's man. For many years he did not hold any official position in the company, a situation he seemed to find appealing, one that complemented his aura of mystery. However, Toshio had decided that his efforts needed to be rewarded with a grand title and had made him company secretary, a moniker that did not sit well with his manly image. I had always seen him as a man of all things, able to deal with all matters, especially those of a sensitive nature. He would know what should be done about my concerns.

Ken was at the front desk also receiving a large sealed envelope. I caught up with him as he was about to take a seat in the coffee lounge. He did not look at all pleased at having his quiet time interrupted, but was gracious as always. I asked him if he could spare a moment, and he invited me to join him for coffee. We were both people who appreciated direct speaking, and I told him straight out what I had seen in the lobby the previous evening. He complimented me on my vigilance but said there was nothing to worry about, as he had been told that they were FBI men assigned to protect Toshio. He went on to tell me that several death threats had been received and no chances were being taken with safety. This came as a great shock to me but was not something that seemed to concern Ken too much. He said the threats were believed to be mainly from crank callers and obviously the work of unbalanced individuals aimed at causing mischief.

I said perhaps we should consider adopting a lower profile for security's sake, perhaps avoiding public spaces such as this morning's breakfast in the Palm Court. Ken said he had discussed this with Toshio but that Toshio would hear nothing of the kind. I could picture that exchange all too easily. Hamazaki was not a man who would compromise his liberty for the sake of some obscure threat. Indeed, only a few days ago I had overheard him say he would like to go on a drinking spree around some of the city's famous bars. Typically, he justified it by saying that in such places you could get the feel of the real New York. Ken said he would ask Toshio to be a little less visible in his daily routine and urge him to be more vigilant.

There was far more we could have said, but discretion always took precedence over expression, and as we were in a public place, neither of us felt it was suitable to talk about some of Mabuhay's more illicit business dealings. In addition, the unspoken fear of being investigated for crimes that would put us all behind bars in some foul penal unit for the rest of our days always loomed large. If Ken could take this in his stride—and he was a better judge of potential danger than I—then there seemed little point in concerning myself any further.

A pile of correspondence awaited my attention, and my morning was already spoken for. Time was, as ever, my ruler, and there was never enough of it to serve my purposes. Perhaps it was time the "secretary" had her own assistant. That notion appealed to me, and I resolved to take it up with Ayumi at an appropriate time. How she would receive such a request I did not know; perhaps she would see it as impudent. Our relationship had from the outset been one of master and servant, but now the parameters had irrevocably changed. As far as I was aware, Ayumi had been deliberately kept in ignorance about my tortured family background. To her I was simply an orphan who had been given a lucky break and as such should be eternally grateful for my lot. Being chosen over her to attend this evening's dinner at the White House was a clear signal that things had changed. Without doubt she would confront her brother and demand an explanation. Sibling rivalry was something a poor orphan like me would never understand.

The Waldorf Astoria's Grand Ballroom seemed monumental in contrast to my room back at the Plaza, where I had spent the morning drafting answers to requests and invitations from a broad and diverse representation of American societies, groups, schools and colleges, and businesses. Toshio had stood firm and instructed me to politely refuse all, citing the rigorous demands of an overstretched itinerary. In truth, he had great chunks of leisure time which he refused to even consider giving up. I knew there were many things he wished to do and certain people he longed to meet. His love of movies and the silver screen had left him with a child-like passion for his idols. This morning his dream had taken one step closer to reality: Buried deep amongst the piles of requests and begging letters was an invitation to attend the Forty-Second Academy Awards presentation in Los Angeles. With a little skillful time management I was sure he could make the event and perhaps shake off the stardust that had glittered in front of his eyes ever since he saw his first movie. I slipped the invitation into my bag and would present it to him when the moment was right.

I travelled over to the Waldorf along with Ken, who was more subdued than usual. He was never the type given to conversation, but now he was more surly and tight-lipped than usual. I could tell something was on his mind. Perhaps it was the fact that he was physically so close to Ayumi and yet could do nothing about his frustrations. Ayumi had Tatsuya in tow, and any flirtations were no doubt strictly off limits. I had known of their affair for years and sympathised deeply with Ken. After all, I was in the same position. We were both interlopers in the same marriage. How simple life would have been if Ken had made an advance in my direction. Although he was nearly thirty years my senior, he was still a handsome man, and I might have found a space in my heart for his affections. He just never seemed interested in pursuing me at all, and I always had the impression he saw me as a little girl rather than as a woman to be desired. In truth, I in turn saw him as a stern uncle, one not to be feared but always there to guide me when my path took an unexpected turn. Ken Miyazaki, a kindly and dependable man who would never harm a soul but shrouded himself in mystery and desire. Today he was my unwilling chaperone to the auction, and he was so distracted, I doubted he even registered my presence.

The auctioneer banged his gavel three times to bring the gathering to attention. "Ladies and gentlemen, on behalf of all the charities represented here this morning I thank you for gracing us with your presence and take the liberty of extending our gratitude for your kindness and patronage. The auction is conducted in a lighthearted manner, and all the funds raised this morning will be donated to the stated charity. We have some wonderful and extraordinary items for your consideration, and I will you all to bid freely and with as much abandon as your generosity of spirit allows. All lots shall begin at one dollar, though of course they all have reserve prices. Now, without any further ado I suggest we get the auction underway."

I looked down our line of seats. Toshio had the look of an eager schoolboy, transfixed and innocent, obviously enjoying every minute of this event. His vanity could be well served here, as it was an opportunity to do some good and to be seen doing it. Ayumi, who sat next to Toshio, had by contrast a face like an Easter Island statue. The severity was pouring out, and I was grateful for the space between us. I hoped she would find some calm before she came face-to-face with me. Tatsuya was seated alongside Miyazaki, who was at pains to be civil and act with as much natural nonchalance as he could muster. I felt for him, as it must be a strain to sit next to your secret lover's son. There were two empty seats, as Azusa and Richardson had yet to grace us with their presence. No doubt the purchase of my evening gown was taking up more time than Azusa had intended.

My attention was drawn back to the auctioneer as he announced the first lot that was up for bidding. "Ladies and gentlemen, our first lot this morning has been kindly donated by

Warner Brothers motion picture studio of Burbank, California, and consists of two casual shirts once belonging to the late James Dean. These are truly authentic and were actually worn by the legendary actor himself. They are accompanied by a signed photograph which features the movie star attired in one of these splendid garments. I believe such a fine lot will raise a princely sum for one of our featured causes this morning. After the auction has been concluded, we will spin this wheel, and wherever it stops, that cause will be the beneficiary."

I looked down the line once more; Toshio was on the edge of his seat, biting his lower lip—a sign that he was determined to have these shirts. The auctioneer's assistant indicated a large wheel which looked a little like an archery target. The room fell silent.

"Do I hear one dollar?" There was a muffled cough. "Thank you, sir, for getting us going. Do I hear one hundred dollars, yes, two hundred, thank you, three hundred?" In a matter of seconds we were up to eight hundred dollars, and the bidding was still coming thick and fast. Toshio's head was swivelling this way and that as he tried to keep pace with all that was going on around him. "Do I hear one thousand?" Toshio raised his arm, and there was a slight gasp as the magical figure of a thousand was reached. Having arrived at this sum the auctioneer took the chance to step up the increments. "One thousand two hundred? Thank you, sir."

The bidding had come down to two people: Toshio and a man at the back, whom we could not see but who was knocking back Toshio's bids without any sign of relenting. The auctioneer saw this as another opportunity to raise the bar. They were now bidding in shouts of five-hundred-dollar increases. We had reached five thousand dollars, and for the first time the unseen man at the back was starting to hesitate in his offers.

"Do I hear five thousand and five hundred?" Silence. The auctioneer's gavel was poised above his podium. "This is your very last chance to make a further bid. Going once, twice, sold to the gentleman in the front row. Congratulations, sir." There was a huge round of applause, and Toshio, unnecessarily, rose to his feet and faced the rest of the gathering, giving a nod or two of thanks. The auctioneer then continued. "Now it is time to find out which cause is to benefit from the sale of the late James Dean's shirts." The assistant gave the wheel a spin, and we all watched as it came to a lurching halt. "Police Widows' and Children's Fund of New York City." There was another bellow of applause, and Toshio too grinned in satisfaction. It seemed as if he approved of the recipients.

The conclusion of the first lot presented Azusa and Richardson with the opportunity to finally take their seats. Azusa was giggling like an excited schoolgirl, and Richardson's face was flushed from the obvious bout of drinking that they had enjoyed. After toes had been stepped on and apologies professed, Azusa clumsily slid into the seat beside me. She whispered that she had bought the most exquisite dress from Chanel and was sure I would be delighted with her choice. I could smell the alcohol on her breath, and it was almost laughable to watch her attempting to follow the auctioneer's proceedings. She studied her guidebook but gave it only a minute of her attention before tossing it contemptuously aside. Richardson had his arms folded across his ample stomach and looked set to take a nap, but if I knew Richardson, I would put his behaviour down to an ill-mannered attempt at nonchalance. His arrogance was difficult to fathom. He seemed to carry an air of aggression at all times, and for the life of me I could not understand why Toshio kept him so close to hand. There was no doubt that he was a bad influence on Azusa, one that I prayed would play out soon. Perhaps she enjoyed the company of uncouth men who were nearly twice her age. After all, she had married Hosokawa, and on the face of it Richardson seemed to possess many of her late husband's less desirable traits.

After the audience had finally settled down and the excitement of James Dean's shirts had been put aside for a moment, the auctioneer went about the business of announcing lot number two. "Our second lot for your pleasure this afternoon is donated by the estate of the late Margret Helmsford, whose generosity is greatly appreciated. Miss Helmsford, as you may know, was a great supporter of numerous worthy causes, and her estate continues her legacy. We are honoured to put up for auction a piece from her private collection of fine jewellery, a pink diamond pendant which has been set in platinum and is ready to be worn as a necklace if so desired. Before we proceed, I am obliged to inform you that such a piece commands a high residual value, and as such its reserve price is set at an appropriate figure. Now, who will make the tentative offer of one dollar?"

I caught a glimpse of Azusa and for a moment thought she was going to raise her hand, but she was not sharp enough, and within moments the auctioneer was skillfully reeling in bids of thousands. At the ten thousand point Toshio raised his hand in a show of support, though I could tell he was not really interested in the piece at all. The little pink diamond was now at twenty-five thousand, and from the grin on the auctioneer's face I guessed that its reserve had been well and truly surpassed. "Do I hear twenty-six thousand for this remarkable piece?" Azusa was about to raise her hand when Richardson forcefully grabbed ahold of her arm and restrained her from doing so. The auctioneer's hawklike attention was drawn to the small fuss in the front row. "Is that a bid I see there?"

Everyone seated along the line craned their necks to see what was going on. I heard Richardson say to Azusa, "It ain't worth it, babe." I knew Richardson had garnered a reputation for being on the mean side but had not realised that it extended to other people's money too. However, he did not know Azusa as well as he thought. She shook off his arm and rose to her feet—a little unsteadily, it has to be said. The auctioneer was momentarily stunned at this rather unconventional break in the proceedings and waited to see what was about to unfold.

Azusa stared at him and shouted out in a trill voice, "Thirty thousand dollars."

The audience took a sharp intake of breath. Even the auctioneer looked a little bemused. I expect he wanted to ask if she could afford it. More fool him. However, good manners prevailed, and after offering the chance for further bids, he brought his gavel down and the little pink diamond belonged to Azusa. Cheers rang out, and a few people even got to their feet and applauded raucously. Even Toshio was beaming like a jovial devil. Only Richardson had the look of a peeved man. He sank low into his chair and closed his eyes. The auctioneer, obviously pleased to raise such an unexpected amount, was beaming with satisfaction as he gestured for the charity wheel to be spun to see which cause would benefit from Azusa's money. The assistant gave the wheel a vigorous spin, and the audience whooped in anticipation as it slowed and homed in to its final click and stop. "American Red Cross, ladies and gentlemen." The applause that filled the room seemed to confirm that this was a popular outcome, and Azusa swelled with self-importance. It was obvious that she had taken the applause personally, when in fact it was all for the charity, though some folk were no doubt keen to find out which young woman was flush enough to throw thirty thousand dollars into the charity pot.

A photographer appeared in front of us and without asking permission snapped a few pictures. I saw Richardson's face fill with anger at this impudence and he made to stand, only to be restrained from doing so by Toshio, who placed a firm hand on his shoulder. Nonetheless Richardson was not to be denied his say. "Run those pictures by me, boy, before you even think of using them." It seemed a petty thing to say, but then again, the man was as irritating as they come.

After the bright start to the event, things took on an air of inevitability, and we had to sit through over an hour of uninspiring lots and cautious bids from an obviously restless audience. Nobody wished to be seen leaving early, but most of us would have welcomed the opportunity to do so, and we all had an eye on the time. A drinks party was planned where the event would be concluded in an informal setting and fellow bidders and the like could be photographed for the society pages of New York's many avenues of self-aggrandisement. Toshio looked ready to call time on his presence here and was without doubt looking forward to having a drink in his hand. So it came as a relief when the auctioneer announced the final lot. "Ladies and gentlemen, our final offering this morning is somewhat unconventional but nonetheless carries a vested emotional value and will no doubt appeal personally to several members of the audience. It is an artefact of deep symbolic historical significance. We are honoured to offer a sword, and no ordinary sword by any stretch of the imagination. This fine artefact once belonged to General Tomoyuki Yamashita of the Japanese Imperial Army and was surrendered to our own General MacArthur on September 2, 1945. It symbolised the end of hostilities and the heralding of a new era and a new world order. The sword itself is of immense historical importance, said to have been made between 1640 and 1680 by the great sword maker Fujiwara Kanenaga, who fashioned beautiful items for Samurai warriors. It is put up for offer today under special conditions by the curators of the West Point Military Museum. I am sure that this piece will appeal to all who are able to see beyond its mere existence here in this room."

So this was why we were here. Toshio had obviously known about this all along. He must have been tipped off that this was in the offing. I was struggling to fathom the implications of such an obvious staging. What could possibly be behind this? My first thoughts were How could they put such an article into the public domain? Surely it was state property. I looked along the line at Toshio, who was trying his best to appear nonchalant, though I could see he was obviously on high alert and had closed in on himself. Richardson caught me staring at Toshio, and he too shot a glance at the great man. It was plain to see that he had been kept out of the loop and was also trying desperately to gain a foothold as to what was going on here. Only one man knew what was unfolding before our eyes, and he was content to give his complete attention to the auction guide before him.

The auctioneer cut in once more. "It is my duty to inform all bidders that this lot comes with certain restrictions and they are nonnegotiable. The successful bidder will not be permitted to take possession of the item, as it must remain on display at the West Point Military Museum. However, your ownership will be recognised and a suitable dedication will be displayed alongside the sword acknowledging your provenance and generosity. In essence purchasing this item will be a supreme act of kind benevolence. One more point that needs to be addressed. The curators have offered this lot with the intention of raising funds for a specific cause. So, in a departure from our usual procedures, bidders will know in advance where their money is destined to go. The American Veterans Association will be the beneficiary of your generosity today. This wonderful organisation helps support our brave ex-servicemen who have found themselves in strained and difficult circumstances. I hope you will find it in your hearts to support this worthy cause. Now, if all is understood, I wish to hasten the proceedings."

Toshio swept back his long greying hair and looked as cool as could be. The audience seemed to have descended into a collective voyeuristic group. It was an unusual lot and one that did not appeal to most of those gathered today, but they wanted to see where this was heading. "Do I hear one dollar?" There was a muffled cough from somewhere way back in the crowd which the auctioneer took as the opening bid. "Thank you, and now let us proceed with the real bidding. I am opening the bidding at ten thousand dollars. Do I hear ten thousand?"

There was a gasp as the audacious first offer was comprehended. For an object that had limited monetary value the auction now presented itself as pure theatre, and the star player had yet to take centre stage. The auctioneer spotted a raised hand. "Thank you, sir." Heads spun round as one to see who was making the running. "Do I hear twenty thousand?" Toshio raised his hand, and there at that very moment began one of the most two-way ding-dong battles in auction history. Toshio and the mystery bidder went head to head, spending away without thinking anything of the consequences. The audience was deathly silent, too stunned to fully understand what was going on in front of their eyes. The auctioneer could barely keep pace and was having trouble drawing breath. After five minutes or so we were witnessing bids in excess of five hundred thousand dollars. This extraordinary scenario was compounded by the fact that none of us in the front could see who the mystery bidder was. Whoever it was, he was intent on fighting his corner to the last, and knowing Toshio, I knew Mr X would have to dig deep if he wanted his name displayed by some antique sword.

The bidding was just short of six hundred thousand dollars, and for the first time I sensed hesitation, as Toshio's bid was not immediately countered. The auctioneer too realised that the financial sparring was about to draw to an end and was desperately fishing for a further increase. Toshio leaned back in his chair and willed the auctioneer to bring the lot to an end. "Gentleman at the back, this is your final opportunity to bid. Going once, twice, three times . . . and sold to the gentleman in the front row for five hundred and seventy thousand dollars. I thank you, sir."

His gavel crashed down, the signal for pandemonium to break out. Several cameramen appeared, popping flashbulbs in Toshio's direction. There were also newsprint reporters seeking a comment or two from our man but to no avail, as he was being swept away by some official-looking men in dark suits wearing the strange earpieces. A compere arrived and informed us all that the auction was concluded, then thanked us for showing support for this, the most amazing charitable event in the history of New York fundraising. His words were drowned out by the excited voices from the crowd as they came to terms with what they had just witnessed.

Our party was in danger of being separated as the throng of people who wished to shake Toshio's hand grew by the second. Their disappointment at his sudden removal from the fray was all too plain to see. One or two fellows mistook Richardson for the munificent bidder, an error he was reluctant to address as he tried to garner a little of the attention for himself. Indeed at one point I heard him say that his company had been behind the purchase. A half-truth here and there, the murmur of feigned involvement, was all it took for Richardson to satisfy his conceit.

As the crowd started to disperse, I caught a glimpse of a man sitting alone at the rear of the ballroom. His head was bowed, and he was wearing dark glasses. There was something so familiar about his posture. I drew on all my feminine instincts, but for the life of me I could not bring myself to believe what I was seeing. It could not be true. I nimbly skirted around the crowd and headed for the rear of the room. I took my eyes off him only for a second, but he was gone. I frantically looked this way and that and felt my frustrations boil over. Where in heaven's name had he gone? I knew it was him. I was convinced that the figure lurking in the rear was Toshio's business partner, Tatsuya's father, Ayumi's husband, but more importantly, my lover, Hideo Tanaka.

My heart lurched north and south, and I had little alternative other than to follow the others to the grand suite adjacent to the ballroom, where a drinks and canapés reception had been arranged and selected press and television reporters were to be granted privileged access. I was now convinced that the mystery bidder at the rear was Hideo, and I could only assume that the "pantomime" we had all just witnessed had been prearranged, although for what purpose I did not know. I realised that such a staging was meant to simply drive up the price—that much was obvious. But why? Toshio must have known that nobody in the room would be interested in paying such an exorbitant fee for a nominal item, one that you could not even truly own.

As I entered the suite, I got an inkling of what this was all about. Toshio was seated on a makeshift stage, slightly raised from floor height to allow everyone a good look at the man who had just "donated" a fortune to a cause that had reason to be extremely grateful. He was flanked on either side by two important-looking men whom I had never seen before. I gathered it was an impromptu press conference, one that had been hastily convened in the wake of Toshio's spectacular largesse. There was no need for a microphone, as the space was quite confined. I noticed that Toshio had not bothered with an interpreter, choosing to rely on his own linguistic skills once more. I prayed that this would not lead us into further shadowy misunderstandings.

From the rear of the room I had quite a decent view, though I had to strain my ears to hear the reporters' questions. Toshio fielded a question from the New York Times. I could not quite catch the reporter's voice, but I had no trouble at all hearing the reply. Toshio's voice boomed out, and I felt his pride and confidence sweep across the assembled gathering. "First I would like to say that I am privileged to be here at this wonderful event and honoured to be able to make a contribution towards the support of such wonderful causes. As you may know, our company, Mabuhay, has a foundation which promotes development and self-sufficiency in certain parts of Southeast Asia, and we strongly believe in offering any kind of assistance where and whenever we can. Today I was presented with an opportunity to personally support a cause that is close to my heart. Servicemen who have returned after serving their country and found themselves in difficult circumstances need all the help that a grateful nation can and should offer. I am humbled by their bravery and honoured to be able to donate. When I heard that a sword which once belonged to General Yamashita was to be auctioned, I saw it as a divine sign and one that presented itself as the perfect symbol of the glorious peace that now exists between our two countries. I am pleased that the sword will continue to be displayed in its rightful place at West Point, and I pray that all who come to view it will now look upon it as a symbol of peace rather than as an item of aggression. Thank you."

Applause broke out around the room, and hands were raised by eager journalists keen to push the story further. I heard the words Mr Mayor, and one of the men seated next to Toshio stood and raised his voice. "All I need to add is the thanks of New York and all its citizens, for the Big Apple is one proud place today, thanks to the generosity of Mr Hamazaki. He has made a spectacular contribution and one that will help the lives of many deserving veterans. I thank you, sir."

Again applause rang out around the room. Toshio smiled in a controlled and somewhat calculated manner, certainly not his usual beam of satisfaction, but one more befitting a humble man who was reluctantly accepting the platitudes rolling around him. Five hundred and seventy thousand dollars, the price for near sainthood in this great nation, for that is what Toshio Hamazaki had achieved if the mood of this room was anything to go by—a complete reversal, given his standing in the eyes of the average American only a day ago. The man was now where he best belonged, adored and feted in equal measure and perhaps well on the way to becoming a celebrity in his own right. It was a shame the James Dean shirts would be several sizes too small, as I was sure he would have loved to wear them right then as a mark of his pride.

Somebody handed the man on Toshio's left an envelope. He ripped it open and quickly scanned the document inside. The man puffed up with self-importance, held the paper aloft, and called for some quiet. "Excuse me, everybody. I have an important announcement to make. I have here a letter from our president in which he wishes to personally convey his thanks to Mr Hamazaki for supporting such an honourable cause and says he is looking forward to expressing his gratitude in person at this evening's dinner at the

White House." Once again sycophantic applause rang out at this, the final and ultimate endorsement of Toshio Hamazaki's social rehabilitation.

I travelled back to the Plaza in much the same fashion as I had left some four hours earlier, with Ken once more acting as my chaperone. I had avoided having any drinks, as I needed to keep a clear mind. My thoughts were racing through the day's events. Had I really seen Hideo lurking in the back of the room? I began to doubt myself. After all, it defied all logic. Perhaps my mind had started to play cruel tricks, preying on my desire and offering up tantalising images of a life that was beyond the bounds of reality. I could hardly ask Toshio. I knew better than to ask about matters that were not in my immediate circle of concern.

We had left Toshio back at the Waldorf to enjoy the lime-light he had so craftily engineered for himself. Ever the one for a party—and this morning had proved no exception—he was taking the early hour drink on board with reckless abandon, regaling the guests with exaggerated tales of life back in "mysterious" Japan. His booming voice and bellowing laughter filled the room, and there would be little point in reminding him that he had an important dinner date in a few hours. I signalled our departure and jokingly tapped at the face of my watch, and in response was rewarded with a glass raised in my direction.

So now here I was once more beside the silent and somewhat grumpy Ken Miyazaki as we made our way back to the Plaza Hotel. I considered asking him about Hideo but quickly dismissed that notion, as it would hardly be tactful. Given his relationship with Ayumi, no doubt Hideo was the last person Ken would want to see here. As I watched the bustling streets flash by the limousine windows, I allowed myself to drift off into a conspiratorial fantasy where Ken and I allied to plot the downfall of our lovers' marriage, leaving us free to finally take up with our beaus and live happily ever after. Reality prevailed, as it always does, when we drew up at the Plaza and the liveried doorman, with practiced ease, swung the limousine door open and with a flourish bade us a warm welcome back.

Ken felt it was his duty to offer up some instructions regarding the evening's preparations. He was still under the conviction that he was my boss and needed to show leadership. We both knew the parameters of our working relationship had shifted years ago, but I was happy enough to play out the charade. "Tanezawa, this evening you are to accompany Mr Hamazaki as his aide, not, as I know you are aware, as his companion. In that capacity please use your judgement wisely, and for heaven's sake try to steer the man into calm waters. I think you understand what I mean."

I said I would do my best to ensure that the evening went ahead without complications.

"Very well. A presidential limousine will be despatched to convey the two of you to the White House. Please remain in your room until called, and Tanezawa, I wish you the best of luck. It will be an amazing experience for you." I saw him smile for the first time that day, and it was a smile of genuine happiness. I was touched by his warmth. I suppose that happens when granite cracks. I was catching a glimpse of what Ayumi saw every day in Ken Miyazaki.

I went straight up to my room and, after fumbling in my handbag for a moment, finally found my key to let myself in. Some call it female intuition of a kind, but my senses told me that all was not as it should be. The atmosphere in my room had changed. I had a feeling that I had been intruded upon, and my instinct told me to turn tail and seek help, but there was something else. My senses told me to flee, and yet something was compelling me to enter. I walked past the bathroom and into the bedroom. Nothing. Yet there was a familiar scent in the air, one that I knew all too well. I was just about to turn around when the hand came from behind and gently covered my mouth. I closed my eyes and bit down on my lip. I allowed him to kiss my ear and the nape of my neck. His words were like golden honey to a starving bear. "Sakura, I missed you. I had to be here. I love you." I let his hands roam over my breasts and hitch up my skirt. I put up a show of making a mock struggle, but I wanted him desperately, and the thrill of having him here, in my room at the Plaza, seemed to heighten the eroticism of the moment and made this illicit encounter too exciting to bear. Perhaps it was the fact that he had come to me before his wife that turned me on even more, another small victory in a war that had played out in my emotions a million times a day.

I wriggled free from Hideo's grasp and turned to face him. Without speaking I gave him a deep kiss, and we fell onto the bed, my hands working to loosen his belt whilst he pulled down my skirt and underwear. In moments he was inside me, thrusting away, releasing his frustrations and primeval urges. I desperately wanted to let my emotions free, but I knew I had to check myself, as too much noise would bring us unwanted attention. It was frantic and over in a minute. Hideo, having spent his sexual energy, rolled off me and lay back, gasping at the ceiling. It was out of character for him to behave in such a sexually dominant manner, his usual style being more long-drawn-out and tentative seduction. Perhaps it was the fact that we had been separated by a continent and he felt he had to reclaim me as his own.

I stroked his cheek and whispered into his ear. "I saw you at the auction. You could have told me you were coming. I have missed you."

He leaned towards me and propped himself up on one arm and started to play with my hair. "Sorry. It was a last-minute thing. Toshio needed some help, and I volunteered. Also, I knew I could see you. But I was never here, do you understand? I leave this evening, flying back to Narita from JFK."

Sadness descended on me, but I quickly realised that given a choice I would have chosen this way. It would have been unbearable to see him every day in the company of Ayumi. I looked at the clock. It was only a matter of two hours before I had to be ready for the president's dinner. Oh, how much I wished I could tell Toshio and Mr Nixon that I had a headache and needed to be excused just so I could spend an extra hour or two in the arms of the man I loved. Again, it was just a wilful fantasy having a run around the meadow of my imagination. "Tell me about America. Is Mabuhay well received here?" That was the Hideo I had come to know so well, business never being far from his thoughts, even though I was a little put out that he chose this for his post-coital pillow talk.

"Well, after a shaky start I do believe Toshio is finally getting to grips with the American way of doing things. He seems to be enjoying the challenges and surprises that fall into our path on a daily basis."

Hideo had always been happy to be the anonymous partner; he hated attention and actively shunned the limelight. One of the wealthiest men in the world in his own right and yet he could be taken as an ordinary "Joe Bloggs" any day of the week. The dourness that seemed to hang over him prevented him enjoying his achievements to the full. Although he had never voiced his dislike of Toshio's flamboyance, I often got the feeling that he found some of the great man's public exhortations a little distasteful.

I filled the silence with another of my own thoughts. "The American media seem obsessed with Toshio's mantle as 'wealthiest man in the world.' It's such a contrast to the way we are viewed back home, where little is made of fortunes and possessions and more thought is given to what the business is worth to the value of the country's progress as a whole."

Hideo considered my words, and for a moment I thought I had said something that disturbed him. He sat up in bed and held his head in his hands. He looked absolutely spent. Travelling on the overnight flight must have been exhausting, not to mention stressful, as he was at pains to keep his presence here a secret. My curiosity rose to the fore, and I was unable to stop myself asking the obvious. "Hideo, why did you have to bid against Toshio for the sword? I know it was staged to push up the price, but for what end?"

He looked at me with resigned weariness and then surprisingly answered me with candour. "It was already a done deal, payback for a favour received long ago. Toshio agreed on the price in advance. He did not wish to make a straightforward monetary donation, but felt he should receive something in return for his generosity. I honestly do not know the full details behind the deal or who was involved, but one thing is for certain: There is some kind of agenda at play here, and I beg you to keep your wits about you and look for anything out of place."

He stood up and went over to the window. He seemed to be carrying the weight of the world on his shoulders. As he looked down at the busy street below, he went on. "Sakura, there is so much you don't know, and most of it I hope you will never have to know. I have a terrible sense of foreboding that we are heading into areas that will bring nothing but trouble. There are people out there who have designs on our business and will use any foul means to get their hands on it."

I pulled the bedsheet tight around me as if it could offer protection of sorts. "Hideo, you are scaring me. Please stop or tell me what it is all about."

He turned and wearily shook his head. "I have a flight to catch, and I hear that you have an important dinner date." He strode over to the closet and flung the doors open. "I believe this is your dress for the evening?" He took out the most stunning long burgundy silk dress. It was utterly breathtaking. I was at a loss for words. Hideo went on. "When I came into the room, it was lying on the bed and there was a note from Azusa."

He passed me the note, which was folded several times. I recognised Azusa's childlike scrawl. "Hope the dress makes Dickie Nixon's eyes pop out. Have a great night. Azusa." The Helmsford diamond pendant was draped on the dress hanger. I smiled, as did Hideo. It was obvious he had read my note, but I could not get angry with him. He came over and put his arms around me tightly and spoke softly into my ear. "I have to go now. Remember, I was never here. Understand?" I nodded, and he kissed me on the cheek. "One more thing: Keep your distance from Richardson. I mean, really keep apart from him. Do not sit or walk near him, and do not ever allow him access to your room. The man is foul and never to be trusted. Try to steer Azusa away from his influence. Can you promise to do this for me?"

Without questioning his reasoning I nodded, for his words did not ring hollow. Richardson was indeed detestable. The only question in my mind was, Why did Hideo think it necessary to offer such a stark warning now of all times?

The woman looking back at me from the dress mirror could not be me, surely! It was unthinkable, and yet there she was, the image of Sakura Tanezawa, adorned in the finest dress courtesy of Chanel, along with matching finery beyond any woman's wildest dreams. Sakura Tanezawa, a once-poor little orphan girl about to step out on the arm of the wealthiest man in the world and have dinner with the president of the United States. So why did she feel so empty inside? Well, for one thing, the love of my life had just snuck out like a thief in the night and left me sad and all alone. I had made myself ready for the dinner amidst thoughts both disturbing and confusing. Hideo's cryptic meanderings had left little room for anything else. As I waited for Ken to call, I tried to figure out what could possibly be behind Hideo's thoughts and feelings. He was not a man given over to reckless paranoia like his late business partner Makoto Hosokawa, who was inclined towards the dramatic. Hideo was the calculating type, a thinker who seldom trusted impulse and a man who rarely took risks. This naturally led me to believe something awful was in the offing, and I could not suppress the feeling that the man I loved so dearly was deeply involved in its orchestration.

The shrill ring of the phone nearly made me jump out of my skin. It also brought me back to reality and the realisation that perhaps the most important evening of my life was about to begin. Ken's brusque no-nonsense tone filtered down the line as he informed me that he would be at my door in two minutes and would escort me down to the lobby, where Toshio would be waiting. I made a few last-second adjustments to my dress, checking myself from different angles in the mirror. This fine dress Azusa had chosen for me was very flattering, though I was a little worried about the amount of cleavage on show. I draped the satin throw over my bare shoulders and waited for the knock on the door which came sooner than expected. I opened the door, and from the look on Ken's face I knew my appearance met with his approval, though he did not extend to flattery but said merely, "Very nice, Tanezawa." We made our way to the elevator in silence, and Ken, as gentlemanly as ever, held the doors apart as I stepped inside.

In seconds we were in the lobby and Toshio was striding towards us, his arms outstretched and a huge beaming smile on his reddened face. He had opted for conventional attire this evening, formal black tie without any of the flamboyant colourful touches that he had made his own over the years. There was no scarlet handkerchief in his breast pocket. Even his usual pink suspenders were supplanted by the conventional plain black. We came face-to-face, and he placed his hands on my shoulders and gave me a kiss on the cheek. I could smell the sweet lingering alcohol on his breath. His show of public affection was a little out of character, and it threw me for a moment. His voice was also louder than need be. "Sakura, my word, you do look splendid, as gorgeous as the trees that bear your name."

He took my arm and we walked through the lobby. I was conscious of the attention we were receiving, the stares burned into me, and for a moment I was overcome by the feeling that I was a fraud who had stumbled into someone else's life by mistake. A man I took to be the Plaza's official photographer began snapping away. Toshio even halted our progress to allow him the opportunity of a few decent shots. I feared the cult of celebrity was getting a grip on my boss and he was embracing his newfound notoriety and fame with open arms. The senior management of the hotel had lined up by the main doors to bid us goodwill on our departure to the White House. Toshio nodded his thanks in their direction; I kept my eyes firmly fixed ahead. A large press pack stood outside the doors, and their cameras exploded to life as we stepped outside and into the waiting official presidential limousine. The flashbulbs were almost blinding, and I was relieved to slide into the rear seat. Toshio made his way round to the other side of the car and was soon seated beside me.

The limousine pulled away at a surprisingly fast speed, and gratefully we left the melee in our wake. Toshio leaned back in his seat and stretched out his long legs, enjoying the space in the enormous car that was bigger than my office back in Ginza. He looked at me and smiled. "Tanezawa, I love this country. You can be anything you like here, and you can be anything they want you to be. It is a wonderful canvas for expression, don't you think? America the brave, so they say. America for the brave, say I."

I did not know what to say, so I merely smiled and said nothing. Toshio patted me on the knee. "Don't worry about a thing, my sweetness; we have it all under control." His voice sounded comically sinister in tone. I looked down at his shiny black patent leather shoes and noticed he was wearing odd socks, one scarlet and one pink. Suddenly, I found myself gripped by a fit of giggles. Surely everything would be fine.

We passed the journey in companionable silence. I was content to take in the views from the rear window as the limousine silently swallowed up the road in front. We were teamed up with two motorcycle outriders, and with an exaggerated sense of privilege we made swift progress. If you are to be cocooned inside an automobile for hours on end, then a presidential limousine is the place to be, as Toshio soon discovered. The small drinks cabinet was enough to raise his already soaring spirits even higher. He helped himself to a large bourbon prepared in his usual style, neat on the rocks, and poured a ginger ale for me. Toshio's drinking was the talk of many a loose-tongued gossip back in our native land, but it seemed to pass without so much as a raised eyebrow on these shores.

I wished I had brought along some paperwork to pass the time, but Hideo's sudden appearance had put paid to any last-minute good intentions I may have held. It was alien to my character to sit idly for hours on end; Toshio, however, had no such qualms. He busied himself by frequently topping up his glass and playing with the radio tuner in an attempt to find a clear signal. He was not having much luck and casually remarked, "It is a pity, is it not, that Hideo could not join us on the tour of this fine country. Is it not, Sakura? At least he would be able to fathom this blasted radio for us."

There was nothing sinister or accusing in his tone, but my heart still missed ten beats as I tried to keep my wits in check. I dared not look him in the eyes for fear that my face would tell a story of its own. I always thought of us all as a big family, bound together by circumstance and necessity, a bond that was too strong for any of us to break. Like all families we had our little secrets, or, in Toshio's case, no doubt hundreds of gigantic secrets. Yet despite everything we were allies, our unspoken devotion coupled with unswerving loyalty. That was our strength. I was not privy to some of the darker aspects of our business, and for that I remained grateful. However, for me to perform my duties efficiently I had been entrusted with sufficient knowledge to realise that Mabuhay was not all it appeared to be.

All that aside, I feared my relationship with Hideo would not be well received, to say the least, if it were ever made public. I knew in my heart of hearts that I could not bear the shame, and it was to this end that I feared I was about to be confronted. Ayumi's bitter stare and cold looks had nothing to do with being overlooked for this evening's dinner. She had found out, and now Toshio was about to deliver sentence on me. Was I letting my inner fears gain too much foothold on my taut nerves?

I looked down at the radio and then back out the window. Toshio carried on with his attempt at engaging me. "I found Hideo way back in 1949, living on the edge of poverty. He was filthy, ragged, and bone thin. I brought him into my house and company. I allowed him to marry my sister. I gave him a partnership in my business. I look upon him as a brother, and I hope he sees me as the same. He is not the man everyone seems to believe he is. He has an almost imperial bearing, do you not think, Sakura?" Toshio had me and he knew it, and I felt an overwhelming sense of shame bearing down on me. My eyes welled up with tears. Without looking, Toshio handed me his white silk handkerchief. I looked out the window, but nothing seemed to register in my mind. I was willing the streets to swallow me up.

His voice cut the space between us like an ice knife. "It would pain me to see any member of my family hurt in any way, and it would cause me enormous grief to see or hear of any of my family hurting each other. Sakura, I look on you as part of my family, as is Hideo, and naturally, of course, my beloved sister. So I think it is an opportune time to assign new posts and new responsibilities. I have spoken with Ayumi, and she is in full agreement."

My tears were now filling my eyes, and tiny sobs were working their way out of my mouth. "Sakura, you are to leave your post as confidential secretary to my sister. Your work at the Mabuhay Foundation is over." His words sent tears cascading down my cheeks. My makeup was ruined, but what did that matter now? My life was about to be torn asunder. All I could do was sit and wait for Toshio to deliver his final coup de grâce. I was grateful for the smoked glass divider that separated us from the driver in front;

at least my shame was kept "in house." Toshio was quiet for a moment. The only sound was the clinking of ice cubes as he swirled his glass, lost in thought. "I have decided that you will work as Hideo's assistant from now on. You will reside in an apartment near his in the new Imperial Hotel, and you will take further direction about the course of your employment from Hideo himself. Ayumi, though far from happy with the situation, is to leave the marital home at the Empire and take up residence in an area of the city of her own choosing. She has indicated that she wishes contact between herself and Hideo to be restricted to business matters and public events only. She will not, under any circumstances, consent to a formal dissolution of their marriage. I am sure Hideo will apprise you of the finer details in due course."

I could not believe my ears. Was my affair with Hideo being somehow formalised? Would I ever be able to look at Ayumi again? I did not know where my place was, and I hated confusion. Toshio looked at me and smiled reassuringly. "You may well be wondering how we came to this understanding. Well, let me tell you, I am no stranger to the cruel tricks our hearts can play. Some years ago I too was fortunate enough to find myself deeply involved with somebody. That person meant the world to me, and for the first time in my life I was able to feel real love. I believe it is the only emotion that makes this life bearable. To be in love is to be able to express your heart's desire without fear. For a time I believed I was the happiest man in the world, until I found out my love was not true to me. I had the most awful of times and even thought about leaving this world behind. The one person who saved me from myself during those foul days was Hideo Tanaka, and I made a promise to myself to repay his kindness in any way I could. That is why I see this as the best way forward for all concerned."

I looked at Toshio, and I do believe he, too, had a tear in his eye. I passed the handkerchief back to him, and he expertly folded it in a way that did not show traces of my mascara. He replaced it in his breast pocket and looked out his window and said, as if he were thinking aloud, "I wonder if President Nixon takes a drink."

We still had a few hours' journey time in front of us, and all I could do was try to fathom the emotionally twisted logic of Toshio's reasoning. Knowing Ayumi as well as I did, I was certain she would not give up her husband so easily, especially bearing the shame of seeing him with me, her own assistant. Was her own love for Ken Miyazaki the key to her decision? Or was it simply Toshio's desire to keep a steady ship at all costs? After all, the stakes were high, and he could have lost four of his key players. Perhaps his desire to "steady the ship" came from his need to keep us all working with as much harmony as possible. Something I believed would from now on be nigh impossible.

I glanced in Toshio's direction. He seemed to have concluded his little tête-à-tête and was settling down to snooze the remainder of the journey away. I tried to work out where I now stood in my new position as exposed mistress, the company's shamed scarlet woman. How could I ever bear to even be in the same room with Ayumi? I had taken away her emotional foundation. I had never wanted this to happen, and now I cursed myself for being so weak willed and open to Hideo's advances. Why in heaven's name I could not have been more resolute I did not know. I wanted to ask Toshio's advice, but I had no idea how he would take my questions. In truth I wanted to be far away from here and heading back to Tokyo, on tonight's flight, sitting next to Hideo and hearing his soothing words. I needed him to tell me that all would be fine.

I came to the inescapable decision that I had to leave this trip as soon as possible. I prayed that Toshio would understand and allow me to return to Japan. Yes, that was what any sane and rational person would do. The very thought gave me some comfort, and I allowed myself to slip into a fantasy of escapism for a few minutes. This day was supposed to be a day to remember, and most certainly I would never forget it, but for all the wrong reasons. I didn't think it could get any worse, but then it did.

Toshio stirred from his slumber. By my reckoning we were about thirty minutes away from the most powerful house in the world. He stretched out his arms and legs and gave out a great big yawn. He looked at me, was obviously not impressed by what he saw, and decided a comfort stop was in order. In truth his own need to look in a mirror was far greater than mine. His vanity dictated that he must look his best for the grand arrival at 1600 Pennsylvania Avenue. Toshio leaned forward and tapped the dividing glass. The fellow in the front passenger seat rolled down the divider, and Toshio told him that we needed a short stop of around ten minutes. "Understood, sir."

These protection officers were the epitome of efficiency. There was some kind of exchange over the radio, and we sank back into our plush seats. Toshio fell silent, and for a moment I feared he had lapsed into one of his foul moods. His drinking had tapered off a little; perhaps it had soured his mood. I silently prayed that this was not the case and not for the first time seriously regretted being the chosen one for this evening. Without warning the limousine pulled over and turned into the forecourt of a rather grand official-looking building. I noticed that it was some kind of courthouse or something similar.

The officer in the front sprang out of his seat and swung open the rear door for Toshio to alight. The driver in turn assisted me. "Mr Hamazaki, facilities have been prepared for you inside. Please allow me to direct you and Miss Tanezawa." We followed the young man up the stone steps and into the building. I was directed to the ladies' powder room and Toshio into the facility opposite. Just as I was about to enter, Toshio whispered into my ear that he needed a private word with me before we continued on to the White House. He seemed a little tense. I prayed that his private word was not going to bring further burdens upon my already shattered conscience.

I took a little over ten minutes to repair my tear-stained face and once more made the effort to appear presentable. I prayed that nobody would notice the dark stains on the straps of my gown. After all they were only black on blood burgundy, which seemed to be an appropriate symbol for my own feeling at this moment in time.

Toshio appeared, freshly groomed and smelling of his favourite scent, Dior's Eau Sauvage—a scent I would forever associate with Toshio Hamazaki. He gently took me by the arm and led me off out of earshot of the lurking officer, who respected our obvious need for privacy. "Tanezawa, listen carefully." Did I have a choice? "I am telling you this here in the corridor because I do not trust in the integrity of our transport. I believe it to be compromised." My first reaction was one of shock. If our limousine had been bugged, then all America knew of my adulterous secret. "One of the people on this evening's guest list is a man named Rushton, Robert Rushton. He is an ex-CIA man who has harboured some form of personal vendetta against my family for years. I believe he was in some way responsible for my father's severe depression, which ultimately resulted in his death. He also played a part in your own father's death. This goes way back to 1945, in the days after the war. I believe he was the officer tasked with the interrogation of your father and was also complicit in his incarceration under the foulest of conditions.

"Now listen carefully. His attendance this evening is no coincidence. Someone is playing a mean hand, and we must be vigilant at all times. Do not let anything slip, however innocent you think your words are. More importantly do not let emotion cloud your judgement. As far as I am aware, Rushton does not know who you truly are. But I cannot take any chances. He may still hold the threads of hate that he has clung to over the years. If the name Kojima comes up in conversation, I pray you will let it float into the night without so much as a flicker of your eyelid. Can you promise me that? Forewarned is forearmed, eh, Sakura?"

Toshio seemed almost wild and breathless as he decanted his words. I barely had time to comprehend what he was saying, let alone the implications of his words, and yet there was a feeling stirring deep down in my soul that this Rushton had caused me a lot of hurt somewhere back in time. If Toshio were correct—and I had no reason to doubt him—then Rushton had affected my destiny. He had played a part in my being orphaned and everything that entailed. I had questions, but it was obvious that I would be denied the opportunity to ask them here and now. Why had Toshio waited until the last moment to tell me this? It seemed last-minute revelations were the order of the day. Perhaps he felt he should be the guardian of all doom-laden news, showing his hand only at the last minute. There was so much to be discussed, and yet words at this juncture seemed somehow pointless.

Toshio placed a sympathetic hand on my shoulder and gave me a warm smile of reassurance. "It's turning out to be memorable evening. Bear up, Sakura, and remember we are a team and that we are all in this together, now and always." I sighed and nodded my agreement. He took that as a sign of my strength. "Right, Sakura. Let's not keep the president waiting, eh?"

We made our way silently back out to the waiting limousine. I was beginning to suffer from the agitation swelling inside of me. In the space of a few hours I had been unmasked as a willing party to adultery, and now I was expected to face a man who might have killed my own father—not to mention be introduced to the most powerful man in the world. I believed any ordinary and sane human being would consider this way beyond the borders of their imagination. It was little wonder that I felt I was going to come apart.

I was beginning to look upon the confines of the limousine as some kind of claustrophobic emotional torture chamber. Our escort informed us that we would arrive at the White House in about twenty minutes' time. Toshio poured himself a large whisky and seemed surprised when I accepted his offer of the same. I needed something to calm my frayed edges. I wished to check my face one final time and whilst looking for my compact came across the Academy Awards invitation for Toshio. Perhaps now was as good a time as any to hand it over, but before I did so, I decided to write one simple question on the back of the envelope. I wrote in Japanese and hoped my words would be cryptic enough to mislead unwanted eyes and yet blindingly obvious to Toshio. A rough translation of my words would appear overly clumsy and prosaic when read back in English, but I hoped it would be sufficient to convey my feelings at this time. "Although the competition may appear strong, true talent will always prevail, and the prize will go to the one who most deserves it. 'To the victor the spoils' as they say here. I hope the path to your destiny is paved with success and will be so for many years to come."

I handed Toshio the grand-looking envelope, and he flipped it over and read my words. He smiled and said in a low voice, "You may rest assured. All is well." His face lit up when he took out the stiff gold-embossed invitations. "How very wonderful of them to invite me. I'm so honoured. It has been my dream to attend ever since I can remember." He looked at me, and I swear there were tears welling up in his eyes. Perhaps it was the liquor that was making him emotional, but for a moment I saw the child in him trying to escape. I knew he had financed some rather expensive Japanese cinematic attempts in the past, but they had largely resulted in dismal failure. Still, the world of Hollywood represented a kind of holy grail, and for Toshio to be invited to pay homage was to be closer to his dream than he had ever imagined. I did not wish to spoil his moment, but I felt certain his invitation had come with a heavy dose of expectation from the movie moguls, who would take every opportunity to pitch projects to him and offer countless executive producer titles in return for his generous financial backing. I knew Hamazaki would be unable to resist the calling his vanity so craved. The glamorous lifestyle and universal acclaim were desired with pitiful desperation and served only to paper over the dark shadows of the past.

I had begun to regret taking that double whisky. My mind was in other places as we drove slowly down Pennsylvania Avenue. As we approached the side gates of the White House, I noticed that an agitated throng of antiwar protesters had gathered on the opposite side of the street. They were penned in by a large police cordon. Nonetheless their chants carried through the air with a sharp degree of menace. Their anger was made even more vivid by the glare of our headlights, and it was obvious that our limousine had attracted their fury.

Toshio did not even glance in their direction; to him they were invisible. He was focused on the moment, and his intensity was infectious. This was supposed to be a joyous occasion, one to remember for a lifetime, one to tell your grandchildren about. However, I was shrinking into myself and trying to make myself as small as possible. I was only a glorified secretary from a poor background. How in heaven's name had I found myself here?

The answer to that conundrum lay in the fact that I was privy to the darkest secrets of an even darker past. Everyone had secrets and a place in the past where they feared to tread, and without doubt the man waiting at the grand double doors, sweating profusely, was guardian of many such darkly shrouded places. He too, without doubt, found himself lost in the maze of morality. It seemed to me that the more power and wealth one accumulated, the more the simple things in life became only a pleasant memory, not quite lost forever but no longer there to be enjoyed.

President Nixon beamed at his guests as they ascended the steps to the Blue Room. His wife, Pat, stood loyally at his side, giving out that little bit of a homey touch that her husband so obviously lacked. I cannot recall the moments leading up to the "handshake." It was as if I were in another world, another life. I was floating on air. The president's strong, confident tones bore into me and brought me partially back to ground. "Mr Hamazaki, it is such a pleasure to meet you at last. Welcome to my home. I hope we find the time to talk more later. Please come in—you are so welcome."

Hamazaki bowed in traditional Japanese style and said how honoured he was to be invited and that the pleasure was all his. The president nodded to me, smiled in a condescending manner, and indicated for us to move on through to the reception room, a kind of grand foyer with a large staircase in the centre. I was surprised at how few guests there were—no more than thirty, I would guess. It was obviously going to be an intimate dinner. This only added to my insecurity, as I thought there would be less opportunity to melt into the shadows.

I tried to stay as close to Toshio as possible, hoping some of his confidence and bravado would wash off on me. He fell into the party with all the ease of a practiced socialite. He charmed his fellow guests with his skilled conversational style, which he had perfected almost as an art form, and soon became the centre of attention in a room full of powerful people. He worked the room well, trying to meet as many of the guests as politely possible before we were all called into dinner. The president was in the far corner and seemed to be busy with a large group of dowdy-looking men, some of whom puffed on fat cigars. Toshio must have sensed my unease, for he sought to draw me into the talk at many opportunities, interjecting his anecdotes with the odd "Isn't that right, Sakura?" or "As Sakura will tell you" and other such conversational leads.

Champagne was flowing freely, and Toshio was topping up his levels without a care in the world. To him it was all so easy; in fact it was almost as if we were back in Ginza in our own grand reception room where Toshio spent so many hours receiving guests of his own. It was fast approaching eight o'clock, and soon we would be called into the dining room. There was a seating plan by the main door, and I noticed that some of the guests had drifted over to see where they had been placed. I was all too aware that a person's seating position was seen as a reflection of their importance or in some cases lack of it, but I was astounded to see that Toshio had been placed only two settings away from the president himself. My eyes scanned the plan, and with a growing sense of panic, I realised that I was not seated alongside Toshio but at a different table altogether and that seated to my left at our circular table was a Mr R. Rushton. A highly unlikely coincidence, I was sure. Having dinner in the White House with the man suspected of murdering my father. How much more my nerves could take this evening, I did not know.

Toshio sidled up to me and whispered into my ear. "Take it easy, eh. Remember, play all innocent and be your usual charming self, and all will be fine." Before I had a chance to gather my wits, a gong sounded, and we all moved into the dining room. It was luxuriously decorated, and the crystal and silverware sparkled under the light from the chandeliers above. The room had an almost seductive quality about it, as if the history of so many grand functions had given it a soul of its very own.

An aged gentleman, tall and classically styled, approached me and bowed courteously. He had the look of an older David Niven, and the manners to match. "Forgive me, but I do believe you may be Ms Tanezawa? Please allow me to introduce myself. I am Robert Rushton. It seems that we are seated together. Please allow me to escort you to the table." I was lost for words, dumbstruck, but, I hoped, managed to conceal my nerves. I bowed, and he offered me his arm and we walked together to our table. Rushton drew out my chair and with practiced ease settled me into my seat. I looked over toward Toshio and saw that he had already seated himself and was making himself known to the characters around him. Rushton busied himself greeting the man on his left; it appeared that they were old acquaintances of some kind. A nervous-looking young man to my right seemed to be in awe of the whole occasion, so much so that he could not seem to stop his staring at the president himself, who was deep in conversation with a man in the doorway. Rushton turned to me and sought to offer some reassuring words. "Ms Tanezawa, we are lucky this evening. This is a more relaxed gathering than usual. Some state affairs can be quite stuffy, you know. I much prefer these casual dinners."

He conspiratorially lowered his voice when telling me that last bit of information. He was also letting me know that he was no stranger to functions like this. I politely demurred as befitted the manner in which Rushton naturally expected me to act. After all, as far as he was concerned, I was just some humble secretary from far away and one who should hang on to his every word. I felt quite comfortable with Western etiquette; after all, I had been Ayumi's "sidekick" for more than fifteen years, during which we had dined at countless foreign embassies and hosted spectacular functions of our own. For a moment I was gripped by a deep melancholy and drifted off into a remorseful daydream. My times with Ayumi were well and truly spent. My work with the Mabuhay Foundation was over, my future now clouded in doubt.

I was brought back into the moment by the arrival of the president and Mrs Nixon. We all stood respectfully while they took their seats without announcement, after which we settled ourselves back down into our own seats. I had heard it said that Nixon hated fuss and pomp but was a stickler for respect; that is to say, he felt he was due it without question. I had also heard it whispered amongst those who care about such things that Nixon harboured grudges against those whom he believed to have slighted him in some way. His was not a happy administration, and there were often reports of discontent amongst his staff. It must be trying to be a president in times of war when hate arrives afresh just as sure as each new day dawns. How much of the gossip was accurate one may never know, but looking across at him right now I would have said he was trying his utmost to be Mr Charm personified.

It was rumoured that no wine would be served at dinner and that this was standard protocol. However, I was relieved to note that it seemed we were to be treated to wine after all, as the wine-glasses gleamed in the light. My relief was entirely centred on Toshio's behalf, as I knew he functioned much better when the wheels of conversation were greased by a steady flow of fine drink.

The president and First Lady unfurled their napkins, and we all followed suit. It was a case of "follow thy leader." This evening we were to be treated to "service American-style," meaning the courses were already served on the plates. Four courses in total. I hoped we would be out of there in no time at all. I turned to Rushton and asked him in the politest of ways what he did for a living. He gave a wave of his hand and said he had long ago retired but that occasionally someone in office sought out his opinion on this matter or that. It seemed his speciality was the diplomatic service, but I was left unsure, and Rushton did not seem keen to enlighten me any further. I put his age at around seventy-five, which would have made him about fifty years old when he tortured my father. I looked at him and then down at his liver-spotted bony hands. Had those hands been around my father's throat? Had he lashed out in violent hate at the man I loved and could now no longer even picture in my mind? The desire to stick my fork into the back of his hand was a pleasurable option that I had to fight hard to resist.

We were served a thin, watery tomato soup for the first course which everyone said tasted delicious but to me lacked spark and imagination.

Toshio was holding court like a true socialite champion. I caught sight of Rushton glaring over in his direction. Something in his expression was unmistakably unpleasant. It was there for a moment, but there it was. Contempt, loathing, disgust, perhaps even envy. I did not know but Rushton did not find the sight of Toshio Hamazaki being the life and soul of the party an easy thing to bear.

Rushton turned to me and said, "Your boss seems to be an easy fellow—charming, too. He is so different from his father, whom I had the opportunity to meet with some twenty years ago." My feigned surprise drew more out of Rushton. "Oh yes, our paths crossed when Hamazaki Senior was part of a trade delegation that visited us here in the States—1949, I believe it was. I found him to be an enlightened soul and an engaging conversationalist, if memory serves me well."

I smiled and said I had never had the fortune to meet Toshio's father but had often heard stories about him from Toshio himself. I also asked Rushton to talk with Toshio, as I was sure he would want to hear about anything to do with his father, whom he still missed dearly. Rushton seemed to give this some thought, and though his eyes were cold, he smiled at me. "I am sure I will get the chance to have a little talk with Mr Hamazaki later, but now let us enjoy this fine evening. Ms Tanezawa, I am so curious to know more about you. I am fascinated by the Far East. You know I had the opportunity to serve my country out in the Philippines during the war. I also got to see a little of Japan. Tell me, where are you from?" We talked a little about this and that. He told me of his memories of Japan and how things had changed. He avoided any talk of Mabuhay business or Hamazaki. It would have all been so pleasant if it hadn't been a charade, a dance around the unspeakable. A waltz with my father's killer.

The meal passed by with surprising uniformity. Each course was allotted twenty minutes precisely. I noticed that the president and First Lady had their timing down to a tee. The wine waiters were efficient but a little miserly in their service. I hoped Toshio was not finding his flow of wine, or lack of, too frustrating. Rushton obviously had no such concerns, as I did not see him take a drop of alcohol throughout the whole meal. He even placed his hand over his glass whenever the waiter was hovering around the table. The absurd notion that he may have thought I would drop something in his drink sprang up in my imagination like a pitchfork-wielding devil. Rushton was a cautious and cunning man, of that I had no doubt. He was party to some hideous secrets, and he may well have believed he was controlling this scenario, but little did he know he was dealing with the master schemer in Toshio.

Good manners dictated that conversation throughout the meal service be equally divided between each guest on either side; convention dictated that you alternate your attention with the arrival of each course. However, the young man on my right was most recalcitrant. His attitude suggested that he was finding the whole affair rather boring if not offensive. Grumpy in the extreme and seemingly only here on sufferance, he did not lend himself to being the ideal dining companion, and little conversation passed between us. His name was Fabian Milton, and I gathered he was an artist of sorts. The name registered slightly with me, but I could not for the life of me recall why. Milton was a good deal younger than most of the guests; I would have guessed we were of a similar age, around thirty. His dark, swarthy looks added to his mystique. He had a wild yet controlled manic aura about him, undeniably charismatic and yet far too surly for closer contact. Despite his failings I quite liked him. He was the polar opposite of Rushton, and for that small mercy I was grateful.

The meal concluded, and we were all invited to move to the music room, where we would have the opportunity to have a photograph taken with the president. The buzz of excitement was palpable, as most of the guests were living the dream of a lifetime. On being asked to move through, Milton gave an audible groan as if he had just been asked to wash all the dishes. His attitude made me smile a little. A rebellious nature, especially in the face of such white-walled protocol, was something to be admired, but it did beg the question. Why was he here at all?

The president and First Lady led the way into the music room, and we all followed at a respectful distance. As I was standing, Milton leaned towards me and said in a low voice trembling a little with drink and emotion, "Miss Tanezawa, do you ever feel that the past is a kaleidoscope of memories, some dazzlingly bright but others perhaps flickering more darkly? We embrace the light with nostalgic love, and yet we run from the shadows out of fear. We are all the same, except some of us have more light to guide us than others."

I looked at him, bemused and yet intrigued by his words. "Mr Milton, thank you for sitting through dinner with me. It has been a pleasure to meet you, and I do hope we shall have the chance to talk more later." I bowed to him, and he rewarded me with a smile that lit up his face and turned that surly young man into one of the most attractive fellows I had ever set eyes upon. For a moment I lost myself in his dark black eyes, which shone like black jade. Fabian Milton was hypnotically handsome. Without doubt a girl could get lost there.

Rushton's drab tone brought my brief reverie to a close. "Miss Tanezawa, shall we go and say hello to the president?" Reluctantly I parted company with Milton, as I had no choice but to walk to the music room with Rushton, but I could feel those dark eyes burning through my back and into my soul.

We stood around in tight groups, commenting on the delightful dinner and politely enquiring as to each other's provenance with regards to being in attendance. It was all a game, a matter of name dropping and power pushing. Some folks were wealthy enough to consider money a vulgar subject, and yet that was obviously a contradiction of sorts. In those brief moments whilst waiting for Hamazaki to rescue me, I was mistaken for a Vietnamese official of some kind, also taken for a waitress when one guest handed me an empty glass. I was dismissed out of hand by a pompous, snobbish woman when I informed her that I was a personal assistant. Many people praised my English, and I had to fend off the temptation to correct the staggering geographical ignorance of those who somehow believed Tokyo to be in China and the belief that the Vietnam War was literally being fought on Japan's own doorstep. In truth, my fellow guests were not the most enlightened of people, and I got the feeling that they believed America was the world and everything outside was just a part of something else. Perhaps they were not to blame, as we are all products of our upbringing and we all harbour insular feeling to some extent.

I watched as several people were ushered forward for a photographic opportunity with the president, who in turn grinned mechanically at the hardworking cameraman. I presumed this would all pay off in the future when the president felt the need to rattle the campaign cash jar. President Nixon was full of flattery, and his guests seemed to be lapping it up. His five-o'clock shadow was so dark, he reminded me of Fred Flintstone from the animation that Azusa loved so much. How I wished she were here now. Her lightness and irreverence would take the sting out of the pomposity and make her the perfect companion for this setting. Then I caught sight of Fabian Milton with his back against the far wall, lighting a cigarette, and I realised that perhaps Azusa's absence was not such a bad thing. I am sure she would have been away with Fabian in a flutter of her doe-like eyes.

Restlessness was setting in. Toshio was nowhere to be seen. He had been gone too long for a bathroom break, and more worryingly, Rushton too seemed to have taken his leave. Those guests who had already been captured on film for posterity were politely ushered on to an anteroom, thus leaving the music room with a dwindling number of guests. I was not sure whether to feel honoured or slighted at being in the last group. I decided to err on the former, as the president now appeared to be more exclusively ours.

Toshio was still nowhere to be seen, and my feeling of abandonment was making me more anxious by the minute. I wished I could break away from my small circle of fellow guests and go and join Milton over by the window, but I felt it was my duty to stand about and smile in agreement at the inanities that were bandied about with such casual ease. Then much to my relief I saw Toshio entering the room. He was with Rushton and one of the anonymous cigar-chomping men I had seen earlier in the president's circle. From across the music room, I could sense that Toshio's mood was not as harmonious as it had been earlier in the evening. There was an aura of defiance about him that I had seen when he faced difficult situations in the past. He spotted me and broke away from Rushton and the other man without so much as a "good evening" to either. He broke into a smile as he approached and said, "Sakura, please forgive my absence, but there was an urgent matter that needed my attention." He gave me a polite kiss on the cheek. I felt my status in the room had been given a boost as the remaining guests were finally able to put a label on me at last. Toshio politely nodded to everyone around, but his usual bonhomie was a little depleted. Perhaps the day's events were finally catching up with him. He looked over to President Nixon, who was having something whispered in his ear by Cigar Man. For a moment I was sure Nixon shot us a dark glance. Was it just my imagination playing tricks on me? Toshio was rapidly becoming bored with kicking his heels, and if it hadn't been the president, I knew for sure he would have already said his farewells. His attention was drawn to Milton, who was still loitering disrespectfully at the back. "Sakura, who is that young chap over there?" I told him his name was Fabian Milton and that I believed he was an artist of some kind. Toshio took a long look at him and then caught his attention and beckoned him over to our little group. Milton reluctantly ambled over and accepted Toshio's outstretched hand. "Mr Milton, I believe, it is a pleasure to make your acquaintance. My name is Toshio Hamazaki. Miss Tanezawa here I believe you already know." Milton smiled and said the pleasure was all his, but his eyes told a different story. I could tell at once that Toshio was more than intrigued by Milton and wanted to know more about this dashing fine young fellow. "Sakura tells me you are an artist. Tell me, what kind of artist are you?"

Milton smiled and looked down at the floor. He seemed to find Toshio's question amusing. "Mr Hamazaki, personally I find the labelling and boxing of my art quite wrong, as it tends to create preconceptions in people's minds and then they find it impossible to enjoy the pieces in the spirit in which they were created. However, much to my dislike I am generally referred to as an abstract portrait artist."

For a brief moment I thought Toshio was going to retort with some offhand remark of his own, but he smiled as if he were talking to the class clown. He placed his hand on Milton's shoulder. "I like your spirit, and I only wish there were more like you, especially in this room. Now, Mr Milton—"

"Please call me Fabian."

Hamazaki smiled once more. "Fabian. Have you been known to take on commissions?"

Milton looked at Hamazaki, his face finally lighting up. "Are you asking me to create for you?"

Toshio returned his smile. "That is exactly what I am suggesting. I want you to paint or, as you say, 'create' me. I want a work that captures the spirit of my visit here in this great country."

It was obvious that Milton was intrigued, and it did not take him long to agree. "Mr Hamazaki. Despite the fact that you may not have seen any of my works, I feel your impetuous offer deserves to be met by my own equally impetuous acceptance."

Toshio smiled in delight. He was back in his element, making deals and on the charm offensive. "Wonderful. Sakura will make the arrangements. We are on the move quite a lot, so I hope you will be able to join us on our sojourn through the country."

Milton gave that heart-melting smile of his. "Of course, and the pleasure would be all mine. I thank you, Mr Hamazaki."

For a moment Toshio was lost for words, even flustered, but his expression did all his talking for him. It was an expression I had seen many times before, but never on the face of a man and always on the face of some awed young girl who had gone weak at the knees in the company of a desirable man. Toshio reddened a little and covered his slight embarrassment by looking over towards the president and muttering, "How much longer is he going to keep us waiting?"

I would never have thought that being back in the limousine would feel so liberating; such was my relief to finally be able to put my evening at the White House behind me. Toshio slid in beside me and gave an audible groan that was somewhere between despair and anger. We had been overlooked for a personal photograph and had to settle for being part of a larger group picture which also included Fabian. I could tell this slight had rattled Toshio's pride and self-esteem, but to his credit he had managed to keep his disappointment well under wraps. It was plainly obvious that Nixon had decided to put some distance between Toshio and his own office.

Toshio stared pensively out the limousine window as we crawled out of the White House forecourt. The protesters we had seen earlier had dispersed, and the sidewalk was littered with discarded banners and signs. Toshio was brooding over the evening's events. I was all too aware that a wrong word here or there would be enough to light the emotional touch paper and send him into a foul diatribe. We travelled along in silence. Fortunately our journey was to be a short one, as we were making an overnight stay at the Washington Hilton. I could not wait to finally be alone and put the day behind me.

As we cruised down Pennsylvania Avenue, Toshio's voice cut the silence and made me start. "Driver, please stop here for a moment." The agent in the front seat looked a little weary and asked if everything was all right. Toshio nodded and muttered that all was well. He was staring at a large, seemingly abandoned building on the opposite side of the road. "Sakura, do you know what that building is?" I shook my head. "That is the once great Willard Hotel where many American presidents stayed on the eve of their inaugurations, including the great Abraham Lincoln, if my memory for history serves me well. Martin Luther King finalized his famous 'I Have a Dream' speech in that very hotel. It has hosted great names from history: P. T. Barnum, Mark Twain, the Duke of Windsor, Houdini, and Charles Dickens, to name just a few. They say walls have ears, but I wish they had tongues, too. My word, I bet that place could tell a story or two."

I craned my neck to get a better look at the place. The agent in front told us that it had closed down two years earlier and that he had heard it was probably going to be demolished. Even he looked a little saddened as he spoke. Toshio looked longingly over at the majestic edifice. "It's criminal that a thing of beauty should be allowed to waste away." I got the feeling he was putting together some kind of emotional rescue plan for the Willard. The agent asked if we could drive on. Toshio nodded, and the dividing glass was automatically raised and we proceeded to the Hilton. Silence once more ruled; Toshio looked dead beat, drained of his usual vigour. I suspected the novelty of being here in America was finally weighing him down.

In no time at all we were pulling up in front of the Hilton. The agent was out of the car in a flash and opened the nearside door for us both to exit. There was little fuss, and our greeting was very low-key. Toshio swept through the lobby as if he owned the place. I had trouble keeping pace with him, as did some of the hotel's staff who had been assigned to settle us in. There was a brief comical moment when Toshio took a wrong turn and headed away from the elevators, but any levity was far away as the tension poured out of him like a boiling kettle. We rode the elevator up to the top floor, where Toshio's suite was. I had a room on the floor below, but Toshio had firmly told me to travel up to his suite. My heart sank. I was so desperate to bathe and get into bed. My thoughts suddenly were with Hideo, and I enviously realised that he must have been airborne on his way back to Tokyo. I would have given anything to be on that plane with him right then.

The elevator came to a smooth halt, and we exited onto a fussily decorated corridor hued in greens and red. Contemporary hotels could sometimes register as a little strange, as we almost always stayed in the finest classic hotels whose furnishings seemed to fit like a couture ensemble and were always pleasing to the eye. The suite came replete with a personal butler, and he was standing rigidly by the doors to greet us and offer some orientation, which Toshio firmly declined. However, true to form, he did request a large bourbon on the rocks. The agent seemed satisfied that all was well, and the attendant staff retreated, leaving us alone in the vast suite, which must have been larger than ten normal-sized bedrooms put together.

Toshio sank into a plush leather sofa, cradling his drink. He looked up at me. "Sakura, you did well this evening. I am proud of you." I let his words sink in and allowed some kind of perverse satisfaction to seep into my soul. "Sakura, I think it is time for you to take a few steps closer to the heart of Mabuhay. I have called an important meeting for tomorrow. I have instructed Miyazaki and Weinstein to attend, and along with you, the four of us will work our way out of a little problem or two." I did not know what to say so I said nothing, just bowed and kept my head down. "Now, go and get some rest. Tomorrow is a new day; let us face it with all the steel we can muster. Good night and sleep well."

Finally I was on my own, and I made my way down to my own room, where I was relieved to find that my overnight case had been forwarded as I had instructed. I locked my door, kicked off my shoes and sank onto the bed, and closed my eyes. My mind had blanked out from sheer emotional exhaustion. Closer to the heart of Mabuhay. Those words were floating around like a ghostly echo sounding out the depths of my psyche.

The ringing grew louder and reached an ear-splitting intensity until suddenly I was jolted awake. The phone by my bed was trilling away, and the shameful realisation that I had slept all night on my bed fully clothed and unwashed was enough to send me into an early morning panic. My God! Had I missed the meeting?

I looked at the bedside clock. Eight twenty-two. I picked up the phone and was surprised to hear Ken's voice. "Tanezawa, good morning. Toshio has set up a meeting for ten this morning in his suite. It seems that your attendance is required." I thanked him for his call and said I would be there. Thank heavens for small mercies. I had plenty of time to refresh before the meeting and to compose myself at my leisure.

I went into the bathroom and turned on the bath taps. Whilst my bath was filling, I turned on the television and dialled for some room service. I ordered coffee and a selection of pastries. I longed for a simple Japanese breakfast of miso soup, pickles, and rice, and wondered how long it would be before I got a taste of my old life. It was then that I realised that I was becoming overwhelmed by homesickness. We had been here only a matter of days, and yet all that had happened made it seem much longer. I was beginning to hate America—or was I beginning to hate myself? Our matron at the orphanage always used to say that the mood you wake up with stays with you like a monkey on your back for the whole day, so it was always important to greet each day with a light heart and a smile on your face. I had neither. In fact I could not remember when I had last smiled. I stripped off my clothes, and just as I was about to get in the bath, the door chimed. Breakfast had arrived. My word, such efficiency. I hurriedly wrapped myself in the voluminous bathrobe and opened the door to allow the waiter in. He was pushing a food trolley replete with silver service. I was a little surprised, as he was quite an elderly man. As he was fussing about changing the trolley into a makeshift table, the phone rang and automatically I answered. It was the room attendant enquiring if now would be an opportune time to make up and clean my room. I found the request a little odd, as it was so early in the morning, but told them that after ten would be fine. The waiter had finished his task and stood about paying unnecessary attention to the layout of the crockery. I knew he was waiting on his tip, so I went over to my bag and took out a five-dollar bill and handed it to him. I thought it was a little overly generous, but I had nothing smaller and he did seem genuinely thankful. He wished me a fine and pleasant day and left me to my breakfast. I decided to bathe first and get myself ready, just in case I was summoned earlier than expected.

A soothing, warm bath does wonders for the mind and body, and I felt my spirits rise a little as I sat down to eat. The television was airing the latest news from the war in Vietnam. It was obvious that political tensions had split the media and the reports of increasing casualties were adding to the unpopularity of the Nixon administration. The violation of a sovereign country, Cambodia, by American forces and the subsequent Kent State University campus killings had swept the tide of public opinion firmly into the antiwar camp. Any reasonable person could see that it was a case of damage limitation for Nixon's government. Last evening I had seen the man up close and the strain was definitely there, inescapably etched into his face like an unwanted tattoo, but there was also something else, a determination and defiance in the face of mounting odds. Nixon was obviously not a weak man. He was being played by events thousands of miles away. He had come into office in 1968, promising "peace with honour." There it was: an implicit admission that the war was unwinnable. I for one was not sure why America had involved itself in the first place. Could it really be to stop the spread of Communism? Perhaps Nixon did not realise that there were no lasting thanks for winning a war. People would always remember the awful things, and they had a very short window of gratitude for anything good. It was always far better to please the people than appease them. Nixon could learn a thing or two from Toshio, of that I was sure.

Finally, I felt ready to face the day. It was fast approaching ten, and I decided to make my way up to Toshio's suite. It seemed like a lazy indulgence to ride the elevator up one floor, but I wasn't sure where the staircase was. Walking along the long corridor I passed Toshio's butler, who was pushing a food cart and making slow progress, as the carpet pile was a little too deep for wheels. He nodded and wished me a pleasant morning. I noticed the remains of breakfast and also two whiskey glasses. Toshio had developed the unhealthy habit of having a shot or two of whisky mixed with warm milk as his breakfast drink of choice. I could hear voices as I tapped on the door. Ken opened the door and waved me inside. Seated around the spacious dining table were Toshio and Weinstein and, surprisingly, Meursault, who had finally arrived from Europe. He looked all in. His eyes were sunken, and the dark circles under them were so heavy that they looked as if they had been drawn on his face by an animator. Weinstein and Meursault both stood to greet me. Toshio remained seated. He seemed to be in deep concentration, poring over some papers spread out in front of him. I felt Ken's hand on my shoulder and turned around to face him. He brought his index finger to his lips to tell me to be silent. He knelt down and took a small pole from out of a bag. It was some kind of electrical device, and he proceeded to move it around the contours of my body. He repeated the exercise several times, eventually indicating that I should remove my jacket, which he took over to the dining table. I followed and watched as Ken extracted a small round black buttonlike object from the hem. He placed it into a tiny tin, which in turn he put into another foam-wrapped container. Everyone watched in silence. Eventually Ken nodded, and an air of relief seemed to spread about the room. Ken looked at me and said. "You were bugged. That was a listening device. Has anyone been near you this morning?" I was about to say no when I remembered the room waiter. It seemed breakfast was not the only thing he had delivered. The phone call must have been to distract me. I told Ken this, but surprisingly, nobody seemed unduly worried. Toshio's voice boomed out as if in defiance. "Occupational hazard, you could say. Better get used to it, Sakura, especially as you are now officially in the inner circle." There did not seem to be an appropriate answer to that, and I got the feeling none was expected. Toshio went on. "Thanks to Ken's little gadget, we can safely assume we are now 'safe' to speak freely."

Ken was fiddling about with a box about the size of a cigarette pack. He seemed satisfied, and nodded. "Even if there are any stray bugs in this room, they are now scrambled."

Toshio smiled. "At least it is good to see that Mabuhay can still make products that keep us one step ahead of the American intelligence services." I caught sight of Weinstein, who looked a little pained to hear his country talked down. Toshio told us all to take a seat, and once we were settled, wasted no time in telling us what was on his mind. "As you all know, yesterday I had the honour of being invited to the White House for dinner, where I had some engaging conversations with some rather unpleasant individuals. There is no easy way to say this, so I will spare us all the small talk and get down to the heart of what turned out to be a rather unsavoury evening."

Toshio had our complete attention. "Rushton was at the dinner, and he had a message for me." The mere fact that Rushton's name did not register any surprise on the faces of the others told me that they were already privy to much more than I had realised. Did they know that Toshio suspected Rushton of killing my real father? Of course they did. These men had known more about the "real" me than I had known myself. What of Hideo and me? Did they know of our little arrangement? I felt uneasy and exposed. My life had been turned inside out and upside down, and it would take time before I felt comfortable with myself again.

Toshio looked grave as he spoke. "Rushton wants us to use Mabuhay leverage to gain more air bases for the United States Air Force, both in Japan and the Philippines. He seems convinced that we hold sufficient influence with the powers that be to secure his demands. They want more access for their war machine and want us to pave the way. In return they will cease all active investigations into Mabuhay and its connections to missing war treasures. An absurd notion, I know, but Rushton seemed convinced that he could turn his deluded fantasies into reality." There was a smirk on Toshio's face as he spoke, and it was plain that Rushton was not the only one weaving a complex web of deceit. "Rushton told me that he met with my father twenty years ago and they reached an 'understanding' whereby my father would be allowed to trade freely back home in his own country in return for information that led to the recovery of wartime artefacts. Unfortunately for Rushton my father 'supposedly' took his own life soon after he returned from that meeting, and I believe Rushton never got the information he craved. It is my firm conviction that Rushton played no small part in my father's death, and now that pathetic, flag-waving so-called patriot believes the same tactic may work with me. I think Mr Rushton has made a huge error in judgement, but he is not to be underestimated. He offered me something—a 'taster,' he called it—and here it is."

Toshio gestured towards the papers spread out on the table in front of him. "I invite you all to study these papers carefully. Digest what you read, because they will be destroyed after reading." There was a kind of manic aura about Toshio that was disturbing me. His audacity spoke volumes, and it was plain to see that he believed he was untouchable. Here we were in the Washington Hilton, openly discussing the unsavoury side of our business dealings, in spite of the valiant efforts of the American government, which was obviously desperate to get to the heart of Mabuhay and the secrets we carried so close to our tainted souls. If they ever managed to unlock the hidden truth, they would find a conspiracy so shocking and incredible, I doubt they would even be able to believe the half of it. Even I, who had been party to some of the more revolting truths of the past fifteen years, could scarcely bring myself to acknowledge the awful reality of what actually constituted the day-to-day dealings of Mabuhay, and here was our leader, driven by the demons that hid deep in his soul, a man who may have been described as borderline psychotic, yet gifted with a certain genius that allowed him to act without feeling, and the cold heart required to make the cruellest of decisions.

The papers were passed around from hand to hand. Nobody spoke, but it was plain to see that what they had just read caused concern, although these men were well accustomed to dealing with the dark side. Even so, I noticed that Ken allowed his steely demeanour to crack, as I detected a trace of disbelief—or was it pure anger? I was the last to get the papers, and I felt all eyes on me as I read the brief note which had been prepared on a kind of official form and was headed "Joel Richardson—Chief Operating Officer, Sonic Enterprises." It was brief and to the point, no doubt prepared in a censorious form for our eyes. It implied that Richardson had offered himself as a kind of informer to the Central Intelligence Agency in return for full immunity from any future prosecutions arising from his information. In addition Richardson had pressed for some form of official guarantee that he be allowed to remain at the helm of Sonic in the event of Mabuhay being legally deconstructed. There was no indication of the nature of the information that Richardson had supposedly given. Farther down the paper it was reported that Richardson had approached the Marios regime in the Republic of the Philippines and offered to help find the locations of sites where stolen wartime artefacts might still be concealed.

I read it through and then handed it back to Toshio, who, lost in thought, had annoyingly started tapping his pencil on the table. "We have to bear in mind that this report may be an entire fantasy, concocted by the Americans to force our hand," he said. "I have started my own investigation into the matter, but for now I think it prudent to take it as true until otherwise proven." He took the paper and, along with a few other pieces, proceeded to set them afire, and then dropped them into the steel waste bin by his chair. We all watched in silence, as we knew that the small whipping flames and charred smell confirmed the verdict on Mr Joel Richardson.

Toshio looked at each of us in turn and finally spoke, not with the arrogance shown a few minutes earlier but in hushed tones, tinged with sadness. "We can only assume that there was a lot of truth in this pile of ashes, but the question we must ask ourselves is, Why would the Americans give us Richardson? Was he not quite the catch they believed? Did they really think he was worth giving up in return for a few more air bases? I think not. The reason lies in their belief that Richardson was doubling on them. His treachery came as no surprise. I first became aware of this 'black agenda' over a year ago, when Romana himself made an initial approach to Richardson. It seemed that our 'arrangement' with Romana no longer satisfied his avarice, and he felt compelled to take matters into his own hands.

"Romana's trusted lieutenant, Hector, who also doubles as our man, has proved himself to be most valuable. He kept us well abreast of developments, and it was his information that allowed us to stay one step ahead of the game. Romana found himself under increasing pressure from his father-in-law, President Marios, to come up with a bounty large enough secure his second term. Elections are an expensive business, and Marios has many pockets to fill. With some carefully planted rumours that we allowed to reach Richardson, we managed to isolate his worth, as any information he was able to give would be totally discredited, resulting in his losing all credibility and looking foolish to boot. Thank God for our eyes and ears in that farce of a government over in Manila. I believe the Americans no longer value Richardson as an asset and they are trying to squeeze the last bit of worth out of the situation. Once more we have cause to thank Ogawa for saving our hides."

The mere mention of his name was enough to send my pulse racing. Ogawa, the man nobody spoke openly about. He was Mabuhay's ghost, isolated and yet invaluable to the continued success of everything we did. A man who operated as if he were still at war behind enemy lines, a man who had sacrificed so much for us all and who in return deserved our unflinching gratitude. I had known of Ogawa's role for quite some time. Five years ago on a foundation visit to Manila I had seen the man himself, though I was not fully aware of it at the time. Only later when I subtly pressed Hideo was I able to get the full picture. Of all the regrettable actions we had been involved in over the years, Ogawa's situation was the one that hurt Hideo the most. They had been war buddies, comrades in arms, but much to Hideo's eternal shame, never comrades in peace. However, such foibles did not trouble Toshio. I doubted he ever lost as much as a minute's sleep over Ogawa's situation. He saw his contribution to Mabuhay's rise as a necessary sacrifice. He had tried to soothe his conscience by taking Ogawa's father into his employ as a chauffeur and later as a butler. Hideo was never comfortable with that situation and found it distressing to see the old man go about his duties, believing his only son lost in action in some Philippine battlefield. Ogawa, in turn, was kept in ignorance as to his father's health, which had deteriorated to the point where he was no longer able to perform his duties. Ogawa Senior was eventually sidelined to a retirement home where he had passed away "peacefully" some four years earlier. Hideo did not know if Ogawa had been informed of his father's passing; he suspected not.

Toshio looked at each of us, as if he were trying to take a measure of our resolve. "Gentlemen and ladies, let us take a few moments to consider our position—or more precisely, that of Mr Richardson. It would be foolish of us to believe that merely forcing him out would draw a line under this sorry episode. No, I think a more final approach would be in order. Ken, I will trust the matter to you. Nothing further needs to be said on the matter. As for the Americans' requests, I do believe we will be able to satisfy their proposal."

Toshio leaned back in his chair, which creaked alarmingly, stretched his arms out wide and put his hands behind his head, and somewhat inappropriately gave out a huge yawn. We all took this as a sign that our little meeting had run its course and we were dismissed. Just as we were about to make our way out, Toshio spoke once more, almost as if he were thinking out aloud, as a kind of afterthought. "This unfortunate turn of events has made me realise that it is time we draw a line under some of our past dealings. I think it is time for certain people to become reacquainted with each other, for this is the 1970s, man has been to the moon and back, colour TV is everywhere, and people actually take vacations. The world is now a different place, and Mabuhay needs to redefine its direction. I do not see any further gain in keeping Romana and his cronies in our employ any longer. It is time to play the end game."

The last sentence hung in the air like frozen ice. It was plain to see that Ken knew exactly what he meant, but Weinstein and Meursault looked as puzzled as I did. "As this is not strictly a legal nor a financial matter, I do not wish to prey further on your valuable time," Toshio said. Weinstein and Meursault nodded and made their way out. I was about to join them, but Toshio stopped me in my tracks. "However, this is most certainly a Mabuhay matter, so I will require you two for a few moments more."

Ken and I both reseated ourselves and waited for further instructions. Toshio did not look particularly concerned as he went on to outline his intentions. "Ken, as you know, we have always kept Romana in the dark about the number of precious sites. If he were ever to become aware that only one final site remains to be liberated, then I believe the old jackal would be unable to resist his natural instincts. If I have his card marked correctly, I know he would stop at nothing to help himself to the final pot of gold, and that is exactly what we want him to do.

"Ken, you need to pay a visit to Manila. The usual protocol will apply—the same financial arrangements and terms. Do not agree to anything unusual that might arouse the snake. However, let it be known that this shipment requires special attention to detail, as it is of 'extra interest.' That should be enough to pique his curiosity. I will arrange for the word to reach Romana's ears that this will be the last of our dealings and that as far as Mabuhay is concerned, will signify the end of all contact. He will barely be able to suppress his anger and frustration, let alone his greed. A delayed financial inducement will be enough to ensure your own safety, at least for the duration of your assignment. If I know Romana as well as I believe, then he will want to grab the lot for himself, and when he does, he will be met with a reception committee most foul. Let's begin by dropping a word into the ear of our own Mr Richardson; after all, he may serve one more useful purpose before taking his final mortal breath."

Toshio was staring directly at me as he said those final shocking words. What was it that he wanted to see? Was he testing me or even teasing? There was no hint of play. He was seriously gauging my reaction. He had just hinted at a man's death and I was sitting there dumbly, like a secretary taking notes. My new domestic arrangement as Hideo's concubine had come at a terrible price. It was obvious that I had now graduated within the company, so to speak. Fifteen years ago I had been helping Ayumi set out places for a dinner party and helped take the guests' coats. Nobody knew or even cared about me. Now I was the confidant of the most powerful businessman in the world, and much to the shame of my ever downward spiralling morality, I couldn't deny that it felt good.

The flight from John F. Kennedy Airport had taken nearly fourteen hours. The huge Pan Am airliner had cruised along, speeding me closer to Tokyo and into my lover's arms, leaving the madness of the past week further behind me. Toshio had ordered my return to Japan, and it had come like a godsend, a divine bolt from the blue. Furthermore it was obvious to Toshio that I could no longer function so close to Ayumi. The guilt ate away at me, and I dreaded the time we would meet face-to-face. Toshio was no fool; he had known all along that this new arrangement would take some time to bed in, so to speak. He had casually tossed my flight ticket onto the table back at the Washington Hilton and with little fanfare merely said, "Give Hideo my regards, and I will see you both soon." I had temporarily lost the ability to speak. I had resigned myself to a month of misery, trailing across the States, living in the shadow of Ayumi's wrath and being treated like some kind of corporate harlot. Now there was to be light at last. I felt the tears roll down my cheeks, and they dropped onto the desk like the big raindrops we get only in Tokyo in June.

Toshio and Ken were not comfortable with my overly emotional state and chose to ignore me by making small talk about how much they both missed "real" food and how lucky I was to be on the way back. Toshio had even slipped into a jokey mood by telling me that I would miss Elvis. I immediately thought of Azusa and how much I would miss her company. I asked Toshio to pass on my best wishes to her, which he assured me he would do. When things happened, they tended to happen quickly around here, and Toshio pointed out that my flight was due to leave in six hours' time. He told Ken to arrange a hotel car to take me to the airport. My personal items back at the Plaza would be packed and forwarded by the hotel concierge.

After a whirlwind of panic, dashing to and fro, I eventually found myself on the flight. I had dozed fitfully for most of the journey; total sleep was still way beyond me. I was a nervous wreck, fraught with mixed emotions. My relief at being back in Tokyo was tinged with a feeling of failure, that I had somehow let the side down by leaving early. I was roused by the stewardess before landing at Haneda. My stomach started to tingle; I was close to my love and the reassurance that all would be well.

As the wheels of the huge airliner bounced down on Japanese soil, I let out a sigh of relief. America was behind me, but I knew it would always be with me. Those few days, crazy as they were, had redefined me as a person and also changed my life. It was no longer possible to fool myself into believing that I was some kind of innocent who had been caught up in crimes so foul. Now I was a part of everything, and when the day finally came for the world to pronounce judgement, I would have to take my place in the dock along with the rest of them.

The formalities of my arrival were dealt with in the brisk, brusque, and efficient manner we had come to expect from the officials trusted to dispense their duty in a manner I had come to regard as uniquely Japanese. How things had changed over the previous decade. The economic boom had touched everyone's life in one way or another. Some said it had "softened" a generation. The older folk were quick to criticise the young by saying they had lost their backbone. The right-wing fanatics cruised the streets in trucks blaring out messages, berating the government for toadying to the Americans, and crying out for the restoration of militarism. The students were showing they did in fact have backbones and were taking to the streets in droves, protesting against the Vietnam War and anything else that raised their ire. These were strange times for my country. We were, once more, in transition and seeking to redefine our identity, which had recently been shaken loose. Toshio had once told me that he loved our new pacifist stance, because as a nation it left us with more time to pursue economic warfare. The new battlefields were the corporate boardrooms; the generals were the tycoons who could rattle governments by merely releasing press statements.

The concept of modern-day power had changed. America and Russia were hell-bent on opposing each other, throwing their resources into a vast bottomless well, each creating a huge arsenal of weapons to scare the other witless. Whilst they were distracted and obsessed with the arms race, Japan had been well placed to do what we seemed good at doing, which was making money and lots and lots of it. My thoughts went back to the States, where I calculated the time difference and recalled the schedule of events.

Toshio and the rest of the party would be about to board a flight to Chicago. More facility visits and hands to shake before going on to Las Vegas. I had the schedule etched onto my heart, as I had been the one who had prepared each and every stop. I too should have been there, loyally standing by my boss's side, but here I was, walking through the new arrivals hall at Haneda airport, allowing the familiarity of being back in my own land to ease my troubled soul.

I had been informed that somebody would be here to meet me, and I anxiously looked about the ranks of waiting cars and taxis for a familiar face. I knew Hideo was unlikely to come himself; it was not in his character. Just as I was about to give up on being greeted at all, a tall and rather shockingly cadaverous-looking man stepped forward and introduced himself. "Miss Tanezawa, my name is Baba. I have been instructed to meet and drive you." I nodded, then handed him my small case and followed him out to the parking bay. A gleaming black Toyota Century limousine was waiting and attracted the occasional inquisitive glance from passersby. No doubt their interest was piqued by seeing a woman climb into the rear seat. These cars were unambiguously associated with the big business moguls of our country, and women most certainly were not represented amongst their number. No doubt any curiosity would be satisfied by pegging me as a wife or daughter of a powerful man. To my sudden dismay I realised I was somewhere between the two. Hideo was twenty-four years older than I was, and although our age difference was significant, it had seldom preyed on my mind, and yet at times I felt a crisis of confidence sweeping over me. I settled down for the hour or so drive from Haneda to the Empire and, should heaven bless me, into the arms of my love.

Baba was not the talkative type; in fact he made me feel a little uncomfortable. I would catch sight of him trying to snatch glimpses of me in the rearview mirror. I wondered where Hideo managed to find these creepy men. Perhaps they fitted his ideal as the perfect chauffeur.

Looking out the window, I was struck by the contrast between what was before me and the country I had just left behind. The comical chaos of the New York streets was still very much in my mind, and I now found the sight of my own country a little disturbing. I had never noticed how grey Japan actually was. The uniformity of the landscape rendered it dull, and despite being designed for practical purposes offered little to stimulate the imagination. In fact the monotony was causing me to doze away as Baba made slow progress. He kept his driving to a constant ten kilometers below the legal limit. I could not help but recall speeding along this same highway with Hosokawa, who would take it as a personal affront if another driver managed to pass him. I had learned the hard way that melancholic nostalgia ate away at any chance of finding true happiness, and I was determined to arrive at the Empire with some semblance of joy, despite all that had happened over the past week.

The Century came to a smooth halt in front of the newly remodeled Empire Hotel. I had still not managed to fully appreciate the effect the new place had on the surroundings and also on our lifestyles. The Hamazaki family had long been connected to this hotel. I had heard that Toshio's grandfather was one of the initial investors in the very first construction more than a hundred years earlier. Toshio's own father had taken permanent tenure of a suite of rooms in the old William Lionel Francis–designed original, which had somehow ended up as Hideo's home, and later, following his union with Ayumi, his marital home. Now that had ended, torn apart by me? The guilt would be with me forever, of that I was sure. I wondered if Ayumi had made arrangements to have her personal belongings removed. Perhaps it was better not to consider those heart-wrenching details, as the devils inside of me would forever be pricking my heart with their little red hot pitchforks.

I waited in the car for Baba to open the door for me, which he did with an exaggerated sense of self-importance. I stepped out of the car and was at once drawn into the familiarity of my surroundings. This place had over the years become a kind of illicit second home for me, but now the parameters that governed my position had changed. I was to be an official "unofficial" kind of resident. Toshio had told me that I was to reside in an apartment near Hideo's suite. I had not given that notion too much thought until now, as I was faced with the awkward decision about where to go from here. Baba stood motionless, like some formal statue crafted from a block of cold grey granite. For a moment I was lost. I had half hoped Hideo would be on hand to welcome me, but experience had taught me to expect otherwise. Corporate bosses do not stand about waiting to greet their assistants, even if they do share beds.

I was not left in a fluster for long, for out of the bustling lobby stepped Mr Noguchi, the new assistant general manager of the hotel. "Tanezawa san, welcome home to the Empire." His words caused my stomach to lurch. Those very same words were the ones he used to greet Ayumi every time she herself returned "home." Had my new position already been formalised with the staff? Noguchi had worked here for many years. He had been a bellboy when Hideo spent his very first night here. In fact, Hideo once told me how he did not even have a few coins in his pocket to tip the young bellboy on that first night and how shamed he had felt. Now Noguchi was one step away from the top job. I knew Hideo and Toshio were both on good terms with him, but I could not bring myself to believe they would share intimacies. However, was it possible to keep anything discreet when you lived in a hotel?

Noguchi bowed politely and led the way in the deferential manner honed out of years of commercial domestic service. I did not have the faintest notion where or to what I was heading, but I knew it was best to follow on and brazen it out. We strode through the gleaming, spacious lobby. Noguchi greeted some of the more familiar patrons as we made our progress to the elevators. The young girl attending the elevator bowed and automatically pressed the button for the fourteenth floor, an action that confirmed that a degree of acceptance had been reached. Hideo's suite was on the fifteenth floor, so at least it seemed we were expected to conduct ourselves with a modicum of decorum.

Noguchi showed me to my new residence. From the doors we passed it seemed I was to be housed in an ordinary room, and the door we reached offered nothing that might lead you to think otherwise. Noguchi opened up my room and bade me to step inside. Words escaped me, for what was before my eyes was a thing of pure delight. My room was in fact several rooms redesigned and refurbished into a vast, spacious, beautiful home. I could not help but smile, and my joy seemed to transfer to Noguchi, who seemed to swell with pride at being able to present such fine accommodation. He did not wish to trespass on my emotions any further and politely left me alone to explore my new home.

After a few delightful moments looking over my residence, I inevitably flopped down onto the bed and stared at the ornate ceiling decorations. I realised at once that it was a play on Toshio's own Harmony Room, which was exquisitely adorned in a similar fashion. Playful koi swam and jumped in vain attempts to catch the sparkling dragonflies that perpetually tantalised them. The murals had been etched in very fine pastels so as not to be too obtrusive to the senses. It was a wonderful piece of art, and for the first time in weeks I felt my heart warm.

As I gazed up at my new world, I began to think of my own life and the pitiful events that had led me here. My father, whom I had never known, taken away from me by a war thousands of miles away, never to return, tortured, abandoned, and murdered by whom? My dear innocent mother burnt to death as she slept peacefully in her bed. I often had memory flashes of my mother praying for her lost husband's soul. Had she prayed the night that evil men came to close the circle? I might never know the real truth behind my parents' deaths, and perhaps it would be better for my own peace of mind if it remained so. I had grown up alone, in an orphanage that was regimented and disciplined. Tenderness and love had been alien concepts to me for so long. Mabuhay was my family now, and whatever events had led me here, I should be grateful. If I were to die tomorrow, then so be it. I seemed to be shaped by events around me over which I had no control. It was futile to resist, so I would not attempt to try.

I did not know if all this was just the start of a new beginning or something which marked the end of my old self. Only time would tell, but I feared it would not all be as joyous as the koi before my eyes seemed to suggest. Being at the heart of Mabuhay had come at a dear price, the ultimate price, paid by others on my behalf.

Since my return from America I had seen far less of Hideo than I would have liked, and much to my disappointment and frustration he had yet to visit me here, in my own rooms. He had been deeply involved with some important business about which he had shown little inclination or desire to share the details. I did wish he would confide in me more often; his reluctance only served to fuel my growing sense of insecurity. For in truth, I did not know what was now expected of me, either professionally or emotionally.

I felt like a lost soul, and the splendour of my new home did little to ease my frustration. I seemed to spend day after day closeted in here, filling my time by reading newspapers and watching news bulletins on television. Occasionally I would venture out on shopping sojourns, but I seldom made a purchase, unable to make the simplest of decisions about which blouse or skirt to buy. It only seemed to confirm that I was a soul in transit waiting for guidance or, mercifully, divine deliverance.

My only hope lay with Hideo, but he too was still coming to terms with our new "arrangement." His natural reticence and inability to express his deepest feelings were things I had heard Ayumi complain about on many occasions. Now it was my turn to feel those same frustrations, though I knew I was not standing on the same solid foundations that she had once occupied. Ayumi was constantly on my mind, and at times I found it impossible to think of anything else. She invaded my sleep and wreaked havoc on my ability to concentrate on even the most mundane of things. It was guilt, and quite simply it was tearing me apart inside.

I desperately needed Hideo to tell me how I was to live, how we were to live. Of course he never did. We would spend quiet evenings together in his suite where small talk was the order of the day. He avoided any subject that might broach the emotional. It was obvious that he too was fighting his demons. I noticed that he had started to work more from his suite and had installed extra telephone lines. His desk was beginning to resemble that of a military officer in command of some huge battle. Antiques and valuable art were moved aside to make way for wall charts and pieces of electronic equipment with which he would spend hours tinkering. It appeared he was losing himself in the only way he knew how; it was his way of escape.

He would instruct me to cancel appointments on his behalf, and to concoct credible excuses, I would find myself telling untruths on the phone about why Hideo Tanaka was unable to attend this function or that meeting. On the increasingly rare occasions he did actually leave the hotel, he would exit from the rear, using staff corridors and avoiding all contact with the normal people who thronged the public areas of the Empire.

Hideo was becoming a hermit, a billionaire recluse, and I was his emotional hostage. That was how life was shaping up for Hideo and me. We had not made love once since my return; he had not even so much as touched my hand. I felt drained of all natural feeling, craving. I needed some kind of rewarding employ, but none seemed forthcoming.

It came as a shock even to me when one evening, and for no obvious reason I found myself unable to contain my tears and completely broke down in howls of primal sobs. Everything before me was black. I had lost the colour from my world. Hideo merely looked up from whatever was occupying his time and with a sigh walked over to one of the phones on his desk. I could hear his voice, though it seemed miles away. "Doctor Kato, please attend to Miss Tanezawa at your earliest, if you please."

The medication I was given helped me move away from the edge, and the world seemed a calmer and more peaceful place for an adulteress to go about her daily life. Not that I actually had a daily life as such. I still went up to Hideo's suite to take dinner with him, even though we sat together in virtual silence. I often felt as if I were floating on a fluffy white cloud, and began to find my lack of purpose quite comforting. I tried to undertake the simplest of tasks, but often gave up after a few moments. The newspapers were left unread, and the television screen remained blank. Doctor Kato attended to me twice a day in my own rooms. He checked my vitals and gave me medication. I wasn't trusted with the actual possession of my own tablets; perhaps he and others had learned a lesson from Hosokawa's tragic demise. My relationship with reality was far from stable, but the tears had ceased and I found myself stabilising, albeit as a slower, thinner, and more haunted version of my former self.

One afternoon, after Hideo's butler had cleared away the lunch service, one of the telephones on Hideo's desk rang shrilly, causing me to momentarily stir from my medically induced placidity. Hideo answered, and nodded solemnly. He strode over to the television and tuned in to a special midday news broadcast. We sat in silence, watching as the news anchor, shuffling papers and being handed updates Cronkite-style, delivered his shocking report in a monotone, as if he were reading us all a bedtime story. "Details are still coming in, and we will keep you informed as we receive them, so please stay tuned. An attempt has been made on the life of Mabuhay president Toshio Hamazaki, who has been traveling in the United States. Around seven thirty local time, Mr Hamazaki was leaving his hotel in Las Vegas, Nevada, when an unidentified man wielding a handgun managed to fire several shots before being wrestled to the ground by security personnel. Eyewitnesses said the scene was one of utter pandemonium, with guests and bystanders screaming and fleeing the area. It is reported that several people, whose identities are yet to be confirmed, were hit by gunfire. It is also reported that security officers and the assailant did exchange shots."

Hideo sat still, staring at the screen. His face remained passive, betraying nothing of what he must have felt inside. We did not talk. The screen held our attention as we waited with morbid personal fascination for further details. The newsman filled his lack of information with a hastily put-together profile of Mabuhay and Toshio and a sketchy outline of what the newsroom knew of Toshio's visit to the United States.

As the news anchor was going into details about the rise of Mabuhay, he was handed another piece of paper by a staffer. He read it for a moment before fixing us with his solemn gaze. "I have just been handed an update on the shootings in Las Vegas. I must stress that these are unconfirmed reports, though they can be attributed to reliable sources. The gunman struck as Mr Hamazaki and his party were leaving their hotel to attend a concert by the legendary performer Elvis Presley. The attack has left at least one member of Mr. Hamazaki's party dead and another wounded. We are getting reports, yet to be confirmed, that Mr Joel Richardson has been killed and Miss Azusa Hosokawa has been wounded. However, Mr Hamazaki himself is unhurt, as are his sister, Mrs Ayumi Tanaka, and her son, Tatsuya. We have just received a report that the assassin was killed at the scene, apparently shot dead by security personnel."

A picture of Joel Richardson in his younger days appeared on the screen. The anchor went on to inform his viewers that Mr Richardson was the president of Sonic, Mabuhay's manufacturing division in the United States, as well as a Mabuhay board member and trusted business confidant of Mr Hamazaki. He also told his viewers that they were waiting on an official statement from

Mabuhay's headquarters here in Tokyo. "We will bring you more details as we receive them."

Hideo stood and walked over to the phone. He picked up the receiver and calmly said, "Wait thirty minutes and then give them the initial release." There was a pause, and then Hideo picked up his conversation. He looked directly at me as he spoke. "Yes, the initial press release—the one we agreed on yesterday."

Chapter 11
Elias Cohen
Washington
1970

"What the hell were you thinking? Are you so far gone in your own little world that you honestly believe you are now the almighty arbitrator of justice? What a fucked-up mess." Robert Rushton shook his head in shocked disbelief at his own use of profanity. He removed his glasses and gave the bridge of his nose a short massage.

Cohen squirmed on the other side of the desk as his former boss vented his anger and frustration, unable to look the man he had once so admired in the eyes. Cavernous silence descended as Rushton looked down at the file in front of him. Cohen arched his neck slightly in an effort to see what Rushton was reading, but it was plain that Rushton was collecting his thoughts and using the paper merely as a prop. "I can't protect you from this." He banged his fist down on the file for emphasis. "All I can do is plead on your behalf, and I do that only out of respect for the service you previously gave, but before I go as far as to even consider helping you, I need to know everything."

Rushton leaned back in his chair and stared at the man in front of him. It was impossible not to feel some kind of pity, and he could not escape the cold feeling that he was partly responsible for what Cohen had become. Physically, his onetime operative was barely recognisable as the man he once had been. Rushton had always thought of Cohen as a portly man, and he remembered him as one who never refused a drink or a second helping. Now the man was almost cadaverous, far more skeletal than Rushton himself. Cohen's suit had obviously been purchased during better times, and it hung off him like a sheet on a ghost. Rushton noticed two of the buttons were missing from the front of the jacket.

Cohen's sunken, dark-rimmed eyes told their own story. Here was a man suffering absolute inner turmoil, in the wretched grip of his own lurid paranoid fear and fantasy. The three previous nights he had spent in the agency's custody "suite" obviously hadn't helped, but Rushton was determined not to let sentimentality get in the way of his work. "I am sending you to Boyd for questioning. It's standard procedure, as you well know. We will talk again later."

Rushton stood, leaving the broken, pathetic, hunched figure in the chair. As he reached the door, he spoke to Cohen's back. "How the hell did you allow yourself to sink this low? My God, Elias. Was it all worth it?"

Cohen felt he was floating in space as he was firmly escorted along the corridors to Carter Boyd's little interrogation room. Was this really happening to him? Surely it was nothing more than a dream, or perhaps some other kind of dimension that escaped all rational explanation. Boyd was his usual self—unshakable and the epitome of all that the service had come to expect from its servants. "Elias, I will ask you straight, and I expect honest answers to my questions. I think you know me well enough to understand that I won't settle for anything less." Cohen nodded and looked down at his arms, which were restrained by light bindings, as was his bare chest, on which were placed several kinds of electronic tabs. He was not worried in the slightest about taking the polygraph. He knew it was an inexact science and that despite this, the results could be used against you. It was just another tool in the armoury of the state. Cohen had seen men sweat out polygraphs before and come through with flying colours, but that was when he was on the other side of the glass. He tried his best to concentrate, but felt nauseated and weak. He willed his thoughts to focus on the pure injustice of it all. It should have been Hamazaki here in the chair. How had this come to be?

Carter Boyd had been an interrogator at the agency since the beginning of time, and Cohen had always respected his methods. He was the epitome of professionalism, a ruthless, cold-hearted bastard, one perfectly matched with his craft. "Mr Cohen, I will ask you a series of questions, the answers to which you will reply with a simple yes or no. Do you understand?"

"Yes."

"Is your name Elias Cohen?"

"Yes."

"Were you born on July 5, 1911?"

"Yes."

"Do you currently reside at 1765 Blue Ridge Road, Fairview, Virginia?"

"Yes."

"Are you married?"

"No."

"Do you have any living blood relatives?"

There was a short pause as Cohen considered his answer before delivering a flat "No."

"Do you know a man by the name of George Isaacs?"

"Yes."

"Have you ever met with Mr George Isaacs?"

"Yes."

"Have you ever received money or financial support from George Isaacs?"

"Yes."

"Have you ever met with Mr Toshio Hamazaki?"

"Of course not . . . no."

"Have you ever sent correspondence to Toshio Hamazaki?"

Cohen hesitated again before Boyd repeated his question.

"Have you ever sent correspondence to Mr Toshio Hamazaki?"

"Yes."

"Have you ever made threats against the life of Mr Hamazaki?"

"Yes."

"Are you familiar with the name Joel Richardson?"

"Yes."

"Have you met with Mr Richardson?"

"Yes."

"Have you received money from Mr Richardson?"

"No."

"Did you kill Joel Richardson?"

"No."

"Were you in Las Vegas on the night Joel Richardson was shot to death?"

"Yes."

"Did you witness the shooting?"

"Yes."

"Did you kill George Isaacs?"

"No."

"I have no further questions at present. I think Mr Rushton is waiting to formally interview you." Boyd stood up and poured a glass of water, which he handed to Cohen, who gulped it down, as he was parched. It had a faint taste of apples. "Elias, I just want to say that I am struggling to understand how you came to find yourself in this position. I always thought of you as a steady kind of chap—a firm hand, if you will. I thought you quite capable during the time we worked together, and if it means anything at all, I was quite against you being let go in the way you were. Shoddy, very shoddy treatment indeed."

Boyd shook his head and gave Cohen a pitying pat on the shoulder before reverting to type and shouting for the guards in a voice that almost sent Cohen's dentures flying over the table. The door opened, and two uniformed strongmen entered and ordered Cohen to his feet. One of them grabbed his left arm and forced it behind his back whilst the other clamped an iron bracelet on his wrist. The absurdity of the situation was not lost on Cohen and he knew it was mostly theatrics aimed at belittling him and empowering his captors, but as he was led down the corridor, he could not shake the notion that he was a man walking down death row.

"Oh, for goodness' sake. Is there any need for this?" Rushton motioned towards the chains that bound the pathetic figure of Elias Cohen. One of the guards spoke in a rehearsed mechanical fashion which suggested he had lost his capacity for emotions long ago. "It is standard procedure, sir, that all cautioned persons be restrained when in transit within the building. Director's Protocol 1223 orders it."

Rushton shook his head in disbelief. "Very well, but the man is not in transit now, so remove these blasted chains at once." There passed a few awkward moments as the guards fumbled with the keys and then untangled the chain that bound Cohen's arms to the side of his body. When they had managed to do so, they forced Cohen into the seat opposite Rushton, then took up positions on either side of the door. Cohen looked around the room, wondering why all the rooms in this building had to be institutional grey; even the windows in this one had been painted over in the same paint. The room was cold; then again, everywhere was cold these days.

Rushton reached under the table and pressed a button. He thought he had been quite covert in his action, but Cohen knew all the tricks. He knew they would be joined by others very shortly. Cohen looked at the vacant chairs which were placed on either side of Rushton. "Expecting company, are we?"

Rushton looked weary and like he was doing his best to control his irritation. "Look, Cohen, we just want to get to the bottom of all this. The truth is all we seek, and I hope to high hell you don't hold out on us. Do yourself a favour and don't offer any reason for us to disbelieve anything you say. It can only help if any of this comes to trial. Do you understand what I am saying?"

Before Cohen could find any words to answer, the door swung open and in strode two men both unknown to Cohen. One of them was carrying a large cardboard box, which Cohen took to mean that he was the one of lesser importance. They took up the seats alongside Rushton. The box carrier dumped his burden beside the chair and spoke first. "Elias Cohen, normally at this juncture we would go through the rigmarole of introductions. However, as you have voluntarily forgone the offer of legal representation, we feel the need to maintain our anonymity at this point. I will convey that we are both concerned with the legal aspects of this situation and with following due process." Cohen could think of a thousand points that would fly in the face of such absurdity, but somehow he felt light-headed, peaceful, and strangely at ease with the whole situation. Then he remembered the drink that Boyd had given him some ten minutes earlier, and all he could do was smile to himself. The "truth serum" often talked about, mythologised but always denied. It seemed that things had advanced in the fifteen years since he himself had been an officer. Where the hell was this stuff when they had Tetsuyo Hamazaki in this very building?

Although Rushton sat in the position of authority between the two suits, it was soon apparent that he was no longer in command of the questioning. Cohen looked up at the ceiling and noted the camera which had been fixed into the far corner. He quickly took in how far technology seemed to have advanced since his days in the agency. There did not appear to be any observation window, but that did not mean they were free from prying eyes. Cohen was certain his interview would be receiving an audience somewhere in the building.

The box carrier started by going through the formalities of identifying those present in the room. He referred to himself as Agent X and his colleague as Agent Y. Cohen suppressed the urge to laugh out loud. When asked if it were of his own volition that he was forgoing legal assistance, he merely nodded. Agent X then asked him to state so verbally. Rushton was looking down at the papers on his desk. Cohen realised that this was his habit and that perhaps he did it to conceal his insecurities.

Agent X asked Cohen to detail his relationship with George Isaacs. Cohen thought for a moment before answering. Then his words seemed to trip off of his tongue with an eloquence that did not match his confidence. It was as if he had become another person and the voice was not his own. "It was in the days following the tragic death of President Kennedy that I first received communication from George. He replied to an earlier unsolicited written communication from me. I suppose that was seven years ago—almost to the day, I would say." Cohen felt a wave of sadness sweep over him as he recalled the elation he had felt when that letter had landed on his doormat all those years ago. His reminiscence caused him to pause in his recollection.

Agent X prompted him along. "Why did you write to Isaacs in the first place?"

Cohen looked at him with a pitying look as if the answer were obvious for all to see. "Well, I had hoped that George would be able to offer me some help in my quest for justice. You see, my efforts had reached something of an impasse and I was desperate for a new direction, and I believed George would be able to point the way. He had gained major recognition for his own crusades for justice on behalf of the innocent, and I admired his efforts. So, quite simply I wrote to him and asked for his advice. In truth, I did not expect much in the way of a reply. I knew it was a long shot, and it was never my intention to involve George to the extent that he became as equally involved as myself."

Agent X looked at Rushton and nodded. Rushton slid a paper across the table. "Is this your original letter to George Isaacs?" Cohen was stunned as he looked down at the paper on the desk. He was so taken aback that he found his mind wandering off to his dusty old office, where he had spent night after night compiling this very same letter, the one that had started in motion the death throes of an eminent man.

Cohen nodded, and Agent X stated for the benefit of any recording that the subject agreed that it was the letter. "What did George Isaacs convey in his response?"

Cohen thought for a moment. "I am sure you also have that letter in your possession, do you not?"

Agent X bristled. "Answer the question."

Cohen squinted. His eyes were becoming heavy, and there was a migraine building behind his temples. "Well, I guess he must have been interested in what I had to say, because he offered to meet with me. He asked if I was able to go to New York for a meeting, but as I was in straitened circumstances at the time, I wrote back to him suggesting we meet here in Virginia. I told him I had a heavy load of sensitive case files and I thought it better to review them here if possible."

Agent X shook his head in disbelief. "So, we are to believe that George Isaacs, well-known, eminent activist, dropped everything and came running to meet you, when at the time you were nothing more than a glorified janitor! I find that pushes the limits of believability."

Cohen felt a dent to his pride, but he tried to deflect Agent X's barb. "I have always seen myself as a former employee of the Central Intelligence Agency rather than the employment that was forced upon me for reasons beyond my control." Cohen looked at Rushton as he delivered this ill-disguised rebuke at his former boss. Rushton's eyes shifted, and Cohen knew he had hit a nerve. There was a brief moment when the unease was allowed to gain a little purchase. From the look on the agents' faces it was plain that they were familiar with the backstory. As always, the things left unspoken said the most. "George came over to my place, and we spent the afternoon talking and discussing my theories and concerns."

Agent Y then spoke. "Your theories and concerns? You make it sound like some kind of mathematical equation you were both pondering. What did Isaacs make of your fantasies and obsessions?" Agent Y leaned back in his chair and folded his hands behind his head, satisfied with his little "put-down."

Cohen looked at him and said, "George was intrigued; he told me there and then that he believed my investigations held substance. He did not hold out any hope that an official investigation would reap any dividends and said the best way forward was to force the hand of those in power into some kind of action. I remember him telling me that the greater the riches involved, the deeper and stickier the shit became. Is that true, Mr Rushton?"

Cohen stared at his former boss. It was plain that his words had struck another nerve, for Rushton was immediately provoked into fury. "Listen here, Cohen, you are the one in the deep and sticky shit, and the sooner you realise that, the sooner we can sort out this mess."

Over the next three days Cohen was interrogated by Agents X and Y. He did not feel the need to hold anything back, for he believed he was on the side of right. He told them how George Isaacs had become as fascinated and involved as he himself was. How, after their initial meeting Isaacs had suggested that Cohen visit him in Washington, where they could go over all the files and develop some kind of strategy. Cohen told them that he had been wary of giving an "outsider" complete access to all his documents, but that something about George invoked trust. George had been quite insistent from the very beginning that his own name be kept out of any correspondence, official or otherwise. He proposed setting up an organisation for justice. He told them how they could never quite agree on a moniker for their campaign, but eventually settled on "9245." Cohen went on to explain that it represented September 2, 1945, the date of the Japanese surrender aboard the USS Missouri. They hoped this would give them some form of credence as well as the platform to raise funds to further the campaign.

Cohen explained how over the next two years George developed what would become their strategy. Isaacs believed that justice always started with the victims, and so they went to those who had suffered the most, the governments of those countries that had been pillaged and looted by Hamazaki's forebears and partners in larceny. Isaacs had promised them nothing but their best efforts and a genuine desire to chase down the guilty. They had their own apparatus for investigating war crimes and in certain cases expressed a willingness to cooperate. "Most of our funding came from those sovereign states," Cohen said. "They saw it as a deposit on the possible return of their treasures."

Cohen was grilled about his dealings with Red China and the extent of his Communist sympathies. He was subjected to personal belittling for accepting "Commie" donations to his crackpot organisation, but it all just flowed off him. He had become emotionally rock solid. Take away the fear, and what is left to hold you back? Cohen went on to tell them about the momentum that 9245 started to generate—not only in terms of financial support, but from all sectors wishing them well in their crusade. The war and its fallout were still fresh in people's minds, and the ongoing conflict in Vietnam only served to keep it in the consciousness of those who cared. Many who had served in the Pacific War had gone on to become leaders in many walks of society; 9245 appealed also to their own sense of propriety. They wanted to do something, even if it was just a little bit of altruism on behalf of their mates who had fallen and would never have the chance.

Once he got talking, Cohen found the process almost cathartic. He spoke with a passion, as if he were trying to sign up his interrogators to the cause, but he knew that their focus would soon bear down on the dark days of the past three months. Darkness that had seen the end of optimism, hope, and all they had worked for, darkness that had shrouded their investigations in accusations of the foulest kind, and darkness that had taken away his friend and co-collaborator George Isaacs forever.

After four days of incarceration, Cohen got a sense that his interrogators were softening slightly, insofar as they had ceased making direct threats to his liberty and guffawing at some of his wilder claims. In truth, they were, or should have been, on the same side, and yet Cohen's distrust of his former colleagues ran deep, and certain information in his possession would never get past his lips, truth drug be damned. They had reached the juncture where they had to take some kind of action. Decisions had to be made, and the covering of one's own ass was moving up the priority scale. After all, there were the deaths of two prominent American citizens to consider.

On that fourth day Cohen was woken earlier than had become the norm. He was shackled in the usual way and led out, sleepy eyed, down the familiar grey-walled corridor to the interview room, which made up the custody suite. Agents X and Y were in their usual seats. Rushton was absent, but in his seat was another man whom Cohen immediately recognised: Jack Nolan, the under secretary of state for political affairs. So, the president's eyes and ears had finally made it into Fairfax County. Cohen suddenly realised that there would be no escape from his situation. The dossier that they were compiling would need a conclusion, and he was to be it. Some poor sop to pin the blame on and who would not be missed should they happen to vanish off the face of the earth. Was that why Carter Boyd had asked him about living relatives?

Cohen knew a little about Nolan's background from what he had read upon his appointment, which had been only recently. When was that? Not more than three months ago, surely. Nolan was one of Nixon's Rottweilers. Outspoken and controversial, he was often in the news, and it had become quite commonplace to see him fending off questions from the press about some overseas government that had felt offended by American state policy. He was nobody's apologist and took no prisoners, a brass-necked New Yorker through and through. Nolan had seen action in the Pacific

War, and for that fact and that alone, Cohen was grateful, as he was sure it would mark him out as a man with a modicum of sense of what Cohen had been trying to achieve.

Nolan did not even bother to introduce himself. After the guards had removed Cohen's manacles, Nolan told him to "get his scrawny rat's ass sat down." Nolan looked Cohen up and down like he was an animal sizing him up for a fight. Satisfied that the pathetic man in front of him was ready for lashing, he set about his business.

"Cohen, you are a disgrace to yourself and your country. Your pathetic arrogance has cost the lives of two men. Who the hell do you think you are? Acting as some kind of self-appointed bringer of justice. You make me sick, and I hope they throw not only the book at you but the whole fucking library." He then banged the table for extra emphasis. For a moment, Cohen felt that Under Secretary Nolan must have forgotten that Cohen had been dismissed from service over a decade ago, as he was talking to him like he was still in the employ of the country. However, Cohen soon realised that it was just how Nolan spoke to all and sundry. Perhaps the under secretary's own wife was seen as someone in the service of the state.

Nolan ranted on. "Now, I don't have all day to waste in your company, so I want you to tell me straight how and why Joel Richardson and George Isaacs came to meet their end—and don't even think of wasting your breath on some fantasy that has been cooking in that weirdo brain of yours." Nolan looked at Cohen with a blank and unreadable expression. It was now up to Cohen to colour his thinking in a way that might give a drop of hope for himself.

Cohen looked straight at Nolan and spoke as if Agents X and Y were not even in the room. "George and I were working on our usual business when we heard that Toshio Hamazaki was planning to make a business visit to the States. This was a major shake-up for us, our adversary on our own sovereign soil. We saw it as a watershed moment and an opportunity that could not be missed. We had to collate all the evidence we had and get it before a prosecutor. It was our initial intention to bring a civil case against Hamazaki. We believed we had enough funding to see that through. Our war chest was bolstered by several generous donations from those who stood to gain from any subsequent repatriation of Hamazaki's loot. We geared our efforts towards the serving of civil proceedings."

Cohen hesitated and was lost in the moment, for he realised that he was recalling the most feverish time of his life. It was a time when finally his prey would be within his grasp, a time when dreams were almost indivisible from reality. "I had placed my uttermost faith in George and agreed to follow his strategy, which was beginning to form on a number of levels. We were bursting with optimism, but even more driven by the fear of failure."

Nolan leaned back in his chair and started tapping his pencil on the desk, a sure sign that he was growing impatient with Cohen's fantastical recollections. Cohen did not want to lose himself in the moment, so he decided to jump in at the deep end, the point where it all became murky and where the distinctions between fact and speculation seemed to hold less and less relevance. "About two weeks before Hamazaki was due to set foot in the country, George called me and said he had astonishing news. We met later that same day, and he told me that Joel Richardson had asked for a personal meeting with George and George alone. Now, I have tracked Hamazaki for over twenty years, as you know, and I pride myself on my intuition. This did not seem right. I mean, ask yourselves, why would the CEO of Sonic America, a man in Hamazaki's inner circle, suddenly, out of the blue, ask for a meeting with 9245."

Cohen looked at Nolan as if he were expecting a reply, but all he got in return was Nolan's icy stare and the sound of more pencil tapping. Cohen sighed and continued. "Well, after lots of soul searching we agreed that George would meet Richardson. It was a short meeting, took place in the Fairfax Hotel, room twenty-two, not more than ten minutes, but it was that meeting that sealed both their fates. I believe the reaper was in that room sharpening his scythe and sizing the two of them up."

That last sentence caused Nolan to roll his eyes and Cohen to quickly focus on a more sensible line. "George came out first and told me that Richardson had asked him for a million dollars in return for a signed statement testifying to Hamazaki's complicity in wartime larceny and other misdemeanours. In addition to the million dollars, which he wanted in cash, he demanded that his name be removed from any future civil actions that might be pending. Well, these outrageous demands only served to further confirm what we have known all along, and that is that Hamazaki is guilty as sin and his judgement day has been long overdue."

Now it was Cohen who leaned back in his chair, a smug look on his scrawny face. He toyed with his five-day growth of beard. Despite going six nights with hardly any sleep, he felt momentarily elated and relieved to finally tell his tale.

Nolan, for his part, looked unimpressed and was quick to say so. "Cohen, all you have is one dead man's word against another dead man's word. What the fuck are we supposed to make of that? Truth or not, where the hell does it lead us?"

Cohen thought for a moment and leaned closer in to his audience. "Well, it tells us who killed George, for a start." He leaned back in his chair. Silence came down, and just as Nolan was thinking of wasting no further time on this madman, Cohen spoke out again. "Richardson killed George or had him killed by someone else, and Hamazaki had Richardson killed for betraying him. I mean, a million dollars, I ask you? There was no chance of us ever agreeing to that. Once the cash was off the table, Richardson must have felt like a cornered rat."

His words were not as eloquent as he would have liked, but they had the desired effect. Nolan stared Cohen down and asked him for evidence, something to go on other than supposition. It was at this point that Cohen felt an uncontrollable urge to shout out—that it was plain to all but the most simple of simpletons that Hamazaki was an evil man, the spawn of the devil himself, and the man was getting away with the foulest of crimes. America was turning a blind eye to the base thievery and murder, and it was the deepest shame of the nation that he be allowed to walk free on God's own earth. But of course, he didn't say any of that. Instead he let his head down and rested on the table, feeling tired, very tired indeed.

Cohen was back deep in the bowels of the building, ensconced once more in the "custody suite" fast asleep, the exhaustion finally coming to bear on his fragile mind and body. Upstairs on the top floor a meeting was in progress in the deputy director's office. Cohen slept blissfully, unaware that the next stage of his life was being decided by three men who had much to lose if Cohen's story were ever to gain momentum. It was agreed by all that Elias Cohen should be certified insane, mentally unfit to withstand any legal proceedings, and be detained indefinitely for care and supervision at a state facility. They were able to come to this conclusion in the cold, calculated manner by which they went about most of their business. Life and liberty were casually tossed aside in much the same manner as they put back the twenty-five-year-old Scotch that cemented their decision. Yes, it would be best if Cohen were taken care of by the state: The man was obviously a lunatic and a danger to himself and others. It would be best for all to draw a line under this whole sordid episode. Those three wise men were Under Secretary of State Nolan; Deputy Director Rushton; and Harold Weinstein, legal adviser to Toshio Hamazaki.

Of the three, only Rushton had the requisite self-propriety to feel any kind of remorse about the treatment handed down to his former underling. He made a mental note to ensure that Cohen was placed in the most comfortable of secure facilities and provided with a modicum of basic luxuries. It was the least he could do to assuage his guilt. Nolan raised his glass and proposed a toast to the end of this whole foul matter. The others drank to his optimism, but in truth they all knew there was a ball of tangled loose ends to straighten out, first and foremost of which was the business of the press. It was agreed that Isaacs's death would remain on the books as an active investigation and, after a respectable amount of time wasting had elapsed, the notion that Isaacs may have taken his own life be introduced. This theory would be bolstered over time and given credence by selected snippets leaked to the press. A man's reputation, built over a lifetime of hard work, could be discredited overnight by a word in the right ear.

As for Richardson, Cohen was bang on the money. He had indeed orchestrated the demise of dear old George, an act that was in all their interests, but not over money. That was just a ruse to see how far Isaacs would go. Richardson had had Isaacs killed because Rushton had ordered him to do it. Richardson had been an agency asset for years. Isaacs rebuffed Richardson and went even further by intimating that he had found compromising details he planned to use to force Richardson into giving incriminating evidence against his boss, Hamazaki, a bluff that played out tragically for

George Isaacs. Of course, after Isaacs had been despatched, it was only a matter of time before Richardson had to follow, and for that Rushton had needed Hamazaki. Dinner at the White House had seemed the most appropriate setting to discuss murder, and a few choice words into the ear of Toshio Hamazaki set in motion the final days of Joel Richardson. Even Rushton was impressed with the staging of Richardson's removal. Mistaken identity, the pure brash theatrical killing, stood be admired, and it left Hamazaki standing with a raised sense of heroism that he basked in for days. Rushton recalled seeing Hamazaki giving a brief interview on TV, expressing his grief about the loss of such a loyal and decent friend and colleague, but the man's eyes had told a different story.

Rushton stretched out his lanky legs and swivelled his head in a vain attempt to rid himself of the tensions of the past week. The drink was numbing the present, and he drifted into a reverie of thought. He looked at Nolan and Weinstein and wondered what they knew that he didn't and of course the opposite. It was a dangerous game they were all playing. Knowledge was indeed power, and it was also what got you killed. It was not always so clear-cut, and to stay in this game you also had to get into the minds of the others because, quite simply, you could die for the thoughts in your head.

Rushton had gotten to the point in life where all he wished for was a simpler way of being. How had he come to this? He tried to justify his actions, but found himself increasingly coming up short. He knew where it had started, no doubt back in '45 when he had sat in front of Major Kojima and questioned the man until he ultimately broke, but then again, surely that was Romana who had done that. Romana, oh yes. Who had played whom? Rushton shook his head at the memory and for an instant had a vision of Romana's head exploding like a shot turnip, spitting his gold teeth across the Luzon rain forest. For Santa Romana, too, lived each day blissfully unaware that his days were becoming increasingly finite. Romana's removal from the heart of Philippine power had become a priority for the policy makers in that region. The agency was merely the tool used, and to this end Hamazaki had promised to oblige, albeit on his terms, how and when it most suited his own purposes.

Rushton raised his glass in a mock toast, a laconic smile on his face as he silently mouthed the words, Hamazaki, you devious bastard. His smile suddenly dropped as he considered the nature of his own inevitable demise, for he was now convinced that he was a dead man walking and that all he could do to keep alive was to stay in this treacherous game of bluff and double bluff. He thought of the two million dollars waiting for him in Switzerland, a futile token of control, insisted upon by Hamazaki himself.

Nolan and Weinstein had drifted off to a corner of the room on the pretence of recharging their glasses, but no doubt they were allaying each other's fears and paranoia, papering over the cracks. Rushton burst into an uncontrollable fit of nervous, hysterical laughter, and through his giggles he mouthed the words We are all dead. Uncomprehendingly, Nolan and Weinstein raised their glasses in polite return.

Chapter 12
Lieutenant Ogawa
Tokyo
1974

The sudden heavy downpour did little to dampen the enthusiasm of the assembled masses who had gathered by the roadside to witness an extraordinary event, one more symbolic than of any particular importance. Standing on that sidewalk in Ginza in the warm April, my face was just another in a crowd of hundreds, straining for a better view of the happenings across the street. I swallowed hard as the bitter acid born of resentment rose from my stomach and momentarily caused me to feel nauseated.

It was near impossible to make out the leading players, who were standing no more than twenty strides away. The rain was bouncing off the road, and the notable dignitaries had their collars turned up. The women amongst them had melted into the background, enjoying the shelter of the awning that had been erected for their comfort. So short a distance, and yet a distance that I would never cross, despite being the one most deserving of a place under that awning. I too, should have been standing shoulder to shoulder alongside Hamazaki and my old long-lost wartime friend, Tanaka. Without me they would be nothing, and they knew it. Yet I was being treated like a leper, kept at a distance and excommunicated from all things Mabuhay.

I had given the best years of my life to Hamazaki. Nearly thirty years of loyal devotion to a cause I believed in and followed without question. I had been sold a dream, one which had required me to surrender so much and had led me here, to witness the delivery of a table. Yes, a piece of furniture. No ordinary table—nothing was ordinary where Toshio Hamazaki was concerned. It was reputed to be the longest table in the world, hewn from the tallest mahogany tree ever felled. It was a gift from President Marios of the Philippines, a token of his undying gratitude for all the good Hamazaki and the Mabuhay Foundation had bestowed upon his nation. The table was said to be so long that construction of the new Mabuhay corporate office building had to be halted for the table to be installed on the upper floor, after which the work could finally be completed.

The new building was still shrouded in canvas tarpaulin and steel scaffolding, which only added to the mystique of this surreal occasion. The newspapers had reported this event from the symbolic angle. The largest boardroom table in the world was another symbol of Japan's corporate success. I looked around at the faces of my fellow gawkers, and sure enough, pride was perhaps the one thing that had drawn them here today.

The mayor of Tokyo had just finished his address to the crowd, his words drowned out by the rain and the inadequate public address system. It mattered little, as we were not his intended audience. The dignitaries offered a smattering of applause as the next speaker, the Philippine ambassador, rose to say a few words. Thankfully, brevity was one of his finer points, and he concluded his short speech with a flourish of his arms.

Then, the unmistakable figure of Toshio Hamazaki stepped out from the crowd and approached the microphone. As if by divine intervention, the rain suddenly eased, and rather suspiciously the sound quality miraculously improved. Hamazaki's voice seemed to float in the air, and the crowd quickly picked up on his words. "Mr Ambassador, Mr Mayor, and all assembled here today, I thank you all for patience and your attendance on this wet but nonetheless auspicious day. In view of the weather I think it desirable that we proceed with haste. I would just like to thank President Marios for his unparalleled generosity in bestowing upon us this remarkable symbol of friendship. As always, at times like this I cannot help but wish that my dear father were here to witness such a milestone in the path from Hamazaki Electricals to Mabuhay. A twenty-five-year-long journey, one that has not always been easy to tread and yet has brought us all great satisfaction. Mabuhay is a company that has stayed true to its ideals, and I believe we have played no small role in shaping the destiny of many people who for no reason other than circumstance have found their life lacking in opportunity. This fills me with the deepest sense of pride in all that we have achieved.

"Today Mabuhay is to take custody of this truly wonderful table upon which I know many papers will be signed into action, thus continuing the great works performed by the foundation. So, without further delay, I think it better to proceed whilst the clouds are being kind to us and ask the deliveryman to put this beautiful table where it belongs."

There was a spontaneous outbreak of applause as the engines of a huge crane cranked into life, dousing us with acrid black smoke which took a few spluttering moments to clear. The chains tightened, and the thick ropes that bound the huge table gave an audible groan. Slowly the heavy table rose from its resting place off the back of two flatbed trucks. The crowd whooped in excitement as it rose into the air. Its true size now revealed only added to the occasion—at least twenty yards in length. It was undeniably spectacular, and yet I was left feeling cold and unmoved, for I alone knew what it had taken to get to the point where a president sent such a gift to a businessman.

Hamazaki had just spoken of a path, one not easy to tread—perhaps because his path was haunted by the ghosts of so many sacrificed souls, the corrupt, the tortured, and, of course, the dead. Murdered out of necessity to preserve the great lie, a lie that would forever live in his mind. Was the man capable of gleaning satisfaction from that foul path littered by the sufferings of so many? As I looked up into the grey Tokyo sky, the table swung perilously, as if trying to free itself from its bindings. The sick part of me wanted the thing to come crashing down. The crowd looked up, silently awed by the sight. I turned up the collar of my long coat, pulled my Homburg down tight to my eyes, and turned my back on the absurd spectacle.

I walked, head bowed to avoid the unlikely event of being recognised, and within a few moments felt relief at finally being freed from the crowd. I hated the hustle and bustle of modern Tokyo. It was an alien place to me and one I had barely known on my return. When had that been now? I could scarcely believe it myself, but I had been back in my homeland for almost two years. Surely that should have been long enough for me to complete my "process of readjustment," as my sympathetic counsellor termed it, but I knew in my heart that I would never be able to find contentment or peace. My soul was infected with resentment, and I found myself sinking into an uncontrollable spiral of despair. I had been used, deceived beyond all credulity, and the most galling truth of it all was that I had allowed it to happen. I had closed my eyes to the blatant evil of my involvement in Hamazaki's great conspiracy, so much so that I had deluded myself into believing we were working towards a brighter future for so many. I had been sold a dream by Hamazaki, and I had willingly bought it. A dream that had cost me the best years of my life, a dream that required me to "die" in a Philippine jungle, my body sacrificed to the great war machine, my very own existence pulped out of all space and time. Except I was not lost to life, even though there were so many times I wished I was.

I had been given a new cause, a new identity. I had become Ramil Tan, a Chinese Filipino mute. As a war-stricken survivor I lived as a destitute beggar on the streets of Manila whilst all the time going deeper into my cover to pursue my covert agenda—or should I say Hamazaki's agenda. As far as the rest of the world was concerned, Ogawa had died along with the hundreds of thousands of poor souls just like him, and in truth I had died, I had died a thousand times. I felt the pain of all my fallen comrades, and it ripped my heart out.

When the warring stopped and the guns had fallen silent, I was ordered to go to ground and avoid capture by the victorious Americans. I had lived like an animal for months. I was instructed to bury the effects of my military past, my uniform, my rifle, even my soiled army-issue underwear. I stole some ragged clothes from a poor family's shack. I walked shoeless until my feet were blackened and hard. It was a necessary suffering for my transformation from Ogawa, proud Imperial Japanese Army officer, to street beggar. I had to endure continued hardships to not only look the part but live the part. The Philippines was in turmoil, and after a few months I was able to take my ragged, filthy, and putrid self to the streets of Manila. Nobody paid me any heed. Life was hell for a while, and there were times when I felt I had been forgotten and my "mission" had been abandoned.

Late one afternoon I lay exhausted under some trees near Roxas Park, unable to fully succumb to sleep, as I had to be vigilant for the military police, who were viciously ridding the streets of vagrants like myself. There were rumours that men like me were being exterminated just like the rats that gave us our only meat. I had not spoken a word for months, my cover was so deep.

That afternoon a face silhouetted by the brilliant searing sunshine stared down at me. It was the face of innocent kindness and pure heartfelt love. Her name was Mary. Sister Mary Delaney, to be exact, and she was from the Convent of the Holy Mother. She peered down at me and offered her words of comfort. "Mr Ramil Tan, it is time for you to come off the streets." She pressed a piece of paper into my hand, and turned and serenely walked away. I watched her walking into the distance until she became a mere speck and I believed her existence was just a trick of my imagination. The paper in my hand told me otherwise. On it was an address written in beautiful script. If any man could ever know how the mark of an angel would look, then this, surely, would be it. My English was poor, my Tagalog even worse, but I was able to read, and I had a vague idea where I was to go.

That day I decided not to venture out to beg. I decided to keep as close to the shadows as I could. It would be reckless and a gross dereliction of duty should I be hauled off the streets now. When you have lived with the sky as your only roof for so long, time takes on an altogether different dimension, and your appreciation of life is forever altered. I would make my way to Sister Mary Delaney's address in my own time, but for that moment I wished to savour the feeling of hope, a feeling that I thought had been lost forever.

It took me two days to find the place. I walked across the city, all the time heading north to Tondo District. The farther I walked, the more broken my surroundings became. I was walking into the most destitute and poverty-stricken areas of Manila. The war had been very hard on these people, but here it looked like they had been especially chosen to bear life's hardships and much more besides. I tramped through stinking corrugated shantytowns. Nobody paid me so much as a blind bit of notice. I was nothing, as worthless as my surroundings. I had to be brave and take a calculated risk, as I had little real idea what my destination was. I would choose dead-eyed old men squatting by the road and show them the paper. Most times they would just shake their head and wave me on my way, other times they pointed farther down the street. I wore a piece of cardboard tied with twine around my neck. It told overly curious people that my name was Tan and I was mute. Nobody ever read as far as the last line, which asked them to please spare me a cent.

I knew there was no such a thing as a formal address here. Sister Mary's paper may well have read "Shithole shack with rusting door and stinking toilet pit made out of old tyres" rather than the words written, which were "Calle Mendoza." Hours of confusion eventually resulted in me standing outside the Convent of the Holy Mother. I was not the only one who seemed to find this space so inviting. I found myself amongst the lowest of all, and we would wait for the convent to open its doors and the sisters to pass amongst us, distributing meagre rations of bread and rice into the grasping hands of the starving people. Others would spend hours on their knees silently praying in the blistering heat. I believe they were asking their God for a miracle, perhaps for divine intervention in the recovery of a loved one who had been struck down by illness or madness. Perhaps they believed they were closer to the hand of God.

I spent two days amongst the people there, and at times I too felt like praying for a miracle. I got more pitying glances outside those gates than I had in my entire life. However much pity I gleaned, it did not stand me in much stead when the food was handed out. The children were wild and feral and would scavenge with admirable ferocity. They would not think twice about seizing from your hand, and I once saw two kids no more than five or six years old actually try to prise open an old woman's mouth to get the bread out as she ate. The stronger devotees would beat off the kids with bamboo poles, which caused me to flash back to the war, when our own noncommissioned officers would resort to that same harsh method to keep the troops in order.

I had started doubting whether I was in the right place when on the evening of my second day there I saw the same angelic face that had smiled down at me in Roxas Park. To my surprise and growing frustration she ignored me as she went about her business of pressing bread into the outstretched hands. As I forlornly looked on, she turned and looked over her shoulder, meeting my eyes. She did not betray any sense of emotion but suddenly looked more purposeful. Her bread basket was empty, and yet she turned and walked towards me. We stood face-to-face, and she took out one hard piece of bread from the pocket of her habit. She spoke in my language, her voice lowered and conspiratorial as she pressed the bread into my palm. "Eat with care, Mr Ramil Tan, for I hope that within, you may find the Lord's sustenance."

She turned and left me standing alone in the dusty track that masqueraded as a road. There were no furtive glances back, she just melted away into the throng and disappeared through the gates back into the convent. I knew we would cross paths again, and I too found myself saying a silent prayer, almost pleading for the time when I would get my chance to speak with Sister Mary.

With the bread tightly clutched in my fist I made my way back down the road and after a few minutes found a place to rest under a shady tree. It was a palm of some sorts, and its leaves were fanned out like a giant peacock. It somehow seemed like a sign, and for the first time in months, if not years, I felt the swell of optimism rise deep within my chest. In this country, experience had taught me that you are rarely, if ever, alone. I had a quick look about, but nobody was paying me any heed. After all, what interest is there in a stinking destitute person such as me?

I dug my fingers into the stale bread and broke it open; there, folded into a neat stamp-sized square, was my sustenance. My clothes did not boast one single trustworthy pocket, so I decided to commit my communique to memory. It was another simple address, only this time I would be heading back into the heart of the city, a good distance from the squalor of Tondo. Quite why I had been dragged through the ordeal of tramping miles to receive it in the first place was unclear. Weariness was a weakness I refused to succumb to, and before my legs told me otherwise, I was up and on my way, heading back into the heart of Manila. Little did I know at the time that I would be staying there for the next twenty-eight years.

The efficiency of modern-day Tokyo still left me astounded. After living for an eternity in a society that set its own pace, I was constantly surprised by buses that arrived on time, public clocks which always displayed accurate times, and the public address announcements that kept its citizens informed of their moral obligations. Life here in Tokyo was also chaotic, but it was organised chaos. People obeyed the rules and knew their place. They gave what was expected of them and were grateful for what they received in return. It was a safe place, sanitised of radicalism, devoid of spirit. The great economic push had come at some cost. I felt we had given away a lot of what had made us unique as a people. My generation had laid down their lives for the Emperor, the army, and the country. I remember my old field sergeant who in the heat of battle lost his left leg and refused all help, insisting he carry on firing towards the enemy lines, all the time screaming his devotion to his beloved Emperor until his final breath wheezed from his body. That took some guts, and now, as I looked about my fellow passengers on the bus bound for Yanaka Cemetery, I wondered how many of them truly knew what it meant to feel alive, not just to be alive but to feel.

Since my return, Yanaka was the only place I had felt a connection with, and I made the trip out to the cemetery whenever I felt the need for a moment of quiet reflection. My father was at rest here. He lay in a regular plot, paid for by Hamazaki. The inscription on his headstone simply read "Saburo Ogawa 1886–1969" and below "A Faithful and Loyal Servant." The first time I saw his grave, a tear rolled down my cheek. His final resting place was in the poorer section, adorned with a Christian cross. I took this imagery personally; it was an affront to what little decency remained in my heart. It mocked and taunted me and made the guilt bleed out of what goodness remained in my soul. I had no doubt that it was a dark reference to the foulness of my own misdoings. Another hurt in a life of pain inflicted by Hamazaki. My father was no more Christian than Attila. My poor, poor father, forced to live out his life believing his only son to be dead, a deception so cruel, it belied belief. I suppose Hamazaki thought it convenient to cut my familial ties, therefore making it easy for me to accept my imposed isolation. My heart was forever scarred, and despite receiving consolations of a kind, I could never rid my soul of that hurt.

I suppose my pilgrimages out to Yanaka had become my only solace. Over my father's resting place I would say my prayers, seek his forgiveness, and repent for the poor souls who found themselves in my path. One face loomed large in my mind and even more so here, when I visited Yanaka. The poor sweet, innocent Sister Mary. In this section of the cemetery I was surrounded by tombs which bore Christian images, the cross of Christ, as worn by Sister Mary. It felt like she was standing beside me and we were praying together. Her kindness the ultimate contrast to my own wickedness. Her image hurt me and burned into my heart, shaming me for all eternity. I did not believe any divine power would ever forgive the evil that lay deep in my soul; my only hope was that they would punish the man who had planted that evil: Toshio Hamazaki.

I said my goodbyes to my father and turned to make my way back into the city. The bus service was so frequent, there was no need to memorise times. What was a wait of ten minutes when you had spent a lifetime waiting? I had been back in my homeland for nearly two years now, and the fanfare and furore that accompanied my return had all but gone away. The "forgotten soldier" had been forgotten once more. It had taken a great deal of planning to enable my repatriation, and once more it had inevitably involved hardships on my part. After living all my middle years as Ramil Tan, I was to be once more reincarnated as Ogawa—the long-lost soldier who had refused to surrender his post and continued to live undercover in the Luzon jungle, fighting his own one-man war. Twenty-eight years after the Emperor had called an end to the fighting, Lieutenant Ogawa had walked out of the jungle and finally surrendered his arms and his unit's colours.

To make this pantomime appear real, I had to actually go back and live the life of a lost, deluded renegade. It was vital that I look the part. My cover had to be able to withstand the inevitable scrutiny that would follow. I needed to be hardened up and grubbed up. My life as Ramil Tan had hardly been played out in the lap of luxury, but even so, it took a great leap of faith to go from Filipino street beggar to long-lost Imperial Japanese Army officer. So it was that I found myself back in the steaming undergrowth, cut off from all society. I found the place where I had buried my army past so many years ago and, wearing my old stinking and shredded army tunic that still bore the bloodstains of so many fallen friends, once more became First Lieutenant Ogawa of the Imperial Japanese Army. It was also necessary that I become reacquainted with my rusted rifle. It was the only thing I had tried to keep in good order. Fine soldiers never bear ill arms.

So it was that I made preparations for what I believed would be the start of the end of my life of hell. I had been briefed on my new mission by Ken Miyazaki, and as audacious as it seemed, he convinced me of its viability. He assured me that President Marios would grant me a full pardon for any acts I had perpetrated as long as they were seen as the acts of a man believing he was still at war. I would be sent back to Japan a free man and welcomed back into the bosom of my country. He told me to expect a certain amount of undue attention which, like all news stories, would eventually blow away in the wind. He was, by and large, correct in his assumptions, but one thing neither he nor I had reckoned on was my becoming a focal point for the right-wing fanatics back in my homeland, who took my sudden reappearance as an affirmation of some true samurai spirit. How saddened they would have been if they had known even half the truth—that Ogawa was in fact a liar, thief, corruptor supreme, and murderer.

I lived off the ground for over a year. I never shaved and seldom washed my clothes. My own stink was so unbearable and so powerful, I believe it destroyed my own natural sense of smell. I moved my encampment every three or four days. At times I would steal from local fishermen who left their catch on their boats. As they got drunk on tubâ and slept the afternoon away, I would take my chance and help myself. I was once the cause of a fight as two gangs of fishermen, each accusing the other of theft, fell into a violent drunken brawl which left a few men down, bleeding into the sand. Little could they know that the real thief was only a step or two away under cover, watching with fascination. I found that my actions gave me a strange sense of pride. It was difficult to explain, but I believed I had been corrupted to the point where I could find satisfaction only in the misfortunes of others.

As a nation we had lost the war, and yet I had been forced to live out my life in the ruins of that defeat. I could not play a part in the contrition process, nor did any healing enter my own soul. I was a lone wolf, cut loose for the purpose of a greater good, a purpose that was to serve others and never myself. I was promised my rewards. Hamazaki's father, the man who had set me on this insane path, had sold me a dream. I was playing a part in the restoration of national pride. Our mission was to make provisions for our nation to be reborn and rise again out of the ashes of defeat with pride and honour. To do this we would need a source of funding that was out of the reach of our conquerors. That was my purpose, simply to assist in the facilitation and removal of vast amounts of war loot. I accepted my orders without question and vowed to do whatever was necessary to see the mission through to its end. To die or to take life, there was no difference. Loyalty was everything.

Through old man Hamazaki's network of contacts I was guided in my duties and became skilled in the fine arts of manipulation, deception, and corruption. Of course a fine pension awaited me, but I had never lived a materialistic life. There was nothing I coveted. During my life as Ramil Tan I was given a simple allowance, in grubby used money. It was enough to keep me in food and drink and to take care of unexpected needs such as new shoes or a haircut now and again. Perhaps more importantly it allowed me to beg on the streets without money being my only purpose. Begging was my cover—the reason, or perhaps the explanation, for my existence.

It was in the autumn of 1947 that I found myself living in my room at the back of an old fruit seller's shop. I had lived in this place for about a year. It was where Sister Mary had sent me all those months before, a simple windowless place with a rickety wooden floor, no water, and a disturbing lack of privacy. It took me a few weeks, but I scoured the dumps for wood and with my military sense of pride managed to make my space a little more habitable. The owner of the fruit shop was a mean-tempered old hag who would have sold her own mother for a few cents. It was obvious that she had been "taken care of" by my Tokyo masters in some way or another. I believe she genuinely thought she was renting her hovel to a distressed war victim and was satisfied with the arrangement that some fool somewhere was willing to pay over the odds for a shithole shack. For the most part, the old crone would leave me be, but she made it plain that she would not tolerate my presence in her shop or in full view of her customers, most of whom looked in worse shape than me. That room was my home for twenty-five years, and in all that time she never once gave me so much as a bite of fruit.

The months passed in agonising slowness. I lived my life as I had been told. Ramil Tan would go out early in the morning and beg, mutely, around the streets for scraps of food. I would clean up parks and richer men's gardens for a few pesos. I made myself available for a day's work and was paid in rice or sometimes vegetables. I managed to survive, and over time I became more Ramil Tan than Ogawa. I picked up street Tagalog, as I forced my ears to compensate for my lack of speech. As time passed, my soul was being worn down. I began to think that Hamazaki's wild scheme had somehow unravelled and I had been forgotten. I was indeed the lost soldier, fighting one long, never-ending war with a merciless enemy, futility.

As hope was being crushed from my heart, I received a visitor. It was April 30, 1948. When you have had no cause to open your door for an eternity, dates tend to stick with you forever. It was late in the evening, and the knock on the door sent me into a mild panic. I scoured my room for anything I might have carelessly left about that would have given rise to suspect that I was other than Ramil. I opened the door just a little and peered out. Behind my back I had in my grip a razor-sharp fruit knife that I had stolen from the hag months before.

I did not need the knife, for the voice beyond spoke softly and with loving concern. "Ramil Tan, it's me, Sister Mary. I have been instructed to check on your welfare. Please open the door."

I hurriedly hid the knife under a pile of rags and stepped back, allowing the door to swing open. She stepped in and took a long look at me. She did not look about my room. She paid no heed to my squalor. I had heard that these women were God's own angels, and at that time I believed it was so. Resplendent in her black habit she looked like divinity itself. She asked me if she could sit, and I put a cloth over an old box that doubled as my table. She told me to sit, and I sat on the floor with my back pressed into the corner.

"Ramil Tan, it seems you have friends in unexpected parts," she said. "I am here to give a message to you. Be resolute in your faith and strong in your convictions. Your diligence will be rewarded in due time."

Hearing my own language was like hearing the joyous sound of water cascading down a beautiful waterfall, and hearing it from the mouth of one so unlikely to know my tongue brought tears to my eyes. I had so many questions, and for once I could not restrain myself from speaking. Of course I was aware that the old crone might be eavesdropping, so I kept my words to the merest of whispers. "Why do you speak Japanese so well?"

She looked at me with a kind of pitying affection and smiled. "Ramil, the war took away so much of what we loved, and yet it left us with unexpected changes. My story is not important, but I will tell you all the same. I was a teacher at the Irish mission in Tokyo. I loved my work. We taught the children English whilst the nuns tried to teach the love of God. The war came, and we teachers were told to pack up and get back to Ireland whilst it was still possible. I wanted to stay, and the only way to do so was to change careers, so to speak. I became a nun, there and then, serving out my holy orders amidst the backdrop of war. There were six of us, and we were restricted to a poor small convent for most of the war.

"Someone eventually found a practical purpose for us, and we were assigned as carers for wounded soldiers who had been fortunate to find themselves back in Japan. It is out of necessity that I learnt your language."

I nodded as if I truly understood the life that had been forced on her. It was obvious she must have had a curiosity of her own to satisfy. Why would a Japanese misfit like me be cast asunder in such surroundings? She went on, and what she had to say was amazing beyond invention.

"I, along with my brave sisters, worked amongst the war stricken, offering what little comfort we could in the face of such valiant sufferings. One fine day our sick ward received a visitor. His name was Mr Tetsuyo Hamazaki; he was the government's minister for armaments. He praised our work and said how grateful he was for our efforts and that one day, in kinder times, we would be fully recognised. Our Mother Superior told him that to be able to serve God was reward enough, and we went about our business. Anyway, the war did eventually end, and it meant changes for everyone. Our mission was to be broken up, and we were to return to Ireland.

"I had seen enough faith-testing suffering to last a thousand lifetimes, and I must confess I began to doubt my own convictions. In the weeks that followed, as I was preparing for our passage back across the seas, I was summoned to the offices of the new government ministry. There I met with Mr Hamazaki once more. He was so kind and understanding. It was like he could read my mind. He told me to consider a posting to a convent in Manila. He needed my help in communicating with a special 'lost' friend. If I agreed, he, in return, would build a fine school back in Tokyo, where I could go back to what I dearly loved.

"I decided to do his bidding, as I know you are doing too. We may serve different masters, Ramil Tan, but I know you too are working out of love for your lost comrades. Mr Hamazaki told me of your bravery. Volunteering to stay behind and help find your lost, wounded, and afflicted comrades is a noble cause indeed. You are a brave soul, Ramil Tan. It cannot be easy living in the shadows, but I hope you find reward each and every time you help the families of the fallen. Their joy is your reward. I know your task is fraught with danger, as there is no sympathy here for men

646

like you. But God's forgiveness is almighty, and he stands with you in your valiant search."

I was dumbfounded. Hamazaki had sold her a tale, and she had bought it. My life as Ramil Tan was beginning to take on a whole new dimension. I was now not only a dumb beggar, but one on a mission of mercy. She gripped my hand and looked into my eyes. "You may rest assured: Your confidences are safe with me. I will always be here to assist you in your heroic endeavour. I will be the guardian of your welfare, just as you are the guardian of so many poor, lost souls." Her blind innocence left me speechless, and all I could do to hide my shame was stare down at the floor as she stepped out and disappeared into the night.

The bus made slow progress through the rain-drenched streets, but I did not care at all. A ride on a cool bus was still a pleasurable novelty for me, and I treated each journey as an education. My country had changed beyond all reason, and I would stare out the windows at strange shops and billboards and be totally clueless about the nature of their business. Young people were a special mystery to me. Their clothes were a world apart, and the long hair sported by some of the wilder boys irritated me for some strange reason. Their freedom had come at a high price, a price paid by men like me. I wondered if they knew that, or if they even cared. When I was their age, I had killed men, some with my bare hands. I suppose that kind of experience unavoidably creates barriers.

Upon my return the Metropolitan Authority had kindly accommodated me in a small apartment which was conveniently situated in the back area of Shibuya Ward. My bus ride back from Yanaka would take me past some of the touchstones of my life. One place held a special kind of nostalgia for me: the Nakano School, which of course is now long gone. I had heard it had been destroyed in the firebombing of Tokyo. Now in its place stood an insurance company building, a nondescript edifice, just like its predecessor.

I suppose Nakano is where all this really began for me. I was taken from the duties of a usual army officer and trained in the arts of espionage and counterintelligence. My commanding officer at the time was Lieutenant Colonel Nishii, a man who would blight my life for years. I had heard he had been killed in action during the Battle of Luzon in 1945, but I knew it was an untruth. I had seen the man with my own two eyes. He had used his knowledge to forge some kind of personal amnesty with the new Philippine government; I believed he had been given a comfortable deal, as I had seen him several times in the company of government officials.

My life as Ramil Tan took me to some fine quarters where I would ply my begging skills, often finding a cane across my legs for my trouble. The military police were not choosy when it came to handing down a street thrashing. The blind, the mute, the sick, the lame, the old, the very young, and the dying were considered an embarrassment to the authorities. If you were on the streets and in the wrong place at the wrong time, your life was worth nothing. I had seen men beaten to a pulp and pistol-whipped until their eyes were out, all for being hungry and wanting. You needed strong wits to survive on those Manila streets, and I guessed Nishii had wits of steel, for he seemed to not only survive but flourish. I wished I could go over and say, "It's me, Ogawa, your onetime soldier." He would take me in his arms like a father coming face-to-face with a son returning from the war and save me from Hamazaki's madness. But I knew that to be pure fantasy. It would mean certain death for me. Nishii had sold his soul to the enemy, and that meant I too was now his enemy. If the traitor knew I was there across the street, watching him coming and going, I would not live to see another sunrise.

My bus soon arrived at the Tokyo station, where I decided to alight and get some air. The rain had eased, and the air was cool; besides, I enjoyed walking past the grounds of the Imperial Palace. It gave me joy to know my Emperor was safe and sound somewhere within those high walls. I was his servant, and deep down, the innocence of my youth still burnt strong. This was still like a sacred place; it was as close to divinity as old soldiers like myself could ever be.

I would never stand beyond those gates, never in a thousand lifetimes—unlike Hamazaki, who, like his father before him, was accepted without question. Then there was my old comrade Tanaka. Hideo Tanaka, bastard prince soldier, for want of a better title. Tanaka, a man who owed me his life, for I had saved his on that fateful night thirty years earlier in the Luzon jungle. On that evening when we said our farewells, we both believed it to be our final night on this earth. Fate proved otherwise, and we both still lived and breathed, although one of us was to enjoy far greater surroundings than the other. Tanaka had made a grand life for himself, of that there was no doubt. I had thought him dead for years. Nobody had even so much as hinted at his continued existence. I had met with Hosokawa and Miyazaki on many occasions as we went about our business, but nobody had ever spoken of Tanaka. So my astonishment was total when, some twenty years earlier, I had found out that he was in fact Hamazaki's partner and was wed to his sister. I had read in a newspaper that Tanaka had become one of the wealthiest men in the country. I suppose his grand entrance on this earth had opened a few doors for him.

It sickened me to think that they were fattening themselves as I lived a life of hell on the filthy streets of Manila day after day, month after month, year upon year. I did not know what had happened to all the loot we recovered, and as I looked up at the now looming Empire Hotel, I felt it was time for me to accept the fact that I had been played for a fool for most of my life. My old friend lived in that grand place, and I lived in a welfare apartment. I had risked my life for years so he and Hamazaki and the rest could enrich themselves. My friend had not even seen fit to meet me, and I had been back in the homeland for two years. I was an embarrassment to them, a stigma, and a threat to all they represented. To be honest, I was surprised I had been allowed to live this long. Had my demise already been planned? Had it been signed off by the man who never left his grand rooms? I, more than any man, knew how they thought and operated, and it would be total folly for me to believe my role had played itself out. I knew in my heart there would be some kind of end game for me. It was my fate.

The rain had started to pick up again, and I quickened my pace. I stopped at the small kiosk on the corner of Chiyoda junction to buy the evening newspaper. The rain was bouncing off the small awning, and the old proprietor was having trouble covering his wares with a plastic sheet. I bent down to lend him a hand in securing the flapping sheet and took a copy of the early edition of the evening's paper. To my surprise the story of the Mabuhay boardroom table had made the front page. My God, they did work fast in this city. There was a picture of the table being raised into the air and in the foreground Toshio Hamazaki, smiling as he took in the full spectacle in all its absurdity. I stood under the awning and gawped at the picture. I had never met Toshio Hamazaki face-to-face, but from his picture I could recall his father. The similarities were eerie. The long angular face, the high cheekbones, and the eyes that for some reason made people feel uneasy. I had heard many an urban legend regarding Hamazaki. I made it my duty to know as much as I could. After all, we were connected by so many toxic bindings. However, I was now Ogawa, the prodigal soldier, and that was my role.

Since my return, my connection to my former life had been virtually sanitised. I had been in contact with Miyazaki on only one occasion. A few weeks after my return he had paid a visit to my apartment. It was a cold encounter and one that left me with no doubt about what was expected in terms of my conduct. I was told to keep my distance from the company and to never allude to any relationships with it. I was forbidden to speak to the media and told I should flatly refuse any requests for interviews. Miyazaki gravely warned me that any loose talk would carry its own consequences. If I were approached by any inquisitive authorities, I must seek his advice. I was told I could gain his attention by placing colourful flowers in my front window, which implied that Miyazaki was having me watched.

He did nothing to foster a sense of well-being or reassurance. Instead he created an atmosphere of paranoia and self-doubt. I had met with him many times back in Manila, and even though we operated in different theatres, I had always believed we shared a sense of mutual respect and admiration. I liked his no-nonsense approach, and his attention to detail was outstanding. I knew little of his background, but it was plain to see that he was from ordinary beginnings like myself. I detected a military sense of duty about him, and we forged a trusting relationship.

Miyazaki was almost the opposite of his drunken predecessor Hosokawa, who was an irreverent, snobbish man and weak to the core. I had thought Hosokawa a liability for years. That man was not cut from the right cloth, and his weaknesses were a danger to us all. Spoilt little rich men had no place in this mean business of ours, and it gave me great satisfaction in 1965 to pass on a communique from Tokyo that signalled Hosokawa's end. Hamazaki had reached the end of his patience with Hosokawa, whose drug dependency had put us all at risk. During the 1965 negotiations to remit one of our bountiful sites, I was told to pass the message to Miyazaki that Hosokawa was to take his final breath there in Manila. I felt it was in some way a small but divine revenge for Sister Mary.

Those were heady days indeed; I had been a trusted and important part of the machine. But now, even I had to admit that I had little of value to offer. What exactly kept me alive? Perhaps even hardened devils had a sense of moral obligation after all. Besides, who would ever believe me? Mine was a story so incredible that any attempt to tell it would see me confined to a mental health institution.

Miyazaki had seen fit to offer me a monthly stipend which was a very generous amount indeed, but it came with a warning not to overtly live beyond my means. My allowance would arrive monthly in an unmarked, plain envelope, each time franked with a different postal mark, an innocuous piece of mail with used banknotes inside. I had never used any of the money, and right now twenty-four brown envelopes sat unopened in my old suitcase.

I had lost myself in the moment, and the kiosk owner brought me back with his attempt at conversation. "That Hamazaki, eh? A man like that will be satisfied only when he rules the world." I nodded and searched around in my pockets for a few coins with which to pay him. As I was doing so, a magazine caught my eye. It was called Spotlight, and there was a strange picture of Hamazaki on its cover. He was portrayed amidst a mosaic of American dollar bills. I picked up the magazine and told the vendor I would take it, too. I folded the magazine inside my newspaper and set off on foot for my apartment, which was a brisk walk of thirty minutes or so away. If I kept my head down, I could avoid the giant hoardings which seemed to grace every available space in this city. Mabuhay was in every person's life, whether they cared for it or not. Beautiful women with pearl-white smiles, caressing some banal domestic appliance, beamed down from huge billboards up high, entering our subconscious and willing us to part with our hard-earned money in exchange for their wonderful product. "Let us take the strain out of hectic living." That was the latest assault on the pockets of the nation, but as always it was the phrase underneath that stung me the most: "Mabuhay. The world's most caring company."

That evening the rain grew into a torrential downpour, which put paid to my evening stroll around the nearby park. I found my new life hard to accept, and certain parts of the day needed to be filled. Perhaps there was still a lot of Ramil Tan in me, as the need to be out and about was verging on the obsessive. Relaxation was nearly impossible to come by. I was not a drinking man, and television was one habit that fortunately had passed me by. I preferred listening to the radio, but it served only as a mere distraction. I had become accustomed to getting by on very little sleep, and though I was now in my sixth decade, I rarely slept more than four hours at a time. So, what was left for a man like me? A man haunted by the memories of a past that constantly lived in front of my eyes, as if it were yesterday.

I sat in my armchair and began to read the magazine I had bought earlier that afternoon. It was a little damp from the downpour, but the shiny pages were still intact. The cover proclaimed Hamazaki to be their "Man of the Decade," and inside they promised revealing insights into the life of Toshio Hamazaki. It turned out to be quite disappointing, as it was by and large a rework of established facts. The story contained a few exclusive comments where Hamazaki paid tribute to Mabuhay's deceased cofounder Makoto Hosokawa and of course to Hideo Tanaka, still very much alive and living a reclusive existence far removed from the public gaze. The mosaic cover picture of Hamazaki had been taken from an artwork by some world-famous artist and Hamazaki consort, Fabian Mills. The article boastfully said that Hamazaki intended to hang the original piece in the main reception of the new Mabuhay corporate offices in Ginza. The picture had apparently drawn widespread disapproval from art circles, but Hamazaki had dismissed those who found the piece vulgar as a collective of inane fools who could not recognise pathos if it struck them fist-first in the face. So, art appreciation seemed to be another facet of the amazing Hamazaki. A small inset picture of Hosokawa was buried in the corner of the page. It had obviously been taken in his younger days, for he still looked quite healthy and undamaged by the cruel whip of time.

Hosokawa: how I hated that man. I only wished I could go back in time and put my hands around his throat and squeeze the air out of his being until his eyes swelled and he breathed no more. I dropped the magazine to the floor and felt my breath fall shallow. I closed my eyes and slowly counted down ten seconds in an effort to fill my lungs. Mary Delaney was, as always, behind my eyelids, her features etched in my mind. My guilt was forever present, as sickening as a satanic tattoo, a constant reminder of the evil man I once was and, as I still lived on this earth, must remain. Yes, the evil seed planted by Hosokawa on the orders of Hamazaki.

My hands fumbled around the inside of my shirt for the simple wooden cross. The cross of Christ, once the simple adornment of one of God's own angels and now shamelessly worn close to the heart of the one who had taken her life. I gripped hold of her cross and said a silent prayer as I had done each day since my hands had squeezed the life out of her innocent being. I prayed not for forgiveness, which would have insulted all decency. My prayers were for her soul and her memory, and I hoped with all my heart she had found her God in heaven and was sitting by his side, for that is where she truly belonged.

The dead hours of night were always the worst time. My spirit would desert me, leaving me adrift with the empty shell of a being who had once harboured ideals of decency. The ghosts of the past would seep into my mind and boil my blood, leaving me screaming out in a cold sweat. Screaming out to whom? I had nobody in my life. There was no chance of redemption for Ogawa. This was my existence.

After my repatriation the authorities had thought it necessary to appoint a counsellor to handle my adjustment and reintegration into modern life. I had resisted, but Miyazaki had told me it would appear a little strange if I refused all help, and after some vetting, he had told me to submit myself to any therapy that was on offer. My appointed counsellor was a man named Kazuki Zenigami, a strange name, but I had never asked him about its origins. Zenigami was too young to have experienced the horrors of the war, but seemed to be well informed and had a sanitised understanding of what we survivors must have gone through. I say sanitised, because you could never know what it felt like to be in the midst of hell. The stench, the noise of battle, and the silence wrapped up in the void that encompassed mass death was impossible to comprehend secondhand. I believed men like me were programmed to shut down the trauma of the heart.

It might take some time, but time was all I had, and I could play the part of bemused and bewildered war veteran with ease. Words would slip out of my mouth almost of their own free will.

I knew they were the words my counsellor would want to hear. I was a consummate liar, verging on the pathological. After all, my whole life had been one long series of untruths. During my sessions with Zenigami I would find myself talking about one thing whilst thinking of something entirely different. Only a week earlier I was telling him about my fear at riding an elevator for the first time, but my mind was back in the Luzon battle and thinking of stripping bloody corpses of their boots. The connection now escapes me, but it was there for a moment.

Zenigami had spent the first weeks of our sessions together probing my memory, and it was quite an effort to keep my story straight. At first he was happy to find that I was not some half-wit who was not of sufficient intelligence to realise the war had actually ended. I submitted myself to various tests and was at all times careful to gauge my responses. As I said, I was a skillful liar, and playing Zenigami became an extension of the game. Part of my mental rehabilitation took the form of educating me about the changes that had taken place in the modern world. I displayed sufficient disbelief upon being informed that man had walked on the moon and that we in Japan no longer had an army. I jostled with Zenigami and said I found the former easier to understand.

I tried to avoid looking back into the past, but it was futile, as the past lived inside of me like a cancerous tumour that fed on what little decency remained in my soul. I had been used, of that there was little room for doubt. The sickening part of it all was that I had allowed myself to be used for the damnable purposes of others who were far more mired in evil than me. In the very beginning my mission had seemed almost noble, and I felt proud to be trusted with such a great responsibility. Nishii had selected me personally to be his chosen one, and although I had serious doubts about the feasibility of his mad scheme, I had been offered no other alternative than to lay down my life if necessary and follow his orders.

I had been ready to die in that Luzon hell, of that there was no doubt. As the battle was drawing to its disastrous conclusion, I had made my final pact with my gods and was ready to allow my spirit the freedom it deserved. However, as fate would have it, I was destined for another role. I was called the "protector," a moniker which was casually hung on me by Nishii himself. I still recall that evening when I was called away from the front line of battle and driven down the lines to the Imperial Army staff headquarters. I thought my conduct had been called into question for some reason and that I was to be punished for some breach of discipline or other. Why else would a lowly officer find himself before his supreme commanding officers?

With the stench of cordite and warm blood still fresh on my foul uniform I found myself stood to attention outside the door belonging to the man I had come to regard as a god, General Yamashita. His chief aide, Major Kojima, brought me up before the great man and told me to stand at ease. The general waved his hand and bade me to sit before him. It was only then that I noticed Nishii was also present. He was sitting against the far wall next to an elderly gentleman with a fine moustache. They were both cradling large brandy glasses in their hands. It is funny how the mind remembers some of the smaller details when exposed to great stress. The general spoke to me without looking up from his papers, which were scattered all over the desk before him. His voice was somewhat feeble and wavering. I strained to hear his words amidst the noise of battle which was raging in the forests outside, turning almost entirely in favour of the enemy.

He briefly introduced the two seated to his left. Of course I was already well acquainted with Nishii, but that evening, there in

General Yamashita's quarters, was the first time I had ever heard the name Hamazaki. The general started to brief me about what was expected. He appeared to be confused and had difficulty arranging his papers. It was easy to see that he had been thrust into the moment, and I do believe he had not been afforded the time to adequately prepare. He was addressing me in loose military-speak, talking about honour and pride in serving our Emperor and nation, but I could see he was losing his train of thought. Hamazaki showed his impatience by tutting and interrupting him several times. At one point he even broke with all protocol and said, "For God's sake, Yamashita, tell the man what he has to do in plain and simple language."

Hamazaki's exasperation left no doubt about who was the senior and who carried the most importance in that feral atmosphere.

I remember the look of disdain on the general's face as he struggled to keep his dignity intact in the face of Hamazaki's insolence. Unfortunately it was too much of a struggle for the man who had the fate of what remained of our army on his shoulders. He calmly turned to face Hamazaki and spoke in a condescending tone that implied he was not willing to be a party to whatever it was that Hamazaki needed. The general stood and gave a deep and respectful bow to Hamazaki and said he thought such a matter would best be served by the one who had created the situation. He said he was excusing himself on the grounds that our soldiers needed to make a final stand before the enemy overran our positions and made it impossible for the minister to be extracted from the battle zone. He left Hamazaki with the ominous warning that his safe corridor of passage might not be intact any longer and should that be the case, the minister might wish to make some kind of final offerings to the gods and his family.

Hamazaki looked coolly at him and told him to go and do what he thought best. The general bowed again and took his leave but not before addressing me once more. He looked into my eyes, and I snapped to attention. His words still remain in my heart. "There is no finer end for a brave soldier than meeting his gods in battle. It seems that this honour is to be denied you, and for that you have my sympathy. Do their bidding with all your ability, but never forget that you are a soldier, and never be anything other than a proud soldier. Be true to your Emperor, your country, and most of all to yourself. May the gods have mercy on your soul."

Perhaps the gods had had mercy on my soul, for I was still alive. I slept on a warm and comfortable futon. I had more food than I deserved and no doubt enough money in those unopened envelopes to see out my days, yet I was still alone in this world. I had nobody, just as Ramil Tan had nobody. Being alone had become my natural state, so much so that I could not bear to be in a crowd. When I was, I feared the onset of panic, and cool, sticky sweat started to trickle down my back. I felt totally inadequate for this modern life. I had not lived apace with this society and sometimes felt an enormous sense of not belonging. I felt homesick for the Philippines; I missed the bright smiles of the ordinary folk and their gay, carefree attitude toward life. I even pined for the food and the language. Of course I knew such thinking was absurd and I could never return. Even admitting to such a longing would cast a long shadow of doubt on my life as a so-called "forgotten soldier."

I wished I could talk to Zenigami about my true feelings, but like so many other things, they had to remain buried deep in my soul. It seemed I was destined to live out my days in this small dank apartment, living my hermit-like existence with the stoicism expected from one who had been to hell and back. As I said, my only contact with anyone connected with my former life had been with Miyazaki, and that had been restricted to a few brief, clandestine encounters that left me in no doubt that any dereliction of duty on my part would result in the harshest of consequences. Did that mean I was under a suspended death sentence? I had once considered making some kind of record of my activities and using it as a shield to ensure my safety, but I knew it would only have the opposite effect. My life was not my own. It never had been and it never would be.

I was fifty-six years old and had never lain down with a woman. The urge had always been there, but the opportunity had always escaped me. I knew you had to create your own opportunities in life, but as far as women were concerned, I felt that part of life had passed me by. Even as Ramil Tan I could not find the comfort of a woman. Even the whores who graced the streets around the Makati area would not take my money. I was too close to the gutter even for the filthiest whore. Living as I did was a hell of my own making. Even on the occasions when it was necessary to become Ogawa, such was my devotion to duty that I could not find it in myself to seek sexual relief. My frustrations were buried, and that was where they stayed. I became an expert in pleasing myself, and much to my shame would spend days spying from afar on the semi-naked fisher wives who would sit on the beaches back in Luzon tying nets. I would glory in their naked breasts, the dark nipples that cried out to be caressed. My seed would find itself spent onto a coconut leaf and buried in the sands or rocks that lined the beach. That experience was the closest I had been to real sexual satisfaction and as close to a real woman as I was ever likely to be. After all, the only woman I truly cared for had been murdered by my own hands, the living breath throttled out of her as my hands squeezed her delicate white throat until her pitying eyes bulged with blood and could no longer see. I fumbled for the cross of Sister Mary as that final scene of her life, burnt into my brain, tortured me with its vivid clarity. The comfort of womankind was something my tainted and undeserving soul would never enjoy.

After my "glorious" repatriation I was in great demand. I was a curiosity, a throwback to a time when the country had lost all sense of reason. I suppose some people saw me as a symbolic being, the manifestation of all lost soldiers. I stood in the shoes of all the brave men who had never returned from battle. I received sacks of letters from still-grieving mothers, wives, and daughters. I read a few, but the effort to make any kind of meaningful response was too much. After all, it would be only hollow words on my part, and meaningless. I gave up on reading them, as their desperation was but another nick on my conscience. The post office had been instructed to hold back all my unsolicited mail, and I had been assigned a box number where my real mail would wait for me to collect it. There would lie the monotony of my new existence. Gas bills, electricity bills, and medical letters all seemed to signal my place as just another ordinary man living in a vast, lonely city.

I would drop by the post office each Friday afternoon at two o'clock. After signing off on all the anonymous mail so that it could be destroyed, I would pick up my bills and head off to spend the rest of the afternoon in a nearby park or, if the weather was foul, maybe take a coffee in one of the new, overpriced places in Higashi Ward. I suppose my strict adherence to keeping time and stubborn military discipline made my routines predictable. So I was not too surprised when the voice of a man seated on the park bench behind me drifted into my ears. "Ogawa san, I trust you are well? Do not be alarmed. I mean you no malice, but I would be obliged if you remained silent. I take it all is sound with you. We have a mutual friend who would dearly like to be reacquainted. If this evening is agreeable with you, then our friend wishes to extend an invitation to his home and hopes you will dine together. Now you may speak. Yes or no will suffice."

It seemed my invitation was framed with a certain amount of expected compliance on my part and there was only one possible answer. "Yes."

There was a pause, and then he continued. "Excellent. Our friend will be most pleased. I would be obliged if you made your way to the clock tower at the Ginza street intersection, where you will be met and escorted. I need not remind you that it is taken as understood that you will be circumspect in your actions. So, this evening at seven o'clock, if you please. Now, I think you should lose yourself in your newspaper for a minute or two. Good day to you, Ogawa san." Silence hung in the air. Even the bird noise had been swallowed up along with the cries of the children playing away in the distance.

The air around me was pungent with the aroma of sweet tobacco smoke. I had smelt that only once before, but I had never forgotten, as it seemed to be forever associated with the heady aroma of malice. Back in General Yamashita's office, old man Hamazaki had filled the room with the same aroma. Hamazaki?

I remained seated, blankly looking at my paper and waiting for my own little world to realign itself. My mind filled with all sorts of thoughts, some fearful, others hard to describe. I was in confusion. Of course the mutual friend must be Tanaka. Who else? I had so many questions, but I knew deep down that whatever lay in store for me had already been decided. There was nothing I could do but hold hands with fate and jump headlong into the unknown. After a very long moment of confusion one particular emotion of surprising intensity started to take hold of me. It was excitement, and for the first time since I had been repatriated, I felt alive once more.

I did not glance back as my messenger walked away. Such an action would have been seen as a display of contrition. Suddenly the vast park took on a different aura, and the solitude it had offered only a few minutes earlier seemed to have disappeared. I felt vulnerable in that open space, and the need to get myself under cover was irresistible. I was Ramil Tan once more, and I was back in the game. There were nearly four hours to pass before my appointment at the Ginza clock, and I decided they would be best spent taking rest back at my apartment. The old soldier in me knew that you had to take sleep whenever opportunity afforded a chance. It was one of the unwritten survival rules of battle.

After a short bus ride and a few hundred yards on foot I was back at my apartment. I looked up and down the street for anything that looked out of the ordinary. All seemed too ordinary, too quiet. What was I expecting? Being careful is one thing, allowing paranoia to take hold is something else altogether. I forced myself to focus on the evening instead of the present and climbed the short flight of stairs to the second floor. Maybe it was the sudden unexpected turn of events that caused me to wheeze, but I was feeling quite breathless, and the tension deep inside me was rising. I fumbled my keys into the lock and pushed the door open, kicked off my shoes, and opened the futon cupboard. I made a quick, rough bed and lay down, closed my eyes, and thought about what this meant to me. I was in that place between sleep and awareness that is frustrating and relaxing in equal measure.

From the way the sun cast shadows on my walls, I knew it must be time to walk over to Ginza and once more throw my lot into the lap of the gods. I had a choice of two good suits and decided on the one that had been given to me by the Japanese consulate general back in Manila. It was the same suit I had worn for my repatriation flight back to Japan and the one I had stood in to face the barrage of cameramen that awaited me at Haneda Airport some two years ago.

As I was taking the suit out of the closet, my eyes were drawn to the cardboard box that sat on the top shelf. For some reason not clear even to myself I took it down and opened the lid. My old uniform was folded neatly in that box. Unlaundered and bearing the stains of death, it was like a precious second skin for me. I had made a request in my final testament that my body be burnt wearing this uniform. I shook it loose, and the urge to wear it once more was irresistible. I slipped the tunic over my head and pulled the baggy shorts up over my skinny legs and tied the twine that held them up. To my satisfaction they still hung on me like the day they were new and adorned with the insignia of which I had once been so proud. Or course my badges of honour had been removed, but in my mind they were still very much there, catching the light and gleaming with pride. I looked into the mirror and for a moment saw a younger version of myself, a twenty-year-old Ogawa standing to attention, ready to fight and die for his country, but then tears welled up in my eyes and the image before me came into sharp focus. A sad, balding, and virtually toothless old fool dressed in a pantomime costume from a show long played out, a man hanging on to his memories because that was all he had to hold on to. I snapped to attention, saluted this pathetic reflection, and made a promise to myself to change my last testament.

It took me around twenty minutes to make the trip on foot to Ginza, and I arrived with a few minutes to spare. Not wishing to look like a loiterer, I spent a moment perusing the newspapers and magazines at the kiosk on the corner, eventually settling on that evening's Yomiuri. I looked at the headline that was splashed over the front page: "Saigon Falls." There was a picture of a helicopter hovering above desperate people who had their arms outstretched and fear etched into their faces. It seemed incredible to me that the mighty Americans had not been able to defeat the North Vietnamese. What did that say about my own army that had been so savagely destroyed by the American forces only thirty years earlier? Of course those of us who had been there knew it could have been different if our belligerent leaders had seen fit to supply us and even feed us. Men lose the stomach to fight when they are hungry, and it is hard to go into battle with nothing more than a belly full of leaves and boiled-boots soup.

As I was staring blankly at the picture, I felt someone take hold of my arm and firmly lead me to a car which had pulled over to the side of the road. I slid into the rear seat without paying much attention to my escort; after all, it mattered little anymore. The inside of the car was cool and spacious. I could stretch out my legs to their full length, and still had room to spare. The man seated next to me stared forward, expressionless. His shaved head and dark glasses added to his menacing demeanour. I had expected us to turn left at the next major intersection and go on to the Empire, but we continued straight. My escort must have sensed my heightened agitation, for he spoke for the first time. "Don't be alarmed, Mr Ogawa, we shall be at our destination soon." I took his opening gambit as a chance to engage him in conversation and asked how long our journey would take, but he was having none of it. I suppose you could call him the ultimate in benign intimidation.

Our driver was a ghostly-looking fellow with deep sunken cheeks and watery red eyes, the kind of chap better suited to driving a hearse. We progressed in silence. My only view was out the front window, as there were curtains draped over the rear passenger windows, but I knew we were in Chiyoda. To my surprise the car made a sharp left turn and we stopped at a small gate which was opened for us by an old man. The ghostly driver moved the car forward slowly, and the gravel crunched under the tyres, sending up a small cloud of dust.

We pulled to a halt, and my man got out and walked around to open the door for me. I stepped out into the dusk and looked at what was before me. I did not need anyone to tell me where we were. The sacred place for all old soldiers, the spiritual home of the fallen, Yasukuni Shrine. I squinted against the final shafts of sunlight and noticed a lone figure sitting in front of the shrine with his back to me. I looked at the hulking figure of my escort, who had removed his sunglasses in a form of deferential respect. He nodded, and held out his hand to indicate that I should join the figure before me. I walked the twenty meters or so down the path, which was sided with lanterns and beautiful cherry trees. The man was sitting on a small blue plastic bench, which seemed a little incongruous with the surroundings.

I stood awkwardly for a moment or two before he spoke. Without turning around he spoke with a cool and relaxed air. "Lieutenant Ogawa. Please accept my humble apologies for disturbing your day. I am honoured to be in your company. I feel we have known each other since time began." He turned around and offered his hand. "My name is Toshio Hamazaki."

I took his outstretched clammy hand, and we exchanged an uncomfortable handshake. The irony of the situation was not lost on me. The wealthiest man in the world and the poorest ragamuffin Ramil Tan, cosying up together as if we were old chums catching up with each other's social calendars. Hamazaki patted the bench seat beside him and I squeezed alongside, feeling diminished against his heaving stature, for he was as impressive in the flesh as the myths surrounding him suggested. The serene nature of this sacred place had a welcoming effect on my nerves, and I felt strangely empowered and in control of my senses. We both stared forward in silence, contemplating the shrine before us. At this point I realised that we had been afforded the place to ourselves. I suppose wealth carried a multitude of privileges.

Hamazaki glanced back over his shoulder. "I do hope Tsutsumi san was not too brusque with you. He was told to display the utmost courtesy; however, I feel he may be lacking in refinement, although he is unswervingly loyal to the core. Those hardened Kyushu men all seem to be hewn from the same rock, don't you agree, Ogawa?" I nodded and told him that some of the bravest men I had fought alongside had hailed from there. Hamazaki smiled and said his own ancestors had originated in Okinawa way back, but he himself was born a soft Tokyoite.

Something about his manner was both disturbing and compelling, and our small banter was drawing me to the latter. Hamazaki looked at me, and for the first time I found myself able to take in his features in more detail. No doubt he had been a strikingly good-looking fellow in his day, but as with all of us, time had started to take premiums from his looks. He was a little jowly, and his eyes were watery. The broken maze of tiny red veins over his nose told a story of heavy drinking, which was confirmed by the bittersweet, acrid smell of stale sake which still lingered on his breath. His hair was long and grey and tied back in an effeminate manner. Despite these cosmetic imperfections he was still a mighty being and had that natural sense of entitlement that all men of his class seem to be born with.

Hamazaki raised his hand and snapped his fingers. After a few moments which we both spent in contemplative silence, the driver arrived, bearing a silver tray replete with a bottle of sake, three small cups, and a small plate of rice crackers. Tsutsumi followed and set up a small trestle table before us. After the tray had been settled, they both bowed towards Hamazaki and made their way back to the car. Hamazaki poured sake into a cup for me and also into the third cup, which he pushed towards the shrine before setting the bottle down. I immediately returned the compliment by pouring a cup for him. We both picked up our cups, and Hamazaki raised his in salute to the shrine. I followed suit. "To all you brave spirits, we drink this for you, in your memory and out of respect and deep love for all your brave sufferings and sacrifice."

We drained our cups in unison and set them down. Hamazaki immediately refreshed my cup and I his. The third cup remained untouched. It was for the gods, omiki sake, an offering, and a communication with the divine kami. It was so simple a gesture and yet heavy in symbolism and meaning. Hamazaki told me that this brand of sake was favoured by brave kamikaze pilots at the end of the war. He looked to the shrine and said he hoped they were still able to enjoy the taste.

With the sake warming our bodies Hamazaki seemed to visibly relax. He stretched out his long legs and put his hands behind his head. "Ogawa san, I have been looking forward for so long to making your acquaintance in person. Although we have worked together for as long as I care to remember, the very nature of our work meant we were separated, and yet I feel we know each other well enough. Would you not agree?" I nodded. "We owe you a great deal. In fact, without you I do not believe Mabuhay would be where it is today, and for that you will always have my profound gratitude. Your loyalty and devotion to the cause has not gone unnoticed, despite the fact that we are forced to play out our lives at a distance apart."

I was happy to let him do all the talking. My only questions were about my father, and I was sure that he would come up in this little talk soon enough. "Ogawa san, there are things I want you to know, and I invited you here this evening to fill in some of the gaps so you may find yourself in a more peaceful state. So if you will spare me a few moments of your time, I will enlighten you a little."

Then he said, "Do you feel his presence?" I looked at Hamazaki, puzzlement etched on my face. "Close your eyes and tell me what you see." I did as I was told but saw nothing except the residue image of the shrine before me, as it seemed to have burnt itself into the back of my eyes. Hamazaki did not seem disappointed with my lack of response. In fact at times it almost felt like he was talking to himself. "Yamashita, General Yamashita. Close your eyes and picture his face. Do you see him before you?"

I did try to conjure up the image of the man himself, but all I could bring into focus was a picture in my mind's eye, an impersonal image, something anyone could recall. I decided to stretch my imagination a little and told Hamazaki that I believed I could picture the general.

Hamazaki's voice lowered. "Tell him we are deeply sorry for besmirching his good name. He has been wrongly bound up in the urban myth that bears his name. 'Yamashita's Treasure,' so unbefitting a mantle as there ever was. For that, I, on behalf of my father, apologise. Ogawa, please tell him that." At this point I was beginning to believe that Hamazaki had lost all sense of reality, but then I remembered something my father had told me long ago. The kami, or spirit, hears those who were closest to them. Now, I was never close to Yamashita, not by any stretch of the imagination. I spent only a brief few moments in the same room with him, but maybe in Hamazaki's eyes I was closer to him than anyone else he knew. I bowed my head and said a small apologetic prayer, which seemed to satisfy Hamazaki.

"Ogawa san, does the general accept our apology?"

Maybe it was the sake coursing through my veins, but I felt myself being uncontrollably drawn into Hamazaki's madness. I said, "I do believe he does."

Hamazaki fell quiet for a moment or two before carrying on. "Please tell the general that we are deeply sorry for associating his good name with a project that he naturally found repellent. If there is any solace to be found, then it is in all the good that has been done since those dark, foul days."

I found it increasingly hard to follow Hamazaki's thinking and was tiring of playing his macabre charade. In an almost comical afterthought Hamazaki told me to tell the general that he himself thought "Luzon Treasure" was a more befitting moniker. I tried to keep the smirk from my face as I passed this gem on to the general. Hamazaki put a hand on my shoulder. "Thank you, Ogawa san. Thank you for helping me communicate my prayers. I feel a little less burdened."

He poured me another cup of sake, and I poured one for him. We raised our glasses. Hamazaki proposed a toast, and we drank to General Yamashita. Hamazaki looked at me. "We have so much to talk about and I have so much to tell you, but first let us talk about your father." My toes almost curled up inside my boots. "Your father was the dearest of men. Loyal to the core. He is missed here." He put his palm against his heart, a gesture I found strangely touching. "However, there is one thing. He was not the greatest driver I have ever known."

We looked at each other for a moment, and then the granite between us cracked. We both fell into a fit of giggles like a couple of schoolboys. Perhaps it was nerves that had kept me together up to that point. Whatever it was came as a welcome respite. Hamazaki, a man I had forced my heart to hate, a man at whose door I had laid all my woes, was in fact a likeable fellow.

He looked at the shrine; his eyes welled up as he got caught up in a haze of nostalgia. "Twenty years ago I came here to this very place. It was a searing hot August morning, and the cicadas were in rebellious voice. I stood alongside Hideo and Hosokawa. We were here for the tenth marking of the end of the conflict. I can still picture, as clear as day, your father standing by the Bentley over there, waiting to drive us back. I am sure he was thinking of you on that day. It hurts me to think of his sadness, and for that I will die a lesser person. I'm so sorry."

He put his hand on mine and stood. "I will leave you for a few moments' solitude so that you may talk with your father." He stood up and took a few rice crackers from the plate and walked off to the side. I kept my head bowed in mock prayer until I felt a suitable amount of reverent time had passed. I looked around for Hamazaki and saw him crouched down, cooing at the pigeons and throwing them bits of rice cracker. The richest man in the world.

Our solitude was eventually disturbed by the arrival of another car, an automobile of a kind I had never seen. It was huge and bore the shining figure of an angel on its front grille. Hamazaki took this as a signal that our time here at Yasukuni was at an end. "Ogawa san, your car has arrived." Confusion must have registered across my face. Hamazaki let out a deep laugh. "Do not worry, my friend. There is someone who is looking forward to seeing you this evening, someone far more deserving of your time than I. Baba here will be your driver for the short ride over to the

Empire. Enjoy your evening, Ogawa san; it was so nice to finally make your acquaintance. Good evening to you."

He gave me a small bow and headed off towards the car that had brought me here. I was directed into the gleaming silver hulk of a car by my driver. "Good evening, Ogawa san, my name is Baba," he said. "I am the personal chauffeur for Tanaka san. He has instructed me to attend to any needs you may have before proceeding on towards the Empire, where you are to dine with Tanaka san."

My heart was lurching here and there. I told Baba that I did not require anything and that we could go straight to the Empire. He held open the rear door for me, and I took a moment to have one last look at this sacred place, a place about which my army buddies had sung songs, a place where at one time we all believed a part of us would find everlasting peace. I knew that honour would never belong to me. The cruel passage of time had no doubt decided where my spirit would finally lie, and sadly it would not be here. I was just about to get into the car when I noticed that Hamazaki was taking a moment to chat with Tsutsumi, who was looking over at me with a kind of manic intensity. Now, call it old soldiers' instinct, but I had the strangest feeling that they were discussing me and it was unlikely they were conferring benefit upon my good self.

A cold shiver ran down my spine. Hamazaki threw down his cigarette and crunched it into the gravel under his heel; he caught my stare and gave a slight bow before getting aboard his car. I left Yasukuni with the feeling that I had somehow missed the true point of our meeting. Hamazaki had always been like a mythical figure in my mind, devilishly devious and ruthlessness personified. Now that we had finally met, I was still no wiser about his true nature, but as I had told myself so many times before, my fate lay in the hands of the gods, and Hamazaki was no god, just a mortal being, as we all are. There was nothing I could do to change my destiny. All roads eventually lead to the same place, but some are less travelled than others.

I felt light-headed from the sake I had drunk earlier with Hamazaki. It was not an unpleasant feeling, and I quite enjoyed the short ride over to the Empire. The splendid white Rolls-Royce was not a common sight on the streets of Tokyo and received more than its fair share of curious stares from the pedestrians who thronged the sidewalks. I knew they could not see me, as I was shielded by the almost jet-blackened windows. Baba was well practiced in handling the vehicle, and I felt myself slide around on the shiny black leather bench seat.

I thought of my father driving around these same streets, and as if by some kind of telepathy, Baba must have read my mind. I caught his stare in the rearview mirror and without preamble asked him if he had ever been acquainted with my father, Ogawa the chauffeur. Baba did not seem unduly surprised and answered my question without flinching. "No sir, unfortunately I did not have that particular pleasure, but I have heard only wonderful things about Ogawa Senior. I am honoured to follow in his footsteps."

I could not think of a suitable response to his blatant flattery, so after a few moments I redirected the conversation to safer, more banal ground such as the unbelievable change in the Tokyo skyline and the crowded streets. We were of a similar age and therefore could make meaningful connections with the past, but it was only talk for talk's sake, and I was relieved to finally see the Empire loom up before us.

Baba nodded to the liveried doorman, who waved us on past the main entrance. We rounded the corner and came to a halt at what seemed to be the delivery area and staff quarters. Baba was swiftly out of the car and around my side to open the door with a bit of an exaggerated flourish. I suspected the man may have been blessed with an understated sense of humour in his leisure time. "Ogawa san, we have arrived at our destination. Please do not be perturbed by the surroundings; Tanaka san prefers your visit to remain as private as possible. We may access the main body of the hotel without attracting undue attention or inconvenience by using this elevator, which is normally reserved for the daily comings and goings of the staff."

Baba leaned into the car and switched off the engine, and then escorted me over to a small, simple elevator. After what seemed like an age it finally arrived and we travelled up a few floors. I was relieved to get out of that small space, as it had obviously been recently used by some kind of seafood delivery service. We walked through a few empty rooms, and Baba produced a key which he used to open a locked door and gain entry to the main body of the hotel. We rode another elevator, far grander and almost palatial in contrast to the first one.

It was obvious we had stepped into another realm—the denizen of the privileged few. I suddenly felt rather shabby in my dress. The cheapness of my clothing stood out here, and I had the strange sensation of feeling physically diminished in stature. Baba was a good head and shoulders taller than me, and even his chauffeur's uniform was a far better cut than my own dreary attire. I resolved not to fret about trivial matters. After a walk of about a minute along the plush, wine-red carpeted corridor, we came to an imposing set of grand doors. Baba pushed the bell button; there was no sound to be heard from within. He gave me a deep reverential bow and took a few steps backwards. "It was an honour to be of service to you, Ogawa san. I bid you good evening." He turned and left me waiting before those heavy doors.

I was just about to try the button once more when I heard what seemed like the sound of a bolt being slid back. The doors opened slowly, and I was greeted by a face which was both shockingly familiar and welcomingly comforting. "Ogawa san, we have been expecting you. Please do come in."

Tanezawa had not changed at all. In my mind's eye she was still the same young woman I had glimpsed back in Manila on the occasions I had picked her out of the crowds as I had spied surreptitiously on my colleagues in this so-called business of ours. She smiled and extended her palms in a welcoming gesture. The mere presence of Tanezawa was enough to settle what remained of my nerves, and I responded by giving her my best smile, which I knew might be slightly off-putting, as my mouth was still missing most of its teeth. A uniformed valet stepped forward and took my coat. Tanezawa thanked him on my behalf and bade me inside.

I had given very little real thought to the purpose of my being summoned here, and my mind was still very much full of my earlier meeting with Hamazaki. This was turning into one of the most extraordinary days imaginable. I had already taken sake with Hamazaki as we played out our little pantomime before the spirits of the brave ones, and now I was about to play a part in another man's world. This time I felt I was due a little more respect, for without me Hideo Tanaka would most certainly not have been here today. It was I and I alone who had saved that man from joining his comrades in glorious death as the war machine ground out its victims and spat out the mincemeat all over the Luzon jungle.

Tanezawa was the model hostess, full of grace and modest efficiency as she led me through to a vast and beautifully furnished room. I had expected to find Tanaka sitting there on one of the large cherry-red leather sofas, waiting to greet me, but the vast room only exuded loneliness. Tanezawa asked me to take a seat and offered me a drink. I was about to decline but did not wish to appear ungracious, and settled on a small Scotch and soda, which she prepared herself and served on a small silver tray. I noticed that she did not prepare a drink for herself. She sat opposite me, and I had a notion that her confidence was slowly melting away. She looked a little uncomfortable and seemed to be at a loss for words. It was obvious that small talk was not her forte and she was in an unfamiliar and equally uncomfortable situation. I guessed she must know how deep my own involvement in Mabuhay had been, but I did not know for sure how far reaching the confidences of Tanaka and Hamazaki had extended to her own good self. I was being very guarded and chose my words carefully and with the utmost discretion. To the best of my knowledge Tanezawa had served as Ayumi Tanaka's assistant, primarily concerned with the charitable work of the Mabuhay Foundation. I had little knowledge about her current role and to be honest was surprised to find her there. I supposed the years of loyal service had brought Tanaka's confidence and that she must be a trusted and loyal servant of the Mabuhay cause, but for now maybe I guessed it would be in my favour to appear ignorant of all that was playing out before me.

"Ogawa san. Thank you so much for being our guest this evening."

Her words spiked my curiosity. "Our guest?" I leaned forward and looked a little more intensely into her eyes, bowing graciously as I did so.

"Hideo has been praying for this moment since the two of you parted on that fateful evening over thirty years ago in the Philippine jungle, and now his prayers have been answered." She glanced over to a side door as if expecting Tanaka to make some kind of grand entrance, but I knew it was the natural modesty in her soul that caused her to look away, as I felt she did not wish her words to be taken as a sign that she was the keeper of secrets. It was now obvious to me that Tanezawa, young as she might be, was as close to Tanaka as one could possibly be. Did she know everything? No doubt as the course of the evening unfolded, we would be furnished with enough clues about the missing pieces in all our lives to fashion a picture of the truth.

We sat facing each other, and an uncomfortable, heavy silence formed a void between us, neither one of us knowing quite what to say for fear of causing offence or misunderstanding. I had sat in on many a volatile meeting over the years. When a man had dealt with the likes of Santa Romana and emerged in favour, then you would expect to be equipped with the experience to handle simple domestic affairs such as this, and yet something about Tanezawa was upsetting my thoughts. Perhaps it was because of the dark secrets that I kept so close to my heart. Would Tanezawa be so welcoming if she knew the depths to which my soul had plummeted? After all, I had stood over her father's corpse and run my hand over the wounds that had cut him down. Major Kojima had been an honourable man, but a man caught up in the birth of all this madness that had resulted in this thing that drove us all: Mabuhay.

I looked at Tanezawa closely; I could see nothing of Kojima in her face, but then, war and its attendant suffering did tend to give us all a new face. As my mind drifted into morbid nostalgia and started to reflect on that day Sister Mary called upon Ramil Tan to inform him of the death of a Japanese officer up at the prison in the north, a gong sounded, and the large wooden double doors were opened by the manservant to reveal a dining room like I had never seen before. The room exuded wealth and opulence but was finely balanced with exquisite taste and feel. I had seen some grand places in my time but nothing as grand as this. Even President Marios's rooms paled by comparison.

Tanezawa stood and led the way. I followed in her wake, feeling shabbier than ever. The vast dining table was set only for four. Intricate flower arrangements were placed in empty places to mask the embarrassment of loneliness or perhaps to enhance the feeling of togetherness. There was no sign of my illustrious host. The servant, whom Tanezawa addressed simply as Murakami, was busying himself with setting up what appeared to be a pair of air bottles which he had wheeled in on a small trolley and placed next to the head of the table. He had a clipboard in his hand which he marked as he tested the functions of the dials on the bottles.

I noticed a surgical mask attached to the rig. Tanezawa caught my stare. "Ogawa san, please do not be alarmed. Tanaka san suffers no serious ailment. However, he finds it best to live in a more controlled environment, and that includes the administration of pure oxygen at regular intervals." She took her seat without offering any further information, despite the incredulous look that had spread across my face. I could not stop gawping at the oxygen contraption, and even before he had made an entrance, I was beginning to doubt whether I would recognise the Tanaka of old. Those doubts were further compounded when Murakami proceeded to replace the utensils at the head of the table with those from a box marked "sterile." The room was eerily quiet, and yet there was a hissing sound from time to time, the source of which took me a few minutes to detect. At certain places in the walls a fine watery mist was being dispersed. Tanezawa again sought to head off my curiosity. "That is a mixture of the purest water on the planet blended with a compound of rare herbs that are found only in the deepest depths of the Amazon rain forest. Its purpose is to soothe the mind and keep the room balanced, thus creating the perfect breathable environment. After all, we are nothing without air. Isn't that so, Ogawa san?"

This only seemed to confirm that Tanaka had indeed lost touch with the reality. Had our wretched business driven his sanity over the edge, allowing his riches to indulge eccentricity to the point where real life no longer carried any meaning? I had read that he was very rarely seen in public, and now I realised why. Perhaps he could not bear the contamination of the outside world. He was a designer and innovator, blessed with a talent like no other in the world of electronics, and maybe he had designed his own personal little kingdom in an effort to forge a divide between what lurked outside and his closeted pure-air rooms. A divide between heaven and hell, and here I was a visitor from hell. One of Satan's minions come to infect his paradise.

Tanezawa and I took our seats at the dining table and kept up a respectable silence as we waited for Tanaka to make his entrance. Murakami had left us, presumably to assist in the preparations for the evening's meal. I caught Tanezawa's attention and asked her if some other person would be joining us for dinner. She looked at the fourth place setting and shook her head. "It is our custom to lay an extra place, and we do so each evening. Hideo insists on it." Despite my obvious confusion she offered no further explanation, but it was obvious that something was preying on her mind. Although she was well within the bounds of rational control, she appeared agitated and at times at a loss about where to direct her stare. It was not my place to pry, and in any case, silence suited me; it gave me time to collect my thoughts.

Tanezawa looked over to the ornate standing clock, which told us it was a little past eight. She glanced at her wristwatch and gave a little sigh. "It seems Hideo is caught up with the final business of the day. I am sure he will not keep us waiting much longer." I nodded and said it was perfectly understandable and that it was a pleasure to be here and to please not have any concerns on my behalf. I passed a few silent moments by counting the intervals between the pure Amazon air hissing into the room. It was exactly one minute.

As I was settling into my surroundings, a small door at the far end of the room opened and out stepped Murakami, who took up his place, standing at attention almost in military fashion with a white cloth draped over his arm. Without any preamble the lighting in the room dimmed by a quarter, and from somewhere in the distance classical music could be heard. It was by no means obtrusive; in fact it blended perfectly into the background. Tanezawa looked at me and whispered, "Wagner. Hideo loves Wagner. It helps him relax." I looked at Tanezawa. She was beautiful in some kind of special way, and in that instant I felt for her. She too had her own demons. What kind of pact had she made to keep the little devils at bay? There was no sound, but we both turned our heads to the small door, and there he was, Hideo Tanaka, gliding across the room with arms outstretched, almost like a spectre. A man I had last seen thirty years ago in the Luzon jungle, where we had said our goodbyes, both of us believing that evening would be our last on this earth. Fate had conspired to prove otherwise, and here before me was the living proof that miracles did happen. For some inexplicable reason I could not rid my mind of Sister Mary on her knees praying to her God. Tanaka walked across the room, his gaze fixed upon me. He was wearing dark glasses, so it was almost impossible for me to gauge his demeanour. Tanezawa and I both stood to greet him. He stopped in his stride a few yards from me and honoured me with the deepest and most reverential bow I have ever received. I felt awkward and uncomfortable. Surely he was the one more worthy of such a greeting.

He stepped forward and grasped my hand between his own cold and clammy hands. "Ogawa san, I thank you from the bottom of my heart. You have made this day the most special day of my life, and you have my unreserved gratitude. I am truly honoured to be in your company."

The three of us stood awkwardly for a short moment, none of us quite knowing what to say next, before Tanaka took his seat at the table and we followed suit. The long dining table, which was designed for grander occasions, looked almost comical as we settled into our places. I had to fight the urge to stare at Hideo, and it was an effort to try to appear at ease. I was beginning to regret being here but alas knew that I had very little choice in the matter. Murakami appeared and with accomplished aplomb poured each of us a measure of red wine from a decanter that seemed to sparkle with many different hues of blue light. Tanaka raised his glass in my direction and simply said, "Welcome home, my dear friend."

I returned the compliment with as much enthusiasm as I could muster and said it was my pleasure to be back amongst friends after so long in the wilderness. I noticed that Tanezawa looked a little ill at ease and was looking down at her place setting. I retraced my words to satisfy myself that I had not said anything untoward. It was plain that none of us were at ease with one another, and my discomfort was further stretched to the margins when Tanaka pulled on a pair of thin surgical gloves and started fumbling with the oxygen mask. He placed it over his mouth and began taking heavy gulps of air. His eyes were invisible to us, as they were shielded by his dark glasses, but an aura of manic intensity about him only served to confirm that Hideo Tanaka was no longer the simple man I had once known. An uncomfortable silence descended as Tanaka reclined into his chair and took several noisy gasps of air. Tanezawa's own discomfort seemed to be on my behalf, as she was no doubt used to Tanaka's eccentric displays. That notion was confirmed when she raised her arm, a signal for Murakami to come scuttling across the room and go about his duty of disconnecting Tanaka from the contraption and snapping off his rubber gloves, which made a comical pop as they were removed. When he had finally finished this bizarre rigmarole, the table resumed some semblance of normality, which was further defined when Tanaka finally removed his dark glasses and I got a look at his face for the first time in thirty years.

Everything about him had changed, and yet he was still the same man. The Tanaka I had said farewell to all those years ago was a man ravaged by years of war, a man deprived of life's basic necessities, a man who did not expect to live to see another sunrise, a living corpse waiting for the reaper to deliver the final condemnation. That was my last memory of Hideo Tanaka, but now here he was sitting opposite me, a different version of the man I once knew. Ruddy cheeks and tired but clear eyes were a possible testament to the benefit of his weird regimen. He smiled for the first time and shook his head as if disbelieving what was before his own eyes. Without doubt he must have been shocked by what he saw, a toothless old man with next to no hair whose skin had taken on a grey pallor that was impossible to lose.

We looked at each other for what seemed an eternity, until Tanaka broke the silence. "My dear Ogawa san, please forgive me if my actions have unsettled you. I'm afraid there are certain procedures I live my life by, and my insistence upon and the taking of pure air before dinner is one of them. I suffer from specific phobias which are best managed here in the confines of my home. Moments of stress and anxiety only exacerbate my condition, and the need to administer relief is then undeniable. I have consulted with some of the best medical minds in this field, only to be left dependent on my compulsion for extreme cleanliness. I believe it is a reaction to our plight of thirty years ago, during those final days of the war when we hid down in the hole and stayed in total darkness for days on end, breathing through bamboo canes and feeling the creatures of the ground crawling over my body, eating me away one micro bite at a time. I honestly believed that death was preferable."

He paused for a moment, looking down at the table as if embarrassed by his own words, or perhaps he had drifted back to his hellhole in Luzon. He looked up slowly and there, for a fleeting moment, I caught the genuine sadness that lay across his face as he continued his humble speech. "Ogawa san, it pleases me to see that you seem to carry the burdens of the past more lightly. It is a true testament to your resilience in the face of such hardship, and you have my deepest admiration and respect." I listened to his words with the kind of forced detachment one reserves for times when the talk makes you feel uncomfortable and almost nauseated. Tanezawa reached over to Tanaka, and for a moment I thought she was going to embrace him. She settled for a consoling pat on the back of his hand. I was lost for words and lowered my head and contemplated my surroundings. Tanaka's opening gambit was hardly the stuff of dinner party conversation. I wondered about his sufferings. His words had brought that time back to life and only served to awaken my own wartime demons which I too found hard to keep at bay and in the confines of my practiced amnesia.

Dinner was surprisingly simple and served with graceful efficiency by Murakami, who I had noted was completely in the trust of his eminent employer, for Tanaka did not make any attempt to censor his conversation when his manservant was in

683

attendance. For the most part we made small talk about how the city had changed and how disrespectful the youth of today had become. The emotive issues that bound us together were like snakes smeared in grease, unable to get purchase and raise their heads, but they slithered around in a complex tangle that soon would become impossible to resist and eventually demand our attention.

As we made our way through trays of Japanese delicacies that were chosen to reflect the various regions of our country and countless varieties of soba noodles that seemed to be a particular favourite of my host, I managed to piece together something of Tanaka's life. It was plain that Tanezawa was more than just his confidante. I had gathered as much from Miyazaki when we had met in Manila some three years earlier, but Miyazaki had subtly failed to tell me that he himself was now squiring Mrs Tanaka. All these changes in bedfellows were bewildering for a man such as myself who had failed miserably in all matters of the heart. I believed I would be able to muster a justifiable defence for my own loneliness, as my circumstances were hardly conducive to forming a relationship of any kind. Indeed, how can a man expect love when the only woman he has had feelings for had to die by his own hands, and for what? So he could sit at a rich man's table and hear how easy it was to lose control of your heart and how the winds blew fate around with such reckless abandon that it was futile to resist. Tanaka said he believed there was no such thing as choice, for whatever we decided on, that was always our intended destiny. Choice was little more than an illusion intended to keep us from going insane, as our fate lay with forces we would never begin to understand.

Tanaka seemed to bear his depression with the stoicism that had helped him survive those dark days of the past. He told me how he had finally given himself up and surrendered to the Americans and how his mind was riddled with the guilt of survival. It was obvious he wanted me to sympathise with his plight, but all I could do was nod and say things like "Really" and "That must have been hard for you." My own heart had turned to stone many, many years earlier. Besides, Tanezawa was his obvious vessel for comfort, as she reached out for his hand and gave him a consoling touch when his conversation seemed to plummet to the depths of despair.

I was relieved when we finally finished dinner and were able to move away from the table, which seemed to serve only as a barrier to genuine conversation and to my ability to think in a meaningful way. I thanked my hosts for their generosity in serving such a delightful and surprising offering. Tanaka said we would be more comfortable in the sitting room, and after he had completed a thorough bout of hand sanitation, which took up a few uncomfortable minutes, he led the way.

If the dining room was a splendid place to behold, then the sitting room was simply breathtaking. I suppose all wealthy men made statements in some way or another, and this room was undoubtedly the work of the finest craftsmen. All four walls were panelled in dark mahogany, and fine murals had been carved into them. Lighting had been placed at specific points to accentuate certain features. It took a few moments for me to take in the scene that surrounded me. The walls were testament to the life of Hideo Tanaka. A picture-scape like none I had ever witnessed. I had been in some of the most beautiful Christian churches of Manila and there was no denying that they carried a certain aura that was fuelled by centuries of belief. It was almost as if the prayers of the worshippers had soaked into the fabric and foundation of those holy places. The air felt heavier, and as Ramil I used to go there, at first to escape the blistering heat but later just to feel closer to something that I had no words to explain. I suppose I was in awe of the fact that pure faith was enough for some people and I desperately wanted to be able to believe that there was something or someone to guide me through those dark days. I needed a form of pure devotion and tried my darndest to will it into my tortured soul. Now I was overcome by those very same feelings, here in Tanaka's sitting room, of all places. This space brought back those feelings of longing. But why? It was obviously very recent but had an ancient feel to it.

Tanaka was studying me closely, looking for signs in my expression. After a few moments he beckoned me over to his side and drew my attention to a particular panel that pictured a man carrying another in his arms like a baby. There were fallen comrades all around, and the earth was disturbed by violent explosions. The detail was amazing, and it was only after a few moments that realisation finally dawned on me: I was looking at my own face, for it was me as a young man, carrying the broken body of Hideo Tanaka in my arms. Closer inspection revealed an elaborate depiction of fine details, most of which would have been lost on those who had no reason to know the sufferings of that time. Bootless corpses whose faces were contorted with fear, agony, relief, or plain nothingness were blended into the ground alongside spent water bottles inscribed with the names of their once thirsty owners. Men whose last mortal moments were captured in heartbreaking details that rendered me at a loss for words. It was a myriad of all possible emotions, a thing of morbid beauty and equally a testament to man's brutality. Poetical letters written by soon-to-be-departed soldiers blew about in the fug of war, sadness, and desperation smattered with hopelessness and loss, some barely literate, others expertly crafted, but all striving to say the same things, to love and be loved, to stand brave and believe that death was more glorious than life.

I could have spent hours gazing at this montage, but was so overwhelmed by its scale and meaning, I could barely believe my eyes. Of course I was drawn to the Luzon battle scenes, but my curious eyes fell upon other scenes as well. There was one of a man curled up in a foetal position, lying on a single tatami in a workroom, surrounded by radios and drying laundry. The door was slightly ajar, and peeping inside was a familiar fellow, bedecked in finery and carrying a walking cane. It was Hamazaki, and I gathered that it must carry some poignant meaning known only to Tanaka. I felt a little like an interloper who had stumbled upon the most secret pages of a private diary. My embarrassment must have shown, for at this juncture Tanaka felt the need to explain his choice of interior decoration. He asked me to make myself at home, indicating a leather wingback chair by a vast unlit fireplace. As we settled down, drinks in hand, brandy for me and barley tea for my host, I began to gain a picture of the life of Hideo Tanaka.

"Ogawa san," he said, "this is my sanctuary, a place where I keep my memories alive and try to make sense of all that has happened in my life. I suppose it is the scientist in me that looks for connections between happenings, and in those rare moments when I identify common threads, I honestly believe I can see the future with a fair degree of certainty. It is a model I have applied to the business side of my life, and it has served me well over the years. I am told there is now at least one Mabuhay product in fifty per cent of the developed world's households, a statistic I find incredible, given that twenty-five years ago I had nothing before me but broken radios."

He glanced over at the panel of the sleeping man. No further explanation was required. "I have never been a man of words, and I find it awkward to express myself. Everything I want to say is here in my mind; it just does not verbalise very well. However, I have come to realise and accept my shortcomings, for I believe I would not be able to create the products I do if I were of any other character. We are all what we are, and there is little purpose to be served by raging against the forces that dictate our existence. When I was younger, I wished I was a little more like Hamazaki, a free spirit able to enjoy the trappings of our wealth, but I knew that was an impossible dream. In truth I felt embarrassed by my wealth, and yet I am no fool. I understand fully where my debt lies. Ogawa san, without you none of this would have been possible."

He raised his hand and gestured around the room. For a moment I thought he was talking about the room itself, but then I realised he meant his life. He fell silent for a moment as if he were steeling himself for some kind of important pronouncement. "My dear friend, let us look out over the grounds." He stood and walked over to a large window, and I followed like some pitiful lapdog. From that window, so high up, was a view of beauty. The Imperial Palace was lit up in all its splendour. We both looked out, silently appreciating the magnificent sight.

Tanaka looked lost for words, but he soon recovered and continued, though he sounded a little subdued, as if he were talking to himself. His hushed words moved me to my core. "I was born in that place, in one of those rooms, to a mother I never knew. I was an embarrassment to a father who did not want his lineage disturbed by an unwanted bastard child. A mere few hours after my birth I was carried out of the palace and handed to Hamazaki's father, who had been tasked with placing me in a comfortable adoptive home. I was given to the Tanaka family, who raised me as their own son. I was their son, they were my parents, and I still grieve their deaths. I would give anything just to see them for one last moment to say goodbye, but alas, American bombs denied me that chance."

He looked over at the panel which showed American bombers high in the skies above Tokyo and for some reason a Metro bus stop and, bizarrely, a herd of rampaging African wild animals. No doubt it carried great meaning for Tanaka, but the symbolism was lost on me. Tanaka looked at me and then back out over the grounds of the Imperial Palace. "I was cast out, so one may only presume my birth was not welcomed, and I joined an elite club of unwanted royal bastard children. There is a certain irony here, don't you think? Anyway, my adoptive father was instructed to report on my welfare, health, and general state to Hamazaki Senior each year on my birthday. In turn Hamazaki would deliver the report to the palace. I can only assume that the circumstances of my birth were such that some person in high quarters felt it necessary to keep a watch on my progress. I was made aware of all this only after I met Toshio. It was he who told me everything. From this I gather I was afforded certain benefits, such as acceptance into officer school when my background dictated I was a natural for the regular conscripts, fewer beatings in cadet school, an initial easy posting, and ultimately the privilege of surviving the war, in no small part thanks to your good self. Also, it no doubt helped ease Toshio's mind when I proposed to Ayumi. So, here I am, bastard prince Tanaka in your debt, my good friend."

I did not know what to say. I went back to my chair and sat down, wishing I could be excused. I felt the need to get out of this room now. It was becoming a little overbearing, and I could not see what Tanaka wanted from me. I had served Hamazaki for nearly thirty years, watched over his loot, reported back, and negotiated its safe passage. Loot which had greased the way for Hamazaki and Tanaka to become two of the wealthiest men in the world. I believed I had earned my rest and retirement. In truth I wanted no further part in this circus of deception called Mabuhay.

Tanaka asked me to look at the panel by the grand piano in the far corner of the room. I walked over, and there before my eyes was my father. He was standing proudly by a great car, looking even younger than I had ever remembered him. In that instant I thought about Tanaka being denied his last goodbye. I too had been denied, by Hamazaki. That was the root of all my resentment. I went about my duties believing my father was well cared for. What I had not known was that he believed I had perished in the carnage of battle. Such a situation suited the cause, and nobody, not even my so-called good comrade Tanaka, ever saw fit to tell him otherwise. I closed my eyes and counted back from ten in an effort to get my emotions under control.

Tanaka's voice was floating in the distance, and it was an effort to fix on his words. "Your father was a fine man. I had nothing but the utmost respect for him. He represented all that was good about our country and lives. He is dearly missed by all of us." I turned to face him, unable to control my emotions. I lowered my head as if I had been chastised, not out of shame but in fear of saying something I might regret. Tanaka picked up on my discomfort and bade me once more to take a seat. Tanezawa appeared from an anteroom bearing a silver tray, upon which were two large glasses of brandy. It seemed Tanaka would on this occasion allow himself a little fortification. In this room, too, the Amazon air hissed at regular intervals and seemed to signal breaks in our emotions.

"Ogawa san, there is one matter I would like you to tell me about: the day the last site was liberated. I want to hear it from your own mouth. I have heard Miyazaki's version, but all the same, I would like to hear how you saw things." I looked into my brandy glass and swirled the amber liquid around as if I were some kind of mystic looking for a vision. After a minute or two I recounted those events that marked the end of my mission in Manila.

"As you know, it was the last site, and I had been told by Miyazaki that an end strategy had been decided," I said. "It was a great relief for me, as I honestly believed I could not have pushed my deceptions any further. Romana was getting greedier by the month and had even started seeking me out to push Tokyo for more money. As I walked about the streets as Ramil, I was often pulled in by the street police and then, unsurprisingly, found myself in the custody of their secret friends. Hector would play the hard man for the benefit of his cronies, but in truth he seldom really did any lasting damage. He was a decent fellow deep down, a man caught up in events that were beyond his control. We had a great deal in common, and I sympathised with his situation.

"Anyway, as instructed I let slip hints and clues that a big deal was on the horizon, something that needed to be handled with great sensitivity. I also hinted that this would be the final round of negotiations and our mutual business would soon be concluded. Of course word soon reached Romana that our twenty-year partnership was to draw to an end, along with his four-million-dollar payouts. He must have figured that our contributions to Marios's election campaigns would also, naturally, come to an end. I waited on word from Tokyo—that is, from you and Hamazaki—to go ahead and confirm the start of the last round of negotiations.

"Of course, Romana by this time had already decided upon one big final payday for himself. He had no intention of honouring the final agreement. Miyazaki and I sat in on a meeting one week before handing over the coordinates and safety precautions that were vital to the liberation of the last site. Romana asked us directly if it were true that this was the end of our business together. He seemed to find it unbelievable that we may have finally come around to the last site. We said neither of us were privy to such information, but I could see in his eyes that he did not buy my words.

"Romana was edgy and tight; he looked under greater stress than usual and did not cajole or try to intimidate us, as was his way. He accepted the usual terms without much fuss and asked for his initial two million in cash the next day. Miyazaki and Meursault delivered the money, and the deal was in motion. Up to this point I had no idea what our strategy was to be. Miyazaki then proceeded to give me a set of coordinates and told me to go in deep cover at that location, complete with seven days' rations, within twenty-four hours. He also told me to take my army kit and all wartime effects, as I would no longer be going back into Manila. It was time to say farewell to Ramil Tan.

"It was a mighty task and I barely managed it, given that these old bones are no longer what they once were. I made it into the mountains and settled into my given location and waited. From my vantage point, which was on high stony ground, I had an impressive view of all before me. I knew I was overlooking the last site. As darkness fell that first evening, I heard a slight rustling in the foliage. Miyazaki appeared, and he was ladened down with some heavy-looking canvas bags. We did not speak, but by this time words were not needed, for I had a fair idea of what was about to happen.

"My imaginings were confirmed when Miyazaki opened up his bags and began to assemble two high-velocity sniper rifles. When he had finished this task, he leaned back and asked me if I still had a little fight left in me, enough for one last battle. It was as if time had gone back thirty years. I was back in the Luzon war with a rifle in my arms, and I can tell you, I had the same fears as I had back then."

Tanaka had closed his eyes and was taking in my story. He nodded and waved at me to continue.

"Miyazaki is a hard man and no doubt has seen conflicts of his own," I said. "He is also a man who does not suffer fools gladly and sees no purpose in humouring old soldiers. There was a job to be done and he wanted it done." Tanaka nodded knowingly. Suddenly I remembered there must be bitterness between the two of them, and regretted talking of Miyazaki. I knew Miyazaki was now Hamazaki's man and that as long as that remained the case, he was untouchable.

Tanaka looked intently at me and urged me to continue my tale. I looked over at Tanezawa and noticed that she was taking notes. This made me feel uncomfortable, and I faltered a little in my delivery and became a little defensive, which Tanaka picked up on. But he told me not to have any concerns, as it was for his own purposes only. He waved his hand towards the far wall, which was still a blank canvas waiting for a record of further milestones in his life. It was then that I realised my recollection of those events was necessary for him to form a picture in his mind.

Tanaka closed his eyes and asked me to carry on; I knew he was allowing himself to go back to that devilish time when every living minute felt like a reprieve from the inevitable. He had seen hell, and its fiery gates had been wide open, inviting him inside, but fate had other ideas for Hideo Tanaka. Now he was taking one last peek into the inferno.

I took a minute to compose my thoughts and then continued. "Miyazaki had brought along extra supplies in case we needed to extend our vigilance beyond what was anticipated. We spent the next day in silence, observing everything around us. The air was so laden with tension, you could almost reach out and touch it. I was reminded of those long days and nights dug deep into machine-gun posts, watching out for an enemy that would appear from nowhere and unleash hell. All our waste, bodily and otherwise, was put into plastic bags and tied tight and stored in our packs for removal later. In the unlikely event of a future investigation Miyazaki was determined that we would leave no trace of our presence. We seldom spoke. Words were not necessary. As dusk fell once more, the sounds around us changed as the creatures of the night began to wake. Truth be told, I was a little afraid. Darkness had always left me feeling vulnerable, as I was the kind of man who liked to see his enemy coming.

"We took turns keeping alert through the night. Seeing was near impossible, as it was a cloudy moonless sky, and it was a constant effort to stop your imagination from playing tricks with your senses. Was that a rogue boot crushing a stick? Did I hear the faint whisper of a faraway voice? We spent the cool night each absorbed in our own thoughts and fears, dug in on that ridge, covered over with the kind of camouflage netting that had not changed since your days in battle."

This little personalisation seemed to jolt Tanaka a little. He opened his eyes and looked at me, but I couldn't read his thoughts. I carried on. "Dawn eventually broke, and the sun crested the mountains to our left. It was like someone had turned a switch. The whole scene lit up before us in that special time when the air felt clean and the foliage was dripping in morning dew. The jungle is truly a beautiful place, but it takes a special eye to see it. I took a moment to say a silent prayer for all the men who had fallen in battle, ours and theirs. Their spirits had fertilised nature's pageant, and I prayed for some of their strength to help me see this mission through. I tried to feel at one with the earth. Perhaps I was more akin with the spirits of this place, as I had lived here on and under this very earth for more months than I could remember.

"Miyazaki was a difficult man to read. He came across as cold, calculated, and methodical, qualities that no doubt go towards making a good soldier. He never looked me in the face and went about his business as if I did not exist. I began to fear his mission extended beyond the obvious. My paranoia, once woken, became a raging beast that had free rein to devour all rational thought. I remember looking out over the dripping green leaves and listening to the shrieks of the tree monkeys and thinking it might be the last morning I would ever see." Tanezawa seemed to have stopped taking notes, and Tanaka too had opened his eyes in concern. This would have been the opportune moment for them to assure me that my fears had been unfounded, but it seemed that neither could find the words to say so.

"The noise shook me to my senses. At first it was a distant hum, but within seconds the canopy was shaking in its wake. Monkeys and birds were sent screeching and crying, dispersing in all directions. We slunk in tight as a Chinook helicopter circled overhead. We did not want to become part of the disturbance, and hung on to our netting for dear life. Having scoured the area for hostiles, the helicopter made a slight descent and hovered above the clearing. We watched as four ropes were thrown out from the sides and men climbed down to the ground. I heard Miyazaki counting them down. Twelve bodies in total, dressed in army fatigues, but these men were not loyal to any regular army. They were mercenary, loyal only to money and part of Romana's private militia. The advance party that would secure the area before the extraction process could begin. Half a dozen men fanned out to form a cordon whilst the others dealt with the heavy equipment that was being unloaded in giant cargo nets from the helicopter's great belly. They had done this many times before and were well practiced in the tasks required.

"As you know, during previous extraction missions Romana would direct operations from a distance, but on this occasion we were banking on him making an appearance. His greed would get the better of his caution, and the desire to check on his final payday would prove too irresistible for his corrupted soul.

"Miyazaki scanned the scene below us with his powerful eyeglass. I too strained my already tired eyes scanning the area. My sweat constantly dripped over the lenses of my Leica binoculars. Romana was nowhere to be seen, but Miyazaki did not seem worried. He spoke for the first time that day. 'All is well, my friend.' Whether he was referring to the mission, Romana, or me I did not know. We were now living on the kind of adrenaline rush you can get only when your nerves are stretched to snapping. We had something real to watch before us, and I was drawn into the fascination of the process. I had been the guardian of these sites for so many years that it felt almost hypnotic to finally be able to see one opened up.

"Well, after the initial burst of activity, things on the ground seemed to settle down and Romana's men went about their task with a surprising degree of efficiency. Honestly, I would have expected a more haphazard approach, but these men were well drilled, and they all seemed to know exactly what to do. Six men had disappeared into the surrounding undergrowth, no doubt to keep vigilance whilst their mercenary comrades went about making preparations for the extraction.

"There was a good deal of measuring, both with rolls of tape and more accurately by a theodolite, which was operated by an elderly man who looked out of place in his baggy fatigues.

Miyazaki seemed to be studying this man with particular interest. I could not get a fix on his face, but something about him was familiar. Miyazaki kicked my heel to get my attention and mouthed his name. It was Nishii.

"At that moment my whole body seemed to tense and pour sweat as I strained to confirm Miyazaki's assessment. My former commander back in league with Romana—it seemed too incredible to be true. My brain was racing through all the possibilities, and I was trying my damnedest to keep my head. Miyazaki, on the other hand, was playing a cool hand. He kept taking water at regular times and every ten minutes or so viewed the scene below through his telescopic sight. It was obvious we would be dug in for some time, and I was beginning to wonder when Miyazaki would brief me about our 'end game.'

"It took the men on the ground around six hours to assemble the rig, which they had situated just off the centre of the clearing. Four other men had been busy digging a shallow channel of about ten metres long in which they had laid a length of detonation cord and now seemed to be covering over with heavy ballast, no doubt to force any explosion downwards. They toiled like beasts in the sweltering heat, stopping only for water breaks and bits of food. I must confess to feeling a little sad on their behalf, as I knew that they must be in the final hours of their lives. No doubt they were looking forward to a generous payday and dreaming about what they would be doing in a few days' time. Some loved ones must be awaiting their return and living on the promise of a better life. As always it would be the ones left behind who would do all the crying. All those dreams were going to be shattered for sure. Did they deserve this? Was that for me to judge? I tried my best to divorce myself and my feelings from such thoughts; instead I told myself that this was the last day of my war."

Tanaka listened to me with intense concentration, at times closing his eyes and taking deep breaths. He seemed particularly moved when I talked about how I had felt at that time, but true to form, he kept his own feelings locked within and did not say anything, choosing to close his eyes and allow me to recount those final hours. I took a draught of brandy and carried on with my tale, not wishing to sound sensational, but to just give a plain recollection of how it happened.

"Without warning the men detonated a small explosion, sending up a huge cloud of dust which obliterated our vision for a good few minutes. The tree monkeys were sent screaming like wild banshees in all directions; one even ran over our hide. Birds too flew off in panic as their usual idyll was disturbed. As the dust settled, we saw that several men had gathered around the centre of the clearing and were peering down into a narrow chasm that had been broken open. Miyazaki was cursing under his breath, as he had to clean his sights of the film of dust that had descended upon us. He tossed the cleaning rag to me and told me to do the same. As I was polishing the optics on my rifle sight, we heard the unmistakable hum of an approaching helicopter. We covered our sights and glasses to prevent reflections and pulled the ground netting tight over our bodies as we lay flat on the ground. The helicopter made several passes before circling overhead and finally making a descent. It was a small craft built for speed and seemed capable of carrying only a few passengers. As it touched down, whipping up the dust once more, we waited to see who would put their boots on the ground. This was the critical moment, and we both knew it.

"We waited with a tension that ate into the pits of our stomachs. The pilot cut his engine, and the blades slowly came to a halt. Two men went up to the helicopter and opened the door; they snapped to attention and threw sharp salutes as the passengers finally emerged. First out was Hector, who ignored the men and strode straight over to the centre of the clearing. We waited and I heard Miyazaki whispering under his breath. 'Come on, you bastard.' Then, like a ghostly apparition before us, came the unmistakable figure of Santa Romana, his eyes shielded by dark glasses and customary fat cigar hanging out of the corner of his mouth. Again Miyazaki's whispered words hit my ears. 'Got you, bastard.' I stared with fascination at Romana as he issued commands to his men, who seemed to have found an extra gear and were now buzzing about like ants on hot tiles. Romana looked smaller and a little stooped compared with his men, who no doubt had been chosen for their physical prowess. A small canvas awning had been erected, and they seemed to be using it as makeshift command post. Romana went over to join Hector and Nishii, who were looking down at a large paper that they had spread out over the ground. All three were in our direct line of fire, and as I looked down the sights at Romana, all I could think about were the times that man had threatened me with beatings, mutilations to my manhood, and even death. The contempt with which he had held me was creating an emotional backlash that urged me to pull the trigger right there and then, but no, we waited for what seemed like an eternity."

Tanaka asked me to pause and excuse him for a moment. I presumed he had felt a call of nature. He stood and left the room, leaving me alone with Tanezawa, who was reviewing her notes. I thought she might take the opportunity to ask me a few questions; after all, we were talking about the man who had sent her father to his certain death. Did she know that? Had Tanaka told her the whole truth about how her unfortunate childhood had been the catalyst for her eventual acceptance into the inner folds of Mabuhay? Did she know that she was playing a part in one of the biggest conspiracies in the history of mankind? As those thoughts raced through my mind, it suddenly dawned on me that this little interlude was for nobody's benefit but my own, and for a moment I felt a little isolated in this vast, fancy, oppressive room.

Tanezawa avoided meeting my gaze, adopting the officious, cold stance she had always reserved for business. She stared down at her notes without looking up, and her voice caught me a little off guard. "Ogawa san, please have no sentimentalities for my feelings. Do not spare me the whole truth, as I have long ago accepted where I came from, and this business of ours holds no sway with delusion. In fact if we cannot be open with each other, then what is the purpose of all this?" She tapped her notepad with her pencil in a manner that reminded me of Zenigami, my counsellor. I felt irritation building from deep within, for I had been nothing but truthful. I wanted to take her words and throw them back into her face. After all she had been a part of the big lie surrounding my father. Her own complicity in that matter was in my eyes unforgivable. I had long ago accepted that these people operated within their own rules and mores.

I leaned forward, my voice hardening as I spoke. "Believe me when I tell you, for I will not disguise the truth for your benefit. I will tell you exactly how your father's murderers met their end."

She looked up, and for the first time I saw that her reservations about me had vanished, and she smiled. Not the smile of an angel, more like that of a sly imp. She placed her hand on mine and said, "Yes, I do believe you will, my dear Ogawa."

With the consummate timing of an old trouper, Tanaka came back into the room offering apologies for his absence. He seemed invigorated, as if he had been given an extra shot of life, or perhaps it just seemed that way in comparison with my own sudden onset of weariness. I wanted this evening to be over and to be excused. My own simple bed had never seemed more inviting. They both sat before me, waiting expectantly for the next installment of my tale.

"I was beginning to wonder when we would make our move, and I remember marking the sun's slow descent, as each minute passed felt like another lost opportunity. Miyazaki hardly removed the spyglass from his eye. It must have taken great fortitude to keep up that level of concentration, and I admired his single-mindedness. I figured we had about three hours of pure daylight left, after which the shadows would begin to play tricks with our minds. The activity on the ground was frantic, and it was obvious that Romana's work team were going about their task with similar concerns. I could not imagine Romana or Nishii being willing to spend a night on the ground if it was at all avoidable. They would be desperate to put as much distance between themselves and their crime as possible.

"I looked over at Miyazaki, who had taken an interest in the mountain ridge to our left. He checked his watch and signaled for me to get closer. I slowly eased myself over to his position, and he gave me my orders in that succinct way he seemed to have made his own. His whispered voice was barely audible over the noise of the parrots cawing overhead. 'Ogawa, you are responsible for Nishii. You will take your shot after I have delivered my own to Romana. We will take them down in the clearing so you will have enough time to sight your target in the confusion that will follow. Two targets, no more than two shots each. After we have confirmed our success, we will stay in position for a few moments before making our extraction on foot. I want you to keep close to me, as there may be hostiles in our path, though I reckon Romana's men will fancy flight to be a safer option than fight. Good luck, my friend, keep a steady hand, and balance your aim with empty lungs.'

"I nodded and shuffled back to my position. I tried to focus my mind. It seemed incredible that I was to deliver the final blow to a man who had set me on this path—incredible but at the same time fitting and just. I felt an exhilaration that was hard to understand unless you have been in the throes of battle.

"Adrenaline coursed through my body. The anticipation was unbearable, and sweat poured out of me, dripping down my face into my eyes. We held our position for another thirty minutes or so. Eventually Romana and Nishii were standing together in the clearing. They were looking into the pit that had been excavated and waiting on something heavy that was being lifted to the surface. The ropes on the rig were straining, and two bare-chested, hulking men were heaving with all their might. Another man appeared from the chasm in the ground and swung the load to one side. It was smaller looking than I had expected, given the effort it had taken to get it to the surface. Then realisation dawned. I had been there before, and so had you, my dear Tanaka."

I locked eyes with Tanaka, whose expression gave nothing away. He merely nodded and said, "That is so, Ogawa san. Your memory serves you well, though I am surprised it took you so long to realise. Perhaps it was the fact that thirty years ago that hellish place was shrouded in the devil's darkness and battered by rain from hell. That, together with our blinding fear, would be enough to wipe the memory of any sane man." Tanaka looked almost apologetic as once again I had been used as a pawn in a wider game and he had been caught cheating like a naughty schoolchild. I chose to ignore his obvious discomfort and continue my tale.

"The load turned out to be a small chest not unlike those you often see in pirate books. It was lowered onto the ground, and I could see Romana ordering his men to stand back. It seemed to take an age as they decided on their next move. No doubt they were cautious, because as you know, many locations and safes were rigged with explosions or gas, but this trunk seemed small and unassuming. One of Romana's men was tasked with opening the trunk as the others took a few steps back for safety. The man worked the lock with a jemmy, and after a minute the top popped open without fanfare. I saw Romana bark an order for the man to step back. The scene below seemed to freeze in time. Romana walked forward and looked into the trunk, and Nishii and Hector joined him. I saw Romana put his hands inside and remove something. It was wrapped in a dark green cloth and looked similar in size to a newborn baby. Romana cradled the bundle as he slowly unwrapped it from its binding. He dropped the rags to the ground and sank to his knees.

"He was facing me, and I had a clear view of his newfound treasure. It caught the dying sun in brilliant flashes of green and gold. It was a statue of some kind and held the attention of all those around it. The frantic activity came to a halt as they gathered around to admire the shining beauty that was being jealously caressed in Romana's arms.

"This seemed to be our moment. Miyazaki raised his voice slightly before squeezing the trigger and said, 'This is for Gloria. May you forever rot in hell, you bastard.' The shot rang out around the whole clearing. In my peripheral vision, Romana's head exploded like a shattered watermelon, and the men on the ground froze in fear. They had no idea where the shot had come from, and their panic sent them scurrying to all parts of the clearing. My sights were now trained on Nishii, who was trying to prise the statue from Romana's death grip. My first shot was not as accurate as I would have liked. I believe I hit him in the buttock. His screams seemed to be in harmony with the birds and monkeys and could be heard even from our lofty position. My second shot was final. It struck him in the face, and the back of his head opened up. Miyazaki kept his calm and merely said, 'Two kills confirmed.'

"We stayed in position for what seemed like an unnecessary length of time. The men on the ground had scattered. The echo of our fire had made it almost impossible for them to get a fix on our position, and in any case Miyazaki's assessment of their unwillingness to engage proved to be the case. Not so much as a single round was discharged in any direction, let alone ours. We studied the scene below as if it were a scientific experiment, and watched as Hector Ramirez slowly gathered up the figurine with a sense of calm that seemed out of place, given the circumstances. He stared directly up at our position, almost as if he knew exactly where we were, but then again, it was obvious he must have."

I looked at Tanaka expectantly, giving him adequate opportunity to add to my recollection, but his expression told me that he was deep in thought. I wondered what was going through his mind. Was my tale what he had expected it to be? After all, he of all people knew only too well what that place truly felt like, for he too had shaken hands with death and lived to see another sunrise.

I closed my eyes to gather my thoughts, as I knew my words were being carefully digested by Tanezawa, who was scrawling her shorthand like the efficient little mite she was. For some bizarre reason the image of her naked and on her knees, her head between Tanaka's legs, fixed itself in my mind like a photographic negative, and no matter how hard I tried, I could not shake it away. It was so distracting that I had to ask Tanaka if I could use the washroom. Being the most hospitable and courteous of hosts, he rang for Murakami to escort me. As if by magic the manservant appeared and stood by the door, waiting expectantly to be of service. I excused myself and followed him out and along a short corridor which connected to several luxurious-looking sitting rooms. Eventually he showed me into a bathroom the likes of which I never knew existed in this world. Fine robin's-egg-blue marble and sterling silver taps glistened in the subdued light. Piles of freshly laundered virgin white linen towels were bound with silk ties. There was a rack of perfumes and colognes and baskets of soaps all wrapped in exotic-looking packages. Even in here, Wagner accompanied one's ablutions.

The irony of all this opulence swept over me; only a few years ago I had been a user of nature's own toilet.

All this, as fine as it was, paled into insignificance when confronted with the actual toilet bowl itself, and to my growing shame I realised that I did not have any idea how the thing was operated. There was a panel of switches and some basic diagrams which I presumed were instructions for rejecting the waste, but I was taken aback when jets of water splayed out and hit me in the nether regions, leaving me looking like a child who had failed to make it on time. There was only one thing for it, and I opened the door and called for Murakami's assistance. A grown man asking another grown man how to use a toilet is a belittling experience for both, but Murakami was efficient and explained the functions in simple language, as if teaching a child.

On the way back to the sitting room I asked Murakami how long he had been in Tanaka's employ, to which he replied a little over ten years. He then told me he had worked for Mr Hosokawa until his untimely passing. There was a distinct moment there that was most certainly uncomfortable and we both felt it, so it was with some relief that I found myself once more in the sitting room with Tanaka and Tanezawa. Neither got up from their chairs to greet me, and from their expressions I gathered they were eager for me to get on with my tale. I settled into my seat once more and took the opportunity for a little small talk.

"That is a mighty fine bathroom. I have never seen anything like it. Electrical functions, heated seat, and all."

Tanaka allowed himself a wry smile. "Actually, you are part of a privileged group, as it is the only one like it in the world. I designed and commissioned it myself. It is a prototype for what I believe will one day be a standard in most bathrooms around the world. In fact Mabuhay has developed an extraordinary range of new cutting-edge items that could only have been the things of dreams a decade ago. I have a vision in my mind where people will use telephones outdoors, televisions will be as big as walls, and we will all enjoy cool air in our homes."

Tanaka seemed to have become more alive when talking of his inventions, and I wished I knew a little more about his field in order to engage him, but my knowledge did not extend much beyond wiring a fuse. In any case his imagination seemed to have left reality in its wake. Tanaka seemed to realise this and shook his head slowly, as if further technical talk was a waste of verbal and cerebral energy. I took his point and continued my tale.

"After a time which seemed like an eternity but could not have been more than five minutes, the clearing became devoid of all activity. Romana's body lay crumpled in the dust below us like a fallen scarecrow. There was a dark stain in the dirt around his head. Nishii's body lay near Romana's; their boots were almost touching. I remember thinking they looked like the broken and bent fingers of a giant clock. Miyazaki never took his eye off his sight. He was ever so clinical in his method and actions. All I could do was wait for him to signal our next move.

"In fact it was not Miyazaki who signalled our intentions but a quick and unmistakable flash from the far ridge on our right side. Someone had used a mirror to catch the dying rays of the setting sun. It flashed four or five times. Miyazaki spoke, his voice more relaxed than earlier, and he seemed to lower his guard a little. 'Ogawa, it is time for us to make our retreat.' He started to dismantle his rifle and motioned for me to do the same. We went about our tasks and cleared our hide, pulling branches across the place where we had lay hidden for the past two days. After Miyazaki had gone over the ground two times to satisfy his attention to detail and to make certain we had left nothing incriminating behind, he turned to me and said, 'Ogawa, it has been a pleasure to serve with you, but this is where our path together ends.' Miyazaki unclipped the holster on his belt and took out his sidearm. He studied it for a moment and then looked at me with an intensity that burnt deep into my frayed soul. I remember thinking that this had always been the place I was to die and to finally do so now would be the natural way of things: a life gone full circle, eventually meeting its destiny after a thirty-year reprieve. I stood my ground and willed myself into silence. I would not plead, nor would I try to reason with Miyazaki. I knew such words would only be ground into the dust.

"Miyazaki slowly shook his head and stepped forward. Placing his hand on my shoulder, he handed the weapon to me. 'Go now, my friend, go to ground and make like you have been lost to the world for thirty years. When you come out of this hole, you will be feted as the lost soldier. Your effects are already in place.' He handed me a small compass with a reference point which was close, no more than an hour on foot. He waved his hand and motioned me on my way. His last words to me were 'See you in Tokyo, my friend, or, if we are lucky, at Yasukuni.' Those same words used to drip from the mouths of desperate men on that old battlefield thirty years ago. The trees rustled in a sudden breeze, and the monkeys had returned to satisfy their curiosity. I turned to walk away. After a few paces I stopped to look back, but Miyazaki had already disappeared."

The three of us sat in silence for a few minutes, each lost in our own thoughts. Tanaka closed his eyes and clasped his hands together. Maybe he was doing his best to picture that final moment in Luzon, or maybe he was trying his utmost to remove himself from that hell. I asked him if he would like to hear about my time living back in the jungle as Lieutenant Ogawa of the Imperial Japanese Army with the façade of a loyal and fanatical nationalist who had refused to accept defeat, who had continued his own personal battle for more years than he could remember. Tanaka shook his head and said that was perhaps a story best saved for another time. He thanked me for my honesty and said he was deeply sorry for all my troubles both past and present. He asked Tanezawa if she would allow us both a moment in private. She did not find this in the least unusual and took her leave with courteous grace.

Tanaka waited until she had closed the door behind her before he spoke. "Ogawa san, you must believe me when I say I owe you everything. Without your loyalty I would be nothing. Your sufferings have been borne on strong shoulders, and no one is more deserving than you." There was a brief silence before he continued, and I knew he was struggling to find his words. "What I am about to tell you does not come easily, and my heart fears your response, but there is no easy way to say this thing."

He looked directly at me, and his words slipped off his tongue as if they were coming from some far-off place. "Your intuition was correct. Miyazaki was ordered to take your life back there on that day in Luzon. Toshio had ordered your death. He believed your continued existence to be a liability to our operation. He told me that there was no further practical purpose in allowing you to live. The sites had all been liberated, and you were of no further value to Mabuhay. Toshio had asked for my blessing, and reluctantly I agreed with him."

Tanaka looked down, unable to meet my eyes. I felt my blood run cold through my veins. He carried on speaking, his voice barely audible across the short distance between us. I got the feeling he was wrapped in a shroud of shame. "Yes, I agreed with Toshio, and I did not reason with him for a different outcome. Miyazaki was tasked personally by Toshio to see to your final moments. I agreed, but I want you to know that I had no intention of letting you go.

"Miyazaki and I have an uncomfortable relationship. I believe you may have gathered that he is my wife's lover and has been for more years than I care to think about. It is an arrangement that is far from ideal but seems to work if we stay away from each other's lives. I had never spoken to Miyazaki after he unofficially took up with Ayumi, that is, until the evening before he was due to leave for Manila on that final mission. I summoned him here and told him in no uncertain terms that he was to ignore Toshio's orders and instead supplant them with my own—those being the lost soldier scenario. He was to tell Toshio that there was no opportune moment in which to kill you and that he had had no choice but to let you loose into the jungle. A thin plan at best, but given my limited options the only one I could put together in such a short space of time.

"Miyazaki sat in that very chair where you are now and listened as I told him what to do. The man was caught between a rock and a hard place. He had no desire to betray Toshio and saw little benefit in agreeing to my wishes until I told him that your life was worth my forgiveness. I would give him my complete blessing to make a new life with Ayumi if that was what he wished. I would allow divorce proceedings to be started in return for your life."

Tanaka looked away, as if he were trying to conceal his expression. I guess he must have realised his words were hardly the stuff of reconciliation. My life had been spared in exchange for another man's happiness. It took a minute or two for the whole absurdity of the situation to dawn on me, and when it did, I found myself gripping the sides of my chair so hard, my fingernails were beginning to ache. Tanaka turned to me and said in a voice that had suddenly hardened. "Ogawa san. Do not judge us too harshly. A tremendous amount is at stake here, and if you were in Toshio's position, I daresay you too would have taken the same course. I know it does not make anything right, but I want you to know nothing is personal."

My continued silence seemed to unnerve Tanaka to the point where he was struggling for words. I now knew exactly what he'd meant when he'd told me he was an inadequate being when it came to dealing with people. After my hurt had subsided a little, I asked the obvious question. "Do I still have anything to fear? Is my existence still considered a threat or embarrassment to you all?"

My words came out with a rawness and hurt that took Tanaka off guard. He seemed genuinely moved. He stood and walked over to the grand window once more, looking out at the palace as if it were the answer to all of life's problems. He spoke without looking back at me. "I have known Toshio Hamazaki for over twenty-five years, and I have never known him to give up or even back down on anything. So I can only say yes, your life is still at risk. That is why you are to leave now and never return. Ogawa san, I am giving you the chance at a new life, a brand-new start far away. I beg you from the bottom of my heart to take this opportunity with all the zeal you can muster."

As I was about to unleash my frustrations, the door opened and in came Tanezawa. She was carrying a large briefcase, which she set down on the centre table. Tanaka walked over to join her, and they both sat down and motioned to me to join them.

Tanezawa was icily efficient as she explained what they had in mind for me. "Ogawa san, here is your new passport. Please examine it. I believe all the details are in order save for your new name, of course." I picked up the thin passport and flicked through the pages. It was maroon in colour, and the words on the cover shouted out at me: "Pasaporte and Republika Ng Philipinas." My birthdate was accurate, but my birth address was listed as Angeles, Manila. The photograph was so undoubtedly me that it could have been taken today. Only the name screamed out from the page. Joe Mendoza.

I looked up at the two of them, who were staring at me as if waiting for praise for their efforts. The only thing I could say was "I would rather die here in my own country than go back and be conveniently stabbed in the back." I threw the passport down on the table and looked to one side, letting out a sneer of frustration.

Tanezawa ignored my petulance and continued her brief. Tanaka leaned back in his chair and studied my face as she did so. "You are not going back to the Philippines. A new life awaits you in a new country far away. Joe Mendoza is to see out his days on his ranch in the Argentine, breeding and raising fine horses. Your past life will be to your advantage. You know the Hispanic ways.

We believe you will be a true fit. There is a well-established Filipino community already in place. All you have to do is keep a low profile and enjoy your early retirement. The ranch is yours, acquired in Joe Mendoza's name with assets you have accrued through a lifetime of shrewd investments in mineral mining. The details are all here." She tapped the briefcase on its side as if praising a child with a pat on the head. "You will have plenty of time to digest the details. Your passage will take a full fifteen days."

I raised my hand and halted her in midflow. "Passage? What in the devil's name are you talking about?"

Tanezawa looked at Tanaka, and before she could reply, he leaned forward and placed his hand on my shoulder. "Ogawa san, you are to leave this very night. A berth has been reserved for you on the Shino Maru, which sails in a little over five hours' time." Tanaka looked at his watch as he spoke those last few words. It was obvious he was trying to hide his discomfort, and Tanezawa quickly picked up on this and finished the conversation for him.

"You will be taken from here straight to Yokohama Port. Baba is standing by downstairs, awaiting his orders." I shook my head as if trying to shake off a cobweb of disbelief. We sat in silence for a good few minutes, each of us lost to our own thoughts.

I was just about to speak but was beaten to the line by Tanaka. "Ogawa san, it is for the best. There is no other alternative. To stay here would be tantamount to a death sentence." His voice began cracking with emotion as he pleaded. "You must see the sense in this—it is for the best. It truly is. Please believe me when I say that if there was any other way, I would do all I could to secure your safety."

I could not bring myself to believe what I was hearing. Surely I was in the midst of some dark, manic dream. I would wake soon to find myself in my small apartment, and life would be as it had been yesterday, but there was no escape from this madness. I looked Tanaka straight in the eye. "Death sentence? For as long as I can remember I have lived with that hovering above my head. So many times I would have embraced it as a merciful release. What makes you think anything has changed? I do not care if I die tomorrow or in ten years' time. The thought of another day in this life does not fill me with joy. One day we all have to answer for our sins."

Tanaka contemplated my words and then stood and walked over to the window once more. With his back to me he spoke, but this time his voice seemed charged with more longing. "Ogawa san. You will be on that ship and you will make a new life and you will find the long overdue happiness you so deserve. Go and fall into the arms of a sultry maiden and outlive the lot of us. That is what you will do."

If only life were so simple. Did life deny me or did I deny life? To my own astonishment I found myself thinking of a new life. I closed my eyes, and there I was, sitting in a rocking chair on a long wooden porch with a wide Stetson on my head, snoozing the hot afternoon away whilst my horses frolicked in dusty pens. The words tripped out of my mouth before I had time to stop them. "I will go." Tanaka turned around and clapped his hands together. His face was a picture of relief, and even Tanezawa allowed herself a little congratulatory smile.

There were a million and one questions that begged for an answer. If a person was to literally disappear from his own life, certain practicalities needed to be addressed. However, each time I raised some possible problem, Tanezawa had already foreseen the difficulty and dealt with it. I was not saying I was of any particular importance, but my reappearance into society and my circumstances had made me into the kind of oddity that would be missed if I suddenly vanished from all public view.

The plan had been laid. My counsellor, Zenigami, was to report me missing after I failed to show up for several sessions. His concern would prompt an investigation, and the authorities would eventually force entry into my apartment, where they would come upon a letter. This letter would be ambiguous in detail but would leave the reader in no doubt that I had failed to adjust to my new life and had resolved to end my days. How or where was of no matter. It would be more convenient for our purposes for the authorities to be blinded by smoke and mirrors.

As for Hamazaki, Tanaka would tell him that regrettably, on this night we had parted on sour and sad terms, and he had feared for my sanity and well-being. Tanezawa pressed me as to whether I had harboured any incriminating materials in my apartment that might need to be dealt with before the police took an active interest. I told her about the unopened envelopes that came every month with my allowance. They both stared at me as if I were mad. Tanezawa thought for a moment and then said it was of no relevance and might work in our favour, especially if the investigation into my disappearance were to be undertaken by a certain senior police figure. I did not ask anything more; some things were better left unspoken.

Tanaka asked me if there were any items of sentimental value that I desperately needed to take with me. I thought for a moment but couldn't think of anything. A lifetime lived devoid of emotional attachment. I did not possess as much as a single photograph. I had no official record of my family or of my own existence. It didn't matter if I never went back into that place again. Tanezawa said that she had prepared a travelling case full of new clothes and accessories that would be most befitting for a well-off new émigré.

Was that what I was now? I suppose it was a step up from my previous incarnation as Ramil Tan. However, the similarities were blindingly obvious. I was again being forced to live my life in the shadows, denying my true existence, and all because Toshio Hamazaki had taken to distrusting me. It seemed absurd. I had been a loyal servant to his nefarious cause and had never given any reason for the burden of distrust to land at my feet.

My indignation could be held back no longer, and before I could check the pitiful words that poured out of my mouth, I said, "Tanaka san. Why now of all times? What has happened to make Hamazaki turn against me? I have been back on home shores for over a year without incident; surely Hamazaki has no reason to fear me." I stood in his grand room feeling lost and betrayed. I desperately needed an answer. Something that I could grasp and wring the reason out of.

Tanaka looked at me and shrugged. "It is not my place to make reason out of the mind of Toshio Hamazaki, but it is my reckoning that he believes you to be under some form of official scrutiny as we speak. He may feel he cannot bear the risk of an investigation into your circumstances. I know Hamazaki owns the ears and eyes of many officials in high office. More than likely something has come back to him." Tanaka and Tanezawa were both looking at me as if expecting me to offer some form of confirmation to this wild theory. All I could do was shake my head in disbelief. "Out of respect, Toshio allowed me this time with you. However, as you know, I have hijacked his plans, and now I fear our intentions may be thwarted if we are not scrupulous in our attention to detail." I looked down at the floor, no longer able to muster the enthusiasm to mount any form of rational counter to all this madness.

My legs went weak under me and I sank down into a chair, the need for social deference now long past. Why should I spare these people the horrors that lurked deep within my soul? I spoke without thinking. "Back in Manila, many years ago I had a special friend, a kind friend, who offered me solace when I needed it most. Her name, as you well know, was Sister Mary Delaney. Well, one hellish night, Hosokawa called on me in person. He told me in no uncertain terms that I was to take her life that very night. He was passing on the orders of Toshio Hamazaki. I guessed Hamazaki wanted to make sure all was right after his father's death.

"It was not my place to reason why. I did as I was ordered. That evening I strangled the last breath out of that sweet angel of a woman. As she was dying with my hands around her throat, her eyes burnt deep into mine. I did not see hate or fear. I saw love and compassion and, in my more desperate moments, forgiveness. When she died, so did I. I had lost all feeling. I gave everything to Hamazaki, to you, and to Mabuhay. You may do with me as you wish. If I am to live in some country I know nothing of, then so be it, I may just as well die there. Quite simply, nothing matters anymore."

A heavy, brooding silence descended, and I saw that my little outburst had upset Tanezawa, who was dabbing her eyes with a handkerchief. Tanaka remained silent, but I could read his thoughts. My words only served to make him believe that perhaps Hamazaki had been right all along. I was a dangerous liability.

After our shared moment of letting emotions gallop away, I expected Tanaka to call the evening to an end and send me on my way with Baba to Yokohama Port, but he seemed to find some inner reserve of fortitude and managed to muster up enough spirit to try to make our time together conclude as companionably as possible. Tanaka said he understood all my frustrations and sympathised deeply. What he failed to say was that he was basically impotent as far as reasoning with Hamazaki was concerned. I wondered what the consequences would be for him if this evening's subterfuge were to come to his partner's attention. Did he really care? After all, he too had been the subject of a duplicitous life.

Tanaka stood, and I thought this was to be the moment of our parting, but he surprised me. "Please, my friend, before you take your leave, there is something I would like you to see. Follow me." He shuffled off towards the far door with me following a few paces behind. Tanezawa remained where she was, picking her way through the documentation of my new life. We passed three closed doors along a dimly lit corridor. Tanaka came to a halt in front of a dark wooden door that was fixed shut with some kind of numbers lock with which he fiddled for a few moments, eventually slowly pushing the door open. It was a small room of no more than twelve tatami in size, but obviously not poor in taste.

Tanaka bade me to enter, and I did so with a little reverence, for the sight before my eyes was like nothing I had ever seen in all my days. Such a thing of outstanding beauty could only have been crafted by the divine fingers of the gods. I had heard that such fine things truly existed, but my eyes refused to comprehend, and I was struck dumb. It was magnificent, truly breathtaking.

Tanaka's words, like a distant echo, seemed to be coming from afar. "The Emerald Buddha, looted by the British from a remote temple deep in the Burmese wilderness and then captured by our own forces at the close of war. She was transported at great risk back to these shores and into the hands of Hamazaki Senior, who took it upon himself to assume provenance. He had heard of the so-called mystical powers that the goddess was supposed to possess. The lure of divine protection was something that even an old sceptic like Hamazaki found irresistible.

"The war had already been lost, and it was merely a matter of weeks or even days before our Emperor finally ceded to defeat. However, one final task fell into the hands of Hamazaki. He was ordered into the thick of the Luzon battle to save my life. An almost impossible ask under normal conditions and certainly suicidal during those last few days, but somehow he pulled it off, because here I am, a living testimony to that miraculous feat. He decided that he would take the goddess along with him in the hope that some of her powers would see him able to complete his mission. It is this very same goddess we buried in the jungle that steamy night thirty years ago and also liberated on that fateful day when Romana and Nishii paid the price for all their evil deeds.

"I cannot question her powers, for she has been nothing if not true to the mystique that surrounds her. I believe, because I have no god of my own, that my soul is lost. This is the only symbol of a life that was once so pure and innocent. Her divinity comes from the breath of those who passed before us, those who lived over a thousand years ago and those who will live for a thousand more."

Tanaka gazed at his goddess, his expression betraying a deep respect for the magnificent beauty before us. The look on his face was almost the mirror image of the one I had seen earlier when Hamazaki had used me as a conduit to talk with General Yamashita. From anyone else, those words would have been sanctioned as a true sign of madness, but these men's wealth deemed them merely eccentrics.

After my initial awe and Tanaka's babbling I began to see the Emerald Buddha for what she really was. Despite her unquestionable beauty she was, like so many others living or passed away, another victim of terrible circumstances. The fact that she now stood in a rich man's home, gazed upon by him and him alone in order to satisfy his conscience did little to appease my own feelings of wrong.

I looked at Tanaka and said, "You said you would do anything for me." Tanaka nodded in affirmation. "I would like you to return the Emerald Buddha to her rightful place. Back to Burma where she belongs, back to the bosom of her people."

Without looking at me he simply said, "Of course, it will be done. You have my word."

Tanezawa escorted me out of the Empire. We did not speak. Words would have been utterly pointless now. I tried my utmost to think things through but found I could not concentrate on even the simplest of thoughts. For a man who was about to say farewell to his homeland forever, I was strangely ambivalent.

We used the same discreet corridors to make our exit, and when we reached the ground floor without having passed a living soul, Tanezawa finally found her voice. "Do not judge him too harshly. He is a good man full of fine intentions, but unfortunately, as you may have gathered, he is not a man who commands his own destiny. From the very day he was born, his life has been shaped by others. His masters are all powerful, and it is to his great credit that he has managed to keep mind and soul together. Ogawa san, we wish only the best for you. I only hope you can find the peace you so rightly deserve. Goodbye, our dear friend." She stopped in her tracks and held out her hand, not to shake but in a gesture that I should carry on alone.

I saw Baba waiting at the end of the dark corridor. My case, the one which contained all the details of my new life, was beside his feet. I turned to say my final farewell to Tanezawa, but she had already gone. An intense feeling of crushing loneliness fell upon me, and as I slowly walked towards Baba and into the unknown, a tear rolled down my cheek. It was the first time I had wept since my father had scolded me for throwing stones at a neighbour's cat. I was seven years old at the time and still remember his anger ringing in my ears. I closed my eyes and said under my breath, "Father, I was not the kind of son you so much deserved. I should have been here for you, and now I am to leave once more. I beg your forgiveness. You are in my heart, always."

Chapter 13
Elias Cohen
Tokyo
1976

Cohen stood in the centre of the great hall of the most famous train station in the world and allowed the architectural extravagance to seep into the pores of his soul. The world around him had never seemed more alive than at this moment. In fact, everything before his eyes appeared unbelievably surreal. He figured that six years of enforced, medicated incarceration could do that to a man. He felt his senses had been heightened to the point where he thought of himself as a starving lone wolf stalking his prey. It was this fitting analogy that had kept him focused during his time at Sunningdale, the place the United States government had seen fit to hold him without charge or reason for the past six years. Over the years he had convinced himself that he was destined to die in that ghastly place of lethargic simplicity, his once sharp awareness cruelly eroded by years of mind-numbing medication, forced to confront the possibility that indeed he was crazy and more than likely to remain so. As hopelessness seemed to have conquered all, a reprieve came in the form of his body, which also gave up the ghost of a future. The doctor had given him six months to live at most, a prognosis that served only to feed Cohen's determination to fulfil his destiny.

The cancer that invaded his pancreas was aggressive and would soon swarm his organs, finally bringing the curtain down on a life unfulfilled. It was decided by all concerned that Elias Cohen should be granted his liberty to enjoy the last few months of his life in the sun, so to speak. After all, this was still America, and sympathetic drama still played on even the hardest of hearts. There was a new administration in place, and its forward-thinking officials had an easier time finding the compassion to grant a dying man the dignity to go meet his maker under the great American sky. Robert Rushton, on the other hand, had grave misgivings, and despite all rationale to the contrary, it was his signature that had finally liberated Cohen. For the life of him, he could not quite understand why he had acquiesced. Was it guilt that tore away at his soul, or could his once willing underling perhaps be manipulated into doing one final task?

Cohen took a seat on one of the benches in the great hall of Grand Central Station and watched the sea of humanity dash past his eyes. Businessmen hurrying to meet connections, brandishing their briefcases in front of them like weapons to part the crowd, people with tickets in hand, lost in confusion as they stared up at the departure boards, harassed parents herding their broods along on the way to unite with family in other parts. Lovers lurked in the shadows, embracing and wishing time would stop, their goodbye kisses frozen in a moment already lost. Cohen knew only too well that today's kiss was tomorrow's memory and that sweet as they were now, those memories would only become the fuel that fired the bitterness of disappointment. It had been a mere four days since he had walked out of Sunningdale, and now he found himself awash in the euphoria of freedom overriding tiredness as he took his first steps on the road to fulfil his destiny.

His mind drifted back in languid reflection. The past six years felt like a constant drag of thousands of grey Monday mornings. Day after day he had remained passive, switched off, blanking all emotion and taking care to show nothing of the obsession that still ate into the very fibre of his soul. His shutdown was so complete that he believed his cancer had grown out of the roots of desperation and bitterness. Now it offered him the ultimate way out. Cohen embraced his disease as a gift from God, the answer to all his prayers. There would be nothing to lose and all to gain. That is what God desired.

During his "lost" six years Cohen had been the subject of much analysis and also the vessel for countless medications intended to subdue and ultimately eradicate the demons that played in his head. As a human guinea pig he played his part well, said what he thought they wanted to hear, and did what he thought they wanted to see, but he knew that if they could read his thoughts, he would be a dead man. He granted himself the luxury of a smirk and a pat on the back, for now he was a free man once more, released into society. Of course the authorities had severe monitoring measures put in place, but he had run through his options a million times. He knew that if he were to have any hope of fulfilling his destiny, the need to act with haste was paramount.

Upon his release the authorities had placed him in a halfway house in upstate New York. He had fifty dollars in the pocket of his ill-fitting suit, which was off the back of one of his fellow inmates and smelt slightly of piss. The state's generosity also extended to a book of food coupons, enough for two days. This miserly approach was obviously another instrument of control to ensure a hungry man reported to the door of his oppressor. He had been "transported" to his new residence in the back of a functional wagon. Although he had been free from restraint, others were not as fortunate, and three manacled and medicated fellows were his travel companions who were being moved to other facilities.

On arrival at his halfway lodging he was shown into the barest of bedrooms on the ground floor by the superintendent and lectured about the times of his curfew. He was not allowed liberty at all for the first three days of this so-called "settling in" period, after which any outside activities would be at the superintendent's discretion and accompanied by a staff member at all times. Compassionate release obviously came with uncompassionate terms, and Cohen was not of a mind to spend a further minute of his precious dwindling time dancing to their tune. Unwilling to establish a pattern that might mark his habits, he knew he must act and act soon. He had told them that he felt overwhelmed with tiredness and wished to sleep.

The moment his door was closed, he was up to the window and cursing the fact that it was bolted tight. The fading voices beyond his door told him the corridor outside was clear, and without a second's thought he stepped out into the unknown. He could not use the front door, as he would pass the superintendent's cubbyhole window. His heart beating like a jackhammer, he went the opposite way, searching for a back door of some kind. He heard the sounds of a TV from behind a door to a room he took to be some kind of communal lounge, then behind him voices getting louder. Panic forced him to open the first door he came to. It was a room not unlike his own, and Cohen immediately gave thanks to God, for there flapping in the breeze was a lace curtain shading an open window. He was halfway out and on his way to freedom when he heard a frail voice from beneath the bedclothes. "Go on God's speed, but the devil is riding on your back." The sickly cackle of laughter that followed this dark prophecy sent shivers down his spine, and he dared not look back over his shoulder.

Cohen was now on the open street for the first time in over six years, and he felt as if he were reborn. However, his exhilaration was tempered by his fear of exposure, for he knew that this was his final chance to answer his "calling" and that he was to meet his destiny, wherever that may lie. He mentally checked off his immediate priorities as he had done a million times over when fermenting his plans as a custodian of the state. Dreams, no matter how hard you may wish them into reality, seldom take into account the harsh realities that obstruct the pure visions from which they were borne.

Cohen was on the streets in early April without an adequate coat to keep out the wind that now whipped about his body. He had the fifty dollars in his pocket, but had been forced to abandon all his personal belongings, including his medications, save for the photograph of his dear Dorothea, which he had removed from its gilded frame and was now in his inside jacket pocket, as close to his heart as ever. Head bowed, he strode down the street, putting distance between him and that wretched halfway house. He kept glancing down the streets for a cab, but it had started to rain, and they were few in coming.

Cohen had forgotten how hostile a place the outside world could really be, and the sounds of a normal morning's comings and goings were beginning to weigh heavily on his ability to think. The hustle and arrogance of the place was intense, but equally afforded him protection from prying eyes. It was with relief that Cohen spotted a vacant cab cruising down the street, and he stepped out into the street, arms waving, to halt it. New York cabdrivers have a natural disposition that allows them to spot a lunatic. It is part of what allows them to survive their job, and this driver slowed down but not to a halt as he looked Cohen up and down before finally stopping and letting him aboard. Cohen gratefully slunk into the rear seat and told him where to drive to.

East New York was an area that most drivers would avoid, but Cohen had struck lucky, and his cab swung out, made an illegal U-turn, and headed down the road. Cohen could sense the driver snatching sneaky looks in the rearview mirror, no doubt assessing whether his fare had the money to pay. Perhaps the driver had picked up on Cohen's anxiety. He took the first opportunity to engage his nervous charge. "Don't get called to take so many folks such as yourself up there; you live there from way back, man?"

Cohen looked at him in the mirror and tried his best to feign disinterest. "No, I'm just calling on an old friend."

The cabbie seemed satisfied with this, but went on to say what he no doubt always said. "Remember when that place was a decent family area, a place for honest working folks to make a start, now it's all gangs and drugs. You be careful there, sir, watch your back. They'll have the shoes off your feet if it means getting them an hour's worth of fix." Cohen said nothing, preferring to stare out the window, until the driver brought the cab to the side of the road a couple of blocks short of Cohen's destination. "This is as far as I go; we had a cab jacked just last week down there, so nine dollars if you will, sir." Cohen handed him a ten-dollar bill and got out. He headed down the street, collar pulled up tight and hands slunk into pockets, to the address he had memorised for years. George Isaacs had always told him that if anything were to befall him and Cohen needed help of any kind, he would find it at Vermont Street. Isaacs had a cousin who lived there, and George had told Cohen that this cousin owed a great debt to the man Cohen had come to regard as a dear friend, dearly departed. Cohen could not ease his mind as images of George played so close to his psyche. He had often cursed himself for dragging George into the hell of all things Hamazaki. He cursed but never blamed himself for the events that had led to George's death. It was God's will, just as it would be when Hamazaki faced divine retribution.

Number 1243 Vermont Street looked a degree better kept than its neighbours on either side. The trash cans were emptied and neatly lined by the steps, which led up to a plain grey door. Lace curtains hung in the window, but there were no obvious hints as to who resided behind them. Cohen took a deep breath and prayed that Thomas Wilson, cousin of the great George Isaacs, still lived behind this door, which his bare knuckles were now rapping upon. After a few moments he heard a noise, and someone made a movement in the hall. The door did not open, but a man's voice could be heard from within. "Who is there? What do you want?"

Cohen steeled himself and replied, "My name is Elias Cohen, I was a friend of George Isaacs, and I need to speak with his cousin Thomas Wilson." The door opened ever so slightly, and a short man, much younger than Cohen had imagined, peered through the gap. "I am Thomas Wilson, and my cousin George has long passed."

"Yes, I know. I was working with him on a special case, and now I need your help. George told me that I could rely on you to help me if ever I needed such. Well, now I need that help." The door closed, and Cohen could hear the safety chains being slid back. The door opened to let him inside.

Cohen followed Thomas Wilson down a short unlit corridor. He noticed that Wilson was struggling with a profound limp and steadied himself using the rail which had been fixed to the side wall. Wilson let Cohen into a side room and offered him a seat in a great leather wingback chair that was drawn up close to a small fire burning in an ornate grate. Wilson eased himself down into the chair opposite Cohen and stared at his unexpected guest with a certain curiosity that put Cohen on edge—so much so that he felt obliged to speak forth. "Mr Wilson, I am desperately in need of your help, and what I am to ask of you no regular man could do, but I know George always told me that you could do anything, and I pray now that is the case."

Wilson said nothing, and for a moment Cohen thought his words had fallen on deaf ears. After what seemed like an uncomfortable eternity Wilson spoke. "Mr Cohen, does this help you need serve the legacy of my lost cousin?" The question took Cohen by surprise, but he had no hesitation in nodding in affirmation. Wilson rose unsteadily to his feet and beckoned Cohen to follow him. They made slow progress up a dark staircase and along a similar gloomy corridor.

The sparseness of Wilson's abode suddenly hit Cohen. It was almost monastic and the air chilled. Cohen could not help but wonder why in heaven's name he would wish to live within such dour walls. He found himself in a large room at the back of the house. There was a single bed pressed up against the far wall, unmade, but with linen neatly folded on top. Underneath the large window was a presidential-sized dark mahogany desk and chair flanked by a tower of steel filing cabinets. Cohen noticed they were all fitted with combination locks. "This was George's room. He often worked here when he felt the need to escape and find a quiet space in which to think."

Cohen was astounded. He had not realised that his deceased partner had such arrangements. Wilson caught Cohen's stare and picked up on his surprise. "George would often spend days on end up here working away on cases, and in the evenings he would come downstairs and we would go over some of the more difficult problems together." Cohen stared at Wilson, urging him to say more. Wilson leaned on the cabinets and went on. "Mr Cohen, or may I be allowed to call you Elias, you see I feel I have known you for an age. There were no secrets between George and myself. I know all about your demons and what stokes your fire. I know that what you are about to ask of me will expose me to risk, but please assure me that your path will not dog tail back to this door."

Cohen said that it most certainly would not. With a deep sigh Wilson fiddled with the dial on one of the cabinets and extracted a large cardboard file box. Cohen noted that it was labelled "Mabuhay." He felt an irrational urge to seize the box from Wilson's hands. The conflicting emotions that raged in him were soon doused by Wilson's matter-of-fact approach, and later that evening the two of them sat at George Isaacs's desk and worked on Cohen's plan.

Wilson had not flinched one iota when Cohen had asked for a handgun and twelve rounds of ammunition, nor had he seemed to think that acquiring a Canadian passport in Cohen's name would prove to be any kind of obstacle; nor did he flinch when asked to help with travel arrangements from Canada to Tokyo. It was Wilson himself who suggested that Cohen might need more than two thousand dollars to cover expenses.

Cohen was warming to the man and his steely efficiency. He found himself envying George's past, having such a solid boulder in Thomas Wilson to lean on. It soon became apparent that Wilson was and had always been George's Mr Fix-it.

It was agreed that Cohen would spend the next few nights as a guest of Thomas Wilson. Cohen felt relief and gratitude; after all, if it was once good enough for the great George Isaacs, then it was pure destiny that deemed Cohen must follow in his erstwhile partner's steps. So it was that Cohen found himself sleeping in the ever so slightly fusty bed that George himself had used on occasion and where he no doubt had stared at the same ceiling, working himself into a funk over the improbabilities of success. Cohen gave silent thanks to a God he had long ago given up faith in. He thanked him for putting Thomas Wilson on his side, and whilst he was feeling reverential, he threw in a prayer asking for some divine protection and the moral strength to see his plan to its final conclusion. That image played behind his retinas, so real he could touch it, hear it and see it, even smell it. If God believed in right, he would fall on the side of divine justice and see Toshio Hamazaki collapse to the ground, his body torn to shreds with bullets, each one inflicting bitter pain and the chilling realisation that his next breath would most certainly be his last.

Cohen was not so distantly delusional that he believed his plan totally workable. He knew that the odds were stacked against him and that it would take more than a fair amount of luck and benign coincidence for it to succeed. However, after Wilson had listened to Cohen and had not derided his ideas—quite the opposite, in fact—he had felt a swell of confidence surge through his veins. Thomas had shrugged aside each major problem as nothing more than just another thing to do. He was going to do it. He was unstoppable. However, there was one major sticking point in the plan that was taxing even the skills of Thomas Wilson, and that was securing some form of official invitation to the annual garden party held within the walls of the Imperial Palace, an event that was attended by "the great and the good" every April to celebrate the flowering of the cherry blossom and its symbolism in the cycle of life. Cohen knew that Hamazaki would be there as he had been each and every year for the last twenty-seven years. Cohen's obsession about all that related to his nemesis stretched to thousands of tidbits of knowledge, from the common to the inane. He made it his business to know his enemy. He knew that Hamazaki, like Dean Martin, never wore the same socks twice, and he also knew that Hamazaki thought of himself as the centre of all things, including the Imperial Cherry Blossom Viewing Party. Cohen knew this would be, as always, a beautiful event, and a focal point of the Tokyoite social calendar which encompassed the epitome of everything Japanese. It would be fitting for Hamazaki's final day on earth.

Thomas Wilson had not shown the slightest interest in any of that theatrical symbolism. He was concerned only with the practicalities and as such garnered even more respect from Elias Cohen. Wilson had said that the logistics of Cohen's plan were easily manageable. The passport was a given, and rail transport arrangements into Vancouver didn't pose a problem. The flight from Vancouver into Tokyo should be able to be booked within Canada to avoid raising the suspicions of eager civic-minded busybodies. Wilson had said that the Canadian travel routes had been less policed since the end of the Vietnam War, as Canada was no longer the destination for peace-loving American draft dodgers. In fact, security was likely to be far tighter coming back into America, as those peace-loving souls were now drifting back in search of some sort of pardon.

After Wilson had shared this snippet of information, he locked eyes with Cohen, and they both acknowledged what had passed, unspoken, between them. Elias Cohen was not coming back. This was a one-way trip. Cohen's personal kamikaze mission was to fulfil a vendetta that tore away at his soul and had no doubt planted the seeds that were ripening into cancerous tubers deep in his guts. He had placed an inordinate amount of trust in the abilities of Thomas Wilson. He realised that he had simply transferred all of his fond feelings for George to Thomas. He had been a free man for less than twenty-four hours, and yet he had connected with Thomas Wilson more than any other human who had crossed his path in the six years of his unjust incarceration. He offered up one final prayer to the God he no longer believed in and asked him to allow Thomas to deliver on his promises, for he knew he could no longer bear another shred of disappointment in this life.

The next two days passed slowly amidst a haze of frustration. Cohen began to fret frantically over the minor details of his plan. He sweated about the things over which he had no control, such as the weather in Tokyo, the possibility of a heavy April rainstorm, and the forced abandonment of the cherry blossom viewing. His lack of a detailed replacement plan caused him to have panic attacks. His confidence swerved by the hour, and he would have welcomed Thomas Wilson's reassurance had he been around the house long enough to give it. Wilson went out for long periods to make arrangements and finalise details. Cohen, for his part, knew that he had little option but to place his faith in this man, and faith was the only thing he had in abundance. In truth that was all he had right now. He was sure of nothing except that his days were numbered and the cancer which was eating away his body and soul was a gift from the God he doubted and the thing which put him beyond the normal and almost caressed his thoughts into focus. So it was that on the third day of pacing the rooms of Thomas Wilson's sparse abode that the man himself finally arrived home and called Cohen to sit down with him, as he had positive news at last.

They seated themselves at the kitchen table, and Wilson brought out a bottle of Asbach brandy and two glasses. Cohen had never been that much of a drinker. Even in his agency days he had shied away from the drink-fuelled get-togethers that were part of his colleagues' lives. Wilson poured two small measures and raised his glass. "Elias, I toast to your courage and your convictions." Cohen lifted his glass in response and, unable to think of a suitable repose, sipped his drink. It was the smoothest hard liquor he had ever taken. Wilson picked up on his approval. "George and I made this a kind of ritual; we would open a bottle of this stuff and go through our plans. It's amazing what an altered state of mind can come up with."

Wilson stared at the bottle of Asbach and for a moment allowed his mind to swim off into the past. He spoke absentmind-edly, as if to himself. "This was George's favourite. To you, George: one last tilt of the wheel." Cohen, too, raised his glass and enjoyed the velvety sensation as the drink tickled the back of his throat.

Wilson seemed to be a little tired from his exertions of the past few days, and his eyes were rimmed red. Nontheless he was in a talking mood, and Cohen was grateful to just sit back and listen as he spoke of the friend they both missed so dearly. Cohen real-ised that Wilson had no chance to speak of his affection for George Isaacs to anyone on an equal level. "George was a remarkable human being, a person to whom I owe my life. You see, he saved me." Cohen was fascinated to hear how these two seemingly dif-ferent souls had found their paths and destiny locked together. He leaned forward and nodded encouragingly. He had already guessed that they were not cousins in the blood sense, more like cousins bound by honour and loyalty to each other, a bond created to bind their mutual respect. Wilson was silent for a few moments, lost with his memories. "It was 1954, upstate New York, a scorching day in August. I was up there to look around a college campus; you see, I had a notion of studying back then, to make something of my life. My teachers thought I had a bit of what it might take for a black man to succeed in a white man's world. Anyway, that's all by the by now." Wilson took a slug of his drink and poured himself another generous shot, waved his hand across his face as if brushing off bitter memories. "It was searing hot and I was gagging of thirst, so I went into a corner store to buy a soda. Handed my coins over to the old lady behind the counter and went out on my way. As I was leaving, a pickup screeched to a halt and out jumped two guys with masks on. They knocked me to the ground, sending my soda bottle smashing over the sidewalk. They were big guys and they stormed into the store. I heard crashes of broken glass as they swept the shelves of bottles and jars, raised voices, hysteria, the men screaming. I didn't know what the hell to do, and I lay on the ground. As I was just getting to my feet, I heard two bangs, gunshots, unmistakable. Then it was quiet for a second or two. I was paralysed with fear. I heard the door slam and they ran right by me, but not before coshing me with a bottle of something. Bourbon bottle, I was told later. Blood flowed out the side of my head. I got to my feet and sat on the kerb, dazed. It wasn't long before the cops arrived, two squad cars, sirens and lights blazing. The suits arrived soon after. The uniforms cuffed me, and the detectives more or less spat in my face. I was taken to a nearby hospital, where they put twenty stitches in my gashed head, and then back to a police station, where I was questioned for three days without a lawyer by my side. They beat me and humiliated me so I would give up my 'accomplices.' You see, they figured I was part of the gang who had robbed the store of twenty-six dollars and shot an old lady twice in the face. The poor old dear had kept a log of her sales.

"I was charged with first-degree murder and robbery. Their case was that I had gone into the store first as some kind of lookout and, being a dumb ass, fallen and smashed my head in the escape and then been abandoned by my mates in the panic. They could not accept that I was just an unfortunate in the wrong place at the wrong time. Even the fact that I had genuine reason to be in that area at that time washed little by them. You see, that was what it was like to be a black man in the wrong place in them days— maybe it still is. Anyway, I was thrown into jail to await trial. The state appointed me a lawyer, and that man was George Isaacs, and well, all I can say is, the rest is history. George blew away their case in court. It took him less than an hour to make me a free man again, but needless to say I never made it to college. A man tarnished by the law finds many doors slammed in his face, but George saw something in me and gave me a chance to help him in matters that needed an eye for detail. Over time we became a great team as each of us honed our skills. I guess you probably realise now that I owe the man more than I could ever repay."

Cohen didn't know what to say, and they both sat in silence, allowing the moment to drink them in. Wilson took a long slug of his brandy and stared at Cohen. "Elias, you say this man, Hamazaki, is responsible for the death of our dear friend."

Cohen looked intently into Wilson's eyes. "Without any doubt whatsoever."

Wilson nodded gravely. "Then he must pay the ultimate price. He must die, and you will be the deliverer of justice." Wilson raised his glass, and Cohen followed suit. "To the death of Toshio Hamazaki, and may it be delivered with haste and yet the greatest of pain."

Cohen smiled and felt a warm glow of satisfaction as the smug vindication of all his sufferings swept his entire being. Thomas Wilson was indeed the finest fellow who walked this foul earth. Wilson leaned down by his side and heaved his tattered briefcase onto the table. "Now, my friend, it is time to get down to business."

That evening the two men turned the crazy thoughts of Cohen's deranged mind into something that resembled a workable plan. Only God would know how Thomas Wilson had been able to lay down the impossible in so short a time. Cohen was in absolute awe of the man. Wilson explained that the most difficult part of their scheme had been securing the invitation to the Imperial garden party. These things were planned a year in advance, and all official invitations had been sent and duly responded to. To get round this, Wilson had first tried to view the official guest list, but all his contacts and discreet delving had drawn blanks. He had to somehow secure Cohen a legitimate invitation, one that would not arouse undue scrutiny. Of course this would have to be in his alias. To add even more credence it was thought that Cohen needed to stay as close to the truth as they dared. Wilson had found out that there existed such a thing as the Canadian Japanese Friendship Society, a collection of individuals from both countries who seemed to admire each other in a sycophantic manner. The society apparently was made up of do-gooders from all walks of life and had one member, a Mr Albert Strassman, whose Canadian passport was now in the hands of Elias Cohen. Cohen marvelled at the document and could not take his eyes off his photograph; even the birth dates were identical. Cohen noted that he was now a retired timber merchant from Alberta. He looked at Wilson. "Thomas, this is remarkable. How the hell you managed to create such a forgery in so short a time I will never know."

Wilson allowed the satisfaction to beam across his face. "My friend, it is no forgery. Save for the photograph switch and a change in the birth date, that is the genuine article. In the unlikely event any overzealous official should care to check, the serial numbers will hold tight and the bearer will be you, Mr Albert Strassman."

He did not offer any explanation for how he had acquired this document except to say it had taken a great deal of favour calling. Wilson had learned that one or two members of the Friendship Society were invited to view the cherry blossoms in the Imperial gardens each year. The real Mr Albert Strassman, this year's fortunate recipient, had originally accepted but then reluctantly declined because of failing health. Now all that remained for Wilson to do was reinvite Mr Strassman. An initial phone call to the Japanese Embassy in Ottawa, explaining that Mr Strassman's health had improved greatly and he felt sufficiently recovered to travel to Tokyo, was met with the expected wall of official dogma. After several hours of frustration on Wilson's part, the embassy had reluctantly allowed Mr Strassman's request to be put forward to the Grand Chamberlain, where it would be referred to the director of protocol and a final decision would be made. However, it was noted that such a request was highly irregular and might ultimately be met with disappointment. Despite the embassy's pessimistic outlook, Tokyo came through with a promptness that took Wilson by surprise. The director of protocol had been delighted to hear of Mr Strassman's recovery, and of course they were looking forward to making his acquaintance in person. They put themselves at Mr Strassman's disposal and wished him a pleasant and safe journey to Tokyo. Even Thomas Wilson had been taken aback by his own audacity. He had pulled off some coups in his time, but this had to be up there as one of his finest. George Isaacs would have been mightily proud of his work.

The fine details were ironed out to the point where Cohen felt he had fully stepped into the shoes of Mr Albert Strassman and they fitted him like a pair of comfortable old loafers. The train tickets from Grand Central bore his new name, as did the flights booked from Vancouver to Tokyo which departed in two days' time. Hotel reservations had been secured for a one-night stay in Vancouver and in Tokyo. Cohen had been a little disappointed to learn that he was not to stay at the Imperial as he had hoped, but at a smaller established hostelry which went by the curious name of Hillside and was said to be quite close to the royal residence. Wilson had thought it better to keep as low a profile as possible, and the Imperial was too close to the centre of the matter. Wilson had made reservations for four nights at Hillside, two of those being before the party and two, somewhat optimistically, for after the event. They both knew that it was important to keep up the façade of normality. George Isaacs had always said that it was the things people had never thought about that usually tore the best-laid plans into shreds. It was all a matter of perspective. We all see things differently, and those who are blessed with real talent are able to see and think as others do. Cohen knew that Thomas Wilson was one of these rare individuals, a man whose talents had been redirected because of a blow on the head from a thug wielding a bourbon bottle.

Then there was the no small matter of concealing the revolver and the six rounds of ammunition. Obviously, this was no easy thing to do, but Thomas felt quite confident that departing passengers' baggage was not subject to X-ray, and he had it on good authority that Japanese customs preferred a visual inspection of arriving passengers' luggage. Besides, he felt certain that the arrival documentation which gave the reason for the visit as a "guest" of the Imperial Household Agency would be sufficient to avert any invasion of privacy. On the other hand there was no cause for complacency, and it was thought best to break down the firearm into as many parts as possible and conceal them, wrapped tightly in polythene and hidden amongst various personal items, such as hair cream and camera equipment. Cohen had come across many agents during his time in the service and reckoned that Thomas would have made it up there with the best of them. He seemed to be in possession of an inordinate amount of knowledge about the workings of virtually any kind of system. From transportation schedules to the smuggling of weapons, it all came with an ease that bubbled with confidence.

They spent the night going through the details, hammering away at points that Thomas believed could be flaky. He drilled Cohen on everything and fired questions at him from all directions. It was necessary for Cohen to know all about Alberta and the lumber trade and the business done between Japan and his illicitly adopted country, Canada. It was tedious stuff, but if the cover was to hold, then it was potentially of dynamic importance. He also had to be aware of his recent health problems, treatments, and subsequent recovery. Thomas had said that the Japanese people on the whole were health obsessed and not averse to inquiring about issues which we would consider beyond conversation with strangers. He and Elias spent the dark hours going through everything and more and then some. Thomas would not countenance the idea of sleep; in fact he believed that tiredness was a friend of those planning perilous activities, his logic being that if you could stand up to the test when bone tired, then you would find it even easier to cope when refreshed. Cohen did not wish to find any holes in this logic, and willed himself forward. They discussed what would happen to the real Albert Strassman once everything came out. Thomas had made absolutely sure that no roads led back to his own door and any investigation into the real Strassman would only lead to a similar dead end. As the dawn started to announce its arrival by peering through the cracks in the curtains, Thomas thought it prudent to catch a few hours' sleep before it was time to say goodbye forever to Elias Cohen. Both men knew they would never speak again beyond this morning, and they both knew that their own fate, despite all the preparation, was now in the hands of the gods.

Cohen snapped shut the lock on his new suitcase, which contained all the new and appropriate clothing for his mission. He had it set in his mind that he was indeed on a mission, one that had been his destiny for thirty-two years. Before closing the case he ran his hand over his morning suit, which was packed on the top and was the requested dress for the garden party. He had put Dorothea's photograph in the inside pocket, close to his heart as always. He ran his hand over the fine cloth and with a morbid vision realised that he would die in this suit. He examined the two lapel pins that Thomas had somehow acquired. One was the maple leaf of Canada, the other, two logs crossed with "C L A" affixed across. Cohen smiled as he thought of the Canadian Lumber Association being forever entwined in infamy. He looked around the once bedroom of George Isaacs for the final time. He took a deep breath as if attempting to inhale the spirit of the great man, checked himself in the mirror, discounted the darkening circles under his eyes, and said farewell to Elias Cohen, as he was now, until death, to exist only as Albert Strassman.

Thomas was waiting in the hall to bid him farewell, and for a moment the two men were beyond words. Not really knowing each other more than a few days and yet the feeling that there was so much between them led them into an awkward embrace. Thomas seemed to be unusually dour, but had he really been any-thing different? Cohen, or now rather Strassman, extended his hand, offered his thanks, and set out into the outside. Thomas pat-ted him on the shoulder in an affectionate way that offered more than inadequate words could ever cover. The two men parted company, one without so much as a glance over his shoulder, the other closing the door without hesitation. A yellow cab had been arranged to wait on the corner of the street, and sure enough there it was. The drive over to Grand Central Station was without event, and Cohen found himself in that great hall, waiting for his train and the long journey to Seattle and then onwards to Vancouver.

Elias Cohen had grown up in a religious family. His parents had been devout, and unquestioningly believed in the power of the Lord and that all things were the result of God's own hand. In fact, one of Cohen's earliest memories was of his father heckling an evolutionist who had been trying to lay science on the minds of simple folk in the street. He remembered his father's face turning puce with rage and shouting the man down with quotes from the Bible as he covered his son's ears. The rather confident man of science and learning just laughed with a smugness that served only to further enrage Cohen Senior. Despite the minor drama of that moment, the thing that had remained forever with Cohen was the impotence of his father's rage. There was no channel for release, no conclusion, and it would be Cohen who bore the brunt of his father's suppressed anger. To Cohen, merely believing was never enough. He very much wished he could point to one thing or another as proof of a divine existence, when in fact all life had taught him was that the contrary was more likely the pointer to the truth. He had questioned his own faith so much that he seemed to be in a perpetual state of confusion, his rationale torn to shreds by what he was about to do. "Thou shall not kill." That was the Lord's command, but Cohen would kill. To kill for the greater good: surely God would understand. As the train rattled along towards Vancouver, Cohen stared out the window at the grey clouds which had just cracked open and dazzling rays of late spring sunshine bore through. It was life mimicking his thoughts, it was a sign. Oh yes, God would understand.

The journey was painstakingly slow. Days melted into nights and back again, but Cohen let the hours pass by allowing his mind to take him places. The dark past was about to be avenged, and for that, time was an irrelevance. He focused all his energy on being Albert Strassman, going over the Canadian's details again and again, until he knew the man inside out. By the time the train finally crossed the border into Canada, Strassman was ready for anything. A train guard walked through the almost deserted carriage to announce that there would be an immigration check and all passengers should have their passports or papers at the ready. This was to be the first official test for the new Albert Strassman. It had been agreed that Strassman had been on vacation for a week or so in New York and was now returning home. His Canadian passport didn't bear an entry stamp, as it was normal for citizens of each country to flit in and out without the burden of formal bureaucracy. In truth the borders were impossible to monitor beyond a token presence. Officials generally were informed to keep an eye out for miscreants who might head their way, but other than that, not much else. Cohen doubted that his own status as a wanted fugitive had made it as far as the Canadian border police. His thoughts were confirmed when an official walked through the carriage shouting, "Documents, please." Cohen held up his passport, only for the official to glance at the cover and pass straight on by. The laxness of it all surprised Cohen no end.

The remaining two hours of the journey were a complete blur as Strassman succumbed to all the pent-up exhaustion that had driven him for the last three days and fell into a deep sleep. He was shaken back into the real world by the train guard, whose voice seemed to be three times louder than usual. "End of the line, sir, please vacate the train." Strassman took a few moments to get his bearings, and after a moment of panic, safely located his suitcase and dragged himself down the aisle and out onto the platform of Vancouver's Pacific Central Station. The confidence he had mustered during that arduous journey had worn thin. He now felt bone tired and shackled by chains of nervousness as he headed for the taxi rank. Strassman noted that the pace of life seemed to be a step or two behind that of New York. There was a distinct lack of hustle and feeling of constant threat that seemed to follow you everywhere in the Big Apple, and for this he was grateful.

It was a twenty-minute, four-dollar taxi ride across town to his lodgings for the night. Thomas had arranged for him to stay at a large traveller's lodge, the perfect place to remain inconspicuous. His documentation once more stood the test of inspection, even if it was only a cursory glance from the receptionist, who insisted on calling him "my dear" without once making eye contact. Within minutes of arriving at the lodge he flopped onto the bed and slept the sleep of the dead. Twelve hours of deep slumber passed before he awoke in a panic, not knowing where he was. He stared at the murals on the unfamiliar walls. The doleful moose head which stared back from a forest of giant maples brought him around to a state of realisation. There were four hours before his flight to Tokyo, enough time to refresh himself and eat one of those famous Canadian breakfasts. He swung his legs over the bed and tried to stand up, but a wave of dizziness and a sudden swell of nausea hit him. He realised that he hadn't taken his medication for more than a day and a half and the tumours deep inside his body were probably rejoicing. He groggily opened up his case, found his medicine box, and fumbled some tablets down his throat washed down with earthy water cupped in his hands from the bathroom tap. He knew he would feel a little better in a few minutes and decided to take a bath before breakfast. As he lay in the warm water, he noticed a new swelling in his left groin, slightly painful and tender to the touch but to Strassman further encouragement if ever he needed it that he must not fail in this, his life's calling.

Despite feeling ravenously hungry Strassman could manage only half of his famous Canadian breakfast. He put it down to too much of a good thing, and yet he knew the truth. His body was slowing down, there was no denying it. He had dressed casually for the flight to Tokyo, in an open-necked shirt, loose slacks, and a plaid sports coat, clothes that Elias Cohen would never have chosen for himself but somehow seemed appropriate for Albert Strassman. The penny loafers he sported were the first pair of slip-on shoes he had ever worn, and he marvelled at their ease and comfort. It caused him to sink into the mire of his past. Had he made life too hard for himself, made too many sacrifices for no reward? He quickly dismissed such thoughts as sentimental claptrap and went to get his things, check out of the lodge, and get the next stage towards his destiny up and running.

The Vancouver airport felt small and provincial, and Strassman had an irrational doubt whether direct travel to Tokyo was at all possible. He had seen busier bus depots than this, and yet there it was on the departure screen: Air Canada flight AC 116 to Tokyo Haneda International. The flight was on time, and check-in was in progress. He approached the almost deserted check-in counter, and the butterflies in his stomach seemed to cry out to be heard. Despite a throat as dry as sandpaper, he managed to greet the clerk with something that he hoped bordered on normality. He placed his travel documents on the counter and hoped the clerk would not engage him in unnecessary conversation, as he didn't have the greatest faith in his ability to sound like someone from Alberta should sound. Luckily, the clerk seemed to be keen on speeding up the procedure and without asking any questions at all, had his case on the belt, weighed, tagged, and disappearing down the belt for loading. Strassman said a silent prayer that his belongings, like himself, would arrive unhindered. The clerk handed him a luggage identification tag and informed him that the plane was scheduled to take off on time and that it was expected to be a quiet flight, as there would be few fellow passengers on board. Strassman nodded his thanks and strode on for the next stage of his façade, perhaps the acid test: passport check.

The departure lobby was almost as deserted as check-in, and to his amazement he breezed through with nothing more than a cursory glance at the cover of his passport. He had almost an hour before his plane would depart, and he spent it in sweet relief, taking a seat looking out on the runways where he could watch the planes take off and land. He realised that his plan was now on an unstoppable course, and yet a certain sadness descended upon him that he couldn't quite fathom. It had nothing to do with impending death, his own or that of another. He tried to pin down his feelings, but they were complex and fleet of thought. A gentle shake of his shoulder brought about a momentary panic attack, for he didn't recognize his surroundings. It was impossible that he had dozed during his wait, and yet there it was. The last call for boarding had been sounded, and he'd had to be roused by a member of the ground staff. Strassman struggled to his feet with the groans of age and the hindrance of a man being eaten away by the disease inside him. He declined the offer of assistance to board, gathered his flight bag, and was on his way.

The flight was a wonderful experience, his first taste of a different kind of life. He was surprised by the luxury of it all: a seat as wide as an armchair, drinks at his beck and call, smiling and polite young ladies, and a soft pillow for his head. Only one other passenger was in this section of the plane, a Japanese man who was engrossed in paperwork of some kind or other. The two travellers did not so much as make eye contact, let alone greet each other.

Strassman looked at the empty seat beside him and longed for his beloved Dorothea to be sat there. He closed his eyes and willed himself into a fantasy life where they were flying together on this very plane, Dorothea drinking champagne and giggling that lovely laugh at the heady excitement of it all. He was again Elias, a young man who pined for all that she was and all that she would become. He allowed the fantasy to take them to places he had never dreamed of. He pictured Dorothea in a beautiful house, greeting him as he came home from a hard day's work and asking him to sit down, as she had something to tell him. He was to be a father, and with an explosion of joy, they fell into each other's arms and danced around the room without a trouble in the world. Of course another child would soon follow, and now he and Dorothea had two beautiful daughters in the image of their mother. The children would grow up, bringing pride and constant love to their perfect life.

As sweet as this fantasy was, Strassman allowed it to run out of control, and of course the spiralling descent into reality was almost too much to bear. He closed his eyes and swallowed back his bitter tears and once more bit down on the bile of hatred that had filled his life for over thirty years.

At what point Strassman had fallen asleep during the flight he had no idea whatsoever, and he was astounded to be told that they were approaching Haneda Airport and he should make preparations for landing. He took a few moments to regain his composure. He looked over at his solitary travelling companion, who was once again engrossed in his paperwork. Strassman could not deny that the Japanese were a diligent race, and over the years he had been forced to accept that they indeed had many fine qualities, but in his mind acceptance didn't run close to forgiveness. Not even close.

As he stared out the small window on his right, he was consumed with a sudden swell of paranoia. He had been foolish enough to let his guard down. What if his solitary traveling companion and presumably some kind of businessman was not what he seemed? Had he spiked his drink and searched his hand luggage? Strassman shook his head at such a ridiculous and irrational notion. His mind wandered back to Thomas's warning that it was the things you never think about that end up being your undoing. He returned his attention to the view and stared at the postage-stamp-sized paddies below. He suddenly realised that he had been digging his fingernails into his wrist and a smear of blood had soaked through his cuff.

There it was below: Japan. Strassman thought of the aircrews who had looked down during the war, maybe even the very same views, more than thirty years ago now. Most people he knew claimed that time sped up as you got older, but for Strassman the opposite was true. For him time had passed in a manner that he could only describe as achingly slow, and yet now that he was in the final days of his life, he felt as if he could almost see his final mortal hours spiralling away as the finger of destiny beckoned him. Time was now like a roaming rabid dog, foaming at the mouth and waiting for the bullet that would bring it all to an end.

Once more the all-too-familiar nerves cascaded through his body and left him coated in a film of sweat that pasted his shirt to his back like wallpaper. He stood in line waiting for the immigration officials to process his documents. He was directed into a short queue of three people who stood under a sign which deemed them to be "aliens." Strassman felt a little offended by such directness;

747

however, it was just another spark in the great fire of hatred that raged somewhere deep within. He craned his neck to see how the officials were dealing with his fellow travellers, only to be thwarted, as there was a dogleg in the line which allowed officialdom to be conducted without scrutiny.

Each arriving "alien" had been required to complete a document on which the reason for their visit was to be stated. Strassman had written quite prominently, "Invited guest of the Imperial Household." He was confident that that would be enough to deflect unwanted attention and his smooth passage would be assured. What he hadn't anticipated was the reverence with which his presence would be received. Upon seeing his documentation, the young official glanced up and then back down at Strassman's documents. Clearly awed, he deemed it necessary to call someone higher up the chain of authority. A more senior official appeared and gave a gracious bow, which Strassman awkwardly returned. The officer then beckoned Strassman around the counter and summoned a further official, who was instructed to assist Strassman with his luggage and onward transportation to his accommodation. Clearly, Imperial might still weighed heavily on those in uniform.

Although Cohen understood the mechanics of the Japanese language quite well, he and Wilson had agreed that it would be best to appear uncomprehending, as his assumed being, Strassman, would be unable to string two words together. So there he was, being treated as an important dignitary, lording his way through immigration and the cursory nod at customs. Within minutes he was placed in the back of a stately taxi that appeared to be brand new, his luggage, which contained his instrument of death, carefully stowed in the trunk. The three officials who had assisted him through the airport lined the kerb and bowed in unison as his taxi pulled slowly out into traffic and made its way towards Tokyo city centre. It took a great deal of self-control to not laugh out loud. He noticed his driver trying to snatch a glimpse of his passenger from time to time. On the occasion their eyes met, the driver bowed his head. It was a sign that he felt honoured to be transporting some-one who was obviously someone!

Although basked in blinding sunshine, there was a distinc-tively cool breeze around Tokyo, something Strassman was grate-ful for, as he hated the heat. He had paid scant attention to the unfolding scenery on the journey into the city, preferring to rest his eyes; he must have slumbered, for the driver was now out of the taxi and holding the door for his exit. They had arrived at the Hillside Hotel, and a bellboy was taking hold of his case and holdall. Strassman reached for his wallet, where he had placed some small yen currency to cover incidentals, but the driver was doing his best to wave away any fare owed. He was babbling on about what an honour it had been to drive him and that alone would be fare enough. Strassman insisted that the man take something for his work and left a thousand-yen note on the seat. A more than gen-erous fare and one that Strassman felt appropriate, given his false status. The driver bowed and remained in that position until Strassman had entered the lobby of the hotel.

The hotel staff were the embodiment of efficiency. The manager was on hand to accompany Strassman straight to his room, where he could complete his registration at leisure. Clearly, they were aware of the reason for his stay and were obliging beyond what normal duty called for. The manager, who spoke basic English although in a somewhat comical textbook fashion, enquired if there was anything that needed his attention. Strassman told him that he would require his morning suit and tails pressed and hung. The manager bowed and said he would send a member of housekeeping to his room to assist with his unpacking. Strassman said that would be unnecessary, as he would see to his own arrangements. For a moment the manager looked as if he was going to dispute this, but he acquiesced with a bow and left Strassman to recover from his journey.

As soon as he was alone, Strassman set about readying himself. He opened the cases and immediately began reassembling his revolver. The parts had been cleverly secreted in various items of clothing and personal effects; the cylinder, for instance, had formed a working hinge on his diary. It took moments to locate the parts, and in no time at all his weapon was in his hand, loaded and ready. He walked over to the dress mirror and looked at himself. His own image seemed to jump out of the mirror and mock him. The long flight had taken its toll. His eyes were heavy and looked more hooded than usual, and his pallid skin seemed to have gained new folds and creases. Strassman had seen pictures of healthier corpses, but it mattered nothing, as his body was merely a vessel, to be used until its purpose was met. He raised the weapon and looked down the sights into his own reflected eyes. A smile drew across his mouth. He was now unstoppable. Hamazaki was as good as dead, and his own sweet release from the torment that life had inflicted upon him was only days away.

Strassman was bone weary, but sleep was not easy to come by. His body screamed out for rest; his mind, however, was racing at full speed. He lay upon his bed and stretched his tired limbs, and stared out the window. The view that greeted his tired eyes was unspectacular. The only hint that he was indeed in Japan was the partially obscured, yet unmistakable sloping roof of a nearby temple. Everything else seemed to have been built in the last decade. Strassman wondered if this area had taken heavy bomb damage during the war and the slipshod architecture was the result. Then in a flash it occurred to him that he was probably only minutes away from Hamazaki's Ginza residence. Without a second's hesitation he was up on his feet and sluicing his face with cool water. Forgoing the temptation to shave his grey stubble, he ran some brilliantine through his hair and was about to leave his room when he remembered his revolver, which he had left lying on the bedside cabinet. Cursing his stupidity, he unlocked his case and placed it in a pair of rolled-up socks, and then double-locked the case using a solid padlock that he had brought for the purpose. Another of Thomas Wilson's foreseen practicalities, one of many that Strassman had come to be ever so grateful for. He decided to dispense with a jacket, as he was sure he would find it plenty warm enough. His nerves alone were a source of body heat. Having placed the "Privacy, Please" sign on the outside door handle, he made his way to the lobby, where the keen-eyed manager who had offered him help on his arrival was immediately on his heels. "Sir, may I be of any assistance?"

It occurred to Strassman that not too many foreign guests ventured out on foot alone. "Actually, I was finding it a little difficult to sleep, and I thought perhaps a stroll around the neighbourhood might help." The manager thought for a moment before beckoning over a bellboy, who looked ridiculously young. "Sir, if you please, this hotel servant—Tani is his name—will act as a guide for you and help you find your way. It can be a little confusing on the streets." Strassman thought about waving his offer away, but then he thought, what harm could come of it? The youth might be able to provide some valuable local knowledge. He agreed that this was a fine idea. The manager delivered a cannonade of instructions as the youth robotically acknowledged the importance of his task. Strassman was able to pick up most of the instructions. Don't get lost, no jaywalking, look after the guest, do not accept any gratuities. After the bellboy had changed his uniform jacket to his everyday attire, the two of them set out.

At first Strassman found it wearing, having to feign a lack of Japanese. Tani, for his part communicated in a mix of concocted English and exaggerated hand gestures, falling back on his native tongue only when frustration got the better of him. It was around five in the afternoon, and the streets were beginning to bustle as people went about their reverse commute. Strassman noticed that they were attracting the odd prolonged stare, but he couldn't give a fig. He felt quite tranquil here on the streets of Tokyo. He told Tani that he would like to walk down Ginza and take a look at the shops. Tani nodded enthusiastically—a simple request easily satisfied. They strolled along, ignoring the leaflets being offered by salesmen. Strassman, despite his best efforts to despise all before him, realised that he quite liked the place. Walking the streets was easy, and despite the crowds, nobody barged into him, unlike in New York, where you were likely to be physically thrown out of the way if you became unwittingly static on the sidewalk.

Strassman found himself pointing out landmarks in order to play the dumb tourist. Tani responded with an almost childlike desire to please, often wittering on long after the point had been made. They came to a large intersection and waited for the crossing light to turn green. Above them was a huge advertising board, perhaps as large as a tennis court. It said simply, "THE FUTURE STARTS NOW WITH MABUHAY," and below, a Japanese script, when translated, read, "Believe in what you buy, because we believe in what we sell." Strassman felt his mood darken as he looked up at the board. It was a grand reminder of why he was here in the heart of Tokyo. They crossed the street and walked on in silence for a few more minutes, Strassman lost in his thoughts. He began to think of Mabuhay after Hamazaki was gone. Who would take over the helm? Would the assassination of Hamazaki wake up the world to the deceit and depravity of this vile corporation? Tanaka would have to step into the breach and face the fire. Strassman considered the possibility of also taking out Tanaka, but as much as he relished the prospect, he doubted the opportunity would present itself. Chance was never so kind. Whatever, all would be settled in a little less than forty-eight hours. Strassman would work all day tomorrow on his contingency plan, which was something he had kept secret from Thomas Wilson, because for Strassman, merely killing Hamazaki was never going to be enough. He wanted the world to understand why the man had to die.

They reached the old clock tower on the Ginza crossing, and Tani was looking to Strassman for a lead on which way to turn. Without making it look too obvious, Strassman strode out towards Toshio Hamazaki's personal residence. Of course, he had made it his business to know all there was to know about Hamazaki's lair. They passed the grand corporate portal that now served as the headquarters of Mabuhay International. Strassman felt the familiar rush of cold anger mixed with something he could not quite fathom. It was with a sense of self-disgust that he had to admit that this unexpected emotion was indeed curiosity. Perhaps it was only natural that he would want to confirm all that had been, up until this time, merely academic to him. He knew everything about Mabuhay that was on public record and a lot more besides. For instance he knew that it was in this building that the world's longest boardroom table was housed, another ill-gotten asset from the depravity that masqueraded as legitimate business. Strassman felt the urge to step inside, but knew this would be tantamount to heresy. He feigned indifference and asked Tani if he knew what the building was. The boy beamed back at him and said, "It is the building of the richest in Japan." The boy's English needed work, but Strassman got his drift. He felt sorry for the youth, as he detected some kind of misplaced pride in his words. Just as Strassman was about to stride off, a black car drew up by the kerbside, its windows shielded by fancy lace. The driver, a chauffeur of some kind, was purposefully out of his seat and at the rear door. The driver remained bowed as his passenger alighted. Strassman held his breath, as he half expected Hamazaki himself to step out onto the sidewalk. For a split second he cursed himself for leaving the revolver behind. However, his feeling subsided somewhat when he realised that it was a woman who swung her legs out to exit the vehicle. She accepted the hand of her driver, looking a little unsteady on her feet, but quickly regained her poise.

Strassman recognised her immediately. Azusa Hosokawa, widow of the long-departed Mabuhay cofounder Makoto Hosokawa. Cursed with a beauty beyond understanding, this woman had been swept up by the much older Hosokawa at a time when he should have known better. Strassman knew that this woman had long been a source of embarrassment to the Mabuhay Corporation. Her countless affairs had been played out in public, and regular exhibitions of public drunkenness had seemed to push her to the fringes of the business. She was the unwanted executive, an interloper who had stumbled into the heart of the business, onetime teenage bride, a few years married and beneficiary of her late husband's wealth. Now she was simply too wealthy to give a hoot what anyone thought of her. It had been widely reported that she had recently sold a great deal of her shares in the company back to Hamazaki, but she still maintained a seat on the board and held enough interest to vote on important matters. That is, if she was sober on the day in question. Today at least, she seemed steady on her feet as Strassman and Tani passed her on the sidewalk.

The rush of excitement that Strassman felt only served to fuel his determination. He felt the theatre and drama of the world of Mabuhay all around him; he could squeeze the life out of it. The power was now all his, and his heart glowed warmly with the knowledge that he and he alone would be the bearer of justice.

A few minutes later they were strolling past the Ginza home of Toshio Hamazaki. It was an elegant building, almost like a grand dame that seemed to emanate offence towards the newer structures that had sprung up on opposite sides. An elegant set of marble steps led to a grand double door. Two magnificent Okinawan Shisa lion statues stood either side. It was widely believed that these icons offered protection against evil. Strassman smiled to himself: the folly of belief in false gods. As much as he wished to do so, he could not be seen lingering on the doorstep of his quarry, and the sudden appearance of a liveried doorman only hastened his stride up the Ginza thoroughfare. He had seen all he had wanted for today. Reality had been confirmed, and now it was time to lie low, gather his strength, make final preparations, and make his peace with God.

His curiosity more than satisfied, Strassman was eager to return to Hillside and make use of what little productive time the day had to offer before he succumbed to the tiredness that was taking over his body. His guide, Tani, was caught off pace as Strassman strode on, no longer willing to play the part of dumbstruck visitor. Perhaps if Strassman had kept up his guard, he would have noticed the black Toyota Century that had cruised slowly past him. The lace curtains that shaded the rear window from prying eyes may have offered little clue about the occupants, but the area and the fact that it now drew up opposite the Mabuhay building would have been enough to warrant a second glance from even the least curious of passersby. The doors opened and out stepped Ken Miyazaki. He glanced up and down the Ginza thoroughfare, as was his habit after so many years, and took a deep breath, as if he could somehow get the spirit of the street into his being. Despite being in the bosom of corporate luxury, Miyazaki had never allowed his street instincts to dull. He was savvy enough to know that tomorrow could always see it all come crashing down. He would have been mortified to know that fifty meters down the road, there was a man intent on making that shocking vision of doom a reality. Miyazaki strode up the marble staircase, satisfied that all was well and good in his world.

Strassman arrived back at his hotel and palmed Tani away with a smile and the offer of a few hundred yen, which the youth flatly refused. They bade their goodbyes in a clumsy fashion, and Strassman went up to his room unaccompanied. Upon entering, he immediately checked the carpet under the swing of the door. Before leaving, he had placed a small wooden bead on an exact spot, and as it was still in place, he was able to deduce that nobody had been in the room during his absence. The simple tricks that the agency had taught still served him well. He went into the bathroom to relieve his bladder. His stream was dark coloured and noticeably smelly, another side effect of his medications and a constant reminder that the inner workings of his body were closing down.

Strassman drew his attaché case out from under the bed, checked it over, and, when satisfied that it hadn't been tampered with, entered the unlock code and clicked it open. He took out two identical, large, sealed, brown envelopes, the contents of which contained the reasoning for his actions. One was addressed to the editor of the Tokyo Daily News, the other to the director of Organised Criminal Activity at Interpol's office in Geneva. These communiques contained all the evidence that Strassman had collated against Hamazaki and Mabuhay. He had also included a letter which made clear that other official agencies had long given up the pursuit of justice, thus leaving him no other alternative than to be the bringer of final reckoning. He had written that this was what God himself wanted and that the world would be, in a small way, a better place when devoid of the scourge of Hamazaki. These letters were his justification and the guarantee that he would not be seen as a lunatic who had gone rogue and taken the life of an innocent. It wasn't enough that Hamazaki had to die; it was important that the world knew exactly why he had to die. Strassman wanted Hamazaki's crimes highlighted across the world. He fell to his knees, closed his eyes and quietly recited the Prayer of Faith, from the Epistle of James. Strassman felt a close connection to St James, whom he believed to be the spiritual brother of Christ himself. Strassman knew deep down in his soul that "James the Just" would accept his supplication and guide him into the arms of Christ. Satisfied that all was well in his world, Strassman began to make his final preparations for the following morning. The day would dawn, and with the dawn there would finally be justice on earth.

In fact the dawn brought a haze of rain which, when he woke, caused a panic attack deep in Strassman's core. What if the reception were to be cancelled at such short notice? He stood at the window, gazing out across the rooftops that now glistened from the fine misty rain. He knew that there was some kind of official wet weather plan and the event would take place in some form or other. However, he didn't like the unexpected, as it wrestled away his control over events. Strassman called down to the front desk and asked for some coffee and toast to be sent up to his room. He also enquired about the weather forecast, only to be met with an uncomprehending reply. Nonetheless, he proceeded to make his deathly preparations in a surprisingly calm and calculated manner. His morning tails were hanging in the closet, and the crisp, starched, white formal shirt lay on the bed. He looked down at it and pictured the dark crimson bloodstain that would mark the end of his mortal being. Strassman was half dressed when the room boy arrived bearing his morning order. With the tray set down on the dresser and again, a gratuity flatly refused, Strassman sat down to what he knew would be his final meal on God's earth. As he poured his coffee, a shaft of sunlight burst through the clouds, the rays biblical in their descent. Strassman looked to the heavens and mouthed a thank-you for what he took to be a divine affirmation of the day's forthcoming drama.

At five minutes before ten Strassman loaded six rounds into the cylinder of his revolver. He gave it a spin as he had seen in so many Wild West movies and then clicked it shut and placed it in the inside pocket of his grey morning coat. He knew that there would be pat-down security, and before entering the palace grounds he would place the weapon in the small of his back, as far down as practicality allowed. He was confident of avoiding detection; after all he was an honoured guest of the Imperial household. He fixed in his buttonhole a white carnation compliments of the Hillside, and next to that the pin of the Canadian Lumber Association—the mark upon which his entire falsehood depended. Finally, the faded sepia photograph of his dearest Dorothea, placed inside his jacket, close to his heart. Satisfied that all was well he picked up his official invitation and the two large envelopes for mailing and set off to fulfil his destiny.

The lobby was quiet as Strassman entered. He rang the desk bell, and the manager appeared as if by magic. He gave a gracious bow to Strassman and once more professed his humble appreciation for Strassman choosing his hotel and what an honour it was to have such an esteemed guest stay with them. Of course, the hotel transport had been made ready, and a glance to the foyer revealed a chap in a smart suit holding his driver's cap by his side in an almost military manner, waiting for instruction. Strassman handed his correspondence to the manager, asking that he mail them immediately. No sooner had the words left his mouth than the manager called for a boy. It was Tani. Did they ever give that boy any rest? He was told to go immediately to the central post office and have the mail franked for delivery. Strassman nodded his satisfaction and thanked the manager. Suddenly, a strange pitying emotion swept over him, as he knew that this kind and generous man and his fine establishment would face extreme scrutiny from the authorities when his most distinguished guest became an infamous murderer. Dismissing those thoughts as sentimental nonsense, Strassman gave a curt bow and walked out to his waiting transport.

The sun was beaming down, and any trace of the morning rain was gone. There was a beautiful crispness in the air. A perfect day to die. Strassman passed the journey lost in a myriad of his own thoughts but unable to actually focus his thinking, as his mind was ablaze with images of the life he had lived, contrasted with the life he could have lived. He no longer held any regrets; his destiny had all but erased any such thoughts. In truth, he would revel in the delight of seeing the end of all his suffering. He stared out the side window, looking but not seeing. The drive across the ward to the Akasaka Imperial Gardens would take no more than ten minutes, and to Strassman's surprise the driver was already out of his car bowing at two official-looking fellows bedecked in the finest morning coats. They spoke to the driver, and Strassman caught sight of them peering surreptitiously in his direction. Good manners obviously prevented any intrusion upon his privacy, and, satisfied, they instructed the driver to proceed along a section of road that had been cordoned off specifically for the vehicles of the Imperial guests.

Strassman felt a trickle of sweat roll down his spine as he gazed through the front windshield. The procession of vehicles was slowing almost to a halt, and he could see there was some sort of checking taking place ahead. This time it was to be the police and security of the Imperial Household. He knew if he passed this hurdle, then he was inside the grounds, and with that thought came the realisation that all his planning had stood firm and Hamazaki's fate would be sealed. Two police officers, accompanied by one suited official, approached the car. This was it, the acid test. The driver once more made to alight from his vehicle, but was told to remain seated. The officers were more concerned with the practicality of their duties than the finer points of protocol, and tapped on the rear window. Strassman wound down the glass and looked directly into their eyes. He had his Imperial invitation at the ready, but was taken aback when the first word he heard was "Passport." He stammered his reply in English, which was that he had left it behind at his hotel. Strassman, although competent in Japanese, gave no hint that he understood the language. He took out the invitation and handed it to one of the police officers, who in turn and without looking passed it to the suited official. Strassman noticed that several cars were being waved past and seemed to be entering the restricted area without the kind of impediment he was facing. He had a feeling that this was not going as well as he had imagined. There was some talk over the police radios that he strained to hear but couldn't quite make out. The police officer ordered the driver forward and told him to stop alongside a small ornate gatehouse where another official appeared, an elderly distinguished man, wearing full morning suit and bearing the gold chrysanthemum lapel badge that marked him as a senior member of the Imperial staff.

Strassman suddenly felt out of his depth, and his nerves were starting to show. He kept his hands by his side, as they were quivering. The gentleman approached the car. "Good morning, Mr Strassman. Thank you for your patience and understanding, but we have to follow certain security guidelines. All is in order, and if you require any assistance in the function, please approach one of our staff and a translator can be arranged. Thank you for waiting, and on behalf of the Imperial Household we welcome you and all your fellow Canadians to the Imperial Gardens." He gave a bow and offered the return of the invitation. The officer waved the driver forward, and they once more proceeded towards the gardens. Strassman was speechless beyond relief. It was real, he was in. A wide road opened before them, and Strassman could see the huge gates ahead. The driver was instructed to halt, and from here it was obvious that progress was to be on foot. Staff members milled about, offering any kind of assistance. His fellow guests were also alighting from their vehicles, and several elderly ones were being placed in wheelchairs. Strassman thanked his driver, who in turn bowed and drove off back towards the public way. Strassman watched him leave. He knew that he would be waiting to transport his guest back to the hotel. A fruitless wait and only soon to be met with the horror that he had driven a killer into the heart of Japan.

Strassman felt as if he were floating on air. His legs were quaking as he passed through the ornate gates that bade access to the gardens. He could barely acknowledge the courteous bow presented by the two courtiers who flanked the entrance. No sooner had he got over the realisation that he was now in the inner sanctum than an official appeared at his elbow. "Excuse me, Mr

Strassman, sir. If you would be so kind as to allow me to escort you to the Canadian reception".." He bowed and extended his palm in a gesture which was both authoritative and suppliant in equal measure. Strassman bowed and followed on the shoulder of his guide. He wasn't so naïve as to expect free wanderings throughout the grounds. Indeed, from what sparse information he had managed to research, he had expected to be corralled amongst guests of similar type.

One aspect for which he was grateful was the fact that he was highly unlikely to be presented to the Imperial family, as he had not been prepped by any officials. It would have only been a further complication. Simplicity in all things, which was one saying Thomas Wilson had often repeated throughout their planning. Strassman now thought of Thomas and wished he could see how far their scheme had been successful. His mind raced back to that house in New York, and he tried to picture Thomas's face as he sat down in the simple kitchen to read tomorrow morning's newspaper. Would Thomas feel a sense of relief as he too had reaped his own vengeance on the man who had orchestrated the demise of his dear close friend, George Isaacs? After all, it was for his beloved soul that Thomas had done his work. Strassman knew that George would no doubt be mortified about what was about to pass, but all the same, he hoped he would also appreciate the resolution.

As Strassman and his guide made their way through the thickening throng of guests, he was constantly on watch for his prey. However, neither Hamazaki nor anyone associated with Mabuhay was at all visible. Strassman stopped walking, explaining to his guide that he wished to take a rest. The guide asked if he was feeling well and whether he would like to sit down. Strassman reassured him that all was fine, but the lines of sweat trickling down his forehead may have told a different story. He took in the scene before him and for the first time appreciated the breathtaking beauty of the perfectly manicured gardens. The symmetry and congruence was a true work of art. For a moment he wished he was here in other circumstances. He patted the pocket in which he had placed the faded picture of his late wife, Dorothea. "Not long now, my dear, not long." The words were spoken as a muttering to himself. He gazed out at the throng of guests, the men all bedecked in the same morning wear like a colony of penguins. The women attired in formal dresses that provided subdued contrasts in colour and wide hats that seemed ridiculously impractical.

His guide waited patiently for Strassman to resume his walk and, satisfied that Hamazaki was so far not to be seen, he waved the way forward. In a matter of moments Strassman found his hand being gripped firmly in a handshake. "Welcome, my dear fellow, my name is Coleman, Robert Coleman. Senior secretary of the Canadian Embassy. Please call me Bob." Strassman thanked him and in a bizarre moment of thoughtlessness nearly introduced himself as Elias Cohen. He quickly got over his fluster and resolved to get his nerves in check. Coleman was a burly fellow and if pressed you would have him down as a typical outdoor type. His cheeks were flushed, perhaps from a little overindulgence of the hospitality. To Strassman's relief, the senior secretary seemed not in the least bit interested in the Canadian lumber business, and after the formalities were done, Strassman sensed that he was scanning for more distinguished company. Indeed, after a few awkward moments, Coleman was off in the direction of an elderly Japanese man who seemed to be of his acquaintance.

Standing alone, with a glass of warm champagne in his hand, Strassman was beginning to wonder if this would all turn into pure folly, but then he remembered the letters he had sent out earlier this morning, and his resolve was steeled. There was no way back for him, it was do or die. Just as he was wallowing in self-doubt, he sensed a change in the bearing of the people around him. He picked up on the demeanour of some of his fellow guests. Although continuing conversations as if nothing had changed, their gaze told a different story. Strassman looked to his right, and there amidst a crowd of smiling and bowing sycophants was the man himself. Toshio Hamazaki. Making his way through the grounds as if he were a champion prizefighter walking through the masses to the ring, shaking hands, smiling, pulling certain faces closer to show favour. His confidence poured out like thick sugar treacle, and it was evident that he inspired awe amongst some guests.

Strassman could not take his eyes off the man, and it was an effort for him to look as casual as possible. His hand strayed to the revolver and, taking advantage of the distraction, he quickly shifted it to his lower jacket pocket. Hamazaki was heading his way, and he could now see the man's features clearly. His silver hair was shot with flashes of platinum and white, shockingly long and pulled back off his forehead. His beard was sharp, like a musketeer. He was a good head taller than most of the people around him, and his waistcoat was like something you would see on an Eton schoolboy.

Strassman wiped his sweaty palm on his trousers and squeezed the butt of the revolver for reassurance. Justice beckoned, and he felt the foul swill of vengeful anger swell in the pit of his stomach. He was about to stride forward when that damn fool Coleman gripped Hamazaki's hand and steered him into a different path. Suddenly, a throng of youths got in his line of sight, dressed in what seemed to be school uniform. It took Strassman a moment to realise that they were probably kids from the Canadian school in Tokyo. Fighting back the primeval urge to kill, Strassman took control of himself. He did not wish to see the detritus of his kill splattered over the crisp uniforms of the innocent. He resolved to bide his time, and watched as Hamazaki coolly moved amongst the kids, ruffling hair here and there.

Hamazaki was now heading in a different direction, bestowing greetings on smiling fellows, moving away from Strassman's view. There was no choice but to follow, so he stepped out of the throng and casually followed in as nonchalant a manner as his nerves would allow. He was aware of the palace officials who were in constant attendance, offering assistance, oblivious to whether it was required or not. Strassman did not wish to stand out in the crowd, but it was difficult, as he had strayed into an area of the gardens where foreign guests seemed to be few. Not wishing to look lost and draw attention, he stood on the fringe of a large group, hoping that strength in numbers would aid his cover. He could still make out the figure of Hamazaki, catching glimpses of his waistcoat as the guests parted to allow him through. He tentatively took a few steps forward, and there before him was a sight that caused his blood to boil and ignited the fires of rage that burned deep in his soul.

Hamazaki stood amongst his own. Strassman instantly recognised Hideo Tanaka, smaller and more aged than he had imagined. The two of them together. Surely that was an opportunity presented by the Almighty himself. It took a moment before Strassman realised that he was now looking at the private area reserved for the Mabuhay Corporation. A party within a party. He saw Azusa Hosokawa, tottering on her pink heels, champagne glass in hand. All her movements seemed to be exaggerated, from the way she threw her head back when she blew out the cigarette smoke to the shrill laugh that drilled through the crowd.

Strassman spotted another familiar face, one that seemed to be all that Azusa Hosokawa was not. Ayumi Hamazaki, serene and graceful, attending to the needs of those around her. Of all the evil souls that had been corrupted by Hamazaki, she was the only one who Strassman believed had any kind of a heart. He remembered seeing pictures of her in some remote African out-post, cuddling sick children. However, any sentimentality he felt was quickly swept away. She was, after all, the sister of an evil man, and all the charity work that she so lovingly wallowed in was undertaken with blood money. For a moment he wished he would live to see her anguish as all her good deeds were exposed to the world as a front for a criminal empire. The image before him was surreal: the corrupt empire, here in the heart of the Imperial Gardens, laughing before his face. Their relaxed, almost bohemian attitude incited his anger, and he braced himself, for it was time to put an end to one of the worst travesties of justice the world had ever seen.

Strassman slid his hand into his jacket pocket and with his thumb pulled back the hammer of the revolver. His instrument of death now primed and ready to deliver, he stepped forward towards his target. Hamazaki had turned his back and was now in conver-sation with a group that had converged on him. There was no more than a shadow's length between himself and his prey. It was time. Under his breath he started to recite the Lord's Prayer. As he was about to take out his weapon, Hamazaki spotted someone in the crowd and turned on his heels, throwing his arms in the air in an extravagant gesture of welcome. This threw Strassman for a moment, and he murmured a curse. Hamazaki was already lost in the crowd.

Strassman noticed the odd stare flashed in his direction. Some of the guests may have picked up on his anxiety, a throwback reaction, animal instinct. He was aware that he was out of place. Not just here in the Imperial Gardens, but in an area of the party where his presence must look very odd. A waiter stepped forward bearing a silver tray laden with drinks. Without as much as a second thought Strassman took a flute of champagne. He thought it would give him a more casual look, even make him look like he belonged. His eyes locked onto the gaiety that seemed to follow Hamazaki everywhere he went.

The voice in Strassman's right ear seemed to come out of nowhere. He had been blindsided by an ancient gentleman who was leaning heavily on a stick. The man was old and wrinkled, and for a moment Strassman was unable to tell if he was a Westerner or Asian. "My fine fellow, here all alone. May I keep you company for a moment or two?" Strassman fought back the urge to be grossly impolite and quickly realised that some kind of engagement would add a little to his subterfuge. The old fellow waved over the drinks waiter and took a glass of champagne for himself. "Shouldn't really," he cackled, "but at my age you have to take your pleasures where you find them." Strassman studied the old fellow closely, but nothing about him sparked any recognition. Yet there seemed to be something unsettling going on. "Let us drink to our host, and drink to every day we live to see another."

The fellow raised his glass, and Strassman did the same. They locked eyes, and as the champagne trickled down Strassman's throat, the realisation that he had been duped came in an instant; his entire being felt as if it had been shocked with an enormous power punch to his temples. Strassman slumped to the ground, his knees sinking into the soft mossy turf. His throat was full of a thousand needles, and his eyeballs felt as if they were fighting to dislodge themselves from his skull. He keeled over onto his side. He saw the old man crouch down beside him and pocket the champagne glass. He felt his face close in as the man rummaged inside Strassman's jacket and relieved him of the revolver, and then he heard him whisper, "No more days for you, fucker." Strassman now saw the man for who he was, his face smaller, but crystal clear as if at the end of a tunnel, the eyes swimming in a mix of hate and delight.

Ken Miyazaki took a step back from the man on the ground, who was now in the throes of convulsions, a thin stream of vomit and blood leaking from the side of his mouth. Strassman was paralysed, the life draining out of him. Unable to breathe, drowning in the air of the Imperial Gardens. The guests had parted and he was alone, stricken. He heard someone shout for a doctor, but the voice was miles away, and then the smell of jasmine flowers and a face so close. He tried to call out to Dorothea, but she was not there. The last thing Elias Cohen saw on this earth was the face of Toshio Hamazaki, the smell of jasmine even stronger. Hamazaki leaned in close with a smile and a whisper. "You bitter fool, you had it all wrong. You understand nothing and you are nothing." His words went unheard, for Elias Cohen was gone, his face swollen and tinged with a blue hue, a trickle of bloody spittle leaking from the corner of his mouth.

Hamazaki stood up and waved the curious and ghoulish guests back. "The poor fellow has been stricken by some kind of a seizure. Let's give him some space and allow the medical experts to do what they do best." First aiders were quickly on the scene, but they knew the task was futile. Nonetheless, they worked on the stricken body of Elias Cohen until a medical team arrived bearing a wheeled stretcher. Toshio Hamazaki watched in silence as the corpse of Elias Cohen was pushed away through the crowd. The shocked murmurings of the great and good could still be heard as they looked in Hamazaki's direction. Hamazaki was talking to an old man, looking to all the world as if he were offering him comfort and solace in this moment of tragedy. The old man turned on his heels and blended into the throng of guests with an agility that belied his years.

Later that morning Ken Miyazaki could be found at his usual table in the corner of the Edo Tea Shop, catching up with the morning newspapers and looking as if he didn't have a care in the world. He barely gave a second glance at the young boy who shuffled nervously up to his table. Miyazaki held out his hand, and the boy handed him two large, identical envelopes. He put them on the table and reached into his jacket pocket, took out his wallet, and slowly handed the boy a crisp ten-thousand-yen bill. The boy's hand was shaking as he reached out to take it. Miyazaki snatched at him like a cobra strike and gripped the boy's hand. "Tani, speak of any of this and they will be your last words. Keep your silence and the gods will smile upon you forever. Do you understand?" Miyazaki released his grip and pressed the money into Tani's sweaty palm and waved him on his way. As he watched Tani disappear through the door, he couldn't help but wonder how great things were built on such fragile structures and the feeble nature of his fellow men. He shook his head and went back to his newspaper.

Around the same time Miyazaki was enjoying his second cup, Rushton was working late at his desk when the phone rang. It was his secure, private line. He had been expecting this call, and lifted the receiver. The voice at the other end was a familiar one. The caller was brief. "The cherry blossom is glorious under bright blue skies. When only one petal falls to the ground, nobody notices, and the sun continues to shine." Then the click and buzz of a line gone dead. Rushton walked over to the window and looked down, for a moment lost in his own thoughts. The late-night traffic was still bumper to bumper. He envied the simplicity of ordinary folk and their mindless routine, swimming in their own ignorance, oblivious to the goings-on around them. They should be grateful, for it was men like him who allowed them the luxury of a simple life. Yet Rushton knew deep down that he had taken the wrong path and was mired in filth that would remain long after he was gone. He had tried to reconcile some of his darker deeds by doing some good. He thought of General Yamashita's sword, and the memory brought a smile to his face. He had insisted that Hamazaki bid a ridiculous amount in a charity auction so the funds would benefit war veterans. He had sold his own soul in a vain effort to ease the guilt that weighed heavily on his conscience. Rushton had become an expert in setting reductive thoughts to one side, and he went back to his desk. He had an important call to make to one of his agents. Mr Thomas Wilson.

Rangoon
1976

The sun had not yet risen. For ten-year-old Au Hih, the beginning of each new day was full of awe and wonder. Au Hih was the youngest of the novice monks and as such was tasked with sweeping the temple floor each morning. He went about his duties with unquestioning diligence. He woke each morning at four thirty, undertaking his solitary prayers before going about his tasks. A short walk up a rough track led to the temple, and given the hour, Au Hih always enjoyed the solitary splendor of everything around him. The insects had started their morning reverie, and Au Hih amused himself by chanting in time with the chorus. Some of the older monks had jibbed him about wild tigers who loved the colour saffron because it was so much like their own fur. They lurked in the shadows, waiting to pounce upon little robed monks. Au Hih laughed at their teasing, but it was in his mind all the same, and he clutched his broom with a mixture of stoicism and trepidation.

The new dawn was breaking, shafts of sunlight danced amongst the elephant leaves and shifted through the tall palms. The vines were blooming, and pink honeysuckle cascaded from high above. As Au Hih got closer to the temple, he slowed his pace, and for a moment felt himself being completely swallowed by all around him. Belittled by nature, he was overcome by a sensation that he was no more important than a fallen leaf, an ant, or even a wild tiger. Seconds turned into minutes before he could trust what his eyes were telling him. He sank to his knees and started chanting. It was a simple mantra, one of thanks which soon echoed far and wide. Au Hih was soon joined by the other novices, followed by their elders. The sound of their chant rippled out wider and wider which alerted the nearby villagers, who jostled their way onto the track. The chant grew louder and became a thing of wonder which served to call the folks from all the neighbouring villages.

As word spread, the dusty track upon which one little novice monk had walked, clutching his broom tight to his chest to fight off tigers, drew people from far and wide. To see was to believe. Their lady had returned. She had been on a journey that had taken many long years, and had seen many things, but she had never forgotten her home. She was back, and for Au Hih and all those who gazed upon her beauty that miraculous morning. All was good in the world, and their unwavering faith in the decency of humankind had been rewarded.

Argentina
1976

The sun was beginning to set over the lush plains of the Pampas. Joe Mendoza leaned back in his chair and enjoyed the cool, fresh breeze, which he thought of as nature's reward for a hard day's work. He looked forward to this time of day, when he sat on the veranda and took a few peaceful moments to reflect. This evening, the children of the gauchos were taking turns showing off their riding skills. The Criollo horses looked splendid and fearless as the kids cajoled them into races and fast turns and rearing up on their hind legs.

Joe lit a cheroot, a habit picked up from the ranch hands, took a long drag, and allowed himself to drift away for a moment. A strong gin was placed on the table beside him, and an affectionate touch on his shoulder brought him back into the moment. The cobalt-blue sky had given way to wispy shades of reds and orange as the sun made its slow descent. The breeze carried a sweetness he hadn't noticed before. He reached for the small wooden cross that hung around his neck, brought it to his lips, closed his eyes, and said his daily silent prayer.

The ghosts from the past were always there, but they weren't screaming so loudly these days. The children were calling his name and waving. He took off his hat, smiled, and waved it in the air. Joe Mendoza had finally found life.

ACKNOWLEDGMENTS

My heartfelt thanks to Laurel, Jane, Simon and Martin.

—Rushton

ABOUT THE AUTHOR

Rushton Medley grew up in Barnoldswick, a small mill town in the north of England. After studying economics and politics at the University of Hull, he moved to Hong Kong and spent the next ten years working and playing hard. He now lives in the beautiful Japanese city of Kumamoto, where he writes, plays guitar, and enjoys the occasional glass of wine.

@RushtonMedley